EVE turned her head to protest but before a word could be spoken his mouth covered hers, gentle but drawing the very breath away from her. As his lips moved over hers, his hands moved down her back, pressing her body against his own. She struggled against his embrace. His lips moved, and against her will she began to feel herself melt in a strange rush of emotion. She had never been kissed like this by a man and even as her body fought against him, her mind whirled with the wonder of it.

IT was not the kiss of a soldier...

A SHIELD of ROSES

Mary Pershall

BERKLEY BOOKS, NEW YORK

A SHIELD OF ROSES

A Berkley Book / published by arrangement with
the author

PRINTING HISTORY
Berkley edition / July 1984

ISBN: 0-425-07020-4

Acknowledgments

Don Mastrangelo, who first said yes,
Chuck Morrell, who showed me how,
Carole Garland, who sent it home,
But most of all:
Carol,
Sister and friend, who never let me doubt . . .
And Wayne,
Who has always made me try harder.

Dedication

To Lee, Greg, and Kip
You never fail unless you quit

In our world, if love there be,
Linger with me.
Waken the emerald dream, of silver threads,
Of shadows to come.

The land grows still,
Anon, the battle is done.
For days that are no more, I reach to thee,
In need, my love, linger with me.

Author's Note

For the benefit of telling a love story, without apology I have played outrageously with history and English climate. There is no evidence that Richard and Eve met before their marriage in the Christ Church of the Trinity of Waterford in the year 1174. Though both lived, as did many of the characters in this novel, Richard, who like his father before him was known as Strongbow, did indeed invade Ireland. With some evidence to support my claim, I should like to believe that his story, and his motivations, are told here.

As for Eve, or Eva, she epitomized the strength of the Irish woman of that time. She brought a broad fifth of Ireland to her marriage bed and she helped to effect, for better or worse, a change in Irish history—as did her father, Dermot.

Since eight hundred years have passed from the time of the events, I have taken the liberty, for the expediency of the story, of condensing almost two decades into three years. Richard's name was, in fact, on the treaty of the battle of Wallingford declaring Henry King of England in 1154. As for the suffering of the peoples of England and Ireland, the mood of the time, and Henry's motives, I have tried to express them accurately in context, though the dates of actual events have been changed.

Richard made good his promise to Eve as they stood together on the knoll overlooking Ferns. To quote Henry Orphen Goddard, professor, University of Dublin, in his book, *Ireland Under The Normans*:

> . . . the untimely death of the Earl of Striguil was a real misfortune, not only for the Angle-Norman colony but for Ireland. If Ireland was to benefit by Norman rule and

Norman organization, and by higher civilization and greater industrial energy of the new colonists there was needed a man whom the other colonists would recognize as being by birth, antecedents, and abilities, their natural superior. It was not a soldier that was wanted, nor even a general capable of conducting extensive military operations, but a statesman actuated by the single purpose of making the Norman rule a success. Richard deClare came of an illustrious house, had thrown his lot with Ireland, had wedded an Irish wife, and his whole future depended on the success of his undertaking. Moreover, to judge by the earl's success in winning over the most of the chieftains of Leinster to acquiesce in the Norman settlement, which he did (after showing his strength) more by persuasion and reasonable treatment than by sword, he was the man best fitted to carry on the work of pacification.

I am deeply grateful for Goddard's research and, most of all, for his communication of an objective understanding of the events that led to the particular changes in the history of Ireland that I have dealt with in this story.

The Prophecy

Within the depths of Ireland the relentless rains bore down on sodden forests of oak and ash, driving at heavy limbs in tormenting, twisting winds. Newly formed rivulets rushed in gathering protest about granite prominences, pulling tides of sandstone into the valley about the drenched encampments of the enemy which lay ominously silent.

Amid the impenetrable mountain marshes, drawn into wattle shelters, the people waited. When the battle of the storm was done they knew it would come, the nerve-shattering war cry of the clans who came from the north to claim Okinselagh and its people for their own. Conditioned by centuries of war their dreams were filled with images of axes and pikes raised, husbands and sons taken, the lamentable wails of women, the never-ending repetition of nightmares realized.

Deep in the center of the high mountain valley, just east of the enemy's encampment, there lay a stone manor larger than the rest. The anguished cries of a woman carried above the tumult of the storm. Unobserved, an old woman stood in the shadows of the room, her spare form concealed in the meager light of flickering torches. Her face remained impassive while she was sharply tuned to the dangers outside as well as to the pain of the young woman whose fingers tore at the fur coverings of the bed during yet another moment of agonizing torment.

As the squalling babe came forth from its mother's womb, the old woman stepped from the shadows. The women gathered about the birthing chamber drew back, averting their eyes as if in fear of ancient traditions, recognizing that it must be done quickly before the men knew what was about.

Gnarled fingers reached out to the babe where it had been placed on its mother's breast. The young woman clutched the babe to her in a moment of hesitation and then, with a gentle kiss to the soft, tender forehead, slowly she gave it up. Exhausted, pain-filled eyes followed the unlikely pair until the door of the chamber closed quietly behind them.

The crone kept to the shadows as she moved with her bundle through the manor, avoiding light which might reveal her to the men who would stay her from her purpose, because of their loss of ancient traditions. Reaching her chamber, she bathed and swaddled the infant, then laid it tenderly in its waiting cradle. As the thunder rolled angrily across the mountains, the old woman mumbled prayers to the ancient ones and hastened to build a fire, sensing their impatience to be heard.

Dragging a chair before the hearth, she sat at its edge and stared intently into the leaping copper- and lemon-colored flames. Her eyes narrowed at the forming scene as the movements of the blaze began to fill her with a deep sense of foreboding.

As the flames licked hungrily at the wood, wavering forms shaped slowly to the wizened eyes and the old woman cried out softly. Her mind filled with the vision. Helmed men ahorse, shielded by iron. Great walls crumbled in a deafening roar of fires and rivers of blood. Shadows of swords and lances never seen before moved in dance about the walls of the chamber, encasing the old woman and the innocent child swaddled nearby. The shriveled chin began to tremble and her eyes darted to the sleeping infant, recognizing the child's part in the coming drama.

The prophecy was clear. Nothing would be changed to circumvent its passing. The land would tremble and nothing would be as before.

PART ONE

The English

1

Ireland
November 19, 1152

Eve spun the wool endlessly upon the spindle as her eyes fixed upon the whorl of bone and she struggled to concentrate upon the menial task. It seemed that life had been always thus. Effort was wrung from her while her mind and energy reasoned and leapt beyond her experience. In a fit of petulance she jerked at the tender length of wool, breaking it, which brought forth a mumbled oath as she set to restring the length. It seemed a monumental waste of time when there were so many important things happening! Her people were threatened. O'Rourke... Her lips tightened as she thought of her father's most bitter enemy, the enemy of her clan, the murderer of her mother.

Frustrated, she pushed aside the spinning and rose from her stool to cross to the window of her chamber. Leaning against the window embrasure she stared out into the courtyard, which was ringed by an entrenchment and a longport, the piked-pole wall that encircled the manor. Evidence of the morning's preparations were strewn about, having been abandoned in departing haste. Her brilliant green eyes narrowed as they moved from smoldering cookfires, grey traces of smoke trailing beyond her window, to an upset iron pot of forgotten cabbage and mutton. A sharpening stone lay where it had been tossed carelessly aside, while amid all were the heavy tracks of carts and horses carved deeply in the mud of the bailey, giving proof of the activity but a few hours past.

They had left before dawn upon learning that O'Rourke's

5

forces had crossed the Wicklow Mountains and now threatened
Ferns itself. Why? Why does it so often take men so long to
come to the only possible conclusion? In the war council she
had spoken against the folly of waiting for O'Rourke to attack
first. A few of the men had taken up her cry, favoring the push
of the northern clan back to Meath, but other arguments had
prevailed and caution was chosen. Now, at last, they had gone
to meet the threat, leaving the women to their waiting—this
endless waiting. The waiting was almost unbearable for they
could not know who would finally appear at the gate of the
ringfort—the returning forces of her father or O'Rourke.

Sighing, she turned back to the room and winced as her
eyes lit upon the spinning. Nay, there was no possibility she
could set to the task again, not this day. There must be something else she could do to occupy her time! Her indecision was
resolved when the door opened to the chamber and an old
woman entered, pausing briefly before she closed the door
behind her. Eve smiled at the interruption, missing the look of
determination in the old woman's eyes. Bent from age, her
face weathered with lines of time, the spare form crossed to
the wardrobe and began stuffing a woolen bag with garments
before Eve realized what she was about.

"Gerda, what are you doing?"

The old woman paused and turned. "Yer Father 'as returned,
lamb. He awaits ye in the common room. He'll be tell'n ye
what needs ta be said."

"He's back?" Eve gasped. "Oh, Gerda, why did you not
say so!"

As Eve rushed from the chamber the old nurse mumbled in
Gaelic, shaking her head as she closed her eyes in prayer. "A!
Mmo truaj tu," she whispered. "Go with my love." Heaving
a heavy sigh she returned to her task, refusing to dwell on the
visions which floated through her thoughts. She had kept her
counsel, revealing to no one what she had seen in the flames
sixteen years before. What would have been the point? Only
the women would have given credence to her ramblings. The
men would have condemned them as superstitions. Worst of
all, Eve's father would have exiled her to her people in the
west. Then who would have guided the child and prepared her?
Gerda prayed that she had done her job well, for she knew that
the lass would need great courage and strength to endure what
was to come.

Rushing from the bedchamber Eve fought back the rising

excitement and fear that pressed at the back of her throat. She made her way quickly down the darkened hallway to the main room of the manor, where she found her father pacing before the fire.

A powerfully built man of middle-age, Dermot Mac-Murrough, king of the provinces of Leinster and Okinselagh, supported enormous shoulders which strained against the jerkin of inverted sheepskin he wore. His beefy arms were clasped purposefully behind his back as he paced. His head, now bent as if to aid the effort of deep thought, was covered generously with a thick ruff of coarse brown hair and, like his closely cropped beard, was as yet untouched by grey. The hardened muscles beneath the rough wool of his leggings and the determined strides which carried him across the length of the hall boldly defied his approaching years.

The hound sleeping by the fire raised its head and whimpered softly in greeting as Eve entered the room. At the sound Dermot spun about and his fierce blue eyes softened for an instant as they fell upon his daughter. The sight of her brought a familiar tug to his chest. God's Breath, he thought, she looks more like her mother with each passing day: the same auburn hair, streaked with gold, the same oval face and small slender nose turned up slightly under graceful arching brows...

"Father! What has happened? Where is Donnell and Enna?"

Her large green eyes, filled with tearful questions, brought him quickly back to the present. "Your brothers are safe, lass," he growled. Suddenly he needed the pitcher of ale which sat on a nearby table.

"But then...why are you here? Where is everyone? Have we beaten O'Rourke?"

"O'Rourke's boldness is exceeded only by his greed!" he spat, as he poured himself a healthy measure of the ale. "He is camped but a few miles from Ferns. He will not stop until he has destroyed us—which he will not!" he bellowed. "Forces from Leinster will come!" He took a long draught of his goblet and turned to her. "But until they do we are in serious jeopardy. There is nothing for it...I am pressed to make a decision I have been considering for some time." He purposely avoided looking at her as he ground out the last words. "There is a Welsh escort waiting without to take you to England."

"England?" she gasped, staring at him in disbelief. "You cannot!"

"I can and I will!" he roared back at her. "Would you have

me allow you to remain—to meet your mother's fate?"

His angry words silenced her as memories she had willed
into the hidden recesses of her mind surfaced with a quickening
shudder. Eve barely remembered her mother. There remained
only flashes, fleeting wisps of her: soft green eyes, a soothing,
tender voice, gentle arms enfolding her when she awoke from
a child's nightmare. There was one other memory: a night filled
with unthinkable pain followed by a hollow emptiness that she
had sensed, even then, would never be filled.

Even now, so many years later, Eve's hand went involuntarily to her throat as she remembered the choking fear she had
felt. In that night long ago she had sensed a presence and had
pulled herself from sleep to find a shadow standing over her
bed. The specter was outlined by an aura of light from the
hallway to the bedchamber she shared with her older sister,
Urlacam. She had cried out against a sudden, gripping wash
of terror, not simply of the figure itself, but of a suffocating
feeling of disaster that the shadowy form carried. Miraculously,
the specter was Donnell. He drew the two little girls into his
arms, and Eve could recall the added shock of seeing tears in
her older brother's eyes. Donnell, her idol, her protector, was
weeping. The tears had frightened her even more but she had
lain stock-still in his arms. His face taut with grief, he had told
them that their mother would not be returning from her visit
with her father in Kildare. Slowly, painfully, he had recounted
the story. Her party had been set upon, her escort brutally
murdered. The beautiful bantinnera had been taken captive by
the men of Tiernan O'Rourke, their father's most bitter enemy.
Before Dermot could extract his beloved queen from O'Rourke's
grasp, she had died from the ravishment she had suffered, the
act setting clan against clan.

Dermot's rage had been endless. He had refused all offers
from O'Rourke to accept hostages or the payment of a fine for
the offense and the war between the clans had intensified as
never before. Twice during the ensuing years the provinces
had almost been destroyed and now, once again, O'Rourke's
encampment was only a few miles from where they stood.

Oh, she understood well enough. If O'Rourke were to take
her it could well be the lever to bend her father to his will.
Among her people the outcome of a battle was measured in
hostages—and O'Rourke knew that Dermot MacMurrough
valued none higher than his youngest daughter. So, O'Rourke
sought to claim Okinselagh and Leinster through her . . . Nay!

She would not leave. This was her home, these were her people. If they had only listened to her and met O'Rourke before he entered Wicklow...

She threw up her hands in desperation against Dermot's will. "I will not go," she cried. "It is unthinkable. I will go to Gerda's people in the mountains. They will not find me there—"

"There is nothing more to be said!" he snapped, turning his deep blue eyes to her. "In the coming days there will not be time to worry about you and I'd have my mind eased! If only you had listened to me and chosen one of the lads I picked for you to wed you'd no longer be my concern."

"Lads? They were old men!"

"Old men, is it? I suppose the son of Cinel Owen you'd be considerin' old?"

"He was a bore and you know it!"

"Perhaps," he snorted. "But at least you'd be safe now and well out of the hands of O'Rourke!"

Fighting to control her anger she lowered her voice and answered grimly, "Aye, Father, but at what price?"

She thought of her obedient and mild sister now safely nestled in her husband's large manor in Dublin, vividly recalling how Urlacam had meekly consented to the arranged marriage with Connell O'Brian. She knew full well that her father's purpose for marrying Urlacam to the fat, old toad was to give himself added protection from the northern provinces.

She had watched her sister lay a trembling hand in O'Brian's that cold, brumous morning in the family chapel as his watery eyes leered down at Urlacam from his pink, fleshy face, and Eve had shuddered with disgust. At that moment Eve had vowed that she would never enter into a loveless union, regardless of her father's wishes. She had never ceased telling him so whenever he broached the subject. More than once he had chosen a suitor and the servants had cringed from the battle which raged, father pitted against daughter, two equally dogmatic wills reaching a voluble crescendo that allowed neither a suitable solution. Eve was firm that the man who took her to the marriage bed would be one of her choosing, someone with whom she could build a life of love and respect.

Dermot's voice remained hard and unyielding as he stared into the fire. His hands were locked behind his broad back in a gesture Eve recognized as one set with resolve. "Well, lass, ye have chosen your lot. Sir Robert FitzHarding is an old friend.

He has arranged for his knights in Wales to meet you at St. Davids and escort you to Bristol. There you will journey on to be fostered with his cousin, Gilbert deClare, the Earl of Hertford."

She struggled to keep her voice calm even as she felt her anger flame, heated by the realization that he had plotted her future without a word to her. "How long must I remain there?"

"For as long as I deem it necessary." He growled.

A prolonged silence followed as Eve's thoughts turned desperately for a way to change his mind, even knowing that this time it could not be done. "Why did you not tell me of this before so that I could have had time to prepare?"

"Prepare?" he roared as he whirled back on her. "Aye, you would have liked for me to give you warning! Warning to slip off into the hills to hide away against my purpose! Nay, this time, lass, you shall do what you are told!"

Eve should have known better but soon her own stubborn temper, so easily met, was pitted against his and the ensuing battle ended with Dermot storming from the room, shouting over his shoulder that she was to be ready to leave within the hour.

Unable to believe what had occurred, before dusk she found herself in the bow of a small boat. Her Welsh escort rowed against the resisting current of the small channel toward the darkened form of a ship that loomed in the heavy fog. Each stroke took her farther from the rugged Irish coast and everything familiar and loved.

2

England
December 3

anctuary, refuge. Somewhere in the world there must have been a place of peace and contentment but Eve had never known it and now all of her senses doubted it. She glanced about the large common room of the inn, her nose wrinkling from the overpowering smell of stale ale and unwashed bodies. The tavern was crowded, a fact that had caused Sir Bowen to heatedly argue that they should spend another night encamped along the road. Her pleadings had softened him until he had conceded to her wishes but now she began to suspect that he had been right. As her gaze wandered about the room she startled at the looks of anger, even hatred cast in their direction.

She glanced at the Welsh knight and his men-at-arms as they wolfed down their dinner of watery stew and course wheaten bread, wondering if they too had noticed the low regard in which they were held by the other occupants of the inn. Her own supper lay untouched as she pulled her cloak more tightly about her, feeling a sudden chill though the heat from the nearby hearth and the press of bodies kept the tavern uncommonly warm.

Safety in England? She smirked grimly at the thought. The first long cold night in England, as they camped in carefully chosen seclusion, she had suspected that such a place of safety was only a myth. Thinking that she was asleep, two of her escort had spoken softly in bitter, anxious voices of their urgency to be done with their task and of their eagerness to return

to Wales. She understood then the impending danger which
lay about them, confirming her suspicions that England's brutal
disobedience was not unlike that of Erin. Glancing nervously
over their shoulders, as if expecting the darkened forms of the
looming forest to come suddenly alive, they had spoken in
broken sentences of England's civil war which had torn at the
country for the past twelve years and left the land at the hands
of unlicensed barons and bands of starving villeins uprooted
from their hamlets and villages.

Lost in her thoughts, Eve gradually became aware that she
was being watched with particular interest by a disheveled pair
who hovered over their cups at a nearby table. As she caught
their eyes the slatternly duo looked quickly away and their own
eyes met for a long moment above slowly drawn smiles. Though
reason insisted that their exchange had nothing to do with her,
Eve felt her skin crawl with an unpleasant tingle. Unsettled,
she turned on the bench and pretended interest in her meal.
Her stomach churned at the sight of the unpalatable stew but
she forced a mouthful, shuddering at the sickening-sweet taste
of the greasy, overcooked mutton.

Sir Bowen finished his meal and pushed back his bowl. The
large, heavily-muscled knight scratched his coarse dark beard,
his brows furrowing into a scowl as his alert brown eyes darted
about. He never should have let her talk him into the inn, he
thought with disgust. He had to admit that comforts had been
sorely lacking since their flight from the small, rocky Irish
beach a fortnight before. Even in that short time he had found
himself susceptible to her coaxing though he doubted that she
was aware of the effect she had upon him, or his men. He
smiled to himself, recalling the shock he had felt when he had
first laid eyes on his charge upon her landing at St. Davids.
They had helped her from the boat, the breezing catching the
hood of her cloak, the intake of breath from the man at his
side forcing his attention to the young woman.

She was lovely—nay, beautiful, Sir Bowen thought. Her
hair, deep auburn with bright streaks of burnished gold, fell
gently about her face, framing enormous green eyes the color
of bright emeralds beneath thick ebony lashes. Her complexion
was as fresh and as creamy rose as a bright dawn of a spring
morning. The men, halting in their tasks, openly gawked until
Sir Bowen recovered. Shouting terse orders he sent them reluctantly back to their duties. She is not even yet a woman full

grown, he reflected. Suddenly he felt very old. Rising wearily he stretched as if to sluff off his years, then made his way about the end of the table to where she sat.

"Milady, we will be leaving at the first light so it would be best if you were to retire early," he said with an unaccustomed gentleness that brought curious glances from his men. "If you have finished your supper I will see you to your room."

Gratefully, Eve rose and smiled up at him as she took his arm, all too willing to be relieved of the room's company. After escorting her up the narrow staircase, he paused at the door to her chamber and cautioned her to bolt the door.

"Do not open it for anyone but me," he warned her sternly.

She closed the door behind her and threw the bolt. As she heard the sound of his departing footsteps she turned away and began to prepare for bed, throwing her garments carelessly about as anger surfaced with a deep, aching fatigue.

"Dermot MacMurrough, what have you done to me?" she thought crossly.

In a moment of honesty she admitted that her father had judged her correctly; had he confided in her she most certainly would have used the knowledge to defy him as she had so many times before. She never meant to anger him, not deliberately, and she knew that she was stubborn and willful. But to send her to England? Surely she could have found refuge among Gerda's people in the hills above Ferns! She would have known how to cope among her own people!

"I should have seen it!" she thought, "I should have known that he was plotting something! A plague on you, Dermot MacMurrough!"

As was her habit when confused or confounded she began to consider her resources and her options, neither of which looked particularly promising. Her early years had been happily spent tagging along behind Donnell and Enna and little Conner, until he had been sent to be fostered with Urlacam. She had wallowed in pleasure as they had included her in their games, teaching her to ride and hunt until she had mastered the bow and knife almost as well as they. After much cajoling, Dermot had even consented to her joining with her brothers in their studies under the rigid discipline of their parish priest. Dermot had been determined that his sons would have the same advantages as the sons of the English peers he had observed, and Eve had benefitted. She had taken eagerly to lessons of Latin,

French, and the ciphering of figures, grasping even more quickly than her brothers as her mind had turned excitedly to the challenge.

Then, suddenly, it had changed. Over her protests, then her silent hurt, Dermot had insisted that such was not seemly practice for a young maid. Soon she found herself delegated to the women's quarters and engaged in pursuits he considered proper. Surprisingly, and to Eve's dismay, Gerda had supported him. Having lost her last ally, Eve reluctantly had conceded, though she had never been satisfied by the gentler pursuits of learning to work a needle, how to play the lyrical Irish lyre, and other refinements expected of her. She knew now that she had been right. What good were those things to her now? Her people were threatened, her family in danger, and she had been sent away! The thought of whiling away her days in some faraway English manor while her father and brothers struggled to hold their lands made her tremble with frustration and renewed anger!

Once unrobed, she shivered in the chill of the frigid room, her fingers aching from the cold as she quickly donned a thin woolen chemise. She slipped beneath the covers and pulled them up to her chin. Waiting for the warmth of her body to warm the bed, she fought against the chattering of her teeth, fed by her unsquelched irritation.

She thought of Gerda with longing; of how she had begged for the old nurse to come with her to England. But Gerda had been firm. She said that her time was spent and that Eve must face the future without her. She would return to her people, to spend her last days in the comfort of ancient traditions that had become lost to most in Erin since the coming of the Church.

Unbidden, idle words often spoken by the old woman floated dreamily through Eve's mind. Ancient words without meaning, but now strangely comforting. As drowsiness played upon her, her anger began to dull and she found herself drifting between moments of fitful sleep and reality until, at last, she slipped into a dark, dreamless void.

Some hours before dawn, Eve awoke with an aching chill. She could feel a breeze drift across the bed from the window on the far side of the blackened room. She sat up and threw back the covers with a jerk, irritated that she had forgotten to close the shutters. She pattered across the room, her bare toes curling away from the icy floor, and pulled the shutters closed. As they snapped shut the sound triggered the certain thought that they had been firmly closed when she retired. Frowning, she turned when a hand leaped out from the shadows and clapped over her mouth, muffling the cry that tore from her throat. Her head was wrenched painfully back as a blanket was thrown over her, stiffling her cry for help. Hands grasped, pawing at her as she kicked and flailed wildly against them. Her mind whirling with heart-stopping terror, she felt herself lifted from the floor. Frantically gasping for breath against the suffocating blanket, she felt a thud against her temples and her head seemed to burst with bright, spinning lights and she heard a gruff voice, coming from far away, "Blimey, ye've killed her!", before the world disappeared into a blackened, closing chasm.

She first became aware of a deep aching in her temples, then a dull throbbing in her wrists which were bound tightly behind her. She opened her eyes, wincing at the sharp spear of hot pain which shot through her head by the simple action. She was lying on the floor of a small wagon covered with a canvas through which she could see the greying light of dawn. The jarring motion of the wagon increased her discomfort and she tried to roll onto her back, only to find that she was wedged among blankets and sacks stacked in the wagonbed. She could just barely wiggle the arm beneath her in a meager attempt to return some feeling to it. Bile began to rise in the back of her throat and she panicked with the thought that she was going to be sick. She forced herself to be calm, breathing slowly and evenly until she felt her churning stomach begin to settle.

Who were they, what did they want with her? Had O'Rourke's grasp reached her even here? What twist of irony that would be! She listened for sounds, something to identify her captors, but the only sounds that reached her were the creaking boards of the wagon and the horses' hoofs as they struck the hard-packed road.

She drifted in and out of a painful, restless half-sleep while marking the time of day by the lightening and eventual darkening of the canvas stretched over her uncomfortable prison. She was jarred awake as the wagon seemed to move from the road onto a bumpier path; then, miraculously, it stopped. She swallowed fearfully as she heard the low, gruff voices of her captors for the first time and the sinking spring of the wagonbed as they stepped down. The terror within her heightened, her

apprehension mounting almost unbearably as she dizzily contemplated the next moments and what they might bring. The
canvas was thrown back and hands reached in and grabbed her,
dragging her from the wagon. She stumbled, almost falling to
the ground on unsteady legs, but hard fingers pressed into her
arms, wrenching her up and twisting her about.

She found herself in a dense part of a forest amid a small
camp of surly-looking men and her breath quickened as the
light of the campfires identified them to be soldiers of the king.
She had noticed their tunics on the docks at St. Davids and Sir
Bowen had identified them to her. At the time she had wondered
why his face had darkened with his answer and now the memory
gave her little comfort.

Her sweeping gaze froze as it settled into the cruel eyes of
a large thick-set man who was striding toward them, his hair
a bright carrot-orange in the flickering light of the fire. As his
eyes swept over her she shrank back involuntarily, realizing
for the first time that she was clad only in the wool chemise
she had worn to bed. The blanket about her shoulders had
fallen away and the man grasping her arm made no move to
retrieve it as he tightened his hold on her while the other undid
the bonds of her wrists. Once free, she tried to reach the fallen
cover but was jerked about to face her captors for the first time.
Gasping, she recognized them as the two who had been watching her with such interest in the common room of the inn.

"I told ye to bring supplies!" the large red-haired soldier
snapped. "If ye found a bit to amuse yourselves, ye had no
business bring'n' her with ye!"

"Our purposes were good, Captain!" the one holding her
enthused. "She 'ad a full Welsh guard as 'er escort and ought
ta bring a good sum fer ransom!"

"That so?" The captain's shaggy brow raised with interest.
His eyes narrowed, then he reached out and grasped her arm,
pulling her from the other man into the light of the campfire.
"Let's be hav'n a better look at ye, girl," he said, spinning her
roughly about. She could hear the sound of his breath drawn
though his teeth as he stared at her in the light of the fire, the
outline of her body showing clearly through the thin wool.
"Well now, Thatcher," he drawled softly. "'Haps ye've done
a good thing after all. Who are ye, lass?"

As she stared into the captain's eyes, her temples began to
pound and her chest constricted painfully until she thought she
would suffocate. Contemplations of what might happen to her

spun wildly through her mind even as she tried to deny the terrifying reality. When she did not answer, he repeated the question with a sharp bark and she jumped. Before she could stop herself, she let out a high, nervous laugh that seemed to come from somewhere apart. The captain blinked at her odd response and he took an unconscious step back from her as his heavy brows drew together in uncertainty. His unsettled movement and expression served to clear her mind for an instant and she claimed a moment of strength she felt only on the surface.

"I am Eve MacMurrough!" she spat, raising her chin defiantly. "Daughter of the king of Leinster, who will cut out your foul heart if you so much as lay a finger on me! I am here by the permission of your king and I demand that you see me safely to Hertford!"

The captain's eyes grew wide, then his frown deepened as he fixed on the coarse material of her soiled chemise. "A fine lady, is it?" he smirked. "A lady's maid or a plaything for the Earl of Hertford, I shouldn't wonder." His eyes passed over her boldly, his hungry regard fixing on her amply-filled chemise where the fullness of her breasts pushed against the thin wool. She felt a dizzying fear wash over her once again as his mouth broke into a black-toothed grin and she realized, for the first time, that he was drunk.

"Aye, methinks ye've done well, Thatcher. She might be worth something to us." He followed her wide-eyed gaze to the others who had gathered about and barked orders for them to be about their business. Disgruntled, they moved reluctantly away to the campfires while casting envious glances at their leader. "You too, Thatcher, and you, Arn, get yerself some food." He snapped to the two who hesitated by the wagon.

"But, Cap'n, 'tis we who found her!" Thatcher whined while Arn encouraged him with a poke in his back. "Ya can't keep 'er all to yerself!"

"Do as I say!" the captain roared, sending the two scurrying away with the others. "Now then, lass, they'll not be bother'n ye." He stepped slowly toward Eve and the bright intentness of his pale eyes made her skin crawl.

"Leave me alone!" she cried, stepping backwards only to find that she was trapped between him and the fire.

"Ah, come now girl, ye be want'n me to see ye to Hertford. 'Tis a favor ye be ask'n, 'tis a favor ye'll be giv'n'." His voice was thick as he reached out to finger a lock of her hair which hung loosely over her shoulder. "It should be making no difference to ye, it'll not be yer fingers ye'll be wear'n' to the bone for them fine lords." He sniggered at his own crude humor as she pulled her hair from his rude caress. "Come now," he repeated less gently. "Be glad it'll be a man's part that'll have ye first and not the meager excuses ye'll find 'neath them fine linens. Be good and we'll be see'n' ye to Hertford, sooner or later."

He snorted with laughter and suddenly reached out and yanked her to him, crushing her slender form to his broad chest as she cried out in protest. She could smell the stale wine on his breath and a wave of nausea choked her with the offense. His hands moved roughly over her body as his moist lips found her throat and she gasped against the outrage. She willed herself not to struggle, a sick feeling of inevitability spreading over her as she wanted to scream, to rail at him, but she knew that it would only add to his enjoyment and prolong her misery. She almost retched as his mouth covered hers while the sounds of his men crowed with approval behind them. He raised his head and his eyes, red with wine and lust, focused uncertainly upon them and he scowled.

"I'll be giv'n' us some privacy, girl," he slurred. "The others can do what they will when I'm done."

She shrieked at his words and began twisting and clawing at his hands in a desperate effort to break free. Effortlessly, he pulled her with him into the darkness of the wood, dragging her into a small glade where he spun her about and threw her up against a tree, knocking the wind from her. Before she could catch her breath he was on her, pressing her against the tree with his huge form as his eager hands moved over her body. An anguished sob escaped her as his lips moved ruthlessly over her face and neck. This couldn't be happening to her, it couldn't! Slowly, he pushed her down on the pine needles, his weight pressing her onto the earth as a heavy hand went beneath her chemise, searing her flesh beneath its harsh search. As she struggled frantically beneath his crushing form, her breath caught and the sound of her scream reverberated through the trees. Laughing, his hand went to the neck of her chemise, rending it from neck to waist to expose her ample breasts to his hungry ~ gaze, the bounty bringing forth a grunt of pleasure as he cruelly pinched the soft flesh between his rough fingers. She cried out against the excruciating pain, the sound wrenching from her in loud, gasping sobs. He managed to loosen his leggings and she could feel the pressure of his swollen member against her thighs as he shoved a leg between her thrashing limbs and mounted her. Shutting her eyes tightly, she sunk down into hopeless inevitability and tried to focus her mind on an abyss of darkness, to block her senses from the feel of his hands and the expected pain.

Dazed, she slowly became aware that his hands were no longer groping at her and his body was still. Why had he stopped? Confused, she opened her eyes to stare at the glint of steel only inches from her face as it pressed against his neck, bringing forth a small drop of blood. She watched with a fixed fascination as the dark serum trailed down the soldier's neck, then slowly she raised her eyes and looked beyond the sword to a dark figure looming over them. It seemed surreal and for an irrational moment she thought that the ancient gods of the forest must have intervened. The voice was no more than a low controlled whisper but it pierced both of them.

"If you move, or utter a sound, you are dead. Do you understand?" The captain nodded stiffly and the voice continued. "Roll off of her. Slowly."

The soldier obeyed and the steel moved with him, pressing against his chest as it pinned him to the ground. The stranger motioned to Eve and she rose quickly, never taking her eyes from the tall figure before her, and covering herself as best as she could with her torn garment. Her trembling legs were barely able to support her as she leaned against the tree. She should have been filled with relief, elated to see her brutal assailant lying helpless beneath the broad sword, but her heart pounded within her chest as her eyes fixed upon the tall, shadowy form.

As she tried to comprehend what was happening, the wood about them took on human form, silent figures emerging from the trees to pass by them toward the camp. Stupefied, she watched as a man paused and knelt beside the soldier and quickly went to work trussing and gagging him. When he had finished he looked up at his leader, who motioned with his blade for him to follow the others. Pausing slightly, the mysterious knight glanced back at Eve. "Stay here," he ordered, then disappeared.

It erupted without warning. The night was suddenly filled with the sounds of screaming men and horses. Her eyes flew to the bound man as he struggled against his bonds and in an unbidden moment of self-pity she was swept with an utter feeling of despair. She sank to her knees, covering her ears with her hands as she sobbed uncontrollably, her senses assaulted by the lamentable sound of dying men.

It ceased as unexpectedly as it had begun, the abrupt silence being even more terrifying than the sounds of battle. Trembling, she raised her head and cried out as she found the knight standing before her.

"Are you all right?" he demanded. The mail of his hauberk gleamed in the moonlight and his eyes shone darkly ominous from beneath his helm, the noseguard landing a monstrous appearance as he towered above her. She crossed herself against the specter, murmuring a prayer and bracing herself against the expected flash of his sword.

"I asked if you were all right?" he repeated impatiently. She nodded weakly. Satisfied, he turned to the men who were joining them.

"What shall we do with this one?" asked one of the men, indicating the bound figure at their feet. "Shall we send him to join the others?" Without waiting for an answer, the man stepped toward the bound soldier and raised his bloodied sword, but the knight stayed his arm.

"Nay, we shall send him back to Stephen. Let him take the message of what has happened here tonight. Untie him."

The soldier was pulled roughly to his feet. As they loosened his binding he wrenched free and lunged toward the mailed knight. "You bloody bastard! I'll kill ye!" he screamed. In his fury he nearly reached his foe, as it took three of the men to subdue and hold him.

The knight's voice was edged with contempt. "Nay, you have a more important duty to perform. Return to your liege lord, your despotic king, and give him a message. Tell him that as long as he is on the throne of England he will never find peace."

The soldier, his face and neck red with rage and hatred as he strained against his captors, spat at the knight. "Let me go and put a sword in me hand, yer cowards. Ye'll hang, all of ye!"

As the knight answered, the sound of his laughter sent chills along Eve's spine where she stood in the shadows. "Nay, 'tis Stephen who is the traitor, to England and to her people. But I will not debate it here. You are free to go—but go quickly before I change my mind and give you to my men."

The soldier was led to the clearing and only one of the men remained with their leader as he glanced at Eve, gesturing a thumb toward her, "What shall we do with the wench?"

Eve found her voice for the first time, her fear melting under her anger. She shrieked at them, determined to fight back while her speech slipped into a heavy brogue.

"I'm suppos'n' ye'll be hav'n' yer way wi' me first? Ye fearless men of England! But ye'll be hav'n' ta kill me first!" She flew at the knight, grabbing for his sword as she tried to wrench it from his scabbard. He caught her to him, pinning her easily against him as she kicked wildly and railed at him with her fists.

"Hold!" he growled. "No one is going to hurt you!"

She fought furiously, venting her outrage for what the soldier had done to her as well as her fear for what this new threat might offer. As she flailed and kicked she screamed a stream of profanities, well learned from her brothers, over the belly laughter of the other man.

"Ah, Richard, 'twould seem that the battle is not yet over! Are you need'n' of help?"

"Nay, you idiot," he shouted over Eve's protests. "Stop your cackling and get the horses! Cease, wench, or we'll leave you to your next folly!"

He managed to pin her arms against her sides, holding her firmly as she twisted to break free. Finally, exhausted by her struggles, she slumped against him. "It would seem that I have already met it!" she spat, her chest heaving from her exertions.

She heard him chuckle and looked up to find him grinning at her. "Do not compare me, wench, to the manner of the one who was enjoying your favors. Though, from what I observed, I am inclined to believe that I would enjoy the game."

She stiffened at his words, quickly finding renewed energy as she flung herself away from him. "You assuming lout!" she shrieked. "If you touch me, I'll . . ." She halted in mid-sentence as she felt his eyes moving over her and she glanced down to where her torn chemise had fallen away, exposing her to his gaze. Horrified, she hurried to cover herself, her cheeks burning as she heard him laugh softly. Binding herself as best as she could, she lifted her chin defiantly and glared at him. "And what are your plans for me now, or dare I ask?"

"We must be away from this place," he shrugged. "I am not inclined to leave you here."

"You need not concern yourself!" she hissed. "I am quite capable of taking care of myself!"

"I have seen ample evidence of that!" he snorted. Without another word he took her arm and led her through the trees

toward the clearing. As they entered the camp her face paled
at the sight before them. The moon shone over the carnage,
the light of the spent campfires lending an eerie quality to the
death and destruction. The bodies of the soldiers lay everywhere
and the low fog drifted about the lifeless forms, shrouding them
in a deathly quiet. Her stomach churned with revulsion and her
legs began to fold at the grisly sight. As she wavered a strong
arm went about her and she was pulled up against her side.

A horse was brought up upon Richard's orders, a mighty
destrier that pawed impatiently at the ground in an eagerness
that lent a strange contrast to the death about it. Glancing down
at her, Richard removed his cloak from behind his saddle and
placed it lightly about her shoulders. Without conversation he
swung into the saddle and reaching down he pulled her up in
front of him. She squirmed uncomfortably, aware of his nearness as he pulled the cloak about her and tucked it beneath her
knees.

"What about those?" she snapped.

"What?" he asked, following her pointing finger.

"I do not see why I should have to ride with you," she said
tightly. "Surely I can take one of those horses. I assure you
that I ride quite well!"

"Take a good look at them," he countered, a bit impatiently.
"Notice their ears. They are nicked, as is done with all horses
belonging to the king. Would you care to be found with one
of them? It might pose questions you would be unwilling to
answer."

"Oh," she said in a small voice.

He shouted to his men and they left the clearing, picking
their way through the trees to the road where they headed north.

The warmth of the sun against her face forced her eyes open
and she blinked against its brightness. Instantly she became
aware of the strong arms about her and the feel of his hard
body against her own softer one. She sat up quickly and would
have fallen from her perch except for his arms, which came
swiftly about her, pulling her back against him. She heard him
chuckle and she turned to find herself looking up into the
greyest eyes she had ever seen.

"Good morning."

"Good—morning," she stammered, her cheeks flushing pink
as she realized that she must have slept the night cuddled up

against him. As if reading her thoughts, he smiled down at her, his mouth breaking into a disarming grin which made her breath catch in her throat. He had removed his helm and pushed back his coif, revealing dark sun-streaked hair falling over a broad forehead. His mouth was strong and sensuous with a firm square chin. The sun had tanned his face to a darkened bronze, paling his eyes in contrast to where they appeared almost transparent. The face, unmistakingly noble in bearing, was ruled by those eyes. They seemed to bore into her, holding her own with an unspoken power, yet touched with a gentleness and humor that startled her.

Aware that she was staring at him, the color in her face rose. She squirmed uncomfortably, acutely aware of his nearness and the difficulty of her situation. "Where are you taking me?"

"That depends upon you." He smiled. "Perhaps, if you would tell me how you came to be in the camp last night, and where you are going, I could help you."

"Help me!" she bristled at the words. "You are a murderer, a miscreant, a . . ."

"Possibly," he answered, clearly amused by her indignance. "But one that you should be grateful to have happened by. Or am I mistaken in thinking that you did not enjoy the game you played?"

"How do I know that I will not fare as poorly with you?" she hissed.

"You do not." He grinned, pulling her more tightly. Gasping, she pushed away from his arms and turned her body until her back was pressed against him.

"Am I your prisoner then?" she gritted.

"Of course not. You are free to be rid of us if you wish." He pursed his lips in thought. "The next village is a day's ride from here. If you keep to the road you should be able to make it in two, perhaps three days on foot depending on how often you stop to rest. I suggest you stay well hidden when coming upon other travelers, and, of course, fight the temptation to avail yourself of unfriendly campfires." He pulled the horse to a halt and looked down at her questioningly, his grey eyes dancing with amusement. "Shall we part company now?"

"Ooooh," she breathed. "You are horrid!"

"Nay," he offered, his mouth twitching with laughter. "Just accommodating."

As they rode, now in total silence, her back began to ache

and her thigh became chafed where it rubbed against the pommel of the saddle. She rubbed the spot gingerly, wincing at its soreness. Sighing softly she turned in her seat and leaned her shoulder against him. She was grateful that he made no comment and she peered up at him from the corner of her eye, wondering what he would do if he knew that he held the daughter of an Irish king in his lap—one that would be worth a considerable sum for ransom. She knew that she had no other choice; she had to stay with them until she could find other means to reach Hertford. But, she was not going to make the same mistake she had made with the captain.

"I—I was running away," she hesitated. "My father wished for me to take a husband and I could not abide his choice." She winced inwardly, knowing that she needed much more practice before she would be an accomplished liar. She wondered if he could see through her meager attempt.

"I see," he answered blandly. "Then our destination should not be a concern to you. That will simplify things, will it not?"

She lifted her chin, turning to look at him boldly, her anger swelling as she realized that she would have to play along with his game. "Aye, milord, 'tis no matter where we be!"

"Ah!" he laughed. "There is that brogue I heard last night! I was wondering what had happened to it! Without it you speak English very well!"

She stiffened, her eyes flashing at his humor. "The brogue is real enough, milord, but I have been taught to speak in your coarse English manner, if you prefer!"

He raised a tawny brow. "And perhaps now you will tell me what to call you, besides wench."

"Eve, milord," she answered tightly.

"Eve," he repeated, ignoring her anger. "It is a good Irish name; it becomes you. But cease calling me 'milord,' Eve. It is not necessary."

She shifted in her seat, her body aching from the forced ride and unconsciously she pressed against him as she stretched. He noticed her movement and glanced down at her, a moment of concern passing over his face before he turned and motioned to one of his men.

"Orlan, the men are tired and the mounts are in need of rest. We will stop ahead." The man nodded and pulled back to tell the others, and she looked up at him, noticing for the first time the lines of fatigue on his face.

"Will we stay long?"

"Long enough for you to bathe and rest if you wish—with complete privacy," he added, noting her shock. "You do bathe in Ireland, do you not?" he grinned.

She glared at the comment. "Aye, we bathe, milord, though ye're 'ardly the one ta be criticizing!" she retorted, wriggling her nose. "'Tis not the smell of the rose on ye!"

He threw back his head and roared with laughter. "Touché, Eve!" His voice lowered as he grinned at her wickedly, "Perhaps I shall join you in that bath!"

Her eyes flew open with horror but he shook his head with a chuckle, "Never fear, milady, I shall grant you the privacy I promised."

3

They took their rest atop a small knoll overlooking a glorious valley where they could see for miles, easily detecting the approach of anyone who might be searching for them. The view afforded a breathtaking panorama of undulating hills ringing the valley, fringed by forests of beech and chestnut. The richness of the soft meadows stunned Eve as she stared, transfixed, at the luxuriously gentle contrast to the harsh and unforgiving granite and high mountain valleys of her home.

"There is a small stream among the trees. You may refresh yourself there and no one will disturb you."

An odd look crossed his face, then he abruptly turned away and returned to his mount. He removed an article from his saddlebag and crossed back to her, handing her a chainse of white linen.

"You had better wear this. I do not think that garment is suitable for this company."

She mumbled her thanks, flinching at the laughter in his eyes as she made her way down the slope, soon forgetting about him in her eagerness to wash herself of the dirt, grime and odors of her experiences.

When she returned the camp was sleeping with the exception of the watch, who nodded and smiled shyly when she strode by. There was a bounce in her step as she felt oddly happy and content, the change in her mood greatly encouraged by the fact that she was clean and comfortable once again, though she was still cold. As she had bathed she had thought about her situation, reflecting on the timely interference of Richard and his men. She did not know what to expect from them, yet her situation had improved over that of the previous night. She remained wary but thus far they had given her no reason to doubt their intentions. While she found herself unsettled by Richard's presence, she felt touched by the kindness he had shown. Suddenly the situation had taken on the aspect of an adventure, and not one that was entirely unpleasant.

She had torn the bodice from her chemise and was wearing Richard's chainse. It fell over her skirt almost to her knees and she had rolled up the long sleeves to her wrists and had tied it about the waist with a strip of wool torn from the discarded bodice. Her skin shone from the vigorous scrubbing and her tousled, damp hair hung freely to her waist and now became the object of her thoughts.

She entered the grove where the horses were tied, their saddles set to one side. Spotting Richard's, she crossed to it and kneeling down began rummaging through its contents in search of a comb.

"Are you looking for something?"

His voice startled her and she jumped up. Spinning about she found Richard standing a few feet away. He too had bathed and changed into a fresh linen chainse under a knee-length tunic of soft dark brown leather split on the sides to his waist; and chausses, a type of loose-fitting hose, of dark green held to his calves by cross garters. Sharing the warmth of her mood she gave him an impish smile, quite unconsciously and totally unaware of the effect it had upon him.

The filtered light sifted through the intertwined branches of the grove, lending an opaline quality to the rosy blush of her skin, and played in dancing highlights on her freshly scrubbed hair, which hung in soft, unruly ringlets about her face. Richard's gaze swept over her with fascination. Her large, emerald eyes shone with a bright expectancy as her sweetly-formed mouth softened into a smile that made his breath catch. With some difficulty, he cleared his throat and gestured to the saddlebag as he repeated his question.

"I assure you that my intention was not to reward your generosity by playing the part of a thief," she said quickly, now embarrassed that he had found her going through his things. "I was only looking for something with which to comb my hair."

Running his fingers through his own damp hair he grunted as he passed by her and knelt by the bags, riffling through them until he found the object of her search. Rising, he handed the comb to her and his eyes held hers for a long moment.

"I will do my best to see to your needs, damoiselle," he said softly while a brow rose slightly. "If you would but ask."

She began to feel self-conscious under the intentness of his regard. She could almost feel the hardness of his body as it had pressed against hers upon the destrier. The unbidden thought added to her chagrin and she flushed deeply. Murmuring her thanks, she brushed passed him and stepped quickly from the glade.

She settled herself on the grassy crest of the knoll to let the warm morning sun dry her hair. As she set to work, patiently untangling the mass, she did not notice immediately when Richard stretched out beside her. He watched her through half-closed lids, appearing to sleep while she worked, his eyes moving slowly over her slender form as he admired her full, rounded breasts which pushed tauntingly against the linen of the chainse and her trim waist and long shapely legs that were outlined so delectably beneath the thin wool of her chemise.

He wondered how she had come to be in the soldiers' camp. He had not believed her story for a moment. This was no wench from an impoverished family. The soft hands that had layed upon his arms held no calluses from strenuous work. From her bearing and confidence he knew her to be more than a lass from a simple borough. What intrigued him even more was her flustered, easily disconcerted confusion by his slightest touch, her awkwardness at his attentions, attesting to the fact that she was no wench of easy virtue. What was she doing alone, unguarded, in times such as these? A delightful and intriguing mystery, he mused, one he looked forward to solving.

She combed her hair until it shone, then deftly twisted it into two thick braids which she tied with strips of wool she had tucked into her belt. Finishing her task, she laid the comb next to him and pulled her knees up, wrapped her arms about them and looked out over the valley, lost in her thoughts.

Seeing her so pensive, he rolled onto his side and leaned his head on a hand. "Have your thoughts returned to Ireland or do they lay in the future?"

She turned to look at him, startled at the odd rush of tingling pleasure she felt by the rich, deep timbre of his voice. Unsettled, she gave him a quick, nervous smile.

"I . . . I thought you were sleeping. I was thinking of home . . . wondering . . ."

She halted, alarmed by the unguarded thoughts she had almost expressed. Averting her eyes from his questioning gaze she lay back on the grass and stared at the sky, watching the small puffs of clouds that drifted lazily overhead.

"It is hard to believe, looking at this beautiful, peaceful morning, that so many men died yesterday."

He sat up abruptly, hooking an arm about a bent knee as his eyes swept over the sleeping camp. His brows furrowed into a scowl at the tone of criticism in her comment.

"Your sympathy is sorely misplaced, Eve," he growled. His eyes fixed upon the valley below, his voice suddenly becoming edged with a sharp hatred. "A small village to the south of here testifies to their actions. They had burned, murdered and ravished, leaving nothing but the old women and small children—and those only because they had been hidden away."

Eve's eyes widened. "But they were men of the king!"

He snorted, a grim amusement creeping into his grey eyes as he looked down at her. "It would seem that you met the measure of that." He ignored her blush as he continued sharply, "Their actions are allowed as there is no longer attempt at just law in England. The structures that old King Henry began to build died with him. His eyres, kept from the villages, are no longer allowed to settle disputes and give recourse to the free-men against the injustices of their lords. Titles are no longer given to men of honor, won by merit, but Stephen bestows them to any who will do him homage. He allows them to do as they please while he looks the other way, as that is how he holds their loyalty."

Listening, her thoughts turned to home and she was struck with the similarity of their situation. Envy stirred within her at the freedom Richard enjoyed in striking back at the injustices he found about him. It reminded her of her own frustrated feelings of helplessness.

"I can well understand your anger," she offered. "My country too is at war and that is what made my leaving the hardest to bear." Her green eyes kindled with anger as she gritted on the next words. "Had I remained, how I would have relished drawing a bow against our enemies! To fight alongside my brothers against those spineless, loathsome, hellhounds."

Tawny brows arched with surprise at the angry string of

torments which followed. Her tirade was abruptly halted by
the sound of his laughter as it filled the still morning air, causing
the men to mumble and stir in their sleep. Her mouth dropped
open in wonder as he fought, evidenced by the shaking of his
shoulders, to control his mirth. His grey eyes danced with ill-
suppressed humor as they swept over her.

"What do you find so amusing?" she queried.

"Merely the possibility of finding a formidable opponent in
one so small and slender of form," he answered with a chuckle.
"Though the possibility, I must admit, would prove an interesting challenge."

"Oooooh!" Now understanding his meaning her stiff Irish
pride was sorely pricked and she sputtered at him with indignation, "How dare you laugh at me! What would ye be 'nowin'
about my ability wi' the bow, or anything else for that matter?"

Her protests only caused him more merriment as he practically choked on his laughter, which made her green eyes spit
with fire. Had he not been enjoying himself so thoroughly he
would have noticed the change in her. Suddenly she threw
herself at him and began pelting him with her fists. Still chortling, he came about and threw up his arms to deflect the blows.
Catching her wrists, he rolled her effortlessly back on the grass
and held her half beneath him as she struggled against him.
Slowly his mirth subsided as he began to notice her green eyes
flashing brightly beneath heavy lashes and her cheeks flushed
with anger. Even in her rage she noticed the change in him,
the amusement which left his eyes as they traveled slowly over
her face. She became rigid, her eyes growing wide with fear
as she stared up into his intense grey ones, their meaning
abundantly clear. There was an embarrassed cough behind them.

"Ah . . . Richard. The men are awake. Will you be wanting
to take leave?"

Richard looked down at her, his mouth twitching as if fighting a smile. "Aye, Orlan, I think it would be best to leave
immediately."

He rolled off of her and stood up, holding out a hand to her
which she ignored as she struggled ungracefully to her feet.
Orlan made his way back to the men who were saddling their
mounts as Richard went to his destrier, leaving her alone in
her humiliation. She brushed the grass angrily from her skirt
and her body trembled and her chest heaved as she sought to
calm her fury. Her mind was vivid with what she had read in
his eyes and it had taken the joy from the morning. The lovely

valley lost its enchantment and became alien and hostile as she looked out over it with resentment. How could she have allowed herself to become comfortable with him even for a moment? Her first impulse was to flee, to leave her fears of the knight behind her. It only fed her anger to realize that her terror of being alone was greater than her fear of him.

She clenched her teeth. First her father, sending her from him without counsel; then the English soldier who would have taken her so brutally with no more regards to her feelings than if she were a bitch cur; and now this knight, laughing at her . . . and his intentions were clear enough! He would satisfy his male needs with her upon his whim and how could she stop him? Did anyone care how she felt? Not in a male world, that was certain! What a fool she had been to think that she was safe, even for a moment! Tears of self-pity welled up in her eyes but she took a deep breath against them, determined not to let him see her weakness. Wiping her eyes with the back of her hand she threw back her heavy braids and prepared herself to face him head-on, with sore-won pride and defiance.

She walked toward the men, noticing as she approached that they were taking dried venison from their saddlebags, and she realized that she was ravenously hungry! She had not eaten for a full day and her last meal was hardly enjoyed. She chewed her lower lip as she stared at the meat, hoping that they would offer her some. At once she realized, with horror, that they would leave Richard to care for her needs!

"I will starve first!" she thought. "God help me if I ask him for a morsel!"

As if on cue, Richard appeared from the grove, leading his mount as he munched on the dried meat and wordlessly offered her some. She looked at the meat with longing but she shook her head indignantly.

"Nay!" she hissed, "I will not take anything from you!"

He shrugged, his grey eyes dancing as they moved slowly over her. Signaling to his men, he swung into the saddle and turned, reaching out a hand to her. She spun on her heels and strode toward the others, who were already mounted, her skirt swishing with her mood. She stood before them, her hands on her hips, as she looked from one to the other expectantly. Seeing her intention, they stirred uncomfortably in their saddles, unwilling to meet her gaze. Her lovely mouth twisted into an angry pout as she realized that not one of them would offer to let her ride with him! Caught unawares, she squeaked as an arm went about her waist and she was lifted off her feet and plopped unceremoniously into Richard's lap. She heard the muffled chuckles of the men as Richard turned the destrier toward the road.

They rode in silence as Eve strained not to lean back against him—an almost impossible feat due to the movement of the horse. She squirmed awkwardly, trying to pull herself forward, only to slip back repeatedly.

"You would be more comfortable if you would stop fighting me and lean back," he said with an irritating casualness.

"I am quite comfortable the way I am!" she snapped.

"Then I would be more comfortable," he countered, pulling her against him. "Now behave yourself."

"Behave myself!" she breathed, aghast. "How can you say that to me?"

Any point she would have made was lost as her stomach growled—loudly. He had the decency to fight a smile as he reached behind him into the saddlebags and pulled out a piece of venison which he offered to her. She looked the other way, fighting with herself, almost faint with hunger.

"Take it. There is no reason to go hungry. Besides, 'tis easier to have pride on a full stomach."

She was about to protest when her stomach growled again, this time bringing a deep chuckle from him. In spite of herself she smiled, and reached eagerly for the meat.

As she munched on the delicious morsel Richard reached back in his saddlebag and extracted something which he laid in her lap.

"Orlan made these for you from rabbit skins."

She blinked with amazement at the objects in her lap then lifted and turned them in her hand. They were slippers, crudely laced but quite suitable and undoubtedly warm. She bent over and drew her leg up to slip one on as Richard's arm went about her for support. Wriggling her toes in the warmth of the rabbit fur she forgot about the earlier antagonisms and turned to him with a warm smile of pleasure.

"You are pleased?" he asked.

"Of course!" she smiled. "They are wonderful! I am touched that he would do such for me."

"You underestimate us, Eve. We have no reason to want to harm you. Not everyone is like the soldiers you had the ill fortune to meet. Which leads us to an earlier problem that should be settled between us."

She had resumed munching on the jerky and a graceful brow arched in question to his words.

"As I said, you have no reason to fear me, I have no intention of raping you." She stopped chewing and stiffened at his bluntness. "I have never forced a woman. If and when I choose to bed you, it will be mutual and you will enjoy it as much as I."

She sputtered at his words, almost choking on the meat, "Of all the conceit! How dare you! I have no intention, or interest in . . ."

"Then you have nothing to fear, do you?" he interrupted with a grin. "Either way."

The fog rolled in even before the sun had completely settled beyond the hills and encased them in its thick damp folds. They stopped for the night, camping a safe distance from the road under huge spreading oaks from which hung heavy moss that granted them natural tents which would help allay the chill.

The wet cold had soaked through Eve's cloak, plastering her garments against her skin. She tried her best to ignore her discomfort as she did her part to make camp, helping one of the men to lay the fires for the evening meal and to prepare the hares caught earlier. The warmth of the blaze and the aroma of the meat as it turned on the spit helped to revive her spirits. Soon she was dry and by the time the meal had finished she began to relax. Their bellies full, and their own humor restored, the men sat about in the warmth of the campfire joking with one another, their easy camaraderie releasing the tensions of the past days.

The pleasantness of the evening was all too soon ended as the men began to spread apart, moving to the edges of the trees, where they lay down under their mantles to sleep. Eve pulled her cloak tightly about her and yawned. Exhausted, but unwilling to leave the warmth and comfort of the fire, she stared into the blaze, mesmerized by the flames. Unaware that Richard had crouched next to her until he picked up a stick and began to spread the coals, she turned to him curiously.

"What are you doing? Surely you are not going to put out the fire!"

"Aye. I am doing just that."

"But I am freezing!"

"It is better to be cold than to awaken to the wrong end of

a sword," he answered calmly.

"Sword?" she whispered, gulping as her eyes grew wide.

He looked sideways at her, his eyes moving over her briefly before he shook his head. "Eve, do you think that they will give up so easily? A fire can be seen for miles. By now the captain may have found aid and I do not relish meeting combat with tired men and horses. The men need sleep. I will not post another guard so that you may enjoy the fire."

"I am sorry, I did not mean . . ."

"I know. Meanwhile, it will be a time before the coals die. You may enjoy their warmth until then."

He began to rise and seeing this she became suddenly alarmed. She knew that he should be the last person she should want as company but suddenly the thought of being left alone was more than she could bear.

"Wait, please, stay and talk with me, just for a time."

He looked at her for a long moment, puzzled by her request, but he shrugged as he sat down, "If you wish."

"Tell me," she said, glancing about the camp. "Why do the men sleep so far apart? Would they not be warmer if they slept closer together?"

"A group of sleeping men make an easy target. They are close enough to give alarm but spread enough to make more difficult a surprise attack."

She considered his answer, turning her attention to the dying coals. They fell to silence, staring into the glowing embers, hot points of brilliant red winking at them among the still grey night. The thick fog covered the wood to lend a feeling that they were completely alone.

"Do you return now, to your home?" she asked softly. "Would they be able to follow you there?"

"Nay, we will be safe enough."

She looked at him from the corner of her eye, noticing for the first time that he wore no coat of arms upon his tunic. From his manner and bearing she knew him to be gently born and she was just as certain that this was not the case with his men. They were good men, hearty and true, obviously completely faithful to him and their cause. But they were simple men, much like the freemen of her truath, definitely not of the seasoned cut that had accompanied Sir Bowen.

"Milord? Forgive me but I am puzzled. If you promise not to laugh I should like to ask you something."

He looked at her and his eyes were unreadable but the smile

he offered was gentle. "Aye, *cherie,*" he inquired softly in his Norman tongue, "what is it that puzzles you?"

She answered him in kind, not noticing the slight raise of his brow as she responded in a smooth, fluent French. "What do you hope to accomplish with such as last night? Surely you will become a hunted man, and those with you also. I reason that you are aware of what you are doing, but what of they?"

He studied her for a long moment. There was something in his look, a guarded hesitation, but it quickly disappeared and his manner was gentle as before. "They understand and believe in the cause, as do I. Their determination is the more fierce since they are closer to the injustices of their king, the more surely wounded by Stephen's whims."

"And you?"

"Me?" he shrugged. "I have seen too much to do nothing."

She watched him and listened to his words, knowing that there was more, much more, than his simple answer.

"And if you are caught? What of your family?"

"That is assuming that I shall be caught," he smiled. "I have no intention of being caught, as the prospects are not very pleasing."

"Nonetheless, your family must be concerned. Think of how hard it must be on them, particularly your . . . wife."

She could not see his face clearly in the light of the nearly extinguished fire but she could hear his deep chuckle and feel his eyes on her.

"Ah, *cherie,* there is no need to play games. If you wanted to know if I had taken a wife you had but to ask."

She could feel her cheeks burn at his jest. Mortified, she flared at him, "I assure you, Sir Knight, I have no interest in such matters! My concern was only for the grief you might cause others by your traitorous actions!" She jumped to her feet, gathering her cloak about her, but before she could take a step she felt his arms go about her, pulling her to him.

"Eve," he murmured gently, "my teasing was well deserved but not meant to hurt."

The hours past had proved a sore trial for him. The memory of the moments spent upon the grassy knoll had played reck-lessly upon his emotions, fueled by the hours of her soft body nestled against his own. The wench was bewitching, and there was something else, a need, a loneliness he read in her that touched something within him he had never felt before.

She turned her head to protest but before a word could be

spoken his mouth covered hers, gentle but drawing the very
breath from her. As his lips moved over hers, his hands moved
down her back, pressing her body against his own hard length.
She struggled against his embrace, her hands pushing against
his chest as she tried to break free, but his arms held her to
him. His lips moved, and against her will she began to feel
herself melt in a strange rush of emotion. She had never been
kissed like this by a man and even as her body fought against
him, her mind whirled with the wonder of it. It was not the
kiss of the soldier. It was soft and gentle and stirring. Her lips
were alive with the sensation, wonderously tasting of his being,
her back burning with the touch of his hands as they moved
lightly searching each part. She was aware of the feel of his
rock hard body pressed against hers. This was her first warm,
intimate contact with a man. She was shocked by the feel of
his maleness, and the difference, yet the familiarity of touching
another so intimately. His lips moved over her face and to the
fragrant folds of her hair as he murmured to her softly. She
felt as if she were being lifted from her feet. Wonderously, the
world began to lose its presence as her mind dismissed the
reality of what was happening, only concentrating on the kiss
itself.

She realized, with a start, that his hand covered her breast
and while the touch was gentle the memories of the English
captain came flooding to shock her into reality.

"Nay!" she breathed, pushing against him sharply to break
free of his embrace. "Do you think that I am so easily got, a
wench to satisfy your male desires upon your whim? Nay!"
she cried. "My value is more than that! If your intent is firm
you will have to do that of which you promised not. You will
have to take me by force!"

He stood there calmly, allowing her to spend her wrath. As
the outburst ceased he spoke, his voice low but with a touch
of anger.

"Damoiselle, I find it tiring to repeat myself. Why would
I take by force what is so easily attained elsewhere? I am judge
enough to know that what just passed between us was mutually
given but I am much too fatigued to belabor the point."

Before she could comment he turned from her, leaving her
to stand alone in the veil of fog which seemed to close behind
him, leaving her in total isolation. The impact of his words
slowly penetrated her mind, her anger in contest with the truth
he spoke. She had responded, there was no use denying it to

herself. She was appalled to realize the ease by which he had brought about the response in her and she trembled with a deep shame more acute from that realization than from outrage over his boldness. How could she, so soon after the terrible experience of the night just past? And with a man she had only just met? The thought terrified her and her only defense was hatred toward the object of her fears. While her mind whirled with these thoughts he was suddenly once again at her side, towering above her like a phantom forming from the elements of the fog. She recoiled, bringing her arms up to protect her as a scream began to gather in her throat.

Sensing her hysteria he grabbed her shoulders and shook her hard. "Eve, stop it! I am not going to hurt you!"

Wrenching herself free from his grip, she stepped back and swung at him with all of her frustration and fury bent into the pass. Before it made good its target he caught her wrist and spun her around against him. His mouth was next to her ear as he growled in a low, angry whisper.

"This is enough! You will wake the camp, or worse, bring anyone who might be near down upon us! I do not think you would wish to see that captain again, or would you?"

His words had the expected effect and she sobered as an anguished sob escaped from deep within her. A firm grip on her arm, he led her toward the trees and sat her down roughly on the blankets he had laid by their base on the soft, moist leaves. She watched him warily as he sat next to her and threw a cover over her before he lay down and turned his broad back to her.

"Now behave yourself and go to sleep," he growled.

In the silence that followed it was all she could do to breathe calmly. Behave herself? He did it again! How dare he! She turned her head to stare at his back and was stunned to realize that he was actually asleep! As if nothing had happened! She pulled the blanket under her chin and stared up into the bluish-black shadows of the tree. Though exhausted, sleep did not come easily as the damp air permeated the blanket in a frightfully short time, causing her added misery and making her shudder with the chill. Soon her entire body was trembling. She heard him move next to her and then he was there throwing his blanket over the two of them and then pulling her against him.

"Do not misread this, Eve," he muttered. "My intent is only that you should sleep warmly."

The length of his body settled against hers but she did not

protest as she felt his warmth ease away her chill. The last thing she remembered before sleep overtook her was the measured sound of his breathing.

She awoke to find Richard gone and the blankets tucked tightly about her. The men moved silently about in the greying light of dawn, breaking camp and saddling their mounts, but there was no sign of Richard or Orlan. She rose and adjusted her garments and rubbed the sleep from her eyes. The uncomfortable memory of last night made her mouth tighten with renewed anger. She was relieved by his absence, grateful that she would not have to face his cocky grin. But her mind recalled the touch of his hands and her breasts and loins tightened at the remembrance as a warm flush swept over her. She shook her head with an anguished gasp as if to clear her mind of such disquieting thoughts. It was as if her body were a traitor mocking her with its own memories. She looked swiftly to the men, afraid that they observed her disquiet and could guess the source, but their attentions were to their own tasks. She heaved a great sigh, wondering what the day would hold for her. She crossed to the campfire where she helped herself to the meat and wheaten loaf she found there. She stood munching on her breakfast when Richard and Orlan returned.

She was surprised to see Richard dressed once again in chain and mail. Their mounts were richly lathered, their sides heaving, indicating that their ride had been hard. Orlan shouted orders to the men while Richard crossed swiftly to Eve, his shrewd eyes observing the activity of the men as they hurried to break camp. Sensing the urgency, she gaped at him, her eyes growing wide with fear at the grim look he held.

"The king's soldiers are near," he said, answering her unasked question. "And they are searching for us."

She paled at his words, her head growing light with fear. The bitter memories of the night in the soldier's camp rushed in and she shuddered. He grabbed her arms for support, his eyes burning at her from beneath his helm.

"The battle must be met, Eve, and for your safety we must leave you here. I would leave you a mount but there is none to spare." He hesitated, unsure that his words were heard, then reaching into the pouch of his belt, he extracted gold coins which he pressed into her hand.

"If we do not return by the time the sun is at its highest, walk to the north. Be sure that you keep from the road when anyone approaches. Let no one see you, do you understand?

There is a small village a half day's walk and with this gold you may buy help there—but let no one see it or know that you have it. Locate a man, a carpenter by the name of Alden. He is a friend and is to be trusted. Do you understand?"

She nodded as she stared at the coins in her hand, feeling nothing. He watched her, his eyes darkening with concern as he noted her dazed look. For a moment he doubted her very sanity. Suddenly he pulled her to him, crushing her mouth against his in a long, harsh embrace. She reeled with the intensity of it, her mind riveting back to the present, and fury burst within her. She pushed against him as he released her and she stumbled away, her eyes wild with anger as she drew the back of her hand over her mouth as if to wipe away the distasteful feel of his kiss. Before she could scream the words that were forming, he turned toward his destrier and swung into the saddle. Pausing before he turned the animal's head, his eyes swept over her.

"I need not fear for you now, Eve." He grinned. "The devil himself could not contain you in your wrath."

With that, they were gone. She stood alone in the center of the clearing with no one to vent her anger upon.

The morning passed as if it would never end. The sun seemed to freeze in its position in the grey morning sky. She glanced at it for the countless time before resuming her pacing where she had almost worn a path near the campfire. Her mind was racked with indecision. Should she abide by Richard's counsel and remain for his return or leave before the appointed time and try to enlist aid in the village? The thought of traveling alone over the alien English countryside was terrifying. Still, she could not fathom why she should follow his instructions and deliberately wait for him to reenter her life! As she paced her thoughts were interrupted by a sound in the trees to her right. She froze as a creeping fear tingled up her back. She rushed to the small pile of wood by the fire and, grasping a good-sized stick, she hurried to the edge of the trees and hid behind a massive oak. Trembling, she fervently prayed that whoever approached had not seen her! She stood motionless for what seemed to be an endless moment as she strained to hear. There was nothing. She swallowed hard, her breathing gradually becoming more normal as the long moments passed. It was probably just a small animal, she reasoned. Finally she threw down the stick with distaste, completely annoyed with herself. As she turned her heart leapt to her throat. With a

whimpering cry she fainted into the arms of the large helmed
knight who stood there.

She awoke slowly, emitting a soft groan. Seeing a form
above her she cried out and brought her arms up protectively,
and blinked with shocked disbelief as she recognized the face
that looked down at her with deep concern.

"Sir Bowen!" she gasped.

"Aye, milady, thank God we found you! I beg your forgiveness for our stealthy entrance but I had no way to know
that you would be the one to greet us!"

She sat up, wondering at his sudden presence. "I had dismayed of ever seeing you again! How is it that you found me?"

He smiled ruefully, glancing at the campfire from which a
stream of grey and black smoke wafted up through the trees.
"A smoldering cookfire can be seen for miles, milady. You
are most fortunate that 'twas one of my men who first saw it."

She gazed dumbly at the fire, Richard's warning of the night
before coming back to her. She groaned, disgusted with her
stupidity.

"I should have squelched the fire," she mumbled.

"Pardon, milady?"

She shook her head. "'Tis nothing, Sir Bowen." Suddenly
she remembered as she looked at him anxiously. "Did you meet
with anyone—a party of men, perhaps, or a battle?"

He looked at her questioningly. "Nay, milady, none. Should
we have met with one?"

He listened gravely as she recounted her story, punctuating
her words occasionally with a black scowl or a mumbled profanity. Being Welsh, he had no regard for the king's men and
cared little what happened to them. His only concern was to
deliver the lass to her destination on instruction of his lord,
then return home to his beloved Wales as quickly as possible.

"You are certain that you are all right?" he questioned.

"I am fine, really."

"Well then, if you are fit to travel we should be rid of this
place." He gestured to one of the men and helped her to her
feet as the horses were brought forward, "'Tis an English manor
where I am to deliver you, and while I am less than pleased
at the prospect, we had best be about it."

As they rode away from the grove, while her relief was
immeasurable to be once again with her trusted escort, a part
of her was pulled back to the camp. She mused over what
Richard's reaction would be when he returned to find her gone

and no word of her in the village. The thought pleased her greatly. She hoped to cause him as much distress as he had caused her.

She sighed, knowing, even as she had formed the thoughts, that she was being ridiculous. He would not give her a second thought. His interest in her had been forced upon him, a whim at best. She would only be a memory to amuse him when he bothered to think about it. She began to visualize him with another, laughing as he recounted an episode in a forest, depicting her as a silly little twit. The woman joined him in his laughter . . . laughing . . .

How dare he! Her eyes shone with wrath and she glared at one of her escorts who happened to chance a look at her at the ill-timed moment. The Welshman startled with surprise. He shook his head with wonder over what he could have done to enlist such a reaction from the maid and quickly dropped back before Sir Bowen took notice, since the knight's protectiveness for his temporary ward was intense.

While her anger flamed, fed by her thoughts, the vision began to take another shape. As if she had no control over the forming scene, Richard began to make love to his paramour. The woman smiled, moaning with pleasure from his caresses. Eve groaned, troubled by her own reverie, bewildered as to why the mere thought of him should bring her mind to torment and her body warm with the remembrance of his touch. Her hand went to her middle where she felt the shape of the coins tucked in the folds of her belt and she struggled to push from her mind the reflections of the tall grey-eyed knight who had pressed them into her palm.

4

In the dream she had been walking in the field near her father's manor at Ferns. It was a warm spring day and she could feel the warmth of the sun on her face as she began running through the knee-high grass, awash with excitement as she knew that this was the day that her father would be returning from Meath. She had reached the steps of the manor, anticipating the feel of his massive arms about her in one of his welcoming bear hugs, when she had awakened.

She snuggled down into the furs and sleepily mused over the precious memories as the door opened and Bridget entered carrying a morning tray of bread and ale in her ample arms.

Not wishing to begin the day with the maid's idle chatter, Eve feigned sleep and snuggled deeper into the pillows. Smiling, Bridget set the tray next to Eve and went to the windows and threw the shutters wide. The morning sun bolted into the room and Eve grimaced, then loudly deplored the deed, to Bridget's pleased grunt.

Bridget bent before the hearth and gently stirred the banked coals until she found a small glow of red buried within. Taking a handful of dried leaves and straw from a basket on the hearth, she patiently added bits of the kindling until a minute spark caught, quickly redoubling into a tiny flame. As the fire caught, she added wood and then hung a kettle of water over the fire for Eve's toilette. She removed the washing basin from its stand, breaking the slivers of ice from its surface before tossing the contents out the window into the courtyard below. Returning the bowl to its stand she filled it with the steaming contents of the kettle, then laid a warmed towel next to it.

Eve slipped from the bed and splashed her face with the warm water as she shivered in the crisp morning air. It bit sharply through her thin chemise, encouraging her to slip hastily into a heavy woolen kirtle of pale yellow and her feet into her thick leather boots. The cut of the gown effectively hid her charms, with its close-fitting long sleeves and a collarless, high neckline clasped with a bone pin. The gown fell loosely to the hemline to swirl about the tops of her boots.

Bridget watched from the corner of her eye as she set about straightening the chambers. Eve's garment brought a deep frown from the heavy-set woman. The outmoded style had not been seen in England since old King Henry's time. Before Stephen's reign, the Empress Matilda had revolutionized her father's court by reappearing from the continent in the tight, close-fitting pelisse, which had a deep neckline and long, trailing sleeves and had remained in the height of fashion long since the Empress's return to Normandy. Bridget shook her head in mute disapproval over the affairs of her young mistress. She had been greatly dismayed when Lady Leonore, the mistress of Hertford, had given her to Eve. She feared that her very soul would be snatched by the spirits known to accompany those from that mysterious land across the Irish sea. But, when she had timidly grown to know the lass, she was touched by the open freshness of her beauty and her sweetness of spirit, something Lady Leonore refused to see. Attentive to her duties, she failed to notice when Eve snatched a piece of bread from the tray and rushed from the room. When she heard the door latch, Bridget groaned audibly.

"Oh Lordy! Lady Leonore will be snatchin' the hair from my poor head when she learns that the lass has left again!"

Gloating over her escape, Eve stepped lightly down the steps of the pentice hoping that the enclosed stairs, which ran along the outside of the castle wall, would allow her to leave without being detected. A smile touched at the corners of her mouth as she considered Leonore's fury when Bridget informed her that Eve had left the castle once more. She knew that she would have to face Leonore's wrath when she returned, but the chance to escape the morning hours with the others was well worth it.

She walked into the bright morning sunlight which had begun to melt the ice clinging to the walls of the castle. The uncertain droplets gathered into tiny streams, quickly gaining

momentum as they hastened down the mortar and cracks of
the keep. As she crossed the courtyard she turned her face to
the welcomed warmth, recalling her dream and thoughts of
home.

She entered the stable, gratified that no one was about, and,
gathering her skirts about her, she climbed into the loft where
she stretched out in the fragrant, clean straw by a window
giving her a clear view of the manor. She rolled onto her back,
enjoying the solitude as she drew in a deep breath, tasting of
the crisp morning air. A small bird hopped along a beam which
crossed the loft and she watched it with interest, envying it its
freedom. She smiled as it stopped and turned its head to look
at her curiously and then chirped as if willing to share a moment
with her from its busy morning.

"You would think that Leonore would be well contented
that I spare her my presence," she said aloud, regretting immediately that her voice had startled the bird. It flew through
the window leaving her once again alone in her thoughts.

She heaved a sigh, wondering how long she was expected
to remain at Hertford before it would be safe for her to return
home. Sir Bowen and she had arrived at Hertford just before
dusk, dusty and travel-weary from their forced ride. The lights
of the manor had beckoned a welcome respite as the Welsh
knight had lifted her from her horse and ushered her into the
great hall, the end of their journey coming as great relief to
them both. Eve had been awed by the vastness of the castle
and the enormity of the room where he led her. Unlike her
home at Ferns which was built of stone and wattle, the Norman
keep was fashioned entirely of stone. The massive cuts fitted
tightly with mortar, rising above tall, beamed ceilings to a
second floor and the crenelated parapets encircling above. She
had marveled at the fortress, its ponderous stone walls which
encircled the stronghold paling the memory of the spiked-pole
wall of Ferns, now painfully spare in comparison.

"Ahhh," she had thought, "How securely Ferns could be
defended against the likes of O'Rourke with a fortress such as
this . . ."

Her thoughts had been dismissed, the relief quickly spent,
as Leonore, who had gathered with her ladies before the evening fire, quickly established her displeasure over their unwelcomed appearance.

The mistress of Hertford had calmly placed her needlework

beside her and, rising, had folded her hands, her dark eyes gleaming with displeasure as she had ignored the timid smile from the lovely young lass standing before her. Her black hair was tinged with grey where it showed from the edges of her wimple. Her alabaster skin was beginning to show the signs of her approaching middle age by the lines at the corners of her eyes and at her mouth, which was drawn tightly as she glanced at the girl, then to the knight who was making his introductions.

"So," she interrupted snappishly, "you are really here. I had but hoped that the need would not be met and that you would be able to remain in Ireland where you belong."

Stunned, Sir Bowen's eyes blazed with anger over Leonore's cruel remark. "My Lady," he growled. "Perhaps it would be advisable if you were to summon Sir Gilbert so that I might discuss the matter with him."

"My husband is away from Hertford. He is settling business in the south and will not return for some time."

Sir Bowen's eyes narrowed at the revelation. "A message was sent of our arrival in due time. I would have thought that Sir Gilbert would have chosen to be here for the arrival of his ward."

"You are incorrect, Sir Knight, and I shall not dispute the matter with you. His business is far too important for him to come rushing home to meet with some . . . for this . . ." Leonore sniffed down her nose at Eve where she stood silently listening to the exchange.

Bowen glared coldly at Leonore, his voice becoming dangerously low. "Did you try to reach him?"

"I saw no need of it, I know my husband's mind," she snapped.

He stepped close to her, towering above her as he spoke in controlled anger, his words reaching Leonore and Eve only. "Then know my mind, woman. I have no choice but to leave her here with you as that is the order of my liege lord, though my thoughts are of another reasoning. But mark me well, you shall see that it goes gentle with her as the child is no barbarian but a gentle and noble lass. If I should hear otherwise I shall see fit to return and counsel with your husband. I know the Earl well and I do not think he would look favorably upon this meeting."

Leonore paled under the onslaught, her composure broken

by the stern regard of the massive knight. Her manner changed abruptly, becoming the perfect hostess as she ordered food and drink to be brought.

Thereafter, Leonore had been graciously generous, providing all of the comforts Hertford could offer during the knight's short stay. Eve had known that he had tarried longer than he had intended, and that it had been due to concern for her, but the morning had finally arrived when he prepared to take his leave.

She had stood at the foot of the steps to the hall when his men had made ready to mount, tears gripping at her throat as she watched his comfortingly familiar movements. A smile tugged at her lips as he bellowed in his gruff manner at those he felt were lagging. He took the reins of his destrier in hand and paused to look back where she stood waiting, looking small and vulnerable. As his brows furrowed into a disturbed frown she could contain herself no longer and she rushed across the spance, throwing herself into his arms and kissing him resoundingly on the cheek. He reddened at the demonstration but gave her a hearty squeeze in return. He looked at her tenderly for a long moment, then his eyes darted about, glowering at his men in case one of them should find the display amusing.

"Oh, Sir Bowen," she wept. "How will I ever be able to thank you for what you have done for me? I shall never forget you or your kindness!"

He grunted and paused uncomfortably as he was unable to express his feelings for the maid. "Beware of that one," he growled, gesturing his head toward the hall. "She means no good for you. If you should . . . ah . . . need anything, send word to me by my lord, Sir Robert."

She nodded and stepped back as he swung into the saddle, pausing for an instant to look at her once again, a look of regret, before he shouted to his men and rode out of her life.

Then it had begun. Eve lay there in the loft, ruminating about the ladies of Hertford as they gathered in the large chamber on the east side of the keep. They met each morning to keep company and exchange gossip while tending to their needlework, music, and other feminine pursuits, all of which bored Eve to distraction. She smiled wryly as she realized what the subject of their gossip was certain to be on this morning. She could almost hear them as they quipped in their waggish tongues over their absent member.

Katherine, the wife of one of Sir Gilbert's knights, was a tall, ash-haired young woman with a fair complexion and large brown inquisitive eyes. Under different circumstances she and Eve might have been friends but she resolutely followed Gwen's lead. Gwen. There was another matter. From their first meeting, the night of Eve's arrival, Gwen's flashing black eyes would gleam wickedly at Eve as if contemplating some malicious mischief. Eve had been stunned by the vicious verbal assaults of the young, raven-haired woman, having done nothing by her reasoning to warrant Gwen's hatred. But it did not take long for Eve to realize that Gwen's attitude was supported, if not encouraged, by her guardian. Leonore ignored her ward's taunting and encouraged Eve's treatment as a lesser member of the household. Eve was made constantly, and at first painfully, aware of the simplicity of her clothes, her plain woolen kirtles lacking in contrast to the richness of the fabrics and design of the noble women's garments. They mimicked the accent of her speech and strained to find fault with her manners until finally Eve rebelled. Outraged, her Irish pride took hold and she resolved to herself that if they were intent upon treating her as an outsider she would remain so—and gladly.

She was suddenly brought out of her thoughts by the sound of a horse entering the courtyard. She rolled over and peered out of the window. A man had ridden into the courtyard and dismounted as Sir Gilbert's steward rushed from the hall to greet him. He wore no hauberk and his leather tunic was besmeared with the soil of his travels. Eve strained to make out his features, curious as to the identity of the stranger, but was disappointed as he handed the reins to the steward and, taking the steps two at a time, disappeared into the hall.

Eve brightened in interest as there was something strangely familiar about the manner of the visitor. She climbed down from the loft and, after pausing at the stable door to brush the straw from her hair and kirtle, she lifted the skirt and dashed across the courtyard. As she entered the hall she found the man standing by the fire, a goblet of wine in his hands, conversing with Leonore, who looked up upon Eve's entrance, her brow arching with displeasure.

"There you are!" Leonore snapped.

As the young man turned, Eve gasped and a hand flew to her mouth to cover her surprise. It was as if her brother Donnell was standing before her. The same fair hair and sapphire-blue eyes, the high cheek bones and ruddy complexion. The look he returned her was warm and friendly—and laced with curiosity.

"Do not just stand there gawking, Eve! And look at you, your face is smudged! You look like a kitchen maid!"

Eve stuck out her chin defiantly, angry that Leonore would speak to her in such a manner before the stranger.

"I took a walk. It was such a beautiful morning I could not bear to be inside."

The young man broke out in a broad grin at Eve's boldness. He stepped forward, grinned roguishly at her as he nodded a greeting.

"You are new to Hertford. I am greatly indebted to Sir Gilbert that he sent me on ahead to see to the ladies' needs, for this fortunate happening has placed me full ahead of the others and first to claim your attentions!"

"Gervase!" Leonore snapped. "She is no common wench to be rutted by you, 'tho she looks the part!" Reluctantly she introduced Eve to Gervase, "She is Eve, daughter of Dermot MacMurrough."

Gervase sputtered at the announcement and his face lit with genuine surprise. "But we had no word that you had arrived, milady!" He glanced with bemusement at Leonore. "As my lord's squire, surely I would have been told!"

"I saw no reason to inform Sir Gilbert," Leonore answered tartly. "Or to call him back from his visit with Lord Severn." She noticed Gervase's speculation over Eve's appearance and scowled. "I am sure that you are fatigued by your journey and I have no need of your services at the moment." Her tone left no room for argument and to Eve's disappointment he placed his tankard on the table and bowed courteously to Leonore and Eve, then left the hall.

Two days passed before Eve saw Gervase again. Leonore had confined her to her chambers as a punishment for her disobedience—something which Eve ordinarily would not have minded quite so much except that she wanted to see Gervase again, so the time was poorly met. But on the third evening Eve was allowed to join the others in the great hall for supper. She took her place at the end of the dormant table, aware of Gervase's eyes upon her. A servant offered the washing bowl and a warmed towel to Eve and as she washed her hands she kept her eyes averted from Gervase, grateful for something to occupy the moment.

Gervase puzzled over her awkward behavior but before he could dwell upon it Gwen and Katherine descended the stairs.

"I see that 'her ladyship' has been allowed to join us this evening, Katy," Gwen cooed. "Now, perchance, we shall be provided with some amusement."

Gervase frowned at Gwen's words and he shot a look at Leonore, who seemed unperturbed by the young woman's shocking remark.

"Methinks, Gwen," asided Katherine, but in a voice loud enough to be heard at the table, "that she would prefer to take supper in her chambers, then Gervase would not observe how awkward she is in the presence of her betters."

They paused behind Eve's chair as Gwen looked at her friend with mock concern. "But think of how it must benefit her to observe our breeding and deportment, Kate! After all, we must make sacrifices for those less fortunate."

Eve stared at the table, her cheeks flushed by the taunting. Gervase shot a horrified glare at the two women, who were taking their places next to Leonore while looking quite self-satisfied by their cruel quips. Recovering from the shock, he found his tongue.

"It would seem that the Lady Eve would benefit more readily from ladies more gently deported and kinder of manner," he snapped.

Gwen flared at his words, her mouth drawing into a tight, angry line, but she quickly passed it off and smiled sweetly at the handsome squire. "Gervase, I forgive you for your speech. I realize you are newly returned to Hertford and know not of what we have had to contend. As my Lady Leonore will tell you, we have earnestly endeavored to help Eve since her arrival but are met with ungratefulness at every turn."

Gervase looked to Leonore but the mistress of Hertford busied herself with the steaming meat in the mazer held by Gaspard, apparently unconcerned by the conversation. He caught the frown that passed over the steward's face but Gaspard set the mazer on the table and hurried from the room. Gervase glanced back at Eve who sat picking at her food, looking as if she would flee the room if given the chance, and his eyes darkened with doubt.

The remainder of the evening passed uneventfully as Katherine entreated Gervase into a game of backgammon and Gwen settled by the fire with Leonore. As he played he watched over Katherine's shoulder, the reticent Eve, where she sat on the window casing, staring out into the night. He remembered the bright smile that had greeted him the morning he arrived and doubt plucked at his mind as he sought to discover the truth of what had been happening at Hertford in his absence.

The next morning Eve entered the hall to discover from Gaspard that Leonore had left the manor with Katherine and Gwen for a morning's ride. She smiled, knowing Leonore's mind. Eve relished a morning's ride over the beautiful English countryside and Leonore's intent to rob Eve of the outing was obvious. But this time she secretly pleasured at the news and was touched by the concern of the embarrassed steward.

"Gaspard, I shall enjoy walking in the gardens this morning," she assured him. "From the feel on the air I warrant that soon such pleasures will be forsworn till spring."

The flowers had disappeared with the approaching winter but the trees and shrubs emitted a fragrance of their own. The garden was like a miniature forest and Eve imagined that one could stand at its center never knowing that there was a castle nearby. She stopped at one of the small stone benches discreetly placed along the path and sat down, slipping off her uncomfortable boots. She wriggled her toes in the crisp morning air and as her mind drifted idly she rubbed her toes in the dirt of the path, tracing designs in the soil.

"Good morning, milady."

Her head came up with a start to find Gervase standing, at the edge of the clearing, leaning against a tree. She wondered how long he had been observing her actions. Her eyes followed his amused smile to her feet, which were now covered with dust, and she winced, chagrined that he had caught her in such an unseemly task.

"Please, do not be embarrassed, milady," he said, sitting down beside her. "It is I who should apologize for spying on you."

"You were spying on me?"

"Aye, but only for a moment. I saw you come into the gardens and I followed as I wished to speak with you. When I saw you here alone with your thoughts, and looking quite lovely, I was hard put to disturb the moment."

She flushed at the compliment as her gaze fell to her feet, which she quickly pulled beneath her skirt. "I am glad that you followed me, Gervase, as I too wished to speak with you."

His eyes narrowed, wondering if she would use the moment to speak ill of the others. He guessed that she had good cause but he refused to involve himself in mere squabbles of women. He would not take her part against his mistress without good reason.

"About what, milady?"

"'Tis nothing, really." She smiled. "Just that you remind me of someone."

His brow arched with surprise. "Who might that be?"

"My brother, Donnell."

He threw back his head and roared with laughter as Eve's mouth dropped open in astonishment, startled by his reaction.

"Forgive me, milady," he chortled. "But a smitten swain laments being told by a beautiful maid that he reminds her of her brother!"

His eyes rolled with the jest, bringing giggles from Eve. He marveled at how fetching she looked when she laughed.

"I beg you accept my apology if I offended you," she smiled. "But I was watching you from . . . when you arrived. At first I was sure that it was Donnell, come to fetch me home. That is why I so rudely appeared in the hall while you conversed with Leonore."

He noticed the wistful look as she spoke. "Are you so sad at heart for your home?" he asked gently.

"Aye," she answered, swallowing back the tears.

He saw the moisture in her eyes and grew alarmed, panicked at the possibility that she might start to cry. "Tell me," he hastened. "Have things been well for you here? Have you everything you need?" His eyes passed over her coarse, outmoded kirtle to her heavy boots.

"Aye," she answered, blinking back the tears. "My needs are met."

He cleared his throat and pursued the question. "I am puzzled by what I observed last night. Do Gwen and Katy always behave thus?"

"Perhaps they feel that they have their reasons," she smiled. "My father always said that when my ire was up my temper was something to reckon with."

"I saw no evidence of it."

She shrugged, not knowing how to reply. She looked away from him, missing the look of understanding he returned.

"Well, milady," he said cheerfully, "now that I have returned we shall have to do something to allay your sadness!"

Gervase was as good as his word, and his attention to the lovely Eve served to enrage Gwen who used every opportunity

to demonstrate her jealousy and spitefulness. Leonore endeavored to account for as much of Gervase's time as possible,
taking it out on Eve in full measure when the young squire
managed to spend time with her.

Gervase was hard put to understand their attitude toward
the maid as he found her refreshingly open and honest, her
manner and bearing beyond reproach. In fact, he was enchanted
by her. If he had only been more worldly in the ways of women
he would have known that this was exactly what rankled the
fair Gwen. Bewildered to how he should handle the women,
he found himself looking eagerly forward to Sir Gilbert's return.

5

ir Gilbert and his retinue arrived at the end of the week. They clattered into the courtyard before dawn, having ridden through the night in their eagerness to be home. Eve sprang from her bed at the sound of the disturbance and rushed to the window, disappointed that the view afforded her only a small section of the courtyard over the parapet of the lower tower. She could hear male voices shouting orders to the servants and laughter carrying over the bedlam in weary good humor over their homecoming. She snatched up a gown and began pulling it over her head as the door opened. Bridget hesitated, then closed the door quickly behind her.

"I thought that you might decide to see what the fuss was about, milady, so I came straightaway. It won't do, it just won't do." She straightened the covers of the bed and motioned for Eve to return. "I will not have my lady appearing at dawn before the men with sleep still in her eyes! Now back to bed with ye."

Seeing that Eve's intent was to ignore the request, she planted herself firmly before her, her hands akimbo on her broad hips. Eve sulked as her eyes fixed on the door.

"I just wanted to see..."

"I know what ye be wanting to do, milady," Bridget interrupted. "And I'll be having none of it! I've been quiet these many weeks though it is the devil I catch from Lady Leonore when you have your way. Now I insist. When ye meet the gentlemen you'll be meeting them fit and proper, not like a servant girl. Now, back to bed with ye."

Disappointed, Eve found herself meekly tucked beneath the covers.

She awoke late in the morning to the sound of Bridget bustling about the room and immediately recalled the excitement of the dawn. Stretching contentedly, she sat up and hooked her arms about her knees. As Bridget poured the hot water from the kettle in Eve's bath, she glanced up and caught the bright, expectant look in Eve's green eyes.

"The gentlemen are abed, milady. It was a long night for them to be sure. You'll not be meeting them until later in the day. But," she added, glancing at Eve from the corner of her eye, "Lady Leonore would be greatly pleased if you were to appear in the morning chamber with the other ladies."

Eve bristled because she well understood the implication. So, she thought, blackmail! Unless she was to abide by Leonore's bidding, she would be kept virtually a prisoner! Pouting, she sat back in the pillows and considered the alternatives.

On this particular morning the attention in the morning chamber was focused on a fair-haired young woman who had traveled to Hertford with Sir Gilbert. She was small-boned and slender. Her fine features held fair brows and large soft eyes which were accentuated by the severe wimple of starched linen she wore, her flaxen hair hanging loosely down her back from beneath the short headpiece. Her gown was of the finest blue silk, matching the color of her eyes, and fit closely about her slender waist. Her father's lands lay to the south, Lord Severn having been friends of the deClare family since the time of William the Conqueror.

"Wait, wait!" she laughed. "You are both talking so quickly that I cannot understand a word!"

Gwen waved her hand at Katherine. "Let me tell her. You always fail to remember the details! Lavinia, you will not believe the manner of the maid! She is completely impossible!" Reading the doubt in Lavinia's eyes she became more insistent. "'Tis truth, her manner is coarse and she speaks with the most appalling accent! Why, consider even now—does she prefer learning her art with the needle, or music? Nay, rather she would spend her days alone in the forest. Lord only knows what she does there! But, whatever it is, you can be most assured that it is something to deplore!"

Lavinia's lovely face shadowed. "Gwen, whatever are you talking about?"

"It is true, Lavinia," Katherine said. "It is said that they believe in frightful things! I have heard that the spirits of wood nymphs and evil forms, little people, wait in the trees and take revenge upon their enemies! That must be why she spends so much time alone in the forest!" she added smugly.

"Oh Katherine!" laughed Lavinia. "You do not really believe that!"

"You would be well to do so, Lavinia," assured Gwen. "Why, Father Petrus was quite disturbed when he learned that she was to foster here. Everyone knows that the church has long had difficulties in Ireland!"

"Gwen," Lavinia sighed, "had you quizzed the good father, you would have found that the difficulties of the Church in Ireland stem not from the people's belief of Druids, but rather in their politics and customs. On the matter of religion the Church has been quite successful."

As if on cue, the door opened and Eve entered, the skirt of her kirtle swaying defiantly as she approached the group, but she stopped short as she spied the unexpected visitor. Katherine and Gwen exchanged glances, then looked expectantly at Lavinia, satisfied at her shocked expression over Eve's appearance. Eve felt self-conscious, knowing the other to be a lady of some refinement. From the looks on the faces of Gwen and Katherine she knew that she was expected to make a fool of herself in front of the visitor and it made her instantly resentful.

"Lavinia," Gwen giggled. "This is Eve."

Lavinia shot a stern look at Gwen but Gwen's eyes were planted on Eve with a decided gloat.

"Please, Eve," Lavinia said kindly, patting the stool next to hers, "sit here by me."

Eve walked past the group, averting her eyes from Lavinia's, to sit on the hearth. Ignoring them, she chose an apple from a small bowl next to her and began munching on it.

"You arrived much before you were expected, Eve," Lavinia offered. "Sir Gilbert has been visiting with us at Lighthurst, but had he known that you had arrived I am certain that he would have been here to greet you. I too would have enjoyed that pleasure."

Eve paused as she bit from the apple and looked at Lavinia doubtfully. The young woman's manner was friendly and warm but Eve could not help but to judge her by past experiences.

Was she toying with her? She glanced at Gwen and Katherine
and caught the sharp looks of annoyance that passed between
them. Uncertain, Eve looked back to Lavinia and a small spark
of hope began to kindle. She had dismayed at the possibility
of finding a friend her own age at Hertford but there was
something about Lavinia that now made her wonder.

"Is your manor far from Hertford?" she asked.

"It lies just south of London," Lavinia answered. "Perhaps,
someday, you might consider visiting us at Lighthurst. It has
been quite lonely there the past few years and I would truly
enjoy the company of another woman."

"Oh, Lavinia, really . . ." Gwen began.

"Quiet, Gwen," Lavinia said sharply without looking at the
raven-haired woman. "Please, Eve, tell me about your home.
I was fortunate to visit Wexford years ago with my father. I
recall how beautiful your country was, the little I was able to
see of it."

Eve suppressed a smile as her doubts about Lavinia faded.
She could feel Gwen's resentment as she and Lavinia, two
newly-found friends, soon became engaged in a warm and
friendly conversation, all but excluding both Katherine and
Gwen, much to the latter's dismay. Gwen glared at them, then
her surly gaze darted to Katherine, who merely shrugged and
turned her attention to her needlework. Annoyed, she picked
up the lace she had been embroidering and set to the task,
trying to ignore the now happy chatter of the other two.

"Ouch!" A finger flew to Katherine's mouth as she pricked
it with her needle.

"'Twould seem that your thoughts are not on your work,
Katherine," Gwen smirked. "Could it be that they lie in another
part of the castle?"

Katherine sighed wistfully, "Yea, Edward took to bed with
the men upon his return as he feared to awaken me at such an
unseemly hour. I sorely miss him. It was naught of sleepless-
ness that I tossed and turned in my bed through the night."

Lavinia's brow raised at Katherine's words and she angered
over Edward's thoughtlessness. It was common knowledge that
Edward's eye roamed beyond his marriage bed and it did not
set well that he refrained from seeking the warmth of his young
wife's bed upon his return from a long absence. She feared
that Katherine's naiveness was sure to lead her to sorrow.

"Of that I am certain," teased Gwen. "Your tenseness has

been apparent these past weeks! Many was the time I feared it would be necessary to bid a swift rider to Lighthurst to fetch Edward home!"

"Look to yourself, Gwen," Katherine countered. "I think that the ride you seek is not that of a spirited mare of a morning over the countryside. I have seen your gaze staring wistfully to the south from the window of your chamber, and heard your sighs as your eyes closed in dreaming."

Gwen's eyes danced wickedly, "Aye, I do not deny it. This manor has been too long without the comfort of men. What of you, Lavinia? Has your travel to Hertford been truly for our company or because you could not bear to part with the company we seek? You would not be blamed. If Richard were my betrothed I would not trust him to be free from my sight!"

"Richard cannot be trusted when he is in sight!" Katy parried, breaking the two young women into laughter.

"Richard is not my betrothed, Gwen," Lavinia answered firmly. "He is like a brother to me. I could never look upon him as a lover."

"Nonsense, any woman would look upon Richard as a lover if he were to just turn his eye in her direction. Besides, it has always been expected that the two of you would marry."

Eve's head had jerked up at the mention of a name so recently connected to her past. They should meet *her* Richard, she thought. Pompous, insufferable, rude. She shook her head to clear it and took an almost spiteful bite of the apple. HER Richard? Indeed! What an incredibly distasteful thought! She half-listened to the conversation as the women continued to enroll the godlike qualities of their mystical Richard and she began musing in spite of herself. If only it were possible that such a man could exist, she thought. I could love such a man. Pah, she thought and grimaced. Impossible. No man is that perfect.

"Nay, Gwen!" Lavinia insisted, the tone of her voice bringing Eve's attention back to the conversation. "Richard is not for me. He has never looked upon me in that way. I know that there was a time, years ago, when it was understood . . . But Strongbow and my father would not expect us to enter a loveless union. The matter has been long since closed and I have accepted it. I treasure Richard's friendship far more than a marriage which would not be based on mutual desire."

"You are foolish, Lavinia! I would take Richard on any

terms, and make him love me!" Gwen's eyes gleamed. "Aye, if a woman were to play her cards well she could make him love her."

Whatever Lavinia would have said in reply was lost as the door opened and Leonore swept in, accompanied by Gervase and two other men. There was no question as to the identity of one, a dark-haired, tall knight with rather effeminate features. Katherine flew from her chair, spilling her needlework over the floor as she rushed into his waiting arms.

The older man was richly dressed and noble in bearing. His dark hair was touched with grey at the temples and his eyes held no hint of kindness as they held Eve's for a long moment before he motioned for her to stand. She rose, feeling suddenly timid under his stern regard.

"Is this the lass?" He scowled at Leonore, never taking his eyes from Eve.

"Aye, milord, 'tis she," sighed Leonore to her husband.

A greying brow arched in displeasure as his eyes moved slowly over Eve. "Your father should have advised us of your arrival."

Eve glanced with surprise at Leonore but the older woman avoided her questioning look.

"I fear that my lady gives disquieting news," he continued. "I expect a young woman of my household to behave in a seemly manner according to her station and my position. And, as for this . . ." He gestured angrily, indicating her appearance, as he looked to Leonore for the answer. "Is she to appear as a serving wench or woman of the village? What is the object, milady?"

Leonore threw up her palms in exasperation, "Nay, milord, do not look to me! It is through no lack of effort on my part. The maid chooses her own manner of dress by her very behavior. Would I provide her with apparel for a maid gently born when she behaves as a wild thing, refusing all that I would offer by way of instruction?"

Gilbert looked back to Eve, his eyes narrowing speculatively, "Is this true?"

Eve swallowed hard, forcing back her anger and humiliation, as all eyes in the room were turned upon her. Raising her gaze she tensed, not from the angry glare of Sir Gilbert, nor the smugness of Gwen and Leonore, but from the open lear of Edward's face. She felt her cheeks burn at his lusty stare, even before his wife, whom he held at his side. Pulling her eyes from his, she looked at Sir Gilbert boldly.

"Aye, milord. It would not be unfounded to say the choice is mine. It has never occurred to me to wear other than I would in Erin."

"Damoiselle, you shall not choose to do so here!" he snapped, causing Eve to wince. "I will have no maid under my care behave in such a manner! You shall obey Lady Leonore in all that she requests of you and cease defying those who have sought to befriend you! I warn you, do not appear before me again until you are properly attired or you will find yourself engaged in a pursuit that befits what you attempt to represent!"

Eve's chin quivered and her eyes filled with tears under the onslaught. Gervase had stepped forward, his expression filled with concern and empathy for Eve, but before he could come to her defense Sir Gilbert spun angrily about and strode from the room. Leonore choose the moment to enjoin the attack.

"Eve, you have brought this upon yourself . . ."

Her words were checked by a glare of hatred from the Irish maid, who, tears beginning to stream down her lovely face, backed away toward the door, until she turned and ran from the room, caring for nothing but escape.

Lavinia called after her, then looked with consternation at the others. She was startled by the look of disgust on Gervase's face. He glanced at Leonore before fixing his disapproving gaze upon Gwen, who wore a most satisfied smile.

Lavinia's brows knitted into a puzzled frown, then slowly a gleam of understanding began to appear in her lovely blue eyes.

"Gervase," she said, "this has proved quite unsettling. Would you be so kind as to accompany me on a walk in the garden?"

"Aye," he nodded eagerly. "I would enjoy that, milady. This room has suddenly become quite close."

Eve flew down the hall and into the courtyard, thinking only of reaching the castle walls and the serenity of the forest beyond. Blinded by tears, she darted headlong beneath the massive iron portcallis of the keep, unaware of the two figures approaching from the opposite direction. The wind was almost knocked from her as she thudded sharply into the tallest of them. His arms went instinctively about her before the impact threw her against the wall. As he swung her about to regain his balance, she found herself staring into surprised grey eyes.

"You!" she gasped. Her green eyes, illuminated by the tears, grew the more at the sight of him. But her stunned amazement was none greater than his own.

"Eve!" he murmured incredulously. "What strange twists of the gods has brought you to Hertford?"

His companion, a huge, burly knight with a fierce black beard and coal black eyes, looked from one to the other with interest.

"You know this wench, Richard?" His eyes swept over Eve with open regard, his appreciation of her attributes apparent in his gaze. "By the truth, Leonore's choice of wenches has improved!"

She glanced at the speaker, then back to Richard, who studied her carefully with a guarded look of concern. She puzzled at the look but her attention was again gained by the other.

"Well, Richard," he boomed. "Where do you come by knowing the lass? Has Leonore unwittingly brought her from Claresta? You, by Satan's wisdom, would know best on that matter!"

"Nay, the lass and I met but briefly a long time past." He paused with a smile. "But the memory of her remains fixed in my mind."

The large knight grunted in appreciation but Eve stared at Richard in wonder at his statement. "But, Richard, why do you say thus when you know that it has only been..."

Her protest was cut short. Richard, seeing her intent, scowled blackly and silenced her comment by swinging his head down to cover her mouth with his own. No warning being given, it took her a moment to realize what was happening. When it registered, the shock over seeing him again fled and the remembrance of a forgotten anger rushed to her senses. She fought him as a muffled scream escaped in an angry squeal and her arms struggled to free themselves from the iron grip that held them to her sides.

Her squirming caused the older knight to guffaw merrily, "Richard, I think you have found a true vixen, full of the devil's own spirit! 'Tis likely more than you can handle. Perhaps it would be better if I were to take the chore!"

Richard raised his head slowly while his arms still secured her tightly against him. His eyes were frigid as they peered into hers, giving her a warning glance that commanded her words to her throat. It suddenly dawned on her as she looked into those iron, grey eyes that his kiss had not been of lust, but of silence! Reading recognition in her own, he relaxed slightly.

"Nay, you old windbag," he countered with a lightness that surprised her. "The day will not see the dawn when I must ask you for help in such matters! Get you to the kitchens where Gilbert's fat cook will better suit your needs."

The knight chuckled appreciatively while Richard held Eve's eyes with his own. As he had spoken his eyes had softened to a warmth that seemed to reach deep inside of her. She felt her legs grow weak while a warmth spread over her loins and breasts pressed tightly against his hard body and her memory returned to a tender, lost moment deep within a forest. As he beheld her bewildered look, his eyes began to sparkle and his mouth twitched as if fighting a smile.

"So," he murmured for her hearing only. "The time has come when I may hold you quietly in my arms."

His words brought her to her senses and she shrieked in outrage, flinging herself from him. His hands went out to catch her but she spun, digging her heel into his soft boot, making him grunt in pain and reach for the offended member. She lost no time in grabbing up her skirt and sprinting from the portal toward the safety of the wood.

As Richard glared, his companion doubled up in laughter, finally having to lean against the wall of the gate to steady himself.

"Go ahead and laugh, my friend," Richard growled as he wiggled the circulation back into his foot. "The moment won was well worth the outcome."

He glanced in the direction of the fleeing maid, knowing the full weight of his words. He cast a troubled look after her as he considered the unexpected problem of finding her here. He meant her no harm, in truth he was attracted to her, but she held knowledge dangerous to him and all who were loyal to him.

The knight rubbed the tears of laughter from his eyes with the back of his hand. "Richard, from what I observed I warrant you are right."

Richard limped a few steps, much to the amusement of his companion, who had the good sense to suppress a smile. But, as they walked, the knight watched Richard from the corner of his eye and his manner changed.

"Richard, we must talk. Hertford is abuzz with stories of your behavior of late. This morning is just an example. Had I not fetched you from the tavern you would have made no attempt to see to your duties. You have strained Gilbert to the end of his patience and now enlist support for him from the others. Your disappearance from Lighthurst caused great embarrassment to Lord Severn yet you refuse to answer for your actions." The hurt in the knight's voice was apparent as he continued. "You refuse to justify them, even to me, and without leave you even took my mount!"

Richard sighed wearily, unwilling to speak on the matter even to his friend. "Enough, Warwick. I am in no temper for lectures this morning."

"Enough? God's breath!" Warwick halted in his steps, a deep red anger creeping up his neck. "You are in no mood for lectures? You are a squire on the verge of losing your chance to spurs and you treat it as if it were a worrisome insect annoying you! You are still my responsibility and I will not allow you to treat it as nothing!"

Richard halted, realizing that he had gone too far, even with Warwick. He reached out a hand and laid it on Warwick's arm.

"Forgive me, my friend, as my mind was elsewhere. Believe me, I do not minimize the importance of what you say. I know your words to be true, and in my best interest, and I take them to heart. I cannot explain but I ask you to trust me, though I have done nothing to warrant it. I will talk with you of this someday, to that I swear."

He held his breath as Warwick ran his fingers through his unruly mane, his face still dark and foreboding. Pushing away Richard's hand he swore under his breath and strode on without another word. Richard let out his breath, deeply relieved that the matter, at least for the moment, had been dropped.

As they passed before the hall Gervase came swiftly down the steps toward them, calling for them to halt. He looked nervously at Warwick, then to Richard before stammering, "The master-of-the-sword does not require Richard on the jousting field this morning. My Lord Gilbert has requested that he meet with him in the hall before mid-meal."

Warwick glanced at Richard, scowling at the news. "Tell milord Gilbert that he will be there."

As Gervase disappeared back into the hall Warwick shook his head and rubbed the back of his neck, "Let us hope, Richard, that it is not too late for your reformation. It would seem that your cousin would have a word with you. Let us hope that it is not his final word."

"Indeed," Richard muttered with a frown, glancing in the direction of the portal.

* * *

Richard descended the stairs to the hall. He had bathed and changed into a light blue linen knee-length tunic over a white chainse and dark blue woolen chausses, with a gold belt girdling his narrow waist. He ran his fingers through his damp hair, his jaw tightening with distaste over the coming event.

Sir Gilbert stood before the fire with Warwick and Gervase, each holding a tankard of ale in sullen silence. Warwick sat on the edge of the dormant table and stared into his tankard as the others looked up upon Richard's entrance.

"Good day, Gilbert, and to you, Gervase," said Richard as he poured himself a tankard from the pitcher on the table. Gervase nodded in greeting while Gilbert only grunted, turning to the fire as if to compose his thoughts.

"It is not a good day, Richard," Gilbert answered grimly. "It is an unpleasant task I perform this morning."

Richard leaned a hip on the table, pulling a leg beneath him as he drank from his tankard, and studying Gilbert carefully over the rim.

"Richard, I do not pretend to understand your behavior of late. To be truthful I have no desire to understand it, as there is no excuse to be given. You bring shame upon the deClare name. You are a squire whose responsibility it is to prepare himself for the glory and honor of knighthood, yet you spurn and stomp upon the opportunity. You are away from the manor, without leave, when it suits you; you miss chapel when Father Petrus would enlighten your soul, and God knows you need it; and you reject the purity you would gain at this important time by frequenting, at every good chance, Claresta and her harlots at the tavern. Your pleasures seem to be more important to you than the vows you are about to take. What have you to say for yourself?"

Richard did not take his eyes from his tankard as he spoke in a low voice, "Is that all you wished to speak to me about?"

"All?" Gilbert sputtered. "All? Is that not enough?"

Richard hid a smile, then looked up at Gilbert and answered him in a voice that showed no contriteness, "You have taken the words spoken about and deemed them to be truth. I shall not dignify them with a denial. You will believe what you will."

"Blood of the gods!" roared Gilbert. He spun his back to Richard, his hand going to his head as if to control his anger.

"And you would push me to make an end to your future!" His eyes darted wildly about the hall as if hoping to see the answer written on the walls and finally he seemed to study the flickering flames of the fire. The room was bathed in silence until Gilbert, apparently once again in control, turned to look at Richard squarely. Richard returned the look unflinchingly as Gilbert spoke in an even, controlled voice.

"Aye, you are of my blood. Strongbow will be here soon and I grieve for his sake, as well as your gentle mother's, to tell him that his son will not wear spurs as given from me. For that reason, and no other, I shall give you another chance. But, and mark my words carefully, Richard, if you fail in your responsibility, even one more time, I shall send you from here to make your own way without the honors and protection knighthood will give you. From now to the day of your vows you will be the supreme example of the squire under petition, do you understand?"

Richard nodded and the two looked at each other. Their eyes locked in unspoken challenge as Warwick could be heard to let out his breath as if he had been holding it the entire time.

At that moment a rustle was heard at the far end of the hall and four pairs of eyes turned upon a small, slender form who had entered from the kitchens and was attempting to cross to the stairs undetected. Gilbert, whose anger was far from abated, turned on the maid.

"I told you not to appear before me again as a common slut! I see that you choose to stretch my patience to its limits, woman!"

Richard shot a look at Gilbert and turned a puzzled eye back to Eve where she stood frozen to the spot. Gervase stepped forward, determined to intercede for her where he had not had the opportunity earlier. He leaned over to the Earl and his story tumbled out in a muffled voice, unheard by the others. Eve strained to hear what was being said but her effort was to no avail. She could not flee as Gilbert's eyes remained riveted on her as Gervase spoke. She was relieved, however, when his face softened and she glanced about, noticing Richard for the first time. Her back stiffened and she returned his regard with an angry flash of her eyes, filled with contempt and utter disgust.

She nearly jumped out of her skin as Gilbert bellowed in anger, looking first to Gervase in disbelief, then back to her.

"My lady," he sputtered, "Gervase has told me a story that should have been told to me by you! Why did you not confide in me when I confronted you this morning?"

Eve lowered her eyes, nonplussed by the question. "You did not give me the opportunity, milord," she answered in a small voice.

Gilbert coughed while the others fought to hide their amusement, turning their attentions to the tankards in their hands.

"It is so. I apologize for that. But the problem no longer exists. You are part of my family for as long as you are here and you shall be treated accordingly. No daughter of nobility shall be treated as less beneath my roof."

Upon Gilbert's words she noticed that Richard's look had changed to one of astonishment and his eyes now regarded her with open wonder. The dumbstruck look encouraged her greatly and she drew herself up. Elated by the change in events, her quick wit came to the surface.

"My Lord," she queried sweetly, "Gervase I have had the pleasure of meeting, but would you be so kind as to introduce me to the others of your company?"

"Aye, milady, forgive me for ill manners." He gestured casually to Warwick, whom he noticed was strangely silent. "May I present Warwick deSheffield, knight to my uncle, Earl of Striguil and Pembroke, and my cousin, Richard deClare, his squire and ward."

She started upon learning that Richard was but a squire. Her mind rushed back to the visage of a man of power and authority. Her brow knitted with a bemused frown as she wondered at the mystery. Slowly, a small gleam entered those emerald orbs as she flushed with secret delight. The look of warning he had given her at the portal took on new meaning, bringing with it the knowledge that she could bring him cowering to his knees and within her power. But, if she had expected him to grovel before her, his eyes to plead with her across the span between them, she found that she was sorely disappointed.

His eyes left hers to travel slowly over the length of her slender form, then back up to her face. He smiled and gave her, unseen by the others, a huge wink.

Flabbergasted, she gawked at him and began to tremble with rage and confusion. She stammered her excuses to Sir Gilbert, anxious to rid herself of this bold, infuriating man's presence. She turned on her heels and ascended the steps of the hall as rapidly as possible without breaking into a run, unaware of the fetching picture she presented to Richard's appreciative regard.

6

Eve slammed the door behind her and looked wildly about the room for something to vent her petulance upon. Cousin to Sir Gilbert and a squire besides! Her memory was vivid with the way he had looked at her in the hall. Those damnable grey eyes! Lit with amusement and raking her body as if mentally undressing her before the others! Her entire body was shivering with rage as she grasped the dressing table and bit her lower lip in an effort to calm herself. Glancing into the small silvered mirror on the table she caught her reflection and grimaced. There were smudges on her cheeks and nose which she rubbed angrily. The discovery didn't add to her mood as she realized, with mortification, the picture she must have presented to him in the hall!

His sudden reappearance had made her realize what she had tried so hard to deny: that the memory of those two days with him had never been far from her thoughts. Like a phantom he would enter her mind when she least expected it, dwelling there, taunting her with the memory of haunting grey eyes, changing from a pale tenderness to a dark anger with his moods. Her very dreams would betray her, the episode by a fog-shrouded campfire replaying itself over and over, because he had stirred a bittersweet awakening of her emotions. But, though often tormented, she had comforted herself with the knowledge that she would never see him again. In time, she had been certain, the memories would dissolve.

Upon leaving him at the portal she had rushed headlong to

the quiet glade that had become a place of sanctuary, a respite from the biting tongues of the women. Reaching it, shaken, she had been able to calm herself and, with clear, controlled reason, face the shock of seeing him. Recalling the discussion between Gwen and Lavinia she had decided that he must be a knight to Lord Severn. The answer had seemed simple: she would make her way back to her bedchamber, undetected, there to remain until Lord Severn returned with his party to Light-hurst.

Eve jumped from the chair and strode to the window, only to turn away to pace the room. He would be living here! She would be forced to see him every day! Her thoughts were halted by a light tapping at the door and she whirled upon it, her eyes flaring as she dared anyone else to disturb her. "What is it?"

The door opened and Lavinia entered timidly, her gentle blue eyes wide with a question. Seeing Eve's distress she shook her head and her voice was soft with apology. "Eve, I am sorry for what happened this morning. Sir Gilbert was quite cruel, he never should have said those things to you. Really, it is quite unlike him. He is a kind man, but he does not understand what has been happening. But I do know and I assure you that he will soon be informed of it."

"He already knows," Eve said tightly. She was curious about the large linen-wrapped bundle Lavinia was carrying. "What is that?"

"It is the manner in which to put Leonore and the others in their place." Lavinia smiled conspiratorially. She crossed to the bed and laid the bundle down. "Open it!"

Eve peered at it doubtfully, glanced at Lavinia, who seemed barely able to contain her excitement, and then slowly unwrapped it. Within the wrappings lay an exquisite pelisse of luxurious hunter-green velvet, a fine woven chemise of sheer linen, white silk hose, and tawny-colored house slippers of the softest leather. Eve stared stupefied at the articles, then glanced up at Lavinia with her mouth agape.

"Well?" Lavinia said expectantly. "Do you like them?"

"They are beautiful," she breathed. "Are they yours?"

Lavinia rolled her eyes with exasperation. "They are yours, ninny!"

"Mine?" Eve stared back at the garments. "Ohhh. Nay, I cannot!"

"Do they not please you?"

"I will not accept charity as if I were a foundling, Lavinia. You must return them to the one for whom they were made. My own garments suit me well enough!"

Lavinia sighed and sat on the edge of the bed. "Is that where the trouble lies? Oh Eve, do you not know? Gilbert had them made for you. That is why he was so angered when he saw you."

"Then it is still charity, Lavinia," Eve said tartly. "It changes nothing! Besides, they are much too costly."

"Listen to me! Aye, they are costly, but the price was paid by one you cannot deny! Sir Gilbert ordered them made on the request of your father and the price was set before the commission!"

"My father?" Eve was completely dumbfounded.

"Aye," Lavinia grinned. "And much more. An entire wardrobe was prepared for you." Her mouth twisted into a wry smile. "That is why Leonore was so displeased when you came— her intent was to keep it all for Gwen. Fortunately, that one could not resist bragging to me of it."

"A wardrobe?"

"Trunks. Oh, and there is something else," she brightened. "But you shall see it in good time."

"But why? I do not understand. It is not like my father to be so free with a coin."

Lavinia shrugged. "I cannot guess to know your father's mind. Perchance he thought that your needs would be different here."

At that moment Bridget entered, her arms full of mysterious objects. Full of business, Bridget nodded briefly to them, then motioned to the open doorway. Two serving lads entered carrying buckets of steaming water which they poured into the tub, then they departed. Without ado, Lavinia and Bridget set about stripping Eve of her garments and ushered her to the waiting tub. Bridget began scrubbing the flabbergasted Eve with enthusiastic vigor. Eve was humiliated at being washed by someone else, but Bridget seemed not to notice. She tackled Eve's hair, humming to herself as she lathered it, working until it shone. Lavinia searched among the fragrances Bridget had brought and, nodding happily, she passed a soft lilac fragrance beneath Eve's nose and proceeded to scent the water lightly. After rinsing her with a pail of warm water from the hearth, Bridget received Eve with a large fresh cloth as she stepped from the tub, rubbing her briskly until her skin glowed with a rosy pink hue.

The sheer linen chemise of snowy white was pulled over her head. It fell to just above her ankles and Eve marveled at the soft garments as it felt like heaven against her skin. They sat her at the dressing table and Bridget brushed Eve's hair to silk, then she stood back with Lavinia as the two of them pursed their lips in careful study.

"It must be special," Lavinia observed, lifting a lock of the silky mass. "Her hair is beautiful. It must be shone to its full advantage."

Bridget took a handful, lifting it to the top of Eve's head. "Perhaps if we were to put it up, with garlands."

"Nay." Lavinia shook her head. "It should be down."

"Down?!" said Bridget. "Without a wimple, milady? 'Tis not decent!"

Eve glanced in the mirror at Lavinia, whose hair peeked from beneath the hem of her wimple.

"Tell me, Eve," Lavinia mused. "In Ireland do you wear your hair always in braids?"

"Aye, nearly always...except..." She brightened, then jumped up from the stool and rushed to her trunk where she threw back the lid and riffled through her belongings until, at the bottom, she extracted a small package wrapped in wool. She laid it in Lavinia's expectant hands.

"These were my mother's, though I've never worn them."

Lavinia gently unwrapped the treasured package and found two breathtakingly beautiful disks of about four inches in diameter, wrought of gold in the finest workmanship she had ever seen.

"They are lovely," she whispered. "How are they worn?"

Beaming with pleasure over Lavinia's reaction, Eve took them and, pulling back her hair, she clamped them over her temples and ears, where they held back her tresses so that they fell down her back in soft waves and ringlets.

"Oh, they are lovely!" Lavinia gasped, clasping her hands happily. The disks highlighted the luster of Eve's hair and made her large, green, heavily-lashed eyes seem even larger.

Bridget looked doubtful and while she begrudgingly admired the effect, there was a strong hint of disapproval in her voice. "But, milady, her hair is not covered."

"It will be fine, Bridget. We will not be going out of doors and besides, she looks perfectly lovely!"

They helped Eve into her stockings, then dropped the pelisse over her head as she wiggled into the sleeves. The inseam of the sleeves hung to the hem of the skirt and the bodice was cut low to reveal a little of the delicate chemise and not a small amount of her rounded white breasts. The velvet was cut narrow at the waist, smoothing over her slender hips before flaring out into a full skirt which almost brushed the floor, accentuating Eve's full curves.

Eve rubbed her palms over the soft fabric, marveling at its feel, until she suddenly dismayed, "But I have no girdle!"

Lavinia smiled as if she contained a great secret. She motioned to Bridget, who retreated to the table where she had deposited her burdens. Bridget brought forth a small casket, which she set on the table as Eve glanced at Lavinia with bewilderment.

"I told you there was something else, now you shall have it. This too is from your father, with much love I would surmise."

Eve slowly opened the lid to the elegant little box and gasped as she beheld its contents. It was filled with treasures of fine Irish gold: rings, necklaces or torcs, armlets, dress fasteners, a filigree girdle of gold links and, lastly, a small dagger in a golden sheath inset with precious stones. She lifted it lovingly from its resting place, turning it over in her hands as she thought of the one who had placed it there.

Lavinia bent over her, her voice gentle as she beheld the treasures. "These too, would be my guess, had belonged to your mother."

Eve nodded, her eyes misting with tears as she fastened the delicate girdle about her waist and hung the dagger from it. The thoughts of both women were the same as they imagined the moment when Dermot had presented the dagger to his wife. Its sharpness attested to the fact that it was not meant for mere ornamentation. Lavinia stepped back and studied the effect. She sobered instantly, awestruck by her own handiwork.

"You are beautiful!" she breathed. "There is not a swain below who will not be dumbstruck by the sight of you!"

Bridget, for once, was silent. She started to snivel, grabbing the corner of her apron to dab the tears from her eyes. "Aye, milady, 'tis true. I fear I shall have to sleep on a pallet at yon door to keep the lads from ye!"

Eve blushed at the compliment and turned to see herself in the mirror. Even for one who had been raised without vanity she was not a little pleased to see the image reflected there. She turned one way, then another, amazed at the transformation she beheld. Why had her father done it? He had never been one to care about another's opinion, regardless of what Lavinia had suggested. But, like most women everywhere, the feel of new and beautiful clothes heightened her spirits and gave her a fresh, undaunted outlook. The color of the gown brought out the vibrant green of her eyes, which she now turned happily to the others. Lavinia smiled at the pleasure she read there and dismissed Bridget, with thanks. She poured a goblet of spiced wine for them both. As they stood sipping it they could hardly keep from giggling as their eyes caught.

"Lavinia, there is no question about it, she will captivate them."

Eve spun about to find Richard leaning against the door-jamb, his arms crossed casually across his chest as he observed the proceedings.

"Richard, what are you doing here?" Lavinia asked, taking the very words from Eve but with a tenderness Eve did not feel. Lavinia crossed to him and he placed an arm lazily about her waist as he brushed her cheek with a brotherly kiss.

"I came to take her to dinner."

"How nice!" Lavinia smiled, returning Richard's hug. "I cannot think of a handsomer escort!"

"You cannot?" Richard smiled down at her, then chuckled at the blush that crept up Lavinia's cheeks. "There is another waiting for you in the hall who grows more impatient with each moment."

She laughed happily and brushed off his teasing with a wave of her hand but her deepening blush confirmed that he had struck home.

"Lavinia," Eve stammered as she avoided looking at Richard. "I do not wish to have an escort..."

"Nonsense, Eve," Lavinia smiled. "Now that the men have returned it would really be quite unsuitable for you to attend mid-meal without one! How fortunate that Richard appeared just at this moment! It was really quite thoughtful of you, Richard, particularly now..." She smiled conspiratorially and stepped by him to the doorway where she turned and glanced back at Eve, giving her a happy wink as she left.

Dismayed, Eve started to call after her but the words died in her throat as she realized it was too late. She stiffened, facing the disarming fact that she and Richard were alone.

"What are you doing here?" she flared.

"I told you." He smiled, stepping into the room. "I came to take you to mid-meal."

"I do not want to go with you, there are anywhere else."

"Would you rather be with Edward?" he asked calmly, stopping to pick up a golden torc from the opened jewel casket. "He has been looking for you. I think he is quite enamored with you, Eve. And he has not even seen you as you are now."

"Edward?" She blinked. "But he is married!"

"He only wishes you for a dinner partner," he observed. He glanced up at her with a roguish grin. "Or so he says."

He laid the torc back into the casket and sat on the edge of the table, his eyes moving over her in careful study. "You really do look quite beautiful. It is decidedly more effective than that of the unwashed peasant girl, though I expect that the real Eve is somewhere in between. In a way I miss her."

She stepped back away from him and swallowed hard. "I really do not care what you think of me! Now, will you please go!"

He looked at her for a long moment, then shrugged. "I could, if that is what you really want. But, keep in mind, Eve, that we will be living beneath the same roof. We cannot avoid each other entirely and I think it best that we reach some sort of understanding, the sooner the better."

She opened her mouth to answer but the retort hung on her lips as the bell rang for mid-meal. Frowning, she glanced at the open doorway. Pondering her decision she flashed on the remembrance of the leer Edward had offered to her that morning and the thought that he would be waiting for her in the hall. Sighing, she nodded in agreement.

As they reached the top of the stairs Eve looked out over the crowded room and her courage fled. If only there were not so many in the hall! Eyes turned upward, fixing on her as silence spread over the room like a breeze wafting through an open window, finally reaching her with an effect like a blast of cold, winter air. She stopped short, her eyes swimming over the gazes which were filled with disbelief, but which in her panic she read as hostility. She wanted to flee back to the safety of her chambers but she felt Richard's hand on her elbow, squeezing gently with reassurance as he led her down the remaining steps to the hall.

Sir Edward, who stood at their base with a small group, followed the stricken looks on the faces of the ladies. Turning in time to find Eve a few steps away, his face fell into unmasked astonishment. He recovered quickly, his expression turning to delight as he stepped away from Katherine and Gwen, sweeping his hand out to Eve at the foot of the stairs, quite ignoring Richard's presence.

"My lady, you are enchanting!" His eyes roamed hungrily over her, pausing as he lustily admired the low cut of her bodice. "I would deem it a great honor, milady, if you would consent to be my partner for dinner."

"The lady has a partner, Sir Edward," Richard said smoothly.

"Richard, I think it would be best if you were to remember that you are but a squire," Edward said with disdain.

"I have not forgotten, milord. Nonetheless the lady had chosen her dinner partner. If you disagree I will be quite content to settle the matter without."

Red-faced, Edward glared at Richard, sputtering over such insolence from a mere squire.

Alarmed, Eve dug her fingers into Richard's arms. "Richard, please," she whispered. He laid his hand over hers where it lay on his arm but he continued to regard Gilbert with an icy calmness that Eve recognized as perhaps none other would. But the danger was not lost upon Edward who, while he continued to regard Richard with haughtiness, did not attempt to delay them as Richard nodded to the ladies and led Eve away.

Gilbert arose as they approached, beaming his approval and motioning for them to sit at the dormant table. It was a singular honor, one that confirmed his pleasure with her since only the knights and ladies of the greatest rank took their places at the Earl's table. Other linen-covered boards were set upon trestles, to be dismantled after each meal: one for the squires who were not attending the needs of their lords, and others for knights and ladies of lesser rank and visitors to the manor.

As they took their places Leonore began to recover from the shock over the change in Eve's appearance. As she spoke, her voice laced with sarcasm, her eyes were fixed upon Eve's garments.

"My dear, you look lovely. I am overwhelmed by such a change. Who . . . what has brought this about?"

Eve bit her lower lip to keep from saying what was on her mind but fortunately Sir Gilbert came to her aid. "My dear, no explanation is necessary. The results speak for themselves and certainly bring pleasure to these aging eyes."

Eve smiled gratefully at the Earl and, as she turned to sit, she caught Richard's grin. As they sat, the others in the hall moved to their places and the social chatter was resumed until the room was again a din of voices and laughter. Eve sighed with relief that their attention was no longer upon her but the realization brought with it another, that Richard was indeed her partner for mid-meal.

In the men's absence the meal had been like any other but now that they had returned she knew it would be much more. She had often heard Katherine and Gwen complain about the absence of the men and the changes forced upon their lives when the manor was inhabited with only the women. Then they had eaten lightly, to return to their needlework or duties about the castle. But, when Hertford was in full residence the mid part of the day was centered about the meal, to become an afternoon of visiting and gaming—a daily celebration from their morning duties often lasting well into the afternoon.

She glanced at Richard as he cut a generous trencher from a loaf, expertly trimmed the crusts and laid it before her. It would be shared by them as a plate and following the meal, when it was soaked with juices from meat and fish, it would be gathered into baskets to be distributed to the poor at the door of the kitchen. The trencher became a symbol of sharing between them and it made her acutely uncomfortable. She stole a sideward glance at him, startling to find him looking at her.

"Are you all right?" he asked.

"Aye," she answered, lowering her gaze self-consciously.

Fortunately at that moment Gaspard appeared, followed by the servants laden with steaming mazers and mets heaped with roasted meat and fish and quenelles, a dumpling made from meat that had been pounded with bread crumbs, stock and eggs and poached; loaves of manchet made from fine flours; broths of almonds and heavy creams; roasted teals stuffed with eggs, spices and grapes; and an array of tarts and pastries which they placed before the guests. Tantalized by the aroma of Gaspard's efforts, Eve found herself ravenously hungry and she began to eat with relish. Thus engaged she wondered at the chuckle from Richard and looked up to find him watching her.

"I am gratified to find that my presence has not stunted your appetite." He grinned.

Self-consciously, she sat back from her meal and reddened. "Indeed, Richard, your presence has not affected my appetite in the least!"

"Good," he said, pouring her a measure of spiced wine. "When you are finished there are some things I would like to say to you."

"You may talk to me while I eat." She shrugged, pointing to the quenelle. "It really does not matter."

He chuckled and served up the dish, then leaned back in his chair to regard her carefully. "I want to apologize for my actions at the gate this morning. I hope that you understand that it was necessary."

Her spoon paused half-way to her mouth from her silver-lined bowl and she laid it down again as she gaped at him. "You think that it was necessary to—to paw me, to handle me as though I were a . . ."

"It was the quickest way to silence you. Do you deny that you were about to blurt out the manner of our meeting?"

She glanced about, alarmed that he would speak of it so boldly but found what he already knew, that the others were engrossed in conversations of their own.

"You could have said something!" she whispered sharply.

"Said what?" he countered. "Eve, my concern was not just for myself but for others who could have been immeasurably harmed."

Reluctantly, she admitted to herself that he was right. It struck her, for the first time, that she was being exceedingly ungrateful. After all, he had saved her honor, and quite possibly her life. Why did he make her so angry? "I have never thanked you properly for what you did for me. If you had not, you would not be in danger now. I do not mean to be ungrateful, it is just that . . . other things got in the way . . ."

"There is no need to thank me, Eve," he said after drawing from his goblet. He set it on the table and regarded her thoughtfully. "My reason for being there was for another purpose, which is what places me in danger. It was merely an accident that I was able to help you."

"Nevertheless, my thanks," she pressed.

"Accepted." He shrugged. His eye began to sparkle as his mouth twisted into a cocky grin. "I must say that I am pleased to find you here, as it gives end to the mystery."

"What mystery?"

"The riddle that has played at my mind these past weeks. I found myself saddled with a succulent young wench, by all appearances a maid from a simple borough, and one so fired in temperament as to arouse my manly impulses. Yet, at the same time she is not what she appears."

"Was I so obvious?" she queried. In spite of herself he had struck her curiosity.

"Love, a maid from a simple village does not meet easily with a fluent French tongue."

"Oh!" Her thoughts turned back to the memory of a quiet conversation by a campfire.

He laughed at her recognition. "You will have to practice the art of deception, Eve."

She smiled. "I do not think it is an art at which I relish becoming accomplished. Perhaps, after all, it is best to hold to the truth."

"To that we agree. However, there are times when it is necessary to let others assume what they will—but enough of that. Tell me why you are here."

"You have already heard part, though you chose to find humor in it," she smirked. "My country is at war, my father's enemies pressing so close that it was necessary to send me here for my safety. In Erin a battle, indeed, a war, can be lost by the taking of hostages. For that reason my father did not mean for me to become the means by which to defeat him."

"And for this he sent you to England?" Richard asked.

She was surprised at the doubt in his voice. "Aye, of course! What other reason would there be?"

His eyes were unreadable as he considered her question for a moment, then he shrugged. "Perhaps nothing."

He turned and set to his own meal. As her eyes wandered about the room to the brightly colored banners that hung from the high-vaulted ceiling, she questioned him about the various coats of arms. He explained that they represented each of the families in attendance at Hertford, and they chatted about the difference of the English formality to the simplicity of her own people, in manner and dress.

"I found no fault in your appearance before." He smiled as he pushed away the trencher and leaned back in his chair. His eyes dropped over her garment. "Fine clothes do not make a lady," he said, his gaze traveling to Gwen, then back to her, where they seemed to warm. "Though when they adorn one gentle of spirit they enhance, like a fine setting for a jewel."

She smiled at his reference to Gwen's disposition, while flushing at the compliment. Fingering the luxurious velvet of her gown she said, a bit chagrined, "It seems a bit out of character for me. I am not used to such finery but I must admit that I like it."

"It is perfectly suitable." He smiled.

The meal was officially finished when Sir Gilbert rose from the table. On the signal many of the company rose to go to the gaming tables or to gather into clusters, and Richard turned to Eve with a questioning look.

"You have a choice, milady. You may withdraw to the ladies for idle conversation, or so we are led to believe, though I reason it is more of gossip, or you may join me in a game of chess. Do you play?"

"Aye," she laughed. "I do play. And I would much prefer it to what I can confirm to be the subject of the ladies' conversation."

He led her to a gaming table near the hearth where the boards were set. They were barely involved in the game when she silently thanked the good priest who had taught her the game, since Richard played in earnest. It was obvious that he could do nothing else because the game was used to train the men for war and the board was a battlefield on which Richard instinctively fought, no quarter given.

In an unconscious moment, Eve made an ill-fated move with her rook and was disconcerted to note the gleam in Richard's eye. But, before he could respond, their attention was distracted by the sound of angry voices behind them.

"William Rufus was sovereign! The men who murdered him were traitors!"

Sir Gilbert glared at Lord Ashby, an overfed, vainglorious lord who was known to be close to Stephen's ear. Gilbert's mouth was drawn into an angry line as he answered with tight control.

"Rufus was a tyrant. He undid everything his father spent his lifetime trying to build. His death was well deserved."

"He was his father's favorite! You cannot deny that! He was heir to the throne!" Ashby's plump face puffed with anger, his cheeks reddening as he glared at his host.

"Favorite he may have been, but the Conqueror had a father's blindness to Rufus' weaknesses. 'Twas England's luck that his reign was short-lived. Besides, it has never been proven that Rufus was murdered. I tend to believe that it was a stray hunter's arrow that caught him. In either case, the arrow could have come from Robert's bow the more readily than Henry's.

As the elder he felt overlooked and had more to begrudge
Rufus."

"Nonsense! Henry had plotted his time well..."

Sir Gilbert began to turn away, disgusted by the conversation. "It was a blessing. England got the best of the lot in
Henry."

Lord Ashby sneered with contempt at Gilbert's back. "It is
understandable that you would say thus, milord, since it was
one of your family that found special favor with Henry."

Gilbert spun back, his eyes flaring with anger. Eve gasped
as Lord Severn grabbed the Earl's arm before it reached Ashby.

"Enough!" Severn barked. "Ashby, let us remember that
we are guests here! This goes far beyond propriety. You owe
your host an apology!"

The room had fallen to a deathly silence as the two men
glared at each other. Finally, Lord Ashby drew himself up
grandly, refusing to note Severn's disapproving frown.

"I do apologize for not acting as a proper guest, Gilbert. It
was ill-mannered of me to partake of your meal and then take
issue with you. However, I do not apologize for what I have
said; therefore, I shall take my leave and not embarrass you
further with my presence."

Without hesitation he strode past Gilbert and departed the
hall, his retinue following swiftly behind, leaving the hall in
a long, awkward silence.

"Good riddance." It was Warwick's booming voice that
broke the silence. He poured a generous tankard of ale for
himself and Sir Gilbert. As he handed one to the Earl, he
wrinkled his nose and looked about in mock question. "The
air seems to have taken on a more pleasing aroma..."

Titters were heard about the hall as Gilbert laughed at Warwick's parry and soon the hall was returned to its former pleasantness, the moment forgotten except by one.

Eve swallowed hard as a feeling of homesickness rushed
over her. While the words had meant nothing to her, they had
brought back memories of Dermot bellowing in argument with
others, and the broad wink he would throw to the small girl
curled up in a chair near the fire. He had loved the challenge
of a heated argument and the memories of those times, now
seeming so far away, filled her with sadness.

She excused herself from Richard, dismissing the look of
concern that crossed his face as she moved away to a window

overlooking the courtyard. She leaned against the cold stone of the casing and watched wisps of breaking clouds. She closed her eyes in dreaming, pretending that she was at Ferns, standing in the hall with her father nearby. She would open her eyes to find him next to her, giving her one of his broad smiles as he did when he was well-pleased, filled with pride and love.

"Eve, you are running away."

She turned to find Richard standing next to her. He was looking at her steadily with a hint of disapproval and she bristled, not only from the boldness of his statement but from the fact that he had interrupted her dreaming.

"Will you please leave me alone!" she snapped.

He sat on the window ledge and looked at her calmly. "You are homesick, are you not?"

"Ooooh! You think you know everything about me!"

"Nay." He smiled. "Hardly everything. But I do recognize what I have felt myself on occasion. Remembrances, a longing for something familiar. You are here now, Eve, and it is a new part of your life. It may seem hard but you must learn to accept it."

She bridled at his attitude of superiority and criticism which she was not prepared to handle. "Oh! Could that be true? Do you always accept, Richard? Perhaps you should not run away. There are those here who would be interested in our place of meeting! Perhaps I should enlighten them, as it would help you to face what you are doing!"

"If it pleases you to tell someone, then feel free to do so," he said calmly.

"It does not worry you?" she snapped, miffed by his confidence.

"Not at all."

"Come now, Richard. You are not concerned about the knowledge we share? You told me that it was from your 'concern' that you kissed me this morning."

"When I first saw you this morning I was concerned." He shrugged. "I had no way of knowing then that you had not told someone of our meeting upon your arrival. If so, my absence from Lighthurst could have been somewhat compromising. However, my alibi has now been well established and it is one they are all to ready to believe. Should you choose to mention it now, when so much time has passed, I am certain that they will feel you are mistaken."

He reached out and lifted a lock of her hair from her shoulder and fingered it thoughtfully. "Accept our friendship, Eve. There is no reason for you to fight it."

His fingers seemed to burn into her where they touched her shoulder, unsettling her far more than the words he had spoken. The sudden rush of emotions she felt by his touch and the gentleness of his words only served to remind her of the intimate moments she had spent with him and it dissipated all understanding she had begun to share with him. Threatened, she pushed his hand from her shoulder and stepped back from him.

"Friendship!" she gasped. "In the future, Richard, I would deeply appreciate it if you would not speak to me at all!"

She whirled on her heels and strode away, her hips swaying with her angry mood. He stood to watch her go as Warwick appeared at his elbow.

"You seem to have an unsettling effect on the lass, Richard."

"It would seem so."

"What did you do this time?"

"Me?" Richard grinned innocently. "I merely offered her my friendship."

Warwick chortled. "Your friendship? I do not think the lady will have any of that!"

A smile touched at the corners of Richard's mouth as his eyes followed her up the stairs. "She will, Warwick. Give her time, she will."

7

A time of peace and serenity was approaching Hertford and England, a time when life could be enjoyed for the sheer pleasure of being. Christmas through Epiphany would mark the longest holiday of the year, weeks of celebration and release from accustomed toils, a pause from the usual energies to maintain and improve existence. As it neared, each member of the household, servant and noble alike, were called upon to do their part; no one was spared from the preparations.

The men dove deeply into the forest, searching until they found a mighty fir for the Christmas yule log. After felling the tree they trimmed its branches and cut it to a desired twelve-foot length. Then, girdling it with massive iron chains, which they attached to the harnesses of two of the largest war horses, they began the slow arduous journey to the manor. The muscles and sinews of the destriers strained against their burden. While unaccustomed to the task their mighty heads stretched forward in instinctive determination to conquer the challenge, accompanied by shouts of encouragement from the men who took turns pushing and pulling the ponderous log. On Christmas Eve, the log would be trimmed to a six-foot length for Hertford's hearth and the remaining timber cut into pieces for the villeins to carry home to their mud-and-wattle huts, there to be burnt as a first fire on their hearths to bring luck in the coming year. Their arrival at the manor, as the sun was setting in a red-gold blanket, was regaled by cheers and pints of ale.

The destriers were not forgotten as their rewards took the shape of apples and the horses nibbled them eagerly from the offered hands.

The women were not idle as seldom-used rooms were opened, cleaned and aired for the expected guests, linens prepared, and extra hands were needed to measure and stitch for the many new garments needed for the celebration. The great hall was thoroughly swept and the molding stone of the floor was scraped and scattered with fresh rushes scented with a generous sprinkling of dried rose petals and herbs. Some decorated the hall with boughs of greenery and red sashes and ribbons while others in the kitchens busily prepared the game brought in daily by the men who had left at dawn to supply Hertford with the vast amount of food that would be needed.

Gaspard carefully checked the pantry and buttery against his ledgers, checking off the preserves, fruits and vegetables stored in brine that would be used, including the carefully guarded imported sugars made of roses. The harried steward fretted over the late arrival of orders he had sent to the coast for cod, salmon, turbot, oysters and eel.

Eager to be at last set to some useful purpose, Eve offered to assist in the kitchens. She had often done so at Ferns and she was eager to learn how to prepare the unusual English dishes. Loaves of manchet and coffins of pastries were prepared to hold the meats and fish. They were made hollow, to accept the addition of fillings later, and she watched with fascination as the dough was laid on the pans, then a hollow straw was inserted and with a gentle breath expanded it to an air-filled coffin. Capons, partridges, mallards and quail were roasted with stuffings of eggs, laced with spices, fruits, onions and pork. Though her day began at dawn and continued well into evening when she would fall exhausted into bed, Eve was happier than she had been since coming to Hertford.

She had been acutely aware of the tension among the cooks when Gaspard had brought her to the large smoke-filled room the first day. Even the young boys whose task it was to mind the ever-turning spits eyed her with suspicion, the room falling to an awkward silence as Gaspard informed them that the Lady Eve had come to help. Rolling back her sleeves, Eve donned an apron and ignored their guarded, distrusting glances and she plunged happily into the work. Shrewdly, she realized that her first conquest needed to be Blanche, the large, ruddy-faced cook who ruled the kitchens with a heavy hand. Her booming voice snapped orders, sending the others scurrying about, just out of reach from the ever-present ladle which she wielded as effectively as a war-club for those she thought were dallying. Plying her with eager questions Eve proved herself to the doubtful Blanche, as she followed the terse instructions quickly and with a deftness that brought an approving glance from the hard-won cook.

By the third day Eve found herself thoroughly accepted, a fact proved as they began to include her in their banter of servants' gossip. Not a member of the household was spared. Occasionally, Eve had to stifle a gasp at the knowledge revealed and she often bit her lip not to giggle when new light was shed upon the stiff-necked ladies of Hertford. Blanche proved her loyalty one afternoon when Gwen meandered into the kitchens, her dark eyes gleaming maliciously with the intention of tormenting Eve. Few peevish words passed from her fair lips before Blanche sent her scurrying, leaving no mistake of who was in charge in that domain and showing she would broach no such behavior to "one of her own."

There were other reasons the hard work added to Eve's contentment. No word had arrived from Ireland and the long hours kept her from dwelling upon this disappointment. When left unguarded, her thoughts would turn to home and her brow would crease with worry. Her mind worked in a chain of events that would take her, once again, from Erin's shores to the memory of gray, mocking eyes and a hard body pressed against the length of her own. Such moments brought puzzled looks from Blanche as Eve's normally happy mood would shift to a sullen, angry quiet. Sensing that the lass was troubled, the cook knew better than to press with questions. The affection she now felt for the young maid was evident as she would throw a protective cloak about Eve and a black frown would answer the questioning glances from the others.

As the days passed, Eve was curious to note the increased traffic from the surrounding villages as the inhabitants appeared each morning at the kitchenyard laden with great sacks of flour, baskets of fruits and vegetables, and cages of fowl. Commenting on it to Lavinia, it was explained that a great feast would occur on Christmas Eve for the lord's tenants, his way of thanking them for the year's industry. When Eve observed that the tenants would be providing their own feast, it brought a startled and slightly disapproving frown from her friend.

The holidays carried an even greater importance for Hertford this year, a fact which brought a particular shine to Lavinia's eyes, which Eve now knew was for Gervase. The knighting ceremonies would be held between Christmas and Twelfth Day. Families of great importance would be arriving to watch their sons enter into the order and the festivities would continue for four days. Eve had to admit that she was somewhat fascinated by the prospect since knighthood and its systems of feudalism had never come to Erin. The few times that an English knight had visited Ferns, Eve had been hustled off to the women's chambers, there to wait in seclusion until the visitor had departed. Curiosity had overcome the better of her when once, as the knight had departed, she had cracked the shutters in time to see the mailed and helmed man swing into the saddle of his war horse. The sight of the destrier was enough to bring a gasp from the watching girl as she had never seen such an immense animal. The gasp also brought Gerda to her side. The nurse snapped the shutters closed and with a wagging finger she pulled the girl back into the room. Eve had railed with disappointment, begging to be told why she was not allowed to meet such an exciting visitor, but Gerda ignored her pleadings and mumbled something under her breath about not wanting the English to see Erin's fair flowers.

Sir Bowen was the first knight she had ever spoken to and while she was hard put to take the whole matter seriously she could not help but to muse about the ceremonies that were professed to transform mere men into that glorious state of perfection.

One morning as Eve was taking loaves of manchet from the hearth, Lavinia swept into the kitchens, her mind bent on stealing a few hours from their labors. She chose a sweetmeat from a tray on the table and nibbled at the delicacy as she watched Eve work, her eyes dancing with mischief.

"Eve, we've not had a moment to ourselves for well over a week, unless you count the hours spent on our knees during mass. I'm of a mind to take fresh air and you look as if you could use it. Dear me, I fear your skin will be permanently reddened by the heat in this room!"

Eve's flour-covered hands flew to her face. They both laughed at the snort of disbelief from Blanche, but the cook then took up Lavinia's part.

"She's right, milady. You've been work'n' too hard and I've been tellin' ye all along. Do ye good to take a break.

'Asides, we're way ahead on our work what with the help ye've been givin'."

Her tone left no room for argument and Eve soon found herself enjoying Lavinia's quips as they walked along the eastern tower of the keep, warmly bundled in fur cloaks against the biting air of the December morning. They paused and leaned out over the parapet, spying on the castle creatures below as they scurried about their morning duties. Intrigued, Eve spotted the jousting field just outside the castle walls, where the men were well into their practice. They took their hand with the sword in pairs, wielding the broad, pressed steels with graceful swing and pass. Lavinia pointed out Kerwain, the master-of-the-sword, as the sound of his voice bellowed in dissatisfaction over the efforts of his pupils.

"Are they really as inept as he would imply?" Eve asked. "They appear quite good to me."

"Nay." Lavinia laughed ruefully. "Our knights and squires are among the very best. Kerwain is never satisfied until they are perfect, though sometimes I think he is particularly hard on . . . Oh look! I think you will see for yourself."

As Eve turned back she heard a bellow of rage from Kerwain and her attention was sharpened as she noted that the object of his wrath was none other than Richard.

"You handle your blade as though it were a cudgel, but then it surprises me not counting for the time you spend with us here!"

They could not hear Richard's answer but the meaning was obvious, as they saw Kerwain angrily draw his sword, sweeping it above his head. Richard reacted instantly, bringing his weapon up to deflect the blow. Shifting his weight quickly to one side, he brought his weapon about as Kerwain barely met the pass before it could deliver a crushing blow to the knees. The clang of metal could be heard across the keep as the two men swung and parried with a fierce intentness. Suddenly Richard tripped and began to fall backwards, bringing a horrified gasp from the two women. Kerwain's next blow would have surely met its mark but Warwick stepped quickly forward, grasping Kerwain's arm before it fell. Richard rolled to one side and came up on his feet, once again in readiness as he faced his adversary but Warwick's angry roar reverberated against the stone walls, bringing the two to their senses. Kerwain waved Richard off with an angry gesture and, shouting gruffly to the others to be about their business, he strode off to another group.

Eve let her breath out slowly. "What was that about?"

Turning to lean against the parapet, Lavinia shrugged her shoulders. "Richard is not among Kerwain's favorites."

"Is he so inept with arms that he should arouse such wrath?"

"Nay, Eve." Lavinia shook her head sadly as the hem of her wimple lifted gently in the breeze that began to stir about the tower. "Quite the contrary. Richard has a natural ability with the sword. With the bow he already surpasses his father and it was he who won the name of Strongbow with his ability."

Eve glanced back to the field in wonder, "Then why . . ."

"Oh, Eve, I do not understand it myself. Richard has changed so much . . ." Her voice trailed off with sadness as she looked to the object of their discussion on the field below. Eve followed the look, then remembered the teasing from Gwen and Katherine the morning they met.

"Do you love him, Lavinia?"

"Not in the way you imply," she smiled. "Richard and I were raised together for a goodly part of our childhood. Oh, there was a time when I looked upon him with a child's worship but it grew into a very special friendship. He and my brother, John, were very close, closer than two brothers could be. John was taken from us by a quick and deathly fever and I found that my feelings for Richard changed then to a sisterly affection as that need was greater, for both of us, and has remained so. It was after John's death that Richard began to change."

"How has he changed?"

"He is . . . different. More intense, brooding and . . . secretive."

"Secretive?" Eve startled at the word. "How do you mean?"

Lavinia's fair brow wrinkled into a frown. "Well . . . he keeps more to himself. He used to be so happy but since John's death he seems preoccupied. Where he used to be attentive and thoughtful, he is now distant. Once," she added wistfully, "he promised to be a great knight of the realm."

"And now?"

Lavinia sighed deeply, "Now he seems to care for none of it. His interest is to lifting a tankard and spending time with Claresta and her harlots at the tavern near here. He disappears from the manor, telling no one of his purpose, to be away for days at a time. Why, even upon his visit to Lighthurst he was naught to stay! At last, after five nights, Warwick came upon him at Claresta's—in most unsavory company."

"You know of this?"

"Father did his best to keep it from me but such a thing is impossible to secret for long. It was the last straw and now he has pushed the matter to where his very spurs are in jeopardy. Gilbert has vowed that if even a hint of scandal touches his name between now and the ceremonies, knighthood will forever be beyond his reach."

"What of his family, have they said nothing about this?"

"Richard is the only son of a great and powerful family, Eve. Their lands at Striguil are rich and vast, held since the time of William the Conqueror. Their castle, Chepstow, would take your breath away, its walls so great, its battlements so massive that no enemy has ever been able to broach them. To their back lies all of Wales, where loyalty from that people was won at a time when other Norman lords dared not enter its borders without massive armies. But, you must know that Strongbow, should Gilbert find Richard unworthy of knighthood, will let the decision stand."

"But if the deClares are so powerful, would the loss of his knighthood be so terrible?"

"Well..." Lavinia hesitated, "it is true that for someone in Richard's position knighthood is not as important as it would be if he were landless. But, I fear that the dishonor could destroy whatever relationship that remains between Richard and Strongbow. It has been strained for many years, although I do not understand why."

Eve looked back to the field where the men had resumed their labors, seeking out one in particular. She watched him as he expertly moved through his practice, her brow furrowing into a pensive frown. She was tempted to tell Lavinia of what she knew but something made her hold her tongue. He had said that her knowledge was useless but even so she could not bring herself to speak of it even with Lavinia. He had helped her and she could not forget that fact, regardless of how she felt about him. Aye, she would give him this and the debt would be repaid, his honor for hers. Then the debt would be cancelled and she would owe him nothing! But, if ever again— ever—he humiliated her, continued to cause her torment, she would also return that in kind! But how? She needed to know him much better, his failings, his weak spots. To achieve that she had to gain his trust...

"Lavinia," she ventured. "What would a man suffer, should he be found guilty of a traitorous action, after he has won his spurs?"

"You mean if he were to break his vows?"

"Aye, what then?" she asked innocently.

Lavinia shuddered, clearly horrified by the prospect. "Why, he would be exclaimed 'val proditor,' his name stricken from the list of knights. His coat of arms would forever be worn turned on his surcoat and all men would look down upon him and his name!"

"I see," Eve answered softly as she rested her chin on her hand and she leaned out over the parapet to watch the activity on the field below.

The morning before Christmas Eve was ushered in by billowy black storm clouds which threatened to put a damper on the festive mood. The winter had been uncommonly warm, the usual white blanket of Christmas snow replaced by occasional rains and sleet, leaving the landscape draped in a forbidding brown. It was as if nature echoed the desolation of its people, refusing the hopeful cleansing a new snow would promise of a fresh spring.

The hunting party returned with early afternoon, the blackened sky having opened in a deluge of rain, defying all attempts to seek the needed game. The remainder of the afternoon was spent in the company of the ladies, pursuing quiet pleasures about the roaring fire in the great hall. Eve sat on a stool near Warwick, watching his rhythmical movements as he worked hewing the edges of his broadsword with a sharpening stone. The steady sound of the stone against metal lulled her into a peaceful, almost hypnotic contentment and she blinked sleepily as she tried to stifle a yawn.

Suddenly, there arose a commotion from without, drawing their attention to the massive doors of the hall. Gervase rushed to the portal, swinging it open in time to admit a party of travelers, their cloaks drenched by the rain that had muffled the sounds of their arrival. As they threw off their soaked outer garments, Eve saw that the group included a small party of men-at-arms accompanying a tall, aging noble of impressive stature. His fair, reddish hair was streaked with grey but his pale eyes held a look that, as they swept over the hall, seemed to devour those who were present. The fragile form at his side set back the hood of her cloak, revealing a noble face with large dark eyes framed by a starched linen wimple. Upon their appearance the hall came alive with a boisterous gaiety in welcome of the visitors. Sir Gilbert leaped from his chair and strode across the room. He threw open his arms in welcome, grasping the arm of the man and then sweeping the woman into a warm embrace.

Eve leaned over to Warwick, who had set his sword aside, and wore a pleased grin. "Warwick, who might our visitors be?"

He leaned forward, his gladdened eyes gesturing toward the strangers. "They be my lord Strongbow, Earl of Pembroke and Count of Striguil, and his lady, Isabel."

Eve's interest snapped back to the arrivals. She glanced at Richard, who had risen from his chair as his mother, brightening at the sight of her son, quickly crossed the few steps between them to be taken tenderly into his arms. Keeping an arm about her, Richard turned to his father, who met his look with apparent restraint.

"You look well, milord," Richard said simply.

Strongbow merely grunted, then reached out and grasped Richard's shoulder. "We have much to talk about." They exchanged a long, silent look before Strongbow cleared his throat and turned away to Gilbert, whom he slapped on the back.

"Gilbert!" he bellowed good-naturedly. "The journey has been hard and I am famished, as is my lady! Think you that worthless steward of yours could provide a proper repast? Gaspard! Where are you?"

Gaspard came rushing into the hall, wide-eyed at the commotion.

"There you are! I shall grant you but a few moments to provide me some proper nourishment before I raid those precious kitchens of yours and set them to ruin!"

Gaspard gasped and his eyes filled with horror as he turned and fled to do Strongbow's bidding. He knew full well that the Earl was as good as his word. The hall roared with laughter at the sight of the fleeing steward and Gilbert took Strongbow's arm affectionately.

"It is good to see you again, Uncle," he chuckled. "I fear that Hertford has been too serene of late, although now I have no doubt that the matter will be changed." He noted the fatigued look on Lady Isabel's face and he added, with concern, "I shall instruct Gaspard to set out supper in private quarters so that you might rest."

An intimate supper was taken by the family in the lesser hall, a small room located behind a partition dividing it from the great hall. It had once been the private chambers of the former Earl and Lady of Hertford before the upper chambers had been added to the castle, a practice common to most of the older castles in England. During the earlier period the lord and lady, indeed the children too, would sleep in the small room off the great hall with only a screen to divide it. The purpose was to draw the warmth of the fire built in the center of the larger room, its long black column of sooty smoke barely escaping through the hole cut in the ceiling for the purpose. The addition of the second floor and the massive chimneyed fireplace had brought a new standard of living to the residents of Hertford.

Gilbert sat at his place at head of the table listening to the light banter between Strongbow and Warwick, while noticing that Richard had taken no part in the discussion but had kept his attention to his mother's needs during the meal. He now sat back in his chair moodily staring into his cup, apparently bored by the conversation. Gilbert shook his head slightly and leaned back, rubbing his forehead thoughtfully as he addressed Strongbow.

"Uncle, I would know what news you would bring from the west. How do things fare at Chepstow?"

Strongbow sobered at the question, his brows gathering darkly as he sipped his ale. "Not well, Gilbert, not well. Stephen's men encourage mayhem and destruction, partaking of whatever pleases them with no regard to property or title. We must continually ride the boundaries of Striguil to thwart their raids. Knights must be sent into the fields to guard the villeins and soldiers must be placed in the hamlets at night . . ."

"You are telling me that they revile Striguil?"

"They have not threatened Chepstow itself but to the lands and the people, aye. 'Tis the reason so few knights accompany me on this journey. I dare not leave Chepstow unfortified for fear that it would no longer belong to the deClares upon my return."

"God's Blood!" Warwick roared. "Are you unable to stop them? If times have arrived when mere soldiers can take what belongs legally granted title!"

"Ho!" Strongbow parried. "Warwick, if you have not witnessed the same at Hertford you are indeed fortunate! Where a soldier's position does not carry enough strength, Stephen provides the title to see to the task. He dispenses Earl and Lord to any man in his service who convinces him that he will ply his deeds with support to the king. The bloodier their actions, the more favor is gained. More than that, they are allowed to build new strongholds without license—and their claim is honored."

Strongbow noticed that his son sat sullenly quiet. "And you, Richard, what are your thoughts on the matter?"

"Me?" he shrugged his shoulders with a bored look of indifference. "Stephen is king. It is his right to grant title to anyone he deems fit."

Strongbow startled, then absorbing Richard's words and manner, his face became washed with anger. "You can sit there, mildly accepting what is happening to England and pretend indifference! Warwick!" He turned his wrath on the unexpecting knight, who had been unhappily following the exchange. "God's Breath! What manner of man are you returning to me as my son?"

Warwick sputtered, looking from Richard to Strongbow. He noted that Strongbow's knuckles had turned white as they gripped the table but before he could form an answer, it came from across the table. Richard's voice was calm, his expression wide with innocence.

"My Lord, was not Stephen's right to the throne established by the peers of this realm? Is his right to rule now lessened because he does not govern as you would have him?"

Strongbow's eyes were black as he regarded his son with disdain. "Are things so simple for you, Richard? Do you feel no anguish, no pain? Can you not feel the people crying out in their misery or are you so content with your pleasures that you cannot look to their need?"

Richard took a draught of ale as the room waited in a baited silence. He stared into the amber liquid of his cup, his fingers turning it slowly. "The nobles of this land, those who truly rule England, chose Stephen in their greed, laziness, and short-sightedness, long before I had a voice in the matter. I will not be blamed for the decision now. I simply choose to live with it."

Strongbow paled as he leaned back in his chair. Never taking his eyes from Richard, he answered in a barely controlled voice, "So that is it. You still will not forgive me for my silence these many years. Your manner to me these past years have said as much but I excused it to the exuberance and rashness of youth. Richard, while we were aware of Stephen's weakness, we hoped that his rule would bring peace to England. I will not justify myself to my own son more than that. To answer your question, it is the duty of the peers of this realm to protect England, not to sit idly by, engaged in their own pleasures while she is devoured!"

As they glared at one another the rage of the elder did not allow him to notice the small gleam that began to stir in Richard's eyes.

"Well, Father, if that is true, the answer seems simple enough. If you feel that Stephen destroys England"—he paused, measuring his father evenly as he drawled the last words—"take his throne from him."

Richard rose, the sound of his chair scraping against the floor, shattering the silence. He lifted his tankard in salute to his sire before he lifted it to his mouth and then, setting it on the table, he left the room.

Gilbert cleared his throat as he rubbed a hand over his mouth to cover a smile while exchanging amused looks with Warwick.

"What do you find so humorous?" growled Strongbow, glaring at the two.

"It would seem, Uncle," answered Gilbert with a raised brow, "that you were handily led to a desired end."

As Richard stepped around the screen he stopped short. Lavinia and Eve were sitting before the fire with needlework and from their embarrassed expressions it was apparent that they had overheard the angry comments. His eyes met Eve's and he startled at their intensity, his own becoming clouded with doubt. He hesitated only for a moment, then he stepped forward and snatched her wrist, pulling her from the chair as her needlework spilled over the floor. The action brought a surprised gasp from Lavinia, as he pulled the startled maid after him through a nearby doorway and down a hall.

No words passed between them as he half-dragged her down the hallway and into the buttery, where he closed the door tightly behind them. He released her and turned his attention to the crocks of wine and barrels of ale which lined the walls. Grabbing two tankards from a shelf he drew ale from one of the barrels and handed one to her before quaffing his in a long draught. Stunned into silence, she stood wide-eyed before him, waiting for an explanation for his astounding behavior.

"Sit down," he ordered.

She obeyed and sat down stiffly on a bench.

"I am not going to hurt you, Eve," he said irritably.

"I know that."

"Then why are you trembling?" he growled, drawing another measure of ale.

"A rather foolish question!" she snapped. "Why have you brought me here?"

"We would have been disturbed in the common rooms. Or would you have preferred that I had taken you to my chambers?"

She raised a brow at rude remark and repeated her question.

"Are you still afraid that I am going to rape you?" he taunted. "It would be a mite difficult in such close quarters, milady, but I reason that it could be managed if you expect it."

"Richard," she breathed, her voice catching. "Why are you trying to hurt me? Have I done something to warrant this abuse?"

He looked at her strangely for a long moment. She thought she read a look of regret in his expression but it was gone so quickly that she reasoned it to her imagination.

"Your crime, my love, was being at the wrong place at a most inopportune time. Your presence here, and the knowledge which you have of matters that do not concern you, now causes some difficulty."

"Oh! Could this be true? You had assured me that my knowledge meant nothing!"

"It did not. But, now that Strongbow is here it complicates the situation somewhat. My father has the capacity of seeing to the heart of the matter, when it suits him," he said bitterly.

Recalling the sharp words between Richard and Strongbow it piqued her curiosity and for a moment she forgot her own anger.

"Richard, why are you so embittered toward your father? What has happened that you cannot tell him the truth about yourself?"

"It does not concern you!" he said crossly. "What does concern both of us is what I shall do with you."

"Do with me?" she gasped. "Are you inferring that you would harm me? I cannot believe . . . How dare you! By what right . . ."

Richard snorted at the last word and his mouth twisted with a short, cruel laugh. "My love, there are no rights for the individual. Everything is taken for the gain and the ultimate purpose justifies any action. Have you not learned that?"

The contempt in his voice drew her up stiffly but reason won out as a hint of a smile touched her green eyes.

"You do not believe that any more than I," she said softly.

"Nay?" A brow raised in question. "And what makes you think not? Do you think me incapable of removing you from the opportunity of being a danger to others?"

"Nay," she answered calmly. "Not if I truly deserved it, but you know that I do not. I assure you that no one shall know of our meeting."

His eyes narrowed speculatively. "I see no reason to trust you, Eve."

"Because I say it!" she retorted, rankled by his doubt. "Do you find it so impossible that I could keep my word?"

He shrugged, running his fingers through his hair. "I have never known a woman to keep her word."

"Richard, I question your judgment of such matters!" she sneered. "Observing the ladies of this manor I wonder that they have ever been intrusted with matters of importance! Do you withhold your trust because they betray the secrets involving the petty gossip of women? Small wonder, with nothing more on their minds, that they have become petty and insignificant themselves! I assure you, Richard, that I have had no chance to live such a simple life!" She fought a small smile as she added the last words carefully. "Richard, I would not betray knowledge of such importance without a good reason. I have come to realize that, should I tell of what I know, you will lose your right to knighthood and . . . and I want you to have those spurs."

His eyes widened with bemusement. "Why should that be important to you?"

She returned his look with forced innocence. "Let us just say that I feel I owe it to you."

He studied her for what seemed an endless moment and she began to wonder, with increasing discomfort, if he could see through her ploy. Her heart began to pound and she almost jumped when he shook his head and chuckled deeply.

"You are quite correct. I have never trusted a woman with a matter of importance as they have always seemed to be free with their gossip. Perhaps the truth of the matter is that I have never wanted to be empowered by a woman."

"Well," she replied smugly, "you are now."

He gaped at her, then threw back his head and laughed loudly, filling the small room with his amusement. She began to smile, gloating as she savored her coup when, without warning, he reached out and grasped her arm, pulling her from her

perch as her tankard clattered to the floor. She found herself
upon his lap. One arm was about her waist and the other was
firmly set at the small of her back. He smiled into her eyes,
his own feasting on the lovely contours of her face.

"Perhaps, *cherie*, I do not mind too much. I think that to
be empowered by you might prove to be a pleasure."

Bristling, she squirmed against his chest to free herself.
"You assume too much, Richard! There was no mention that
this came as part of the bargain!"

He gave her a wicked leer. "But, *cherie*, we have struck an
intimate bargain, you and I."

"Intimate? But I do not see how . . ."

"What is more intimate than my life? You hold it in your
hands, so it most certainly belongs to you."

Without further warning his hand pulled her head down to
his, his lips cruel and demanding as they crushed against her
own. Before she could react he drew back and smiled at her
stunned expression, his eyes mocking her outrage.

"May I still assume your faith, my love? Is there nothing
that will shake your conviction?" he taunted.

Her first reaction was to strike back at his insufferable boldness. With great effort she caught herself in time, as the intent
of her purpose overcame her anger. In her wish for vengeance
she knew instinctively that he must trust her intentions. The
thought gave her renewed determination.

"Richard," she whispered, "are you so bitter, so unreason-
ing, that you can trust no one? What purpose can you see that
I should betray you? If naught else, can you not accept my
gratitude? What have they given me here that is greater than
what you did for me?"

His brows cocked in wonder as her arms went slowly about
his neck with what she thought to be a seductive smile. She
lowered her lips to his but was totally unprepared for the response it brought from him, as he pulled her against him, his
hands moving easily over her back. It was a deep, passionate
embrace that, to her utter amazement, shocked her senses. He
coaxed her tenderly, encouraging her response as his tongue
flicked over her mouth and entered, probing and teasing until
she became washed with a warmth that left her lightheaded.
She gasped against his lips for breath.

"Nay, Richard," she breathed. He ignored her soft plea,
twisting her across his lap to cradle her in his arms. His free

hand cupped her face as his lips moved to the sensitive corners of her mouth and eyes, then traced a fiery path down her neck to her bare shoulders. Her intent seemed to fly to unknown regions as she responded to his touch, her body betraying her as if a more powerful purpose invaded reason. She moaned softly as his hand covered her breast and stroked it gently through the thin silk of her pelisse. His hand slipped beneath her bodice to search for a soft mound and, as his fingers began to tease its rosy tip she gasped, suddenly burning with a bitter-sweet pain that was almost unbearable in its pleasure.

"Richard," she gasped.

"Hmmmm?" he nuzzled against her ear.

"Gaspard may seek more wine."

"Tell him that I have all that I need," he murmured.

His lips moved to her ear, nibbling that tender lobe as she fought to bring her emotions under control, knowing at the same time that she did not want him to stop.

"Richard, please, we shall start a scandal."

Her words sobered him instantly, bringing a soft groan from him as he leaned back against the wall. "My love, you seem to have a faculty for saying words that strike to the heart of the matter."

She sat up, inwardly struggling not to show him how deeply he had affected her. "My lord? You seem to have a change of mood. Could it be something I said?"

He groaned again, acutely aware of the fetching picture she made as she sat primly on his lap, her large green eyes bright with mischief, her skin still flushed with passion.

He stood up suddenly, lifting her to her feet but putting his arms about her waist to pull her back to him before she was able to step from his reach. "You sorely test me, wench." He grinned. "The moment won is yours though I think you lose as much as I."

She flushed at the truth of his words, bringing a chuckle from him as he pulled her closer. "The day will soon come when I shall not have to hide my feelings for you," he whispered hoarsely. "And as I once promised you, when the moment comes you will pleasure in it as much as I."

She tensed at his words, his confidence touching off her anger. She wanted to throw the words back to him but instead looked up through her lashes while inwardly amazed at her capacity of playing the game.

"That has yet to be proved, Sir Squire. Methinks you speak of what only a knight's vow will prove out. Though, I must admit I find myself contemplating the matter with much curiosity."

"In that event, my love, I cannot be but grateful for the delay, as it serves to strengthen my suit. Meanwhile, I shall take every opportunity to remind you of what is to come."

His words brought a strange, aching throb to the pit of her belly. She forced a smile and slid her arms about his neck. "And how shall you remind me, Richard?"

She yielded to his kiss, while acutely aware of his hard body against her own. Her lips quivered under his with trembling anticipation when he released her abruptly. Confused, she blinked at the scowl he offered.

"You are a vixen. Can this be the same frightened maid I discovered in the forest? Whatever has brought about such a change?"

"You, milord." She smiled.

"Me?" His brow arched with the question.

"Aye, milord."

Amusement crept into his eyes but there was something else that lingered in those warm, grey orbs that she could not read. They seemed to pierce into her soul, extracting the very truth from its depths. Unsettled, she dropped her gaze from his, smarting under his answering chuckle.

"I am beginning to realize that I am getting more than that for which I bargained, Eve. Be as it may, I had best return you to Lavinia for, if I do not, I fear I shall break my promise and involve you in that scandal of which you spoke—here and now."

He turned her and pushed her gently toward the door. As they left the room Eve decided to seek the solitude of her chambers, unwilling to face Lavinia or the others in her present state of mind.

As the young couple exchanged a brief kiss at the buttery door, black eyes watched them from the shadows, then followed Eve as she disappeared down the darkened hallway. When Richard returned to the main hall Warwick stepped from the shadows, the light from the flickering sconce set into the wall revealing the unhappy smirk that crossed his face. His first impulse was to follow Richard and confront him with what he had seen. Damnation, the scoundrel had no business toying with the lass, not now! Thinking better of it he muttered a profanity under his breath and continued on his way to his chambers.

"Not in front of Strongbow and Gilbert, lad," he reasoned. "But we will face it, I promise you that!"

8

Warwick threw the covers aside with a grunt and sat on the edge of the bed. As the frigid night air pricked his skin he shuddered. Half turning he pulled a fur off the bed and wrapped it about his shoulders. He sat there for a moment, scratching thoughtfully at his beard until, with a deep sigh, he rose from the bed and moved to the window. Sitting on the ledge he leaned back against the cold stone of the casing, pulled a leg beneath him and tugged the fur more closely, his eyes wandering over the moonlit landscape. The ground-clenching fog had settled about the valley, hugging to the forest beyond. The dark forms of the trees hovered in a saw-toothed outline against the blue-black sky.

Running his fingers through his thick hair a deep sigh escaped him once again.

"Richard," he growled, "I do not believe that you have changed this much. What has come over you?"

He thought back to the years when Richard was a small boy. He smiled ironically, recalling the anger he had felt when Strongbow announced that the child was to be his charge, even though he knew that Strongbow worried for the boy's safety— with good cause.

When old King Henry died, Stephen had snatched the throne from his uncle's deathbed and Strongbow had reluctantly given him his oath of fealty. While raving to Warwick that Stephen was a mindless weakling, he nevertheless concurred with the majority of nobles that it was no time for England to feel a woman's hand in rule. Matilda, Henry's daughter, had taken issue with the decision. Henry had promised the throne to his widowed daughter and she brought her armies across the channel from Normandy, tossing England into a vicious civil war.

It was not long before even the most apathetic of nobles had become disturbed by the changes brought about through Stephen's ineptness. Strongbow's peers pressed him for support of Matilda but the Earl had answered them with silence. Warwick could still visualize Strongbow as he strode about the hall at Chepstow, bellowing his anger.

"They all wanted that mindless fool on the throne—but only because they thought that he would let them go their own way as Matilda would not. Now let them stew in their juices! God's Breath! I will have no part in a war for England! She has seen enough!"

Warwick knew that Strongbow also had second thoughts but that he fervently hoped Matilda would withdraw her claim and leave England in peace. Only Warwick knew of his deep concern when he was ordered to take the child from his nursemaids and guard him well. If Richard was taken into the wrong hands, it would be the lever needed to induce Strongbow to take sides.

Strongbow's position of silence was further complicated when Stephen, in a move of surprising profundity, bestowed him with the Earldom of Pembroke. Naturally it appeared that Stephen was rewarding him for his support and the new Earl was placed in the impossible position of not being able to refuse the honor, which would have insulted the crown, yet not wanting to accept it. He had no choice but to continue his silence.

Warwick's thoughts turned to those early days with the boy. To his surprise his original anger and resentment over feeling that he had been reduced to a nursemaid changed to a sincere affection for his young charge. He found the boy to be bright and full of enthusiasm for whatever challenges Warwick presented to him. It was impossible to be angry when Richard would look to him with genuine awe and respect, hanging on his every word as if it were unchallenged law.

He recalled the day when Richard rode his first horse and the time when he taught him to use the bow. He chuckled to himself remembering the moment when Richard had dragged the broadsword up to him, determined to become its master even though he could barely lift the massive steel. Remembering his pride at watching Richard grow to manhood and prepare himself for knighthood under his careful tutelage, Warwick suddenly sobered. Feeling the sharp pangs of reality, he was recalled to the present. As if the pain were physical, he rubbed his fingers across his furrowed brow.

His head came up sharply as he heard a sound from below. Peering down he spied a figure moving through the night at the foot of the wall. He watched with interest as something triggered a subtle spark within him. The figure moved across the courtyard, leading a horse until it stopped at the outer gate. As the moonlight passed over the figure Warwick tensed with recognition. Richard swung into the saddle and swiftly rode from the gate, leaving Warwick stunned for an endless moment.

Regaining his composure, he sprang from the sill.

"This time, lad, we will see what you are about."

Warwick rode through the night, following Richard's direction to the nearest village. Upon entering he spotted Richard's palfrey where it was tied beside the tavern. He slipped from his destrier and crept silently to the low building.

In a few moments he was at the back of the thatched structure and, easing himself to the window, he peered into the room.

At a glance he saw Richard standing at its center, his foot propped up on a chair by a table surrounded with men, most of whom Warwick recognized. Claresta moved about the table, filling the tankards. Sitting at the head of the table was a ruddy-complected stranger, his garments dusty with travel. He was glaring at Richard and his mouth was drawn into a tight, angry line.

Warwick leaned back against the wall, his ear near the window as his eyes darted about, assuring himself that he was unseen. His head came sharply about when a raised voice carried from the room.

"I tell you I am sure of what I am told! Do you question my word?"

"Nay, Rolf, not you," Richard answered. "I question your source. Where did he receive his information?"

"From the wife of the Lord Chamberlain. She detests the old man and would do anything to spite him."

"Did he pay her well?"

"The lady is not in need of coin. I believe that payment was given beneath the covers."

There were chortles and rude comments from the other men which Richard cut short. "You base your information on the word of a disgruntled wife?"

"Richard, that is the point. The lady is happy, for the first time. She was convent-raised and married off at the ripe age of thirteen to the old goat. Her affection for my informant is real, and returned."

Warwick heard a chair scrape and footsteps approach the window. He drew in his breath and leaned closely against the wall, his hand going to the hilt of his sword. He relaxed as the steps halted short.

"Then we will go with what we have. On the chance that it is true, the information is too important to ignore. If it is also true that it will happen before Twelfth Day, we have not much time. I know that no word of it has reached Hertford.

"Rolf, you return to London immediately. I do not want anyone to see you here. The rest of you, do not fail to keep me informed. I suspect that Stephen will deploy his men before the announcement is made. For now I must return to Hertford before my absence is discovered. I fear that my, ah . . . behavior of late has caused a certain amount of discomfort for my cousin."

The comment brought a raised eyebrow from Warwick but before he could dwell on it the men began moving about. He returned quickly to his destrier and, swinging into the saddle, he moved quietly from the tavern. As he reached the road he turned and spurred his horse toward home.

Richard opened the door and silently entered his chambers. He rolled his shoulders wearily before removing his sword and cloak, hanging them on a hook by the door. He began to unbuckle his hauberk when he suddenly tensed, sensing another presence in the room. Spinning, he grasped the hilt of his sword, pulled it from the scabbard, and turned back in a single motion.

"Ah, Richard, there is no need for that."

At the sound of Warwick's voice, Richard relaxed. He slid the blade back into its resting place.

"It is a late hour to expect visitors—and why do you sit in the dark?" He lit a candle, then knelt before the hearth, adding kindling to the nearly dead coals until the wood burst into a small, eager flame. He rose and poured two goblets of spiced wine, handing one to Warwick, who ignored the questioning glance that came with it.

"Were you waiting long?"

"Nay, not long." Warwick's eyes traveled to Richard's cloak, still damp with fog. "It is a cruel night to be about."

Richard shrugged, then a grin spread. "You know my reputation—undaunted even in the face of adversity, when the lady awaits."

Warwick's only comment was a grunt as he stared into his goblet idly, swirling the ruby liquid. He was determined to bring Richard to the truth and have done with this idiotic farce but he knew he must tread softly. Richard had stripped down to a linen chainse and chanuses and now stood before the fire, letting its warmth dry his damp clothes.

"Is there some particular reason for this late visit?"

"I thought we might have a talk, like we used to. It has been a long time, lad, and I have missed them."

"Aye, it has, and I am sorry for that." Richard plopped down in a chair across from Warwick, propping a foot on the edge of the hearth. They sat, each waiting for the other to speak. The silence grew longer, neither knowing how to begin. Warwick began to grow angry, knowing that the unusual strain between them had been put there by Richard's secretiveness. He coughed, clearing his throat uncomfortably, his voice cracking slightly as he spoke. It was so totally out of character it brought a slightly raised brow from Richard.

"Your, ah . . . mother looks well, Richard. I am glad that they did not choose to winter at Pembroke."

Richard leaned on the arm of his chair with his chin resting on his hand, his face hidden in the shadows of the room as the flickering fire played its light over Warwick's strained face. Richard studied his old friend, his own face remaining expressionless as he pondered the real reason for Warwick's being here.

"Aye, Pembroke can be cruel this time of the year."

Warwick took a long draught of his wine, emptying the goblet, then leaned over to refill it. As he sat back, he propped his feet on the hearth, exposing them to the light of the fire.

Richard glanced down and his eyes turned cold. Warwick's boots, which supposedly had brought him the short distance from his chamber, were flecked with fresh mud, the red clay found only outside the castle walls. The change in Richard's expression quickly disappeared as he raised his goblet to his mouth.

"Now tell me why you are here."

"What?" Warwick looked up, startled by the question. "I told you, I could not sleep."

"I know, so you came to talk."

"Aye."

"Then explain the mud on your boots."

Warwick's eyes followed Richard's to his feet. As Richard's meaning registered he suddenly became overwhelmingly sick of the entire episode, angry with Richard and with himself for the pretense. He slammed his goblet down on the table next to him, his black eyes blazing with anger as he glared at the younger man.

"Damnation, you are right! I am sick of this cat and mouse game between us! Let us have the truth and let it begin with you!"

"Me? I am not aware that I have lied to you," he answered calmly.

Warwick stared at him in amazement, the anger momentarily gone from his face. "Not lied?" he whispered. He jumped from his chair and paced between the door and the chair before stopping in front of Richard. Before he could speak Richard regarded him evenly.

"You have been spying on me."

"Ahhh. Do not try to put me on the defensive, Richard. Aye, I followed you tonight, but for good reason. For months you have done all you could to make everyone think the worst of you. Did you really think that I would let such behavior pass?"

"I have never lied to you, Warwick, nor to anyone else for that matter." Richard's voice was icy calm.

"You lied tonight! You said that you were with a woman!"

"Aye, and I was. You assumed the reason."

Warwick bellowed with frustration. He slammed his fist on the table, upsetting the goblet, which rolled onto the floor with a clatter. "Stop bantering with me, Richard! Everyone has believed exactly what you wanted them to! It was no mere assumption!"

"For everyone except you, is that it?"

"Aye, Richard, everyone but me. What I do not understand is why you left me out of this!"

Richard knelt before the fire, adding wood to the hungry flames while Warwick waited for an answer. He exercised what little patience he had left, sensing that Richard was struggling to find the right words. He picked up the fallen goblet and refilled it along with Richard's. Richard was mute as he took it, avoiding Warwick's questioning stare, and he carried it to the window without drinking. He stood there for a long moment in deep thought, then finally turning, he leaned against the wall and looked at Warwick openly for the first time since entering the room.

"How much do you know?"

"Enough."

"And you still wonder why I kept it from you?"

"Aye. We have been together a long time. How could you misread me so badly? Did you think I would betray you, and to whom?"

"Do you not know?"

There was a long silence as Warwick's mind tumbled with the question, then slowly the answer cut through his brain. "Strongbow? You think that . . . you really think that your father would betray you?"

"Why not?" Richard answered bitterly. He raised the goblet to his lips, missing the horrified look on Warwick's face, which quickly turned to sheer frustrated anger as Warwick spun away, shaking his head.

"Sweet Jesus! Where does it come from—this lack of understanding between father and son!" He stood facing away from Richard, afraid that if their eyes met he would lose his temper completely. For some unspoken reason he blamed himself for what was happening.

"Richard, today your father asked me what sort of a man I was returning to him. Ahhh, there was anger—but pain too! He gave me a look I shall never forget."

"Pain!" Richard snorted with disgust. "He is only angry because he feels that I have shamed him, in a manner that he cannot accept. It was all too easy for him to believe the worst."

Warwick spun back. "Richard . . ." He almost choked with his fury. "Richard—sit down!"

Richard hesitated but, when he saw the storm that had gathered in Warwick's face, he complied.

"Richard, you claim the rights of a man. It is time you developed the understanding of one!" Warwick took the chair across from him and his voice was incensed. "Your father has always been proud of you, until the past few months. During that time you have given him nothing—except what you have *wanted* him to believe. For him you have added an almost unbearable burden, that he has failed you also."

Richard looked up with surprise as Warwick raised a disgusted brow. "Aye, your father already carries the heaviest burden that a man can: that he failed everything he spent his life protecting through a mistake in judgment. Frankly, I think he is too hard on himself, and I have tried to tell him so. Matilda would have been no better than Stephen, only different. She is a cold and cruel bitch. She cares only for the power that was taken from her—that was proven when she had the throne in her grasp, only to throw it away in London, all because the merchants would not cower before her."

As he spoke, Warwick watched Richard warily, waiting for an outburst of defense for the empress. But none came. Richard just sat there, his expression noncommittal as Warwick searched his mind for the answer to the puzzle: He plots against the king, deservedly or not, but not for the empress. Then who? The dawn slowly came up in Warwick's agonized brain, the truth striking like a bolt.

"The son! My God, you've thrown your spurs to her son!"

A smile tugged at the corners of Richard's mouth over the dumbstruck expression on Warwick's face. He withheld comment, waiting for the answer he needed, knowing that this was the moment when Warwick would either support him or be the cause of his undoing. Inside he began to feel a sick knot growing in his gut, knowing what his action must be if Warwick decided against him.

"Holy Blood!" Warwick fell back in his chair and stared at Richard. He did not notice that Richard's knuckles had turned white where they grasped the arm of the chair, nor that they relaxed slightly as Warwick threw back his head and burst into a bellow of laughter. The knight wiped his eyes with the back of his large hand, then picked up his goblet, raising it to Richard in a salute before taking a long draft, wine escaping from the sides of his mouth and into his beard. Richard picked up his goblet and swirled it slowly as he stared into the cup, his voice belying what was in his eyes.

"And what will you do now?"

"Do?" Warwick considered the question with surprise. "Join you, of course! If I am to be included now!"

Richard raised the goblet to his mouth, relief flowing through him as the knot began to disappear, leaving a dull ache in the pit of his stomach. "It seems that you already are," he muttered.

Warwick slapped his knee and jumped up. He began pacing the room again, feeling more elated than he had in years. He was not sure whether his excitement was more from the fact that Richard had justified his confidence or the thought of seeing action again, committing himself to a purpose, fighting for an ideal. The memory of past battles raced through his mind, bringing him to a halt in midstep.

"Richard, what of Strongbow?"

"What about him?"

"You mean that you are not going to tell him? You would let him go on believing that . . . even now?"

"Warwick," Richard began in a tired voice. "You answer the question. I am committed to what I am doing—totally. What if I were to tell him and he did not agree? If he tried to stop me . . ."

"He would not. He may not agree with you but he would not try to stop you from doing what you believed in!"

"I cannot take that chance."

"Richard . . ."

"No." The look he gave Warwick unsettled the older knight. Richard's eyes were as hard as stone with a resolve Warwick had never seen in him before.

"Warwick, old friend, you are welcome and I am glad to have you at last with me, but only under my conditions. If I decide to tell Strongbow, it will be *my* decision, and only when I am sure of his feelings. Can you accept that?"

He waited while Warwick sat down again. The knight leaned his elbows on his knees, giving a deep sigh as he answered wretchedly, "Aye. But only because your betrayal could never serve him."

"Fair enough."

Their eyes met in a long, fixed look of understanding, then Warwick broke into a huge grin. "Now, in God's good name, will you tell me what is going to happen before Twelfth Night?"

Richard lost his composure for a moment, then chuckled. "You did your work well tonight." A tawny brow raised as he added, "I am glad that you are on my side."

Warwick guffawed at the quip as Richard leaned over and poured more wine, handing one to Warwick, who was still merrily pleased with himself.

"There is a lot to catch you up on, old friend."

Warwick accepted the wine and leaned back comfortably

as he sobered. Puckering his lips in thought, he studied Richard through narrowed eyes. "There is just one thing, before you begin . . ."

"Aye?"

"What would you have done, had I opposed what you are doing?"

Richard gave him a slight smile. "That, my friend, you will never know."

"The difference is simple, Gervase. In Erin my father, as king, gives a taurcrec, or gift of value, to the represented clans, the acceptance of which is a gesture of loyalty to him. It is his assurance that they will support him in war or other times of need."

Gervase frowned as he understood her meaning. "The tallages which the villeins bring to my lord are due him, milady. He owns the land on which they live and protects them in their endeavors without which they could not survive."

"Indeed?" Her graceful brow arched with the statement. "If this is so, then it would be true everywhere, but I assure you that it is not the case in my country."

Lavinia fingered the azure silk of her gown nervously as her blue eyes darted from Eve to Gervase to Thomas. She did not care for the tone the conversation was taking and sought to temper the remarks.

"Gervase, I am sure that Eve does not mean to be critical, do you Eve? Customs vary but there are good reasons for both."

"I do not expect you to understand our ways, Eve," Gervase continued, ignoring Lavinia's efforts. "But, I must assure you that without Gilbert's direction and the protection of our knighthood, order would become chaos and no one would be served."

"Is oppression the only means to seek that end, Gervase? My father's position as leader of our people is guaranteed by election of the clans and their right to do so is fiercely held as free men. Accordingly, his acceptance of them and recognition of their freedom is what assures their loyalty . . ."

"And has your system guaranteed their protection?" Gervase interrupted.

"Nay, no more than your own, from what I have observed. But, should they perish, at least they will have lived as free men."

To Lavinia's relief the conversation was brought to an abrupt halt as Leonore and Gilbert rose from their places to signify that the banquet was at an end. She jumped up and moved to Eve's side, almost pulling her from the chair. Upon a signal from the Mistress of Hertford, Gaspard and the servants rushed into the room to clear away the remains of the feast and to dismantle the trestle tables for the dancing that was to follow.

As the small group moved through the crowded hall, Eve ignored the glances of admonishment from Lavinia. She had no intention of apologizing for her remarks but she was sorry that she had put a damper on the festive mood. She was about

to say the same to Lavinia when she felt a touch at her elbow
and turned to find Gervase at her side. His blue eyes were
filled with suppressed humor as he bent his head in a slight
bow.

"I am quite surprised to find that you aruge politics with
such fervor, my lady!"

"Then you are not angry with me, Gervase?" she smiled.

"Nay, though I admit that you caught me off guard. One is
not accustomed to hearing such thoughts from one so lovely."

She began to open her mouth in protest but catching a
warning glance from Lavinia she snapped it shut. It took some
effort but for the sake of peace she wrapped her arm in
Gervase's and smiled brightly. "Then let us put our differences
aside and enjoy the remainder of the evening."

As the floor was cleared the strains of lute and chord were
struck by the musicians in the gallery above the hall. At the
first refrain the villagers formed a tight circle in the center of
the room, the men on the outside facing the inner circle of their
women. Eve watched with fascinated curiosity as they began
to dip and turn to the music. As the others with her began to
clap in rhythm to the dancers Gervase leaned over to her, a
pleased grin answering her delighted expression.

"The dancing is begun by the serfs in their own tradition,
a Celtic circle dance called the carole. It is one of the few
things we Normans have not changed," he teased.

Her foot began tapping to the stimulating refrains of the
music which built until the dancers spun wildly about, drawing
the nobles into their revelry as the knights grasped their ladies
and pulled them into the circle. Her eyes shining brightly as
her foot kept time to the music, Eve giggled over the missteps
of a few of the nobles. Suddenly her breath caught and her
chest tightened with pain as she spotted Richard across the
room. She attempted to shake off her disquiet and wondered
to her vexation as Gwen hung suggestively to his arm, pressing
against his side while whispering into his ear.

It hardly helped matters that Eve was acutely aware of how
handsome he looked. He wore a long sleeveless tunic of deep
blue velvet fitted closely about his muscled frame over a snowy-
white chanise of linen. The wide sleeves were slashed to reveal
a stark white underfabric, and the garment was trimmed in
silver braid with a silver-linked belt about his narrow waist.
His tanned face smiled down at Gwen as she fawned over him
and at that moment he threw back his head, his white teeth

flashing with laughter. An unreasonable fury grasped Eve as she noted the self-satisfied look on the black-haired maid as she smiled coyly up at him through her lashes. Eve spun and grabbed Gervase's arm.

"Please, Gervase, show me how to do the dance!"

Startled, the squire blinked down at her, then quickly recovered as he broke out into a grin. He grasped her about the waist and spun her into the circle of dancers. It took but a few moments of following his steps and watching the other dancers before she was moving in the rhythm of the circle. Soon she had forgotten the object of her discontent. Caught up in the exhilaration of the moment she was unaware of the grey eyes that were fixed upon her as Richard watched with open admiration, entranced by the bewitching picture she made moving lithely through the steps.

The last notes of the dance had just ended when the musicians struck a chord for the next, barely giving Eve time to catch her breath before she was swept into another and yet another dance as each of the young swains bid for her attentions. As the evening progressed the suggestive dances of the Saxon peasant eventually gave way to the more sedate ones of the Norman, the lords and ladies taking the floor to express their more polished expressions of love.

Eager for the chance to dance with her again, Miles offered his arm to Eve but when he glanced over her shoulder his brow furrowed into a bemused frown, then changed suddenly to a smile. He bowed courteously to Eve and turned on his heels, leaving her completely baffled by his odd behavior.

"You have been avoiding me, love," came a resonant voice. "I think now it is time for us."

As she spun about, Richard caught her in his arms and drew her into the line of dancers, leaving her no alternative but to take his hand. They turned about each other in the movement of the dance, circling each other like two fighting cocks. Her haughty regard only served to humor him and, as their shoulders touched, he grinned down at her, her answer being a flash of bright anger.

"Ah, *cherie*," he whispered, bending his lips to her ear, "you must smile or they will think that you do not enjoy the dance."

"Humph!" she retorted. "I am amazed that you found the time to spare! Are you certain that you would not be more well pleased with the company of a darker-haired wench?"

He followed her gaze to where Gwen danced and chuckled. "Would you have me rude? 'Tis only for appearances, that I bid the lady's company."

"Ha!" she rejoined. "For one who merely seeks to serve appearances the lady's wit pleases you well!"

"Better a wit than a waspish tongue," he countered, turning his broad back to her as her mouth opened in an angry gasp. When he turned back, his arm went about her waist, pulling her a bit more tightly than the dance warranted. His touch seemed to burn her flesh beneath her gown and she felt suddenly light-headed, her anger weakened by his nearness.

"I noticed that you have not been wanting for partners, love," he smiled. "I feared that I would have to challenge the lot of them to win but a moment of your company."

"Would you have deemed the favor so great?" she countered as she turned in his arms.

"Are you baiting me for compliments, milady?"

The dance ended as she curtsied to his bow and she answered his question with an impish smile that took him aback. Laughing, he placed a hand lightly on her waist. "Come, I shall fetch you some wine."

From the tables set along the wall he poured two deep goblets of hippocras, a wine made of grain and spiced heavily with ginger and cinnamon. She accepted it eagerly. As she held out the goblet for another measure, he warned her of its potency but she begged him for more and, shrugging, he refilled the container. A golden brow arched as he watched her quickly down the second helping and he noted that her eyes brightened and her complexion flushed to a rosy hue as she happily watched the dancers, her foot tapping in time with the music.

"There you are, Eve! We thought we had lost you!"

Gervase approached with Thomas and Miles in tow. A buxom young wench hung possessively from Thomas' arm, apparently in raptures over her good fortune to have snagged such a prize. Her presence and manner brought a doubtful look from Richard, which was not missed by Thomas as he chortled.

"Yon maid has seen fit to honor us with her company," he beamed, obviously in his cups as he added in a loud whisper, "After we fairly 'natched 'er from under 'er father's very nose!"

The words sent the girl into peels of giggles. She pressed against his arm and toyed suggestively with the laces on his tunic.

Richard frowned blackly, knowing that Gilbert held strict

rules about the manner of treatment of his serfs. While Gilbert was not above claiming his rights as lord of Hertford—and many a maid had caught his eye—he did not allow his squires and knights to freely avail themselves of the maids of unwilling fathers. The serf who knew that his lord would treat him fairly and give protection to a marriageable daughter was more likely to produce a better yield. They were also less likely to spirit their daughters away and marriageable young women attracted able young men who would offer their services to a lord.

"My lady!" Gervase cried with mock horror. "You are out of wine!" He rushed to fill Eve's goblet, missing Richard's stony glare.

She accepted the offering, unaware of Richard's growing ire. He observed the mild-mannered Miles, obviously over-wrought with wine as he stood gawking at Eve, making no attempt to hide his lustful intentions. Richard was relieved to note that she now sipped her wine but he continued to watch her guardedly as she laughed a little too loudly at the repartees of the young men and the earthy comments of Thomas' minx, who brushed boldly against the squire's arm.

Finally, as he noticed that Eve leaned a bit too closely to Gervase, a fact which the latter did not miss as he spied the swell of her lovely breasts above the low cut of her gown, Richard had had enough. Ignoring the startled looks of the others, he caught her about the waist and drew her with him toward the open doors leading to the gardens. He noticed, with no small satisfaction, that the possibility that the others might follow promised to be thwarted by an angry-looking middle-aged man trying to make his way toward the small group.

"Where are you taking me!" Eve demanded, a bit slurred.

"For some air, milady," he answered firmly. "I think you are in need of it."

The threatening storm had left the air thick with a heavy mugginess but nevertheless it gave sharp contrast to the warm, crowded hall. The shock of it hit Eve at the top of the stairs and she halted, pulling her arm from Richard's.

"I do not need your help, thank you!" she snapped. "I can do very well by myself!"

She took a step and faltered and would have tumbled down the steps but that Richard caught her about the waist. She leaned against him to the path below, then broke away to walk ahead, her arms outstretched as she breathed deeply of the cooler air of the garden. They walked along the path, the music from the hall growing gradually fainter until she stopped at a widening among a cluster of large oaks where small stone benches were placed beneath each to form a half-circle. The branches of the trees had been trimmed to allow the moonlight to enter the grove and she stood at its center, her arms outstretched to the bright moon, and as she turned in a slow circle, her lovely face shone radiant in the moonlight. He stopped and watched her calmly, shaking his head when she broke out into another giggle.

"You look so serious, Richard! Are you not happy on such a wondrous night?" She ran to him and grabbed his hand to pull him into the clearing. "Oh please, Richard, dance with me!"

"Eve, I do not think . . ."

"Nay? Then I shall dance by myself!"

She spun away from him, dipping through the steps of the carole, when suddenly she halted, her smile fading as her eyes grew wide with horror. Even in the moonlight he could see her complexion take on a slightly green tinge and he stepped quickly to her side as she groaned miserably.

"Oh, Richard, I do not feel well."

"I am not surprised," he chided gently. "Come with me."

A light hand at her waist, he led her through the trees along a narrow path to a small stream which ran through the gardens. He sat her down gently on the grassy slope, then extracted a kerchief from his tunic, dipping it into the cold water to dab her cheeks and brow.

"Eve, the fault was mine. I should not have let you drink so much of the brew since I knew you had not the palate for it." He watched her with a concerned frown and was relieved when her normal color began to return. "Do you feel better now?"

"Aye," she whispered, embarrassed by his attentions. "Oh, Richard, you must surely think me wretched."

"Nay," he chuckled softly. "It is not the manner of my mind. It was a human error that caught you tonight. You are a lovely, bewitching woman. Just, I fear, a bit sheltered."

"Sheltered?" She bristled. "Is that what you think of me?"

She sat up on her knees, setting her hands on her hips. "Richard, do not compare me with one of your delicate court ladies, closeted in their tender years by overprotective guardians fearing for their virginity!" The anger in her voice grew with denial as she saw the amusement creep into his face.

"Richard! I was raised among war, in spite of the humor you once found at the prospect! Sheltered? My grandfather was hacked apart and buried with dogs as insult! My mother was taken to die from the ravishment she suffered by my father's enemies! My brothers have never been left alone for a moment in their lives for fear they would be taken hostage and blinded or murdered and now, when the boldness of our enemies has become such that I was sent from my father's side for fear that I would be used against him, you say that I have been sheltered!"

"Eve, wait!" He had listened patiently to her outburst but as she began to jump up, he reached out and grasped her arm to stop her. She tried to pull away but his grip was firm. He pulled her back against him.

"Richard, let me go!" she shrieked.

Her struggles were useless as he turned her with ease and pushed her down onto the grass, holding her squirming body beneath him.

"Eve, stop struggling and be still! You cannot always be running away whenever someone disagrees with you!"

She held but he could feel the tenseness in her and he knew that she was ready to spring at any moment. He eyed her suspiciously and his voice was guarded. "Eve, if I let you go, will you listen to me? Will you sit quietly so that we may talk?"

She nodded slightly, knowing that she had no choice but to agree but her mouth drew into a decided pout. Warily, he released her and allowed her to sit up, wondering as he did if she would keep her word. Refusing to meet his gaze she stared past him, folding her arms across her chest in a gesture of defiance, unaware of how the action pushed her breasts to where they strained against the fabric of her pelisse. The situation did not go unheeded by Richard as he forced his eyes away from the vision, trying not to look upon the bounty she lay before his gaze.

"Eve," he began patiently, "I do not seek to minimize what you have suffered. Your losses or your grief. Your life has been hard, I do not deny it, but what meaning do these things have for you? Can you learn by them to find a better purpose or do they merely lie within you as food for bitterness?"

She peered at him uncertainly. "What do you mean?"

"Well, as a beginning, ask yourself this: Why did your father send you to England? He told you that it was for your safety, but can you think of nothing else?"

"Nay! What other reason could there be? Are you inferring that my father had some devious purpose for sending me here?" Her eyes sparked with angry denial. "Being the Englishman you are, how could you possibly understand my father's mind?"

"Eve," he sighed, "You make quick judgments, based upon your emotions without any conviction to purpose, rushing headlong into a cause without considering the results."

"Are you quite through insulting me!"

"I am not trying to insult you! I only want you to begin to see the world through a woman's eyes, not that of a spoiled child seeing only what she wants to see."

"Ha!" she cried. "That again! Let me tell you, Richard, what these spoiled, unseeing eyes saw today! A saddened people, oppressed by their betters, whose responsibility it was to protect and care for them but who are so involved with their own pleasures that they did not, or cared not, to see the suffering!"

There was a sudden stillness as he regarded her thoughtfully. "You saw this?"

"Aye," she answered gloatingly. "I said as much to Gervase. Shall I now return to the hall and press the issue—with conviction to purpose?"

"It is well to criticize an injustice, Eve," he admonished. "But before you do be quite certain that it is very important to you, that you are prepared to give up a great deal to defend it. Perhaps everything."

"How would you know . . ."

She halted in mid-sentence as she realized what she had been about to say to him. The truth about Richard began to focus, what he was fighting for, the risks he took, and, indeed, how sheltered she had been for all the terror she had seen. He was right. It was as if her life had happened to her but she had never really been involved with it. She simply moved through it while others formed its path.

"What choice have I been given?" she snapped, using her anger as a wall against the unpleasant truth he was making her see. "It is so easy for you to stand in judgment from the viewpoint of your man's world, shielded by your armor! I am a woman. Is it not expected for me to blithely accept without complaint what is given me?"

He said nothing as he leaned over and reached behind her to snap a winter rose from its bush. Turning it in his fingers he regarded her steadily. "Eve, this rose is soft and fragile,

bruising easily. By all appearances it must be handled gently
if it is to survive. If it is nurtured well, its roots go deep, its
bark withstands even winter's chill. While it is only the flower
we choose to see, its inner strengths are what protect it and
allow it to blossom."

For a long moment she said nothing. Then she took the
flower from him and turned it slowly in her hands. Finally,
she looked up and her eyes were sparkling with mischief. "While
its blossom appears to be its coat-of-arms, Richard, its thorns
are truly its shield—if they are sharp enough."

"As long as they do not prick too sorely," he parried with
a grin. "For in such an event one would cease to care for the
beauty of the flower." But then his smile disappeared as his
eyes softened. "Tell me, Eve, what is it that you want?" he
asked gently.

She was startled by the question, so simply stated. She had
expected more accusations, more criticism, anything but the
tender way he was looking at her. For once his gaze was void
of the accustomed mocking challenge.

"I—I do not know," she stammered in a half-whisper. "I
have always felt that I was in control of my life but now I
know that I have never been. The realization is not very pleasant."

"Truth seldom is," he said flatly. "But once faced it's a
beginning. One thing I've learned is that until you understand
and know yourself, who and what you are, you are of no use
to yourself or anyone else. I too have my demons which chase
me and often they cause me to forget how I might be hurting
others."

"As I meant to hurt you," she said quietly. When he made
no reply she forced her gaze up to his and was surprised to
find a hint of a smile on his lips. "You knew!" she breathed.
"All along, you knew!"

"I was certain that you were plotting something," he grinned.
"The change was much too sudden, my love, and in that I have
not noticed compliance to be one of your virtues, there was no
reason to expect that you would suddenly offer it to me. I must
admit that I was awaiting the outcome with great interest."

"The buttery. . ." she gasped, her cheeks reddening with
the sudden realization. "It was a game for you! You—Oh!"

All along he had known what she was about, that she was
deliberately plying him with her wiles that she had thought to
be so successful! How childish she must have appeared to him!

The enormity of it was too much to bear. She struggled to her feet, intent on fleeing those laughing eyes, unaware that he was sitting on the hem of her gown. As she turned to escape up the slope, the skirt caught and jerked back. Her soft slippers slid out from under her on the dewy grass and she plunged backwards, landing in his lap. His look was no less startled than her own and as they blinked at each other, he braced himself for the outburst he knew was coming. To his complete amazement her eyes began to crinkle at the corners and she leaned her head back against his shoulder and started to laugh. A happy, infectious laughter that caught him up in her humor.

Spent, she lay helplessly in his arms, gasping for breath. Slowly he became aware of the soft, supple form that lay pressed against him, her face flushed with laughter and her eyes sparkling happily beneath thick lashes. Giving in to a strong impulse he drew her into his arms and lowered his mouth to hers, kissing her tenderly. As they drew apart he looked into depths of green full of wonder and a hint of curiosity but fixed on his own. Silently, his hand cupped her face and he raised her mouth to his once again, his tongue flicking lightly over her lips, which quavered under his in a tentative response.

Her lips molded to his, her mind fixed upon the feel of him, savoring the rushing warmth that began to spread over her. She became aware of his hands on her shoulders as he lowered her gently onto the sweet-smelling grass. She moaned softly while his lips moved tenderly over her face to caress her eyelids, to the corners of her trembling mouth, to travel with deliberate slowness to the nape of her neck, when she closed her eyes to the unfamiliar rush of ecstasy his touch brought. Murmuring gently to her he loosened the clasp of her bodice and his hands slipped beneath the garment, pushing it aside as his lips traced a molten path to the tip of her full white breast. She gasped, arching her back against him, her mind spinning in wonder as his tongue teased its tip and a deep, swelling ache began to consume her. Her arms went about him with unreserved emotion, encouraging his suit, finding herself awakening to a vague awareness of his own impassioned needs.

They lingered there, his hands and tongue causing wonders that set her emotions to a raw edge. She could feel her heart pounding beneath his fingers, spiraling her mind to another plane where the grassy knoll and the gardens seemed to disappear. His arm slipped beneath her head and his lips covered hers once more. The kiss seemed to draw the very breath from her, even as she became aware that he was readjusting her bodice. He rose on an elbow and looked down at her, his eyes roaming tenderly over her face for a brief moment before he bent down and kissed her.

He rose to his feet, pulling her with him and into his arms where he held her closely for a long, quiet moment. Slipping a hand under her chin, he turned her face up and looked down into her confused eyes with regret.

"This is not the time, nor the place, *cherie,*" he murmured. "Besides, I have made a promise and it shall be kept."

Unable to speak, she watched while his eyes moved over her slowly, as if memorizing each part of her, until they came to rest on her bodice where it had again fallen open. She followed his gaze to the objects of his hungry regard and flushed deeply as her hands flew to rebind them. She fumbled awkwardly until he gently brushed her hands aside and refastened the clasp. The backs of his fingers lingered against the straining velvet.

"Oh, Richard, I do not understand," she said in a small voice. "How can I be so angry with you one moment and yet the next . . ." She blushed on the unfinished comment but turned her face up to him. Her eyes were open and vulnerable with question.

"Perhaps it is that you are not really angry with me but are only frightened of emotions you do not understand." He smiled gently, tracing his finger down the softness of her cheek. "Nay, I think that there is something else besides anger between us."

His words gave her pause. As she looked up into his eyes, which were full of tender warmth, she realized that she felt a comfort in his presence she had never felt with another. Moreover, it had always been there, even through the anger and hostility. A security, a bond that seemed to tie them together from the moment of their meeting . . .

"Ah, love," he smiled ruefully. "I fear that the next few days shall prove a sore trial."

Missing her puzzled look, he took her by the arm, pausing as she bent to retrieve the fallen blossom and tuck it into her bodice. Then he led her back to the clearing beneath the oaks. Stopping under the bright moonlight, he helped her to adjust her coronet and settle her appearance to rights before their return to the hall.

"Richard, what did you mean, about the next few days?"

"I mean that I shall miss you."

"Miss me? Are you going somewhere?" The disappointment was heavy in her voice.

"Not far." He smiled. "Tomorrow shall be spent preparing for the knighting ceremonies and three days hence I shall enter sanctuary for the purification that must precede my knighthood."

"And then you shall be transformed beyond mortal men," she quipped. "Is that not so?"

"I expect to be the same man, *cherie*. If you wish more I fear you will be greatly disappointed."

"What is it that you expect, Richard? What is it that makes knighthood desirable for you and the others?"

"Oh, I think they look forward to dedicating themselves to an ideal. There are many who seek the protection knighthood will give them and a few who have been given the chance to provide for their families in a more secure way."

"And you?"

"I doubt that I will live my life differently than I do now." He shrugged. "Perhaps it is the training for war that knighthood provides that I find of the most value."

"And the authority that it will give you?" she pressed. "To do what—ah—you are attempting to do?" She glanced about nervously to see if anyone had approached.

He smiled at her caution. "I do not think that any amount of authority would justify my actions to His Majesty, *cherie*."

"Oh, Richard, why do you pursue this course? It can only lead to . . ."

He silenced her alarm with a finger to her lips and he shook his head. "Hush. Do not question me on this matter for I will not discuss it with you. Nay," he added firmly as she began to protest. "For your own safety it is better that you do not know."

He drew her into his arms and soon the thoughts were dismissed from her mind as she reeled in wonder.

10

Eve stretched languorously, then let her body go limp as she stared at the canopy above the bed, her thoughts moving dreamily over the events of the previous night.

"Richard," she thought, rolling his name over and over in her mind. Her green eyes flared slightly as the thought struck her; she was in love with him! Totally, completely. Good Lord, what would her father say, or her brothers, if they knew she was in love with an English knight! But they must have considered the possibility ... aye, they must have!

So then, this is what it is like to be in love. She felt warm thinking about him. There was a flush of excitement when she thought of seeing him again, and an almost physical pain from not being with him now, at every moment.

But did he feel the same? He had said that his night was to be spent in prayer, his thoughts kept from all worldy contemplations. Could it be so? Not one thought for her? She had nothing in her experience that could relate to such control, certainly not in relationships between men and women. In Erin, love was simply taken where it was found and treasured.

If only she could have talked with him after their moments alone in the garden! He was a normal, full-blooded man, to that she could attest. Could he dismiss the tantalizing promise of their budding relationship? The thought passed through her mind that it had only been a passing interlude for him ...

Disturbed, she leapt from the bed and laid the morning fire, shivering in her chemise until the flames grew to a warming height. She splashed her face with icy water, then laid out the garments she had painstakingly chosen for the coming day. She had selected an exquisite silk brocade of delicate buttercup yellow, embossed on its hem, sleeves and bodice with roses of a slightly darker hue and pale green leaves. She would have Bridget garland her hair with matching roses of silk, since she still refused to wear the stiff linen wimple, even out of doors.

Her toilette was nearly completed when Bridget entered with her breakfast tray. The kindly maid's eyes widened with surprise to find Eve up and about.

"Ye had better eat something, lass! It will be a long while before ye have another chance, as mid-meal will not be taken until after the ceremonies."

Eve was much too excited to eat but bowed to Bridget's good sense and she sat obediently at the table where the tray had been set before the fire. She stared at the food with distaste and wondered how she would be able to force even a bite, until she spied a small linen-wrapped bundle on the tray and a square of parchment lying next to it.

"Bridget, what is this?" she queried, picking up the note.

The maid looked over her shoulder from where she stirred the fire and shrugged. "'Twas laid in me hand by Sir Warwick and he bade me give it to ye."

Puzzled, Eve opened the note.

> My love, you shall never be far from my thoughts.
> Wear this today so that I may know that you think
> of me.
>   Richard

Her heart soared with happiness, her doubts washed aside as her eyes lingered lovingly on the signature. Her fingers trembling, she opened the package and gasped audibly at what lay within the thin wool wrappings.

"What is it my lady?" Eve's gasp had brought Bridget quickly to her side and the servant's mouth dropped open in astonishment when she beheld the object that lay in Eve's hand. It was a magnificent emerald suspended on a delicate golden chain. "Oh, milady! 'Tis beautiful! Sir Warwick must truly be smitten with ye to . . ."

"Oh, Bridget!" Eve laughed. "It is not from Sir Warwick! But you must keep this to yourself, do you understand? I will not have this a source of common gossip in the kitchens!"

"Aye, milady," Bridget said stiffly.

Eve sighed, knowing better than to hope that the servant would hold her wagging tongue. From experience Eve knew that it would be general knowledge by nightfall.

"It is time to dress my hair, Bridget," she said a bit crossly as the woman was still gaping at the jewel. "We had better hurry or I shall be late for mass."

The sun broke through the overcast skies to illuminate the open-sided tents which stretched in a large half-circle about the jousting field in a riot of bursting color. Rows of banners hung from the blue and red stripes of the canvas tents, boldly declaring the families represented. At the center of the circle was a raised platform covered in an azure-striped cloth where the ceremonies would take place. Behind the platform stood a straight row of iron-tipped lances hewed of ash, impaled in the ground, from which hung fork-tailed pennons lifting in unison in the slight breeze, each bearing the coat-of-arms of the soon-to-be knights. The velvet green of the grassy field was dotted with the brightly colored gowns of the women and tunics of the men who meandered about, the excitement of the morning evidenced in the tinkling sound of laughter that easily carried across the sharp morning air, its current charged with anticipation.

Eve walked arm-in-arm with Lavinia across the field toward the tents, her mind still fixed in dreaming upon the vision of Richard as he had knelt before the altar in the crowded chapel with the other squires. How handsome he had looked! His grey eyes, for once solemn, were stark against the white garments which were girdled about his narrow waist with slender links of gold. As the priest's voice intoned in the steady Latin of the mass, Eve's thoughts had wandered in remembrance of the way Richard's eyes would crinkle at the corners when he smiled and how they would turn to a warm, deep gray when he would catch her looking at him during their dancing after their return to the hall. She recalled the memories she had once tried with such effort to push to the back of her mind: the moment of awe she had felt when she first laid eyes on him towering above her in the forest; his strength in command and the loyalties he drew from those who served him; the gentleness he was capable of showing, the concern he had shown as he had pressed the coins into her hands. The desire he could stir within her even upon a look, a touch. She smiled as she realized that such thoughts had once brought anger and resentment and now filled her with feelings of warmth and security.

"Oh, Eve! Is this not but the most glorious of days!" Lavinia squeezed her arm, bringing her thoughts back to the present.

"Aye, Lavinia, it is that." Eve returned her friend's smile. "I must say that you seem to be basking in it."

"I have a most special reason to feel so," Lavinia answered in a half-whisper, a blush touching her fair cheeks while she glanced at Eve. "Gervase has asked me to join him on the dais today."

"Oh?" Eve looked puzzled.

"Each newly-vested knight brings a lady of his choice to the dais with him to share his honor banquet," she explained. Her gaze fell to the emerald which hung from its slender gold chain between Eve's breasts. "Has Richard not asked you yet?"

"Nay," Eve answered softly.

"Well, I am sure that he will," Lavinia assured her, patting her hand where it lay on her arm.

As they approached the tents a message was brought from Lady Isabel informing them that she wished for them to sit with her during the ceremonies.

"My goodness," Lavinia observed as the harried servant bustled away. "That should stir Leonore's nettle."

Lavinia's meaning escaped Eve but she did not dwell upon it as they slowly made their way to the center tent. Gervase had asked Lavinia to sit with him on the dais but Richard had made no mention of it. Had he asked another? The thought struck a painful chord and she had to swallow back a lump in her throat.

As they reached the center of the main tent, Isabel rose and greeted them, her warmth in sharp contrast to the cold and disapproving stare Eve received from Leonore, who sat on Isabel's right. It was obvious that the mistress of Hertford took great issue with the favor Isabel was bestowing upon the Irish maid by asking her to sit with them. As Eve took the offered chair next to Isabel, Leonore pointedly drew the older woman's attention.

"We are so proud of Richard," she purred. "I daresay Gwen has been beside herself with excitement!"

So, Eve thought, Leonore sets her sights upon Richard for Gwen! Could it be that the suit was well received and he has asked her to sit beside him on the dais? Her heart twisted with the reasoning and her hand went involuntarily to the emerald. The gesture brought Isabel's eye to the jewel.

"Eve, what a beautiful stone! I do not think that I have seen one so lovely!"

Eve flushed at the attention but the cold look from Leonore stirred a reckless courage. "It is beautiful, I agree, milady. But it is all the more precious to me because of the one who gave it to me." She smiled as she felt Leonore's eyes riveted to her. "It was a gift from Richard."

An audible gasp came from Leonore but Isabel merely smiled and patted Eve's hand. "My dear, I find that my son's taste in jewels is surpassed only by that of his taste in maids."

Warmed by the compliment, Eve murmured her thanks and glanced at Lavinia, who was beaming with satisfaction. At that moment their attention was drawn to the field as horns sounded and she saw Gilbert enter the field followed by Richard, who was flanked by Strongbow and Warwick, while Gervase, Miles and the others walked behind with the knights they had served, to where they stopped at the base of the platform.

Richard paused at the foot of the steps. Gilbert and Warwick mounted the platform and at its center turned to face him. After Gilbert nodded, his cousin ascended the steps to stand before him. With Warwick's help they assisted Richard into his vestments of knighthood. They armed him with a corselet of leather, then a hauberk of double-woven mail, and shod his feet with boots of double mesh. A golden tunic of linen, lovingly fashioned by Isabel, was pulled over his head and on his chest was emblazoned the three red chevrons of the deClare coat-of-arms. A helm was placed upon his head over the coif of the hauberk, the crest of the helm in the red and gold plume of his colors, and golden spurs were girded to his feet as symbols of his honors. Lastly, they lay his shied over his arm, the great deClare coat-of-arms on its gold background. He bent to one knee and looked up at his cousin with the reverence due the great Earl. Gilbert turned and lifted the sword, freshly brought from its blessing in the chapel, from its resting place on the altar. He held it before Richard, who reached forward and grasped the hilt, bringing it to his lips in homage to the holy relics contained within. The task being done, Gilbert aided him in fixing the scabbard to his belt, then stood once again before him in solemn regard.

"Richard FitzGilbert deClare, go forth!" His voice rang out loud and true as deep emotion touched upon his words. "Be

forever courageous in the face of thine enemies and that of
England! Be thou upright and true that God may forever love
thee and be never false upon the vows you have uttered this
day!"

Richard's answer rang out, his voice firm and strong, "Aye,
lord, so shall I, with God's blessing!"

Eve's eyes misted as she beheld the beauty and solemnity
of the moment, when suddenly, to her total horror, as Richard
knelt still before him, Gilbert raised his hand and dealt Richard
a stunning blow, almost knocking the young man from his
knees.

"He struck him!" she gasped, half-rising from her chair.

There were titters from those within hearing as Lady Isabel
leaned to her, merriment apparent in her voice as she whispered, "That is the colee, Eve. It is given as an aid to memory
so that Richard will never forget his vows. It seals the moment
of knighthood."

"Oh," she murmured, greatly embarrassed by her outburst.

The moment following the colee there was a great roar of
approval from the assembly as Richard stood to be warmly
embraced by his cousin. Warwick slapped him on the shoulder
as he brushed by them and descended the steps, whereupon he
disappeared between the tents. Richard descended the steps
slowly, his eyes meeting Strongbow's for a long, silent moment. Richard sank to one knee before his father, his face
upturned as he spoke with feeling.

"It is my most fervent wish, my lord, to bring none but
honor to the name I carry."

As Strongbow reached out and laid his hand on his shoulder,
Richard was startled to see a hint of tears in his father's eyes.

"You need not fear, my son, for it does not occur to me
that you will do less."

As Richard arose Warwick emerged from behind the tents
leading a magnificent war horse of coal black, with trappings
of the finest leathers over a blanket of gold edged in red.
Murmurs rippled across the gathering in appreciation of the
exceptional destrier while Richard walked slowly forward.
Warwick grinned broadly as Richard took the bridle in his hands
and stroked the neck and nose of the fine animal, unable to
speak.

"Well, Richard," Warwick laughed good-naturedly. "Think
you that you can handle such as this? At the least you will not
see the need to borrow my mount in the future!"

"Aye," Richard whispered. "I can handle him, for if I cannot I shall never deserve another."

"And what shall you call him?"

Richard hesitated only for a moment before he murmured, "I shall call him Taran, for I think it shall be like riding rolling thunder."

The war horse began to paw the ground and snort through his nostrils then tossed his massive head as if he approved of his name and his new master. Richard needed no further encouragement as he took the reins from Warwick and swung into the saddle. He spun him about and galloped to the back of the platform where, upon the pass, he grabbed his lance from its place in the line, wrenching it from the ground. Holding the shaft beneath his arm, its iron-tipped point held before the head of the horse, he bore down on the quintain set up at the end of the field. The well-trained animal tensed, instinctively ready for the impact as he carried his master to the target. Richard speared the quintain neatly, knocking it from its stand as a cheer of approval reverberated across the field. He spun on to the next target and the next until he came once again before the platform and pulled the horse to a stop before Strongbow, the dirt spraying out beneath the planted hoofs. He swung from the saddle and grasped Strongbow's arm warmly, the antagonisms of the years passed forgotten in the moment.

Warwick led Taran from the field while Richard and Strongbow took their places in the circle, for the ceremonies were to proceed with Gervase, then each in turn, lasting well into the early afternoon.

The knightings completed, they moved into the tents to receive the well-wishes of their families and friends. Richard took his mother into his arms as her eyes brimmed with tears of pride, her heart tight with the pleasure-pain of seeing her son full-grown and a man now responsible to himself.

Eve stood to one side with Lavinia, not knowing how she should react. Richard had made no attempt to acknowledge her presence. Indeed she could not even be certain that he knew that she was there. She wondered if she should slip away while everyone's attention was centered on Richard and Gervase, who stood nearby with his family. Gervase spotted Lavinia and held out a hand to her and Eve found herself standing alone and feeling more uncomfortable by the moment. She stared at Richard's profile as he held his mother at his side and accepted the congratulations of the well-wishers gathered about. Though she stood close enough to be able to smell the scent of the musk he wore, he laughed and joked with the others without even so much as casting a glance her way. Mortified, she began to doubt his feelings and wanted nothing more than to disappear before he noticed her standing there. As she turned to leave, he reached over and took her hand in his, drawing her to his side. Surprised, she looked up at his profile as he laughed heartily at a jest from Lord Severn and he gave her hand a gentle squeeze, which sent a rush of warmth to her very nerve endings.

He leaned down and brushed Isabel's cheek with a light kiss as she moved away with Strongbow, that noble lord accepting congratulations from the others like a father of a newly-born. It was then that Richard looked down at Eve for the first time, grinning at her as he slipped an arm about her slender waist, his eyes warming to a deep grey as they moved over her raptured face.

"Whose tender voice could it be that I heard cry out on the colee?" he teased.

She drew in her breath as she dropped her gaze with embarrassment. "I am sorry, Richard. I did not understand, it was so sudden!"

He laughed as his arm squeezed her gently. "Do not apologize, love. It was well worth the startled look on Gilbert's face!"

She smiled back at him, suddenly feeling gloriously content to be in his arms.

"I see that you wear my gift," he said, obviously pleased.

"Oh, Richard, it is beautiful! But what meant even more were the words you sent. I had wondered if your thoughts were the same. I did not want to believe that you could put me from your thoughts so easily!"

His eyes filled with amusement, "It was not easy, my love, though I found myself equal to the task."

He laughed at the quick pout that appeared and, giving her a gentle hug, they joined the others to cross the field to the hall.

Tankard upon tankard was raised in toasts of celebration, good cheers and laughter abounding into a boisterous revelry. The tables were laden with a succulent repast, attesting to the efforts Gaspard had given to the momentous occasion.

Her worries put aside, Eve felt she had never known such happiness as she sat next to Richard on the dais. There had been a moment of confusion when they had entered the hall. In her uncertainty of where she was to sit, she had held back, drawing a quizzical look from Richard. When he had understood her hesitation, he had shaken his head with disbelief and with a firm hand on her arm he had escorted her to the place next to his.

The afternoon passed as though in a dream, each moment building upon the one before, bringing her the first real peace since coming to England. As she listened to yet another toast, Richard laid his hand over hers on the arm of her chair, and absentmindedly caressed it with his fingers while he listened to the happy banter that crossed the tables. His touch sent a pleasurable tingle up her arm and she breathed a deep sigh of contentment. He seemed to sense her feelings and she looked up to find him smiling down at her, his eyes dark with emotion.

"You look well content, my love," he murmured.

"I am, my lord. Problems seem not to exist when you are near."

He raised her hand to his lips and brushed them across the tips of her fingers. "Then I shall have to keep you near to me."

"Do not make promises that you cannot keep, Sir Knight, for I shall attempt to hold you to them," she teased.

"The attempt shall not be hard won, *cherie,* for I shall never willingly break a vow to you. Each promise shall be seriously met."

The intentness of his gaze fairly drew her breath from her, suspending the moment into an endless space. As Eve turned her attention to the laughter at the table, Gaspard appeared at Richard's shoulder and leaned down to his ear to whisper a message. Richard's face drew into a black scowl and he glanced at Eve briefly before nodding to Gaspard. As the steward departed, Richard made his excuses to their dinner partners and rose, holding out his hand to Eve.

"My lady, Strongbow would have us join him in the lesser hall."

He stated the request calmly but Eve tensed as she noted an underlying guardedness in Richard's manner. She allowed him to usher her from the dais but her mind rushed with disquieting thoughts. She glanced to the empty chairs, confirming that Sir Gilbert, Warwick and Strongbow had indeed left the banquet. What could they want with her? An unsettling fear played upon her as she held tightly to Richard's hand, gaining no comfort from that source because she could feel the tension in his touch. She stole a glance at him and became alarmed at his grim profile as he pushed back the screen to the small room and stood back for her to enter. She drew in her breath, her fears becoming realized as Strongbow and Warwick turned to greet the pair with grave looks. Sir Gilbert stood at the end of the table which centered the room and with a nod of his head, gestured for Eve to sit.

She did as she was bid and she looked nervously from one to the other, taking a small comfort from the fact that Richard stood at the back of her chair, his hand laid protectively on her shoulder.

"My dear," Sir Gilbert began, clearing his throat uncomfortably. "I fear that we have grave news. Word has reached us from across the sea . . . It is in regards to your family . . ."

"My family?" she cried, terror filling her eyes. "What has happened? Have they fallen?"

"Nay, they are safe," Strongbow assured her hastily. "But I fear that your father has committed an act so grievous in nature that the situation in Ireland has worsened."

She looked from one to the other, trying to comprehend their meaning, then turned and looked pleadingly to Richard for an explanation.

"What has he done?" Richard asked.

Strongbow answered grimly, "It would seem that he has formed a powerful alliance with two other chieftains, Murtough O'Loughlin and Turlough O'Conner. Together they have made a new division of Meath, restoring Murtough over the western half and his son Melaghlin over its eastern portion."

"But that means Tiernan O'Rourke has been defeated!" Eve cried. "For it is he who has claims upon Meath, as given by the high-king!"

"Ah—not quite, milady." Strongbow hesitated. "Rory O'Conner, according to our sources, had not given his blessing to the alliance, nor does he recognize their right to Meath. That is wherein the problem lies. He has joined forces with O'Rourke to squelch the alliance. I fear that Ireland has been reduced to a trembling sod."

"But why did my father do such a thing?" Eve breathed, more to herself than to anyone in the room. "It was never his ambition to take Meath, or any other. It was only Leinster and Okinselagh that he sought to secure!"

"We can only guess as to his meaning, milady, but I believe

that it was for another purpose that he formed, and used, the alliance," answered Strongbow.

"There is something more?" Richard peered at his father.

"Aye," Strongbow sighed. "There was a great battle at Tiernan's stronghold, Dai ngean Bona Cuilinn. Upon burning it to the ground Dermot carried away Dervorgil, Tiernan's wife, and all of her wealth."

Eve stared incredulously at Strongbow for a long moment, then suddenly her hand flew to her mouth and, to everyone's confusion, she began to laugh. Startled, the men exchanged doubtful looks. Fearing that she had become hysterical, Richard sat quickly down beside her and grasped her shoulders, his eyes boring into hers with concern.

"Eve!"

"Oh, Richard!" She laughed. "I cannot believe it! O'Rourke's bantinnera taken! Do you not understand the justice? After all these years my father has had his revenge!" Her laughter stopped sharply and she became grim as a sharp edge of bitterness came into her voice. "Though my father will not be as cruel as O'Rourke. You may not be aware of it but Melaghlin, the new king of East Meath, is Dervorgil's brother. If my father chose to form an alliance with him, he will not use her the way O'Rourke used my mother. At least not to death." As she glanced about at the others, an almost satisfied smile played at the corners of her mouth. "Though I wonder if the lady did not go willingly. Her husband is not known for his gentleness. Moreover, his nickname is 'one-eye'—and it is the most pleasing thing that may be said about the brute's appearance."

Richard lowered his hands from her shoulders. Their shock over her response was apparent as the men exchanged disapproving looks. They had expected her to be horrified by her father's actions. That a young maid should be so elated, so coldly calculating over the rape of a bantinnera, even though the wife of her father's enemy. And she was pleased at the prospect that the lady went willingly! It began to occur to them that the manner of this maid was not as the gently reared examples they expected to find in their own households. The disapproving looks of the older men caused Richard to squirm uncomfortably.

"Eve," he asked patiently. "Do you understand the gravity of this situation?"

"I understand that it is sweet revenge!" she answered grimly, her eyes glowing with satisfaction. "And if Dervorgil is pleased to come to my father's bed, then it is all the sweeter."

Richard winced upon her words as embarrassed coughs were heard about the room.

"I am sure that milady speaks from grief for her mother's death, so cruelly given . . ." Gilbert sputtered.

Eve glanced from one to the other, confused by their embarrassment. She would have said more on the subject but for the warning frown shot at her. She stared at the folded hands in her lap as she chose her words more carefully.

"My lords, if it is true that my father has been successful in battle against his enemies, then perhaps I may now return home, to be with him . . ."

"It is out of the question!" interrupted Gilbert as he shook his head. "Did you not hear my lord Strongbow's words? The provinces are at war and there is no way to determine the outcome! Nay, I could not allow you to return now when there is such danger!"

"Danger?" Eve flared, stung with disappointment. "My lord, you speak of danger, yet how can you assure me of safety knowing what I have suffered here?"

Four pair of eyes widened at the outburst but Eve rushed forward, encouraged by their silence. "You find the taking of Dervorgil abhorrent to your sensitivities, yet I myself nearly missed experiencing that cruel game. Aye, and by one of your own English soldiers when but a few days within this land of my sanctuary! Why, if I had not been rescued by . . ."

She had almost blurted out Richard's part in her recounting when she noticed that he had suddenly paled. She froze, the words almost spilled, fairly choking her as they sought freedom. The men stared at her in stunned silence.

"Fortunately," she continued in a tempered voice, "Sir Bowen rescued me in time."

She looked at Richard, relieved to see that some color was returning to his face and she dropped her gaze once again as she shivered over what she had almost said. She cursed silently, furious with herself that her uncontrolled anger had again gotten the best of her. This time she could have caused grievous damage to one for whom she deeply cared.

"My lady." Gilbert's voice was strained. "Are you telling us that on your journey here you were the subject of an attack?"

"Aye, milord," she answered, willing her eyes not to look at Richard.

"Why was I not told of this before?"

"There was no occasion to do so, milord."

"God's Blood!" he roared. "No occasion? Did you not re-count the story to Lady Leonore? It was she who greeted you upon your arrival!"

Eve glanced nervously from one to the other, not knowing how to respond as they looked at her intently. It was Warwick who spoke, for the first time since Eve had entered the room, and his manner was gentle with understanding, "My lady, did you have occasion to recount your story to Leonore?"

Eve did not answer but chewed nervously on her lip as Gilbert's eyes narrowed with anger. He sat down at the table across from Eve. His eyes were cold but his voice kind as he prodded her to tell the story of her journey to Hertford. Care-fully leaving out Richard's part, she answered his questions, feeling the anger of the older men as she timidly told of the moments in the soldier's camp.

As she finished there was a heavy silence in the small room. Gilbert rubbed his forehead painfully. "Sweet Jesus, and I promised your father that you would be safe in England."

"Why should her safety be guaranteed when our own people do not enjoy that privilege?" Richard stated the question flatly. "What happened to Eve was far less than what others suffer under Stephen's rule."

Warwick's ears perked up upon Richard's words and he stepped forward to take the moment. "Aye, Richard strikes to the heart of the matter. If Stephen's policies continue, or the lack of them, England will decay into a worse state of anarchy than is seen in Ireland."

"Stephen grows old." Gilbert shrugged. "England will not see his weak hand forever."

"God's blood!" Richard gasped. "Is that what you wait for, Stephen's death?" He glanced at Warwick and his jaw tightened as a firm determination appeared in his eyes. "And what of his son?"

"Eustace? What of him?" Strongbow looked at his son with interest. "What are you saying?"

"Just that we should consider the possibility that Stephen may not wait to name his heir. After all, inept as he is, he may be wise enough to realize that England's peers will not accept Eustace. Unless, of course, it is established while he has the power to enforce it."

Strongbow stared at Richard, considering the comment for

a long moment. "Are you suggesting that Stephen might now relinquish his throne to Eustance?"

"It is a possibility."

"Nonsense!" Gilbert blurted. "Even if Stephen were that shrewd he is too greedy to consider doing so!"

"Perhaps," Richard answered calmly. "But the queen is not."

Gilbert snorted in rejection of Richard's premise but Strongbow studied his son as he considered the possibility. He had to agree that Queen Matilda's wisdom far exceeded even that of the other Matilda across the channel harbored in Normandy. The queen was a force to be reckoned with.

Eve, who had sat silently listening to the exchange, stirred uncomfortably in her chair. In her silence the physical drain of the past few hours began to play upon her. Remembering the purpose of their meeting Gilbert rose from his chair.

"My lady, I fear that this has been a most exacting day for you and I am certain that you would wish to retire. Richard, please see Lady Eve to her bedchamber. I doubt that she would now wish to rejoin the festivities."

As the young couple left the room, Strongbow's gaze followed his son, then shifted to Warwick. As their eyes met Strongbow's narrowed and his lips pursed in careful thought.

When they approached the door to her bedchamber, Eve tensed, knowing that Richard's anger was held just beneath the surface. Nothing had been said between them while he had accompanied her up the stairs but she knew that he was furious with her. She hesitated at the door and murmured a good night while refusing to meet his eyes. As she placed a hand on the latch, hoping that he would be silent in his displeasure of her, his hand covered hers and he pushed open the door. She winced at the edge in his voice.

"I think that we have a few things to say to each other before you retire."

He closed the door behind him and stood leaning against the frame as she paused in the center of the room. Swallowing, she turned to face him.

"You are angry with me. You have good reason to be," she said softly, staring at the floor. "What I did was inexcusable. I came dangerously near to jeopardizing you, and everything you are trying to do, through my anger. You were correct when you told me that I jump headlong into a situation without considering the consequences."

"Eve, that is enough."

"What?" She blinked. "But I am trying to apologize! I—"

His look silenced her. He crossed to the hearth where he stopped before the fire and stared into the flames as if to compose his thoughts. She waited nervously, biting her lower lip as she braced herself for the well-deserved reprimand. But, when he turned to her his manner was calm and it was only the bright anger in his eyes that betrayed his feelings.

"You are correct in one thing, you have good reason to apologize—but not to me. You have no conception of the innocent people you could have harmed with your self-indulgence. I can understand your anger and your disappointment but until you can learn to control your emotions, you will be capable of doing irreparable harm to people who have very little control over their own lives." A brow raised in emphasis as he noted the bewildered look she gave him. "It still has not occurred to you that you were born to a position of power, has it? Will you have to cause serious harm to others before you come to realize it?"

She cringed at his words. The fact that the criticism came from him hurt her deeply. She searched for a way to right the wrong she had done while absentmindedly fingering the stone which lay between her breasts, as if it could give her the comfort and reassurance she sought, while wishing instead that his arms were about her.

"Eve, there is another matter."

She looked up at him with surprise, wondering what else it could be that she had done to displeasure him. His manner and voice were filled with forced patience.

"Eve, you must understand that it is not considered suitable for a maid to register such—such pleased satisfaction at the prospect of your father's abduction and rape of the wife of another, even his enemy."

"What?" she cried. She could not believe what she was hearing. "Do you condemn my happiness for my father's success against his enemies?"

"Do not take me for a fool, Eve. It is not of your father's success in battle to which I refer. Certain things do occur, in time of war, but this is not the situation here. It is clear that your father's first intent at Shannon was to take Dervorgil from O'Rourke and for that your people will suffer."

"Richard, I cannot bring myself to be unhappy, or shocked, that my father did such! I told you there is no doubt in me that the lady went willingly! Rape is the only name you have chosen to give to the act!"

"And you feel that her willingness justifies the action?" He gaped incredulously. "You feel that it is permissible for a wife to leave her husband's bed for another's—under any circumstances?"

A deep anguish caught in her throat as she realized the meaning of his criticism. It was obvious that to Richard there lay a deep moral gap between their two peoples. It was not the prospect of rape in time of war that bothered him but that Dervorgil would willingly give herself to another.

"Tell me, Richard," she asked softly. "Which disturbs you the more, that I speak openly on the matter or that I feel as I do?"

"Both," he stated flatly.

Tears of anger and hurt stung her eyes. Could he not understand? Affections were not given lightly by her people. When love was given, it was given completely and for as long as that love existed, it would never be betrayed, but held sacred.

"Ah, you condemn easily, Richard! Think you that what I have seen here is better? It is permissible to give your affections to another as long as it is kept secret and you are most careful to keep a pretense of virtue! You look down upon my people, condemning them as amoral because they are open in their feelings while you play at your game! Ah, yes, it is true. In my country when a man and a woman can no longer love each other, even as husband and wife, yet they find another to serve that need, they enter into that new relationship freely without the burden of the false morality you insist upon! While you, on the other hand, unable to accept the prospect, play at your vows, keeping the objects of your heart a secret so that openly you may appear to be moral! I ask you, Richard, since you insist upon honesty, which is the better, the more true? Your way or mine?"

"Eve," he answered with cold anger, "I am not questioning you, or your morality."

"Aye? Is that true? Perhaps you should!" she cried. "Do you not wonder, Richard, how many lovers I have had before you?"

His eyes turned to a cold, steel grey and the muscle in his cheek twitched as he seemed to fight for control. Without saying another word he turned and strode from the room, swinging the door behind him with a resounding slam. She stood there for an endless moment staring at the door. As her anger slowly abated, she began to feel the weight of what had occurred and a single tear escaped and began to slip down her face.

11

As the first rays of sun appeared over the parapets, Hertford was thrown into turmoil, the planned festivities put aside with the arrival of a messenger from the king. The roused lord of Hertford had greeted the weary traveler in his bedclothes. His hand set to trembling as the parchment's message stunned him into wakefulness.

By the time Eve left her bedchamber the castle was abuzz with the news, the members of the household and its guests having gathered into sympathetic groups to discuss the implications of the king's proclamation.

Mystified by the goings-on, Eve found Lavinia in her family's chambers with Strongbow and Lady Isabel. She was relieved to find that Richard was absent, for she was not ready to face him, but she could not help but wonder at his absence since Warwick was present, as were Gervase and Miles.

"Lavinia," she whispered, "what has happened?"

Overhearing her question it was Strongbow who answered, his voice strained as Eve could not help but notice how aged he seemed to have become in just a few hours.

"My lady, a message has come to us that the king has declared his son, Eustace, heir to the throne. And, moreover, that he will abdicate within a very short time."

"My lord, I do not understand." Eve glanced at Lavinia, puzzled by their obvious distress. "Is this not the way the heirs to your throne are established?"

"Not exactly. Normally the death of a monarch occurs before the throne is given," he smirked unhappily. "In this case there is ample reason for the actions of the king. Many of us here who have been . . . somewhat less than enchanted by his rule had looked forward to a new monarch, one with different politics."

Eve considered his statement thoughtfully, "You fear that the son will be the same as the father."

"Aye. That is the whole of it. We had naively hoped that Stephen would be followed by a stronger, better hand. But now . . ."

"Another matter should be considered," Gilbert interjected as he looked at Eve sternly. "You are part of my family; therefore your place is here. However, you must realize that not everyone shares our feelings. There are those, even now at Hertford, that do not agree that this news is devastating. Anything that you hear in this room shall be kept at close counsel. Nothing shall be repeated, do you understand?"

"Aye, milord. I would do nothing to harm anyone here."

He grunted his approval and turned back to Strongbow. "What I wish to know is where Richard got his information."

"Indeed," Strongbow agreed with grimness. "I cannot believe he merely surmised what was going to happen."

"Perhaps that is just what he did," Lord Severn offered. "It is not impossible."

A tingle of fear pricked at the back of Eve's neck.

Strongbow turned to Warwick, who had been sitting to one side trying to look as unobtrusive as possible. As he stood up and faced his lord, Eve wondered why he looked so uncomfortable.

"Do you know of Richard's whereabouts? I sent Gaspard to look for him but it was said that he left the manor early this morning soon after the messenger arrived."

"Nay, milord, he did not confide in me."

"Humph!" Strongbow snorted, his anger rising. "What is he about? I am certain that he knew of Stephen's plans!" He struck the table next to him with his fist, causing everyone in the room to jump. "How did he know?" He spun back on Warwick, who paled slightly under Strongbow's regard. "Find him! I want to see him now! By the Holy Cross I shall get to the bottom of this!"

Warwick nodded and quickly left the room, leaving it in an oppressive silence. Strongbow slumped into a chair and rubbed his forehead, his words directed to no one but filled with concern. "What is he up to? My senses tell me that he plays a most dangerous game."

Listening, Eve's anger and hurt toward Richard receded behind fear for his safety. She seemed to be the only one who knew what he was up to. If he was with Orlan and the others, and they were to find him there... She should not care. But she did, even now, and whatever else, he did not deserve to fall as a traitor! Whatever they had begun to have was over but at the very least she owed it to him to warn him! But where was he? She recalled the conversation she had with Lavinia the morning on the parapet and suddenly an idea began to play at the back of her mind. When he had covered his disappearance from Lighthurst he had been found at a tavern...

Excusing herself she left the chamber and made her way to her own, where she grabbed her cloak and ran down the hall to the pentice.

As she sat outside the tavern, her mare moved nervously beneath her as if sensing the tension of her mistress. Finally gaining the courage to dismount, Eve tied the reins to the standingpost, took a deep breath, mounted the steps to the tavern door and entered.

The room was bathed in darkness and she blinked at it to adjust from the bright morning sun. As she stood there the odd thought struck her that the atmosphere certainly lent itself to clandestine meetings and dangerous plots. Realizing how ridiculous she was being, she braced herself and approached the counter where a huge, black-haired man was setting kegs of ale for the evening's business. He looked up as she approached and startled at her sudden appearance. He frowned to note the fine cloak she wore, its rich fur trimming drawn closely about her face so that he was unable to make out her features properly.

"May I speak to the proprietress?" she asked, knowing full well the identity of the tavern's owner.

"And who is it that be wanting to see her?" he asked gruffly.

"My business is with her," Eve countered firmly.

The man grunted and left the room, shaking his head as he wondered of Eve's identity. What was the world coming to when a lady of refinement could stroll casually into such a place—and demand to see the owner! Without even so much as an escort!

As she waited, the moments dragged on and she glanced about the room. The place was almost empty but even at this early hour there were a few customers. She was alarmed to note that three men who sat at a table on the far side of the room had fixed their attention upon her. One of the men bent to the others and made a comment that caused the others to guffaw loudly. Eve tensed as the man rose from his bench and began to advance toward her, his eyes raking over her. She backed up against the counter, her stomach churning with revulsion at his leer when, to her immeasurable relief, the barkeep returned. He said nothing but gestured with his thumb toward the staircase. She stammered her thanks and made her way hurriedly to the stairs, nearly tripping on the bottom step in her haste. Her face burned as she heard the chortles of laughter that followed her.

With difficulty, trying not to trip over her skirt, she picked her way up the dimly-lit, narrow staircase. As she reached the landing she looked up and drew in her breath sharply. There in the shadows stood a tall woman who was apparently waiting for her. The woman stepped forward and a small smile played at her mouth while she unabashedly looked Eve over. Eve reddened at the careful examination but her own feelings turned to astonishment. This was not what she had expected. She had envisioned that this woman would be coarse, hardened by years of her trade, her beauty long since marred by giving pleasures to men.

She was beautiful. Her skin was smooth and fresh, flushed with a rosy hue that was completely natural. Her hair, long and gently curled, was of a deep rich brown that shone with highlights that played against it from the flickering sconce on the wall nearby. Her body flowed with youthful lines, her hips slim and her breasts full and firm, clothed in a close-fitting rust wool gown of simple, but tasteful, simplicity. Her voice startled Eve as much as her appearance. It was not harsh as she expected, but soft and feminine.

"This seems a rather strange place for one gently born, milady. Why have you come here?"

"I must see Richard," Eve answered, trying not to show her nervousness. "I am certain that he is here."

"Oh, you are?" Claresta laughed. "And how do you know that?"

"Do not play games with me!" Eve said angrily. "I must see him! It is on a matter of the greatest importance!"

Claresta smiled as she studied Eve openly, interested brown eyes flickering over her, then back to her face, where they narrowed. "Tell me what it is about."

"I cannot discuss it with you. If I must I will search each room until I find him!"

"I do not think that such a search would suit your delicate tastes, milady." Claresta laughed.

"What makes you assume that I am so delicate?" Eve asked coldly.

Claresta smiled and tilted her head at the point made. "Perhaps I should have said unknowing. So," she added as her look changed to open interest, "you must be the one."

"The one?"

"Aye, the one who has struck Richard's interest. I knew that there was someone. Ah well, I am sure that it is just a passing thing."

Eve gasped but, before she could respond, Claresta gave her a short laugh and turned away, motioning for Eve to follow. She was led down the hall to the last door. Claresta tapped lightly, then opened it, resting casually against the frame.

"Richard, there is someone here to see you." The humor in her voice irked Eve but she said nothing as Claresta stepped back and allowed her to enter the room.

The room was sparsely furnished with only a bed at the far side and a small table with roughly made benches placed near the window. Richard sat at the table with two men of rather dubious source and the three turned as Eve entered. Richard's first reaction was unmasked astonishment but he quickly recovered and his face became rigid. The other two looked at her inquisitively, then glanced to Richard with unasked question.

"Richard, I must talk with you!" she blurted. He ignored her comment and murmured something to the others which she could not hear. They rose from the table, peering at her with interest as they passed out of the room. Eve's stomach knottted when she saw Claresta note the angry look on Richard's face. A smile played at the woman's lips as she closed the door behind her.

Once alone, Richard whirled upon her, his face taut with rage. "What are you doing here?" he demanded.

Eve drew in her breath, her good intentions swept aside by his anger. She should have known that this would be his reaction and that the moments of their last parting would still be vivid within him.

"I assure you, Richard, that I am here only because of the concern I feel for others," she said haughtily. "The same ones that you so pointedly reminded me of last night!"

"Go on," he said coldly.

"A message from the king arrived this morning."

"I know of it."

She returned the coldness of his gaze with her own. "Do you also know that Strongbow is at this very moment looking for you? He knows of what you are about."

She saw a glimmer of concern pass over his eyes but they remained cold as before. "How do you know of this?" he asked evenly.

"I was with him this morning. You told me once that he has the faculty for seeing to the heart of a matter and it is so. He fears that you play a game of great danger."

He said nothing in response but turned away from her and stared out of the window. After a long moment he turned back to her. "What of Warwick, where is he now?"

"Strongbow sent him to find you."

"What were his words to my father?"

"He said that he did not know of your present plans. Why?"

"Nothing. Tell me," he asked, with a look of guarded interest. "How did you know that you would find me here?"

"That was easy," she smirked. "A tavern seems to be your source of refuge."

"Aye," he laughed with a cruel edge to his voice. "Perhaps that is true. I know what to expect from those I find here and most of all, they are honest."

His words struck her like a razor-sharp dagger and she paled at the intensity with which he spoke them. Tears blinding her, she spun and flung herself toward the door. As her hand fumbled for the latch, he was there twisting her roughly about to face him. His face was inches from her own and she stared with trembling into pale grey eyes which were deadly cold with anger.

"Do you claim that you have been honest with me, *cherie?* All of this time while I have been endeavoring to protect your precious virtue, you have been playing me for the fool!"

"Nay. I have not!"

He reached out and unfastened her cloak, flinging it to one

side, smiling down at her with eyes that seemed to grow impossibly colder, and she stiffened with fear. There was a deliberate edge to his voice that made her shudder. "Now that you are here, there is no reason for a hasty departure. No one will disturb us and surely I have earned the right to sample what you have so freely given to others. I even recall moments when you desired it."

Suddenly his mouth covered her protests as he carried her to the bed. His hands seemed to be everywhere. She felt the fabric of her pelisse give away and it was pulled from her as in an instant his own garments seemed to miraculously disappear. She was afraid and fascinated, too.

"Richard, please!" she cried. The sounds were soon muffled against his shoulder as he brought his body to hers. A low moan escaped her lips which he ignored as he lowered his shoulders to hers, pressing her down beneath his weight.

Richard had blocked everything except the desire to hurt her. Since that moment in her chamber when she had thrown careless words at him, an anguish had consumed him, leaving him incapable of reasoning little else. Yet, as he felt her body beneath him, and her cries filled his senses, he felt an inexplicable softening overtake him. That moment of hesitation allowed him to realize the pressure of resistance that he met as his body began to fill hers and his eyes flew open to look down into hers with surprise. Withdrawing suddenly, he pulled away and rolled off of her with a deep groan, his body shuddering in protest of what he had almost done, coupled with the agonizing torment of unfulfillment. She turned onto her side as he rolled away and pulled her legs up as she gave in to her despair.

He lay on his back, staring at the ceiling while the sound of her gentle sobbing brought a spasm of deep regret. He stole a glance at her. What was there about this maid that could arouse such fury within him? There was no denying that she had attracted him in a way that no other woman had done, but he had always prided himself on his control. He realized then that he had known what was going to happen from the first moment she had entered the room.

"Why, Eve?" he asked with a heavy voice. "Why did you lead me to believe that you had been with other men?"

"I was angry—and hurt!" she choked. "But that did not give you the right to . . ."

"Do you believe that you are the only one that can be hurt?"

he said sharply. "You played a cruel game, Eve, and you came dangerously close to winning your prize." He sighed deeply. "I would not have it be this way for you."

"Why? Because it is my first time?" she cried. "Why should that make a difference?" She twisted about to glare at him.

"Eve, no woman has aroused such anger in me before. I wanted to hurt you as you had hurt me. You look surprised. Did you believe that I was incapable of being hurt?"

"I did not know that you cared that much," she sniffed.

"Nor did I." He said simply. "But I find that I do."

"You do?" she sniffed, blinking at him through a veil of tears.

"Aye," he said softly, rolling onto his side, "That is why I cannot leave things as they are. You mean too much to me for that."

She wondered what he meant but her eyes grew wide as he turned her over gently and pushed her back into the bedding. He kissed her tenderly as his hand touched her face, coaxing her to his embrace. Her senses filled with the softness of his voice as she felt herself relax and begin to focus upon his hands as they moved gently over her. Her skin became alive, new meaning given to her body as he touched her. Sensations startled her with deep pleasure as his hands found spots she had not been aware of before this moment.

So, this was what it was about. Her mind spun with new knowledge, knowing that it would not be the same with another. She focused on the exquisiteness of his touch as his fingers found her breast and she drew in her breath sharply. Her senses were pulled to his touch, the explosion of feeling brought by his hands and fingers touching her so familiarly, gently teasing as waves of sensation undulated through her body. She moaned softly, overwhelmed by the feeling even as she tensed with anticipation, even as she could not reason more pleasure.

Impossibly, he gave it to her. She gasped as his lips replaced his fingers, his tongue gently teasing the tender tip, circling, his lips pulling at her breast until she cried out against the wave upon wave of sensations that filled her. Yet, even as she thought that she could not bear more, she felt the exquisite pleasure of his hand as it trailed over her sensitive skin to her legs, stroking her trembling thighs to move between. His fingers tormented her, seeking, boldly claiming her body with a intimacy she could not have known in her wildest imagining.

Softly, she cried out as he touched a part of her she had not been aware of, and he stroked gently with a possessiveness that caused her hips to writhe involuntarily against his hand as if she had no control over her own body. Waves of heat spread over her, bringing a tension that made her hold still in fear that he would stop even as a part of her mind begged that he would never cease. Then, suddenly, she came in a rushing tension which pulsed over her in a bittersweet shattering.

Her arms went about him, pulling him to her. "Richard, please," she cried softly, aware only of a deep aching need, wanting, needing to feel him within her.

He pulled her beneath him and he kissed her deeply as he held her to him, his hand going beneath her hips as he spread her thighs with his legs. Gently he entered, pushing with gradual, easy strokes, and he almost sighed with relief. He had held back, wanting to give her pleasure, hoping that she would give him easy entrance. After everything, he did not want to cause her more pain. He held her to him for a long moment, kissing her deeply, trailing light butterfly kisses over her face to her cheeks and neck to the tender spot beneath the lobe of her ear.

Slowly, he began to move within her, waiting, drawing until she began to respond. He thrilled to the sound of her soft moan and the movement of her hips beneath his as he drew her with patience, then brought them both to a final fulfillment, knowing the moment as she cried out his name and he gave himself release.

As she opened her eyes, she became aware only of Richard and the pleasure, the soft warm pleasure, of his weight upon her and the all-consuming pleasure that filled her with a tingling that seemed to reach to her toes.

He kissed her tenderly, then released her from his weight and pulled her into his arms. Holding her close, he brushed her hair back from her face and smiled into her eyes, which were still softened with passion. "Do you understand now why I could not leave you to remember only the pain?" he murmured gently.

She smiled up at him and closed her eyes as she nestled up against him but he drew away and left the bed, to return a moment later with a kerchief he had dampened from the wash bowl. Turning her gently he washed the blood from her thighs, then he pulled her back into his arms, smiling at the flush that had crept up her cheeks, and lowered his head to kiss away her embarrassment.

She awoke with remembrance and snuggling back down beneath the covers, she reached out for him. But the bed was empty. Sitting up abruptly, she called out his name and he came quickly from the window, hearing the note of fear in her cry. He pulled her into his arms, laying a gentle kiss on her tousled hair.

"Did you think that I had left you?"

"Aye," she answered softly.

"I won't leave you." He placed a finger under her chin and lifted her face to his as he brushed her lips with a light kiss. "In fact, I would like to pass the day with you here but there are matters I must face at Hertford."

She sat up, pulling the bedclothes about her as she hugged her knees. "Richard, what is this anger that exists between you and Strongbow?"

He tensed, the muscle in his jaw tightening at her question and his eyes became clouded. "I told you once, it does not concern you."

"Ah," she said softly. "It would seem that anything that concerns you so deeply would also concern me."

He frowned at her, then stood up and crossed the room to the window. He folded his arms across his chest and peered intently from the window. After a time she rose from the bed and, wrapping the coverlet about her, she went to stand behind him. She reached out and touched his shoulder and as he turned she noticed that while his face was taut and hard his eyes were a deep soft grey and filled with pain. He sat her at the table and, taking the bench across from her, he leaned back against the wall and propped his foot up on the edge of the bench. He drummed his fingers on the table for a moment, then stopped suddenly to look up at her as if finally making a decision.

"Has Lavinia told you of her brother?"

"John?" she asked with surprise. "Aye, she has mentioned him."

"What did she tell you about him?"

"Only that you were very close, and that he died suddenly of a fever."

"Humph," he snorted with disgust. "So she was told."

"You mean that he did not?"

Richard sighed deeply and looked out of the window as if composing his thoughts. When he spoke his voice was full of pain, and seemed very far away. "John and I had known each other since we were very young. We grew up together and two brothers could not have been closer..." His voice began to trail away as if his thoughts had taken him to another time, but he cleared his throat and looked back at her. "Severn was visiting us at Chepstow when it happened. Fortunately Lavinia was then at Hertford. I remember laughing at the time when Severn told me why John had not accompanied him to Chepstow. Seems that there was a buxom young wench that had caught his eye..." He paused and shook his head. "So he was alone at Lighthurst when they came."

She saw Richard grip the half-empty tankard which sat on the table and his knuckles became white as he stared into the cup. "Who came, Richard?" she asked softly.

"Our revered Majesty, Stephen, King of England," he answered, his eyes burning. "He and his party were returning to London after a particularly nasty encounter with Robert of Gloucester, the empress' half-brother. The battle had left Stephen's forces decimated and I assume that our liege lord was not in a particularly good frame of mind," he added sarcastically. "In any case, it seemed that one night, as they took dinner, John said something to anger him. The morning found him hanging from a tree in the courtyard."

Eve drew in her breath as her eyes flared with horror.

"When the news reached us at Chepstow I begged my father to avenge John's death—to gather those who were sympathetic and strike before Stephen could reach London. He refused. He said that while he too grieved for John, his death would not be served by bathing England in the blood of its people—that the war with Matilda was devastating enough." He took a deep breath and his voice was thickened as he continued. "I accompanied Severn back to Lighthurst. When we arrived we found John where Stephen had left him. He had forbidden anyone to cut him down."

They sat in silence as Eve's heart twisted painfully to Richard's suffering. She wanted to reach out and touch him, to comfort him, but she knew that his grief would only disappear with time—much more time.

"What of Severn?" she asked at last. "Why did he not try to avenge his son?"

"Because he agreed with Strongbow," he shrugged.

"Richard, will you ever be able to forgive your father, to mend this breach between you?"

"I already have." He smiled a bid sadly. "But I cannot allow him to ever interfere again in what I feel is right."

"You are a man now! I do not think he will."

Richard smiled and looked at her for a long moment, "Someone else said the same thing to me recently. Perhaps it is true."

He stood up and held out his hands to her. She came into his arms and held him to her, wishing that she could wipe away the grief and pain from his heart. She turned her face up to his and as their lips met she felt a full rush of a woman's emotions. To give, to want to protect, to shelter from pain, or when all else fails, to give comfort. At that moment she wanted nothing else than to be loved by him, and to love.

"I wish that I could help you," she whispered.

"You already have. Besides, the pain is not so great anymore. For a long time after John's death I would not allow myself to think about it. I realize now that I used my feelings toward my father to that end. I became angry and bitter toward everything around me—blaming everyone for what happened to John. Then, without realizing it at the time, I came to recognize that what happened to him was happening to countless others—and they were much less prepared to defend or protect themselves."

"That is why you became involved."

"Aye," he smiled ruefully. "And I have been the one who has gained. Grief festers when it is held inside and you do nothing to exorcise it. Each time I strike out against Stephen, a small part of me is healed. It is not for vengeance, hopefully I am beyond that, but to stop him from causing others such pain."

Her arms went about his neck and she pulled herself up to him, kissing him deeply as the intensity of the moment began to stir within both of them. She longed to have him sweep her into his arms and carry her back to the bed but with great effort he put his hands on her shoulders and drew her away from him.

"It is time that we go," he sighed regretfully. His eyes moved over her face as if to memorize each part. With a sudden grin he turned her away and slapped her buttocks, chuckling at the glare she gave him over her shoulder as she squealed and jumped away.

He watched with amusement as she crossed back to the bed while struggling to keep the coverlet about her. He folded his arms across his chest and leaned back against the wall, his look

changing to interest as she tripped a few times and almost lost
the coverlet and he anticipated the results. Much to his disappointment, she reached the far side of the bed intact and
began to search for her garments, but they were nowhere to
be found.

Puzzled, she shot a questioning look at him. He shrugged.
"I fear that your pelisse was, ah, rather the worse for wear. I
gave it to Claresta and she assured me that it could be mended
sufficiently to see you to Hertford."

"What!" Eve cried, "Oh Richard, you did not!"

He startled at her cry. "There is nothing to worry about, the
garment will be cared for. She assured me that one of her girls
was most handy with a needle."

"Oh, Richard, you could you!" she moaned, burying her
face in her hands. "Now she knows everything!"

"Knows what?"

"She knows what has happened between us!"

Dumbfounded, he stared at her then shook his head. "Eve,
Claresta is no stranger to these matters. She thinks nothing of
it."

She gaped at him in disbelief, then moaned again as she
looked away, wondering if he could possibly believe what he
said.

"Eve," he said with exasperation, "I will fetch the garment
for you so that you will not have to face her. Will that satisfy
you?"

She groaned again, refusing to look at him before she shut
her eyes and whispered, "How smug she must feel! Knowing
that you forced yourself on me!"

He blinked at her incredulously. "What are you talking
about? Why should she care?"

She spun on him, her eyes bright with anger. "Do you deny
that she loves you!? I saw the possessive way that she looked
at you!"

"What?" he blinked. "Eve, she is a friend, nothing more."

"You have never been lovers?" she spat accusingly.

He sighed as he turned for the door, stopping to throw a
stony glare at her. "My past has nothing to do with us. I will
fetch your garments."

She stared at the closed door, then squealed with anger.
Men! She recognized his attitude, all too well. She had not
been brought up surrounded by men for nothing! What he

thought about her past had almost destroyed them yet his past was to be no concern of hers! Yet, she knew that she could accept his feelings. What she could not accept was Claresta's knowing and her laughter. She recalled Claresta's comment about her relationship with Richard being a passing thing and she wanted to scream, to throw something. She was not to dwell upon it long because he returned presently with the folded garment over his arm. He flung it on the bed offhandedly and motioned.

"Dress quickly. Warwick is waiting for us."

"Warwick?" she gasped.

"Aye, he has been waiting for some time, so hurry."

She shrieked in horror and fell back against the bedding, pulling the covers up over her head. "Does no one not know of what we have done!" she cried.

His mouth dropped open, then the room was filled with his laughter. Hesitatingly, she lowered the covers to look at him in wonder. "What do you find so amusing?"

"You, my sweet love," he gasped, nearly choking. "You, my fair lady who professes to believe in love freely given! You deride me for caring about your virtue yet you hide there beneath the covers for fear that someone will know that you are a woman!"

She threw an indignant retort at him. He crossed to the bed and threw back the covers, bringing a shocked squeak from her as he pulled her off the bed and into his arms. His eyes were still alive with his laughter as he bent his head and kissed her resoundingly. She melted weakly into his arms, her head floated dizzily from the kiss and she fought to catch her breath. He raised his head and looked down at her with a grin while his hands hungrily stroked her back and hips, pressing her against him.

"You had better dress, love," he whispered huskily, "or Warwick will have to wait a good time more."

As they descended the stairs to the common room, Warwick pushed his tankard aside and stood up. His eyes flickered over Eve with interest, as did the others in the room. He said nothing but Eve dropped her gaze and reddened considerably. A smile played at the corners of Richard's mouth but he gave her a reassuring squeeze on her waist.

"If you have finished your brew we can go," he threw at Warwick with good humor.

"Humph," the knight grunted. "I'm into my fourth cup and it does not serve well to keep Strongbow waiting."

"My father will have to adjust to the fact that I am no longer at his beck and call," answered Richard grimly. "There were other matters that I found more pressing." Warwick glanced at Eve and shifted uncomfortably as she flushed at Richard's comment. "I have information to add to what Strongbow learned this morning," Richard continued, apparently not noticing Warwick's and Eve's embarrassment.

"Is that why you are here?" Warwick blurted.

"Aye," Richard answered, feigning puzzlement to the looks exchanged by Eve and Warwick. "My lady came to warn me of Strongbow's reaction and that you were looking for me. She has known for a long time, Warwick. In fact since our first meeting weeks before she came to Hertford. But I will tell you of that later. Shall we go?"

Relieved, Warwick picked up his tankard and drained the contents. "Then let us be away. I have no doubt that your father has worn a path in the floor at Hertford by this time."

They left the tavern, all three blinking at the rush of bright sunlight that greeted them. Warwick untied Eve's mare and offered his hand to help her mount. She stepped forward and pushed back her cloak to make the task easier as she smiled up at him. The smile froze upon her face at Warwick's expression and she glanced down to where his shocked gaze was fixed. The mended rents in her pelisse glared at him in the bright morning sunlight. She flushed as he shot a startled look to her and then to Richard, who was already mounted. His eyes fixed angrily upon the younger man.

"God's Breath, Richard, what is this?" he bellowed, but Eve cut him short, laying a hand upon his arm, pleading with her eyes that he not cause a scene.

"Please, Warwick, are you not going to help me?" she asked.

"I fear that I am too late," he growled. Sensing her mood, he said nothing more and helped her onto the mare.

The ride back to Hertford was silent but Warwick cast disturbed glances at the couple. A few times it appeared that he was about to speak but the words seemed to die within him. As they entered the courtyard he leapt from his mount and came quickly to Eve's side to assist her, almost pushing Richard out of the way. Eve fought a giggle, her eyes dancing with laughter as the older knight presented himself to her, his arms outstretched possessively to lift her from the saddle. Richard rolled his eyes heavenward.

"Thank you, Warwick," she said demurely. "It is such a relief to encounter a gentleman." As she took his arm she glanced away so that he would not see her smile but he misread her meaning and shot another deadly glare at Richard and turned away to escort her up the steps.

Grey eyes watched appreciatively as she allowed Warwick to escort her into the hall. Passing through the massive portals, she could hear a deep sigh from behind her and she cast her eyes downward in a struggle not to laugh out loud.

12

Richard had touched her heart, soul and body as none other had dared to do. Her childhood disappeared as he brought her to that sacred place only a woman enjoys, to a fulfillment bonded by the knowledge that one is loved and is capable of giving love. The sharing of his body and his mind had brought with it a certainty that she was unique and capable of giving to him what he had not found in another. She felt renewed, expanded.

Richard was gentle and caring, keeping her at his side at every possible moment, though such times were all too brief to suit either of them. There were moments in a dimly lit hallway where he would sweep her into his arms and they managed a brief but impassioned embrace before they were disturbed by approaching footsteps; and precious hours spent near him in the company of others where her heart was warmed by an occasional touch of his hand and tender looks. There was an unspoken understanding between them of an unwillingness to share their feelings with others and they were reassured by the fact that Warwick would keep their counsel, trusting them to expose their feelings when the time was right. They knew he was cautious in his feelings about their relationship, an occasional doubtful frown cast in their direction betraying his doubts, but he kept his silence. For now their love belonged to them alone and it was all the sweeter for it.

Outwardly, the manor had recovered from the stunning news from London and the festivities continued with great banquets, troubadours and players for entertainment, and an early morning hunt to begin each day. In the frantic activity, and the birth of their own private emotions, Eve had not asked Richard about what had occurred between him and Strongbow upon their return to Hertford. She was relieved to note that the tension between them had apparently eased as the relationship between father and son progressed with a new understanding and she assumed they had been able to settle their differences at long last. The final morning of the celebrations came and the men left at dawn to drive the game from the upper woods. The ladies were to meet them on the commons later in the morning for the hunt.

Eve rose early that morning, knowing that her toilette would take longer than usual. The night before Eve had noticed, with some alarm, that Bridget had looked tired and wan. Against the maid's protests she had ordered her to keep to her bedchamber for the next few days to rest. She worried that Bridget's duties were too much for the aging woman and she was angered that Leonore did not notice and assign her to lighter tasks in deference to her advancing years. She made a note to speak to Leonore about it at first chance.

She had chosen a pelisse of deep lavender velvet to wear for the hunt and while slipping it on she noticed that there was a small rent in the seam at her waist. She removed the garment carefully and hastily dressed in one of her old kirtles. Folding the velvet over her arm she left her bedchamber to find the seamstress.

Humming to herself she made her way downstairs and through the hallway, a soft smile tugging at the corners of her mouth as she passed the buttery. Her heart seemed to skip a beat as she recalled the moments spent there with Richard. Oh, to have his arms about her now... She stopped short as she spied a man talking with Gaspard at the end of the hallway. Orlan! What was he doing here? She quickened her step but before she could reach them Orlan had turned and left.

"Gaspard! Who was that man?" she gasped. "What was he doing here?"

Gaspard blinked with surprise at Eve's manner. "Just a man from the village, milady."

"What did he want?" she demanded.

"To speak with Sir Richard, milady. I told him that he had left the castle."

"Did he say why he wanted to see him?"

"Nay, milady." The steward hesitated. "He wants a favor, perhaps. I told him to return tomorrow. Is there something wrong?"

She darted past the startled steward and rushed through the kitchens and onto the steps of the kitchenyard just as Orlan was approaching the eastern gate of the keep. She called to him, relieved when he halted and turned, his mouth dropping open in astonishment.

"Eve, lass! What are you doing here?" he blurted as she approached. "So, Richard found you after all!" He grinned as he recovered from his shock of finding her here. "I have been away for a time and no one had told me but I am not surprised."

"What do you mean?" she gasped, slightly winded from her rush.

"The way he carried on when we found that you were gone and not a word of you in the village. He was—ah—highly out of sorts, lass, I'm glad that he found ye."

His words brought a quick gladdening to her heart and she flushed with pleasure. "Ah, and is that true, Orlan?"

"Aye, lass, he was a difficult man to be with those days. He ranted and cursed, he did. And I see that he has found a place for ye here," he added, noting the pelisse folded over her arm. "I approve. A lady's maid is much more proper for ye."

"More proper than what?" she smiled.

He chuckled deeply, rubbing his forehead as he recalled the memory. "He swore that if he found ye, he'd take ye to Claresta's. Lordy, he was mad, he was. Said that 'twould be better than a nunnery for keepin' ya in yer place!"

Her happiness dissolved as his words slowly penetrated . . . Claresta's! she thought wildly. He wanted her to become a . . . to keep her in her place!

"Ah, lass, I was wondering—the steward said that I would not be able to see Richard until tomorrow but I have something important to give him and it cannot wait."

Her mind was numb with hurt and though he pressed something into her hand she found herself staring dumbly at a folded parchment as he curled her fingers over it.

"Please, lass, you could do a great service if ye were to see that Richard gets this today without fail. Will ye do it?"

Seeing the urgency in his look she forced herself to smile. "Of course, Orlan. I will see that he gets it."

Relieved, the man touched his cap and began to slip through

the gates, but paused to glance back. "Tell him that the men are ready to do his bidding."

With that he was gone and she was left alone, staring at the note which had Richard's name inscribed in a delicate feminine hand.

She paced the floor of her room, glancing occasionally at the note on the table as she fought with herself not to rush and open it. The signature under the seal seemed to scream at her. She knew, without recognizing the hand, who had sent the note. Finally, standing it no longer, she ignored the pleading of her conscience and grabbed it. Warming the wax of the seal she pried it open.

The first part of the message was gibberish, a code of some sort, and it meant nothing to her. But, as she read the last part, clearly written, a cry caught in her throat and she thought she would suffocate from the pain that grasped her.

> . . . as for other matters, Dear Heart, reflecting upon
> your new interest, is it necessary that you play the
> part so well?
> Claresta

"So it is true!" she cried. Orlan's words and what Claresta had written tumbled into a surge of anguish. To have her out of the way he would have placed her at Claresta's! Made her into a . . . But, nay, those plans were thwarted by Sir Bowen's timely interference and he had to find other means! Had Claresta plotted with him, laughed with him, as they had decided her fate? His tender looks, his loving caresses, and she had believed him! She had let him use her when all he wanted was her silence! And to control her.

She picked up the note where it had slipped to the floor and it seemed to scorch her fingers as she stared at it with sheer, barely controlled hatred. Glancing about she spotted her jewel box and she crossed swiftly to it. Her jaw quivered with tears she refused to shed as she hid the note under her jewels. As her eye caught a glimpse of the emerald, lying on a bed of rose petals, she slammed the lid shut as if to close off a part of her life.

"I too can play the game, Richard—with conviction to purpose," she said to herself grimly. "Let us see how you fare without knowing what is written on that page."

*   *   *

Strongbow bellowed in greeting to the knock at the door of his chambers. As the door swung open and Richard entered, he noted at a glance the grim look on his son's face.

"There has been no word from Orlan," Strongbow said, stating it as a fact rather than a question.

"Nay, none. I sent Warwick to look for him."

Strongbow grunted, then pointed to the place across from him with his knife. "Sit down and eat some breakfast. There is nothing more you can do until they arrive."

Richard glanced at the table with distaste and started to pace. "I cannot understand. It is not like him. There should have been some word by now. He should have been here days ago."

Brooding, he crossed back and forth between the window and the table, the only sound in the room being the click of his heels on the floor's wooden planking. He did not see the gathering storm on Strongbow's face. Stretched to the limits of his patience, Strongbow threw down his knife.

"Stop that confounded pacing!" he roared. "I will not have you ruining my breakfast!"

Richard plopped himself into the chair across from Strongbow and hooking his arm about the back of his chair he looked at the food with disdain. "I think I liked it better when we were not speaking."

Strongbow fought a smile and pushed a bowl over to him with the tip of his knife. "Here, try the meat pie. The cook outdid herself."

Richard picked up a piece of the pie and bit at it, chewing it absentmindedly for a moment before dropping the remainder back into the bowl. Strongbow glanced at his son with the hint of a smile which quickly disappeared as he speared another biteful of pie. Washing it down with ale he leaned back in his chair and studied his son.

"Richard, what is your purpose?"

"What?" Richard looked quizzically at his father.

"We have never spoken of your personal goals and I would know of them now."

Richard picked up a knife and toyed with it as he pondered. "To do what I can to bring England to peace. To aid Henry Plantagenet to the throne . . ."

"By war?"

"If need be," he answered evenly.

"And that may be necessary," Strongbow snorted unhappily. "But, my son, it is not a forgone conclusion. England has been at war for almost twenty years and she has not seen peace come of it."

"Apathy has not aided her!" Richard snapped, immediately regretting his words and his tone. "I did not mean—I apologize. I thought I was beyond that."

"Richard, I have never been apathetic to England, or her needs," he said patiently. "She will always have her soldiers—those who are ready to raise their weapons for her, eager to plunge into battle for ideals, misguided or not, and for profit. What she is sadly lacking, and what she will need for her survival and growth, are statesmen. Men who can look beyond their own grasping drives for power and wealth to her needs. Men who can control their impulses, who know that the immediate solution to a problem is not necessarily the best one. They will look far beyond the now to grander dreams. This will take men of the greatest strength and wisdom and I pray that she finds them.

"Richard," he sighed, "the hardest thing of all is to spend you life working for goals that you know will not be realized in your lifetime, that you will never see them to their finish. But the work itself must satisfy you. Do not minimize it. It is a grand thing to know that what you have contributed has built and strengthened, not destroyed. Even though there are many times you must remind yourself that others may not understand your purpose. With the dedication to achieve you must have patience. While others can exercise the luxury of reacting to emotions, of seeing their dreams realized—wrong or right— you must wisely bide your time, patiently waiting for the right moment. This, and only this, will grow and survive."

Richard felt a warm surge of respect as he listened. He knew that he had never understood his father before; perhaps he hadn't tried. He did not know how to respond. Years of bitterness, so recently removed, left him unable to express his feelings. His eyes fell to the food before him and, smiling broadly, he reached over for the pie and helped himself to a generous piece.

Strongbow chuckled and poured himself some ale as he watched his son wolf down his breakfast. "I wish that I could plead to the barons as successfully."

"When you have heard the right words they ring truth. They do not have to be studied upon, or reasoned with, to make them truer." Richard paused and winked at Strongbow. "One only argues with an idea when it is at odds with personal goals."

Strongbow raised a brow and smiled. "You may make a statesman yet."

The servants cleared away the remnants of the meal and the two men sat enjoying each other's company as they had not done for many years. They talked of the past, of things long forgotten, and pleasured in remembering.

"Do you remember that horse you gave me against Warwick's raging protests?" Richard chuckled.

Strongbow guffawed at the memory. "Aye! I was determined to make a man of you—besides, I could not resist your pleadings."

"I thought I could ride anything—I had not the sense to be afraid. I almost broke my neck! And I almost wished I had when mother found out about it. Seems to me we both had to make ourselves scarce for a few days."

Strongbow chortled, "Aye, your mother is something to handle when her nettle is up."

"We . . ."

The door shot open, crashing against the wall, as Warwick stormed in hauling a very frightened Orlan by the neck of his tunic.

"Richard," the man squealed, "I did not understand. I thought . . ."

"God's Breath! What is going on?" Strongbow bellowed as he jumped up. "Warwick! Release him and calm down, both of you!"

Warwick let go of the man's collar, nearly dropping Orlan to his knees as his grasp had lifted him from the floor. Richard ushered Orlan to a chair and poured him a tankard of ale.

"Here, drink this, then tell us what has happened."

"I will tell you what has happened!" Warwick growled, his face bursting red with anger. "This fool, this nitwit, came here three days ago with the message . . ."

"Three days?" Richard and Strongbow said in shocked unison.

"Where is it?" Strongbow demanded.

"Aye, where is it indeed?" repeated Warwick angerly. "He gave it to someone here."

"Who, Orlan?" Richard asked impatiently. "Who did you give it to?"

"Eve," Orlan whispered, afraid to look at the others.

"Eve?" Richard repeated dumbly. His mouth had dropped open in disbelief.

"Richard, I am sorry!" Orlan pleaded. "I thought she was here with you . . . I mean I thought she was loyal, that it would be all right to . . ."

"What is he blathering about?" Strongbow demanded. "Why should he give it to Lady Eve?"

"Lady Eve?" Orlan glanced incredulously from one to the other.

Richard had been half listening, his look changing from disbelief to anger, until he murmured out loud, "That must be why she has stayed in her rooms for the past three days, refusing to see anyone, even me. I assumed that she was not feeling well, too much excitement . . ."

"Richard!" Strongbow broke in angerly. "What is going on? Why would she keep the message to herself?"

"I do not know," Richard answered grimly, "but I intend to find out."

He threw open the door to her bedchambers and found her sitting on the windowseat. She froze, her eyes widening at the fury he was so obviously attempting to control.

"Where is it?" he demanded, slamming the door behind him.

"Where is what?"

"The message that Orlan gave to you—three days ago!" he roared.

She met his glare while trying not to show the sudden fear that crept over her. "I do not know what you are talking about."

"Eve, dammit, do not toy with me!"

"Oh!" she breathed. "Do not toy with you? Richard, I am tired of your one-sided rules!"

He crossed to her and yanked her from the windowseat. "I have no time for any nonsense, Eve!" he said in a low voice as his fingers gripped into the soft flesh of her arms. "The message Orlan gave you is vitaly important and I will have it now! Will you give it to me or must I take apart your chambers until I find it?"

"Richard, please, you are hurting me," she gasped.

He released her and stood back, watching her unsympathetically as she rubbed her arms. From the look he gave her it was glaringly apparent that he would make good his threat, so she went to her jewel box and retrieved the note. As she turned he snatched it and tore it open, quickly scanning its contents.

"Eve," he groaned. "Do you know what you have done?"

"Nay, Richard," she hissed. "What have I done?"

He looked up at her and studied her for a long moment, his eyes cold and hard with disdain. "You really do not know, do you?"

"I know that I will not act as her messenger! Dear Heart!"

He blinked, then scanned the rest of the message, then closed his eyes while he shook his head. "Is that what this is about? Is that why you kept this message from me? Because it came from Claresta?"

"Oh, that and more!" she cried. "Orlan told me of what you had planned for me! How unfortunate for you, Richard, that you had to go to so much trouble to keep me quiet!"

"What are you talking about?"

"Are you denying that you planned to send me to Claresta's. Better than a nunnery, I believe you said!"

Dumbfounded, it took him a long moment to realize what she was talking about. When he finally grasped her meaning, he sighed with exasperation. "Eve, you cannot possibly think . . ."

"I am very serious, Richard! And I do not care to talk with you about it! To hear any more of your lies—about that or anything else, ever again!" she shrieked.

His eyes narrowed, turning to an icy grey as he answered her coldly, "Then you will not. But, I fear that you will hear more about what you have done this day, for the repercussions will be tremendous." He started for the door but halted when she screamed after him.

"I do not care about your precious message or anything else that happens in this hateful country!"

He turned back to her and a flicker of sympathy crossed his face. "You should."

The look he gave her, the quick moment of unconcealed pity, shook her resolve. "What do you mean?" she stammered.

"Just this," he answered calmly. "Did you ever answer the question I once put to you, about why your father chose to send you to England?"

"Be-because he wished for me to be safe from our enemies," she snapped, suddenly feeling uncertain.

"Was there nowhere, in all of Ireland, that could have done as well?" He waited for her answer, which did not come. "You are the ward of the King of England, my lady, first of all. He will take great interest in whom you marry."

"Marry?" she asked weakly.

"Aye. You will have little to say in the matter. But, never fear, you may be assured that the one he chooses for you will be of great advantage to your father."

"Nay!" she cried. "My father would not do that to me!"

Richard's eyes pressed into hers. "Wouldn't he?"

As the door closed behind him he heard her shriek and the sound of an earthen pitcher as it crashed against the frame.

13

The mud-spattered rider slipped from his mount and took the steps three at a time into the hall. He paused at the doorway to allow his eyes to adjust to the dimness of the hall, then crossed to the three men who sat warming themselves by the fire.

"My lords, I carry a message from London for the Earl of Striguil. Would he be here?"

"I am he," Strongbow answered as he reached for the message the man had extracted from the pouch on his belt. He unrolled the parchment and read it carefully, smiling with satisfaction as he glanced at a puzzled Warwick, then at Gilbert. "She has been successful," he grinned.

Gilbert slapped his thigh and beamed as he addressed the stranger. "Go to the kitchens. My steward will see to your needs. You have brought us most welcome news this day."

As the man left the hall Gilbert and Strongbow exchanged satisfied glances, which only added to Warwick's confusion.

"May I ask what is going on?" he asked.

"Aye, Warwick, you may." Strongbow smiled. "Lady Isabel has been tending to a most important mission in London these past three weeks and I am pleased to report that she has been successful. Here, the message will explain her efforts."

He handed the message to Warwick and the knight scanned its contents, paling as the message became clear. "What have you done?" he gasped incredulously.

"We have satisfied our need," Gilbert said simply. "We

now have the solution to our problems."

Warwick reread the message, shaking his head as his brow furrowed. "Does Richard know of this?" he asked softly.

"Nay," Strongbow answered. "There was no need to tell him unless Isabel was successful."

"How do you think he will react? Do you actually think that he will accept this, without question?"

"He will do as he is told," Strongbow said firmly.

"He is a man now and makes his own decisions on such matters!" Warwick protested. "It is not only his life that is involved but the Lady Eve's as well! Their relationship at the moment is rather—well, they have not even spoken to each other in weeks! Do you honestly expect that they will accept this marriage?"

"Richard will understand what we have done," Gilbert interjected. "As for the Lady, she has no say in the matter."

Strongbow silenced Gilbert's retort with a wave of his hand. "Warwick, this decision was not entered into lightly. Eve's withholding of the message caused Henry and his forces to miss the tides and his sailing from Normandy, as you know. If we could have informed him in time that his support here was sufficient, things might have been different. As it is, the only chance we have to now delay Eustace's claim to the throne is by withholding the baron's oath of fealty. Stephen knows that his position is too weak to extract it by force and that without it Eustace's crown would be a farce. We are blessed in that Archbishop Theobald is in sympathy with our cause and has sent a clerk from his office to intercede with Pope Adrian. With the Church's support Henry's succession is almost assured. The only element missing to our plan was a plausible reason for the meeting of the barons, one that would not be suspected by their majesties. A gathering at Chepstow for the marriage has given us that reason and it is all the sweeter considering that their approval was given to the match."

"I am amazed that Stephen gave his consent," Warwick observed grimly. "How did Isabel manage it?"

"It was through the queen that Isabel pleaded." Strongbow stood and moved before the fire, turning to warm his backside as he rubbed his hips. "As you know, when Isabel spent her early years at court she was in a position to give many favors to the young wife who is now our queen. Her Majesty was more than eager to return the favors, or at least that was our hope and it appears to be so."

"Is that all there was to it?" Warwick asked doubtfully, his eyes narrowing as he studied Strongbow. "You have ignored the entreaties of their majesties for many years yet the queen seems to have persuaded Stephen to grant you this favor quite easily—too easily."

Strongbow sighed wearily then took his chair again. "You have known me too long, old friend. Aye, concessions had to be made. In return for their consent I have pledged to give my oath of fealty to Eustance."

"What?"

"Aye, Warwick, but only mine. It will be of no consequence if we are successful. Those who meet with us will know of the reason."

"Even if Richard agrees, what of the lady? I do not think that this is a case whereupon the bride can be dragged into the chapel, bound and gagged. And I cannot imagine her going willingly."

"She shall go willingly," Strongbow muttered. "Her father gave his consent to whatever husband the king chose for her. That was agreed upon before she left Ireland. Dermot is in no position now to antagonize His Majesty, not when he looks to England for aid."

"When will you tell him?"

Strongbow rose heavily from the chair. "There is no reason to put it off. Find him and send him to me in my chambers. I think it best if we talk with him there."

Richard stared at his father with disbelief, then to Warwick who merely shrugged and dropped his gaze to the floor.

"You cannot be serious!"

"I am quite serious," Strongbow answered. "Your mother in now on her way to Chepstow to begin preparations for our guests. I have explained the situation and my reasoning. Surely you understand that there is no other way to achieve our goal as quickly as time demands."

"I too was at first doubtful, Richard," Warwick added. "But I must admit, now that I have had time to consider it, it is the right thing to be done, for more than one reason." He exchanged an even look with Richard and his meaning was all too clear.

"Nonsense," Richard bristled. "I will agree to a betrothal, as it will be effective for our purpose, but I will not force Eve to marry me against her will. As far as I am concerned, once the barons have met, she is free to break her vows."

Strongbow considered Richard's words thoughtfully. "I think that is agreeable."

"Nay!" Warwick growled. "It is not! I do not understand why you are adverse to forcing the lady to marry you, Richard, since I have observed that force does not seem alien to your nature!"

"Warwick, what are you saying?" Strongbow's face darkened with question as he looked from one to the other and became aware of the ill feelings that were passing between them.

"Tell him, Richard," Warwick said coldly. "Or I will."

"There is nothing to tell." Richard returned Warwick's glare but avoided his father's burning eyes.

Warwick's face reddened with anger. "Are you going to deny that you forced the lady, that you took her against her will?"

"What?" Strongbow bellowed. "When was this?"

"It does not involve either of you," Richard said coldly.

Strongbow's eyes flashed with anger, his fury mounting against the horrifying news Warwick had revealed and against Richard's mild reaction. "Richard! Did you, or did you not, force the lady to submit to you?"

"Aye."

Strongbow stormed about the room, taking his wrath out against the walls in a stream of profanities until finally he spun back on his son. "The lady is here under Gilbert's protection!" he roared. "She is the ward of the king and whatever you think of him, she is a royal ward! Not to mention her youth, her innocence! And you—you dared to—that a son of mine should do this thing! You *will* marry her, Richard, and as soon as possible!"

"You have not faced her yet with this news," Richard said calmly. "I do not think she will be eager to protect her good name by marrying me."

"She has no choice in the matter!" Strongbow shouted.

Richard smirked at the irony, remembering the similar words he had said to her, not realizing at the time how closely they would strike.

"You will be ready to leave for Chepstow within the week," Strongbow gritted.

"There is just one thing that I would ask."

"You dare to ask a favor? I hardly think that you are in a position to do so!"

"It is not for myself that I ask," Richard sighed. "It is for the lady. Let me be the one to tell her."

"You? I think not!"

"Even with everything that has happened it would be best if I were to tell her," he persisted. "It involves the two of us and she should be given the courtesy of hearing this news without anyone else present." He read the dubious looks of the other two men and added with exasperation, "Do you fear that I will harm her? God's Breath, you are going to marry her to me. If you have any fears on that score you had better reconsider your decision!"

Strongbow hesitated, then nodded thoughtfully. "Aye, perhaps it would be better if you told her. But do so quickly as we must be prepared to leave by the end of the week. If there is any problem I will speak with her."

Richard shook his head grimly. "There will be no need. As you say, she has no choice."

As Richard approached the door to Eve's chamber he heard her laughter coming from the end of the hallway. She came about the corner, arm in arm with Lavinia. The two giggled but Eve stopped as she saw him standing in the shadows. At the sight of him her face flushed but she held her tongue as he nodded greeting to the ladies.

"Lavinia, I must ask you to excuse us. There is an important matter I must discuss with Eve."

"There is nothing that would cause me to be alone with you, Richard!" Eve snapped. Richard ignored her anger and, nodding to the doubtful Lavinia, he brushed past her and opened the door to Eve's chamber. Taking her by the arm he assisted her into the room. As the door shut behind them, Eve spun on him with eyes flared.

"How dare you! What right have you to push your way into my chambers, to be so rude to Lavinia! You have not even spoken to me in weeks, not that I wanted you to. Indeed, it has been an immense relief to be saved your company! But now, you force this meeting with no regard to my feelings or wishes! What could you possibly have to say that I would be interested in hearing?"

He let her vent her anger as he walked across the room and stood by the fire, feeling suddenly chilled in the winter air that permeated the manor, even against the roaring fires that were kept going day and night throughout. His constitution was such that he had never seen the need to bundle in the layers of fur mantles worn by most, but suddenly he found that the heavy wool of his tunic and chanuses was not enough. He wondered, wryly, how much of his chill came from the winter air and how much from the prospect of revealing his news to Eve.

"Well?" she snapped.

"Eve, please sit down. You are not going to be pleased by what I have come to tell you." He gestured to the chair by the fire and sighed as she stood firm. She clasped her hands in front of her and glared at him.

"I would be surprised, nay, amazed if anything you had to say did please me!"

"Eve, please," he said wearily. "Let us not make this more difficult than it has to be." He rested his elbow on the mantle and ran his fingers through his tousled hair as he stared into the flames.

She flinched at the movement, recognizing the action as something he did when he was deeply upset. Her stomach tightened painfully at the recognition and she was surprised at the emotion it stirred within her. It was odd to realize, now when things had become so estranged between them, that she knew his moods so well. Awkwardly contrite, she moved to the chair and sat down.

"I was rude," she conceded softly. "I know that you would not be here unless it was important and that it must be as difficult for you as it is for me. What have you come to tell me?"

He glanced up at her with surprise, then shook his head slightly, always amazed by her quick change of moods. When he did not answer, she took a deep breath and looked at him squarely.

"This has to do with the message Orlan gave me, does it not? So then, what punishment has been decided for me?"

He flinched at her choice of words. "I appreciate your honesty, and I hope that your courage sustains you, Eve, though I doubt that you are prepared for the results of our actions. We are both responsible and we shall both have to live with the consequences. Ah, I am putting this badly. Perhaps, just a short time ago, this would have been happy news, something that would have brought us both great pleasure. Now . . ."

"What is it, Richard?" she pressed.

He hesitated with a ragged sigh. "You have a right to know that the message you held was the answer to our struggles against Stephen. It would have brought Henry across the channel. Because of the delay we lost the advantage and another had to be found to stop Eustace's ascendancy to the throne. Eve, I assure you that I had nothing to do with the decision that has been made but I agree with the purpose. A few weeks from now many of the most important peers of the realm will gather at Chepstow. At this gathering we will be able to make plans for Stephen's defeat. To avoid suspicion the reason given for the gathering is—is our marriage."

His words hit her like a bolt and she jumped from the chair and leapt back from him, shaking her head with disbelief. "You cannot be serious! Nay, Nay! I will not marry you! They cannot make me marry you!" she shrieked.

"They can, and they will," he said coolly. "I told you that you would have no choice in whom you married and the irony is that it will be me."

"But my father!"

"Your father has given his consent. He agreed to comply with Stephen's choice before you were sent to England. It was a condition of your fostering, Eve. I tried to tell you that."

"Nay!" she cried as tears began to well in her eyes and trip down her cheeks. "Why would he? Why did he not tell me?"

"I think you know the answer to that better than I. Do you still not realize the importance of your marriage for your father? He is in need of allies and he cannot afford to ignore the help that can come to him through your marriage."

Her eyes smoldered with hatred as she glared at him. "What are your plans for me now, Richard? To lock me away at Chepstow where I will be forced to keep your secrets?"

"Eve, don't be absurd," he admonished, his own anger growing. "I told you that I had no hand in this decision." He managed to duck just in time as the candlestick barely missed his head and crashed into the wall behind him. He grabbed her wrists just as she was about to impart a similar missile and pulled it from her hand, setting it on the table.

"I will give you time to absorb what I have told you but, nevertheless, you must be ready to leave for Chepstow by the end of the week. You may speak to Strongbow or Gilbert about this if you wish but they will only confirm what I have told you. The king has given his consent and there is no way to turn back, so resign yourself as I have."

He looked down into her large green eyes which were vibrant with anger and hatred. He was startled by her beauty, which constantly overwhelmed him, her face now flushed to a pink hue that only served to enhance her loveliness. He was struck with the impulse to sweep her into his arms, to urge her against her certain protests to remember their passion. His blood, warming to the moment, surged through his veins as a subtle instinct told him that the moment could be won, that her hatred and distrust could be swept aside to a reawakening of the desire he knew lay just beneath her anger. As he started to pull her toward him, she sensed his meaning and the anger in her eyes changed to fear and she tensed.

Unprepared for the unmasked terror he read in her, his desire faded as quickly as it had appeared and he dropped her wrist.

"Be ready to leave by the end of the week," he said icily. "Lavinia and Bridget will accompany you as companion and maid, so you had best consult with them about what you will need." He crossed by her to the door where he paused and added mockingly, "You need not concern yourself about having to share my company. I shall leave for Chepstow in the morning."

Eve lay in the wagonbed and stared at the stars that winked at her through the opening in the canvas as she listened to the even sound of Lavinia's breathing. There were no more tears to be shed; they were expended before she left Hertford and she left with a dry, hollow feeling of resignation. She grieved for the lost love, so nearly caught, and for herself as she thought of the years ahead, should she marry Richard, loveless years married to a man who did not love her, who only wanted to possess and control her.

The barons were now on the way to Chepstow. It would make no difference if the betrothal was broken due to the lack of a bride—they would have their meeting and everyone would be satisfied. And they would be out of each other's lives.

She sat up very slowly, careful not to wake Lavinia, and silently drew the bundle out from behind the boot of the wagon where she had hidden it. She almost swore out loud as she broke a nail on the tightly cinched knots which held the bundle together. Cautiously, she removed a woolen kirtle and as she slipped it over her head a small, knotted kerchief fell into her

lap from the folds of the skirt. She picked it up and fingered
the coins tied within. Renewed tears tightened in her throat as
she recalled the moment, long before, when Richard had given
them to her. Damn him! Was he to invade her thoughts even
now, when she had far more pressing problems to contend
with? She pushed him away with angry determination and she
gathered up her cloak and the retied bundle and slipped from
the covered wagonbed to the ground.

As she glanced about the sleeping camp, she felt her stomach
flip-flop with a spasm of fear when a guard passed by only a
few feet from where she stood. She stifled a gasp and pressed
herself back into the shadows of the wagon, freezing until the
man was well past. When the way was clear, she edged herself
along the side of the wagon to the trees which ringed the camp
and made her way toward where the horses were tethered.
Pausing in the protective shadows of the foliage she peeked
out to see if anyone was near. To her dismay, a guard had
stretched out under a tree between her and the horses and from
where she stood she could not tell if he was sleeping. She
cursed silently, moved back into the trees and turned to face
their black depths, shuddering at the prospect of traveling alone
through their dense mass. Her courage began to fade but, as
she remembered the alternative, she grit her teeth and plunged
forward, determined to be far away from the camp, and the
future Richard had threatened her with, as soon as possible.

With very little skill, and a great amount of luck, she managed to find her way through the trees to the road. Branches
had torn at her kirtle and her face and arms were smudged and
bruised. She had been concentrating so thoroughly on making
her way through the underbrush that it was not until she found
herself in the open freedom that her solitude, and what she was
attempting to do, struck her with full force. Dispirited, she
glanced about with consternation at the once friendly maple,
elm and ash that now hovered menacingly as if their tentacle
arms were only lingering for the moment to strike. She thought
about the "little people" of the forest her people once believed
in and for once she wished that the tales were true. She could
use her own small army of friends on such a night. She knew
the danger of letting her thoughts wander in such directions,
so she focused her attention on counting her steps, each long
stride taking her farther away from the sleeping camp and
toward freedom.

The ploy worked so effectively that she was not prepared

for what happened next. Her mind had so withdrawn into the total silence of the forest that she was not struck by the oddity of the silence itself. There was no movement at all, not even the soft rustling of the little forest creatures who scurried about the dried leaf floor in their nighttime duties and especially not those creatures—because instinct had awakened them to the presence of another.

She had just taken her eight-hundred-and-sixty-fifth step when a shadow swooped down within inches of her head on silent wings. She let out a shriek and brought her arms up in defense of the night-spirit, the total silence of the deadly spectre only adding to her terror. She melted to the hard-packed road as her knees buckled with fright and she covered her head protectively with her arms, bracing for the impending attack. When nothing happened, and the blood began to flow through her veins again, she lowered her arms tentatively and peered out into the night. The road was empty. She looked around and since she could see nothing, she began to wonder if it had only been her well-developed imagination. As she stood up she spied a movement on a low tree branch which hung out a few feet over the road nearby. There, perched on the branch, sat the largest owl she had ever seen. Its feathers, white, tipped in brown, ruffled as it shook out its body before settling more firmly on the branch. Its stark yellow eyes were fixed upon her with a look that seemed to be filled with interest and certainly no fear.

She laughed nervously in soft greeting as her fear began to disappear. "Well, owl," she whispered. "What are you about? Surely you did not mistake me for a rabbit or a mouse!"

The bird made no move to flee at the sound of her voice and it continued to regard her with what could only be considered as a rude stare. She edged her way past it, watching from the corner of her eye until she was on the other side. Its head moved with her and, when she stopped and turned back, it was still regarding her carefully.

The eeriness of that night was to remain with her for years to come. Strangely, her silent companion was to remain with her throughout the night, moving by her on silent wings to perch in a tree-top or a low-hanging branch until she had passed, remaining with her in comradeship each time she paused to rest. It was not long before she accepted its company with gratitude although she couldn't fathom why it was doing this particular thing! As she sat beneath a tree at the edge of the road during a rest, with the bird on a low branch a few feet away, she found herself talking to it.

"Who—ah, what are you?" she asked as if she expected an answer. "Why are you following me? Or am I following you?"

It blinked.

"Why do I feel that I am safe with you here?"

Mysteriously, as the grey light of dawn began to outline the shapes of the trees, it disappeared so quickly that she was left to wonder if the entire event had been her imagination. But, imagination or not, it had seen her through the night, the comfort of its presence having put aside the terrors she would have faced if left to her own dreaming.

As the sky began to lighten she slumped down at the edge of the road, knowing that she could not walk another step until she had rested. She reached into her bundle and extracted the wheaten bread she had managed to secrete away. Exhausted, she chewed on the stale bread, leaned her head back against the tree trunk and closed her eyes against her abused muscles and joints. She had almost fallen asleep when a sound came from beyond the turn in the road and she leapt up and stumbled back into the trees. Recognizing the sound of creaking wheels she peered out through the foliage and was relieved to see that it was not one of her party in search of her, but a small cart pulled by a single horse. She quickly removed a single coin from her pocket and tucked it in her belt, then taking a deep breath, as her heart pounded, she waited for the stranger to approach.

The creaking cart seemed to plod impossibly forward on ancient wheels pulled by a gaunt horse who had long seen better days. A scrawny, withered old man sat on the wagon seat, a tattered cloak pulled tightly about him against the frigid morning air. His shoulders were humped and he appeared to be half-asleep, apparently trusting the nag to see them to their destination.

Chewing on her lower lip, Eve made her decision and, grabbing up her bundle, she stepped out onto the road. The horse, startled by her sudden appearance, swerved away from her, nearly upsetting the cart and its occupant.

"Ho!" the old man shouted as he frantically grasped to his perch, while trying to bring the frightened animal under control. He leapt from the cart with surprising agility and grasped the bridle of the horse, bringing it quickly to a standstill. He stroked the horse's muzzle and talked to it quietly, then turned to where Eve stood and scowled at her.

"Wa' do ya mean, near scar'n' me animal ta death! Do ye not know better than to leap out upon a man and 'is 'orse?"

"'Tis sorry, I am," she pleaded, slipping easily into a brogue. This time she was determined to be more careful and not give herself away by manner or speech. "'Twas not my meaning. I was hoping ye'd give me a ride in your cart."

He grunted and peered at her suspiciously. "There's naught room," he snapped.

She reached into her belt and extracted the gold coin, causing his eyes to gleam as he spotted it. "Please, I'd be paying for the favor."

"Well now," he drawled. "That would change things, wouldn't it now." He snatched the coin from her offered hand, biting it to assure himself of its worth before tucking it away into his pocket.

He pulled the horse about and checked the harness, then climbed back onto the cart seat as she waited by the side of the road.

"Well, what ye be waitin' fer? Are ye comin'?"

She threw her bundle into the back onto the kegs that were stacked there and drawing up her skirts, she struggled up over the wheel to the seat. He made no move to help her but seemed amused by her awkward struggles. As she plopped down on the seat with a grunt he clucked and flipped the reins, slapping the haunches of the animal, which jerked forward and almost upset her from her perch. They rode for more than a mile with neither of them speaking, though she noticed that he watched her from the corner of his eye. He broke the silence at last as his eyes moved over her, boldly fixing on her breasts and moving down to her waist and hips before returning her stare.

"Where ye be goin', lass?"

"I be looking for work," she answered off-handedly, perturbed by his bold regard.

He peered at her speculatively, wondering what such a fine beauty was doing wandering about the countryside. Was she running away to escape the attentions of some eager lord, or had she been cast out? It was hard to imagine that she was a mistress to tire of quickly, though perhaps her disposition did not match her beauty. These Irish were known to have swift tempers, he mused. Perhaps she had exercised hers once too often. Well, no matter, this could prove to be your lucky day, ol' Finlay, he thought to himself. Garnock would pay a pretty penny for this one, if he played his cards right. And, if he were able to manage to talk with him without that meddling old bag of a wife about, aye, perhaps it could turn out to be a good day, after all.

"What kind of work were ye lookin' fer?" he asked.

"Why? Would ye be knowing of something?" she looked at him cautiously.

"I might. There's an inn hereabouts, run by a friend. I know he be lookin' fer someone to help his woman with the cleanin'— if that work be suitin' ye."

"Is this place far?"

"Not far," he answered, quite satisfied with himself. "We be headin' that way now."

By the time they reached the inn every muscle in her body ached from the jerking motion of the crude cart. The journey had passed in silence, as apparently Finlay was as unwilling to answer questions as she, though her uneasiness with the old man had grown with each mile, as she would catch him leering at her with a nasty grin, causing her to wonder if he was not as old as he seemed.

By mid-morning they turned a wide bend in the road and the inn came into view. It was a large whitewashed frame structure with a thatched roof settled at the edge of a wide meadow. A long row of stone buildings stretched out behind, a barn and what she guessed to be chicken coops and a root cellar. A board hung from a post before the inn, painted with a single red maple leaf. It was not hard for Eve to imagine where the inn got its name, since huge winter-bare maples towered over the buildings and stretched out on both sides of the meadow to the forest beyond.

The inn was apparently the main point of a small village that ran along the road to the far side, a cluster of mud-and-wattle huts, a blacksmithy and various buildings surrounded on three sides by a low stone wall open to the road. There was smoke coming from the roof holes in two of the huts and the smithy's and a couple of urchins stood under a tree curiously watching the approach of the cart. Their garments seemed above the stamp of what she had seen on Hertford's serfs and the faces of the children shone pink and healthy under the dirt and grime, their eyes bright with interest as the cart passed.

Finlay pulled the horse to a halt in front of the inn and leapt down from his seat to tie the reins to the standingpost. He came around to her side but waved her back on the cart as she made ready to dismount.

"Ye best be lettin' me talk to them first. The missus is a mite strick in 'er ways but I think I can convince her that ye be just the one she be lookin' fer."

He slipped around to the back of the inn and, as she watched him go, a vague feeling of uneasiness began to play at her but she could not honestly reason why. What choice did she have but to trust him? What could he possibly gain by lying to her?

As Finlay slipped in the back door to the kitchen, he glanced about the room for a sign of Garnock's wife, Sophie. He breathed easier to note that she was nowhere in sight and he crossed through the kitchen and into the main room, where he found Garnock engaged in a heated argument with a disgruntled guest.

The owner of the inn was a large, heavily muscled man of middle age. He had a heavy shock of coarse greying hair over a pair of prominent, dark, bushy brows and a face attesting to long hard years of struggle. No matter how many times Finlay met Garnock the thing that could set his knees to quaking was Garnock's sheer meanness. There was no other description for it, the man had a mean streak and seemed to enjoy it. He certainly made no apology for it. He pleasured in watching others cringe and tremble with fear under his assaults, both verbal and physical.

Finlay approached the men gingerly, not wanting to direct Garnock's present anger upon himself. For a moment he was tempted to forget the whole thing and slip quietly away but the prospect of profit urged him forward and he braced himself for Garnock's fury. As if on cue Garnock's attention was drawn to the little man and the sight of him increased his foul mood because he had never cared for Finlay, equating him with a weasel he had once cornered in the chicken coop and had greatly enjoyed killing.

"What do ye want?" he bellowed, temporarily forgetting the other man as he pleasured in the way Finlay cringed in terror.

"I—I—have brought ye something, Garnock," the little man squeaked.

"Humph!" Garnock snorted. "What could ye have that I would want?" The guest who had innocently approached Garnock to complain about the size of the bill left the money on the bar and slipped gratefully from the room.

"Shhhh," Finlay whispered, a finger to his lips as he looked quickly to the stairs. "I do not think ye would want Sophie to come down at the moment! My business is with ye!" He smiled wickedly at the innkeeper, whose interest became aroused by the mystery. Anything that would deceive his nagging, shrewish lump of a wife interested him. He would not admit it to anyone, but Sophie was the only thing he feared. The woman was formidable, for all of her size. True, he could have squashed her in an instant, with little effort, but he recognized that she had the one thing he had not—intelligence. It was by her efforts that the inn was kept out of debt and he could not bear the thought of losing it. It was the only thing he loved.

"What is it?" he growled. "Make it quick, I have things to do."

Finlay smiled and crooked his bony finger for Garnock to follow him to the window. "How'd ye be wantin' to have the likes of that 'neath yer roof?" he asked innocently, jerking his thumb to where Eve sat on the cart.

Garnock whistled softly as his eyes widened. "Where did ye find 'er?"

"Ah—she be placed in my care," he lied. "Right away I thought of ye, knowing how ye be needin' a girl to help poor Sophie with 'er work."

"What's wrong with 'er?" Garnock asked suspiciously. "Why would anyone be givin' her to the likes of ye?"

"Just happen' to be in the right place at the right time." Finlay shrugged as small beads of sweat began to break out on his shriveled forehead. "And I be promisin' not to tell where she came from. Let's just say that her previous master found her presence to be—ah—rather compromisin'. But, bein' fond of the lass he wanted 'er safely placed."

Garnock frowned at the obvious lie but, as he looked back at Eve, he knew that he had to have her. The mere thought of having such a beautiful young and tender wench living beneath his roof heated his blood and he could feel his manhood stir as he stared at her. Aye, the thought of having Finlay ride away with her was more than he could bear, Sophie or no Sophie.

"How much ye be wantin' fer her?"

"Ah, I was thinkin' a thruppence would be fair."

"A tuppance, and not a bit more!" Garnock growled with malice.

"A tuppance!" Finlay whined. "But I could get more any-where!"

"Could ye now?" Garnock raised a brow. "How fer do ye think ye could go with her before 'er lord changed his mind?" he said evenly.

"Ah—perhaps a tuppance is fair. At least she'd be off me hands."

Garnock grunted and he dug into his pocket, extracting a coin which he flipped to the little man. "Fetch 'er, quickly."

Finlay hurried outside to fetch Eve. She looked up as he came out of the inn and brightened at the pleased look he wore.

"Well, lass, 'tis done!" he cackled. "Step down, step down!" He grabbed her bundle from the back of the cart and pushed it into her arms as she stepped onto the ground. "One thing, lass, I don't know where ye be comin' from and I don't want to know but I told Garnock that ye be sent from yer lord to find work and it be best if ye told the same story."

He waved her toward the door and hurried up onto the cart seat and chucked to his horse, leaving Eve to wonder as to his hurry. She turned and looked at the inn, wondering as to the manner of the people within and what awaited her. Finlay's haste unsettled her but she knew that her only alternative was to set again upon the road and the few coins in her bundle would not last her long. She had stitched her mother's jewels into the hem of her cloak but she had no intention of spending them for her keep. She had to earn money if she was ever going to reach Erin again. She chewed her lip nervously as she set back her shoulders and walked to the inn's door and entered.

The main room was empty but she could hear angry voices coming from somewhere on the second floor. She set her bundle on a table and sat in a chair, not knowing what else to do but wait until someone appeared. It was a large airy room with huge windows letting in ample sunlight to add to the cheeriness of the room. She liked what she saw. There was an obvious woman's touch to the room, which gave Eve a welcome sense of security. There were sturdy tables placed about and com-fortable high-backed chairs and the bar was a long piece of solid oak polished to a mirror finish. She heard footsteps and her attention was drawn to the stairs as a short, heavy-set woman appeared, followed by a huge man, his shirt sleeves rolled back to reveal enormous hairy arms.

"Nay, nay!" the woman was saying angrily as she waved

off the man's protests with obvious disgust. "I cannot be be-
lievin' this sudden burst of concern! Since when, me fine husband, have you suddenly become so concerned with the hours
of toil I put in here when . . ."

She stopped suddenly and the man almost barreled into her
from behind. The woman's mouth dropped open at the sight
of Eve, then snapped shut as she turned to glare over her
shoulder at her husband. "So this is the way of it? I should
have guessed! A girl to help me with the work, heh?" She left
the man sputtering as she walked toward Eve, appraising her
carefully until Eve blushed. "What be yer name, lass? And
where do ye be coming from?" she snapped. "My good-fer-
nothing husband tells me that it's a kitchen-helper ye want ta
be. Do ye have training as such?"

Eve gawked at the woman momentarily, stunned to silence.
She was a small woman, a full three heads shorter than the
man, yet she was obviously in control. Her wide girth and
ample bosom attested to her talents as a cook, which was
seconded by the appetizing aroma which drifted into the room
from the kitchen. The woman was spotlessly clean, her greying
hair peeking from beneath a starched linen cap, and her plump
hands were folded over a matching white apron. Her small blue
eyes peered intently at Eve as her disapproval and her doubt
of Eve's qualifications were openly evident.

"Well?" she pressed. "Are ye just going to stand there or
are you going to answer me?"

"My name is Eve MacMurrough," Eve answered as she
tried not to show her nervousness. "I was sent from Erin to
stay with me father's relations. They wanted to marry me to
someone I could not abide, so I was wont to stay. As for the
work, I spent many an hour helping the cook at home and what
I do not know, I can learn. I need the money and I am willing
to do whatever ye ask of me."

The woman looked at her with surprise, but not nearly as
much as Garnock who stood silently behind his wife.

"Well now," said the woman, a glimmer of respect in her
eye as she began to smile. "Perhaps you'll do, though how this
one managed to find ye I'll never know, and I don't think I
want to." She indicated her husband with a flip of her hand.
"One day he's bellowing that there's no money to be paying
help and the next he shows up with ye. Well, well, we'll give
ye a try. But mind ye, if ye don't work out, ye'll be sent
packing." She picked up Eve's bundle and thrust it into her

husband's arms. "Here, she can be having the small room at the end of the hall. I'll be seeing her get started now. Heaven knows I could use the help with mid-meal. And don't be thinking of getting any ideas!" she added, pushing him on his way. "I know what's on yer evil mind, don't be thinking I don't! Ye'll be staying away from the lass 'cause I'll be watching ye like a hawk, I will!"

Garnock disappeared obediently up the stairs as Sophie ignored his grumbling and, setting her cap, she jerked her head for Eve to follow and marched toward the kitchen. Eve smiled to herself as she glanced up at the disgruntled innkeeper, and said a silent thanks for her good fortune. There was no doubt that she would be perfectly safe from any untoward attentions from that source, and most likely any others, while the capable Sophie was within hearing distance.

14

Eve pushed her unruly locks from her eyes with the back of her hand, then paused to tuck the wayward curls beneath her cap before setting back to her task of peeling the vegetables for the mid-meal. She tossed another turnip into the steaming pot and smiled to herself as Sophie's whip-cracking voice carried from the barn through the half-opened kitchen door.

A week had passed since Eve's arrival but it had only taken a few days for her to become deeply fond of the mistress of the Maple Leaf Inn. She discovered that Sophie, despite her hard exterior, had a heart as soft as lamb's wool. She had taken Eve under her ample arms without hesitation, showing her nothing but kindness and warmth as if sensing Eve's loneliness and need for love. She was a strict taskmistress, demanding a job quickly and thoroughly done, but the moments spent around the kitchen table with a cup of hot, honeyed ale and a warm fire were many. Sophie seemed to sense when Eve was spent and she would protest her own fatigue and encourage the maid to rest, joining her in happy conversation and a tasty morsel put aside for such moments. She was free with riotous stories about her life with Garnock. Her sense of humor seemed to touch on even the direst of times, but she was careful never to pry into Eve's past.

While stirring a pot of one of her succulent soups the day before, she had explained the odd name for the inn. She had come from Scotland while a young girl, accompanying her family and footloose father. She had been struck by the magnificent array of brilliant reds, oranges and yellows of the turning oaks, maples, and ash that first cold, crisp fall, and they had never stopped being a source of pleasure and amazement to the Scotswoman. Hence, when she and Garnock had built the inn, she had insisted upon the name.

"That ol' fool insisted upon naming something daft like the Boar's Head, or other such nonsense!" she had chortled. "Why, every second inn in England is named the Boar's Head, and I was having none of it!"

She had filled Eve with stories of her childhood, of the people that lived in the village, and the ol' laird, as she called him.

"The Ol' Laird's a good one," Sophie had grinned. "Not like some I hear of. He's good to us, and the young laird too, never demanding the impossible and concerned about the people hereabouts. Well liked, he is, no reason to worry on that account. Besides, seems he's still struck with his lady, even after all the years they be married. Odd for the likes of him, to be sure."

Lost in her thoughts, Eve startled when the door swung open and Sophie strode in, plopping her girth into a chair as she shook her head with disgust.

"That man'll be the death of me! Come lass, sit with me. Ye look as if ye could use a cup of something hot! I know it'll be doing me no harm. The beds are made and the rooms are clean, so let's see to ourselves!"

"But supper will be late if I don't finish this stew," Eve protested.

"Let'm wait," Sophie scoffed. "The Good Lord knows they don't have to do that often! Demanding this and demanding that! You'd think they was fine lairds, or something! Come on lass, the time is ours—don't make an ol' body feel guilty for resting!"

Eve smiled and fetched the ale and, taking a place across the table from Sophie, she couldn't resist a sigh at the pleasure of sitting. She poured a measure for each as Sophie jumped up and went to the cupboard. "I know I put some biscuits by for us, unless that ol' scoundrel got them first. Always snooping in my kitchen, he is. He'd let me starve, he would!"

Eve glanced at the woman's broad hips and smiled at the unlikely prospect. Sophie fetched the elusive biscuits and set them on the table, snatching one before she had barely sat down and she began munching.

"Ah, lass, 'tis a sorry woman I'll be when yer gone," she sighed. "Though you've only been here a week I can hardly bear the thought of not having ye about."

Eve startled at the statement as she set her ale back on the table. Her horrified look of denial was not missed by the older woman. "Ah, lass, I'm not pryin', but I'm not a fool. I know you're only counting the days, and yer money, until ye can be gone. I'd pay ye less on that account if my conscience would not play the devil with me for doing it." Her manner became grave as she waved off Eve's sputtering protests. "Lass, I know ye be doing yer best to hide it but 'tis a lady too fine for this job you'd be. Ol' Garnock," she said, gesturing with her thumb toward the barn, "he be too dumb to notice it, but not I."

"Sophie, you're wrong!" Eve protested, finally getting a word in edgewise. "I like it here just fine! You have no idea how blessed I am to have found you!"

"Ah," Sophie said, her eyes narrowing. "You'd best be cautious, your brogue is slipping." She cackled at the observation and Eve's crestfallen expression. "It's all right, Eve, I knew it from the first. And I'm still not asking any questions. I know what it be like for a young, tender lass in this world. I see and I hear and you'd be surprised at what that is, running a place like this. Whatever the reason you left your last place, I know you must have had a good reason."

"Nay, Sophie," Eve said sadly, "you could not imagine. It is not what you think. I am here by my own choice but for your kindness I want to be honest. I am here to earn money, enough to see me home to Erin. That will take a long time, I fear, so you need not expect me to leave soon," she sighed.

"Well, lass, you can be sure that your time here will be well spent, and glad that I am to have ye. I'm here to talk with if ye want it, but I'll not be pryin', as I said."

Eve smiled at Sophie gratefully, not sure how she could answer such open kindness. In the long, awkward silence that followed she sought to change the subject.

"Sophie, how is it that you met Garnock. You seem . . . so . . ."

"Ill-suited?" Sophie laughed. "It's a common enough story for our kind. I loved it here, more than anywhere else since leaving Scotland. There was not a chance to return there, seeing as how there were those who were more than eager for me father to return, and no good fer him. So, when he began to get that wandering look to his eye again, I said nay, not this time, and fixed me eye upon that poor specimen of a man in the barn. Ah, but he was a sight to turn a young lass's eye in those days—strong, tall and handsome, he was, with a gleam to his eye that could set a heart to flutterin'. He's really not such a bad sort, if ye know how to handle 'im," she added with a chortle. "And I can! And see what we've done, not a bad place this!"

"Nay, it is not!" Eve assured her. "It is wonderful!"

"Aye, that it is, if I do say so myself, and I do!" she laughed. "And here I am, and here I'll stay for as long as the Good Lord allows!" Her manner became sober and she looked at Eve uncomfortably. "There is something else I would speak to ye about, lass. Garnock has a wandering eye. Don't say I can exactly blame him," she added with a chuckle as she rubbed her girth. "But I'd not have him look in your direction! You'd best be keeping yer door locked and don't trust 'im for a moment! As long as I'm about I'm not really worried—but the fact is that I do another service here, besides running this inn. I be midwife for those who need it and that is often the way they come with their bairns. There's a young lass nearby, hardly more'n a bairn herself and in not too good of health. She's due any time and I've promised to be with her during these last days before the birthin'. I'm leaving in the morning and I might be gone a few days so I wanted to warn ye. Keep to yourself and lock yer doors at night. I don't know why, bless me, but I love that brute. But I'm wise enough not to trust 'im."

Eve minded Sophie's warning and did her best to avoid Garnock that next day. Fortunately, the inn was crowded with travelers and there was little time left for Garnock to turn a head her way. The few times he appeared in the kitchen she noticed that he would dally longer than necessary before returning to the main room. She would turn to find him staring at her and she chilled at the way he would goggle her when his eyes came to rest upon a part of her body where they had no right to be. Otherwise he posed no threat and she felt safe enough, though she looked forward to Sophie's return.

On the second day Eve fetched and carried until she thought she would drop from exhaustion. Garnock spent the afternoon in the main room, swilling ale with the more disreputable guests, and left Eve to see to the wants of the inn's occupants. She could hear his boisterous laughter joined with the others as they lifted tankard after tankard as if bent upon making the most of

Sophie's absence. At last the supper mess was cleaned up, the kitchen was scrubbed down, and the last of the guests seemed to be settled for the night. She dragged herself up the steps to her room and, swinging the door closed behind her, she collapsed onto the bed, too tired to bathe or even remove her clothes.

The revelry downstairs reached a rowdy pitch as another keg was tapped and its tawny contents were sloshed into eagerly presented tankards, while Garnock passed around the brew without attention to payment, playing well the drunken host. A rider was heard to approach a point passed unaware by the innkeeper as the door to the tavern opened and a tall, heavily cloaked knight entered the room, his face well-hidden in the folds of his hood. A few of the more sober guests noticed his entrance and shifted uncomfortably in their chairs, wondering as to the identity of the solitary knight but, as they could feel his gaze settle upon them, they turned back to their own affairs. The newcomer did not speak to anyone and did not approach the innkeeper, who was still not aware of his presence, but moved to a chair in the shadows by the far wall, where he leaned back and propped his feet on the table, appearing to go to sleep.

Garnock finally rose from his chair and staggered a bit while his companions bellowed with laughter, the two nearest reaching out to right the brawny innkeeper before he found a place in a luckless lap. Garnock lifted his tankard in a drunken salute, sloshing its contents on his nearest companion and being met with good-natured profanity that went unpassed by his host.

"Methinks ye've all have enough of my hospitality," he slurred. "An ye may be thinkin' I don't know how much of me brew ye've had but a bill will await ya in the mornin'!" He hiccuped and belched loudly as he wiped his mouth with the back of his hairy hand. "But now I've other matters to tend to, as there's a green-eyed wench awaitin' me. Me ol' lady 'as been guardin' her door but now I be deprivin' the wench of me pleasure no longer! See to yourselves, lads." He leaned forward unsteadily to whisper loudly, "If ye be hearin' screams it'll only be her cries of pleasure, so there's no need to come runnin'!"

The men broke out in laughter while one of them slapped Garnock on the back. "If it be good sport ye find, give us a share!"

"Aye, per'aps I will," he slurred. He turned and as best he

could, he staggered toward the stairs. He managed to hit both sides of the wall on the first two steps, much to the great amusement of the other men. He paused, studying the challenge of the staircase, then half fell up the stairs, unaware of the icy grey eyes that followed his ascent.

Somewhere in the back of her mind, Eve heard a door open and the sound of a man's voice. Groggily, she pulled herself up on her elbows and looked back over her shoulder, her eyes flying open as reality brought her fully awake. She began to scream but a large hairy hand was clamped over her mouth and she could smell the stale ale on Garnock's breath as he bent over her.

"Kind of ye to make it easy for me and leave yer door unlocked, lass. Thought I'd have to break down me own door. I've waited a long time for this, girl, but no more. Tonight, yer mine."

She pulled back against his grasp and squealed uselessly against his hand, twisting her head frantically as she struggled to catch her breath. My God, this could not be happening to her again! Enraged, she thrashed at him wildly, pulling at his face and hair as she felt her bodice give way in a rending tear. He laughed drunkenly and threw his weight upon her. His hands grasped at her breasts and pulled at her skirt. She thought, wildly, that she would suffocate as his massive weight pressed her down into the bedding and for an instant the insane thought pushed through her mind that he would pass out on her in his drunken stupor and she would die there.

Suddenly, from nowhere, a large hand clamped on Garnock's shoulder and Eve saw the disbelieving expression on the innkeeper's face an instant before he crashed to the floor. Sobering, he bellowed in rage and leapt to his feet to confront his assailant. He started to lunge but froze in a crouch. Eve saw his face drain of color as it crumbled into a mask of astonishment.

His back to her, the large, helmed knight stood over him, making no move to draw his sword from its scabbard but his voice was cold with deadly intent.

"This woman is mine and no one shall lay a hand upon her but me. Count yourself among the most fortunate of men that you did not see further in your pursuit, for in that event I would have no choice but to end your worthless life. See yourself to the hall, Garnock—now!"

"Aye, milord!" the stricken innkeeper groveled. "I did not

know. I had no way of knowin'!" He fairly tripped over himself as he rushed from the room and Richard slammed the door behind him, then turned to Eve who lay wide-eyed on the bed. He walked over and looked down at her, his face tight with fury, but he said nothing as his eyes moved slowly over her before coming to rest on her bodice. She looked down to her exposed breasts but before she could cover them, he grunted with disgust and moved to a chair near the hearth and sat down. She sat up and pulled her bodice together as best she could and waited for him to speak. She avoided his eyes, aware of the fury that was certain to be lingering there.

There was a long, heavy silence as he removed his helm and cloak, setting them on the table before pushing back his coif. He ran his fingers through his hair, then finally looked over at her.

"You, milady, are a fool."

Words caught in her throat as her thoughts rushed with retort, but she kept her silence and waited for the onslaught of recriminations she knew were coming. But they did not. At long last, he finally did speak but his voice was low with icy calm.

"Change your gown, and gather your things. We are leaving."

Still silent, she rose from the bed and went to the wardrobe, where she removed her only other kirtle and, with trembling fingers, laid it on the bed. She paused as he propped his feet on the table and calmly watched her. Setting her mouth defiantly she turned her back as she pulled the ruined garment over her head and tossed it on the floor. She could feel his eyes burning into her back, knowing that her body lay open to his appraisal under the sheerness of her chemise. She pulled the kirtle on as quickly as possible and then, humiliated to her very depths, she turned on him, her eyes flashing.

"Why should you be angry, Richard? He did nothing more than what you yourself have taken the liberty to do!"

A muscle twitched in his cheek but his voice was smooth as he answered, almost lightly, "The difference is, my love, that you are my betrothed. Therefore, for as long as I shall choose, you belong to me. Very simply, you are my possession." He ignored her gasp and rose to walk slowly across the room to her, holding her eyes with a sheer will of his own. His look was hard, without a hint of tenderness as he stopped before her.

"The simple fact is that before God and man you belong to

me. You have no rights of your own," he said evenly. "Now, you will gather your things and with as much dignity as possible, leave with me through that room downstairs. You will return with me to Chepstow and two days hence you will stand with me in the chapel and give your vows of marriage—without bringing any further shame upon me, my family, or yourself. Do you understand?"

"I will not marry you!" she shrieked. "You cannot make me marry you!"

"If you cannot manage this with proper dignity, there are other means," he continued, ignoring her outburst. "You can be gagged and bound and dragged to the altar, your consent given by another, if you prefer."

"You cannot!" she gasped.

"It has been done," he shrugged. "The choice is yours. Though I should think you would not want to bring further dishonor upon the MacMurrough name. Now get your things."

He turned and went back to his chair, plopped himself down and waited for her to do his bidding. She gaped at him incredulously, then squealed with outrage. Spinning about, she began to throw things from the cupboard. She stuffed her meager belongings into a bundle as she struggled for a solution but she could find none but to comply with his demands. How could he do this? Would he actually make good his threat? Aye, she reasoned, he probably would!

"How did you know where to find me?" she hissed.

"You gave us a good run, I will admit," he drawled. "When they found that you had gone, they struck west, thinking that you would set out for the coast. Why did you choose to go south?"

"Did I?"

He shook his head with disbelief. "Aye, Eve, you did. We would not have discovered your whereabouts when we did if Warwick had not come across that little weasel Finlay. He could not resist bragging in his cups about how he had recently come into coins by selling a beautiful Irish wench with flashing green eyes to a particular innkeeper."

"He sold me? Why, that . . ."

"What did you expect?"

She did not answer but with a heavy set of her shoulders she looked up at him as he rose from the chair. "Will it take us long to reach Chepstow?"

"You truly do not know where you are, do you?"

"Nay, I never asked. I thought they would think it odd."

Richard raised his brows and sighed. "The fact is, had Finlay carried you a little farther he would have brought you to my waiting arms. You are on Striguil's lands, Eve. Chepstow is only a few hours' ride."

He smiled at her dumbstruck expression but it disappeared quickly. He picked up her cloak and set it about her shoulders. Silently, he took her by the elbow and escorted her from the room and down the hallway but, as they descended the stairs, he leaned down to her and whispered tightly, "Do not say a word as we leave, do you understand? No matter what I might say, hold your tongue."

She glanced up at him, wondering as to his meaning, but his fingers tightened on her arm in warning when they reached the foot of the stairs. The room fell to silence as they appeared and all eyes were turned to them with expressions of guarded curiosity. The tension could be felt and Garnock, who was standing behind the bar fortifying himself with ale, paled at the sight of his lord, fully convinced that his end was at hand.

Richard paused as he reached to the pouch at his belt. He tossed it to the stricken man and smiled good-naturedly. "This is for the trouble the wench has caused you and for her keep. I shall see to it that she is set to tasks in the future that will keep her from causing further mischief." He winked at Garnock, setting the room to laughter as Garnock looked as if he would faint with relief. Richard could feel Eve tense under his fingers but his expression did not change and he walked her casually toward the door and opened it for her.

As he closed the door behind them she wrenched free and spun on him. "How dare you say that to them! They think I am your . . . your . . ."

"They think what I wanted them to," he answered, grasping her arms again as he pushed her toward Taran. "Should I have told them that the bride-to-be of their lord makes a habit of frequenting common inns and working as a kitchen maid?"

"How did you know that?" she demanded.

"Some of the men pleasured in talking of the succulent wench that prepared their supper—and congratulated Garnock on his choice of help," he answered grimly as he tied her bundle behind Taran's saddle.

"What purpose has been served by lying to them? Eventually they will know."

He paused and glanced down at her, his mouth twisting into

a smile that did not meet his eyes. "By that time you will be my wife and no one will dare broach the subject. In fact, I do not expect to hear of it again."

The night had turned to a bitter, crisp cold that bathed the landscape in a sheet of icy frost. The bright winter moon shone over the blue-black forest, which hugged tightly to the narrow road, glistening the icy particles that hung from the bows of the trees in dancing lights. The only sound that could be heard was the sharp click of Taran's hoofs and the occasional snort of the destrier's smoky breath. Pretending sleep, Eve snuggled into the warmth of Richard's arms. She had wisely chosen silence as a preferable alternative to his anger. She had tried in vain to remain aloof but she found it impossible with his arms folded about her and the feel of his hard body intimately pressed against her own. They had but covered a few miles when it had struck her in a clear but jolting moment of rationality, that she had known that she would see him again. Had she wanted it? She recoiled from the thought. Nay, nothing had changed except now it was worse than ever! Knowing that she had no choice, she was almost resigned to the marriage since there now seemed no doubt that it would take place. But, his property? No rights of her own? It was at odds with everything she wanted or had expected from a marriage!

In Erin, a wife had rights of her own, her own wealth apart from her husband's, and her body belonged to her, to be freely given. How could she expect less? How could she now live with him on his terms, in a relationship void of everything she held most dear. Nay, she would not be his chattel, a virtual prisoner to be used, or forgotten, at his whim! Yet, as she felt his arms tighten about her in an unconscious gesture of familiarity, something within her stirred, an emotion she desperately wanted to decry. Unwillingly, her memory returned to the other time he had carried her away from near disaster. Unlike then, his arms were familiar and, in spite of everything, gave her a welcomed feeling of security and safety. She peered up at him cautiously, perplexed as to how this could be so. She could not accept the life he had promised her, yet a vague, growing feeling told her that she could not live without him. The realization stabbed at her, causing an almost physical pain as it tumbled over and over in her mind. Biting her lower lip she drew a deep breath against the tears she refused to shed. She closed her eyes in feigned sleep and mercifully it soon became reality as she leaned her head against his shoulder and drifted off into its welcomed release.

As Richard felt Eve nestle against him, his glower softened into a pensive frown and his mind turned to his own grim thoughts. When word of her disappearance had reached Chepstow he had taken to horse within the hour, riding to the northeast with Warwick in an attempt to retrace her steps. As the days passed with no sign of her, the deep, flaming anger for her foolhardiness gave way to worry for her safety. He began to imagine her in the hands of Stephen's men, whose number had increased with the king's declaration, and his accustomed calm gave way to frantic thoughts, images resembling the moments of their first meeting.

Eve shifted in his lap, snuggling closer to him in her sleep and he drew his cloak more tightly about her. Damnation, he thought crossly, was he to spend the rest of his life rescuing her from foolish, impulsive behavior? Did she hate and fear him so much that she would prefer the likes of Garnock to a marriage with him?

When he had left Hertford, he was determined to speak again with Strongbow, this time to make him see the wisdom of releasing her from her vows. No purpose could be served by bounding them both to a lifetime of a loveless marriage. As for the matter of their, ah, indiscretion, if the situation in Ireland kept her from returning home, he was certain that another, more agreeable match could be found for her. He was prepared to press it with a considerable dowry from his own purse, if necessary. He owed her that much. Such had been his thoughts as he had ridden toward Chepstow with Warwick, Gervase, and Raymond FitzWilliam, a young cousin of his mother's whom he had taken for his squire. And, he would have remained resolute had it not been for an off-handed remark from Gervase as they had camped on the third night out.

Their bellies full, Richard had stretched out under a broad spreading oak near the campfire and was listening through half-closed lids to an animated discussion between Gervase and young Raymond. The latter was holding forth with youthful exuberance, extolling his good fortune in becoming a squire to the house of Striguil, and of his eagerness to see combat where he was certain to gain great name and good fortune.

"All things will come in time if they are fated to be," Gervase assured him patiently while stretched out lazily before the fire.

"Though the fact that you have become Richard's squire at this time may give fate a helping hand. I doubt that Stephen will look kindly upon the affairs that are developing, or anyone involved." Gervase dismissed further conversation and rolled onto his side and was moments later snoring in his sleep as Raymond was lost to dreams of mighty battles and glorious conquests.

But, while the others dreamed, Gervase's casually thrown words had assured Richard of a sleepless night. Why had it not occurred to him before, he gritted. There had never been any doubt in his mind as to Stephen's reaction to their plans. Indeed, he was looking forward to the prospect of finally bringing the matter to a head with even greater, if not grimmer, enthusiasm than his young squire. But how could he have been so blind? Stephen's fury would not be narrowed to a few, but to everyone involved!

Eve was a royal ward. If their part in the coming drama were discovered, and it was almost certain to be, Stephen would stop at nothing to take her from the clutches of the deClares, including marrying her off to one of the despotic nobles in his favor. Even worse, if he suspected that she had been in any way part of their cause, the results could be dire. He knew then, with a heavy certainty, that the only way he could protect her was with his name. She had to marry him, and as quickly as possible.

Now, holding the object of those thoughts nestled in his arms, the reality of the decision sharpened unpleasantly. Would she never learn to trust him or would she always react with such hot-headed impulsiveness? With her warm, soft body curled up against him it was becoming harder to think clearly. He smiled grimly as he realized that at least life with her mercurial moods would never prove boring. If he could only help her to realize her importance, and the necessity for her to understand her position. Ironic, he mused, but she struggled so valiantly against the reality that she was a woman, when she was the most fascinating and desirable woman he had ever known.

The horizon began to lighten to a golden hue as Richard pulled Taran to a halt on the crest of a hill. When the destrier pawed impatiently, the movement stirred Eve awake.

"What has happened?" she yawned. "Why have we stopped?"

Richard marveled at her beauty as she turned her face up to look at him. Her expression was blissfully serene with a hint of a smile on her lips. Her hair was tousled and hanging loosely

about her shoulders and the eyes she turned up to him were
warm and inviting, without their usual guarded suspicion or
anger.

"We are here," he said simply. She couldn't know the impulse he was fighting not to kiss those rosy lips which were
curved so delectably into a tender smile.

She looked about with curiosity and gasped. From the crest
of the hill Chepstow loomed before them, the soft rays of dawn
illuminating its battlements in a majestic glow. It seemed to
reach endlessly along the river Wye, which laid at its back,
shrinking her memory of Hertford in comparison. Massive towers were spaced along its walls, each appearing to reach into
the sky over rows and rows of parapets topping walls which
telescoped into the inner courtyards. The brilliant dawn revealed miles of rich farms and meadows stretching to the horizon, with the wide-flowing river cutting through its breadth
like a winding snake to the dense forest, and the fierce, craggy
mountains of Wales, just beyond.

"Oh, Richard," she breathed. "Is that Chepstow?"

"Aye," he answered quietly with pride in his voice. "It was
built by my uncle, who also founded the abby of Tintern, which
is not far from here. It was thought that such a fortress would
be needed to defend us from Wales but fortunately that proved
unnecessary."

He urged Taran forward and the destrier picked his way
down the narrow path of the hill. As they reached the battlements Richard guided him along the far side of the castle to a
narrow path that led between the river and the wall. He slipped
from the saddle and led Taran along the path to a centermost
point in the wall, where he stopped. Eve looked about and
seeing no reason to halt at this particular point, she looked at
Richard with puzzlement.

He lifted her from the saddle and, tying Taran to a ring in
the wall, he answered her unasked question. "No one, with the
exception of your escort from Hertford, knows of your disappearance. It has been said that you were not feeling well and
preferred to keep to your chambers, giving us time to find
you."

Without further explanation he turned and pressed a spot
on the wall. She drew in her breath as the wall seemed to move
under his touch and a section swung away to reveal a hidden
door.

"This entrance proved quite handy for my uncle during

siege," he said as he took her hand to lead her into the opening.
"Be careful," he cautioned, "there are loose stones."

Once inside, the wall closed behind them, plunging them
into total darkness. Her skin crawled as she imagined what
creatures must live in such a place, but he took her hand, its
strong warmth giving her comfort, and he led her carefully up
a steep, narrow staircase. They stopped at the top and she heard
a latch click before the wall opened and she blinked against
the sudden rush of brilliant light. He took her hand again and
led her forward into the most beautiful room she had ever seen.

A warming fire crackled on an enormous hearth across from
a huge bed covered with luxurious furs and robes. There were
winter roses placed about to welcome her on rich tables of
heavy oak and the chairs and walls were covered in tapestries
of soft, muted colors of blues, burgundies and gold.

Transfixed, she was not aware that Richard was speaking
to her. "Eve, I will fix the passage so that it cannot be opened
from this side," he said. "So do not attempt to leave by it."
Seeing her stiffen, he added wearily, "I have not ridden all
night just to see you disappear again. Later in the morning I
will come for you. You will appear with me for mid-meal the
very essence of the eager bride-to-be. Do you understand?"

"I am not a child, Richard," she snapped, as her eyes flashed
rebelliously. "Do not treat me as such!"

A brow arched at her warningly as he opened the door to
the passage and, before she could utter another word, he was
gone.

15

Late in the morning Lavinia and Bridget pounced into the room to wake Eve from a druglike sleep. She sat up in the middle of the monstrous bed and drowsily fended Lavinia's questions while Bridget fussed about the room, clucking her tongue in disapproval over Eve's disappearance. Sleepily, Eve answered Lavinia's prodding vaguely, saying only that she had stayed in an inn nearby, that she had not come to any harm, and Richard had brought her to Chepstow.

In spite of their efforts, Eve would not say more. She was still deeply confused about her feelings and, as she listened detachedly, she managed to avert their questions with half-given answers while her groggy mind slowly awakened to remembrances of the night just past. Lavinia chatted away happily but Eve was aware only of the thundering storm on Richard's face when she had gaped fearfully at him from the bed in the inn; the threats he had made with such menacing conviction; and his arms as they had enfolded her through the night's ride, warm and comforting and in such contradiction to everything else. Her scattered, confused thoughts focused into shock at a soft knock on the door and she brought her head up, certain that it was Richard coming to fulfill his threats.

As Lavinia went to answer the door, Eve jumped from the bed and snatched the linen wrapper nearby and turned to face him with renewed defiance. If his purpose was to humiliate her before Lavinia and Bridget, to see her cower in submission, then he would be sorely disappointed! To her amazement, and complete chagrin, it was not Richard who entered but Lady Isabel. Eve dropped her gaze to the floor, her cheeks reddening. She bit her lip in embarrassment before the mistress of Chepstow, knowing the difficulties she must have caused for this most gentle of ladies who had never shown her anything but kindness.

She felt her cheeks burn as Isabel bid a good morning to the others, and then graciously, but firmly, informed them that she wished to be alone with Eve. As the door shut behind them, Eve braced herself for the well-deserved chastisement and was all the more startled by Isabel's kindness.

"Please, come and sit with me, Eve. There is ample time before you must face your duties this morning."

Eve looked up to find that Isabel had taken a chair near the fire and was holding out her hands to the crackling flames to warm them from the morning's chill. Nervously, Eve took a chair across from her and self-consciously folded her hands in her lap, still unable to meet Isabel's gaze.

"My—my lady," she stammered. "It was never my intention to cause you grief. I . . ."

Isabel surprised her by reaching over and patting her hands. "My dear, I am not here to make you uncomfortable, nor to reprimand you. In fact, I have come to tell you a story."

She smiled at the astonished look on Eve's upturned face, then she laughed softly as her eyes were warm and without a hint of the accusation or disapproval Eve had expected. "Do you think that we are all so unfeeling that we do not suspect what you have been through? Oh, my dear, I above everyone understand the demons that drove you to do what you did. That is why I am here. Now," she smiled, leaning back in her chair as she smoothed a wrinkle from her gown, "I should like to tell you that story. Please bear with me and perhaps you'll understand the ramblings of an old lady. When I was young and full of the enthusiasm and faith of youth, not unlike yourself, it never occurred to me that anything would happen to change the path I had set for myself. In due course Richard's father entered my life and I fell hopelessly in love. He was strong and handsome, everything I had dreamed about, and we set upon our life together without an inkling of what was to come. Our marriage was announced. It was to be a magnificent wedding as befitted the marriage of the Earl of Striguil to the daughter of the Earl of Leicester."

"But you did marry him!" Eve blurted, then flushed at her interruption. In spite of herself she had been caught up in the mystery of the story and had leaned back and pulled her legs up under her.

"Not for a long time," Isabel corrected. "You see, I was to be presented to court before the wedding. I found it a tiresome nuisance as I only wished to be with Strongbow but my father reminded me that it was my duty and it could prove to be of aid to my future husband. So I went and it proved, instead, to be my undoing."

"Your undoing?" Eve parroted. "How?"

"How shall I say it?" Isabel sighed. "There is no delicate way. His Majesty took a fancy to me and pressed his suit."

"You mean Stephen?" Eve breathed, remembering Stephen's other abuses.

"Oh, nay!" Isabel laughed. "This was long before Stephen's time! 'Twas Henry, Stephen's uncle, who was then king. The third son of William the Conqueror. Ah, he was a magnificent man. And brilliant. If it had not been that I was so completely in love with Strongbow perhaps . . . But then, I was in love so it was nothing short of a tragedy."

"Could you not have refused?" Eve asked innocently.

"Refused the king? I could have, my dear, but it would have had dire results for my father and for Strongbow. So, when I realized that he was firm in his pursuit I submitted. I thought I would perish. In fact more than once I considered taking my life. I think that the only reason I did not was because of Strongbow's understanding—as much as he was hurt. He was a man caught between his loyalty to his king and his love for me. Only much later did I come to realize the pain he suffered, as for me he had only strength." She sighed with a deep ragged breath for the remembrance, even after the passing of so many years. "Sometimes, nay, most times, it is hard for a woman to be aware of how a man suffers when the pain is within. They seem to feel compelled to bear it silently while we are allowed to wail and moan when we are hurt. Well, much later, when Henry's eye turned to another, I was allowed to leave court and marry Strongbow. Never once, in all these years, has he ever shown me other than complete love and support. Never has he reminded me of that time. He showed me how to truly love someone and has been the source of my happiness."

Eve remembered Sophie's remarks about her laird and his

lady. "Aye, it is obvious that he loves you very much," she said softly.

"I have never doubted it. Eve, you are going through a difficult time. I told you my story in hope that in some way it might help you. Things do not always happen as we plan them but they can work out. Richard, too, is feeling pain..."

"I know," Eve sighed. "He does not desire the marriage. He has told me why it was arranged."

Isabel peered at Eve and her lips pursed as she studied the younger woman. "Eve, were you aware that Richard told Strongbow that he would not force you to the altar? Once the barons had met he would have released you from your vows. 'Tis Strongbow who will not allow it."

"He did that?" Eve asked with surprise. "Nay, he did not tell me!"

"I thought not. I will never understand why but men feel they have their reasons for not being explicit. Will they never learn that this is what leads to misunderstandings?"

"But, why should Strongbow insist on our marriage if Richard does not? Surely once the barons have met..." The look in Isabel's eye halted her question.

"Warwick informed him of Richard's abuse of you, Eve." Isabel's voice carried a tightness born by a mother who has felt disappointment in her son. "There are no words that I might speak that would undo what you have suffered at my son's hands but I agree with Strongbow that he owes you the protection of his name."

"But I have not asked for it!" Eve was mortified that Isabel should know of what had passed between her and Richard but she could not let Isabel think that the fault lay completely with him. "It is true that at first he—he forced me, but the affection he then gave me was not one-sided. I—I fell in love with him, milady, and if circumstances had not changed our feelings, perhaps..."

As Isabel listened, her face softened as if a great weight had been lifted from her shoulders. "If this is true, then perhaps my little story might help you even more than I thought. Eve, you are going to have to live with the unhappiness and pain in your life. You will face choices each day and make decisions upon them, and you will have to live with the results. Now you are confronted with a very important one. The trick is to recognize it as a challenge—and one you can handle. Your attitude will make the difference and I think you have the inner strength to face it. Moreover, your decision will affect many other lives, including my son's. I cannot pretend that is not important to me. Somehow, out of all of this, I want you both to be happy."

She rose from the chair and drew Eve into her arms, giving her a reassuring hug. "I shall say a prayer for you both that you are able to find a basis for that happiness, my dear. Both Strongbow and I find nothing but joy in that you are to be our daughter. If ever you should need us do not hesitate to come to us."

After Isabel had left, Eve paced the floor and her mind was in conflict over what Isabel had said. Was it possible to find a basis for happiness with Richard after everything that had happened? How could they? She found herself thinking about Urlacam's husband and comparing him to Richard. What a silly thing to do, she thought as she paused by the window and leaned against the stone casing. But she did nonetheless as she wondered if Urlacam had been able to find contentment with O'Brian. Did they fight, or was their life one of peace and contentment—or boredom? She fought a smile as she realized that life with Richard was not likely to prove boring! Ah, but it could, she reasoned heavily, if he were ever to place her aside. Isabel had meant to comfort her with the knowledge that Richard would have released her from her vows but it only confirmed his wish to be rid of her! And why not, she mused bitterly. He had lain with her, her body was no longer a mystery to him, something to anticipate, to desire! And now this marriage was being forced upon him as well as her!

She glanced at the door as she listened for the sound of his approaching footsteps. Soon he would come to fetch her. What would his attitude be? Would she be the object of another lecture on deportment and duties? He would probably expect her to argue with him and give in to her temper . . . Suddenly a small smile tugged at the corners of her mouth as an idea began to dance across her mind.

One thing he had taught her, and taught her well, was that respect was not taken for granted—it was earned. And, she knew with a clear resounding moment of truth, that it was respect, and only that, which would keep him to her. She could not accept a life without it. Nay, she determined grimly, it might be a loveless marriage, he might not even desire her, but he would not cast her aside!

With a satisfied glow, Eve dressed in the gown Bridget had

laid out for her, a pale green satin embroidered with delicate flowers of white and green leaves of a darker hue. The sleeves, which hung to the hem of the skirt, were lined in a deep green velvet matching the dust band that swept the floor. Knowing that she was to be presented to the barons and their ladies, she covered her shining tresses, which were brushed to their full length and almost reached to her waist, with a soft green wimple matching the gown. Eve smiled, knowing that Bridget would greatly approve, and she herself was not unhappy with the effect as the headpiece made her eyes large green pools, though the sparkle that shone from them came from her thoughts. She bit her lips to redden them and with a last pat to her gown, she waited . . .

Richard came for her as the first bell rang for mid-meal. She opened the door, her face set in a soft smile, and she inwardly laughed at the jerk of his head as he regarded her with surprise.

"I see that you are ready," he said, though his voice sounded doubtful.

"Of course, Richard, did you not bid me to receive you for mid-meal?" she said demurely.

"Aye, I did," he answered suspiciously as he regarded her with a curious frown.

She took his offered hand and kept her eyes modestly lowered while they walked down the hallway, though she could feel his eyes upon her.

"Did you sleep well?" he asked.

"Aye, milord."

A long, silent moment passed as he gave her a sideward glance. "You look lovely."

"Thank you, milord," she answered pleasantly. "It was my hope that you would be well pleased."

"Indeed," he grunted, as they paused at the head of the stairs. "I would be more well pleased if I knew what you were up to."

"What I am up to?" she repeated with innocence. "Milord, I only seek to comply with your wishes!"

His head drew back as a tawny brow arched but he said nothing, laid a hand lightly at her waist and escorted her down the stairs to the waiting guests.

She captivated them. She completely charmed every man in the hall and gained the begrudging respect of every lord's lady. Their initial surprise, as they had expected an untutored

lass of unrefined culture, was swept away by the brightness of
her smile, her graciousness, and a warm, ready wit. She was
presented to many of the greatest families in England and to
Chepstow's knights who had not accompanied Strongbow
and Isabel to Hertford. The latter quickly beamed their
approval, with obvious pride, that she was soon to become
Richard's lady. Eve's nervousness, though carefully hidden,
vanished as she caught an approving glance from Isabel, one
filled with affection and warmth, and soon she was thoroughly
enjoying herself as she was swept from Richard's side and
passed from one clustered gathering to another.

Richard's face had darkened into a doubtful scowl as he
watched her. He had made excuses to those in his company
and time and time again tried to cross the room to her side but
she was always a step ahead of him. He watched her guardedly,
from where he half-listened to those who would engage him
in conversation, nodding absentmindedly, as he pondered the
questions that had raged within him from the moment she had
opened the door to her chambers.

Feeling Richard's eyes follow her about the hall, Eve gloated
with satisfaction. She was determined not to allow for moments
alone, giving him no opportunity to chastise her, or chide her.
Surely, once she had shown him how gracious she could be,
and once she had gained the approval of his peers, he would
be pleased with her, and it would be a beginning.

When Strongbow and Isabel, who were obviously delighted
with the presence of their future daughter-in-law, took their
places on the dais, she allowed Richard to catch up with her.
As she felt him approach she turned and gave him a dazzling
smile.

"Richard, have you been avoiding me?"

Gray eyes glimmered with suspicion as he regarded her with
a slightly disapproving frown. "Whatever game you are playing, Eve, I will soon know your meaning, I promise you," he
muttered, as he took her by the arm and led her to their places
on the dais next to Strongbow and Isabel.

When they were seated, she turned to him with a flash of
ill-concealed anger. "Did you not wish for me to be compliant,
Richard?" she hissed under her breath. "Will you never be
satisfied with anything I do, or must you always find fault with
me?"

"Ah," he smiled. "That is more of what I would have expected! Let us just say that I find your sudden, overwhelming

compliance to be a bit out of nature."

Seething, she turned to her meal, refusing to show him how much he had unsettled her. She had let her composure slip, but not again! Nay, no matter how much he goaded her she would not make the same mistake! She smiled secretly, realizing suddenly that he was as unsettled as she. She could sense the tension in him. He obviously did not know what she was going to do next—and that was exactly where she would have him!

The rest of the afternoon passed without an untoward event. Eve continued to be the essence of graciousness and charm, bringing the attention of every man present, and the envy of every woman. The men hastened to assure Richard of the fact with much back-slapping and good-humored jocularity and, when out of the ladies' hearing, ribald remarks of how his future evenings were to be spent and whether or not he would be man enough to handle it.

Richard found himself growing increasingly irritated by their jibes, though well-meant, even when aimed by Warwick and Gervase. He grew moody, and began giving undo attention to the tankards of ale passed to him. He winced when he heard her light laughter carry to him across the room as she bantered with another of the lords or knights that would have her attention, too much attention by his reasoning. He thought of their wedding on the morrow and he sought to reason the conflict it stirred within him. It is a duty, he reasoned, nothing more. His eyes settled blackly upon the hand that a lord had settled upon her waist and his impulse was to set the man apart with a cracked skull, and he was about to do so when she stepped neatly aside, turning her attention to another.

He swore softly to himself and left his surprised companions to share the company of the lovely daughter of the Earl of Sussex. The flabbergasted maid reddened at his sudden attentions, but she quickly concealed her surprise and soon melted in his attentive company.

It was not long before Eve followed nervous glances in the direction of the pair and her chest tightened painfully as she glanced quickly away. Though exceedingly difficult, her manner did not change and soon the uneasiness about her dissipated and the cheerful banter returned. As she half listened to her gallant company, her mind wandered achingly to the other side of the room, and she could not help but to agonize that she had gone too far. What does he want of me? she thought,

nettled by his behavior. The throbbing pain moved through her
until she could not concentrate on what was being said. Unable
to suffer more humiliation, she gave her apologies and made
her way to the stairs to seek the comfort of her chambers, all
the while forcing herself not to cast an eye in Richard's direction.

As she reached the foot of the stairs she felt a touch at her
elbow and she turned to find Warwick at her side. The look
of understanding he gave her made her flinch and she flushed
uncomfortably.

"My lady, do not leave," the burly knight growled.

"There is no reason for me to remain," she answered tartly.

"Aye, but there is." His stormy gaze darted to Richard. "If
you leave now, you lose the battle and forfeit the war."

"What war?" she snapped.

"The one that rages between you and Richard," he answered
simply, his black eyes softening as they pleaded for understanding.

She stared at him for an endless moment but he returned
her look with patience, a smile playing at his mouth as his
beard twitched.

"Warwick," she said, finally understanding his meaning,
her voice carrying a renewed determination, "I think I should
like to beat you in a game of backgammon."

He chortled in answer as his dark eyes danced merrily, "Aye,
milady, you may try. But I warn you, it will not be easy."

"Nothing is," she returned.

The ceiling of the family chapel rose in high-beamed arches,
crisscrossed over heavy stone walls whose narrow slit windows
cast bright spears of light on selected points of the shadowy
room. Eve knelt beside Richard before the narrow altar, feeling
light-headed from the natural stuffiness of the sanctuary, which
was worsened by the heaviness of her rose brocade gown and
jewel-studded coif, and the press of the multitude that had
gathered as witness. She took deep breaths, attempting to dispel
her dizziness, and only vaguely heard the words of the plump
family chaplain, Father Benet, as he enumerated the many
admonishments regarding the keeping of the marriage vows.
She felt Richard's shoulder brush hers and she stiffened at the
touch as it sent a shock through her, his nearness intensifying
each nerve in a wave of sensation. He took her hand, encasing

it in his larger one. She stared at their hands detatchedly as his deep voice recited his pledge to her and to the god he served, while her mind wandered in limbo. She suddenly realized that he was gently squeezing her hand and she looked up at him in wonder. His look was strangely gentle but a tawny gold brow arched in question and she then realized that there was total silence in the chapel. They were waiting for her response. She was surprised at the voice she heard, that she could speak in a firm, clear voice, as she pledged herself to him and to God in kind. And then it was over. He stood, a strong hand at her arm to help her to rise, then he bent and brushed her lips with his own to seal the vows.

Upon arriving in the hall the lords and ladies converged upon the couple to offer their hearty congratulations and best wishes. Richard's manner seemed to lighten and he took their offerings with good-natured smiles, bantering with the men and accepting the kisses of the women, some of whom Eve suspected lingered a moment longer than was necessary. The young maid of Richard's previous night's attentions offered him a subdued brush on the cheek under the stern eye of her father, but Gwen took the opportunity to throw her arms about his neck and fully press herself against him as she held him in a long, lingering embrace. Eve eyed the display with disgust but was soon involved with her own most attentive well-wishers. The men began to pass her from one to the other, each protesting Richard's good fortune, while dismaying that it could not have been they.

Warwick kissed her almost shyly and when she gave the huge knight an affectionate hug she noted, with humor, that his ears reddened. She was passed to Gervase, Miles, and Raymond, who begrudgingly restrained themselves under Warwick's watchful eye, and suddenly she found herself passed back into Richard's arms.

She tensed as his arms went about her, to the encouraging hoots and cheers that resounded from the rafters of the hall, but in spite of the fact that she tried to pull away from him, he lifted her up to him and kissed her resoundingly, nearly bruising her lips in the fierceness of his embrace. There was a roar of approval and her head swam from the intensity of the kiss but when he released her, she gasped as his eyes looked down with a mocking gleam into hers. Her teeth gritted, and she tried to push away from him but he held her to his side as his hand moved freely and familiarly over her back and hips.

He kept her possessively near his side, as toasts were made, and laughter abounded, giving no opportunity for anyone to take her from his side. Finally, to her relief, he led her to the dais for their wedding supper. Handing her into her chair, his brow lifted with amusement at the stony glare she threw at him. Slipping into his chair he leaned over and covered her hand with his as he smiled, to all appearances the loving bridegroom.

"Are you not content, my sweet?"

"Should I be, my husband?" she gritted, as if the words were distasteful. "When, on the eve of our wedding, you should find favor with another?"

"Do not attempt to dictate to me, Eve." He was smiling but his voice held no question as to the seriousness of his meaning. "You are my wife and you will do what I will, which most certainly includes behaving yourself."

He turned away from her and her retort hung in her throat. Unsated, it was all she could do not to stand and scream at him. She clinched her teeth as her mind raced with all of the things she so dearly wanted to say to him! Behave herself! What was he accusing her of? She smirked bitterly at the irony. She had only sought to please him and he had sought the attention of another, yet she was to stand accused of some offense she could not define!

She picked at her food and kept her eyes carefully averted from his. Her ears burned at the sound of his deep laughter as he jested at the table and she was filled with a sinking sensation as she reflected upon the certain conclusions the end of the day would bring. She had willed herself not to think upon it before but, with the realization that her efforts had failed, the inevitability of what would happen came rushing in upon her. She could still feel the harshness of his brutal embrace and the cruel, mocking look he had given her burned in her mind. She could not help but compare it with another time—tender, exquisite moments in the inn at Hertford when he had awakened her to love. But, she knew now, with a shudder, that this would not be the manner of their wedding night. Did he despise her so? Even when he had first taken her, it had been in anger, but anger born of love. But now she sensed a cruelty in him— and there was nothing to be done for it. They were wed, before God and man. She could not hold herself from him, no rights, he had said. He could use her at his will, then leave her for more tender pursuits when it suited him, and she would have no recourse but to suffer his indignities in silence.

He touched her hand at that moment and she jumped in response, turning a startled look at him that was filled with unmasked fear.

"Eve, what is it?"

Recovering, she ignored the look of concern he wore and the gentle tone to his voice, knowing that it only masked his true intent: that his concern was only for the benefit of others.

"Nay, my lord," she said icily. "How could anything possibly be wrong?"

He frowned at the edge in her voice and his concern quickly changed to a cold regard. He raised her hand to his lips and frowned as her fingers trembled at his touch. "Are we not fortunate to have found one another, my love?" he murmured.

To the others in the room it appeared as a tender embrace between a loving couple but none could know of the fierce vibrations that passed between them.

She did her best to delay their departure from the festivities but in an unguarded moment she stifled a yawn and, to her dismay, it did not go unnoticed. He rose and held out a hand to her. She bit her lip, knowing there was no way to refuse and that all eyes in the room were upon her. Rising slowly, as her stomach tightened into a knot, she lay a trembling hand in his.

The men rose, lifting their tankards in toast to the couple. When they reached the foot of the dormant table, to her total shock—expressed in a cry rather akin to a squeak—Warwick took her from Richard and swept her into his arms, spinning her about. There was uproarious laughter as she was passed to Gervase, then to another and yet another, until she was finally placed into Richard's arms where he waited at the foot of the stairs.

There were cheers as he swung her into his arms and began to ascend the stairs, and playful ribbing and ribald comment that followed them to the top. Richard chuckled at her embarrassment and her cheeks flushed to a rosy pink as she squirmed in his arms and shot an angry glare at him.

"You may put me down now!" she snapped when they were out of sight of the others.

"Nay, my love," he grinned. "I find that you do not strain me unduly. You seem light as a feather, at least at the present.

Of course, I have not had the opportunity to observe the women in your family, so I have no inkling of what the future might bring."

As she wriggled and squealed at him, he lifted the latch easily and pushed the door open with his knee. He carried her in and put her down, turning to latch the door as a swift glance about the room told her that the room had been filled with his things. Seeing her dismayed look, he fought a smile and crossed to the hearth where he added another log to the fire.

"I chose this room for us as it is larger than mine and I thought you would be more comfortable here." Then he added simply, with a shrug, "It was my grandparents'."

How strange, she thought, to see his things mingled with her own. Her eyes came to rest on the massive bed, its coverlets turned down, and her stomach churned queasily. She felt him at her side and she tore her eyes away from the bed as he took her hand and pressed a goblet of warmed, spiced wine into it.

She sipped the ruby liquid, shutting her eyes against the burning path it made down her throat. Perhaps, if she drained it, and more, she would be able to see herself through what was to come. Concentrating on the fiery beverage, she missed the amused look he wore as she forced it down, and startled as he took her hand. To her relief, he merely led her to the chairs before the hearth, where they sat before the leaping flames, the silence between them lengthening as they sipped of the heady brew.

Since she had not eaten much, she rapidly felt her head begin to grow light and some of the tension melt away. When he reached over to refill her goblet, she looked up at him to find him watching her and her cheeks, already flushed from the wine, grew warmer. His long legs were stretched out casually before him, his goblet held on the arm of his chair while he rested his chin on the heel of his other hand. His look was not unkind but there was a certain transparent look to his eyes, now almost silver in the firelight, that made her wonder what he was thinking.

The thought occurred to her that if perhaps she did nothing more to anger him, he might be gentle with her after all. She set her goblet down on the table, nearly knocking it over in the process, and rose unsteadily. Even in her dizziness, she noted, with relief, that he remained where he was but followed her with his gaze across the room to her dressing table. She pulled off the heavy coif, sighing with relief as she dropped it on the table. Awkwardly, she pulled the combs from her hair and the dark-auburn mass tumbled about her shoulders to her waist. Kicking off her slippers, she tried to then reach around to the back fastenings of the heavy brocade gown but the full, hem-length sleeves made it difficult and her fingers, which trembled, made it impossible.

She groaned softly, then drew in her breath sharply with a shudder as she realized that he was undoing the fastenings. She swallowed hard as a rush of cold fear washed over her, her mind following each steady movement of his touch down the back of her gown.

He pulled the pelisse from her shoulders and it dropped to the floor, and even in her semi-drunken state she was aware that her body was only barely concealed in the sheerness of her chemise. She closed her eyes as he pulled her back against him and kissed her bare shoulder. She moaned softly as his lips traced a fiery path to the nape of her neck, his lips lingering tenderly, causing her body to respond in a pleasurable rush of tingling that spread to her toes, which wiggled involuntarily. In spite of her resolve to remain placid and unyielding a small whimper escaped her. Misreading the sound as a cry of fear, he tensed and dropped his hands as if they had been burnt. Puzzled, she turned around to find that he had returned to his chair. She blinked with confusion at the storm that had gathered in his face as he poured himself another measure of wine. She stood there, frozen to the spot, as he looked up at her and she blanched at the silvered ice of the gaze that moved over her slowly. She closed her eyes, wavering slightly under his careful inspection, wondering if this was part of his plan to punish her, to humiliate her, and how long she was expected to display herself, and what he would do next.

"Go to bed," he said calmly.

Her eyes flew open and she wondered if she had heard him correctly. "Wha—what?" she stammered.

"I said go to bed," he growled as he turned his attention to the wine.

She glanced at the bed, confused, then back to him.

"Eve," he said without looking up, "I have no intention of making love to you."

"But—but you are here," she said, barely above a whisper.

"Aye," he smirked, as he raised his goblet in a salute, his eyes cruel and mocking, "to all the world, and for Stephen's hearing, we are a happily married couple."

"But . . . where shall you sleep?" she choked.

He glanced up at her and laughed shortly. "In the bed, of course. My love, I have no intention of playing the gentleman and sleeping on a pallet on the floor. The bed is large enough for us both. Now go to bed and give me some peace."

She glanced at the bed hesitatingly, then back to him, but he had settled back in his chair and was studying the fire as if he had already forgotten her. Before he could change his mind she crossed quickly to the bed and slipped beneath the covers, pulling them tightly under her chin. Almost afraid to accept this stunning turn of events, she stared up at the canopy and her mind tossed for understanding of what was happening.

He sat there for a long time, waiting for her to sleep, his mood darkening with each passing moment. Though he tried to disavow his thoughts, he could still see the way she had looked, standing there in her chemise, the flickering light of the fire playing against her lovely body, turning it to a golden hue, each rounded curve of her breasts and hips, her long, beautifully turned legs accentuated by its light. He tried to turn the vision of her from his tortured mind but it would not leave him. Damn! Why did she have to look like a lamb being led to slaughter?

He smirked unhappily at the irony. They had shared the most fulfilling, the most sensual moments he had ever known with another, and he knew that it had been as good for her. And now, as his bride, she was afraid of him! If she had been angry with him, had fought him, he knew that he could arouse her to respond to their lovemaking, to bring her to remembered heights. Now, she lay a few feet from him yet she might as well be in another room with a tightly locked door against him!

The night was nearly spent when he finally left his chair. Removing his garments he slipped under the covers on the far side of the massive bed and lulled himself into sleep while listening to her soft, measured, breathing.

16

Eve awoke to an unfamiliar movement as Richard stirred in his sleep. Reminded that the bed was now shared by another she peered over at him cautiously, careful not to wake him, and she was filled with renewed wonder as she recalled the events of their wedding night and that he had left her untouched. When had he come to bed? His weight had not awoken her as it sunk into the mattress and now, as she lay on her side watching him in the greying light of dawn, she marveled at how peaceful he looked, almost childlike. If his eyes were to open now, what would they hold: anger, amusement, or, the thought tightened her throat, passion? Whatever his reasons were last night for rejecting her, would they be the same when he awoke to find her beneath the covers with him, her body only a short reach away?

Unwilling to test such a prospect, she slipped carefully from the bed, taking a cover to wrap herself in, and stirred the embers on the hearth to rekindle the fire. As she nursed the tender flames, huddling near its meager warmth, she tried to sort out her feelings about what this new turn in her life would bring. The answers eluded her as surely as Richard's reasons for his behavior, or the lack of it, but she felt as if the morning were the eye of a hurricane and the storm was not far behind.

As the fire caught, she rose to glance about the room. His hauberk and mail hung by his sword on a hook by the door, his war chest and wardrobe placed about the walls among her own. They confirmed the fact, by their silent presence, that

the cards were played and she would have to make the best of
it. Her nose wrinkled from the smell of stale wine and she
lifted the pitcher from the table, her brows knitting thoughtfully
to find it empty. She glanced back at the sleeping figure in the
bed, knowing now that he had stayed up until late in the night.
What had been his thoughts as he sat by the fire with her
sleeping only a few feet away? The empty pitcher attested to
the fact that they had not been peaceful. What manner of man
had she married? She sighed and wondered what she should
do next. The morning was growing light and, as her mind
turned to old habits, she thought of how wonderful it would
be to take a morning's ride, alone, in the open country as the
world awoke, at a time when the world seemed new and un-
cluttered.

She entered the stable as a cock crowed from somewhere
in the loft. The horses stirred at her entrance, snorting and
blowing through their nostrils in greeting. The war horses were
separated from the palfreys by a sturdy wall and she spied
Taran as he turned a curious head and watched her cross to
where her mare was tied.

She stroked the mare's soft nose in greeting, then grabbed
a handful of hay from a pile and threw it into the manger to
occupy the animal while she saddled her. Retrieving her saddle
and blanket she set to work quickly. As Eve began to step
away to fetch the bridle, she found to her great dismay that
the animal had stepped on the hem of her skirt, imprisoning it
beneath its hoof.

Eve muttered an oath under her breath, reached down and
tried to lift the mare's hoof, but the mare reacted by stepping
toward her, securing the skirt even more firmly. Eve leaned
and pushed against the animal's flank with all of her strength,
only causing the mare to swing its head to her, its huge soft
eyes unconcerned as it munched on the hay.

"You worthless nag!" Eve hissed as she reached down in
desperation and grabbed the skirt in both hands and pulled with
all of her might, ignoring the possibility of irreparable damage
to the rust wool. As she tugged, mumbling oaths about the
doubtful future of the mare, her feet suddenly slipped on the
straw-covered floor. She was helpless to stop herself as she
landed with a sharp thud on her bottom.

"Oooff!" Her hands flew to the offended part, rubbing it
gingerly as she heard a deep chuckle from behind her. Twisting,
she saw Richard outlined in the brightly lit doorway, leaning

casually against its frame. She reddened, wondering how long he had been standing there witnessing her plight.

"Ah, my love. Is this an example of fine Irish horsemanship?" he mocked lightly. "Such control, such deftness."

She squealed with fury and threw a nasty retort that only caused him to chuckle the more heartedly.

"Ah, what is this? You wish my help? With such a pretty request I cannot refuse!" With a huge grin he strolled over to the mare and ran his hand down the offending leg, effortlessly lifting the hoof from Eve's skirt. He offered his hand to her, which she pointedly refused, struggling ungracefully, but unaided, to her feet. He leaned back against the post of the stall, hooked his thumbs in his belt and watched with amusement as she brushed the straw from her pelisse. Catching the unconcealed humor in his eyes, she returned a scathing look of bright anger, unaware of the picture she made with straw clinging to her hair and smudges on her face.

"I thought you were sleeping!" she spat angrily.

"Thank you, Richard," he grinned, bowing to an imaginary figure. "If you had not happened by, kind sir, perchance I would have been trapped beneath the beast forever! Ah, but do not thank me," he added with a wave of his hand, his grey eyes dancing. "'Tis not necessary."

"I have no intention of thanking you!" she hissed. "You are supposed to be in bed!"

"As are you," he parried. "Imagine my dismay to awaken, expecting the warmth of my bride, only to find that she had flown the love nest. If I did not know better I would think that you did not wish to share my attentions."

"Did you think that I was running away from you again?" she threw at him, not unpleased that he might have felt some concern.

"It crossed my mind," he answered casually. "It would be rather tiresome to have to take chase again. May I ask where you were going? It is not an unreasonable question for a husband to ask of his wife."

"I assure you that I was not running away again," she answered dryly, piqued by his humor and the casual way he referred to their marriage. "I only wished to take a ride. I thought it would give me the chance to think, to sort out my thoughts."

"Eve, this is not Hertford." His manner became stern and his eyes darkened with a frown as he determined to make his meaning clear. "Chepstow's lands border on cruel mountains, yet untamed. It is winter and the game is lean, packs of wolves have come down seeking food. You, and that mare," he gestured his head toward the animal, "would be no match for them. You are never to leave Chepstow without an escort, is that clear?"

She swallowed hard, remembering the huge Irish wolves and their snarling mouths when they were brought down by her father and her brothers, and she nodded weakly.

"Good." He smiled at her and his manner became gentle once more. "If you wish to ride I will take you myself." Disarmed by his sudden tenderness she was surprised when he reached out and took her arm, pulling her gently toward him. Every fiber of her body tensed and she began to tremble as she realized that he was going to kiss her. Instead, he reached into his tunic and extracted a kerchief which he dabbed gently at the smudges of her face. "It would not do for you to return to the hall looking as if you had rolled in the dirt." He frowned at the blush that crept over her cheeks and the look turned to a question as he regarded her carefully. She lowered her gaze in an attempt to hide her thoughts from him, certain that those penetrating grey eyes could see to the cause of her embarrassment, but he put a finger under her chin and lifted her face to his. Had he seen her lips part ever so slightly, and invitingly, and something in her eyes that was not akin to fear? Perhaps, another moment given, the answer would have been found and the basis for a new understanding begun.

"There you are!" came a growl from the doorway. They turned with surprise to find Warwick striding into the stable, his manner urgent. He nodded a greeting to Eve. "I have been looking for you, Richard. The nobles have gathered in Strongbow's chambers since he felt it would be best to meet now before the castle has arisen."

"Of course," Richard replied and Eve could see the change in his face as he stepped to Warwick's side. He threw back over his shoulder, almost off-handedly, "Return to your chamber, Eve. The outing will have to wait until another time."

She bit her lip against the surge of disappointment she felt from Richard's attitude and the fact he could dismiss her so quickly—even though she knew the importance of the meeting. So close, she knew that a tenuous, vital moment had been missed and it felt like a small death. She half listened to their conversation and her feet seemed frozen to the ground as if something nebulous would not allow her to obey. Before she realized what she was saying, she heard a voice cry out.

"Nay!" It was only when they stopped talking and turned two wide and startled pairs of eyes toward her that she realized it had been her voice. "I—I mean, nay," she said more softly. "I will not be sent to my chambers like a wayward child to work a needle or pace the floor until you return."

"Eve," Richard growled as his astonishment turned to a warning frown.

"Richard, I am now the wife of an English knight and, moreover, the future mistress of Chepstow, am I not?" She drew herself up and faced his stormy gaze squarely.

"Aye," he conceded guardedly, wondering where this would lead.

"The nobles have been gathered, aye, even our marriage occurred because of something I did." She continued, her courage increasing with her words. "But the fault is also largely due to you, Richard, and even to you, Warwick. While I admit it was done from anger and spite, I had no inkling of the importance of it, nor the damage it would cause. Will you forever treat me as a child, sheltering me from your life, indeed, as you normally treat your women? If this is your life and what you are committed to, I will be part of it. I want to go with you to the barons, for at least then I will understand what you are about and will not commit another folly because of my ignorance."

Warwick cleared his throat and stared at the floor as Richard's expression passed through a gamut of emotions, first surprise, then disapproval, anger and at last, doubt. Had she confronted him before any but Warwick, the outcome might have been different. He conceded that an element of truth lay in her words, however spoken, and that it might prove useful for her to understand what was happening.

"You may come if you wish, but I expect you to behave yourself. You will say nothing, nothing at all, do you understand?"

"Aye, Richard!" she cried happily. "They will not even know that I am in the room!"

"I doubt that." He grunted. Warwick merely smiled and scratched his beard.

They walked back to the hall with Eve, a light, happy bounce to her step as they exchanged bemused glances over her head. Richard was grateful that Warwick had withheld comment and he even began to suspect that his friend approved. Good Lord, she is even bound to now involve herself in politics, he thought. The hall was empty except for a servant carrying a tray to one of the guests and Richard stopped him, taking some biscuits from the tray and handing one to Eve for the breakfast they had missed. She accepted the offering gratefully, looked up at him with a bright smile and took an eager bite. His brows knitted at the warmth in her eyes and he shook his head, silently wondering, for the countless time, about her quickly changeable moods.

As they entered the room, all eyes turned toward them. Strongbow started to greet them but the words lumped in his throat when he spied Eve. He glanced at Richard but his son just shook his head and shrugged as he escorted her to the far side of the room and handed her into a chair. Amused looks were exchanged by the nobles as they obviously accounted her presence to a besotted bridegroom who could not bear to be parted from his bride and Richard did not miss their meaning as he squirmed uncomfortably.

"Well now," Strongbow cleared his throat as he glanced at his daughter-in-law, "now that we are all here I would tell you that there is another purpose for this gathering other than the marriage of my son to the Lady Eve." He nodded to her, then tore his eyes away to the others. "You are all aware that Stephen has named Eustance as heir to his throne. What you may not know is that Stephen plans to abdicate in favor of Eustance in a very short time." There were angry murmurs among the knights and nobles, which Strongbow silenced with a wave of his hand. He proceeded to tell them of the happenings of the past few weeks and, much to Eve's relief, omitted her part in the story. She glanced up at Richard, who stood at her side, warming as he placed a hand on her shoulder reassuringly, though his eyes remained fixed upon Strongbow.

As Strongbow finished his recounting there were bursts of questions from the men, the first from Lady Isabel's brother, the aging Earl of Leicester. "What of the church? If the Holy Father supports Eustance how can we justify withholding our oath?"

"I believe that Richard has come upon the answer for that." Strongbow glanced at his son.

"The archbishop is at odds with seeing Eustance on the throne," Richard answered. "He has suffered Stephen only in that he hoped, being Stephen's uncle, he would have some influence for good. Also, he recognized that Matilda was not the answer to England's problems. Therefore, he has pledged himself to Henry Plantagenet and has sent a clerk in his office to intercede with Pope Adrian for our cause. Upon arriving at Chepstow word reached me that he has been successful. The pope will support Henry when the issue is pressed."

There were murmurs of approval from the barons with a few exceptions as with the Earl of Leicester. "I have heard nothing of this. Who is this clerk, Richard? Can he be trusted?"

"His name is Thomas Becket and his reputation is impeccable. Theobald trusts him and I have certainly no reason to doubt it."

"There, you have it," Strongbow said grimly. "Now, what is your position? Do you withhold your oath of fealty from Eustance and do you support Henry?"

There was unanimous agreement among the gathering and the room became solemn as they realized the moment was a turning point for England. All thoughts turned to the young man waiting across the channel and they wondered, with good cause, the manner of the man, and the future he would bring with him. The die was cast, tankards were filled, and the bargain sealed. Each raised his cup in salute for the promise of a better time and an end to the more than twenty years that England had seen war. It was entirely possible that with their support, and that of the church, Stephen would surrender his throne to Henry without conflict. At least that was the hope that began to be nurtured within each man's heart.

Throughout the morning Eve sat on the edge of her seat, engrossed in the discussion, a part of her firing to the heat of the conversation as her mind quickly grasped the interworkings of the plans. A few times she wanted to make comment but she wisely held her tongue and at those moments she would feel Richard's eyes upon her and she would look up to find him watching her, his silvered grey eyes warning of silence. Was it so apparent to him, the urge she felt to involve her opinions? How could he read her so well, her feelings, her emotions, yet understand nothing!

After the bell for mid-meal was rung, Strongbow ordered food to be brought to his chamber. As the men relaxed and their conversations turned to other matters, Richard knelt beside her chair and took her hand.

"This will go on for some time, Eve. Perhaps it would be best now if you retired. I fear that everyone is not completely comfortable with having you here."

It was on the tip of her tongue to ask if that included him but she bit it back, knowing that was unfair. She had made ground and she sensed that it was unwise to press further. Rising, she smiled graciously at the men nearby, who nodded to her, and allowed Richard to escort her to the door. As they paused at the doorway it was on her mind to ask him if he would be long but she knew that it was the wrong moment to appear possessive. Instead, she smiled at him and swept through the door, leaving him to wonder at her thoughts.

She spent the remainder of the afternoon attempting to work on a tapestry she had begun with Lavinia at Hertford, a scene of the knights and squires as they practiced upon the jousting field, but much of the time the work lay idle in her lap as she listened for the sound of his returning footsteps or pondered what she had heard in the meeting. She had so many questions she wished to ask him, so much she still did not understand. His eyes had reflected an undeniable excitement as they had laid their plans and, while she was proud of the reverence the men gave him and the respect he had gained, even from the older barons, when Strongbow recounted the part Richard had played over the past few years, she could not help the sudden rush of fear over the possibility that he would be going to war—indeed, wanted to.

The door opened and Eve nearly leapt from her chair but she sunk back down into it, disappointed that it was only Bridget come to see to her needs. She took a light supper in their chambers, as he had not returned by evening, and she was in no mood for the light banter of the women in the main hall. Besides, she could not speak of what was occurring in Strongbow's chambers and she would not leave herself open for the certain speculative titters from Gwen or the others about why her husband would choose to leave her unattended a mere few hours after their marriage.

Finally, undressing by the warmth of the fire, she retired and lay ruminating about the day. For a brief, flashing moment in the stable she had thought . . . He had been tender with her, considerate. There was no doubt that his brief anger had been for her safety, and well deserved. But, what had been his thoughts when he awoke to find her gone? Would he have really cared if she had disappeared again or would it only have been a wound to his pride. His pride. How much did it have to do with his treatment of her, his threats, or was there truly no love in him for her anymore, or had there been, ever? And why had he been so tender . . . Her scattered thoughts wove in and out as she yawned sleepily and soon they made no sense at all and she gave in to her exhaustion.

The coals of the spent fire spread a dim glow over the darkened chamber when she awoke with a start to find Richard curled up against her back. His long legs were tucked under her hips and an arm was thrown casually over her as his face nuzzled into her hair. A gasp caught in her throat as she tried to turn onto her stomach but she found that her hair was caught beneath him and she was imprisoned beneath his arm. As she struggled, he moaned and rolled away from her. She rose up on an elbow and peered at him, the measured sound of his breathing filling the chamber as she realized, with a start, that he was asleep! She moved carefully from him and lay on the other side of her bed. Her heart pounded so hard she could almost hear it and her skin still tingled from where he had touched her. She ached from a strange, gnawing frustration that would not leave her. He was no longer interested in her as a woman, he had made that perfectly clear. Had he taken her into his arms because he dreamed of another? The name came to her involuntarily and she grit her teeth with fury. Claresta! She moved to the edge of the bed and lay with her back to him, her mouth set tightly as she stared into the darkened room. Respect be damned, she thought. She would have more of him than that! Aye, somehow she would have it all!

She did not remember falling asleep but as the room lightened she awoke to the sound of someone moving about the chamber. She rolled onto her back and rose on her elbows to find Richard standing at the end of the bed, fastening his girdle about his waist. He was dressed for riding, in wool chanuses and a dark leather tunic over a brown wool chainse, and he looked up at the sound of her stirring.

"'Tis not yet dawn," he murmured. "Go back to sleep."

"Where are you going?" she blurted, forgetting her anger of a few hours past.

"Hunting," he answered casually as he crossed to the pegs by the door from which he removed his cloak and sword. "We should return by mid-afternoon."

"Hunting?" she repeated dully. "But I wanted to talk with you!"

"I'll return early, in time for us to take an early supper, here if you wish. We can talk then. In the meantime, find something with which to occupy yourself. Perhaps you could visit with Lavinia. You've hardly had a moment to see her since you left Hertford."

She fell back on the pillows, feeling the same gnawing disappointment she had felt the day before, but she said nothing. If he preferred the company of his cohorts to hers, she would not be the one to argue it! Then she recalled the moment that had passed during the night and her eyes flashed to him, wondering if he too remembered, but his manner gave no evidence of it.

"Fine!" she snapped, her curt reply bringing a curious glance from him. "It makes no difference to me, stay as long as you like!"

As he closed the door behind him, her anger was replaced by a pressing emptiness. She pulled the covers tightly about her and turned over, piqued by her own disquiet.

She rose much later than usual and after a bath she searched for Lavinia and found her in the great hall. Fortunately, the other women were not about and though Lavinia was delighted to see her friend she sensed that Eve was on edge. They walked in Chepstow's gardens and because the day was cold and clear, they were bundled in their cloaks against the chill. Lavinia attempted to engage Eve in small talk, deliberately avoiding the subject she knew was on both of their minds, though it was exceedingly difficult for her not to broach the matter. Finally, it was Eve who spoke of it.

"He went hunting."

Lavinia said nothing as they continued walking, preferring to let it come out in its own way.

"Oh, Lavinia," she sighed. "Will it ever change? Does he hate me so much that he now cannot even bear to be with me?"

"He does not hate you. I do not believe it! You know that there are matters he must see to—things that must be done while the barons are here. The fact that it coincides with your marriage . . ." She stopped and flushed at the unfinished comment and Eve smiled grimly.

"It is all right, Lavinia. But can you not see? The fact that you remember proves out what I know his feelings to be. I'll never be allowed to forget what I did, even if I have been forgiven." She laughed softly but there was no humor in her tone. "Do you know what his vows were to me, besides those given at the altar? That I would obey him in all things, that I would have no rights of my own . . ."

"But that is no different than any wife would expect!" Lavinia protested. "How can you . . ."

"But I am me!" she cried. "I do expect more! Lavinia, you are used to your ways but I am not, nor do I think I ever could be! Besides," she added bitterly, "perhaps you are right in that he does not hate me but one thing is certain, he does not want me—as a wife or a woman."

She soon left Lavinia, their conversation becoming awkwardly muted after her shocking revelation, and returned to the isolation of her chambers, finding its solitude strange comfort. Richard did not return by early evening, as promised, and she ordered a light supper brought to the chamber. But she only picked at the food and soon abandoned it to the table near the fire. Looking about for something to do she noticed that Richard's chainse lay on the wardrobe at the foot of the bed and that it held a slight rent in the sleeve. She took a needle and thread from her basket and set to work mending it by the warm fire.

Night prevailed with the winter's mist smoothly drifting over the chilled landscape as if tucking it away against another day. Far away a lone wolf cried mournfully in protest over his solitude as Richard opened the door to their chamber. Closing the door quietly behind him, his tired gaze fell upon Eve where she slept in her chair by the fire.

He moved silently to her side, grey eyes widening with wonder when he spied his chainse folded across her lap, the rent he had made in its sleeve now neatly mended with small, careful stitches. He lifted it from her lap, fingering it thoughtfully between his fingers, then set it aside, his gaze returning to the sleeping figure. Her lovely features, so peaceful in sleep, touched a spot deep within him. His day had been absorbed in the matters of men but he had found his mind turning at inopportune moments to the remembrance of flashing green eyes or to the fear that had shone from them on their wedding night. He had found himself to be short of temper with his companions, enlisting curious looks from them as he snapped unduly at some minor offense. While he had wondered how she fared, his arrow had missed its mark on two occasions, bringing doubtful looks from Strongbow. Richard smiled. Never once had he pictured her sitting before the fire mending his chainse!

"Ahhh, my lady," he whispered, "whatever are we going to do about us?"

Eve stirred uncomfortably, her stiff muscles aching, as she

awoke to find Richard sitting across from her. He had stripped down to his chanuses and chainse and was sipping from a tankard and watching her.

"Richard," she observed sleepily, covering a yawn with the back of her hand.

"You should be in bed."

She let the comment pass and watched him as he turned to stare into the fire. No explanation of why he had returned so late, she thought, or inquiries of what her day had been like. "Was the game plentiful, my lord?" she asked, a definite edge to her voice.

"It was given up early and the time given to discussion of other matters." His voice was weary but she did not choose to notice.

"Tell me, milord, do the others not find it strange that you keep yourself from your bride?"

He fixed a narrowed gaze upon her, wondering where this would lead. "This is a difficult time, Eve."

"Ahh, aye," she replied with forced pleasantry, "the future of England rests upon what you do here. A future that was almost lost because one Irish maid—ah—correction, I would have forgotten that I am no longer a maid. 'Twas so handily done that it was almost overlooked. It is easy to understand why your interest is elsewhere, Richard. The conquest done, your mind would look to more interesting matters."

She rose from the chair and stood before the fire, hearing, with inner satisfaction, the intake of his breath. At least he is now not ignoring me, she thought ruefully. "I think that I shall go to bed." She said it almost to herself as she began to undo the laces on her gown while only vaguely aware of what she was doing. She had not plotted it and felt mildly shocked at her actions but something urged her forward, an instinct older than time guiding her, a deep sense of survival overriding her reason. She knew only that she wanted to cause some emotion in him other than indifference—even his anger would be better.

She slipped the gown from her shoulders and let it fall to the floor, stepping out of it without looking at him. She closed her eyes, biting her lip as she felt, through the thin chemise, the heat from the fire against her skin.

"Eve," he said hoarsely, "go to bed."

She tried to force herself to walk to the bed but she was fixed to the spot, immovable on legs that would not obey her. Suddenly, she heard him utter an almost animalistic growl of

rage and she found herself swept into his arms and crossing to
the bed in a few strides. He tossed her onto the furs and stood
looking over her, his eyes dark with a terrifying anger.

"By all that is holy, Eve, what are you trying to do to me!"
he said with tight control. "You tremble at my touch, aye, even
a look cast innocently in your direction, treating me as if I
were a monster! Then you parade before me, clothed only in
your chemise to arouse my manhood, pressing me to exercise
my rights though I know you think the prospect the worst you
could imagine! I have not demanded those rights but you press
it! You played a game once that drove me to force myself upon
you. Do you again seek that fate?"

As he turned away, something inside of her snapped. She
threw herself from the bed at him but he saw the movement
from the corner of his eye and caught her just before her flailing
arms could reach his back. He took her about the waist, and
with her legs kicking wildly, he threw her back on the bed like
a sack of discarded grain. Her chemise had caught on his belt
and as she fell there was a loud, rending sound. They froze,
both pairs of eyes fixed dumbly on her ruined chemise, open
from neck to waist. Richard's attention was not on the ruined
garment, however, as he turned with a moan and sought only
the comfort of his chair. But Eve's mind was of another matter.
He had torn her chemise! As she stared, transfixed, a feeling
of outrage began to swell within her, unmitigated anger over
having her clothes ripped from her. Even a harlot got better
treatment! She was fed up with men using her, abusing her at
their will! Oblivious to the consequences, she lunged again at
his departing back. This time he was unprepared as he felt her
hands upon his chainse and before he could react he heard the
tear and spun about. But she lunged at him again, this time
catching the front of his shirt, tearing it to the waist.

She backed away, her eyes filled with the horror of what
she had done, and as a hand flew to her mouth, she gaped at
his shocked expression. He looked down at his ruined chainse
dully, then back where she stood by the bed, her eyes large
round expressions of horror. Then, suddenly, he laughed. He
threw back his head and laughed. She started to giggle, as
much from relief as from the sound of his humor. He did look
ridiculous standing there with his shirt in tatters!

"Well," she gloated, "how do you like it?"

"I don't," he chuckled. He pulled the garment over his head
and tossed it carelessly across the room. He looked back at her

with a smile but then something else entered his expression as he regarded her thoughtfully.

"Eve, are you afraid of me?"

Her head jerked at the abrupt question. Swallowing, she forced herself to meet his eyes. "Is that not what you wanted?"

"Your fear? Nay!"

"What then, Richard? Submission?"

"Of course, as my wife."

"And to be your wife I must be meek, obeying in all things?"

"Is it meekness to expect you to stay with me?"

"I only ran away from you because I could not bear a marriage with someone who hated me!"

"Oh God, I've never hated you!"

"Not even when I kept Orlan's message from you?"

"Nay, Eve, not even then. I was angry, of course, but that has been long forgotten."

"Have you truly?"

"I have said so! And I have answered your questions, but you still have not answered mine. Are you afraid of me?"

"I—I am afraid of you, Richard. Of your indifference."

"Indifference?" It was his turn for his head to jerk back. "You think that I feel indifference for you?"

"It is understandable. You have known me, what mystery is there still for you?" She let her gaze fall to the floor, unwilling to see the answer in his face and she missed the look of incredibility which flickered over his expression and changed to amused tenderness.

"Eve." He cleared his throat. Oh Lord, was she truly so innocent? The realization brought a warm rush of tenderness but also a dull kind of fear. "Desire does not end—that is, it only heightens with knowing... Have you not known desire since that day at Hertford?" He tensed as he waited for her answer, as a fearful awareness struck him. Had he destroyed all feelings of desire in her, what had he done?

She recalled the gnawing frustration she had felt when he touched her, the stirring knot that... She looked up at him cautiously and her cheeks flushed at the remembering. No desire? She knew now, with him standing only a few feet away, his face filled with a strange look of urgency, that it had been a driving force that had fed her anger toward him. Could it be possible that he too... She was almost afraid to give her answer and when she did it was barely perceptible, a slight nod with closed eyes, but it was all that he needed. He crossed to her and took her face tenderly in his hands, lifting her lips to his. Her mouth parted under his and though they trembled they were warm and giving, molding to his in a perfect understanding. He raised his head and looked down into her eyes, which were moist with tears, then brushed his lips lightly at each corner.

"I have wanted you since that first moment when I carried you away from the camp," he murmured hoarsely, "and I never stopped, never. But nothing compares with the feeling I have for you now—I love you, Eve, as I have never loved anyone else."

He heard her utter a soft cry but then her arms were about his neck and she was covering his face with kisses, laughing and crying interchangeably as she clung to him. He laughed happily, his own heart soaring with hers as he lifted her into his arms and spun her about, then carried her to the bed, laying her down gently into its softness. His garments were gone quickly and as he lay at her side, he hesitated, and looked down at her with a moment of doubt. "Are you sure?" he whispered, almost afraid to ask the question.

She laughed softly, her eyes filled with happiness and love as her arms slid up around his neck and pulled him down to her. "I am sure."

He made love to her, suspending them both in an exquisite, private time. There was no urgency, no feeling of theft, but a time belonging only to them. He gave his love slowly, deliberately, exploring each part of her and her pleasures, allowing her to discover her feelings, her emotions, laying one upon another as a new triumph. His hands moved over her satin body as he delighted in the feel of her as if discovering it for the first time, taking delight in the pleasure he gave her. She moved with him, whispering her love, and marveled at the intensity of her feelings. She let him lead her, then pushed his hands aside to investigate the wonder of him and his maleness, which she knew now belonged only to her. He moaned and stirred under her searching hands and she marveled at her ability to arouse him and wondered what other secrets she might learn. He rolled her onto her back, his hand moving down between her thighs and her back arched up against him and she moaned with pleasure at the shock it brought, as a deep surging tension grew from her depths to wash over her. Pulling her under him, he took her gently at first until she began to move with him, then built into a passion that engulfed them both into a final bursting intensity that left them both drained as they clung together breathlessly in its shattered aftermath.

He held her to him and kissed her face and hair with a gentle tenderness while she lay nestled in his arms. She sighed contentedly and he smiled at the peacefulness of the sound, pushed her tousled hair from her face and kissed her again in a soft, lingering embrace. He amazed at the warm protectiveness he felt as he held her in his arms and the pleasure he felt as he realized that when he awoke she would still be there. Always before, with other women he had known, he was content to leave, his mind would turn almost immediately to other matters. But, now, he wanted nothing more than to have the moment last. As she stirred in his arms and stretched contentedly, he moved apart and leaned his head on his hand. He looked down at her, smiling as he read the pleasure in her beautiful eyes, which almost glowed in the dim light of the fire that played across their bed.

"Oh, Richard, do you truly love me?" she whispered.

"Have I not shown you?" he smiled. "Is there something I've forgotten?"

"I cannot imagine what." She giggled, as her finger traced a loving path down his cheek.

"There are other ways," he grinned. "Eventually I expect to show them all to you. Are you curious?" He could see her blush in the firelight and he chuckled, leaning down to plant another kiss.

She awoke to his nearness and the warmth of his body even before the dawn's light had filled the room, its first promising rays turning the chamber to a soft grey. She smiled at precious memories as a delicious feeling filled her body with a contentment and peace she had not thought possible. She stared at the shuttered window, at the streaks of light that invaded its cracks, and wondered what new happiness the day would bring. To be with him in their newly discovered love was all that she asked for. How could one person bring such complete bliss to another? She wanted to turn over, to look at him, but she was afraid to disturb the moment. If he awoke he might leave her and she could not bear it. She sighed softly and closed her eyes as if to suspend the moment, but her eyes flew open again with shock. His arms had gone about her waist and he pulled her against him where his face buried in the nape of her neck. She giggled and squirmed against him, then gasped as his hand moved down to search for tender game, his fingers boldly

finding what they sought. She flushed and tried to pull away
but he pushed her shoulders back against the bedding and rose
on his elbow to smile down at her.

"Good morning," he grinned, then bent to kiss her resoundingly, fairly taking her breath away before she could make a
response. She felt his hands push away the covers and the chill
of the morning air as it hit her skin and she gasped. She tried
to recover the disappearing blankets but he caught her hands,
pinning them at her side.

"Richard, it is freezing!"

"It will not be soon," he countered as his eyes gleamed
wickedly. They moved over her hungrily in the open light of
morning, feasting on her body as it lay open to his appraisal.

"Richard, please!" she gasped as she reddened with embarrassment.

"Hush." His lips moved across her shoulder to her breast,
where his tongue teased its darkened tip, and his hands caressed
the soft length of her body until she soon no longer felt the
cold, or her discomfort. Her body warmed to his attentions
until she was consumed with a need that matched his own.

Sated, she lay in his arms with the covers once again drawn
tightly about them. They slept until the sun boldly entered the
room, the dust motes dancing across its rays in a path to the
bed, waking them to the late hour. He rolled onto his back to
stretch and without warning he flung himself from the bed.
Pulling on his chanuses, he washed quickly from the icy wash-
bowl and her heart sank as he donned a chanise and leather
tunic, then fastened on his sword without casting a glance in
her direction—as if eager to be about without another thought
for her.

"Will you be gone long?" she ventured, dreading the answer.
She did not know how she could bear to spend the entire day
without him and she fought the tears that threatened to come.

"I shall return when the mood strikes me," he shrugged.

His answer stabbed at her and she turned her head away so
that he would not see her tears.

Finished with his dressing he stopped at the end of the bed
and looked at her with an amused grin. "Well, milday, are you
going to lie abed all day or are you going to come with me?"

It took a moment for the words to register. When they did,
her face filled with flushed happiness and she flew from the
bed into his waiting arms and she laughed with delight. "Then
you are not going to leave me!"

He grinned down at her ecstatic face as he marveled afresh at her beauty. "You do not know me well, Eve, if you think that I would wish to be apart from you today. I thought that it was time for that ride I promised you. Besides, it is time for the people of Striguil to see their new mistress."

They rode out across the green rolling hills of Striguil's lands, finding joy in each other's company as the horses seemed to sense their mood and stretched out their long limbs, happy to be away from the confines of the stable. He took her through the many small hamlets and villages that crossed the countryside, pointing out, as they rode, the rich farms, soon to be planted to add to Chepstow's immense wealth. They paused along the way to chat with the farmers and villagers and Eve noted the warmth and mutual respect that passed between lord and villein as he inquired of their families, mentioning each wife and child by name. He introduced Eve to them in turn and was obviously pleased both by her easy gracious manner to them and the open approval they showed for their new mistress.

The sun was positioned high overhead when they rode into a familiar village and Eve looked at Richard with question as she spied Maple Leaf Inn where it lay directly ahead.

"I thought you might want to visit an old friend." He smiled, and his eyes began to dance at the look of horror on her face. "Sophie, that is. I imagine she has wondered what became of you."

"Oh, Richard! What will they think when they know who I am?" Her eyes filled with doubt, and not a little embarrassment.

"I doubt that it will be mentioned." He grinned. "'Tis my guess that it will be carefully forgotten, except by Sophie, of course. That one will expect a full story and it might as well be done with."

He tied their mounts to the standingpost and, as he helped her to dismount, he gave her a reassuring kiss, then took her hand as they walked around to the kitchen door. The top half of the door was open and the succulent aromas that drifted into the kitchenyard reminded them both that they were famished. Richard rolled his eyes in pleasure and anticipation, causing Eve to giggle happily. They stepped into the kitchen to find Sophie standing at the hearth, stirring a pot as she hummed happily in rhythm. She turned and gasped, dropping her spoon at the sight of them.

"Eve, lass!" Wiping her hands quickly on her apron, she crossed the room and took Eve into her ample arms in a fierce hug, laughing at the pleasure of seeing her again. She stood back and held Eve at arm's length, her eyes widening at the sight of her finery, the rich burgundy wool of her riding clothes, the fine starched linen of her wimple, and the stunning garnet cluster at the neck of her bodice.

"Well, lassie, I see ye've been farin' well!" Her shrewd eyes took in the glow of happiness that shone from Eve's face, then she glanced over Eve's shoulder to Richard who wore an amused grin, and her eyes narrowed. "And this one," she motioned with a nod of her head. "'As he been treating ye well? If he hasn't, tell me, as to me he's still the tyke that used to hang about me, begging for a treat from my cupboard, and he's not so big that I can't handle 'im!"

Eve smiled up at Richard and nodded happily, "Aye, Sophie, he's been treating me well." Richard put his hand familiarly on Eve's waist, which Sophie noted with an arch of her brows, and he smiled affectionately at the buxom woman.

"The lady is my wife, Sophie." He grinned.

Sophie's mouth dropped open in astonishment and her eyes flew to Eve, who nodded with happy affirmation.

"Sweet Jesus!" Sophie gasped. "We had heard that ye had taken a bride, Sir Richard, but the lass? And here I be thinking ye had her for yer mistress! Bonny!" She laughed delightedly and hugged Eve to her full breasts, then planted an approving buss on Richard's cheek. "Come, come," she ordered, ushering them to the chairs about her table. "I'll be fixing some spiced ale and vittles for us and ye can tell me the all of it!"

They spent a happy afternoon devouring Sophie's meat pie and manchet dripping with fresh butter and honey, and creamy custards hot from the oven. They delighted at Sophie's astonishment upon learning Eve's identity, her wide-eyed interest as they recounted moments of their meeting and, under her prodding, the events that had led to their marriage.

"Where would Garnock be?" Richard asked during a lull in the conversation.

"Oh, he's about, to be sure!" Sophie chortled. "But I'm sure he'll not be showing himself until your well gone! Ah, wait until I be telling 'im who the lass be, he'll near pass away, he will! Do'm good!"

The meal finished, Sophie rose to clear the table and waved off Eve's offer of help. "Nay, lass, ye sit there and enjoy the

company of your husband! I'll not be having a lady so fine
help with the kitchen work, not now that I be knowing who
ye be!" She clucked at Eve's protests and set happily about,
apparently enjoying waiting on the young couple and pleasuring
in the fact that they had chosen to spend the afternoon with
her. As she completed her tasks she wiped her hands on her
apron, poured them all another measure of ale and slipped into
her chair.

"I've been meaning to ask ye, Richard, why the king's
soldiers have been about of late."

Richard, who had been staring at Eve, brought his head
about with a jerk, his eyes darkening at the innocently posed
question. "What? When did you see soldiers?"

"Why, yesterday. Eight, maybe ten of 'em, rode through
here like they was bent for hell. I guessed they were on their
way to Chepstow."

Seeing Richard's face darken, Eve felt a sickening alarm of
dread stir within her middle. "Richard, what is it?"

"Nothing we could not have expected," he said grimly. He
stood up abruptly and held out a hand to Eve. "It is nothing
to worry about—yet. But we best be going."

They thanked Sophie for the meal, promising to return soon,
and made their way back to the horses. Eve saw that Richard
was deep in thought and from his grim look she knew that
Sophie's innocent revelation had borne the worst possible news.
As he helped her onto her mare and fixed her feet in the stirrups
of the sidesaddle he glanced up and took note of the troubled
look upon her lovely brow. "Sophie's news just tells me that
things will be brought to a head sooner than we expected," he
said to her unasked question. "But I should have known better
than to bring you out without an escort. I'm afraid that I've
not used good judgment, Eve, and we had best be back to
Chepstow as quickly as possible."

"But perhaps it does not mean anything," she offered hopefully, but from the grim smirk on his face she knew better.

"If they were up to any good they would have come directly
to Chepstow and made their presence and purpose known." As
he glanced she forced herself to smile, trying not to show the
terror she felt and the premonition of dread that passed through
her.

They arrived back at Chepstow, riding into the courtyard at
dusk, and hurried into the welcome warmth of the brightly lit
hall. Their ride had passed without event and as they had neared

the castle Richard's manner had relaxed, his good humor returning, though Eve suspected that it was given for her benefit.

The remaining guests were gathered with the family before the fire and welcomed eyes turned to them as they entered through the massive portal.

"There you are," observed Strongbow. "We wondered what had happened to you."

"I've been showing my lady to Striguil." Richard smiled as he unconsciously placed an arm about Eve's waist and drew her to his side. "And it is no surprise to me that she has enchanted your people, father."

The tender looks exchanged by the pair and the familiar way Richard held her to his side did not go unnoticed as pleased looks were cast in their direction.

"It never occurred to me that it would not be thus," Strongbow chuckled. "And you, my lady, what did you think of your new home?"

"It is beautiful, milord!" she blurted happily. "It is almost as beautiful as Erin!"

The room broke up in laughter as Eve blushed, realizing what she had said, "I only meant . . ."

"I take such praise as a compliment!" Strongbow chortled.

The evening was still early when Richard claimed his bride, feigning exhaustion, which was met with polite acceptance—except from Warwick, who Richard noticed offering a huge wink to Strongbow, an act which fortunately went unnoticed by Eve.

"Did you have the opportunity to tell Strongbow about the soldiers?" Eve asked as they walked down the hallway to their chamber door.

Richard smiled and looked down at her warmly. "You do not want to discuss that any more than I."

It was true. A nervous anticipation tingled within her as she thought of being alone with him. She turned her face up to his, answering him with a sparkle in her eyes. Their chamber door closed behind them and he swept her into his arms. All thoughts were driven from her mind as his lips covered hers and his fingers began to work at the fastenings down the back of her gown.

17

The guests returned to their manors about the expanse and breadth of England, their banners in the great hall replaced with the coats-of-arms of Gervase and Thomas, who had chosen to pledge their service to Richard and the deClares at Striguil. Miles had returned to Wales, more specifically to St. Davids, where his uncle was bishop, though he had done so reluctantly because he was drawn to remain with his comrades and it was only due to the fact that he was the last male heir of his line that he was persuaded to go.

The manor settled into a comfortable routine and Eve filled her days with the unaccustomed position of being Richard's wife. Isabel seemed content to defer her position as mistress of Chepstow to her new daughter-in-law, insisting with firm but gentle persuasion that Eve aquaint herself with the large staff necessary to operate a manor of Chepstow's size—and the list was endless. Compared with the simplicity of Ferns, Eve was awed by the list as presented by the thin-lipped Waverly, Strongbow's able steward. It was his duty, he explained with reserved patience, to oversee the domestic staff. He administered the estate, including the routine financial and legal matters, and directed the servants. Simple enough, until he droned in a bored manner—that clearly evidenced his impatience of giving precious time acting the mentor—that there were porters, brewers, cupbearers, slaughters, candle makers, cooks and brewers, and, of course, beneath his careful eye was the keeper of the wardrobe. That harried soul, while responsible to Waverly, supervised the laundress and her staff, who would boil the linens in deep wooden troughs, then pound and rinse the garments before hanging them to dry, a necessary process that added little life to the fabrics and kept the seamstresses working day and night with their needles to provide for the household, and often the guests.

Father Benet, Waverly explained, cared for the souls of Striguil, both noble and serf, besides aiding the steward with matters of business. He wrote letters for Strongbow and Richard, kept the lord's seal and acted as almoner: gathering the leftovers from the table and distributing them to the poor. Protection for Striguil was provided by the household knights, squires, men-at-arms, yeomen and the watchmen who patroled the battlements both day and night, and the porters who guarded Chepstow's doors.

The accounting left Eve slightly breathless and she ventured a remark to the effect that the king's own household could hardly be larger, a comment that brought a sputter from the steward who assured her that Chepstow would pale by comparison, though the remark caused him to puff a little with self-importance and it served to enhance her, however little, in his eyes.

Though her days were filled, Eve often found her thoughts returning to Erin as she wondered about the welfare of her family. No word had come, indeed not even a message from her father on the subject of her marriage to the house of Striguil. Well, she had mused somewhat ruefully, bad news always traveled quickly, it certainly had in the case of Dermot's rape of Dervorgil, so she surmised that there had been no recent trouble.

Her thoughts thus, she could not help but compare Richard to her father and it brought a reluctant smile as she considered their first meeting. Both strong-willed and forceful, she knew that when the time came she would find herself caught squarely in the middle and she faced the prospect with both curiosity and a certain amount of dread.

It was at such moments that she missed having a friend her own age to talk with, since Lavinia had left, following a tearful farewell, with her father for Lighthurst. Eve knew then that Lavinia's reluctance was not only for her, but for the sandy-haired knight who stood to one side watching her go, his blue eyes filled with grief and longing. Eve had caught the looks

that crossed between them and as Lavinia stepped forward for
a final hug she whispered her own encouragement to her departing friend. The saddened, tear-filled eyes Lavinia returned,
though bravely borne, wrenched at Eve's heart. Pressed by
earlier questions, Richard had patiently explained to her, against
her outraged argument, that howevermuch deserved, the pair
was ill-matched. Gervase was landless, a third son who would
never inherit, and Lavinia was heir to vast estates and title.
Lord Severn would never approve the match. Eve had stormed
about their chamber, against Richard's sighs, decrying the
entire matter and deriding Richard for even suggesting that
Gervase did not measure up to Severn's unreasonable standards. To gain peace, Richard suggested that there was always
hope and that if Gervase were to gain title and land, then
perhaps it might be possible. Eve picked up on the comment
readily and she turned to him with a look of determination and
snapped, "I will not believe that this is the end for them!
Something will happen to make it possible, I know it!" Perhaps
then, if she could have realized the truth of her prediction, she
would not have spoken it with such fervor. But then, neither
she nor Richard had a way of knowing that with her wish
Gerda's prophecy had gained another step toward fulfillment.

Except for such brief and rare moments, the days passed
with more than mere contentment as Eve relished the never-
ending joy she felt with Richard, the excitement that stirred
within her at the sound of his voice or when she turned to find
him near. At such moments their eyes would meet and, even
in the presence of others, they would be filled with unabashed
pride and love and her heart would tighten in a bittersweet
sweep of pain until she could hardly breathe for the love she
felt for him. As he conversed with others and she caught his
eye, his gaze would travel over her with a love and hunger
that he made no attempt to conceal. The vibrations between
them were electric, the anticipation building until they were
alone behind the closed door of their chambers and they could
finally express the passion they felt for one another, the torment
of their feelings exploding into welcomed release.

The days passed contentedly to the end of February and the
fields, which had been bound by the winter frost, were first
drowned by the rains, then warmed by the sun, releasing them
at last to an important event that would mark the beginning of
Striguil's year. The wealth of Ireland was measured by cattle
and in caring for their precious stock Eve's people were un-

surpassed. Wealth, fines and tributes were given in cattle and the cultivation of crops were kept at a minimum. They took what nature offered, growing only that which took the least care, such as oats and barley, and that only because of the value of such as feed for the livestock. Their knowledge compared to the English serf was limited and harsh winters often brought hardships that were too often realized in the Irish year. Therefore, Eve awoke with a barely contained excitement on the morning tillage was to resume on Chepstow's lands, eager for the festival that would accompany it and for the anticipation of learning something new that could be immensely valuable for her people.

Richard watched her with an amused smile as she bustled about their chamber, washing at the icy bowl on the side table, then picking through her wardrobe as she sought to choose a gown, throwing one and another on the end of the bed. He lay abed, stretching against the pillows at his back, and watched her through half-closed lids as she moved about, as his mind turned to remembrances of a night enjoyably spent.

"Richard," she mused abstractedly, "which do you find the more suitable? I cannot decide."

"Bring them closer," he answered. Intent on her problem she did not notice the twinkle of mischief in his eyes as she brought them around to the side of the bed. Once there, he reached out and grabbed her about the waist, pulling her across his lap as the garments flew about and she squealed in protest. Her outburst was drowned in his laughter, the bed strewn with clothing, as he rolled her beneath him and she struggled against the vise of his grip. She looked up at him, his meaning clearly written in his eyes which were filled with a hungry leer, and she protested loudly.

"Richard, we shall be late for mass. Please, I must dress!"

"You will only need to dress, love, if you plan to leave this chamber. My mind is of another reasoning." He buried his face in the nape of her neck, drawing mingled moans and protests from her as she weakly struggled against his advances.

"Richard, please, let me up!" she gasped.

He rose and grinned down at her. "And if your husband determines that you shall remain? Must I remind you that you are under the rod, my every wish your command, my every pleasure to be met?"

"My Lord," she flipped, her own eyes growing with mischief, "are you not curious to visit Irish sod? There are things

about women I think you should learn there, particularly about
the manner of wives."

His eyes darkened with puzzlement. "Aye? And what would
that be?"

"Things that I think would not please your Norman reasoning." She smiled.

They arrived at the planting fields to find that the household
already settled beneath the massive oaks where trestle tables
had been set up for the feast of celebration that would be laid
out in the early afternoon. The villagers and tenants were there,
having arrived at dawn to support and encourage the men who
were to participate in the plowing contest. Each year, when
the early spring sun had warmed the ground sufficiently to
release its surface from the frost, the contest of Plow Monday
was held. Each man would plow from sunrise to sunset, the
earth he was able to till during those hours becoming his to
farm for the coming year. They worked ceaselessly, the muscles
straining from their arms and bared backs, the sweat of toil
glistening on faces and shoulders even in the still cool morning
air as they labored to the limits of their endurance, knowing
that each square inch of land they were able to call their own
would mean the more they would provide for their families in
the coming year.

The knights lolled about and Eve watched the contrast with
amusement, wondering how they would fare in a like contest.
She glanced at Richard and Gervase, who stood on each side
of her watching the endeavors on the field, and with a wry
laugh she told her thoughts. The two men exchanged looks of
surprise before Richard's brows knitted with a disapproving
frown at his wife.

Gervase cleared his throat. "My lady, a knight's position,
as I have told you, is one of protection and security. Each of
us has a function to contribute and . . ."

"It is not necessary to justify our position to my lady,"
Richard interjected curtly. His eyes flashed angrily at Eve.
"Eve, it is not your place to question our customs but to accept
them."

Indignation burst forward and shone from her face and Richard braced himself with a steadfast determination that this time
she most certainly would obey him. To his surprise whatever
comment would have come forth from her was apparently dis-

missed as her gaze dropped to a point beyond his shoulder and her expression turned to delight. He turned with question to find that his mother had approached and he watched, with mixed feelings of relief, as the two women hugged affectionately. Isabel had journeyed to a neighboring manor the past week to visit with friends and the awkward moment passed as Eve's attention was drawn to the older woman. Rolling his eyes at a clearly amused Gervase, Richard sighed as he knew, with a resigned certainty, that the subject would be broached again. He wondered if life was always going to be a continuing battle between them or if she would ever adjust to their ways and content herself with being his wife, resigning herself to what was expected of her—and nothing more.

As the sun arched into the deepening blue of the afternoon sky, the observers took refuge under the protecting shade of the spreading oaks that surrounded the field. Insects, newly hatched from their frozen egg prisons, now warmed to life, buzzing and darting about as if to make up for their lost time in frantic activity. Brushed aside, they sought out other prey, those intent upon their labors, biting cruelly at the glistening arms and backs as if knowing that there was no time to be taken from the handles of the plows and reins to stop the annoyance. Women: wives, sisters, and lovers, would rush forward with buckets of cool water and ladles to quench parched lips and tongues, and cloths dipped into the water to refresh brows, lastly dripping the liquid in rivulets down the straining backs for temporary ease from the bright sun.

The air became rich with the aroma of the newly turned soil, broken by the crude iron wedges of the plows to bring forth its richness to soon receive scattered seed, which would bring new life to the land and food to ease hunger in the coming season.

Richard sat with his back propped against an oak, barely hearing the banter about him as his gaze lazily followed Eve moving among the farmers who were waiting to replace a spent family member in the field. His expression was hooded beneath half-closed eyes and did not reveal the admiration with which he watched his bride. Aye, she exasperated him, tested his patience to the limit, and he could not fathom why she was so interested in the manners of men. Even now she spent the hours in the hot sun with the serfs, questioning them endlessly to the methods used to farm the soil, instead of lolling in the shade with the other ladies. She seemed oblivious to the fact that her amber silk gown, which she had fretted over only a few hours past, had now become soiled about the hem, or that her hair had escaped in wringlets from the severe confinement of her coif. He watched her brush an elusive wisp back from her face but her attention was fully directed to the men as they, at first with awkwardness and doubt, then caught up in the sincerity of her questions, gestured to the field with their hands and arms in explanation, and even stooped up to scoop up a handful of earth, which was received eagerly by her own slender fingers, delving in great detail into the knowledge they had gained from centuries of experience with the land. As he watched her persistence, an element of pride stirred within him. He startled at the feeling, his brow furrowing with puzzlement, as he sought to come to grips with it. Aye, she was different from other women he had known but was that not the essence that had drawn him to her? Would he have been so drawn had she been mild and consenting, those very elements lacking in her that he was wont to remind her of, at every opportunity?

He watched her as she straightened up, rubbing the small of her back with her fingers to betray her fatigue, and her eyes moved over the gathering as if seeking one in particular. Her lovely features wrinkled into a puzzled frown as she apparently did not find the one she sought, then she turned and walked across the clearing and up the grassy knoll to where he lay and he wondered about the disturbed look she wore. He sat up as she joined him but she did not sit down but instead looked out again across the gathering.

"Richard, have you seen Sophie? I have been looking for her all morning but I do not think she has arrived."

"Nay, I have not seen her." He stifled a yawn and leaned back against the tree.

"She told me that she never missed a plowing. She even promised to bring something special for the feast."

"Ah, is that the reason for your concern!" he chuckled. "I too should be concerned, I would hate to miss one of Sophie's meat pies, or custards, or tarts, or . . ."

"Oh, Richard, be serious! I am worried about her! Perhaps she has taken ill!"

"Eve, I am sure that you are worrying for nothing. She will be here."

As he started to stretch out again, Eve persisted, the worry heavy in her voice. "You have known her for much longer than I. Have you ever known her to break a promise?"

Reluctant to leave the comfort of the shade or the easiness of the afternoon, he started to wave her off but something in her tone caught him, her words playing uneasily at the back of his mind. "What would you have me do, my love? I am sure that you have something in mind." She did not answer but the pleading in her expression made him groan as he knew full well her intention. "I will take some men and see to her, though I am certain that everything is well. She has probably just forgotten about the time."

But even as he said it, a vague discomfort began to gnaw at him. He rose to his feet and gathered up his scabbard. As he turned, his eyes narrowed because he saw her intention. "And where do you think you are going?"

"I am going with you! She may be ill, Richard, and if she is, she will need more than what you and your men can offer her! Certainly there is no reason why I cannot go, since you are so certain that nothing is amiss!"

He grunted, too relaxed to argue with her, and, besides, he mutely reasoned, a long dusty ride might be just the thing to take a little of the spirit out of her. He walked over to where Warwick was stretched out, snoring in a relaxed slumber, and shook the knight's shoulder, bringing him out of his sleep in a sputter. He mumbled something to him, then rose and went to Gervase and Thomas and several other knights who were lolling about, stirring them to their horses tied among the trees in the grove.

Now bent to action, as they rode toward the village, Richard's earlier casualness was replaced by an uncomfortable edginess. As they had taken to saddle something undefinable had caught at the back of his mind, something amiss about the past morning that Eve's concern had brought forth to his consciousness. His mind turned back to the gathering as he replayed the past hours' events and attempted to seek the answers for his misgivings. Eve caught his pensive look and rode nearer, her earlier alarm growing tighter within her.

"Richard, is something wrong?"

He looked at her absentmindedly, then all at once his thoughts became defined. He reined Taran in abruptly to allow Warwick to come abreast of him. "Warwick, do you recall seeing anyone from Sophie's village this morning?"

The knight's brow knitted in thought as he pondered the question, then quickly became grim upon realizing the answer. "Nay. None were there."

"That is what I thought," Richard gritted. "Something is amiss."

Without another word they spurred the horses to a faster pace and a deep heaviness settled on them as they plunged toward their destination.

"Look!" Just before the turn in the bend, Gervase reined in his horse and pointed toward the sky.

A long column of black smoke curled into the sky above the trees which still obscured Maple Leaf from their vision, freezing the hearts of the riders as they stared, transfixed.

"Eve, remain here!" Richard shouted as the knights spurred their horses and plunged forward. If he had looked back, he would have seen the horrified look she held, quickly replaced by grim determination. She had no intention of remaining where she was when Sophie was concerned and she urged her mount forward.

As they rounded the last bend and the village came into view, their hearts were seized with horror. Their hands, clenched on drawn swords ready for the expected confrontation, now gripped the hilts in anguish. Richard heard a cry and turned to find Eve, her face drained of color and filled with wide-eyed horror. He moved Taran quickly between her and the village, attempting to block the sight from her.

"Eve," he said hoarsely, "I told you to wait behind."

She swallowed the nausea that pushed at the back of her throat, as her head swam with lightness, her mind contesting what it had seen. She looked up at Richard and saw the anguish in his eyes and instantly she managed to suppress her own feelings, knowing the pain he was feeling. The last thing she wanted at this moment was to be an additional burden.

"Richard," she said, her voice surprisingly strong. "See to your people."

They moved slowly into the village, their swords still drawn, but they knew that no enemy would be met. The mud-and-wattle huts stood with their leather-hinged doors askew, their meager contents scattered about the road as evidence of the wanton destruction. Lifeless bodies lay where they had been struck, in grotesque positions of flight or struggle. The knights dismounted and walked among the bodies, turning each over with the dull hope that a sign of life might be found. An agonized moan was heard and Gervase rushed to its source, the large form of Almer, the village smithy who was crouched in a strange bent position, but still alive. As Gervase rolled him over, Eve gasped and turned her head away with anguish as beneath the large man's body, there where he had fallen and where his father had obviously sought to protect him with his own form, lay the lifeless and mutilated body of his small son. Mercifully for the moment, Almer passed out once again and Thomas rushed to help Gervase remove the small form before the smithy regained consciousness.

The scene was repeated again and again: the weaver, the tanner and the village carpenter, even the poorest of the villeins, the cottars who had spent their existence repairing the village walls and digging the ditches to receive the waste, each soul Richard had known by name since childhood, each so much a part of his own life.

He looked to Eve, still astride her mare, and followed her hardened gaze to where it was fixed upon the charred ruins of the inn and its outbuildings. He knew that her thoughts were as his, upon the time spent in its warm and cozy kitchen with its mistress. He started to cross the clearing to her but was halted by Warwick, who had silently approached. The knight, his face drawn with grief, laid a hand on Richard's arm.

"Richard," he murmured, his black eyes moving over the carnage as if to confirm his thoughts. "Where are the women?"

Startled, grey eyes moved about the decimated village to confirm Warwick's observation. He began to reply but was cut short as he heard Gervase's shout from the far side of the road. They found him standing by the opened door of a hut, his face pale as he gestured to the interior with his thumb. Richard grit his teeth and stepped into the doorway, drawing in his breath sharply at what he saw in the dim light. Sophie sat on a wooden bench, her eyes staring vacantly at the far wall as she rocked methodically back and forth, clutching a small child in her arms. He could see at a glance that the child was dead. Its eyes were staring lifelessly ahead in a death mask, dried blood covering its small body and the front of Sophie's garment. He ducked into the hut and crossed quickly and knelt before her.

"Sophie, what has happened here? Who did this?" His voice was firm, knowing that her mind had taken her far from what had happened, yet it was filled with tenderness and sympathy. She did not seem to hear him but continued to rock back and forth, staring blankly ahead.

He heard a soft cry from behind him and he turned to find

Eve standing in the doorway. He stood up and tried to stop her but she pushed past him and knelt before the Scotswoman and took her hand in her own.

"Sophie," she pleaded, her voice filled with pain for the woman's silent suffering. "Sophie, it is Eve." Sophie turned her head at the sound of Eve's voice and she stared at the younger woman as a flicker of recognition crossed her face. Her expression turned to puzzlement, as if trying to remember something just beyond her grasp. Suddenly her face became twisted and contorted with remembrance and she let out an anguished wail which sent chills down the backs of the men that watched her in open horror. Richard stepped forward and quickly took the dead child from her arms and passed it to Gervase, who carried the small, lifeless form from the hut. Richard turned back to find that Eve had taken Sophie into her arms and was stroking the greying hair, murmuring softly to the now sobbing woman.

Cautiously, Richard pressed his question. "Sophie, where are the women?"

Sophie's anguish halted abruptly at the softly-put question and she looked up at Richard, then to the other knights as if seeing them for the first time. She cringed into Eve's arms like a frightened child and whimpered in terror at the sight of them.

"Richard, take them out of here, everyone!" Eve whispered urgently. "Let me be alone with her!"

They did as they were bid, and outside their faces reflected the frustration and helplessness they felt as they glanced about the devastated village. Recovering, Warwick called to one of the knights, "Beaumont, return to Strongbow and tell him what has happened here. Tell him that we will need help to bury the dead."

The man nodded and left quickly, all too eager to be away from the deathly place, but dreading the news he would carry to his lord. Warwick turned back to find Richard's eyes fixed upon the door of the hut, their silver coldness spelling his anger and hatred.

"We do not need Sophie's confirmation of what has happened here, Warwick. You know it as well as I. We both know who was the cause of this."

"We cannot be sure of anything," Warwick cautioned, growing uneasy at the stark anger in Richard's expression. He had seen the look once before, when Richard had learned of John's death. Rage had ruled Richard's emotions then and, remembering, Warwick felt an involuntary shiver of fear.

"Who else could be responsible for this?" Richard spat. "And I ask you your own question, where are the women? I think that you know the answer as well as I."

Eve appeared at that moment and motioned to Richard but when he went to her she stopped him at the doorway with a hand on his chest. "She will talk to you now but please be gentle with her. I fear that her mind is fragile."

Richard and Warwick motioned for the others to wait where they were and they slipped into the darkness of the hut. Eve sat down on the bench next to Sophie and took her hands as she spoke to her gently.

"Sophie, Richard and Warwick are here to help you. They would know what has happened here today and they must know where the women have gone."

Sophie turned her face to the men and the look she carried in her tormented eyes caused them to shudder.

"They are gone," she whispered. "They took them with them."

"Who took them?" Eve prodded gently. "Who took them, Sophie?"

"Stephen's men. Aye," she murmured. "They were Stephen's. They boasted of it . . ." Her voice trailed off and Eve rubbed the limp hands, urging her not to drift away from them. Sophie's eyes brimmed with tears as she continued in a faint and anguished voice, "They came without warning, there was no time to stop them, they laughed, enjoyed it . . . Garnock . . ."

"Sophie, what about Garnock?"

"He tried—he tried to reason with 'em—they laughed, dragged him between their horses . . ."

"Where is he, Sophie?" Eve recalled that she had not seen his body. "Where is Garnock?"

Sophie looked at Eve with vacant surprise. "Why—they put him inside. They locked him in . . . They did not see me go to the back. I tried to go with him—but the flames, the flames would not let me go with him . . ."

Eve's eyes filled with horror and she glanced back at Richard and Warwick, whose faces were grim and set with hatred.

"I—I could hear his screams. They laughed, they watched and laughed as it burnt—with Garnock . . ." Her voice cracked and she covered her face with her hands and began to sob uncontrollably, rocking once again in her immeasurable grief.

Eve clasped her to her as she glanced up at the men, tears streaming down her face in silent anguish for Sophie's pain.

Richard and Warwick stepped out into the sunlight, having heard enough, the brightness of the morning seeming to defy in silent mockery what they had heard. The faces of the other knights confirmed that the words had carried to them. Richard whirled on Warwick. "Do you need more?" he asked through his teeth.

"Richard, my grief is as great as yours, my anger of equal measure," Warwick began cautiously. "But we must wait for Strongbow. It is only on his word that we might act."

"Wait?" Richard bellowed, disbelieving. "There is only the faintest chance that the women still live, even now!" He spun to the others without waiting for Warwick's comment. "Who will go with me? I will not force anyone. The choice is yours, but I will not wait!"

They did not hesitate but ran for their mounts and, as Richard would have followed, Warwick grasped his arm. "Richard! You must not do this. We must wait for Strongbow!"

"Nay, Warwick," he growled, pushing the knight's hand from his arm. "Not this time. The choice is mine and I will not live with yet another memory of . . ." He bit off his words and glanced at the door of the hut. "Stay with them and take them back to Chepstow."

Gervase rode up leading Taran and he passed the reins to Richard, who swung into the saddle. Helplessly, Warwick watched as the men rode from the village and his own feelings were mixed over Richard's decision. With a last sweeping glance at the village he took a deep sigh and turned to duck into the doorway of the hut.

Warwick's gaze followed Strongbow as the earl paced the floor before the hearth. His hands were folded behind his broad back and his fingers worked at each other as he turned for the countless time in his silent anxious vigil. The lord of Striguil turned and glanced up the stairs to the chamber where Eve and Isabel sat by the bed tending to Sophie, who was tossing and turning in tortured delirium, in contest for her mind as it sought to erase its horrors and return to the living.

The empty hall was as silent as a mausoleum, its engulfing stillness pressing on the minds and spirits of the aging warriors. Warwick poured a tankard of ale and rose to carry it to Strongbow, while he sought the words that could ease his lord's mind. But none came, as they had not for the past two days of tedious waiting. Strongbow took the offering, knowing that it was given for more reasons than mere refreshment, and he emitted a deep sigh as he slumped heavily into a nearby chair. Warwick poured a measure for himself, then returned to his own place, where he sat peering into the liquid, seeking solace for his own mind.

"How much of the fault is mine?" Strongbow said suddenly. "Would it have been different if I had opposed Stephen in years past?"

"You cannot know that, milord," Warwick answered with conviction. "Hindsight always brings doubts, questions as to whether or not it could have been done another way. Had you made other choices the same questions would remain."

"Aye, we always question the past," Strongbow snorted. "But my concern is not for myself but for..."

"You have always been concerned for others more than yourself," Warwick interrupted. "If you had thought only for yourself, you would have taken up arms against Stephen years ago, we both know it."

"Perhaps, but it is my own son who may now pay for my indecision—and those loyal knights who have followed me unfailingly these past years, and their sons. What can I say to Richard's mother and the other women who wait for their men, should they not return?"

"You will not need to say anything, milord. Our women are strong and they understand what is at stake. Do you not believe that Lady Isabel knows that her son, as well as her husband, must follow his conscience?"

"And Lady Eve? How can I tell that tender young bride that she is a widow before she is hardly a wife? She has not even a babe to comfort her through the years."

"I think that lass is the strongest of them all."

With the last word there was the sound of horses in the courtyard and the two men leapt from their chairs and exchanged quick hopeful glances as they faced the portal expectantly. The door swung open and the knights entered, led by Richard, dusty and travel-weary but a swift apprehensive glance from both Strongbow and Warwick affirmed that none were missing. With a great sigh of relief Strongbow bellowed for Waverly, who appeared almost immediately, followed by servants laden with food.

Richard collapsed into a chair next to Gervase and he threw

down a measure of ale to refresh his parched throat, then poured himself another before he allowed himself to meet Strongbow's questions.

"We found them a day's ride from the village," he muttered, leaning back in his chair. "They had the women but I fear we were too late to save them insult." The knights had paused in their meal to listen and from the uncomfortable looks that passed between them Strongbow knew there was more but he waited for Richard to finish. "Two escaped," he added grimly. "We looked for them throughout the night but they could not be found."

Warwick paled at Richard's news and drew in his breath as he glanced at Strongbow with alarm. But, the earl never blinked an eye as he regarded the men.

"You have my full support for what you have done and your actions were by my authority. No man here is personally responsible but acted as a knight in my service. For now, refresh yourselves, then see to your ladies. Their assurance to your safety is the pressing matter at hand."

Though his words left no room for dispute, the men received them with downcast looks, their appetites having fled and the joy of their homecoming now dampened as they knew that the consequences of their actions would now fully be his own. Each in turn, they rose from their chairs and left the hall quietly, each carrying the burden of unspoken thoughts as they considered what effect it would have upon Chepstow and its lord.

Richard remained in his chair, sitting back heavily as he stared at the table, his expression brooding. He missed the silent interchange between Strongbow and Warwick as the earl motioned with his head for the knight to leave him with his son. Warwick began to protest but he checked himself with great effort as his fists clenched tightly on his tankard. He set it down on the dormant table and walked slowly to the stairs, pausing once to glance back at the two men he loved most in the world, his heart weighing heavily as he ascended the stairs, sensing what Strongbow would say to his son.

Strongbow refilled Richard's tankard, poured himself one and took the chair next to him. His expression held a serenity that defied what had happened, as if the years of indecision had now been focused into a single-minded purpose that brought with it a peace and welcomed contentment. But Richard, involved with his own self-castigating thoughts did not notice and it was he who finally broke the silence, his voice weighted with self-loathing.

"What was done was necessary and I would do it again given the same circumstances," he said sullenly. "But in allowing the two to escape I have failed you. Regardless of what you said to the others, the responsibility is mine and Stephen will hold me alone accountable."

"Richard, you are heir to Chepstow but I am still its lord. I find no fault with your decision to pursue those men. By their actions Stephen has attacked me personally and I will not tolerate it! I am accountable for the actions of my knights, and that includes you."

His voice held an unmistakable authority and with it a finality Richard knew was resolute. "They are certain to come," he observed grimly. "We must prepare for siege and I for one . . ."

"Nay, there will be no siege." Strongbow shook his head firmly. "If we were to do so, it would force the nobles to take sides openly, thus exposing their hand. You know as well as I that to do so now could well spell disaster."

Richard gaped at him, their eyes meeting for the first time. "Then what would you do? Would you hand Striguil to him without raising a hand to stop it?"

"I will go to London. It is possible that the attack upon the village was without Stephen's knowledge or consent. Obviously we had no choice but to defend our people and return our women."

"That is suicide!" Richard gasped. "Even if you are right, and I do not believe it for a moment, you are putting yourself into his hands!"

Strongbow sighed and rubbed his forehead thoughtfully, ignoring the red flush of anger that had spread over Richard's face. "Richard, have you forgotten so quickly what I have tried to teach you?" His voice was low and it held an unmistakable weariness that made Richard wince. "Lasting victories are seldom won by the sword. It matters little what happens to me—" He heard Richard draw in his breath sharply and he dismissed his son's reaction with a wave of his hand. "I have come to peace with myself, Richard, and you have helped me to that end. You, Gervase and the others, even Warwick if he is fortunate, will see the results of what little good I might have done and the knowledge satisfies me. Never expect more than you are capable of giving, Richard. It will only cast your soul into torment and undo whatever good you might achieve. I know that you will never shirk your responsibilities, but do not overlook those turns in your life, however subtle, that are placed there for your own destiny. Never become so fixed upon a path of action that it blinds you to a greater purpose. Your way may prove to be far different than mine, keep your mind always open to find it.

"Those unworthy of power, like Stephen, gain strength when they can convince us that our small efforts cannot affect them, that we are insignificant. They frustrate us, take away our hopes and our dreams, stop us at every turn until we give up, then they have won. But, if we persevere, if we refuse to be beaten and hold together with each doing just what he can, but with conscience and to the best of our own, unique ability, together we are unbeatable. We can topple unjust governments and build nations."

"Then let me go to London, it was my actions that brought this about."

"Nay, Richard, you have much to do, but not this. And you are wrong, I am as responsible for what has happened as anyone. This has only brought about a confrontation with Stephen that was bound to come, sooner or later. I am lord of Chepstow and unless Stephen has completely lost reason he will recognize the power that I have behind me. In fact," he added with a grin, "I find myself looking forward to it, regardless of the outcome."

"And if he has lost reason?" Richard asked grimly, not sharing his father's optimism.

"It could be the catalyst to bind the nobles together, as each will be forced to face the tenuousness of their position with Stephen in power. Would you take that opportunity from me? In the event that I do not return, Richard, you will be my sword, to complete what I have begun, but in your own way."

Richard let out a frustrated moan, knowing that Strongbow's argument was undeniable, though fear for his father set a sickening tightness within him. They exchanged a long look of final understanding and love, the moment turning back the years to a time when father and son trusted each other without antagonisms and competition. Remembrances of his childhood passed through his mind, more by feelings than by form, and for a startling instant he saw a vision of his future. An awareness of impermanence gnawed at him as his senses confirmed that his path would be far different than Strongbow's, yet he knew, as he raised his gaze to his father's, that he would forever draw on that strength and somehow find himself equal to what lay before him.

The knights of Striguil sat about the fire in the great hall, unwilling to exchange glances for fear of seeing each other's deep concern. Richard swilled the ale in his cup, his own mind unyielding with a deep sense of responsibility for the gloom that had descended upon Chepstow. He heard some activity on the floors above and his mind turned to Eve, the reflection acting as soothing balm. Upon his return her opinion, for once, had been silent. She had broached no questions, showing only relief for his safety. They had laid in each other's arms throughout the long night following his return, their positions oddly reversed as she held him to her, his head nestled against the softness of her breast, stroking his hair tenderly and giving him the comfort and safety of her arms. If she suspected the danger that threatened them all, she said nothing. A few days later, when Strongbow announced that he would travel to London, she had quietly appeared at his side and, laying a hand gently on his arm, had reassured him that she understood the turmoil that tore at him.

Would he never understand her unpredictability? And her strength? She had nursed Sophie back to health and sanity, governed Chepstow with a calm but swift efficiency to take the burden from Isabel, who had become totally distraught since Strongbow's departure, and somehow had managed to remain a loving comfort to Richard in their time alone, her serenity helping to calm the raging torment within him.

He looked about him now, reading the thoughts of the others who sat about the hall, knowing that their emotions were set to a fine, and dangerous, edge from the waiting. Their tempers were sharp and they had begun snapping at each other with the least provocation and he wondered how long it would take before a real brawl would occur to release the tension. He smirked wryly, wondering if he should kindle a brawl and wondered if he did, would he be able to stop it?

He stretched his long legs out before him and wiggled his feet to keep them from going to sleep. He fought the impulse to rush from the hall and take to horse, not stopping until both he and Taran dropped from exhaustion. But he knew it to be a meaningless gesture—the problems would exist upon his return. There was nothing to do but to wait. On the other hand...He jumped from his chair, startling the others, and stretched.

"Come, get up, all of you. This inactivity helps no one. We'll see to the needs of Striguil and..."

Gervase groaned loudly and seemed to melt into his chair. "Richard, take pity! I'm of a mind to vegetate before this fire."

"Gervase, if you do not remove your backside from that chair I will do it for you. When Strongbow returns he will find a secure holding. Besides, if we sit here for another moment we will be at each other's throats and I'll not have it! Get up!"

They rode hard, with an unspoken sense of urgency, each finally conceding to Richard's wisdom as they felt themselves relax and then surge with renewed energy by action. They saw to Striguil's needs, checking each hamlet and village and even seeing to tasks normally reserved for others, such as the rebuilding of Maple Leaf's stone wall. They stripped their armor, setting it to one side while they labored alongside the villeins, their bare backs sweating in the hot sun, welcoming the release from tension that the hard physical work offered them. They saw to the needs of the devastated village, hunting for game to feed the remaining villagers and giving what comfort they could.

They returned to the hall well after dark, exhausted but again in control of their emotions, the day's efforts seeming to restore a feeling of hope. But, as they entered the brightly lit hall, their spirits abounding, fate played its final, cruel hand. The oppressive feeling permeating the manor seemed to escape the returning company, except for Richard and Warwick who felt it strike them like a swift blow as they crossed the portal. There is something about tragedy that often passes everyone but a few, affecting only the souls of those most deeply involved, transmitting itself like a messenger, understanding received however unwanted, where no words need to be spoken.

They exchanged meaningful glances, dreaded feelings of horror passing between them as the others set to a welcomed and happy homecoming. Then, without words, they looked to the empty staircase and to what they sensed was awaiting them above. Silently, they crossed to the stairs, each step with a heavy burden, a weight that was almost impossible to carry. Richard hesitated before the door to Isabel's chamber, suddenly unwilling to face the other side of it, until finally Warwick reached across and pushed it open.

As they entered, Eve and Isabel turned to face them. They were sitting before the window on the far side of the room and stood when the men entered. Prepared as they were, Richard and Warwick paled at the expressions on the faces of both women. It struck Richard how aged his mother had become in the past few hours. His eyes fixed upon her, he was unaware that Eve had come to his side and had laid a hand on his arm. He looked at her with question, noticing that her eyes were moist. Warwick stood to one side, helplessly, his black eyes darting from one to the other as he waited for someone to speak. It was Isabel, her shoulders slumped with resignation.

"Richard, my dear son . . ." she whispered, her voice barely audible. "Your father—" Her voice seemed to grow impossibly lower as she spoke with great effort. "Your father is dead."

He felt Eve's hand tighten on his arm as Isabel's words floated meaninglessly within him. Finally, slowly, they settled and took shape. "Dead?" he repeated quietly.

Warwick groaned with a sound slightly unhuman.

"Aye," Eve whispered softly. "Word came while you were gone. It was said that he died suddenly, from unknown causes." She would not add that Stephen had sent his sympathy.

Richard looked at her dumbly, his gaze fixing on a single tear that was slipping down her face, and something inside of him suddenly snapped. All the years of torment, anger and frustration tore from him in his implacable grief as he spun from her and in a movement sent a small table flying across the room to shatter against one far wall, his fury exploding in a howl of savage anguish. He spun back upon the women, straining, but something in their horrified expressions brought him under control, though his face remained blood-red with his rage. "Mother, he will be avenged, I promise you upon my soul. He has gone to his death for the want of protecting me and I shall not rest until I have seen revenge!"

"Richard, no!" Isabel's recovery was miraculous as she crossed with amazing swiftness and took Richard's arms in her hands, the strength in her small frame surprising him as she gripped him tightly, her eyes burning. That is exactly what Stephen wants. You must not play into his hands! He would take no greater pleasure than to destroy Striguil's last heir— and all that your father had worked, had dreamed for! You owe it to him to fulfill the dreams that you began together!"

He pulled her hands from his shoulders gently and held them as he sought to make her understand the force that was driving him. "Mother, can you expect me to forget his murder—aye, we know it was that—and still be able to live with myself?"

"By living!" she cried, her eyes filled with a fiery brightness. "If you die without realizing your dream, how can you avenge him, truly? Would he be avenged if you were to give yourself into Stephen's hands? Nay, Richard, you must go to Normandy! Join with Henry and return victorious—take Stephen's lands, his very kingdom, all that he holds most sacred, take them from him! Only then will your father be truly avenged. Give his memory what he most wanted—England's peace, its future!"

Isabel and Eve watched as Richard struggled with her words, wanting to throw them off in his deep-seated desire for revenge yet unable to dismiss their truth. Fearing that he was losing the battle, they saw Warwick step forward and lay a hand on Richard's shoulder, the knight's eyes filled with unshed tears for his wasted lord, his own grief held tightly in check as he sought to give comfort and support Isabel's wisdom.

"She is right, Richard," he murmured. "Listen to her, I beg of you. There is no other way. Our time will come, I promise you."

He glanced at Warwick, their eyes holding for a long moment before he sighed wretchedly and turned back to Isabel, feeling beaten. "If we are to run we will have to do so quickly," he said bitterly. "Stephen's forces may well be on their way here now."

"You will go." Isabel drew up her head bravely, her voice firm. "I will remain here. This is my home and I shall not spend my last days in any other place. Do not fear for me," she added quickly, seeing the alarm in Richard's eyes. "Stephen will not dare to harm me. Even if he should forget my position as wife of the lord of Striguil, he will not forget that I was Henry's favorite—the barons will not allow it. But you must take Eve with you as he would not hesitate to revenge himself upon her. She will only be safe with you in Normandy, if you would not return to find her married to another.

He glanced at Eve, uncertain of involving her in the life of an outcast that soon would be his and anyone who chose to come with him, but Warwick settled it."

"She is right, Richard, in this also. If you leave her, Stephen will most certainly use her against you. We must take her with us."

"Us?" Richard turned to Warwick with question. "Warwick, with all that you have done for me, and my father, I will not ask this of you."

"Who is asking?" Warwick growled. "I make my own decisions, and continue to do so now. Of course I shall go with you, as will the others."

"We cannot leave Chepstow unfortified!" Richard protested, but once again Isabel took the matter in hand.

"Richard, they will go with you, each one. Word has already been sent, arriving on the tail of—of the other—from Leicester that knights are arriving for my protection. My brother's position in court allowed him to know of my needs even before we were suspect of it and understands what is involved without being asked. Moreover, I am certain that he will do what he can to delay Stephen. Nevertheless, you must leave immediately, tonight! We cannot be certain how effective Robert will be—and you must take all with you who may be held accountable. I will not have one more lost! Perhaps," she added wistfully, "your father gained in his death what he was not able to achieve in his lifetime, for this will certainly force the matter to a head, once and for all. I shall wait, Richard, and dream for the day when you shall return with Henry, victorious!"

PART TWO

Henry

18

May, 1154
Anjou

Sophie watched Eve with an evergrowing eye of deep concern. Her worry over the increasing listlessness of her young mistress grew more with each passing day and she muttered under her breath as she noted the untouched tray left on the small table next to Eve's chair.

For a long, agonizingly lonely year the two women were in almost total isolation, cloistered in the small castle in Anjou. Sophie had been grateful for the opportunity to accompany them to Normandy, and had broken to tears when Richard had come to her chamber, soon after Strongbow's death, to ask her if she would consent to become companion to Eve. There was nothing but painful, bitter memories left for her in Striguil and her total love had become focused on the younger woman who had nursed her back from her nightmares with such tender care. Now, in the year that had passed since their flight from England, it had become Sophie's turn to give comfort in Richard's long absences. As she watched Eve staring in lonely silence from the window of her bedchamber, a sadness etched into the lovely young brow, Sophie felt a rage stir within her full breast toward Richard and his thoughtlessness. Laboriously, she swallowed back the impulse to say something, knowing from past experience that Eve would not discuss it, and that any effort to draw her out would only drive her further away into the shell she had made for herself.

If Sophie could have read Eve's thoughts at that moment perhaps she would have understood why Eve would not share

her feelings. She had been lonely, almost unbearably, but that
was the lesser reason for her unhappiness and her worry. The
true reason she could not share with anyone, not even Sophie
and least of all, Richard. She distrusted Henry.

Upon their arrival to the Normandy coast the youthful son
of the empress was engaged in convincing the argumentative
nobles of Normandy of his right of inheritance to the dukedom.
Richard's appearance with his knights had been met with enthusiasm as they were pressed almost immediately into Henry's
service. Richard and the young duke had met well, an instant
bond cemented between them—that was not shared by Eve—
and Richard's faith in Henry was complete from the moment
of that first meeting. She recalled the portentous moment as
they were ushered into his presence, only hours after their
landing. Word of their arrival had preceded them and a generous and flattering escort had been sent to see to their comfort.
Barely giving them time to breathe, they had been taken to the
manor where Henry awaited.

He was a muscular, broad-chested man of Richard's age,
with a leonine head. His pale eyes had burned with a fiery
brightness as they swept over her appreciatively before settling
upon Richard. His power seemed to instantly possess the new
arrivals, and particularly the young Earl of Striguil who knelt
before him, laying his lips in homage upon the ring of the
extended hand.

If only there had been something tangible Eve could have
objected to, perhaps she could have approached Richard with
her concern. But, it was only a feeling she had been left with,
beginning that first evening. How did you explain a feeling?

Henry had paced about the room as he had listened to Richard's recounting, his intense energy disallowing him the comfort of a chair for more than a moment, but he had listened
intently, bellowing with anger upon mention of Stephen's
treachery and pausing as he cast a sympathetic eye upon Richard on learning of Strongbow's death.

He had ordered a sumptuous feast for the weary travelers
and gave them their first unsettling experience of dining with
him. He could never sit still during a meal. He would tear off
a piece of roasted meat and walk about the tables, munching
at the morsel while he paused occasionally to converse with
the various knights and nobles, throwing a comment here and
there before he would return to his chair to grasp another handful. Richard had watched the proceedings with amazement,

finally turning his eyes to Eve, rolling them with barely suppressed humor, causing her to painfully stifle her laughter behind her hand as the duke's eyes had settled upon her at the unfortunate moment.

They both recognized the brilliance of man but, while Richard admired his quick wit and his ability to pierce directly to the heart of a matter, there was something that began to gnaw uncomfortably at Eve. Looking back she could recall exactly when it had begun, the precise moment, coming like a bolt of warning.

She had been listening attentively as he set forth his plans for England's future, recounting the events just passed in Normandy, chortling with the others as he detailed, in riotous fashion, of his recent meeting with the French king, Louis, and his beautiful young wife. He had first met them two years before when he had accompanied his father to France, for the elder to renew his loyalty to the king as Count of Anjou. While in France, both father and son had managed to draw the attention of the beautiful and vivacious Eleanor. All of Europe, it seemed, was alive with talk of the French queen and Eve had listened with fascination as Henry recounted the exploits of the lady and her amazon army that had accompanied Louis on a crusade. His description of their masculine uniforms, with bright red boots, and their order and drill had the room in hysterics as his own eyes welled with tears of laughter. They had sobered as he finished the story grimly, telling of Eleanor's insistence to camp in a narrow, ill-chosen valley, pressuring the king and his generals until they gave in against their better judgment. His disgust with the men in charge was evident as his voice became edged with anger. Seven thousand French soldiers perished that night as Sacren forces struck from the surrounding mountain into the narrow pass, screaming inhuman battle cries of "Allah, Allah!"

In the silence that followed Warwick was heard to mutter a chosen profanity regarding the waste of manhood given to the crusades, bringing Henry's head about with a jerk. Eve glanced at Richard and was alarmed to see that his eyes had turned silver-grey. She could sense the knot that was growing inside of him, knowing that he agreed with Warwick and would defend him if it proved necessary, perhaps destroying their alliance with the duke before it had begun. Striguil's men had not supported the crusades, one point in which Richard had always been in full agreement with his father. They had viewed the crusades as a folly, leaving it for the French to pursue, but had kept silent with the other barons who were in agreement so as not to enlist the pope's wrath at a time when his support was so desperately needed for England.

Henry walked slowly around the end of the table until he stood abreast of Warwick, his expression an unaccustomed blank. "May I assume, Sir Warwick, that you do not agree with His Holiness in his pursuance of the Holy Grail?"

"If the Holy Grail exists, milord," he answered evenly, "it should most certainly be returned to those who value it the most greatly. However, it has not been proven to exist and I for one doubt it. While the French may feel that they can afford to expend their manhood in the quest, England cannot."

A long, tense moment passed as the Duke's eyes narrowed upon the knight and Richard wondered, as did every man present, if they were going to have to fight their way out. The duke reached out and placed a hand on Warwick's shoulder as a hint of a smile drew on the corners of his lips. "On this matter at least, my friend, we are in agreement. Moreover, I fear that the Holy Father may not be pleased when he discovers other plans I have for the Church in England. His priests overstep their bounds and attempt to rule where only the throne should have jurisdiction. When the throne is mine, changes will most certainly be made."

He proceeded to launch into his plans for England, the visions he saw for her, his lands of Normandy, and upon his father's death, Anjou. Richard visibly relaxed and leaned his elbows upon the table, his attentions fixed upon Henry and his dreams. Eve could see his excitement, and feel his enthusiasm, and at that moment something inside of her, a voice of caution, began to stir. She looked at the young duke intently, wondering at her disquiet as she sought to understand her uneasiness. He was clearly brilliant, powerful, a master of men and, without doubt, kingdoms. He would restore England and bring justice to her people. He talked of those justices without self-glory but with honest conviction and belief, his anger raging at the results of Stephen's inept reign. His spies had done their homework well and though he had not been to her shores since a young child, his knowledge of England's plight was greater than their own, his words stunning the new arrivals though they had just recently left her.

"Richard," he bellowed from across the hall, "how many new baronages do you count as added to England's roles during the time that Stephen has been on the throne?"

"Many, my lord," Richard answered grimly. "There is no way to count them."

"You think not, my friend? Let me enlighten you! While the tally is not accurate there is well over a thousand! And when the authority is mine there shall be a census to determine the exact number and, by God's Breath, each and every one shall be dissolved, restoring the lands to their rightful owners!"

"A census, my lord?" Gervase asked innocently. "How can such a thing be done?"

"The same way the Romans accomplished the feat, Gervase! Each one shall be visually accounted for and a record made. But, more than that," he continued over the murmurs of the knights, "the injustices, the slaughter of the people shall cease! More than a full third of the people have been tortured and killed in the past ten years by the lawlessness of Stephen's powers." He startled at the amazement of the knights. "Did you not realize the scope of what has happened? Could you truly not know?"

"Nay, milord," Richard answered, chagrined. "We have seen and heard only what has happened in our own domains, and there we have done our best to halt the slaughter. But you must understand, the barons have been unwilling to travel from their manors for fear that they will be homeless upon their return. Only recently did the barons unite . . ."

"Aye," Henry winked as his gaze settled upon Eve. "I know of it. I hope that the sacrifice you made, milady, was not too great. It was for the good of England."

She blushed as the men joined Henry in his merriment but they sobered as Henry continued. "I grieve for the death of your father, Richard, but I promise you that his death will be revenged. Join with me, give me your oath of fealty, and I will see you to that end."

"You have it, milord," Richard said quietly as his eyes met with Henry's.

Warwick rose, raising his tankard as his voice filled the room. "To my lord Strongbow and to the day when Striguil and all of England shall be avenged and she shall see Henry Plantagenet, Duke of Normandy, upon her throne!"

The knights rose in unison, raising their tankards with a roaring salute, each draining its contents to seal the toast. Eve watched the gesture, then turned her gaze to Richard as he joined with the others. Feeling eyes upon them, she turned to find Henry watching Richard, yet not drinking. Was it modesty that kept him from joining with the others? Somehow she could not believe that modesty was one of his virtues. His grey eyes, so like, yet unlike, Richard's, held an unguarded look of interest, as his lips pursed in careful thought. Though she believed the honesty of his ambitions, how much of what she had seen had been an act? She was not to know it then, the reason for her disquiet, the gnawing uneasiness she felt while she watched Henry, for it would not come to her until much later that Henry reminded her of her father.

The memories of that night invaded her thoughts as she stared from the window, only vaguely seeing the lush Angevin countryside or hearing Sophie's bustling behind her as she cleared away the untouched meal. She smiled unhappily at the irony that struck her. The past year had brought fruition to her most dreaded fear, that Richard would put her aside, but it had not been brought about by another woman, but by Henry. Each time Richard had returned to her, those moments becoming steadily fewer and briefer, he had seemed to change, to draw further away from her. His thoughts he held within himself, sharing little with her and she had learned not to press him as his temper was the quicker to flare with each instance. Even his lovemaking had changed, becoming urgent and demanding, with even a hint of cruelty, as if he wanted to hurt her. Henry demanded complete loyalty from him, and he gave it, leaving little of him for her. She knew that this caused intense conflict within him, hence his anger, and it was fed by restlessness over his forced exile.

Slowly, as she stared sightlessly from the window, her mind began to fix upon something beyond the castle walls, drawing her thoughts back to the present. She squinted against the morning sun as she attempted to focus on what she now recognized as riders approaching the castle. She tensed as her heart began to beat wildly, and she jumped up from the chair and called to Sophie.

"Sophie, it is Richard, and Warwick and Gervase are with him!"

She rushed through the gates as the riders approached and was not disappointed as he left the saddle, meeting her halfway. He swept her into his arms and covered her face with welcomed kisses against her delighted protests. The others pulled up their mounts and sat grinning at the happy pair.

"You make a returning knight feel most welcome, milady."
Richard laughed. "Is this the way to greet all who approach
your gates?"

"Of course!" Eve bantered happily. "If he is so fair as the
one who holds me now! I am simply overwhelmed at the prospect of company!"

"Well, milady, you will then be pleased to learn that the
problem will be remedied for a time."

"Oh, Richard!" she cried. "Will you be staying?"

He pulled her against him as they started walking toward
the gate, leaving Taran to be caught up by Raymond, who had
dismounted and was following behind. "Come, we have not
eaten and you will have to feed us if you will hear the story.
I have much to tell you."

She held back her questions and was content to sit quietly
by, savoring the peace she felt by their presence and the luxury
of letting her gaze settle on their faces. She kept the servants
busy, making sure the knights had filled goblets and heaping
mazers. She plied them with the excellent light wine they had
found to grow in the Angevin vineyards as they amused her
with anecdotes of their travels and life in Henry's masculine
court, while Raymond lamented, with a great rolling of eyes,
over their unavailability of female companionship. Matilda,
after years of estrangement from Henry's father, Geoffrey, had
finally established an almost cloistered existence in Normandy,
finally content to leave future conquests to her son. Henry
welcomed her sore-won noninterference and celebrated his release from her by establishing all-male company at his court,
though Warwick noted, with a hearty chuckle, that he knew
the gesture would be short-lived since the duke had hearty
appetites that were not filled at the banquet table. On that note
he seemed to defer to Richard, who ignored the opening and
finished his meal before settling back into his chair. He picked
up Eve's slender hand and brought it to his lips and caressed
her fingertips.

"I have missed you, love," he murmured. "It is good to be
home."

Her brow raised slightly to his reference of home but she
warmed to his words and the way they were spoken, her heart
feeding on them as though long starved. "I too, milord," she
whispered. "I have missed you greatly. Is it well then, with
the barons?"

"Aye," he smiled. "They have given total allegiance to Henry at last and I do not expect that there will be further trouble."

"Our journey to Bordeaux will see Henry more trouble than all the barons of Normandy could have hoped to!" Gervase chuckled. "I hope that he finds himself equal to his new conquest!"

"You were in Bordeaux?" Eve gasped, wide-eyed. "What were you doing in France?"

"We accompanied Henry on a rather—ah—delicate mission, my love." Richard's eyes danced as he fought a smile.

"And the French let you go, just like that?" she asked incredulously.

"I do not think that they would have, if they had known," he laughed. "But, as it was, we were disguised as very proper French gentlemen."

"But for what purpose?" she breathed, glancing from one to the other.

"For the rather sensitive issue of Henry's marriage, one that Louis hardly approves of."

"Richard, what are you talking about?" she cried impatiently. "Henry's marriage? Who did he marry, when, and why should Louis care who he marries?"

Richard laughed at her tirade of questions and squeezed her hand gently. "Because, my love, his bride is none other than Eleanor."

"The queen of France?" Eve gasped, stunned by the news. "But how could that be?"

"The former queen of France," he corrected. "Louis divorced her two months ago. As you might expect, the news has caused some dismay in the French court, not surprising, considering the lands our Aquitaine duchess brings with her to the marriage bed."

"Oh, Richard! Will this mean war with France?" She was almost afraid to hear the answer.

"We were prepared for it and if Louis' counselors had their way, there would be." He shrugged. "But, it seems that Louis is content to rant and rave with blustering threats but no action. Henry has taken her to the castle at Rouen and that is why we are here. You, my lady, are going to Rouen to be companion to the future queen of England."

"Me?" she choked.

"Aye, love. I know that you have been lonely here and that

I have had little time to spend with you. I hope that Henry's marriage will settle him down for a little while, though I doubt it. In any case, the lady has need of female companionship at this time, so . . ."

"Surely she does not travel alone?" Eve said with surprise.

"Nay—" Richard hesitated as he glanced at the others, a small smile beginning to appear. "But she brought only a few, most trusted servants with her, since the next few months will be spent in seclusion. There is further news that must be guarded for a time."

Eve glanced at Warwick and the others with confusion and it was the older knight who answered her silent question.

"Eleanor is with child, milady."

"She married Henry when she carries Louis' child?" she blurted, not believing what she was hearing.

"Nay, milady," Warwick answered with a cough. "The child is Henry's."

As Eve met the amusement in each man's eyes the truth slowly became clear and her brow arched with the revelation. "Oh," she said in a small voice, then her eyes began to dance with mischief. "'Twould seem that my lord Henry has visited France more than once of late."

The evening ended early and as Richard and Eve ascended the stairs to their chamber they did so silently, feeling strangely awkward in each other's presence. It had been a full six weeks since they had been together last and, each time he had returned over the past year, it had come to seem more and more like a new encounter. As the door closed behind them Richard pulled her into his arms and kissed her hungrily and she found herself responding, the moments of shyness on the stairs melting away with his familiar touch. His hands went to her breasts, caressing them through the silk gown and he moaned softly next to her ear, "Oh, God, I've needed you." His manner became urgent as he swept her into his arms and carried her to the bed, undressing her and himself quickly to lie beside her. His words had warmed her as much as the feel of his hands and his body as it pressed against the length of her own, and her own need was undeniable while she stroked him and held him to her. But as he made love she felt something missing, something withheld that was obtruse, yet vital. It was as if his body was there, making all the right moves, touching her, caressing her, responding to her physical needs and drawing her body to satisfaction, but his mind, or soul, was constrained.

As they lay together afterwards, their bodies sated and wrapped together comfortably, Eve tried to dispel the nagging feelings that overlay her contentment but they clung like leeches, claiming her thoughts. Her mind pushed her to say something to him, to bring it out into the open where it could be tended to, corrected, but she could not bring herself to speak. An obscure feeling of fear held her back, as if to speak would shatter whatever tenuous understanding they had left between them. She felt his arm slip from her, ever so slightly, and from the measure of his breathing she knew that he was asleep. She almost felt relieved, at least the decision had been taken from her, for the moment. I'll face it tomorrow, she thought, or the next day when we've had some time to renew our feelings. Or possibly never. Perhaps whatever was happening between them would correct itself in time; it would pass, never having to be faced.

19

"**O**h, Richard, what if she does not like me?"

Eve pulled at her skirt before the long silvered mirror in their chambers. Her nerves were hewed to a fine edge, her fingers trembled slightly on the amber silk of her gown over the anticipation of meeting Henry's bride, the glamorous and worldly Eleanor of Aquitaine.

Richard came to stand behind her and pulled her gently against him as he admired her reflection in the mirror, his eyes passing ardently over her graceful form. "She will love you, as I do, Eve," he murmured against her hair. A light fragrance filled his nostrils, making him feel slightly heady.

"It is not the same!" she answered irritably, pulling away from him. "She is a woman and will most certainly not regard me in the same way!"

"Henry finds complete favor with you," he shrugged, amused by her fretting. "I am sure that Eleanor will also. You are upsetting yourself for nothing." He grabbed her again and nuzzled his face in her hair as his hands fondled the fullness of her breasts and one hand sought the deep décolletage of her gown.

"Richard, please!" she snapped, squirming away from him. "Stop pawing me!"

"Pawing you?" his brows arched with surprise, then his eyes clouded. "I think you're making a bit more of this than you need to."

She regretted the hastiness of her words but his reference to Henry had piqued her anger. "I didn't mean that, Richard," she said more softly. "I'm just out of sorts. There is something quite distasteful about being presented to someone like a parcel for auction!"

"Then it is best to have done with it." He smiled.

As they paused before the door to Eleanor's chambers, Eve drew in a calming breath and took reassurance from Richard's hand held tightly to her own. He knocked lightly and as they were bade to enter, he pushed the door open. Across the room, seated before a backgammon table, sat a tall and slender woman with the reddest hair Eve had ever seen. She was intent upon the game, and to Eve's surprise she was quite alone, causing Eve to wonder who her partner might be. She held up the palm of her hand to them as she pondered the board and Eve glanced questioningly at Richard, who bent to her ear.

"It is a habit with Henry and Eleanor to have a running game, each trusting the other to play fairly," he whispered.

"Do they?"

He shrugged with a grin and at that moment Eleanor exclaimed with satisfaction and proceeded to move a number of her stones to her table. "There!" She laughed with another glance at the board. "That should cause some dismay!" She dismissed the game and rose, her attention now drawn to them as she crossed the room, her shrewd eyes quickly assessing Eve in a sweeping glance. "Richard, you devil, however, did you capture this lovely creature? She looks much too innocent for the likes of you!"

Eve caught the look of familiarity that passed between Eleanor and Richard, the obvious comfort they felt in each other's presence, and she felt an unwanted moment of jealousy. For a year she had been kept from Richard's side and the fact that this woman had obviously spent part of that time with him, as evidenced by her ease with him, unsettled her. The fact that she recognized the feeling as jealousy only increased her irritation and she found herself glaring at the duchess. But if Eleanor noticed, she did not show it. She waved Richard toward the door. "Leave us now, Richard, I would have her all to myself! Go on, go on, your presence is superfluous!"

As the door closed behind him Eleanor turned to face her and suddenly Eve felt unsure of herself when she looked into green eyes that were so much like her own, but void of any of the doubts that she felt. Eleanor startled her by grasping her arm and gesturing to the chairs near the warming fire. "Now, we shall sit down and come to know each other, without male interference!"

Eleanor stunned her further by waiting on her, pouring spiced wine from a delicate golden decanter on a table between them. This obviously was a woman who did not stand on ceremony except, Eve suspected, when it suited her. She handed one goblet to Eve, then took a sip from her own while Eve waited for her to speak.

"We have been cast together at a time when we may find great comfort in each other, Lady Eve," she said at last, "considering this male world and its many confinements!" She laid a hand on her belly and chuckled at her own jest.

Eve stared at her, then realizing that she was being rude, lowered her gaze to drink from her goblet, wondering what was to come next from this remarkable woman. Eleanor did not give her long to wonder.

"You feel jealous about my familiarity with Richard," she smiled, her blunt words catching Eve off guard with their accuracy. "I do understand. You have been cloistered away for the past year in that horrible little castle while he has been galavanting about Anjou and Normandy." She smiled at Eve's shocked expression. "I know what you have been going through. They have been to war, with all of its dangers, but men thrive on it, do they not? Yet, we are expected to sit patiently, whenever and wherever they deem fit to leave us, and not complain. Which is the hardest, do you think, the action or the waiting?" None of her questions seemed to require an answer as she rushed forward. "And, if they should die? They have passed to whatever, if anything—more adventures I shouldn't wonder, as it is bound to be their luck—while we face the nightmares of loneliness and insufferable indignities."

Eve was totally overwhelmed by Eleanor's frankness. She had never before heard these thoughts echoed by another woman. Hearing them, she was left breathless. "You have felt this way?" she asked timidly.

"Of course!" Eleanor exclaimed. "Every wife of a knight or a soldier has felt so if she is honest with herself! Sometimes I think that the wives or lovers of a villein are truly the fortunate ones, for all of their disadvantages, for they, at least, see the return of their men each night and feel the comfort of their bodies beneath the covers! I, for one, have never accepted it but then I am sure that my story has been recounted to you.

Why should men experience all that life has to offer while it is our lot to await their return? My life is what is important to me since I am the only one that has to live it! I shall not live one of regret and indeed I regret nothing I have done! As for Richard, you have nothing to be jealous about." She waved off Eve's embarrassed protests. "Oh, I would be guarded if I were you. He is an extremely handsome and virile man and there most certainly will be those who will try to take him from you. I must say that he is a favorite of Henry's and mine. The man is enchanting and a good friend, one we depend upon greatly. It is unusual to find such loyalty in the best of times. He is valued, so you must be prepared to share him."

She left Eve breathless. Even in the silence Eve was not sure if she was expected to say something or if the duchess was merely catching her breath. Seeing her dilemma, Eleanor burst out laughing, obviously delighted by Eve's impasse. "Oh, Eve, speak to me! Say what is on your mind! I thought for a moment, when you stood there glaring at me, that I had a glimpse of someone who did not fear me and I daresay I found it refreshing!"

"I do have something I would ask, Your Grace." Eve hesitated.

"Aye, and what is it?"

"When will Henry go to England?"

Eleanor looked dumbstruck for a moment. "By the gods, is that all you would ask me?"

"Aye, Your Grace," Eve pressed emphatically. "Do you think it will be long?"

"But, Eve, it will mean another most dangerous campaign and more months of loneliness! I should think that you would not want to even consider it!"

"Your Grace, I fear more that it will not happen. It is what he dreams about. Until it comes to pass..."

"He will never truly be yours. Is that it?" Eleanor interrupted, her eyes narrowing.

Eve lowered her gaze under the intentness of Eleanor's regard, confused as to the sudden darkening of those piercing green eyes. "Aye, milady, while I dread the thought of his going, I know that it must happen before we can find peace together."

Eleanor sat back in her chair and continued to regard Eve carefully. She liked what she saw. She had grown quite close to Richard in the past months and through his eyes and the obvious love he felt for this young woman, she felt as if she had also grown to know her. She had sensed Richard's need for his young wife, though Henry had been oblivious to it, and in her own need for female companionship she had pressed for Eve's company. And she was quite pleased with her decision. But Eve's words disturbed her and she suddenly found herself caring very much that this young woman not be hurt. She rose from her chair and crossed to the window at the far side of the room, staring from it. The room was left in a protracted length of silence before she turned back and gestured for Eve to join her. Without speaking Eve rose, her expression one of puzzlement, and went to stand beside her, following her gaze from the window. The morning was turning brightly warm, the meadows and hills running in velvet shades, emerging from the early morning fog to blend in a blanket of green and yellow hues from the brilliant touches of scattered yellows, whites, and reds of the wild flowers sprinkling the countryside beyond the castle walls.

"What do you see?" Eleanor asked, finally breaking the silence in a hushed voice, her own expression transfixed upon some secret.

"A beautiful morning, milady."

"Is that all?" Eleanor turned to peer at her.

"Aye, is there more?" Eve answered, perplexed.

Eleanor smiled as she turned back to the window, her eyes filled with a gleaming brightness. She seemed to devour that which lay before her. "Land. People. A world of it. Understand, Eve, look and see what they see! Battles won, accomplishments, power, memories. It is a place of belonging! And, my dear, those drives are never satisfied. If one is achieved, another comes to take its place. Only the peace of age can replace it, if they are lucky, or death. Do you think that one more battle will satisfy Richard? What then—that he will be content to settle down and satisfy himself with being your husband?"

Eve glanced up with alarm as she began to understand Eleanor's meaning. "Are you saying that he will never be content unless he is at war? Is there no time to hope for when he will be happy with me?"

Eleanor turned and leaned back against the sill with a smile of tender understanding. "Nay, Eve, not necessarily war. But you must realize that you will never completely have him. There will always be a part, a large part, of him that will be out there. If you cannot accept that you will forever be in conflict, with him and with yourself."

"But—you just said that you cannot accept being left alone."

"Ahhh, you misunderstood me. I can well accept a man's needs and desires. I can accept that what he gains out there can only enrich our relationship. But, I also understand and accept my own needs, and they do not include whiling away my hours awaiting his return."

Eleanor saw Eve's brows draw together in thought and she led the conversation on to other matters, sensing that the subject was best left for the moment. She knew, wisely, that it was a lot to digest all at once, so they spent the better part of the morning sitting on the wide sill in the now warm sun, chatting happily on lighter subjects. Until the conversation invariably turned to Louis. Eleanor's face darkened at the mention of his name but she did not avoid it.

"Louis was a weakling and my strengths threatened him." She shrugged. "I was glad to be rid of him and his whining and pouting when he could not have his way. It is impossible for a strong woman to be happy with such a man, Eve, and he will be far happier with that vapid girl he has taken for a bride." For an instant Eve thought that Eleanor's expression had become wistful but it passed quickly as she turned to look from the window. Eve wondered if the gesture was more to conceal a hidden sorrow than sudden interest in the view.

"Actually, Eve, I would have been happier had I not needed to remarry." Her voice seemed to hold an unaccustomed tone of defeat. "A lover, when I needed to satisfy my desires and pleasures, the company of men when I wanted it, would have been the better lot."

"Then why did you remarry? You are a titled, wealthy woman. Surely you could have made life as you wished."

"Oh, Eve, you are innocent, aren't you?" Eleanor laughed. "Aye, Aquitaine is rich and vast! How long do you think I would have been allowed to hold it for my own? Oh, I chose Henry, and do not doubt it, and he was more than anxious to add my lands to his own. But, had I not, there were others who would have chosen me!"

"Against your will?"

"Securely bound and dragged to the altar with a priest well paid to secure the deed! But, I count myself fortunate! Henry is young, handsome and virile and pleases me much! And, I have the consolation that we both approached the marriage bed willingly, a better beginning to a marriage, is it not?"

Eve was disturbed to hear Eleanor's words echo Richard's threats of so long ago, events of that time touching a painful spot within her she had thought forgotten. But she could not imagine now being wed to a man she did not love, and in such a manner! Even in their worst moments of past anger and distrust, the love was there, well concealed though it was. She found it strange that her own situation was so much better than this beautiful and powerful woman. Or was it?

Her first morning with Eleanor ended soon after, when the duchess left for other duties. As she walked slowly down the long corridor toward her bedchamber, Eve mused on the strange morning and the things Eleanor had said. She passed an open window and glanced out into the courtyard below and halted as she spied Richard and Warwick standing by their mounts, conversing with Henry. She paused, leaning out over the sill, and watched him as her mind turned with raging questions. As she felt herself stir at the sight of him she wondered if it would always be so. His handsome face, tanned by the endless hours in the sun, made his pale eyes almost startling transparent by comparison. His ever-tousled hair, streaked by the same sun, hung slightly on his forehead and he pushed it back absent-mindedly as he concentrated on Henry's words. Her eyes passed leisurely over the broadness of his shoulders and his muscular arms, which she could almost feel about her, and a raw, aching desire grew in her. She smiled at that—that the mere sight of him could arouse such feelings in her. At that moment he laughed at some comment from Henry and for an instant his face lost the tenseness she had become accustomed to seeing, his demeanor changing to an easygoing lightness she had almost forgotten. It struck her just how much he had changed since coming to Normandy, particularly in his attitude toward their relationship, and with it came a disturbing vision of the future.

A sound from behind her startled her from her thoughts and her heart skipped a beat as she whirled about to find a tall, dark-haired knight standing behind her.

"Forgive me, milady, I did not mean to frighten you," he said smoothly. "It was only my intention to speak with you."

She recognized him to be a knight to Henry, Sir Gail deMathiew, for she had been introduced to him briefly on their first night in Normandy. "There is no need to apologize, Sir Gail." She sought to step past him but he neatly blocked her exit and flashed a quick smile.

"Do not be in such a hurry to leave. I have been wanting to speak with you since the moment of our meeting. I understand that you have been brought to Rouen to keep company with Eleanor. Have you met her yet?"

"Aye, I have just had that pleasure. Now, if you will forgive me . . ."

He put out an arm and leaned against the wall as she would have passed. "Perhaps you would like to walk in the gardens with me, milady, it is a beautiful day and . . ." He saw her glance from the window and he followed her gaze to the courtyard and smiled. "Ah, your husband. Do not worry on that source, milady, he is well occupied with Henry and will be for some time. Now, about that walk . . ."

She gaped at him, astounded by his attention, and she could only sputter. "I—I assure you, Sir Gail, that my husband's proximity has nothing to do with it! I have no desire to take a walk with you, or anything else! Now, will you let me pass?"

"You need not be coy with me, Lady Eve. I know that it is customary of a lady to feign protest but I assure you that it is not necessary. A young and most beautiful wife, left to endless hours without companionship is apt to dream. But it should not be, you should live in reality and the present. However, I do understand and shall be patient until you feel more at ease with me."

"Sir Gail!" she gasped. "I obviously did not make my point! There will never be a time, however long we may be of acquaintance, that you will have license to say such to me! Now let me pass!"

She hurried past him, her composure shattered by his boldness, though she fervently hoped that he had not seen how much! It took all of her effort to walk down the long hall with dignity she did not feel as she fought the impulse not to look back to see if he followed. As she reached her bedchamber door she flew inside and closed it quickly behind her, then leaned against it as she sought to calm the rapid beating of her heart. "My Lord," she muttered out loud. Whatever had possessed him to speak to her so boldly? It had seemed almost like he had been confident of his pursuit! And then it hit her, the truth that came swiftly in its ugliness to leave her feeling sullied and unclean. He had thought her to be approachable— and why not? He was aware of Richard's long absences, he had said as much, and something in his tone had implied that Richard had preferred it so. The realization shook the foundations of any security she had known in her marriage and she felt open and vulnerable. Damn him, how could he do this to her? Did he care so little? She took a deep breath and forced herself from the door just as she tried to force the thoughts from her mind. It couldn't be, she was reading too much into an innocent encounter! She had been alone too much with her own imagination and now it was getting the best of her! But, somehow it continued to lurk at the back of her mind like an invading, menacing demon.

She went about the bedchamber to set it to rights, placing away her garments that had been strewn about the room in the morning tirade over selecting the right gown to wear for her audience with Eleanor. She was completing the task when Richard came into the room and she breathed a tired sigh as he removed his hauberk and mail and tossed them carelessly down.

He collapsed into a chair and stretched his long limbs, motioning for her to come and sit with him. "How was it with Eleanor? As bad as you feared?" His mouth twitched with a smile. "I think she likes you."

"Aye, apparently she did," she returned listlessly. "I think the lady has need of another woman for company. She was certainly frank!"

"That is Eleanor," he chuckled. "She says what is on her mind. But do not underestimate her—she has great power, perhaps that is why she does not feel that her thoughts need to be guarded. Though often, I think, Henry wishes she would hold her tongue—these rafters tremble when those two are in disagreement, though he loves her passionately. Speaking of that, come here, wench. I've been in the saddle too long this day and I have need of a softer ride."

She stared at him silently, noting his confidence, his almost lackadaisical attitude, his remiss awareness to their problems. And the demon escaped. "Is that all that I am to you, Richard?" she snapped venomously. "An object to ease your comforts and provide you release when you would will it?"

"What?" His mouth dropped ajar and he looked at her with puzzlement.

"You stride in here and plop yourself into a chair, issuing your demands without a word as to my feelings!"

"Eve, what are you talking about?" he said sharply. "I inquired how it went with Eleanor."

"And now on to other matters, is that it?" she cried.

"Enough, Eve," he growled warningly. "If there is something you would know of me, ask it. But cease this shrewish prattle, for I'll have none of it!"

A retort failed her and she faced him calmly while inside she was still raging. "Who is Sir Gail?"

"Who?"

"Sir Gail," she repeated. "Who is he?"

He considered her suspiciously. "Why should you ask? He is no one you need to know."

"I have no desire to know him," she said icily, "but he spoke to me today."

"Did he bother you?" his face darkened.

"Nay," she lied. "But I sensed ill of the man and he made me extremely uncomfortable. I just wanted to know about him."

"Your instincts were good. You would do well to stay away from him," he answered gruffly. "He is the son of a lesser French marquis who obviously thought his fortune could be made in Henry's service."

"Why do you dislike him?"

"Because you cannot trust the man. He is ambitious without loyalty, even to Henry. He is never present when the fighting is at its fiercest yet he manages to be at the front when the battle is won and the accolades are given. I do not trust his kind."

As he spoke, though she listened, she had begun to pick up his discarded things. He leaned his chin on his hands and watched her as she moved about, wondering as to her sudden show of temper. He knew that he had been neglecting her. The knowledge had been gnawing at him for a long time in a nagging guilt until, on the few occasions he had found time to return to her, he had arrived foul of temper and expecting to face her raving accusations over his absence. But she never complained, not once, which had driven the guilts even deeper. The ugly thought struck him—had her calm understanding over his absences been due to another source? Was there another? He glanced up at her sharply where she was bent over his wardrobe. Nay, he reasoned, she detested such duplicity. Indeed, it had been the cause of their first quarrel. If she sought another he would be the first to know. The idea brought a wry smile. In such an event her lover would not live out the hour. But why then the anger?

"What happened today, Eve?"

She straightened up from refolding his garments and turned

to look at him as she smoothed out one of his tunics. "What do you mean?"

The corners of his mouth began to turn up. "It was not my loving bride that met me when I returned. Something must have happened to annoy you."

It was the wrong choice of words. She had thought herself calm but as she saw the amused smile he wore, something snapped. "Is that what you think of my problems, as some mere trifle?"

His humor disappeared and he glared at her. "Eve, I do not wish to fight with you. Can you not tell me what is bothering you without these accusations?"

"And why must I tell you how I feel?" she cried. "Why, after all of this time, do you not know? But then, how could you, counting for the time you choose to spend with me! Or is it that you have found another?"

Letting out a roar he leapt from his chair and strode across to her, snatched the garment from her hands and flung it to the bed, then grasped her shoulders and shook her. "By the blood of the gods, what is the matter with you?"

"Me?" she shrieked, flinging herself from him. "Why can you not face what you have done?"

"Face what?" he flung back at her, "Do you think that I enjoy having you act like a fish-wife?"

"A fish-wi—" Her mouth snapped shut and she spun about, determinded to flee his insults, but he grasped her arm and whirled her back to him.

"Nay, you wanted to talk, now let's have it!"

"What is there to say that you will listen to, Richard?" she cried, now almost on the verge of tears. "I was wrong not to speak of it with you before and to hold it inside of me these past months until I cannot speak except with anger! But what will you hear now except the echoes of your own guilt?"

He wanted to strike her, and she saw it in his eyes, but she held her ground, glaring up at him defiantly while trying to ignore the pain in her arm where his fingers bit into it. She watched the muscle in his jaw twitch as he fought to gain control of his emotions, his eyes burning into her in cold fury. Suddenly, he released his grip, almost causing her to fall backwards, and spun away from her, running his fingers through his hair.

"Dear God, but you try me, woman!" he said hoarsely when he was again master of himself, though barely so. "Eve, I do not know how to help you, or even myself! Neither of us is here by choice and what can I offer you except a life of exile with only a slim hope of something better? Do you think that I never consider the life I have given you, that I am not aware of your loneliness? What would you have me tell Henry, that I cannot see him into battle because I must stay with the women?"

"Ohhh, aye, your precious Henry!" she snapped, too angry to hear his words or his plea. Before she could stop herself the thoughts she had guarded so long came tumbling out. "How can you follow him so blindly? Can you not see his ambitions, his greed?"

"Ambition is not a fault!" he raged. "If you feel so you will have to include me in your criticism, or do you?"

"You only seek to restore what is yours! Or so I thought! Henry sees himself as emperor with the world as his domain! No one will stand in his way and he is using you, can you not see that?"

"No more than I am using him, Eve. But I will not discuss this with you!"

"Why must you shut me out so completely? Have you married some dull wit who has no mind to see into your problems? Who cares more for you? Why must my thoughts be rejected out of hand merely because I am a woman?"

"I have not done that!" he growled, turning back on her.

"Have you not? It is as if you blame me for losing Chepstow! As if every time you look upon me you are reminded of your loss!"

His face turned blood-red and for an instant she knew fear but he strode past her to the door and snatched his scabbard from the hook. "By all that is holy," he shouted, "I have had enough!"

The door slammed behind him, nearly wrenched from its hinges, leaving her standing in the deathly silence that followed.

The great domed hall of Rouen, built by Henry's namesake and grandfather, loomed in high arching spires over the immense round room, sided all around in tall glazed windows. Henry sat alone at a table in the center, bent over charts and maps. He was so engrossed that he was unaware of Richard until he was at his side.

"Here are the tallies of the weapons-room," Richard said,

tossing them on the end of the table.

"Excellent," Henry grunted, his attention still fixed on the charts. "I could use your help with these maps. They make no sense at all! I swear that the dunce who drew them has never set foot on English shores! See if you can decipher them."

Richard leaned over the maps and they spent the better part of the morning redrawing and shifting the positions on the charts. Eleanor had joined them soon after they began and sat listening to their deliberations as she worked a needle but her attention was particularly fixed on Richard. When they had finished Richard leaned back in his chair and stretched, unaware of the looks that passed between Henry and his wife.

"Tell me, Richard," Henry said suddenly, "have I been too demanding upon your time?"

"Nay, milord," Richard frowned. "Have you found my work wanting?"

"Not at all," Henry assured him, "but you have seemed rather preoccupied of late."

"You should know the answer to that, milord," Eleanor grunted as she shifted in her chair to seek comfort from her growing belly. "While there is no other in your service who seeks with more earnestness to restore England to your line, even Richard has other matters important to his life."

"Aye, and what would such matters be?" Henry's brow arched in mock innocence. "I cannot imagine such that would interfere with the events of history, endeavoring as we are to rewrite it!"

"It is of a personal nature, milord," Richard said grimly.

"Indeed?" Henry snorted, "And for this you would bring the course of history to a halt?"

"My lord jests," Eleanor laughed, placing a hand on her belly. "It is obvious that even the great duke finds time for other matters! Too often," she said, glancing at Richard, "we forget what is truly important."

"Insensitive am I?" Henry chortled. "Well, perhaps I have overworked you! Richard, I have just received a number of Norway falcons and tomorrow we shall take the entire day to try their wings!"

"Good lord!" Eleanor laughed. "He's gone daft!" She rose from her chair heavily and picked up her needlework. "Well, milords, now that you have managed to take your minds from work I shall leave you to discuss whatever it is that men do." As she turned to leave her expression became serious and she exchanged a portentous glance with Henry that was not missed by Richard.

"Not entirely subtle," Richard said, turning his gaze to Henry after Eleanor had left.

"It was rather obvious, wasn't it?" Henry chuckled. But his demeanor became more serious as he regarded Richard carefully. "Richard, you know that I am not one to listen to gossip except when it serves me. A certain matter has come to light that I find disturbing. I understand that you have taken separate quarters from your wife." He saw Richard's face tense but he did not respond. "Is it true?"

"Aye, your sources are correct," Richard answered.

"Would you care to talk about it?"

"Nay, milord, I would not."

Henry smirked unhappily but his eyes became determined. "Well, I do. Surely things have not reached an unmendable impasse!"

"Matters are rather strained between us, milord. I cannot honestly say what will come of it." He gritted, wanting to change the subject.

"Do you still love her?" Henry pressed bluntly.

Richard frowned but he hesitated only for a moment. "Aye. Very much."

"Then there is no problem!" Henry brightened. "Take her in hand!"

"Obviously you have never lived with an Irish temper." Richard grimaced.

"You are speaking to the man who lives with Eleanor of Aquitaine!" Henry laughed. He saw Richard's mouth work until it gave into a grin. "Ah, that is better. I was beginning to think that this was really serious!"

"It is."

"My friend, it may seem so but I am certain you will find a way." He paused for effect and a slight edge worked its way into his voice. "I would be most unhappy if this matter were not settled amiably. I am quite concerned about both of you, as is Eleanor. Also, we have enough problems ahead of us without straining a budding relationship with connections in Ireland which your marriage has brought. I expect you to work this out."

Though it existed for only a moment, Henry caught the hardness that took Richard's eyes and its meaning did not escape him. He smoothly moved the conversation to other matters briefly, then dismissed him, watching his departing back with thoughtful appraisal. It was then that Eleanor returned.

"For all of his loyalty, the man will not be easily controlled," he mused to his wife. "Damn, doesn't he realize the importance of an alliance with Ireland?"

"An alliance, milord?" Eleanor asked quietly.

Henry ignored the comment as he continued to stare at the empty doorway. "Well," he said grimly, "there is more than one way to accomplish a goal." His eyes narrowed, and his tone had been one of conviction, with certain knowledge born to one who was used to having his way. He knew, without doubt, that the opportunity would present itself. He had only to wait.

20

Summer prevailed as the sun warmed the earth; tender shoots uncurled their heads to push into the sunlight, blossoming into joyful colors against the reaching mantle of grasses, wild oats, and rye; and nature repeated its grand design for permanence, and assurance that life was a continuing, ongoing chain which could be denied only by man, too occupied, or morose, to observe.

Of all watchers, Eve was the least. Her being remained ensnared into winter's bent, her spirit suspended in its glacial chill. Never had she felt so alone, so isolated, her separation from Richard plunging her into a despondency void of her usual vibrant determination for life. In the week he had been gone she kept to herself, seeing no one but Sophie and occasionally Eleanor when the duchess sent for her. Sophie, as always, had tried to reason with her, to convince her to find Richard and settle the differences between them. "He knows where I am," Eve said tightly. "After all, he is the one who chose to leave." But, at least she had gained her attention as Eve laid down her sewing and sighed, "He has changed, Sophie."

"Nay, lass," the Scotswoman had said softly, "he is the same man. Life has not treated him kindly since Strongbow's death and he still blames himself for what happened. And now, for the first time, he has little control over his life. I spoke with him this morning, lass, and I know that he regrets what has happened between you. He asked about you and the look he gave me was one of love and concern, not anger."

"Did he?" Eve looked wistful. "Then why does he keep himself from me?"

"I think that he fears that until he can resolve his own conflicts he will only add to yours. Give him time. Soon he will be the same man you knew, but even stronger and more self-assured."

"If I had not handled things so badly I would be with him now to support him through this time," Eve said sorrowfully.

"Then seek him out, Eve. Let him know how you feel."

To Sophie's shrewd and emphatic eye there was a glimmer of hope, however slight, in Eve's wavering resistance. A few more days, she had thought, a little more time to salve the wounds... And it might have happened but for Eleanor's appearance.

Eleanor astonished them by rapping lightly on the door, then sweeping in before either could answer, bringing both women to their feet. "Your Grace!" Eve blurted with surprise. Eleanor nodded, her expression grim, as she fixed her attention upon Sophie.

"I would have a word with your mistress."

Sophie cast a doubtful glance at Eve but, as she had no choice but to obey, she gathered up her sewing and departed the room.

"Please, sit down," Eleanor said as the door closed and she took Sophie's chair for herself. She smoothed out her gown and glanced about the room, noting that Richard's things were absent, and regarded Eve, who was waiting with a perplexed look, with careful thought. "I see that you still have not mended your rift with Richard."

"Nay, Your Grace, I fear that we have not."

"Have you seen him, spoken with him?"

"Nay, Your Grace."

Eleanor drummed her fingers on the arm of the chair and her face seemed to be working on some problem. "Eve, I have come with news for you," she sighed suddenly. "Word has come to us... and Henry and I felt it advisable that I should tell you alone. There is no way to say what I must and not cause you pain; therefore, I will say it quickly. Eve, Stephen has taken his final revenge upon Richard. His cousin Gilbert is dead and Stephen has confiscated Richard's lands, giving them, along with Hertford, to a deClare cousin, Rodger."

Eve's face drained of color. Oh God, her mind screamed, how much more was he expected to take? "What of Lady Isabel?" she breathed, terrified to hear the answer.

"Lady deClare? No harm has come to her. Stephen has

allowed her to remain at Chepstow and Rodger sees to her comfort, or so we are led to understand."

"Generous of him," she gritted bitterly, though she was washed with relief that Isabel was safe. "Does—has Richard been told?" she asked, her eyes filling with tears.

"Henry has just told him."

"I must go to him!" she sniffed, trying not to cry as she rose from her chair, but Eleanor stopped her.

"Eve, wait. I fear that there is more."

"What else could there be?" Eve choked with disbelief, dropping back in her chair. "There is nothing left!"

"But I fear there is." She paused as she looked at Eve regretfully, then plunged forward. "We have received a message, a papal decree signed by the Holy Father. It was issued on the bequest of Stephen, we have no doubt, but nonetheless issued by the Church and thus it cannot be ignored, however much we may wish to. Moreover, the decree has been received by your father, and accepted, so I fear that it is final. Eve— the pope has seen fit to annul your marriage to Richard."

It came like a broadside and for an interminable moment she could not breathe. Her temples began to pound and as the room began to spin she had to grasp the arms of her chair to keep from falling. Her brain screamed with denial, and her body went numb, the only feeling left being the searing pain that wrenched at her chest and into her throat. "Oh, sweet Jesus, nay!" she cried, and buried her head into her hands as she gave in to deep, wracking sobs that tore at her entire body. Eleanor came to her side, sitting on the arm of the chair. She took Eve into her arms and stroked her hair, murmuring to her softly until the agony dulled and the tears began to spend themselves. Slowly, aware of Eleanor's arms about her, Eve drew in her breath deeply and the room began to settle again and she straightened to look up at Eleanor blankly. As the dizziness passed, something deep within her began to harden, forming like a spreading wall of hatred that seemed to reach every part of her body.

"Why did he do this?" she whispered in almost a hiss.

"Stephen?" Eleanor asked, taking the chair across from her.

"Nay!" Eve shot at her. "My father! How could he have sided with Stephen against me? How could he do this?"

"It seems obvious, Eve," Eleanor shrugged. "Either on his own, or by Stephen's encouragement, he believes that your marriage to Richard was wasted. By annulling it he frees you for a more suitable match."

"I will not accept it! I cannot!"

"Eve, it is not something that can be ignored."

"I will write to him, contest it! He must relent!" Eve said wildly.

"Ah, but you overlook how easy it is to ignore such a request. A message, tossed aside, is as never written. However..."

Eve's head jerked up at the tone in Eleanor's voice. Her head was tossing crazily between unreality and thoughts of what Richard must be feeling, but something about Eleanor's manner caught her attention. "What—what is it?"

Eleanor shrugged again. "It was just an idea that occurred to me. Nay, it is too much..."

"What is it?" Eve pressed, her voice rising.

"Well—it would seem to me that your only hope is to confront him, face to face, to plead your cause."

"Return home?" Eve gasped, stupefied. She could not handle it, it was too much to think about all at once. All she wanted was Richard. "I must go to Richard," she breathed. "He will know what to do..."

"Eve, do you think that is wise?" Eleanor asked quietly. She paused as the question registered in Eve's face. "Must I remind you of what has happened between you? Now, with his further losses, and this matter added to it, how can you expect him to react? What would you have him say to you? I know that you want to be with him now, to work this out together, and so you should. But what can he do? Indeed, I see no hope for it until Henry has the throne, and has, therefore, the authority to intercede with Pope Adrian. Unless your father relents. Can Richard help you with this? With everything that has happened to him, would you place the burden of this decision on him? Would you ask him to let you go?"

Eve stared at Eleanor as her mind tumbled with confusion. What was Eleanor suggesting, that she leave without even seeing Richard? Now, when he must be going through such pain? But, his self-doubt had built a wall between them. How could she expect these additional burdens not to heighten it? She knew that he still loved her, but could this be the final stroke, the one that would sever even that?

"How?" she heard herself whisper, though her mind was

still full of doubt. "How could I manage it?"

"You would need someone to escort you, someone we could trust." Eleanor appeared to ponder the question for some moments, then she brightened. "Sir Gail!" she exclaimed. "Of course, he is the very one!"

"Gail!" Eve shuddered. "I could never . . ."

"But of course! Eve, you certainly could not ask anyone in Richard's service, as close as you are to them! They would go to him in a moment! Gail is ambitious, he would do anything for money. And," she added with a smirk, "I am certain that I can convince him to treat you honorably." She watched Eve work with the problem, then added another thought, "It must be kept secret from everyone, Eve. I will not even tell Henry. Men have a tendency to stick together, you know. And, there is one more thing. You must not tell Sophie of this."

"Sophie?" Eve gaped. "I trust her completely!"

"Of course, but, Eve, she has been with Richard for a long time," she warned. "You told me yourself of her history. There is no doubt that she would go to Richard."

Long after Eleanor had left, Eve sat curled up in the chair. The sun began to set, casting the room in a dusky pale, the only other light being from the fire on the hearth, which lent a soft glow to the walls and furniture. She ignored the growing darkness as she sat with her arms folded protectively about her knees, her mind raging with what was happening to her and Richard's life.

They were no longer married. It was as if it had never been. A few words on a piece of paper, by someone she had never met, and it had been destroyed. She was fully prepared to defy them all and live in sin with Richard, if necessary. But, even as she considered it, she dismissed the possibility. His lands and title were gone, but somehow she felt that he would regain them. But what would be left for them? What of his pride, his honor? Would she become a constant reminder of what he had lost? This had already become a threat to them. And what if a child came? A—a bastard. He would know that if something happened to him before his titles were regained the child would not be protected . . . Nay, she knew that, no matter what other dreams he might realize, he could never live without his honor, and she could not be the source of destroying it.

How she longed to see him, to go to him right at his moment! What was he thinking, feeling? How she wanted to feel his arms about her! But she knew that if she did, she would be lost. What were her alternatives? To stay, possibly to watch their love die. After all, who knew how long it would be, if ever, before Henry claimed England? To go? Their separation had been intolerable, and now she was considering leaving Normandy? And she knew that it was almost certain that if Dermot would not relent he would never allow her to return. Could she take such a risk? "Oh, sweet Jesus," she whispered in prayer. "What is the answer?"

Sophie found her sitting in the darkened room, staring into the fire, and it was all that the woman could do not to burst into tears as she mutely cursed Dermot and Stephen. She had heard about the news moments after leaving the room as Rouen was abuzz with it. As Eleanor was with Eve, Sophie had sought Richard out, finding him in his chambers where he had withdrawn after speaking to Henry. He had been in control but his face was etched with new lines of grief and sadness as he mourned for Gilbert and the others who had lost their lives, and they sat together, sharing their mutual grief. "Does Eve know?" he had asked, finally. When she told him that Eleanor was with her, he had taken the news quietly. "I never thought to bring her such unhappiness, Sophie," he had said sadly. She dismissed the idea. "You have also brought her joy," she reminded him, "and she loves you very much. Nothing has changed that. Give her the night to accept the news, then go to her. You will find a way together, I know it." But he had said nothing more and after a time she left him to return to Eve.

As she helped Eve to prepare for bed, Sophie urged her to try to sleep, though she suspected that she would see little of it. "A new day tomorrow, lass, new beginnings," she said with little conviction.

But Eve did sleep, falling into a druglike slumber as if other forces would have their way with her against her will. Images of Eleanor and Henry passed through her dreams, their faces contorted and laughing. She found herself bound in a chair in a long, narrow room and Eleanor and Henry were standing at one end watching her, whispering conspiratorially, then Henry nodded to someone just out of sight. She felt terror build within her as Gail appeared and he began to walk slowly toward her, his face twisted into a smile as he approached. She struggled against her bonds to no avail as he came to stand before her and reached out to touch her face. She screamed and was suddenly gone from the room.

She was standing in an open field in the midst of a fierce

battle. The combatants were faceless and they seemed to be
unaware of her presence as they fought savagely. Then Gerda
appeared before her. The old nursemaid turned to walk away
through the mayhem but paused and motioned for her to follow.
She led her through the fray to the edge of the field and turned
back to her. To Eve's shock she held a sword in her hand. She
smiled and held out the blade to Eve, urging her to take it.

Over Gerda's shoulder she saw Richard standing at the edge
of the meadow, a sword in his hand and the blade bloodied.
Gerda followed her gaze and when she turned back her face
was filled with a terrible sadness but she smiled. "Take it,
lamb, you must take it." Compelled, Eve stepped forward and
took the sword as she looked up at Gerda questioningly. "What
shall I do with it, Gerda?"

"You will know what to do with it." Gerda raised her hand
and pointed to a place behind Eve. She turned slowly and found
Henry standing behind her, his own blade drawn as if to strike.
Impulsively, Eve grasped the hilt with both hands, though the
weapon seemed to have no weight, and swung it at the threatening figure. It seemed to cut through him without striking,
but he crumbled at her feet. She stood, transfixed, staring down
at Henry's face, then she turned back. Gerda and Richard were
gone and the field was empty. She looked back at the fallen
duke, and screamed. The face staring up through lifeless eyes
belonged to her father.

She awoke, sitting up in bed, and her body was cold with
sweat. She was trembling and she could feel her heart beating
with a terrifying pounding. She knew it had only been a dream
but she could not keep herself from shaking. She could still
hear Gerda's voice and it was as if she could feel her presence,
even now, fully awake. Shaken, she peered about the darkened
room. The fire had died out completely, and she began to shiver
from the cold. She slid from the bed, pulled a wrap about her,
crossed to the hearth and bent to rebuild the fire. She knew
that there would be no more sleep and she resigned herself to
awaiting the dawn in a chair before the fire. As the flames
caught to the kindling she added some small pieces of wood
and settled into the chair, pulling her wrap about her and staring
into the leaping flames.

It was a dream, nothing more, she reflected, trying to convince herself. As she stared, the fire began to trap her interest
and her eyes seemed to penetrate the flames. Slowly, unreally,

she saw the image of Donnell's face begin to appear. His expression was fixed with sadness and she sensed a grief emanating from him as she felt herself pulled to thoughts of home. His image began to disappear but as it did he appeared to turn and look directly at her, his blue eyes pleading with her, before he disappeared completely. Unnerved, she closed her eyes and opened them again but there was now only the dancing flames and the sound of dry, crackling wood. To her surprise, a sudden peace descended over her, not of contentment but one of resolution. She knew that she had to return to Erin. No matter how slim the chance, their only hope lay in the possibility that she could convince Dermot to relent. That could only be accomplished if she confronted him with it. And, there was something else that pulled at her, a feeling, nothing more, but it was so strong that she could not deny, or resist it.

She paused at the end of the hallway and swallowed hard, wondering if she could go through with it. The remembrance of his burning eyes and his crude advances made her shudder, but what choice did she have? There was no one else, to that she had to agree with Eleanor, and the duchess had promised that the knight could be bought to silence.

She found him in the hall where he sat drinking with his cousin and she could not help to reflect, with disgust, that he tarried while others worked. She pushed back her revulsion and stopped a passing servant, requesting him to inform Sir Gail that she wished to speak with him.

She watched apprehensively as the man bent to Gail's ear and she tensed as she saw the pleased expression that crept over his face. She sat down on a window seat at the far end of the hall, afraid that her trembling legs would no longer support her. As he rose and walked toward her, his step unpleasantly eager, she drew in her breath and prayed silently that her courage would not fail her.

"Milady, I have awaited this moment with great anticipation," he purred smoothly as he bent over her hand. "Of course, I have heard of the papal decree, but do not sorrow as I shall soon help you to forget."

"That is not why I have asked to speak with you!" she snapped, irritated by his self-confidence. She bit off her anger and forced herself to appear calmer than she felt. "Please, sit with me for a moment. There is something I would ask of you, something of the greatest importance that may benefit you as well." He looked at her with interest but said nothing as he sat beside her. While it struck her odd that he did not show more surprise, she pressed on, "Sir Gail, I have a proposition to make to you. A business proposition," she added with emphasis.

"A business proposition?" he parroted with amusement. "And what business would you have with me? I rather think that one of a more personal nature would please us better."

"Do you wish to hear what I have to say or shall we quit the matter now?" she flared.

"You have my full attention," he grinned, his brown eyes dancing.

She paused for a moment, then plunged into it with a deep sigh. "I wish to return to Erin. To do so I will need an escort, one that can assure my departure from here and my safe delivery to Leinster. Can you do this?"

"You are serious, aren't you?" His dark eyes had continued to sparkle with humor as she spoke. "You want me to secrete you out of Normandy, from under the nose of your hus—ah—from under Richard's nose, and across the breadth of England . . ."

"I assure you, Sir Gail, I am deadly serious," she interjected. "I realize what I am asking but I assure you that you will be well recompensed for your efforts."

"I am sure that I will be." He murmured as his eyes moved slowly over her, coming to rest on her breasts, where they lingered for a moment. Reading his thoughts, she glared at him.

"That is the one thing you will never have," she said bluntly. "If you return me to Erin safely, my father will pay you handsomely. But, if you harm me, in any way, I assure you that he will reward you in kind."

"What would keep me from, ah, having my pleasure in you then, shall we say, losing you along the journey? In other words, why this sudden trust, milady?"

"What would be your purpose, Sir Gail? For then you would receive nothing for your efforts except a passing, momentary pleasure, which I reason is not enough for you."

He looked at her intently and she wondered, uncomfortably, why there was humor in his eyes though his face was solemn. Suddenly he stood up and she rose to face him as he turned to her, "I will need time to consider this, milady."

"I do not have much time. If we are to go, I wish to leave tonight."

"If we are to go," he answered with a smile, "I will come to you tonight."

She turned and walked from the room and his eyes followed her, then he walked slowly back to his chair, wearing an extremely satisfied expression. Taking his chair, he leaned his chin on his hands and rubbed his lips in thought.

"Well, cousin," D'Arcy said, "I congratulate you. It did not take the lady long to seek your company. I envy you, Gail. She looks like as tasty a bit as I've seen."

Gail reached over and took up his tankard, pulling a long draught before he leaned back in his chair. "She wants me to take her to Ireland."

D'Arcy nearly choked on his ale and spun to Gail in astonishment. "Ireland? You cannot be serious!"

Gail pursed his lips in careful thought as he stared at his tankard and turned it slowly in his fingers. "Quite the contrary, cousin. I am considering it quite seriously. In fact, the matter has been decided."

"Gail, you've gone mad!" D'Arcy snorted as he lifted his tankard to his lips. "There is no way you could see her out of Normandy, much less across England without being caught. Besides, Richard would be on your trail before you were barely away from Rouen."

"Aye," Gail said softly. "It will please me to bring that bastard down a peg."

"I repeat, you are mad." D'Arcy smirked. "You'll loose your head as the outcome."

"You are quite correct, dear cousin," Gail answered coolly, "if I were to attempt it alone. Fortunately, that is not the case."

"What are you talking about?"

"Nothing at all. Now, if you will excuse me, there is someone I must see."

He left D'Arcy staring quizzically after his departing back and made his way down the long hallway to the council chambers. He paused before the door for only an instant before he knocked.

"Come in!" came the deep reply. Gail smiled to himself, pushed the door open and closed it quickly behind him.

* * *

Eve sent Sophie to bed early. It had been difficult to move through the day as if nothing was happening, under Sophie's watchful eye, but it would not do for the Scotswoman to be there if Gail came with his answer. Sophie! How would she be able to get along without her? She wished that she could take Sophie with her but she knew better. If she even suspected what Eve was planning she was certain to rush to Richard with the news in an attempt to stop her.

The waiting was unbearable and each passing moment threatened her resolve. She busied herself by packing her few things and as she pulled the drawstrings closed she smirked ironically at the bundle, realizing that she would be returning to Erin in much the same way that she had fled. There was only one more thing to be done, and it was the hardest. She crossed to the writing table where a candle burned by the parchment and pen she had laid out. Sitting at the table she stared at the blank paper for an interminable moment, then slowly picked up the quill and dipped it into the ink, posing over the parchment as she swallowed back the lump of tears that welled in the back of her throat.

"Please let him understand," she prayed silently as she began to write, pouring out feelings to him that she knew would be impossible to relate if he were standing before her. She told him of her thoughts over the past weeks and how hopeless their situation was as it existed. She asked for his forgiveness for leaving him but begged with him to understand that it was the only way, that she had to convince Dermot that he had been wrong. Finally, painfully, she ended the letter:

> . . . You tried to warn me, but I would not listen.
> I trusted him. Now, it is up to me to undo the
> damage he has done. Trust me, believe in me, and
> know that I will never stop loving you.

She signed the letter and sprinkled it with sand, watching through blurred eyes while the ink dried. Then, blowing the sand gently from the paper, she folded it and sealed it with the hot wax before inscribing Richard's name across the face above the seal. With a trembling hand, she set it against the candlestick where Sophie was sure to find it, then leaned over and blew out the candle. She sat in the dark, the firelight flickering at her back, with her gaze fastened on the note as if it were her last link with the person she loved most in the world.

She was brought out of her thoughts with a start by a soft rap at the door. She tensed, then felt a sinking sensation as she realized that it was time. She rose slowly and crossed the few short steps to the door, wishing with all of her heart that there was an alternative, even now. Taking a deep breath, she opened the door for Gail.

"Richard!" she gasped.

He stood in the doorway, his face set with determination, yet with a longing in his eyes that made her soften. "Eve, this has gone on for much too long. We are going to talk. Now."

She stepped back in confusion, all of her resolve fleeing at the sight of him. "Oh, Richard! I cannot! I do not want to see you now. I must not!"

"But you will," he said firmly as he closed the door behind him, "I am not giving you a choice."

She turned away from him and her plea came out in a low moan. "Richard, you do not know what you are doing!"

"And you do?" he asked softly. "Do you think that we can go on like this?" He drew her back into his arms, relieved that she did not pull away but instead turned in his arms and clung to him as if she never wanted to let him go. "We will find a way, Eve, I promise you." He murmured, holding her tightly. "You must be patient and trust me."

"I do trust you," she sniffed. "I have never stopped. I . . ."

She never finished what she was about to say because there was another knock at the door and he felt her tense in his arms. He looked down at her questioningly and, seeing her face grow pale with obvious panic, he glanced at the door, doubt growing in his eyes.

"Are you expecting someone?"

"Oh, Richard, please!" she pleaded as her eyes moistened with tears.

He set her from him, his pale eyes growing with suspicion as he peered intently into her own. "Come in," he said calmly.

The door opened and Gail stood in the doorway, his obvious surprise over finding Richard in the room quickly disappearing to be replaced by a cold gleam of pleasure. He glanced at Eve, ignoring the desperate look she threw him, and smiled. "Richard, did Eve not tell you that she was expecting me? How awkward."

The look that Richard turned on her sent her senses reeling with a pain that left her breathless. "Nay, Richard, it is not as it seems!" she cried.

His eyes turned silver and his voice was barely controlled with hard-won restraint. "And how would it be?"

She began to answer but the words held in her throat as she realized, with horror, that she could not tell him the truth. But he mistook her silence and stricken look for guilt, confirming his suspicions.

"Forgive me," he said icily. "I was suffering under the illusion that you still belonged only to me, but I see that you have released yourself from that burden. I will bother you no longer."

He ignored the cry of anguish that escaped her and, crossing to the door, he paused before Gail, who was wearing a most satisfied smile. "Gail, under different circumstances, I would take great pleasure in wiping that smile from your face," he said calmly, though his eyes glittered with danger. "As it is, I will not bother." He glanced back at Eve. "I do not hold you accountable for taking what is so freely offered."

As Richard strode through the open doorway, Gail closed it quickly behind him and turned back to Eve, who was gaping with a vacant gaze at the now-closed door. She wanted to rush after him, to throw herself at his feet, begging for his understanding, but she could not move. All she could feel was the way he had looked at her as he had turned to leave. Then she remembered the note. Glancing at it, where it leaned against the candlestick, its presence gave her a little comfort. When she was gone, Sophie would give it to him and then he would understand. He must!

Gail followed her gaze to the note and he glanced back at her quickly. "Milady, it is better this way, for the parting will be easier for both of you. In time, he will forget. But now we must go quickly. Are you ready?"

She nodded, feeling completely numb inside as she turned and reached for the bundle she had laid on the chair. Thank God, Richard had not seen it, she thought! He lay her cloak about her shoulders and gestured to the door.

"The others who will go with us are waiting by the gate. We must hurry."

As they left the room Gail paused by the doorway and reaching over he picked up the note from the table. He glanced at the name inscribed over the seal and, smiling, he tucked it into his tunic and left the room, closing the door behind him.

PART THREE

Ireland

21

Ferns, Ireland

ve watched her father pace back and forth across the room as he bellowed in rage at her brother. Donnell, who stood quietly by her chair, patiently waited for Dermot's anger to expend itself.

"Damn that O'Rourke!" he exploded, waving an arm in the air, "He crosses me at every turn!" He barked at a servant who would have come into the room to tend the fire, sending the poor fellow scurrying away as he spun back on Donnell. "Have you no control over your men?" he shouted.

"Father, had I not pulled them back, they would have been slaughtered," he answered reasonably. "We were outmanned by at least four to one."

Dermot crossed to the table and poured himself a tankard of ale, splashing the amber liquid over the table and his hand, which he wiped absentmindedly on his tunic. He took a long draught and Eve's eyes fixed on a small stream of liquid that escaped and trickled into his beard. In the months following her return she had looked upon such moments with revulsion, any feeling for her father masked by her anger and frustration. He had laughed at her efforts to dissuade him of his opinion of Richard and vowed to speak of it no more. His energies were completely taken with the defense of Leinster and Okinselagh, even delaying their reunion for three days as he counseled with the urrighs, or sub-kings, at Offaly. He had sent Donnell to greet her and she had been shocked by her brother's appearance. He had aged considerably in the almost two years she had been gone, his once-youthful face now lined with worry.

He had grasped her to him in a fierce welcome of brotherly affection, then held her at arm's length as his eyes filled with pleasure at having her home again.

"You are more beautiful than ever, dear sister," he beamed. "Damn if you are not a woman full grown!"

"It has been two long years, Donnell," she reminded him, "and much has happened."

"Aye, I know." His face softened with compassion and understanding. "Do not be too hard on him, Eve. This is a bad time for us. He had little resistance to Stephen's urging and you know father, he always thinks he knows what is best for us."

"So that is it; it was Stephen," she said quietly.

"Aye, and with great promises of aid if father agreed."

"And has he given it?"

Donnell snorted as he turned about and poured himself a tankard, then collapsed into a chair near the fire. "What do you think?"

"Tell me what has happened, Donnell," she had asked as she took the chair next to him.

"Where shall I begin," he sighed wearily. "Father put all of his hope in Murtough, and while he was secure as ari-ri everything was fine. We actually managed to see a year of peace."

"Uncle O'Loughlin is ari-ri?" she asked with surprise.

"Aye, since Turlough's death. And he has been a great friend. Together we have done much to unite our clans. For a while we thought it might succeed."

"What happened?"

"Rory of Connaught set his sights upon becoming high-king. And our old friend O'Rourke has given him his oath. There is no doubt but that he sees it as his opportunity to avenge himself upon father."

"Speaking of that, where is Dervorgil. Is she here?"

Donnell smirked at the question. "As soon as it looked as if father's position was weakening she bolted like a frightened rabbit straight back into the arms of her husband. But all of the news is not bad, Eve," he added shyly. "The clan has elected me tanist."

"Oh, Donnell!" she exclaimed. "That is wonderful news!"

Pleased by her reaction he grinned broadly but then the

worry began to creep again into his handsome face. "I fear that I have not been much help to him. So far my total contribution as his right hand has been to retreat. We met with Tiernan's forces in Ulada and were forced to turn back."

"Was it bad?" she asked softly.

"Aye, it was bad."

He had gone on to tell her that while the people of Okinselagh remained loyal, those of Northern Leinster followed Dervorgil's lead and began to sway to Rory and O'Rourke's forces, weakening Dermot's forces considerably. It was to be expected as the peoples of that province had always been jealous of the power held in Okinselagh and they were all too quick to change loyalties when they saw the advantage.

Eve's reunion with Dermot had been cool, each reserving emotions they knew boiled beneath the surface. Eve struggled to control her temper, knowing the burdens he carried, but she could not forget the reason for her return any more than she could forget Richard. She had tried time and time again to broach the subject calmly but each time he had dismissed it curtly, until one morning she lost her control and her temper. She had railed at him and thrown threats wildly, warning him that Richard would come for her. Dermot had begun to laugh, the sound of his cruel merriment filling the hall as he extracted a parchment from his tunic and waved it at her. As she finally recognized the note she had left for Richard, she felt as if the world began to crumble under her feet and she had grasped the end of the dormant table to keep from falling.

"Where did you get that?" she cried.

"Where indeed?" he laughed. "Why from your escort, Sir Gail, of course. And he made me pay handsomely for it. Well worth the price, is it not? Now, will you finally understand that your precious Richard will not come for you? You have now but to serve your father, and that you shall!"

Nothing would dissuade him, not even when word arrived that Henry had met Stephen's forces at Wallingford and a treaty had been signed proclaiming that Henry would become king of England upon Stephen's death. The battle between father and daughter had peaked upon the news from England. Even Donnell had tried to intercede on Eve's behalf, insisting that surely now Richard was worthy, as his name had been signed upon the treaty and he was obviously in Henry's favor. But Dermot was firm.

"Henry will not become king until Stephen is in his grave—

that too is in the treaty!" he had raged. "Stephen is in his prime. It will be years before England has a new king!"

But, with all of her frustration and anguish, at least Eve could console herself with the fact that Dermot never mentioned another husband. He left her to herself where she could pass her days in relative peace. She would spend hours at her writing table, pen in hand, while she struggled to compose a letter to Richard. She wanted to explain and beg for his forgiveness and understanding, but each time she finally laid the pen down knowing it was hopeless. Even if such a letter were possible, Dermot would never allow it to be sent.

She wanted to hate Dermot. She should have hated him, but try as she might, she couldn't. Whatever he had done, he was still her father and she could not forget the years growing up, his tenderness with her while he relished his reputation of fearsomeness with others. His care and concern for his people lay behind a facade of toughness so that they would not mistake his concern for weakness. And that was where, she knew, the truth really lay. His weakness. He was not a cruel man, but he was weak to the ploys of others, continually misjudging them and their intentions. Moreover, he had the bad habit of taking the wrong side and not realizing it until it was too late.

So, she had built a shell for herself. A safe haven where she could no longer be hurt, determined to remain there, where no one could touch her, particularly not Dermot. Now, as Dermot raged, she withdrew into her memories, and was only brought back to reality as she heard a commotion from without.

"By the Blood of Mary!" Dermot cursed. "What is goin' on?"

Eve's eldest brother, Enna, entered the room followed by his lieutenants, their garments flecked with the thick mud of the marshes which lay about Ferns to the west. From the grim looks upon their faces, it was certain that the news was not good.

Eve brightened as Enna entered, as she had not seen him since her return. His position as Rahdamma, the elected heir to Dermot's throne, had kept him at his duties. However, her heart sunk as he glanced in her direction and nodded curtly before looking away, his attention on the message he carried. She glanced at the others quizzically, noticing now that they too would not meet her eyes, each looking away uncomfortably though she had known them since childhood.

"Well, what is it?" Dermot snapped.

"Four days ago a ship landed at Wexford bearing news from England," Enna began grimly. "I fear it is grievous news for Erin..." He took a deep breath, glancing briefly at his sister before continuing. "Stephen is dead. Henry was crowned king of England in Westminster on Christmas day."

The intake of Eve's breath could be heard about the room in the heavy silence that followed and all eyes turned to her.

"What has this to do with us?" Dermot growled, regaining their attention. His expression was black as he threw a glare at Eve. He turned his back to the others as he calmly poured himself another tankard. "This is hardly news to bring you from your duties in Okinselagh."

"Nay, father," Enna answered irritably. "We would not have ridden for four days except on a matter of the greatest importance. There is more."

"More?" Dermot's brow raised in question as he perched himself on the edge of the table.

Enna's voice filled with anger. "Aye. A council was held soon after the coronation. Henry laid out a bull from Pope Adrian sanctioning an invasion of Erin. In short, the pope has given us to England."

Dermot paled visibly as his knuckles turned white from their grasp of the tankard.

"Chorp an chriost!" Donnell swore as he took a step forward and gaped at his brother. "Are you certain?"

"Absolutely," Enna replied bitterly. "It would seem that we have only the new queen mother to thank that the expedition has not already begun. The empress has convinced Henry that he cannot spare the forces now, for Louis is giving him trouble in Normandy."

Eve was stunned with disbelief. But, even while her mind tumbled with rejection of what he was saying, a voice inside of her said it was true. That element, that vague uneasy feeling of mistrust she had carried within her since first meeting Henry, now focused.

"Aye," she said softly, not realizing that she had spoken out loud. "It is true. He would have done this."

She looked up to find all eyes upon her and she cringed at the doubt and suspicion she read in them.

"Did you know of this?" Enna demanded.

Now she understood the look he had thrown at her when

he had entered the room, and the uneasiness of the others. "Nay!" she protested. "If I had, do you think I would not have told you?"

Enna looked at her with a pained expression, the doubt clearly written in his eyes. "I do not know, Eve. You have lived with them for two years. Are you saying that in all that time, even in the year you lodged beneath Henry's roof, Richard never once gave you even a hint of Henry's plans?"

"Richard?" she gasped. "He is not part of this, he would not..."

"Richard, Richard," Dermot mocked, his anger exploding savagely as he glared at his daughter. "Do you expect us to believe that one so close to Henry would know nothing of his plans? Or, that you could live with him without ever suspecting?"

She trembled with rage as her eyes moved slowly about the room and she stood up to confront their accusing stares. Her only ally seemed to be Donnell, who watched the others guardedly, ready to spring to her defense.

"Aye, I lived with him, my English husband, through a marriage forced upon me. When have my feelings ever been considered, when have I been allowed the freedom to choose that is the right of any man in this room? What decisions have I made that you should question my loyalty? I do not deny that I loved Richard, or that I love him still, but then I was lucky to be thrust upon such a man, for again, it was not my choice. But the love I bear him is for the man, not because he is English! I trust him, without question. You, father," she flung at him, "did you mistrust him when you married me to him? Why did you send me to England? I will say it only one time and you will believe what you will, I care not. Never, at any time, was there mention of such a plan! Moreover, had Richard even suspected it, he would have told me, for..." She forced her chin up as she struggled to complete the thought, her voice trailing, "...for there was a time—when he loved me."

Donnell stepped forward to play on the uncertainty he read in the men's faces. "Eve, there is no one here who doubts your loyalty. The fact that you are here proves the matter—would you have returned if you had been part of the conspiracy? Besides, there is not a man here who has not known you since childhood and knows that you are incapable of such treachery. Let no more be said of it."

There were murmurs of agreement among the men and Eve

saw the doubts fade one by one. Her composure shaken, she left the room with as much dignity as she could muster, wanting now only the solitude of her chambers to think about what she had heard.

Once alone she slumped into a chair and drew herself up, hugging her knees in a gesture of self-pity. She leaned her head on her knees and allowed the tears to come, now overwhelmed by the accusations of her people and her fear of Richard's. She could not even imagine the horror of that event. The loss of freedom by her people, to live under the tyranny of another and—would Richard be among them? If only Gerda were here, she thought desperately. Someone who would understand her feelings! But, she learned upon her arrival, to her great sadness, that the old woman had died not long after Eve had departed for England. She felt completely alone, here in the place of her childhood, but somehow it was as if she no longer belonged. She had been caught in a vacuum, with no place to rest.

On an impulse, she raised her head and stared into the fire's leaping flames. It had become a habit, since that last night in Normandy, and she often took comfort as she imagined she could see Richard's face in the flames, sometimes with Warwick and the others, once in battle just before the news came from Wallingford, and sometimes just he alone as he seemed to be gazing off in thought, his face filled with discontent. But, she stared until her head began to ache and nothing came, now when she needed it as never before. Finally, she lowered her head to her knees and wept.

No one was to dwell upon the news from England for long. Before many days had passed word arrived that Rory's forces had entered Leinster and had taken it handily, and were now approaching the royal city of Ferns. Dermot moved swiftly, issuing orders to move the household deeply into Okinselagh, which he placed under Enna's command. Dermot moved to the south and attempted to stay Rory's forces at Fid Dorcha, a dense wood which bordered Okinselagh's northern gate. Greatly outnumbered, it was soon evident that O'Conner would force the pass, so in a last act of desperation and in order that there might be less for the enemy to plunder, Dermot fired the city. On a small rise to the south he sat upon his mount, his lieutenants gathered about him as they viewed the burning city. Dermot's face betrayed no emotion as he watched the angry flames lick and devour what he had spent a lifetime building. Finally, in a flat, calm voice, he issued orders of retreat and pulling back on the head of his mount, turned and rode to the south.

Rory seemed satisfied by Dermot's flight from Leinster and was content to leave him Okinselagh. Upon viewing the charred city he returned home to Connaught, taking with him hostages from Leinster to assure their continuing loyalty. But not so Dermot's old enemy, Tiernan O'Rourke. Without Rory's counsel, he marched with his forces to the Fews of Armagh where they came upon Murtough who, taken by surprise, was poorly guarded. They murdered the ari-ri, thereby eliminating Dermot's last support.

"He is gone, father." Enna watched Dermot carefully, unsure of the effect his news would have. "O'Rourke found him at Armagh."

"We must send for Conner," Dermot said quietly. "It is time that he came home."

Enna started at the mention of his youngest brother and he wondered for a moment if Dermot had lost his senses. He glanced doubtfully at the others but it was Donnell who spoke. "He is safe with Urlacam, father. It would be doubtful that he would make it through O'Rourke's lines."

"I would have my sons with me!" Dermot roared. "I want him home!"

Eve knelt by Dermot's chair and laid her hand over his larger one, ignoring her own grief as she attempted to keep her tone light. "It would be foolishness to bring him home now. Besides, what would we be bringing him to?"

Dermot looked up at her and his eyes moved about the small room located in the west wing of the Augustinian abbey where they had taken refuge.

"Aye, you are right. It would be foolishness," he agreed, patting her hand. He rose heavily from the chair and walked to the small slanted window which overlooked the square below. He watched the neat procession of monks walking in column to their time of prayer, their serene attitude of devotion in sharp contrast to the turbulence that existed beyond the abbey walls.

"Father, we must make plans," Enna pleaded. "O'Rourke is only a few days' march from here. The men await your orders and they are prepared to do whatever you request."

Dermot half turned and smiled at his eldest son. "To do

what? To sacrifice the last of Okinselagh's blood to his victory? Without help from the other clans we do not stand a chance, and you know it as well as I."

"Should we submit without a fight?" Enna cried. "The people are willing to die before they see him on Okinselagh's throne! Rory may be able to hold him for a time but you know it will come!"

Dermot ignored the outburst as his attention was again fixed upon the monks in the square. When Enna began to speak again, he waved him off with his hand as his mind began to turn with an idea. At last, he turned back to the others, smiling at their earnest looks. His gaze fixed upon Eve in particular and he pursed his lips in thought.

"I will not sacrifice Okinselagh when there is no chance for victory. But, I have an idea that there might be someone who will help us."

"Who?" Enna snorted his disbelief. "The clans wait to see who will emerge the victor. There will be no aid from that source."

"Not from the clans, Enna," Dermot murmured as he stared from the window once again. "Our Holy Mother, Church, seeks to bend us to her will. Let us see if she will help us."

"The church? She will do nothing to help us now, short of this poor abbey where we have found refuge!"

"Ah, but she has given license to someone who can."

They exchanged puzzled looks, then suddenly Donnell paled as he understood Dermot's meaning. "You cannot!" he cried, his expression filling with horror. "You would ask Henry? He would devour us. You would be handing Erin to the English!"

Dermot laughed bitterly. "We hand them nothing! Once Henry settles his quarrels with France, he will turn his eyes to Erin! It did not begin with him, have you forgotten? When our people sent William Rufus the lumber to aid him in building Westminster—a gesture of goodwill between our two countries—he bragged that he would use it to build a bridge to Erin over which his armies would march! The only reason we have not seen the English on our shores before was due to France or their own civil war! Now, with Henry, our time is spent! Or do you think we can resist them? Hundreds of clans, fighting among themselves and you think we can hold off his armies? But, just perhaps, if we choose the time. If we can use him to gain strength—we might turn it to our advantage!"

Donnell's voice was shaken. "Father, I warn you. If you

do this thing you will be remembered by our people, for all time, as the one who betrayed them to the English!"

Dermot snorted as he raised a scoffing brow. "What do I care for what history writes? 'Tis the life I live now that I care for!" He turned his gaze to Eve who sat mutely listening to the exchange. "And what of you?" he asked quietly. "You have lived among them, you know them better than all of us. What do you say?"

"What would you have me say?" she replied. "Would you have me tell you that Henry will be merciful? I do not know if he will help us, but I do know this: I have been with Henry, I have seen his ambitions and I know them to be endless. Eventually—Erin will be his—no matter what is decided here."

There was total silence in the small room as they digested what she had said, and the determination with which she spoke, and their stomachs twisted with a sickening inevitability.

"There is nothing else we can do, save deliver Okinselagh to O'Rourke and that I will not do!" Dermot said firmly. "We will leave for England on the first tide."

"Nay, father," Enna said slowly as he sorted his thoughts. "I must remain here. You will never be allowed to board that ship unless O'Rourke is held back."

"Aye," Donnell agreed. "And I shall remain also, for the same reason. We will hold Okinselagh until you return, we promise it."

Dermot thought upon the matter for a time, his unwillingness to allow his sons to possibly sacrifice themselves to his oldest enemy apparent in his tortured expression. He knew that they were right, and that the moment they had gone, there would be no one to lead those who remained loyal. He looked at his sons with regret and nodded silently.

"And what of me, Father?" Eve began. "I could . . ."

"You will come with me," Dermot answered. "There is more that you can do in England than here."

She gaped at him, stunned. "There is nothing that I can do there!"

"Donnell, Enna, leave me with your sister," Dermot said gruffly.

As they left the room, and the door closed behind them, Eve spun on Dermot. "Nay, Father! You will not make me return to England! Richard hates even my memory, it cannot be less!"

"You will return," he said evenly. "You will do so, as it

makes my position stronger. Aye, he may think he hates you but he will have to accept you. He is still your husband."

Her mouth dropped open for a moment and she was convinced that he had truly lost his sanity. "Have you forgotten that you had our marriage annulled? Or do you think that merely because it is now inconvenient you can ignore what you did?"

Dermot remained placid, then a small smile began to play at the corners of his mouth. "I have forgotten nothing. But, you and Richard have. The annulment was a first step that was never concluded."

"What do you mean?" Eve stammered, as her heart began to beat wildly.

"Your cobiche, Eve. I did not demand it—and it was never returned by your husband. Therefore, you are his wife still."

"My dowery?" she breathed, dumbstruck. It had never occurred to her. "But—but it was left at Chepstow! You cannot expect . . ."

"I can, and I will. You are still legally married."

"You planned this from the first!" she accused breathlessly. "That is why you never mentioned another for me! You were biding your time in the event that you needed him! You kept me here, let me think—let us both suffer!" For the first time in her life she hated him, and recognized his capacity for cunning, as he looked at her calmly, neither confirming nor denying her accusations. "Father, please! Do not do this thing! Do not force me. If you have any love for me, do not ask me to face him now! It is too late!"

His expression grew hard as he answered her. "Okinselagh is falling, Ferns is burnt to the ground and Leinster lost and you expect me to consider your feelings?"

"Nay!" she spat. "Not when you are concerned with your own! You speak of Okinselagh and its people falling to O'Rourke's hands when you plot to give them to the English! What bothers you the most, Father, that Okinselagh falls or that O'Rourke will become master of it?"

His face flushed and he raised his hand to strike her but, at the last moment, held himself in check. Lowering it slowly, he brought himself under control. He had never struck her before and as he peered down at her the vision of a small, trusting child flashed through his mind, and a face of a woman, the only one he had ever loved. Besides, it would not do to have her come before Henry, or Richard, with bruises on her face. "You will do as you are told or I swear that I will give you to O'Rourke as concubine! Now go and prepare to leave. We go to England!"

Later in the afternoon, Donnell found her sitting on a bench in the small garden behind the abbey. "There you are, Eve. I have been looking for you!"

She did not answer but gave him a wistful smile and she patted the empty place next to her.

"Father told us," he said gently as he took the offered seat. "It must be very hard for you to go back there now. Do you think that you can handle it?"

"Do I have a choice?" She smiled, but it was one of sadness. She leaned back against the bench and closed her eyes for a moment, then opened them to stare out over the garden. "Donnell, do you believe in fate?"

Donnell looked at her oddly, then shrugged. "I believe that we make our own fate, Eve, and we usually get what we deserve. Why?"

"Do you include me in that?" She smiled. "Do I deserve to face Richard again, knowing that he must hate me?"

"I don't know if it is right to think of it as a punishment. Perhaps it is just something you have to do. Besides, it may not be as bad as you think. You might even find that he does not hate you. It may be a new beginning for you."

"Perhaps." She sighed, with little conviction, then added thoughtfully, "I have been sitting here thinking about Gerda. I am so sorry that I was not with her when she died. It was not right, Donnell. She gave me so much and I should have been with her."

"She went home to her people, Eve. It was where she wanted to be. You do not have to feel any guilt, she was not alone."

"I know, but—" Her voice trailed off and she bit her lower lip. "She once told me that we all have a purpose, things we are to achieve in our lifetime before the gods will release us to our peace."

"Gerda was full of tales, Eve," he laughed. "Do not tell me that you took them to heart!"

"There was much wisdom in what she said," Eve insisted. "Do you not feel that you have a purpose? Have you not an inner drive to accomplish something dear to you?"

"Of course. To see O'Rourke's neck beneath my battle-ax and to drive the northern clans home with their miserable tails between their legs!" He saw the seriousness in her eyes and his voice softened as he reconsidered the question. "Aye, to see peace between the clans and for Erin to prosper. Do you not want the same?" Her hesitation startled him and he frowned as she avoided looking at him. "Well, what do you want?"

She shrugged her shoulders and fixed her gaze on a distant point. "To survive, I think, with my principles still intact."

"Is that all?"

She returned a smile to his horrified expression. "That is quite a lot, I think. In fact, perhaps it is the hardest of all. I've watched principles being battered until they are almost unrecognizable. I've seen great and powerful men compromise what they believed in, or laid claim to, while they rationalized that it was for the common good. Henry is such a one. But I am not criticizing, Donnell. I cannot, for I have been guilty too."

"You? What have you done that was so terrible, little sister?" he teased.

"Refused to accept responsibilities," she answered. "Each time I have been threatened with something I did not understand, I've run away. Instead of facing it, seeing it through."

"That is reasonable. No one wants to be hurt."

"That does not mean it is right. Besides, you are humoring me, Donnell. I watched you and Enna facing what is coming with such courage and I'm ashamed for the way I've behaved. I am a MacMurrough too! In the morning I am to leave with Father for England. I could run away again, right now—every part of me wants to. I cannot believe what he is doing is right, but—I have decided that I've done enough running. I must see it through, whatever it is, and whatever pain it may cause me."

"With your principles still intact?" he smiled.

"Hopefully."

Donnell rose from the bench and pulled her up into his arms. He hugged her tightly to him, feeling a sudden wash of love for his little sister. Little sister? Aye, he could call her that, though she was no longer the lanky, awkward little girl with a trace of freckles running across the bridge of her nose, who would chase after him. But, the freckles were gone and, he knew, so was the little girl.

22

Normandy

Eve drew in her breath as she and Dermot followed the chamberlain down the long corridor toward the solarium where they would have audience with Henry. The past weeks had frayed her nerves until now she wondered if she would be equal to what was expected of her. Thus far their journey had been one of frustration. They had arrived in England only to learn that Henry had left for Normandy. Once the channel had been crossed matters became more difficult since no one seemed to know Henry's whereabouts.

Dermot was enraged. Convinced that Henry was avoiding him, his anger turned to stupefaction when he finally became convinced that no one knew where the King of England was lodged. Eve remained unruffled by the crisis, knowing that it was common practice for Henry to move swiftly from place to place, arriving at each new destination unannounced, throwing the owners of the manor he had chosen to occupy into a turmoil over the sudden appearance of their king. As for Henry, he never seemed to notice the commotion he caused. His mind was always occupied with purposes and he thought nothing of setting to work among wide eyes and pale-faced confusion.

Now that they had finally found him, in a small manor in Bayeux, Eve secretly hoped that he would deny their requests and send them packing back to Erin. She had no desire to see Henry again but the true reason for the nervousness and dread she harbored was from the prospect of coming face to face with Richard.

The moment arrived as the chamberlain stopped before the doors to the solarium, pausing only for a moment to tap lightly before he pushed them open and stepped back for them to enter. Dermot saw her hesitation and he grasped her arm firmly and took her into the room. She dropped her gaze to the floor, unwilling to look about, certain that if she did she would look into angry, cold, gray eyes.

She heard Henry rise from the table and move to greet Dermot. The men exchanged pleasantries while Eve still kept her eyes downcast and her head began to swim lightly. She despised herself for her cowardice but she could not bring herself to look up.

Henry stepped before Eve and when her eyes fixed upon the bright silver buckles of his slippers she dipped a curtsy.

"Eve, how lovely you look, my dear. It is good that you have returned. Eleanor will be greatly pleased!"

"Thank you, Your Majesty," she murmured, forcing her eyes to his. "I look forward to seeing her again."

"And you shall." He caught her look as she glanced nervously about the room. "He is not here, Eve," he said quietly and saw the relief that flooded her face. "He is in Bristol on my business. In fact, you were very likely passing through the city as he arrived."

Henry ordered the steward to bring refreshments, then invited them to sit as he returned to his place behind the table which was littered with rolls of parchments and maps. He made polite small talk until the steward had returned. Then he dismissed the man with orders that they were not to be disturbed. An uneasiness pricked at Eve at the gesture. She thought it odd that they were to be afforded a private audience.

"I assume that you are here over the matter of your daughter's marriage," he addressed Dermot suddenly. "You must realize that Eve's—ah, sudden departure has not left Richard exactly affable to the liaison. Of course, I do have some influence with him but I try not to interfere with such matters."

Eve's face burned at Henry's words and she stared at her hands which were tightly folded in her lap.

"That is not why I am here, Your Majesty," Dermot answered. "Although, since you have broached the subject, I would mention in passing that regardless of the earl's feelings my daughter is still his wife. In fact, it would be my guess that he has chosen to have it so in that he has never returned the bride-price."

Eve glanced up at Henry involuntarily, wondering what his reaction would be, but he showed no emotion and continued to regard Dermot evenly. "If what you say is true, and I have no reason to doubt your word, it could, of course, throw a different light on the matter. But, you said that your reasons for being here were of another purpose."

"Aye. I am sure that you have heard of what has happened in my country. I am here to discuss a matter with you that may prove to be for our mutual advantage."

"Indeed." Henry regarded Dermot carefully, then turned to Eve with a smile. "Eve, my dear, I am certain that if your father and I are to discuss matters of state, it would only bore you. Eleanor awaits you in her chambers and I am certain that a visit with an old friend will prove to be of greater interest than what we will discuss here."

It bothered her that Henry's intention was to closet himself with Dermot, with no witnesses, but she was grateful that she would not have to hear her father grovel before Henry. She rose and dipped a curtsy to Henry, avoiding his eyes so that he would not see the humiliation written in her own, then left the room, all too glad to be rid of them both.

Eleanor was delighted to see her, and her greeting was warm and affectionate as she ushered Eve into the nursery to show her Henry's little son, William. After a great display of motherly pride, Eleanor ordered a light meal for them to be taken in her chambers and the two old friends sat down for a visit.

"I was greatly pleased to learn of the coronation, Your Grace, though I would imagine that to be a queen once again certainly must not give you the freedom you once longed for."

"I am much happier than I have a right to be," Eleanor smiled. "Though I know that you never thought you would hear that from me and you never shall again. But, a moment of honesty is good between friends, is it not? And now you shall give me some. How goes it with you?"

"I am fine."

"Eve," Eleanor admonished. "I said honesty. We know what has been happening in Ireland, and I can surmise the reason for being here."

Eve glanced up at Eleanor and she could not help but to show the anger she felt. "I am sure that you can! We know of Adrian's bull!"

"I suspected it." Eleanor sighed. "I wish it could be different, Eve, I truly do. However, you must understand that there is nothing I can say on the matter. Whatever must happen will happen and nothing you or I can do will change it."

Eve's anger faded as she realized the futility of challenging Eleanor, and that she must not do anything to jeopardize any advantage, however small, that Dermot might achieve with Henry. She turned her attention to the meal and realized suddenly that she was truly hungry. The knowledge that Richard was in Bristol had returned her spirits considerably and she found herself enjoying the food. As she began to relax, Eleanor jolted her again.

"Did Henry tell you that Richard is not here?"

"Aye," she answered, the food suddenly tasteless in her mouth. "His Grace said that he is in Bristol." She paused, unwilling to hear the answer but compelled to ask the question. "Does—does he hate me so very much?"

"He is a man who loses himself in his work." Eleanor shrugged. "I will be honest with you. On the surface, at least, you are for him as someone who never existed. He has been very hurt, Eve, and he is not a man to forgive easily."

"Is—is there someone else?"

Eleanor began to reply, then thought better of it and seemed to change her words. "No one important. I think it will be some time before that knight looks upon another with real interest."

Changing the subject, Eleanor talked of other things, not noticing when Eve had stopped eating and laid her spoon down. Her appetite was completely gone and she was glad that Eleanor led the conversation because she was unable to speak. She had thought herself prepared for the worst but to hear Eleanor speak of it, to confirm it, was almost too much to bear.

Once alone in her room she tried not to think about it or to dwell on Eleanor's words. She was grateful that Dermot returned almost immediately and upon hearing his footsteps outside the door she rushed to open it for him. He strode by her and went directly to the decanter of wine on the table near the window and poured himself a goodly measure, which he downed in one long gulp, then bent to pour another.

"Well, what did he say?" she asked impatiently.

Dermot's face was noncommittal as he reached into his tunic and extracted a paper which he held out to her. "He has given me this. You may read it. I would say that it is much more than we could have expected and much less than we hoped for."

She took it from him and opened it, tilting it toward the light from the window to make out Henry's finely set hand upon the parchment.

> Henry, King of England, Duke of Normandy and Aquitaine, and Count of Anjou, to all his liegemen, English, Normans, Welsh, and Scots, and to all nations subject to his sway, greetings. Whensoever these letters shall come unto you know that we have received Dermot, Prince of Leinster, into our grace and favor; wherefore whosoever within the bounds of our territories shall be willing to give him aid, as our vassal and liegemen, in recovering his dominion, let him be assured of our favor and license in that behalf.

She lowered the parchment slowly and let the words settle as she digested them. Now, at least, she understood why Henry had granted them a private audience.

"Father, he has given you nothing."

"He has given us permission to recruit aid within his dominion," Dermot corrected.

"You mean the permission to go begging for aid!" She cried. "He has promised you nothing! What is more, he can decry this as a forgery if it pleases him—there is no seal upon it! And, no witness to its signing!"

"All the more reason why we must seek aid of those who will recognize his hand upon the letter."

She walked to a nearby chair and slumped helplessly into it, the letter still in her hand. "And if they please, they can deny its authenticity."

"Aye, that is why we will seek out one who will not deny it—for if it is in your hand, you who knows Henry's signature as well as he—he cannot deny it."

She looked up at Dermot helplessly, and saw the look of determination on his face, knowing that behind it there was fear and hopelessness. She faltered, wanting to point out that Richard was the least likely to help them, but she knew that Dermot would not listen. She faced the realization that since that fateful morning in the abbey in Erin when Dermot had told them of his plans, that she would not escape England without seeing Richard again. Sighing deeply in what was almost a moan, she nodded and accepted the inevitable.

They left Normandy by the first light of dawn as Dermot was anxious to reach Bristol before the end of the month. He feared that Richard might prove as elusive as Henry had been and he knew that time was growing short. His sons would not be able to hold out against O'Rourke's forces forever.

They lodged in a small inn in Bristol, a thriving commercial town near the English coast, choosing the inn as it was near the fief of Berkeley and Bristol Castle wherein resided Robert FitzHarding, Dermot's old friend. He dispatched a message to Sir Robert immediately upon their arrival in hopes that he would know of Richard's whereabouts. Before they had finished their unpacking a message was returned, to Dermot's delight and Eve's dismay, that Richard was indeed lodged with Sir Robert.

"He gives no mention of Richard's frame of mind," Eve observed. "I wonder if Sir Robert told him of our arrival."

"I am certain that he has been told," Dermot answered gruffly.

At that he apparently dismissed further conversation with her as he bent over the papers on the table and left her with her thoughts. She felt slightly nauseous as she contemplated actually facing Richard, not in some far distant point in the future, but in a few hours' time, a day at the most. She imagined herself standing outside of the room where they would meet, staring at the iron-bound portals as if they were Pandora's box—filled with all of the wonders of the world, and all of its terrors. Would she be able to pass through the doors, or would her courage fail her? She glanced at her father who was writing to her brothers and she knew that he would give her no choice. She wanted to see him again, there was no denying it. She still loved him but she was terrified. What was he thinking now? What would his reaction be towards her? Anger? Indifference? She would soon know.

Richard's first reaction upon learning that Eve had returned to England, and was now in Bristol, had been stunned shock, followed by a surge of furious anger, which he had suppressed with immense effort under the intent regard of Sir Robert, who had peered at him with curiosity. Outwardly, he remained calm, passing the information with a casual remark. Once alone, the knowledge sent him into a turmoil of unwelcomed emotions. He could not fathom why she had returned, or what she had hoped to accomplish by such an action.

The months following her disappearance from Normandy had been torture. When those first, horrible moments after

finding her with Gail had passed and his mind had cleared, he
found that he could not comprehend Eve's being attracted to
the likes of the insufferable French knight. He knew that she
was torn with indecision and confusion over the pope's decision, but that had nothing to do with unfaithfulness. He had
derided himself over his lack of faith in her, realizing that his
reaction had been due to frustration over his own inadequacies
in solving their problems. The following morning, after a fretful
night, he had returned to her chambers, determined to convince
her to forgive him, only to find that she was gone.

At first he had searched for her, unwilling to believe the
obvious. By the following morning, upon learning that Gail
and his knights were also missing, he was forced to face the
truth—that he was a fool. All of the hours that he had spent
deriding himself for not believing in her, the anguish and self-
hatred, only to find that she had misled him—that was the
hardest to bear.

He would discuss it with no one, though those close to him
tried to help. They could not understand the extent of his anger,
or his grief. He was haunted by the remembrance of Gail's
expression, the satisfied, pleased expression to Richard's surprise; and the guilt that Eve wore, confirming his suspicion.
No woman had played him so falsely, hurt him so deeply, and
it could not be forgotten.

The first terrible hurt receded into depths well beyond his
conscious mind. After a time he ceased feeling that particular
catch in his throat when he thought he saw her among a crowd
or when his mind deluded him into hearing the soft sounds of
her approaching footsteps. After repeated betrayals he eventually learned not to listen and soon he did not hear at all, but
built a barrier against his memories.

He threw himself into Henry's conquest, and his own, as
the object that became the most important was the recovery of
Chepstow and the lands that his family had struggled to build.
Following the coronation, he returned to Chepstow to find it
reduced to disorder and the beginning of decay due to the
inattention of his cousin whose lands lay far to the south. He
had set himself to restoring Chepstow and its lands to their
former greatness, and lending encouragement and aid to Striguil's people. It had not been easy. He dipped into his coffers,
almost to the last sovereign to accomplish the task, and did so
unhesitatingly as the needs were great.

When word reached him that his holdings in Wales were

threatened, the news did not concern him overmuch. The fact that Rhys ap Gruffund, a Welsh prince, had risen to arms against the English, was to be expected, as the Welsh had historically used each change of power in London to their advantage. Besides, Richard knew he had nothing to fear since many of the Welsh were counted among his closest friends. However, an event occurred soon after that caused him to rethink his position.

Henry had made good the promise made in Normandy: his first act as England's ruler was to obtain and record exhaustive and accurate census of the lands given by Stephen and the unlicensed castles built during the period. Richard had known that Pembroke would be involved but he was prepared to concede the estates, asking no favor from among the barons. Stephen had given Pembroke to Strongbow; therefore Richard held it in little value except for what moneys it could bring to Chepstow. However, when the census was posted, Richard was stunned to learn that Caermarthen, a manor built by Strongbow during Old King Henry's reign, had also been confiscated.

Assuming an error had been made, Richard wrote to Henry. When the king replied, the doubts that Richard had harbored with him for so long could not be denied. Henry had rewarded his loyalty by confiscating Caermarthen along with his other Welsh holdings. To lose Caermarthen was unthinkable. Strongbow had built the manor for Isabel as a wedding gift and it was there that they had spent the first years of their marriage, and it was there that Richard had been born.

Isabel had waited only until Richard returned victorious before she had gone to join Strongbow and now Richard was glad that she would not have to add this to the crushing blows she had suffered in her last years. He again wrote to Henry but the king answered that there was nothing that he could do at the present. Rhys' claims had set Wales to turmoil and he feared that such a claim by Richard would only worsen the problem. Of course, he had suggested, if Richard were to use his influence with the Welsh and plead for peace with Rhys, then perhaps something could be done. His letter confirmed Richard's suspicions and, though the ploy was transparent, Richard knew that he had no other choice.

Thus, he had come to Bristol to work with FitzHarding in dealing with the Welsh—and learned that Eve had returned to England. He had dismissed Sir Robert's suggestion that he join them in the main hall upon Dermot's arrival, insisting instead

that he meet with them alone in the morning chamber, with
only Warwick in attendance. He had no intention of giving
Dermot, or Eve, the support of others at their first meeting;
the advantage was to be his alone. Only one other besides
Warwick attended the meeting that morning, and he allowed
it upon her entreaties, finally conceding that he could see no
harm in it. On the contrary, recalling certain memories from
the past he found himself taking cruel pleasure in the prospect.

Though he had braced himself, as Eve entered the morning
chamber on Dermot's arm and the soft light from the window
at his back cast gently over her, the memories he had fought
so diligently to suppress came rushing back to his senses. The
emerald green velvet of her pelisse was cut narrow at the waist,
accentuating to his gaze the fullness of her breasts and her
slender form he remembered so well. She looked at him questioningly from under her thick lashes, her eyes deep pools of
green filled with emotion she was never able to suppress. Damn,
he thought, had she deliberately chosen that gown when she
must know what it did to her eyes, not to mention her figure?
He was struck, even as the first time, with her breathtaking
beauty, the remembrance of the softness of her body, and the
way she responded to his touch . . . He fought back the unwilling
thoughts angrily, disgusted with himself that she could creep
back into his feelings with such ease, and he fought the impulse
to send the others from the room to confront her at last—alone.

But, his manner was coolly polite, his voice lazily indifferent as he invited them to sit. He took a chair for himself
before the window where he knew that the bright morning sun
behind his back would make it difficult for them to read his
expression.

Though she had tried to prepare herself, she was stunned
by the coldness with which he greeted her. She had expected
anger, even hatred, but not the icy contempt she read in his
stony glare. He is older, she thought. The man before her now
was a hardened knight, composed and rigid as he greeted Dermot. There was none of the softness, the tenderness he had
once had, though physically he was even handsomer in his
maturity. He wears his titles well, she mused, though something
within her mourned his lost youth.

Her attention had been fixed upon Richard when she entered
the room and though she had noticed Warwick standing to one
side she had been unaware of another who had been standing
in the shadows. As she turned to take the offered chair she

found herself looking into large brown eyes watching her with open interest.

"Claresta!" she cried silently. The insult was complete, the punishment more than she could have imagined. She had the impulse to look at Richard but she sensed that he was watching her reaction so she gathered herself together and looked at him with a cold, unflinching regard while she fought not to betray her agitation.

"We are here at Henry's behest," she heard herself saying, surprised that her voice was firm and sounded amazingly calm. "I assure you that we would not be here if it were not on a matter of the greatest importance."

"I believe you," Richard drawled. "Please continue."

Dermot stepped forward, distracting Richard's attention from Eve as he extracted Henry's message from his tunic. Eve sought a chair at the far side of the room, with the intention of not interfering beyond this point. She would not humiliate herself further, regardless of Richard's or her father's intent. Warwick appeared at her side, saying nothing but handing her a goblet of wine, which she accepted. To her surprise, he turned to stand at her side.

Richard had ignored the fact that she had moved away but as he read Henry's letter his senses filled with the lingering scent of the lilac that she wore. It was a sharp contrast to the heavier fragrances Claresta preferred and its familiarity unsettled him. By the time that he finished the letter, his mood was foul and he found it difficult to maintain his cool pretense with Dermot.

He laid the parchment in his lap and his eyes flickered with anger as he looked up. "Why did you bring this to me?"

"Is it not obvious, Lord Richard?" Dermot began easily. "I am here to ask you for the support King Henry provides. To raise an army to drive back the forces that plague my people."

The extent of Dermot's gall amazed Richard. The man stood before him with no reference to the past, not a hint of an apology or regrets, and was asking him to take up his banner and fight his battles!

"You ask this of me?" he said calmly. "It is not my war. Why would I want to help you?"

"Nor is it Henry's," Dermot countered, "yet he has seen fit to support my request."

Richard looked at Dermot shrewdly, then laughed. "He promises no support! He merely gives you permission to find your own means. Indeed, there is not even his seal upon the parchment. How can I be certain that it is by his hand?"

"You know it to be his; you cannot deny it," Dermot said flatly.

"And pray, why not?"

"Because you are a man of honor and you would not deny what you know to be the truth, whatever you may think of me."

Richard gave him a begrudging smile but then glanced to where Eve sat and his demeanor changed to a frown. "Why do you bring your daughter with you? If it was meant to influence me to take your suit, I fear you have grossly erred."

Eve froze at the comment but Dermot remained unruffled. "My daughter is here because she is a comfort to me. Moreover she speaks the language more fluently than I. But since you have mentioned her, I am impelled to bring up a subject I am wont to mention, my lord, particularly in view of our present discussion. But it is of importance to me as goodly amounts will be needed to finance my efforts against my enemies. I am embarrassed to speak of it but . . ."

Eve drew in her breath sharply as she realized that Dermot was going to play his hand. She started to rise from her chair but Warwick laid a hand on her shoulder and frowned with caution to be silent.

"Get to the point," Richard said irritably.

"A small thing, my lord," Dermot stammered, which Eve knew was for effect. She had to admire her father's acting ability. "I am sure that it will be no problem for you but, well, it is the matter of the bride-price. You have not as yet returned it and as it is customary . . ." He deliberately let his voice trail off and awaited Richard's reaction.

Richard stared at him for a long moment and Eve saw the muscle in his cheek twitch. "It was an oversight. You will have it as soon as possible, I assure you."

"Oh, there is no problem, my lord," Dermot assured him. "It is just that until it is returned, as you know, you are still legally bound. And, I know that you would like to have this matter settled as soon as possible." He glanced pointedly at Claresta, who seemed to be more than a little upset at the news.

"You will have it," Richard growled. "As for the other matter I will give it some thought. As soon as I have reached my decision I will send for you."

"That is all that I ask, my lord," Dermot smiled.

As the door closed behind them, Claresta was heard to murmur a profanity as to Eve's heritage. Her eyes were so intently fixed upon the closed door that she missed the darkening look on Richard's face.

"Claresta, leave us now. I would have a word with Warwick."

She began to protest but seeing Richard's expression she meekly complied, shutting the door quietly behind her.

"Well, what do you think?" Richard growled as the door shut.

"About what? Eve or Dermot?"

Richard threw a stony glare at Warwick. "Both! Damnation! How could I forget about the dowery?"

"How indeed," Warwick muttered but his comment went unheard by Richard, who had begun to pace about the room.

"I swear he must know! He knows that I do not have the means to repay it now! Rodger must have helped himself to it as it is not at Chepstow!"

"Even if you had not forgotten, would you have chosen to pay it when so much was so desperately needed for Striguil?"

Richard ignored the question and continued to pace. "That old goat! He must have known! It is blackmail, nothing more! He will press me for the dowery or force Eve upon me, threatening ruin if I do not comply—unless I agree to help him, of course!"

"Richard, as long as we are discussing it, and I am now allowed to mention her name, there is something that has been bothering me since her disappearance from Normandy. I think it warrants consideration at this moment."

"What is it?" Richard barked. "Get on with it, you sound like Dermot setting me up for the kill!"

"Just this. Did you ever wonder how Gail was able to return Eve to Leinster?"

Richard looked at Warwick as if he had lost his senses. "What are you talking about?"

"Gail." Warwick sighed. "He had never been to England, and we are both aware of his abilities, or the lack of them, yet he managed to secrete her from Normandy, from under our very noses, and take her across the breadth of England, apparently without difficulty. How did he do it? The only conclusion I can draw is that he must have had help—by someone very powerful, someone in a position to lay the way for him."

Richard snorted with apparent uninterest. "Stephen must

have had his hand in it. He merely concluded what he began."

Warwick shook his head over Richard's blindness to the subject. "Then how do you explain how they managed to disappear from Normandy without a trace? Stephen had no influence there."

Richard peered at his friend and his eyes began to darken with new interest. "Are you inferring that Henry had something to do with it?" he asked quietly. "Why would he do it?"

Warwick merely shrugged. "He would not have unless he thought he had something to gain."

Richard walked slowly to the window and stared out into the courtyard below as he considered the question. The moments trickled by slowly and the room was bathed in silence until Richard finally whispered, as if to himself, "Perhaps the answer to that question has come to us today." He turned and looked at Warwick. "By helping Eve to leave Normandy he saw the opportunity to control Dermot—and me." To Warwick's amazement Richard started to laugh but just as suddenly he stopped and turned back to the knight and his expression was hard and bitter. "Unfortunately for Henry he planned on my love for Eve—that I would rush to her cause and settle him firmly in Ireland! However, he did not reckon on the duplicity of a woman!"

Warwick's brow furrowed into a puzzled frown. "What are you talking about?"

"Eve chose her future before she left Normandy. The night that she disappeared I made the ill-timed mistake of going to her. I say ill-timed in that I chose the very moment when she had planned a liaison with Gail. Frankly, I could not care less of what happens to her now—or her father."

Warwick listened with stupefaction to Richard's bitter words. "You found her with Gail?"

"Nay," Richard spat. "He came to her room while I was there. But the looks on their faces spelt their guilt."

"She gave no explanation?"

"I gave her no chance to lie to me, if that is what you mean."

"So that is why you would not listen to Eleanor's and Henry's suggestion that she had been kidnapped," Warwick muttered. He glanced up at Richard, who had taken his chair and had picked up his tankard. "There may be more to this than you suspect, Richard."

"I know all I need to know," Richard growled in answer.

Warwick opened his mouth to protest but he wisely shut it

again. He knew there would be no way to make Richard see reason in his present state of mind. "What are you going to do about Dermot's request?"

Richard rolled his tankard slowly between his fingers as he considered the question. His lips worked in thought, then slowly drew into a smile. "Dermot wants the dowery, and while he may not realize it, that is exactly what he is offering—coin. As for Henry, I will allow him to use me until I have what I want. It is time, my friend, that we had some new adventures, and perhaps a new future. Send a message to our disposed king and tell him that I will see him on the morrow—alone."

"What if Henry disclaims the letter? He must have had a reason for not affixing his seal upon it."

"I will worry about Henry, Warwick. Trust me, before I am through, he will believe that whatever I may do, it was done with his blessing."

23

ve had waited throughout the long morning in the small room at the inn for Dermot to return from his meeting with Richard. There had been little to occupy her time: the mending of a chemise, a letter written to Donnell, and by the time Dermot returned she was ready to wring her hands. Richard had wasted little time in sending for Dermot, only a day had passed since the fateful meeting in the solarium. Her remembrance of Richard's cold regard and his cruelty, not to mention Claresta's presence, had gnawed at her until her emotions were raw and vulnerable. Now, Dermot's news severed what little control she had left.

"You insisted that I come with you to England and now you tell me that I must remain here while you galavant about Wales! It is too much. I will not go to him!"

"Those are his terms, and they are firm." Dermot slumped back in his chair and rubbed his eyes wearily. The meeting with the Earl had proved a tense, sorely won trial and a scene with his daughter now was the last thing he wanted. "I will hardly be 'galavanting' about Wales, Eve, and it would not be safe to take you with me. As I have explained, Rhys ap Gruffund holds Richard's constable, Robert FitzStephen, as hostage in Ceredigion. I will be carrying letters from Richard requesting FitzStephen's release. If Rhys agrees, FitzStephen and his men will accompany us back to Erin."

"Why should Rhys agree to release FitzStephen to you?"

"Because we have no quarrel with the Welsh. It is hoped

that this will be the excuse Rhys has been seeking to release his prisoners. It would set him in good stead with Henry while allowing him to keep his honor."

Eve was still unwilling to concede to Dermot's logic. "Under those conditions Rhys should welcome you with open arms! It hardly sounds like a journey wrought with danger!"

"I also have a letter for Miles FitzDavid in Ty Dewi. Even with FitzStephen's small force the way will be perilous..."

"Miles? But he is an old friend!" Eve grasped at the news hopefully. "That proves that I should go with you! I could help to convince him..."

"Enough of this prattle!" Dermot barked. "I told you that it has been decided that you shall stay!"

"You mean Richard has decided! Without giving either of us a say in the matter! Father, how can you expect me to live here with him and that—that—harlot! Can you not see that this is to be the manner of his revenge upon me?"

Dermot sprung from his chair and glared down at Eve. "Then you will bear it, whatever he demands of you! We came here as beggars, pleading for these English to aid us in a cause not their own! Do you expect them to be generous with us?"

"Why should they not?" she cried. "You are giving them your country! At least you could do it while salvaging some measure of pride!"

"Pride?" He nearly choked on the word as his face flushed to a dangerous red. "Would I be here if I was allowed the luxury of pride? I left that in Erin and I do not expect to know it again in my lifetime! Even if I wanted to change my mind it was too late the moment we stepped foot upon this shore!"

She drew in her breath hopefully, her anger abating as she sensed some doubt in Dermot's resolve. Was it possible that he regretted his decision? "Would you change your mind now if you could?" she asked softly.

"There is no use discussing what cannot be," he answered firmly. "If we do not return with help, your brothers and our people will be lost. All that is left to us now is to bargain for whatever little we can. I am leaving in the morning and you will remain with your husband."

She saw Dermot on his way at the first light of morning and returned to her room to pack her things. She folded each garment carefully into her trunks while trying to keep her mind void of the thoughts of what she would soon be facing. With little success. He had insisted upon her remaining with him—the reason could only be one of revenge. He would force her to live under the same roof as Claresta, humiliating her with the constant presence of his mistress. What other forms would his revenge take? She closed the lid of her wardrobe chest and stared into space, remembering the cold, grey ice of his glare. The remembrance made her shudder. He would be merciless, she was certain. There was a soft tap at the door and a serving girl entered with two men-at-arms who had come for her baggage. At the stern look on Eve's face the girl backed away.

"Mi—milady," she stammered uncertainly, "yer escort is waiting below."

Eve sighed and pointed out her things to the waiting men and then grabbed her cloak and left the room. The time had come and she steeled herself against her dread as she descended the stairs to the common room. As she stepped into the room a large cloaked knight who was standing by a far window turned and, seeing her, broke out into a pleased grin.

"Sir Bowen!" she gasped happily.

The knight crossed to her and bowed low over her hand, brushing it with his lips, then straightened to look down at her, his brown eyes warm with his greeting. "I requested the privilege to escort you, milady. I hope that you are not displeased."

"Nay, Sir Bowen, I am well pleased. It is good to see you again." Her pleasure was genuine. He had grown older, his black hair and beard were now edged with grey but his presence was warm and reassuring as it had been a long time before. Eve felt relieved that Richard had not come for her as it would delay the moment of confrontation but she could sense Sir Bowen's embarrassment in being sent in her husband's place.

"My Lord Earl is occupied with other matters most pressing, milady, and he asked that a reliable escort be sent for you. Those matters are why I am here now in England and they are most urgent," he said uncomfortably.

"I understand, Sir Bowen, and I know something of the matters you mention," she assured him with a smile. "It is of no concern. Shall we be on our way?"

They made their way through the narrow cobbled streets and Eve was distracted by the rows of shops and merchants hawking their wares. She wished, wistfully, that there was time to pause for her to do some shopping. Such a pleasant interlude would be welcomed but she sensed Sir Bowen's urgency so she did not ask. She wondered if she would ever be allowed such pleasantries or if it would be Richard's purpose to hold her a virtual prisoner.

Upon arriving at Bristol Castle, to Eve's relief she was shown immediately to her chambers on the second floor. It was a large cheery room with windows facing the river Avon. Her trunks were set about the room and, anxious for something to do, she set immediately to the task of unpacking, aided by the young serving girl Sir Robert had sent to help her. Barely fourteen, the timid young girl held back uncertainly as she eyed Eve with wide-eyed caution that touched on fear. Seeing the girl's dismay, Eve paused and smiled.

"What is your name?"

"Anna, milady." The girl dipped a curtsy and dropped her gaze to the floor as she twitched nervously.

"Is there something wrong, Anna?"

"Nay, milady," Anna stammered. "That is—I've never been maid to a lady 'efore. I've been 'elping in the kitchen, an' . . ."

"I will show you what needs to be done, Anna," Eve assured her kindly. "Here, take this gown and hang it in that wardrobe." She noticed the girl's hand tremble as she took the gown and she realized that Anna had been expecting a cuff for her dallying. She knew from Dermot that there was no mistress of the household, Sir Robert's wife having died some years before and he had never remarried. She had to assume that the household was run by Sir Robert's steward and the women servants and judged that Anna's treatment had been none too kind under that hand. With some gentle prodding, soon Anna began to relax. It was not long before the unpacking was almost completed and Eve sent Anna for some refreshment and she smiled to herself as she realized that the girl was humming to herself as she left the room. Eve was bent over into a trunk, lost in thought, when she stiffened at the sound of Richard's voice.

"I trust that the room is to your liking."

Eve pulled herself from the trunk and spun about to find him standing just inside the doorway. It was eerily like their first meeting, strange and foreboding, his sudden presence unexpected and somewhat frightening. But, unlike that meeting, she could see him clearly. There was a hint of grey at his temples, or was it only a trick of light from the windows at her back? Why had she not noticed it yesterday? It had only been months, not years! His shoulders were broad in the grey velvet of his tunic, its tightness attesting to the hardness of his

body, which had not changed. Indeed, why should it in such
a short time? But the months did seem a lifetime and he appeared the stranger. So much had happened . . .

"Are you comfortable?" He was still awaiting an answer to
his question and she drew her chin up to look at him squarely,
piqued by the edge of polite irritation in his voice.

"It is quite suitable, milord."

"Good," he grunted. He stepped to the center of the room
and absentmindedly fingered the silk of a gown lying on the
bed. "I have no desire that you should be uncomfortable. If
you need anything . . ."

She bristled at his words, the reality of them bringing her
back to the purpose of her being here. "Indeed?" she snapped.
"Is that why you have brought me to live beneath the same
roof as—as—that woman?"

An icy brow drew up at her outburst, and he smiled coldly.
"So much for the amenities."

"Why, Richard?" she asked bluntly, ignoring his barb. "Why
have you insisted that I come here? Would it not be better if
I were to remain at the inn until my father returns?"

"You are forgetting that you are the one who sought me
out," he answered evenly. He leaned back against the post of
the bed and regarded her calmly but she recognized the smoldering anger in those grey eyes she remembered so well. "As
your father so pointedly reminded me, you are still my wife.
Therefore, you are my responsibility."

"You have everything you want!" she railed. "Why do you
not simply return the cobiche and have done with it—and me?"

"I have my reasons."

"I can well imagine what they are!" She slammed the lid
of the trunk. "I am to live under the rod, as you once threatened,
all because of what you think I did to you!"

"What I think?" He repeated with a short, angry laugh.
"Would you now tell me that I dreamt of our last moments in
Normandy together? Perhaps you have forgotten. Shall I remind
you?"

"Nay, I have not forgotten." She felt tears begin to threaten
her throat and she swallowed them back quickly, angry with
herself that he could affect her so easily, in spite of her reso-
lutions.

"You will believe what you will about that moment, and
all others, yet understanding nothing!"

"I understand all that I need to," he said shortly. "I will speak no more of it."

"Oh, nay, Richard! We will talk of it! I will know what you expect of me!"

They stared at each other in wordless challenge, then his eyes changed slightly, a glint of cruelty flickering across them. "I did not ask you to come back into my life. But, you are here and you will remain my wife, for all the world to see, the mistress of Chepstow, wife to the Earl of Striguil. You shall be what I want you to be. Your life will be as I mold it, with no freedom, no dreams of your own. Aye, even those I will take from you."

She raised her eyes to his and he could see how much his words had shaken her. "And what of your heirs, milord," she said quietly. "Surely Striguil will need heirs and none will be born to such a union. You will lose much for your revenge."

"I will lose nothing, madam." The corners of his mouth lifted cruelly. "Your body is but a vessel to be filled and bring forth my sons as I will it." His eyes traveled over her body slowly, humiliating her with his leisured appraisal. "It shall suit the purpose."

"Richard, you cannot!" she cried, as her voice broke with emotion she was no longer able to conceal.

"I cannot?" he laughed. "Who is there to stop me? You should have thought of this before you forced yourself back into my life. Do not look so stricken. If you play your part satisfactorily, you will find that I can be most generous."

"Richard, if you insist upon this travesty, you had better guard me well," she whispered, her eyes flashing with hatred. "I shall never cease seeking an escape from you, whatever that release might be!"

"I would not expect less," he countered lightly. "I have never known you to surrender willingly. To that end there is another matter you might consider."

Her eyes clouded with fear at the tone in his voice and when he saw her cringe, he smiled. "Your father has made a request of some importance. More so to him than to me, of course. When he returns I have promised to give him my decision. Whether or not I decide to help him in his quest fully depends upon you. Or would you rather see your family and your people perish?"

"Dear God," she breathed incredulously. "That is to be the

condition of my surrender?" Her shoulders slumped in a gesture of defeat and the unwanted tears began to trip from her eyes. "Richard, do you hate me so completely?"

Her defeat caught something and twisted within him but he flung the emotion aside. "The decision is yours. If you take any measure to escape me—any measure—you alone will be responsible for the fate of your people. Do we understand one another?"

She nodded silently, knowing that he had found the one element that could defeat her and she loathed him for it. She turned her face away, refusing to give him the satisfaction of seeing her tears of compliance. Her innermost fears had at last come to pass: he could use her, even abuse her, then set her aside, and she could do absolutely nothing about it.

She heard his footsteps cross the room and the sound of the door closing behind him. The sound of the click as the latch struck home echoed in her head. It was the sound of finality, a desperate decision made and now it must be borne. She turned and looked silently about the room at the disarray left from the unfinished packing. She would bear it. She would finish the unpacking and then order a hot bath. Then she would think about Richard's threats. But she would not crumble, she would bear it.

As she sank into the hot, sudsy water she sighed with pleasure as its warmth enveloped her in soothing comfort. As the water lapped against her shoulders, she closed her eyes and relished the quiet moment, letting her mind drift blankly. The steam from the water drifted about her face, bringing beads of perspiration to her cheeks and forehead. She wiped the glow away with the back of her hand and opened her eyes, letting the reality of the room, and Richard's threats, enter at last. No rights or privileges of her own. He would force her to submit to him and bear his children. No dreams of her own. She knew that he was perfectly capable of carrying out his threats. Nor would anyone question it. Her father did not even have that right. "Dermot MacMurrough, you have erred once more," she thought ruefully. He had brought her to England to help him but had instead handed her to him and given him his revenge. She knew better than to ask him to return her to Erin. She would not give him the opportunity of refusing her; it would give him too much pleasure. Nay, she would give him nothing to use against her. She would play her role, but he would have only her body, never her mind or her soul.

She heard the door open and she twisted about in the tub to find Claresta standing in the doorway, her hand resting on a hip and she was smiling.

"What do you want?" Eve snapped.

Claresta closed the door and walked slowly across the room, her full hips swaying under the beige wool of her skirt, her large brown eyes fixed upon Eve.

"What are you doing here?" Eve repeated the question with growing irritation. "Could you not have had the courtesy to knock?"

"If I had, would you have bid me welcome?"

"Certainly not!"

"Then you have your answer," Claresta said as she trailed her finger in the soapy water. She stopped before the fire and turned as she rubbed her haunches against its warmth. "I think you and I should have a talk."

"We have nothing to say to each other. Now please leave!"

"Ahhh, but we do. To put it bluntly, milady, you should not have come here."

"It was not my wish!" Eve flung at her. "But then, I am sure that you know that."

"Aye, I am aware of it." Claresta shrugged. "I tried to tell him that his feelings are misguided but he evidently feels honor-bound to see to your welfare."

"I am quite certain that you did your best to talk him out of it! How unsettling for you when you found that you could not!"

"Unsettling? Why should it be?"

"Do not play games with me, Claresta. The fact of the matter is he may ease himself upon you, taking his pleasure when it suits him, but he will never belong to you." She paused as Claresta sat on the edge of the tub.

"Go on, this is quite interesting."

Eve grabbed the towel on the table next to her and wrapped it about her as she stepped from the tub. She struggled to control her temper as she wondered how Claresta could remain so infuriatingly calm! "No matter how Richard and I may feel about each other, I am still his wife. And only I can be presented as such."

"How terribly simple you are still!" Claresta laughed. "Do you believe that I entertain such thoughts, that I imagine myself ever being his wife? My fine lady, I have never deluded myself with such! Moreover, I am quite content to be what I am to him—that is where I have the advantage. You see, I have loved him since we were children but I have never expected too much; therefore I have never been disappointed."

"Really?" Eve returned Claresta's smile. "Not even when he married me? Was there not some doubt in you then?" She saw Claresta wince and she knew that she had struck her mark.

"Whatever he may have felt for you it is gone! You made certain of that!"

Eve slipped into a fresh chemise, ignoring the glaring looks from Claresta. "What exactly is it that you expect?"

"I want you to leave here! Now, before you do further harm!"

"Harm? To whom?"

Eve noted with satisfaction that Claresta's composure was shattered as her mouth twisted into an ugly sneer. "Him! Can you not see that? He is intent upon hurting you and it twists inside of him until it can only destroy you both!"

"Are you certain that it is not yourself that you are worried about? He may come to love me again, you know."

"Leave!" she shrieked. "You must, you know it. It is the only way for either of you!"

"I have no say in the matter, I have told you that."

"But you could! I could help you! I have friends that would take you to the coast and you could return to Ireland!"

"Nay, it is impossible. I will remain, no matter what happens."

"If you stay, you will regret it, I promise you," Claresta hissed with such vengeance that it startled Eve, her mouth twisting with each word. "I vow that we both shall be rid of you, once and for all!" She spun and ran from the room, leaving Eve to stare after her. A tingle of fear ran down Eve's spine as the angry words hung in the room long after Claresta had left. She shook her head to dispel the atmosphere, then walked slowly across the room to shut the door. The unreality of the past hours pressed its way into her and she shuddered involuntarily. This is all just a bad dream, she thought. But she knew that it was not. It was real and she would have to see it to its certain end, whatever that would be.

Richard tossed and turned in his bed, muttering an oath as he attempted to settle his body against the lumps and knots that seemed to materialize to disturb his sleep. He flung his arm out from him, only reminding himself of the emptiness of the place beside him. He rose angrily from the bed and, as the chill of the blackened room assaulted his bare skin, he swore again, grasping a cover which he pulled about him. He sat back on the edge of the bed as the blanket fell loosely about him and his mind fixed upon his disquiet.

As he had fought for sleep, each time beginning to drift into its release, his mind had been filled with the vision of flashing green eyes and thick, silky auburn hair as it lay spread over the pillows, jolting him back into wakefulness. He felt an impulse to seek out Claresta where she lay in the room next to his, wondering if her night was as restless as his own. He smiled wryly, realizing that his room lay between that of Claresta's and Eve's, like a buffer, too much like the truth. He recalled the look of surprise on Eve's face when she confronted Claresta in the morning chamber and, while she managed to conceal it quickly, the open pain when she turned to him had not been missed.

"What did she expect?" he growled out loud. He got up from the bed and crossed the room to the fire where he poured himself a measure of wine and plopped into a chair, at last giving in to his own grim thoughts.

Claresta had appeared within hours of his return to Chepstow. She had asked no questions, there was no need as word had spread quickly that their lord had returned home alone. They had stepped into their old relationship with ease. He had taken her without ceremony that first night, his lovemaking cruel and demanding, and he realized later, with some amount of guilt, that he had hurt her. She never made mention of it but continued to be there when he needed her, yet slipping quietly into the background when his mind and efforts turned to his work.

It had never occurred to him that he was using her. Indeed, he would have been surprised to find that she thought of him as anything more than a casual lover. He provided for her well and she was free to come and go as she pleased. He knew that her position as his mistress had elevated her considerably and was looked upon most enviously by her peers. He never considered anything more.

He thought of her now, and the eagerness she would greet him with if he went to her bed. He felt himself begin to stir at the prospect of those soft arms and full breasts and hips. But suddenly, his mind turned to other, fairer game, and his ardor cooled as quickly as it began.

"Damnation! Is she to spoil me for other women?" He sloshed another measure into his goblet and sat brooding into the fire. He had been shocked, and disturbed, by the amount of emotion he had felt when he had first seen her again—and that he could still find her desirable. How much had that knowledge played upon the decision he had made? Why not? he thought; she is still my wife, ironically, and she shall remain so. The thought gave him pleasure and he set the goblet on the table, realizing that there was no better time for her to learn what it meant to be his wife and how things were going to be between them. Why should he deny himself his pleasures as her husband? He rose from the chair and slipped on his chanuses, then left the room.

He gave no pause as he swung open the door to her chamber but, as he did, a vague awareness flashed through the back of his mind—that she had not bothered to latch the door. He made no sound as he entered, his habit of moving silently brought about by years of practice moving through the lines of the enemy. He paused as his eyes became adjusted to the blackness of the room, the only light coming from the moonlight which seeped through the cracks in the shutters. He looked to the bed where she lay sleeping and his large body tensed automatically as he spied another form leaning across her bed.

A sound came from deep with him, an almost animalistic guttural growl as he took the expanse of the room in a few strides, and before the intruder could respond, he was upon him. He clenched the outstretched fist as a gleam of moonlight flashed on silvery metal before it could reach its mark and he twisted the arm about as they locked in deadly struggle. Eve came awake at that moment, the sound of her scream muffled as Richard fell across the bed with the attacker. They thrashed about and Richard pulled him from the bed as his feet regained the floor and his fist found its target, smashing the smaller form to a heap at his feet. The knife clattered against the stone floor.

"Light the lamp!" Richard barked, reaching for the collapsed figure as it began to stir.

Her fingers trembled as she struck the flint again and again until it caught a spark against the wick. As it flamed, she twisted about to find Richard standing by her bedside, crouched over the form of a man who was groaning as he struggled to get to his feet.

"Who is it?" she gasped.

Richard drew the man up by his collar and twisted his face to the light of the candle. She recognized the man to be one of those who had escorted her from the inn that morning.

"Who sent you to do this?" Richard roared, his voice boring into the senses of the man as he struggled against Richard's grasp.

"No one, milord!"

"Tell me now who put you up to this or I swear that you will end your miserable life, here and now!" Richard shouted.

"What is going on?" Warwick appeared in the doorway from his room across the hall, his face still filled with sleep and clad only in his chanuses. Seeing the scene by the bedside, he came fully awake. "God's Breath, what has happened?"

"It would seem that this one was bent upon murder," Richard gritted. "Though I do not think it was by his own reasoning. Who paid you to do this?" He demanded once again as he twisted the collar of the man's tunic.

Warwick stepped between them and laid his hand upon Richard's arm, which would have squeezed the life from the underling's throat. "Richard, enough! You will kill him and then we will never find the answer. Leave him to me. See to your lady!"

He dragged the man from the room and Richard turned to Eve for the first time, finding her crouched wide-eyed on the bed, the covers drawn up about her in an instinct of protection, her expression filled with terror and child-like question. "Who was he, Richard? I mean—why would he want to harm me?"

A surge of protectiveness overcame him, her vulnerability touching him where other emotions had been held in careful check. He sat on the edge of the bed and pulled her into his arms, nestling her against him as he smoothed her hair back from her face. "I cannot imagine," he murmured softly. "You are not to worry; no one is going to harm you."

She snuggled against him, her fear dissolving with the feel of him, her senses filling with his scent, his maleness, and she drew from his warmth and comfort. It had been so long.

"Thank God I came when I did," he whispered, holding her tightly. "Another moment and it would have been too late."

She closed her eyes, savoring his tenderness. "Why did you come, Richard?" She felt him stiffen slightly and she pulled back to peer up at him but he sat back on the bed and shrugged, avoiding her eyes.

"The important thing is that I did. Had I not, the question would be moot. The important question at hand now is why he wanted to kill you."

She watched his face and, as he spoke, suddenly it became clear. With the realization came renewed anger. "The answer is not far from your bed, Richard," she snapped.

"What are you talking about?"

"Your mistress! She made it perfectly clear to me that she would go to any lengths to be rid of me! It would seem that I should have taken her at her word!"

"Claresta?" Richard glowered. "Do not be ridiculous! She would not have had a hand in this. What would she gain?"

"Why do you not ask her?"

"I have no intention of accusing her of such an act," he growled, standing up. "It would be my guess that your father's enemies have followed you here and would be the ones to gain by your death."

"Then go on your fool's errand, Richard! Please, just leave me alone!" she shrieked.

He started to speak but held his tongue in the wake of her fury. She would not listen in her present state of mind. The only way he would be able to convince her would be to prove the identity of her attacker. He strode from the room, pausing at the door to warn her to latch it behind him, and made his way back to his chamber to finish dressing. He found Warwick in the hall with the man-at-arms and Sir Robert, who had been summoned from his bed. They were standing over the hapless man who sat cowering in a chair before the hearth. "He insists that he alone is responsible," Warwick said.

"Impossible," Sir Robert growled, never taking his eyes off of the man. "I warn you, Lucas, to speak. You have been in my service for almost two years and I have never known you to be less than loyal. Why have you done this? Be glad that I have not summoned your knight, but I may still. When Bowen finds out what you have attempted to do he may strangle you with his bare hands." When the man did not speak, Robert lost what little patience he had left. "Blood of the gods, man, the only answer for a crime so horrendous is the gibbet but at least come clean and I will see that your family is cared for! Would you rather that they be cast out? The decision is up to you! Now speak or I shall turn you over to Bowen to extract the truth!"

"Ye mean me wife?" the man laughed suddenly. "Ye would

cast 'er out? I could care less what 'appens to that bitch!"

"I am grieved that such a thing should happen beneath my roof, Richard," Sir Robert said, feeling abashed. "Is the lady Eve all right?"

"She is fine," Richard gritted. He glanced at the man who was peering up at him with a satisfied smile and the look of intense hatred on the man's face startled him. He reached down and grasped the neck of the man's tunic and pulled him from the chair. "Talk, damn you! You might just as well now, for I swear that you will eventually. Did O'Rourke send you?"

"Ye'll never know that!" The man choked.

Richard threw him back into the chair and watched with disgust as the man rubbed his neck. When he had caught his breath, he looked up at Richard and sneered. "Ye don't remember me, do ya, melord?"

"Remember you? Why should I?"

"Aye, why should ye? 'Twas me brother ye killed. His face ye looked down upon as ye stuck yer sword inta 'im. I was lucky, I got away—to make ye pay part of yer price for what ye did. Me and other—King Stephen was glad to hear the news we brought to 'im."

"You!" Warwick bellowed, grasping the man's meaning first. "You were at Maple Leaf with the others?" This time it was Richard who stayed Warwick's arm as the knight reached for the man.

"Nay, Warwick," he said grimly. "He will die soon enough, and not just for what he has done tonight. I still do not believe that he was alone in this. In any case, we will find out before he dies."

"Aye, Richard, I promise you that," Sir Robert agreed. "And within the hour. Warwick, take him to the cellars and see that he is well guarded, then send for Bowen."

Warwick grasped the man roughly and pulled him from the chair. As they started to leave, Sir Robert called them to a halt. "Wait. Take his pouch and I will see that it goes to his wife, whatever the man thinks of her. She deserves it for having to live with him."

"Nay!" The man struggled to stop Warwick and showed the first real alarm since he had been taken. "Nay, it is for another—a woman I know in Bristol!"

"You are in no position to ask for favors. Take the pouch, Warwick."

"Let me have it," Richard said calmly. He had been watching the exchange with interest and now, seeing the man panic, he reached for the leather pouch. He pulled open the draw-strings and dropped the contents into his hand, his head jerking with a start as his fingers immediately folded over the object which had fallen into them. When he looked up, his eyes had turned to a cold, steel grey.

"There will be no need to torture him," he said with control. "I know who paid him."

"What is it?" Robert asked.

"Nothing that I cannot take care of myself. I am aware that this happened beneath your roof, Robert, but the offense was against my wife. I ask you that you allow me to take care of it."

"If that is what you want," Robert answered, puzzled.

"It is. I will tell you of it later."

When the others had left, Richard glanced up the stairs, drawing in his breath. He left the hall, taking the steps slowly, each weighted step setting his resolve for what he knew he had to do. Pausing before the chamber door, he took a calming breath and opened the door, stepping silently into the room.

He crossed to the bed, pausing at its edge as he looked down at the sleeping figure. The light of dawn crept in from the window, turning the room to a soft grey so that he could make out her sleeping features; the thick lashes on fair, rosy cheeks, her hair tumbled in disarray about her lovely face. With a passing moment of regret, he reached down and threw back the covers, bringing a sleepy gasp from the bed's occupant.

"Get up," he ordered, stepping from the bed.

"Richard, it's you! You startled me!" Claresta gasped, but seeing that it was Richard, she lay back on the bed and smiled sleepily, her eyes warming dreamily as she reached out her arms to him. "You frightened me, Richard. That was not a very nice thing to do. If you are very nice, I shall forgive you."

"Get up," he repeated.

Her eyes grew alarmed at the menacing tone of his voice and she rolled over, slipping from the other side of the bed. "Richard, what is it?" she stammered nervously as she turned to face him. A tingle of fear began to creep up her back from the way he was looking at her. He rounded the bed and came to stand before her, his eyes peering down into hers with an anger that made her tremble. Silently, he took her hand and pressed an object into it. Glancing down, she gasped and in-stinctively stepped back from him.

"Aye," he said quietly. "It is the broach you begged me for, the one you spied in London and said that you could not live without. Why, Claresta?"

"Where—where did you get it?" she stammered. "I lost it—I . . ."

"Oh? Why did you not tell me?"

"I—I thought you would be angry."

"Do not lie to me, Claresta," he drawled disdainfully. "We both know how the broach came to be in Lucas' hands. But you should know that your plan failed. She is safe in her room."

Her face fell at his words and, panicking, she threw herself at him, pulling at the front of his tunic. "Richard, I only did it for us. Nay, for you! I only wanted us to be as before! You will never be happy so long as she is here. Remember how she hurt you . . ."

He pried her fingers from his tunic and moved back a step. "Enough. You could be hanged for what you attempted to do tonight. Be glad that the knife did not find its mark or I would hang you myself. As it is, I should thank you in a way for you have helped me to find one who was ultimately responsible for my father's murder. However, what you did cannot be forgotten. You will pack your things and be gone within the hour."

"Nay!" she cried. "Please do not send me away from you! I promise that I will never do anything again to displease you! She is safe, there was no harm done!"

"Take the broach," he continued calmly, ignoring her pleadings. "It will more than see to your needs. You may go anywhere you wish except to Striguil. Do not return there, ever, or anywhere else that Eve resides. Do you understand?"

At the mention of Eve's name, Claresta's eyes suddenly flamed with hatred. "Richard, I pity you! You are so filled with hatred for what she did to you that you are bent on your own destruction! You will destroy yourself because of her!" Her voice suddenly broke into brittle laughter. "The worst of it is that you don't even know that you still love her! That love will keep the hatred alive for both of you, feeding upon itself until you are both consumed by it!"

He turned from her and strode to the door, pausing with his hand on the latch. "Within the hour," he said quietly, then closed the door behind him.

He returned to his chamber, drained by the confrontation. He found Raymond kneeling in the pre-dawn light as he laid the morning fire and he looked up as Richard entered the room.

"Do you wish me to order some breakfast for you?" he asked as he stood up.

"Nay," Richard answered wearily. "But pour me some ale. I could use it just now." He slumped into a chair before the hearth and held out his feet for Raymond to remove his boots. He rested his head on the back of the chair, his fatigue easing slightly from the warmth of the fire. Then he remembered Eve.

"Raymond, go to Lady Eve's chamber and tell her that I wish to see her."

Raymond nodded and left the room while Richard sipped on the ale, the liquid rushing through his body, easing the battered feeling he had been left with from the hours just past. He sat staring into the flames, composing his thoughts of what he would say to her. He would apologize, he owed her that much. For once he would control his anger with her, no matter what she said. Presently, Raymond returned and from the look on his face Richard could guess the manner of Eve's response.

"Is she coming?"

"Nay, milord," Raymond answered reluctantly, his barely whiskered face flushing with embarrassment. "She—she refused to come."

"What did she say?" Richard watched Raymond struggle with the answer. "Go on—tell me."

"She—she told me that she would not be bidden like a servant. She said that—that she would not leave her chambers until her father returned."

Richard's sigh could be heard across the room as he rubbed his eyes. "You may go now. See to your own breakfast. I will call you if I need you."

After Raymond left, Richard sat for hours staring into the fire, sipping occasionally from his tankard. The events of the night had built into a crescendo, causing a climax that had allowed him to see more clearly than he had in a long time.

How much had he contributed to Claresta's actions? Had his own anger given her reason to feel justified in what she had planned for Eve? She had said that he hated her so much that it would destroy them both. It was true. Even when he had sought to bring Stephen from the throne, which had begun with John's death, he had not been so blind to his feelings of revenge. He had understood its threat and had come to grips with it. But now, with Eve, he had been acting on pure emotion, wanting to hurt her no matter what it cost. Why?

He recalled the other words Claresta had screamed at him.

Were they also true? Did he still love her? Was it possible?

For the first time he began to think clearly, without anger, about the events in Normandy. Warwick had suggested that there was more than met the eye about Eve's disappearance. He knew now that Henry had been involved with her departure, that he had used both of them. Had he also used Gail? It was reasonable. Warwick was right, Gail could not have carried it off without help. What part had Eve played? Had she been duped as he had been? After all, she had returned to Erin, to her father. She would not have done so if her purpose was to run away with Gail. What a fool he had been! If only he had known that she had returned to Erin!

He had never believed that she had been kidnapped and now he realized that Henry had not expected him to. The time was not right for him to go chasing after her into Ireland. Henry only meant to keep him in doubt. If Dermot had not played into his hands, what means would Henry have used? Perhaps it would never be known, but for Henry the results were the same. How amused he must have been when Dermot showed up in Normandy with Eve in tow.

All of his life he had been so sure of his decisions, confirmed in his purpose and those he followed. What happens when heroes become mere mortals, with all of the frailties assigned to them? He smiled grimly as, from the recesses of his mind, he recalled Strongbow's words to him long ago. His father had the courage to admit his mistakes and turn them to better purpose. Could he do the same? Henry was right for England but he was not infallible. Could he live with Henry's greed for power, the personal insults inflicted upon him for those purposes, even to taking Eve from him? There had to be more in his life, something that could allow him to regain a measure of the altruistic dreams he once harbored, now tempered with reality.

Eve. His thoughts returned to her, now with a warmth he thought lost to him, and he reveled in it. She was as guileless as he had been, and as much used. Nay, more. What had she suffered, and now under his own hand? He wanted to go to her and tell her of his thoughts but as he imagined the scene he smiled in spite of himself. Nay, too much had happened to think that she would fall into his arms just because he had finally come to grips with reality—his reality. He feared that she would insist upon returning to Erin with her father and it would be the end of it. He could not even be certain that she still loved him. Why should she, after the way he had treated her? She had to learn to trust him again, to remember what they had before, and to want it again.

And, there was the Eve he had known before to consider. Unsure of herself, distrustful, quick to anger with impulsive reactions. If the plans he was formulating were to have any chance of success, she would be an important part of it. But, she would need a courage and strength he was not sure that she possessed. Nay, he could not force it upon her. She had to come to him of her own free will, by her own decision. If she had the will.

Renewed by his thoughts, he rose and stretched. A few hours of sleep were in order, he thought, as he pulled his tunic over his head, though his body was recharged with a hope and an eagerness to the future that he had not felt in a long, long time.

24

Eve pushed the untouched tray aside with distaste. Sighing, she leaned back in her chair and contemplated how she was to spend the endless hours that lay before her.

Over two weeks had passed since the night of the assault and in that time she had not left her room, nor had she seen Richard. The door had not been latched against her; the decision had been her own. She had spent the first two days in self-imprisonment because of an unwillingness to face him, yet fully convinced that the door would open and he would be there—to fulfill the promises he had made to her.

As the days passed, and he did not come, she began to relax with a guarded optimism. Perhaps his hatred of her had stilled his threats and he was now content to leave her to her own devices—his punishment to be endless days of loneliness and uselessness. Her initial relief over his absence waned as the empty days and nights began to wear on her mind and spirit. The four walls of her room became hated objects as she memorized each mark and line of the stone and mortar, the objects in the room becoming symbols of her captivity.

In the past few days she had begun to nurture a new hope, faintly born from her growing restlessness and frustration. Her father would be returning soon and if his mission was successful, perhaps he would not need Richard's help. If he could be persuaded to forgo the bride-price then she would be free to return with him to Erin, and free at last from Richard's anger.

Her only hope, she dwelt excessively upon the possibility, her hours spent in rehearsing the moment with Dermot, countering every objection he was certain to throw at her, building upon the reasons to support her request. In the agonizingly empty hours her mind played upon itself in fruitless hope and she began to see her thoughts as reasonable. The plan nurtured and grew until her entire being focused upon it.

Now, her mood was lighter and she actually turned a smile upon Anna, who had entered to remove her tray. The girl returned the smile timidly, wondering as to Eve's good humor and what had happened to effect such a change. There had been considerable speculation among the servants in the kitchen—that effective chain-work of castle gossip—about the handsome earl and his beautiful, melancholy lady. It was common knowledge that they kept separate rooms and that Eve had not left her chambers since coming to Bristol Castle, and that the earl never visited his young wife. Conjecture formed around the assault upon Eve's life and her blaming the earl; but many insisted that the presence of the earl's mistress had caused the strife between them. Anna agreed with the latter premise; it was not fear she read in Eve, but a deep, abiding sorrow.

In Anna's position as Eve's personal maid, the servants had looked to her as a source of information about the mystery and it had not put her in good stead that she had nothing to offer. Watching Eve as she now sat by the window looking almost peaceful and content, Anna shook her head in wonder. Something had happened to change her mood. Could there have been a change in her relationship with the earl? Anna wondered if she could press Eve to come out of her shell and inadvertently offer a hint to the mystery. She mused excitedly about what it would mean to be armed with such knowledge; to be the object of interest in the kitchen instead of always in the background, ignored by the others. She imagined herself dangling the knowledge tantalizingly before them as they begged or bribed her with a succulent tidbit from the hearth, all the while she taunted them with her secret, until finally she told them at long, long last.

Eve noticed then that Anna was still in the room. "I am not hungry, Anna," she said, but noticing the girl's thinness, added, "You may have it if you wish."

Anna thought of the meager breakfast the cook had given her before dawn, nothing more than scraps left from the previous night's supper, and she picked at the tray eagerly, choosing a tasty piece of cheese. As she munched on it she watched Eve's profile and pondered over what she could say to draw Eve out. Her mind had never been trained to subtleties and she finally decided to plunge right in.

"Milady, ye seem cheerier this morning," she said with her mouth full. "I'm glad, as 'tis been sad to see ye so long of face, all shut up in this room. 'Tis not right, a beautiful lady like ye." Anna washed the cheese down with the warm watered wine on Eve's tray, then wiped her mouth with the back of her hand. Fortified by the fact that Eve had not reprimanded her for speaking, she pressed on, "Aye, 'tis a crime that ye've been shut up in this room with nothing to do and no one to talk to. But, ye was right to insist that 'e send 'er away. No good can come of it by having 'er here while yer in residence. Men think they can get away with anythin' if ye don't put yer foot down now and then."

Eve had only been half listening to the girl but Anna's last words caught her interest and she turned from the window. "What did you say, Anna?"

"That ye were right to insist he send 'er away," Anna repeated as she chose another morsel from the tray. "Things are better now that she's gone. Sir Robert did not like her much, the way she would lord 'erself over all of us when Earl Richard weren't about. Though she sure seemed to act different when he was! Never tried to act the high and mighty when he was here! Knew her place then, she did!"

"Claresta?" Eve blinked. "She is gone?"

Anna paused with a bite of tart halfway to her mouth as she realized that Eve had not known.

"Aye, milady," she said wide-eyed. "Had no one told ye?"

"When did she leave?" Eve pressed.

"Why—the day after ye arrived! She left at dawn she did, bag and baggage." Anna noted Eve's stunned expression and she tried to hide her pleasure over extracting such a tasty piece of gossip with such little ease. So, the earl had conceded to his wife's wishes and had sent his mistress away but he had refused her the satisfaction of telling her. Just like a man, the girl thought, to let her sit alone in her room to fume until she finally found out from someone else! If she had only mentioned it before! Well, at least there would be no reason for her to continue to stay in her room.

Eve had turned back to the window, not wanting Anna to see the confusion on her face. Claresta gone! She must have been behind the plot, after all, and Richard had sent her away! Ironic, she thought, it was Claresta who had left Richard instead of her. They had both lost. She slowly became aware that Anna was speaking to her. "Were you saying something?"

"Just that I suppose ye'll be taking yer meals in the hall with the earl now."

"Nay, Anna," Eve answered absentmindedly. "I shall continue to take them here."

Anna could not hide her surprise. "But why? Now that you know there is no reason!"

"I will not be here for long, Anna. Only until my father returns from Wales and then I shall be returning to Erin with him. Until that time I shall continue to have all of my meals brought to my room." She saw the girl stiffen at her words and her thin pale face seemed to blanch as she set the unfinished tart back on the tray.

"What is it, Anna?"

"No—nothing, milady," Anna stammered nervously. She averted her eyes from Eve and picked up the tray, suddenly anxious to leave.

"Anna, stop!" Eve heard the tray rattle in the nervous young fingers and she went quickly to the girl's side and took the tray from her, setting it back on the table, then grasped the girl's shoulders. "What have you heard?"

The girl panicked. She now wished she had minded her own business and she whimpered piteously as she thought of the fury that was certain to come down upon her head when she answered Eve's question.

"Anna, tell me what you know!" Eve demanded, determined not to let the girl leave the room until she answered her question.

"Yer father, milady," she flinched. "He—he has gone."

"Of course he has gone!" Eve said with exasperation, "Why should that upset you?"

"Nay, milady, ye do not understand. He was here and now he has gone."

Stupefied, Eve stared at Anna and her own face paled as she began to understand what the girl was saying. Her hands fell to her sides as her expression changed to disbelief. "He was here?" she whispered. "When?"

"Two days just passt, milady," Anna answered, rubbing her arms. She wondered why Eve had gone to a deathly white.

"And he is gone, he left?"

"Aye, milady. 'E left with a small body of men. I heard

them say that it had begun, whatever that means."

"Where were they going, Anna, did you hear that too?"

"Aye, milady, they were going to St. Davids and then 'cross the water to Wexford."

Eve slumped into a chair and stared off into space, her face working painfully with the information. Frightened, Anna backed away from her, pulling at her skirt nervously as she stammered, "Is that all, milady? I know nothing else, I promise you!"

When Eve did not answer, Anna picked up the tray quickly and fled from the room, anxious to escape while Eve remained fixed in whatever thoughts had distracted her attention. Eve was unaware that the girl had left as her thoughts whirled with the discovery that her father had returned and had left for Erin without her—without even seeing her! Why was she not told, why was she not even allowed to see him? But the answer came as quickly as the question was formed and her rage flared with the knowledge. She recalled Richard's cuttingly brutal remark about taking her dreams from her and with the remembrance her despair and compliance dissolved under a paroxysm of Irish fury and wrath. Impulsively, she gathered the blue wool of her skirt into her hands and dashed headlong from the room, intent upon finding Richard and having it out with him.

She paused halfway down the stairs. Her eyes swept over the hall to the men who were gathered, until she spied Richard talking with a small group. She was momentarily surprised that Gervase was among the group, and that the hall was filled with strange knights, but she passed it off, the objects of her thoughts only for the tall, dark-haired knight who sat with his back to her.

The knights paused in their conversations and their mouths dropped open in stupor at the sudden appearance of the extraordinarily beautiful young woman and at her manner as she strode across the large room. Her cheeks were flushed with anger and her eyes were boring into Richard's back with open fury. Puzzled glances were exchanged and a few murmured comments were heard as the room became hushed to a deathly silence when she came to stop behind the object of her rage.

"Richard, damn you, look at me!" she shrieked, unaware and uncaring about the gasps of the men.

Their faces froze in shock at the outburst. Richard turned and his face hardened with anger as the knights waited with baited breath to see the outcome of such a display. By now

even those newly arrived had guessed the identity of the outraged young woman. They watched with fascination as Richard
rose slowly from his chair to tower over her but they were
more absorbed by the fact that she did not cringe before him
but stood with her feet firmly planted and her anger matching
his own.

"Behave yourself, Eve, and return to your room," he gritted
quietly. "I will not tolerate such a display of bad manners."

"Nay!" she hissed as her eyes burned into his. "I will not
return to my room! I want to know why I was not told that my
father had returned and why I was not allowed to see him!"

"This is not the time nor the place to discuss it," he said
flatly and began to turn away. "Return to your chambers and
I will speak with you of it when you are calm."

She reached out to grab his arm. "Nay, you will talk with
me now! I will not let you put me off again, not this time!"

Meeting the limits of his patience, he spun back on her and
suddenly felt the force of her hand as it struck his cheek, the
sound of the slap reverberating about the silent hall. The force
of her blow made him flinch and, seeing the cold anger in his
eyes, she braced herself for the returning blow. But the blow
did not come. He grabbed her wrist and spun her about, half-
dragging her across the room as she stumbled to keep up with
his long strides. As he pulled her across the hall and up the
stairs she railed at him in a long stream of Gaelic profanities,
some of which cast serious aspersions on the manner of his
birth. While her words could only be translated by a few, who
were heard to cough, their meaning and intent was all too clear
to the men, who were exchanging wide-eyed looks of astonishment and not a little embarrassment.

Richard pulled her down the hallway and pushed open the
door of her room, practically throwing her inside and slamming
the door behind them, a sound which could be heard in the
hall below. She barely regained her footing and spun back to
lunge at him, intent upon using her nails on his face, but he
caught her wrists before they could reach their target and
wrenched her arms back behind her.

"Stop it!" he roared, his voice breaking through her shrieks.
"Stop it or I swear I'll strike you!"

"Do it!" she screamed. "It would be the least of what you
have done to me!"

He grasped her shoulders and shook her, then released her
suddenly and she fell back stumbling.

"If you wish to talk with me, you will lower your voice and calm yourself!" He glared, ignoring the red welts on her wrists which she rubbed as she continued to glower at him.

"Why did you keep me from seeing my father?" she cried.

"No one kept you from seeing him, Eve," he gritted. "You had but to leave your chambers and you would have found that he was here. You chose to remain cloistered. The door was never locked."

"I did so to avoid seeing you!" she hissed, her lips curling with contempt.

"Then the decision was yours. You cannot blame anyone else for it," he said dryly.

"Did he not ask for me?"

"Aye, he did. And I told him the truth, that you preferred to remain in your room. Oddly, my love, he did not ask after that but seemed content to leave it so."

Her eyes widened at his words and inwardly he winced at the pain that crossed them momentarily. "He left without another word about me?" she whispered, her voice breaking.

When he did not answer she turned and stepped away, her anger sinking into a wretched knot in her chest as she knew full well the answer to her own question. Dermot's mission had been successful and once he had gained his purpose he was all too willing to leave her with Richard. She had probably even been part of the bargain. Richard watched the slump to her shoulders, sensing the hurt and betrayal she felt.

"It is time that you grew up," he said to her defeat. "Stop playing the small child vying for her father's love."

"Oh! You are horrid!" She spun back, her face filled with hatred. "Tell me, Richard, what did you give him, what promises of encouragement to sprint across the water thinking Erin would be his once more? Did you ply him with men and weapons, promising your support, playing upon his greed when you know full well your true intent?"

"My true intent?" he parroted with an arch to his brow. "And what would that be?"

"Don't toy with me! We both know the answer to that! You see my country as part of your dominion, my people as subject to your own greed and that of Henry's, their freedom lost to the building of your own wealth! How long shall it be before you crush his dreams, Richard, as you have tried to do to mine?"

"Tried?" he asked sardonically. "You mean that I have not

been successful? I shall have to try harder."

"Oh, you are vile!" she cried.

"Actually, my love, none of this concerns you. You are the wife of an English peer and your time will be spent fulfilling those duties. I doubt that you will have time to wonder as to the fate of your mother country."

"I may be the wife of an Englishman but I shall never cease being Irish!" The words rolled off her tongue as if they were bitter to the taste. "My blood, aye, the breath of my very life, lay across that water and it will never change, Richard, no matter what you may do to me! This land will never be my home and your people will never be mine! You may be able to force me to live with you, to make me comply with your wishes each day; aye, you can even destroy my dreams of returning to Erin, but you will never make my heart, or my soul, English!"

"Are you so certain?" he asked. His eyes were unreadable as she stared into them and his calmness infuriated her.

"Aye, Richard," she breathed. "I am certain! Your intent is to make me your slave, your purpose to mold me into the form you see as the perfect English wife, eager to please your every whim, denying nothing to her lord and master! Yet, you will be defeated as you have me too late! My people prize their freedom above all else, something you could never understand, thinking as you do that freedom can only be understood by the most powerful and well-born. You, like all of your kind, delude yourselves into thinking that your ways are best and without you the average man could not possibly survive! Nay, Richard, you will not conquer me, nor will you ever fully conquer my people!"

"That is quite a speech!" he laughed. "But I do not recall asking for your heart, only your obedience! And that, madam, I shall have."

He turned from her, ignoring the scathing look of hatred that followed him to the door. As if in afterthought, he paused with his hand on the latch and turned back to her. His voice was cool and calm but his eyes had once again become an icy grey of warning.

"I will not tolerate another display of ill-breeding as the one you gave today. You are welcome to join us, now or at any time, but only if you behave yourself. The alternative will not be pleasant, I warn you. Do you understand?"

She set her mouth tightly and lifted her chin with defiance.

His face darkened at her resistance and he walked back to her slowly, stopping before her as his eyes bit into hers with deadly intent.

"I asked if you understood my meaning?" he said deliberately.

"I understand you, Richard," she scoffed. "But I will not promise to obey you!"

"Nay?" His eyes burned down into hers and inwardly she recoiled from his gaze but she stood her ground. "I think, my love, it is time for your first lesson." Without warning, his hand went behind her back and he crushed her against his hardened body, his other hand tangling into her hair as he brought her surprised mouth up to his. His mouth moved over hers, bruising it beneath the fierceness of the cruel embrace, as his arms held her firmly against escape. She squirmed frantically as she kicked against him ineffectively and she tried to twist her mouth from his. She gasped for breath as his lips found the nape of her neck and his hand left the silkiness of her hair to slip to her waist where she felt him begin to pull apart the fastenings from the back of her gown. She would have cried out in protest but his mouth took hers once again, muffling her cry as she felt her gown being pushed from her shoulders, cascading to her feet to be joined a moment later by her chemise.

His mouth moved demandingly over hers as it forced her lips to part and a hand cupped a breast and his fingers teased its tip until it hardened and he could feel her breath quicken under his touch.

She moaned in anguish as she could begin to feel forgotten and now unwanted feelings begin within her, the tightness in her loins and the tension spreading up over her middle. Desperately fighting the betrayal of her own body, she groaned as she felt her determination begin to melt under the burning heat of his lips and fingers that seemed to scorch wherever they touched her. Unconsciously, her arms went up about his neck and she pressed her body against his as she began to respond to his kiss and her pulse quickened with anticipation, everything forgotten except the feel of him and her own raging emotions.

His hands went behind his neck to take her wrists and he pulled them down in front of him as he set her apart. Confused, she opened her eyes to find him smiling at her.

"I think that is enough for one lesson," he said dryly. "Though I think you will prove to be a quick study."

Her face, still flushed with passion, reddened deeply and she pulled back from him, now filled with self-loathing for the betrayal of her body and the ease by which he had brought about the response. "I hate you!" she sobbed, bending to retrieve her torn garments, quickly covering herself the best that she could.

"Do you?" he chuckled as he watched her struggles. "I would believe that the moments just past would suggest otherwise. Do you understand now that I mean what I say?"

The lesson had been well learned. The next morning Eve dragged herself from her bed and gave special care to her toilette and the choice of her gown. It galled her to submit to his demands but she could not find an alternative. He had made his point, he would not hesitate to use his body, and hers, to bend her to his will. She knew that nothing further could be gained by remaining in her chambers. Besides, Gervase was at Bristol Castle and she hoped that through him she might learn something of Richard's plans and of his last meeting with Dermot. As she dressed she tried to keep her thoughts from what it was going to be like to face the others. You do make your own problems, she gritted to herself, and she recalled Richard's last words to her. They had been spoken softly and she had barely heard them as he had turned to go.

"It is time that you began to control your emotions, Eve. If you do not you will continue to be hurt—and to hurt others."

How often had he said the same thing to her before? And why should he care now? Only to save himself further embarrassment, she reasoned. Had he not said it? She was to be the supreme example of the dutiful, submissive wife.

There was considerable speculation upon her appearance in the hall but out of deference to Richard it was kept mute. In fact, her now docile and mannerly behavior confirmed their opinions that, while she had acted the role of an unruly wife, she had been tamed by her husband, and rightfully so. Indeed, hardly a man there had not had a similar experience, if perhaps not quite so embarrassing to her lord. They sympathized with Richard's position, though it was apparent that he was fully prepared to handle such a feisty mate.

Richard rose from his chair as she approached the table and handed her into the chair next to his, his eyes narrowing with speculation as she turned her gaze from his. He placed her between Sir Robert and himself, the former clearing his throat uncomfortably, but he made polite comment as to his pleasure of having her join their company, and he solicitously asked if she was feeling better this morning. He was dismayed that such a scene should have happened at his table and he now reasoned he understood the events that must have led to their separation. He commiserated with Richard for having taken a foreign wife, unschooled in proper deportment, and his mind traveled back to the memory of his own lady, remembering her tender gentleness and breeding. On the other hand, he mused, as did many another in the room as they noted Eve's exceptional beauty and recalled her wild behavior, perhaps there were other consolations . . .

The meal passed uneventfully although Eve knew Richard was watching her guardedly and suspected that his attention to her was something more than politeness. His hand would rest possessively on hers as he talked with the others, his fingers toying with hers as if to remind her of his possession, his domination. She resisted the impulse to draw it away for fear it would also draw his attention. She knew that there was no way to stop him from doing whatever he wanted but she had promised herself not to give him reason for another "lesson." As soon as the meal was finished and the men drew apart from the tables, she rose, forcing a smile to Richard's unasked question, and wandered from the table. She appeared to make her actions seem casual but she walked slowly across the room and found Gervase where he was talking to two other knights. To her relief, he seemed to sense that she wanted to talk with him privately and, making some small excuse to the others, he drew her apart.

"I am glad to see you again, Eve," he offered kindly. "I have often wondered how you fared."

"I am well as can be expected, Gervase. But what of you . . . and Lavinia?"

"I have heard that she is well."

She did not miss the look of sorrow that passed over his blue eyes. "I had hoped that you would have found a way," she said softly.

"Nay," he shook his head, "I fear that there is little likelihood of that."

"One should never give up hope," came a resonant voice from behind her, "but then, perhaps it is best that you remain unfettered, Gervase. What you deem now to be the object of your dreams could possibly only become a source of regret."

The pair turned to find that Richard had approached and

was wearing a sardonic smile as he nodded to Eve. She reddened at his cruel comment but she kept her temper under control as she turned back to Gervase, ignoring the grey eyes which were now watching her with interest. "Gervase, I was told that my father has left for Erin. Do you know of his plans?"

Gervase looked uncomfortably past her shoulder to Richard, and he was obviously puzzled by her ignorance and was not sure how to answer.

"Your father left because he was recalled," Richard answered bluntly. "It seems that your volatile countrymen of Leinster have seen the errors of their ways in giving their oaths to O'Conner and now seek the comfort of their former lord."

"They sent word of this?" she gasped.

"They did."

"What if it is a trap?" she exclaimed. "It was said that he took only a small force with him. Why did you not send a suitable body?"

"Eve, the conflict is first and foremost Dermot's own. I have no intention of mounting a major force and sending it across that blasted sea if there is no reason for it. The word came in your brother's, Enna's, own hand and your father assured me that he could not be forced to write it, even on pain of death. Therefore, it seemed prudent to let Dermot have his way." As he watched her expression change he cocked his brow and smiled. "Or would you prefer that English armies enter Ireland before they are needed?"

Her eyes sparked with indignation as she replied icily, "I would much prefer, my lord, that no Englishman ever sets foot on Erin's soil!"

"Then you should hope that things go well for him, Eve," he returned evenly. "Then you may have your wish, at least for a time."

Eve looked to Richard, Gervase and Warwick, who had joined them. "Are you all part of Henry's plans to occupy Erin?" she spat.

"No one here plots with Henry to conquer Ireland," Richard answered wearily.

"You deny that is your plan?" she pressed accusingly, her eyes darting to each of them.

"We would not deny that Henry has kindled the idea for some time, milady," Warwick offered. "He has received the Pope's permission to do so, but I assure you that no man here has supported him."

"The thoughts are not original, milady," Gervase interjected. "English sovereigns have long had their eye upon Ireland. You have only the French to thank for your sovereignty."

"That is to satisfy me?" she flared. "I am to be thankful for the troublesome French and now complacently accept our English overlords?"

"No one is expecting you to be satisfied by the prospect," Richard cautioned. "We only want you to accept the inevitable."

"Accept! I accept nothing!" she exploded.

"What do you propose to do about it?" Richard's face darkened. "It was your father's idea to ask for Henry's help. He knew what you have not yet faced, that it would only be a matter of time before Henry made his move. He had very little to lose by playing his hand now, and much to gain."

It startled her to hear him echo Dermot's thoughts but she stifled her surprise and continued to glare at him. "What possibly could be gained?"

"Nothing, if Henry had opted to lead forces into Ireland. However, now there is a chance. The small force I sent with Dermot could enable him to gain control, *if* the people of Leinster and Okinselagh truly wish his return and *if* he does not make an error."

"Do you expect me to believe that you have no designs upon Erin for yourself?" she spat contemptuously. "I find it difficult to imagine you aiding my father out of great love for him!"

Richard's expression hardened and his grey eyes flickered with anger. "Careful, madam. You are showing your temper. I have no intention of discussing my motives with you, particularly in your present frame of mind."

The room had become quiet as attention was drawn to the heated conversation and they were being watched by curious glances. Noting it, Gervase quickly attempted to change the conversation. "Richard, I meant to tell you that everything is ready for the journey." Warwick picked up on the interruption and they drew Richard into discussion of details of the mentioned journey, giving both Eve and Richard time to regain control of their anger.

"Journey?" Eve drawled, when the others had gone. "Could I be so unfortunate to find that you are leaving me for a time?"

"Never fear, my sweet," he countered with an unhumorous smile, "I would not dream of depriving you of my company. We are leaving in the morning for Chepstow and of course you shall accompany us. Are you not anxious to see your home once again?"

She knew that he was baiting her and she forced herself to smile and she meant to answer pleasantly, though she was unable to keep the venom out of her voice, "Of course, milord, I can not think of anything that would please me more!"

25

s they approached Chepstow's gates the overcast skys darkened into a threatening storm. Eve's heart lightened as she spied a short, plump figure standing at the top of the steps to the hall. Sophie squinted to make out the identity of the riders though the red and gold pennons of the deClare coat-of-arms identified them to be friendly. Her plump, rosy face broke out into a huge grin as she spied the small cloaked figure astride the dappled mare which rode next to Richard's Taran. Richard had barely set Eve upon the ground before Sophie had covered the steps to the courtyard and swept Eve into an enormous bear hug. The two women were soon laughing and crying, intermixed with Sophie's admonishments of how much she had missed Eve. Giving her another fierce hug the Scotswoman took charge of the arrivals, ignoring the grumbling of the men as she ordered them about, giving sharp words to the ones she felt were lagging with the unpacking. Begrudgingly, they did as they were bid as even the burliest of them smarted under Sophie's tongue lashing. They threw pleading looks at Richard, who stood to one side, his amusement plainly written on his face as he watched the proceedings.

"Well, don't just stand there with a smirk on yer face!" she snapped suddenly at Richard. "Help yer lady into the hall, can ye not be seeing she's plainly wore out?"

Eve had to smile at the frown Richard threw at the Scotswoman. "Sophie, one of these days I'm going to lock you in a tower room and throw away the key."

"Go ahead, if ye think yer man enough to try it!" she threw back at him.

Richard took Eve's arm and bowed in mocking obedience to Sophie but as they passed he drew back her arm and slapped the amply-rounded buttocks. Eve giggled as Richard laughed at the sharp comment that followed them into the hall but their was no sting in it as Eve could hear her chuckle.

"I see that she has not mellowed in my absence!" Richard laughed. "In truth I do not know what I would have done without her. She runs Chepstow without a fault and I have no complaints."

"My lady Isabel?" Eve asked, glancing about the hall. She thought it odd that Isabel had not come to greet them.

"She died soon after my return to Striguil, Eve," Richard answered quietly.

Eve froze and spun about to look at Richard with horror. "Oh, Richard, I did not know!"

The awkwardness of the moment was saved as Sophie came bursting into the hall. "Sweet Mother Mary, Richard, why did you not tell me that you were returning? Nothing is ready and I had no idea that Eve was returning with you!"

"Everything is fine, Sophie," Richard smiled. "You need not work yourself into a dither."

"Humph! So much you know!" Sophie snorted. "Well, we will do the best that we can! Come, lass, I'll be seeing you to your chambers and you can freshen up. We'll be having to do some mite of rearranging later but I suppose we can make the laird's chambers suitable for the time being."

"Nay, Sophie. Eve shall have Lady Isabel's chambers."

Sophie's shrewd gaze darted from Richard to Eve and from the flush on Eve's cheeks it took her only a moment to understand the situation. "So, that is the way of it?" she shook her head. She started to say more but from the imploring look on Eve's face she bit back her comment and headed for the stairs. "Come on then, lass, and I'll be settling ye in."

Though it was apparent that Sophie was fairly bursting with questions, it was not until Eve had bathed and her trunks were unpacked that Sophie dismissed the serving girls and, shutting the door behind them, she turned to Eve. From the expression on her face Eve knew that the respite had come to an end.

"Well now, lass, it's been a good long time since we've been able to talk!" She took the chair across from Eve where their supper had been set but for once the older woman's attention was not on food. "Well now, I've been patient. Out with it."

"I do not know where to begin." Eve sighed.

"For a beginning, tell me why you left Normandy!"

Knowing there was no escape, Eve explained her reasons for her disappearance, Gail's involvement, and the part her father had played. To her relief, Sophie listened quietly, digesting what Eve was saying without comment.

"I do not know what else I could have done, Sophie! I could not remain as things were! Had I told him of my plans he never would have let me go! If only Gail had not taken my letter, he would have understood and everything might have been different."

"I wonder," Sophie mused as she mulled over what Eve had said. "If you had taken me into your confidence, child, I would have warned you that nothing can be accomplished by running away."

"I know that now, Sophie," Eve said quietly.

"You gave yourself into the hands of another, Eve. Can you expect Richard to forgive that easily?"

"But nothing happened!"

"I do not doubt you but then I am not the one who has to be convinced. You allowed your pride to become more important than his feelings. Now, I fear, his pride and honor are involved, and his distrust. Once lost, that is the hardest to regain."

"Aye, and his pride and honor are so much more important than mine!" she said angrily. "Do you know that he would have forced me to live beneath the same roof as Claresta, humiliating me with her presence as his mistress? If she had not taken it into her hands to do away with me, she would be here still!"

"What are you talking about?"

Sophie's eyes widened as Eve recounted the story and whistled softly as Eve finished. "So. I wondered what had happened to her. Well, good riddance to that one. Now that she is gone perhaps the two of you . . ."

"Nay!" Eve shook her head in angry denial. "There is nothing for us, not anymore!"

"But Eve . . ."

"Nay!" Eve jumped up and turned away as she set her hands on her hips. "Sophie, I know you mean well but I will not talk

of this anymore! You do not understand the situation and I am
not going to explain it! He refuses to return the bride-price—
which is the only solution for either of us! He means to keep
me here as a—as a chattel!" She spun back to Sophie, enveloped in her bitterness. "Please, Sophie, do not speak of it
further! There is nothing you could say that could convince me
to accept what he has planned for me!"

The following morning Eve found the hall empty but for the
servants who moved through the hall on their way to other
tasks. Relieved by Richard's absence, Eve tore a chunk of
bread from a mazer on the table and sat on a stool near the
hearth as she munched on the breakfast. It was there that
Waverly, Richard's steward, found her moments later. The
small, portly steward's arms were laden with massive leather-
bound books, which he dropped on the dormant table.

"When you have finished your breakfast we can begin,
milady," he said in a businesslike tone. He took a chair and
opened one of the ledgers, then looked back at her with an
expectant expression. Seeing that Eve had just popped the last
of the bread in her mouth, he pulled the chair next to him out
from the table and nodded toward it. "Shall we begin?"

"Begin what?" she asked, puzzled.

"Perhaps it is too soon," the steward frowned thoughtfully.
"Lord Richard said that we were to begin immediately. If you
wish to wait until another time, I could speak with him."

She went to stand beside him, her curiosity deepening as
she glanced at the ledgers. "What is this, Waverly?"

"Why—the accounts, milady!" Waverly said with surprise.
"Did milord not tell you? As mistress of the household you
must acquaint yourself with them. There is much to learn,
milady. A manor of Chepstow's size requires a great detail to
organization. But do not fear, I assure you that you will find
the ledgers in good order." He glanced at the books with pride
as he touched one with a gesture akin to affection.

"Richard said this?"

"But of course," he answered, looking at her strangely. "Is
there something wrong?"

She shook her head as she took the chair next to his. Her
surprise over Richard's request was soon forgotten as Waverly
took her patiently through the ledgers, explaining each entry
with painstaking detail. He was delighted with her interest in
the accounts and her quick grasp of the entries. He gradually
warmed to the task, answering her poignant questions with a

warmth in his smile seldom seen on his usually staid face. He would never have presumed to question Richard's orders, serving him with a steadfast faithfulness as he had Strongbow before him—but he had wondered as to the advisability of placing such a responsibility on the Lady Eve. He had remembered her only as a flightful, spirited young woman and he had serious doubts as to her capacity for taking the position as Chepstow's mistress. After all, her background had to be considered and she could not hope to take Lady Isabel's place, that lady had been born to the position. He had begun to suggest his opinion to the earl but Richard had dismissed it, most firmly.

They were into their work barely an hour when Richard and his knights entered from the courtyard. Eve wrinkled her nose as the smell of sweat and horse assailed them and she rolled her eyes at Waverly, who merely smiled and closed the ledger.

"Perhaps we might finish this later, milady."

"Aye, Waverly, when things are again quiet." She laughed over the bedlam that had begun in the hall.

Grey eyes looked up with interest at the sound of Eve's laughter. Richard unbuckled the belt of his sword and dropped it on the edge of the dormant table. His eyes widened as Waverly leaned over to Eve's ear and whispered something that caused them to break out in laughter before the steward rose to take his leave.

"It would seem that you are getting on rather well."

Eve looked up to find Richard standing by her chair. "Aye, milord. Did you think that we would not?"

"I did not consider it at all, but I have seldom known Waverly to display a sense of humor. I think you have won him, madam."

She wanted to ask him about his decision to involve her in Chepstow's business but her question fled as she became aware of the intent way he was looking at her. Her breath caught and she looked up at him with uneasiness but he merely smiled and turned to join the others who were diving enthusiastically into the mutton and cheese set out by the servants.

Shaken, she forced herself to be calm, yet wondering why she was trembling so. She rose to help the harried servants serve the men, pointedly avoiding Richard. If he noticed that she was keeping her distance, he gave no evidence of it as he set to his meal and conversation with those on either side of him. It seemed only a short time later when he grabbed up a piece of mutton and rose to take his leave, the signal leaving the others to groan but they quickly followed suit. Suddenly they were gone and the hall echoed with its emptiness. Their short-lived company left it emptier than before and Eve thought she could almost hear her heart beat. Or was it his absence that made her heart beat so? If he had been angry, or threatening, she would have been prepared for it—but to face that there had been something else in that look, however brief, was more than her confused emotions were prepared to handle. Leaving the rest of the disorder to the servants, she left the hall to seek out Waverly and his accounts.

The men had not returned before evening and Eve joined Sophie in the hall for a light supper. The two women sat at the end of the side table, enjoying the peace of each other's company and they had just finished their supper when the men returned and slipped wearily into their chairs. The servants bustled about to see to their needs, supervised by the capable Sophie, who pressed Eve back into her chair when she had attempted to help. Alone, Eve forced herself not to seek out Richard though she knew if she looked to the center of the dormant table he would be there. The thoughts of the morning came rushing back and she feared if she looked up she would find him watching her. Thus engrossed, she jumped at his touch when he appeared at her side and took her hand, bringing her from the chair. Wordlessly, he led her to the chair next to his and handed her into it, ignoring her questioning look of surprise. Glancing about she caught the smiles on the faces of Chepstow's knights as they bent back to their suppers and she felt her color heighten. Richard poured her a measure of spiced wine before turning to his own supper. She sat rigidly, her hands folded in her lap, ignoring the goblet he had poured for her and as he reached across her to the salt cellar his voice was low, and surprisingly gentle.

"Are you feeling well?"

"Why, Richard?" she gritted.

"You are my wife, your place is at my side," he answered calmly.

There was nothing she could say in rebuttal, not even to his tone as there was no anger nor mocking to his voice. Almost immediately he had turned his attention to Warwick who sat on his other side and Eve toyed with her wine as she listened to their conversation. Where was his anger, or at least his accustomed teasing? Was he playing with her in some new game? Were all of his threats smoldering beneath the surface, waiting for her to make the wrong move, to say or do something that would give him cause to strike? By the end of the meal she was a self-imposed bundle of nerves.

As he finished his meal and leaned back in his chair, he glanced down at her and his brow lifted in mild surprise. There were high spots of pink blush on her cheeks and her large green eyes were bright with anger.

"Is there something wrong, my love?"

"With your permission, I would like to retire," she said tightly.

He leaned an elbow on the arm of his chair and rested his chin on his hand as he regarded her thoughtfully. "Is there something you would like to talk about, Eve?"

"Nay!" she gritted.

"We do not have to talk here," he offered, following her nervous gaze about the room.

"I wish to retire, milord—alone!" she whispered angrily. His meaning had not missed her and she panicked at the thought that he would accompany her to her room.

When he did not answer, she forced her eyes to his and found him smiling but his eyes did not match the curve of his lips. "Fortunately, milady, your wishes are not in contest with my own. If they were, I assure you that you would not have any choice in the matter."

As she left the table her back stiffened; she could feel his grey eyes boring into her back. She kept her chin up and smiled at the few faces that looked up as she passed, avoiding only Sophie's inquisitive stare as the Scotswoman paused at the kitchen door, her hands full of a large steaming mazer.

In the days that passed Eve found that each confrontation with Richard became more unsettling. He was solicitous in his attention of her, coolly polite and, to her surprise, his demands were few. The greater part of her time was taken with Waverly as she learned the mysteries of Chepstow's accounts that were to be added to her other duties in running the large manor. But while learning to be Chepstow's mistress kept her mind from her problems, it was also a reminder of who was its master. In her duties, she would often have to consult with him on some matter and while she would approach each encounter with considerable deprecation, she found his manner irreproachable. He met each instance with his full attention and some manner of kindness but she sensed that he was waiting for something. She would catch him watching her thoughtfully but, when he confronted her gaze, he seemed to draw a veil over his eyes and they would be as before, noncommittal and distant.

What did he want? What was he waiting for? How long could she go on like this? It was like finding herself alone and unarmed in a forest and waiting for an angry, circling wolf to spring.

Two weeks after their return to Chepstow she entered the hall of a morning and found Gervase and Warwick having their breakfast. It surprised her to find them there, since she had risen later than usual. She had awakened early but, faced with the prospect of another day of the same, she had rolled over and gone back to sleep. The sameness, without prospect of change or even answers, was too much to face. When she had finally risen, and gone listlessly through her dressing, she had descended to the hall with an unaccustomed heaviness of spirit. As she found her old friends in the hall, she had greeted them with a half-smile to their pleasured welcomes.

"Milady, are you ill?" Gervase asked with genuine concern. She looked pale and wan and a little thinner than normal.

"I am fine, Gervase," she answered as she poured herself some ale from a table near the buttery. As she strolled over to the men, who were exchanging concerned looks, she sipped from her tankard and glanced about. "Have you seen Waverly?"

"He rode out early this morning," Warwick offered. "I believe he had matters to see to at Caerwent. I do not think he will be returning before the end of the week."

"He did not mention it to me," Eve said, pouting, as she sat by the knights. "Well, perhaps I can be of some use to Sophie this morning."

"She is riding with us to Maple Leaf," a deep voice came from behind them. Richard had entered from the kitchens and he was munching on a piece of bread and cheese as he came to sit across from her and propped his feet on the table.

He noted the look of disappointment on her face as she turned away, sighed and looked about the hall.

"If your duties are not too pressing, perhaps you would wish to join us," he offered casually. Stretching, he pretended not to notice the happy change in her expression as she turned to him.

"May I?" Her listlessness had suddenly faded and the unguarded look she gave him was washed with a childlike excitement.

"Of course, if it would please you," he answered. As he watched the animated change to her face, he had to fight a smile.

"Oh yes!" She jumped from the table, barely containing her excitement at the thought of a morning ride, delighted with the sudden rescue from what had promised to be a dull morning. She started from the room but halted at the foot of the stairs and looked back with hesitation. "Can you wait for me? I must change."

This time he could not contain his amusement. "Aye, we can wait," he laughed.

She hitched up her skirt and fled up the stairs. Richard watched her go, openly grinning as he absentmindedly reached for his tankard and looked up to find both Warwick and Gervase watching him with interest.

"What do you find so amusing?" he growled.

"Us? Nothing," Warwick answered as he looked at Gervase in mock surprise. Gervase answered in kind and the two returned their attentions to their meal but both were grinning broadly. As they finished their meal, Eve returned. The men turned as she reached the foot of the stairs and they saw Richard's eyes sweep over her appreciatively and linger on her narrow waist of the tight-fitting corn-flower blue wool of her gown, the smooth neckline accentuating the fullness of her breasts which caught his eye. She had fixed her hair into two thick braids and wrapped them in a coronet about her head, covering them with a shoulder-length coif of transparent white gauze.

"You look lovely, milady," Gervase offered first, his own gaze fixed involuntarily upon the inviting cut of her gown. Hearing Richard clear his throat, he pulled his eyes from her and ignored the perturbed and angry gaze of his lord. Richard took Eve's arm and escorted her from the hall, throwing back over his shoulder to Gervase that he was to find Sophie. Warwick was mounted when they reached the foot of the steps and he held the reins of Eve's mare as Richard lifted her into the saddle. A few moments later Gervase and Sophie emerged carrying two large baskets, which Gervase affixed to the back of the saddles.

Eve's spirits were lifted as they rode out along the banks of the river Wye, the sharp hooves of their mounts clattering over the bridge. They crossed to the east and made their way along the irrigation canals. The morning was bright and warm,

adding to Eve's pleasure as she turned her face to the soothing
warmth. For the first time in many months she felt almost
content and she made her mind up that nothing, not even Richard, would be allowed to spoil such a beautiful morning. The
hills were rolling blankets of velvet shades sprinkled liberally
with gold and white wildflowers that seemed to have blossomed
to fit her mood. The air was fresh and clean and she drew of
it deeply, closing her eyes momentarily to savor it, unaware
that Richard was watching her, entranced by the rapture on her
lovely face.

They would pause occasionally and the men would dismount
to talk with the serfs working the fields. Eve only half listened
to another exchange as her mind wandered lazily and her mare
munched on the grass at the edge of the field. While she looked
out over the planted fields, something began to play at the back
of her mind, something she had seen at each farm that struck
a small discord within her but had yet not formed in clear
thought. She shrugged it off and yawned behind her hand, her
attention brought about again, as the men swung into their
saddles.

As they rode toward the village, Eve spied a small boy
sitting under a tree at the edge of the road. He jumped up as
they approached and stood back to watch them as they passed.
He was dressed in sturdy trousers and shirt and his face wore
the normal smudges of a boy who has been playing but as they
passed Eve saw him closely and the smile she had offered the
lad froze on her lips. She recognized him as the son of one of
Striguil's tenants but the change in him since she had seen him
last was startling. Then, he had been a happy youngster with
plump rosy cheeks, cheeks which were now sunken below
gaunt eyes that haunted her long after they had passed. She
turned to look back at him but he had disappeared into the
bushes that lined the road.

Gervase and Sophie were engaged in a happy banter and
seemed unaware of the boy or the change in his appearance.
Eve glanced about the countryside, her eyes sweeping over the
fields as a subtle spark nagged at her that there was some
connection between the boy and whatever had been bothering
her. Richard rode a few lengths ahead and she was about to
push her mare abreast of him with her questions when they
turned the road and rode into Maple Leaf.

The village had been rebuilt, with the exception of the inn,
whose grounds was grown over with grass and weeds, only

small bits of charred timber remaining here and there to remind Eve of what had happened.

They dismounted in front of one of the larger mud-and-wattle cottages and tied their mounts to the standingposts. Almer, Maple Leaf's barrel-chested smithy, left his forge in the three-sided structure next to a cottage and wiped his soiled hands on his heavy leather apron as he came forward to meet them. His enormous arms and shoulders glistened with sweat. He wiped his dripping brow, and came to a sudden halt as he spied Eve next to Richard.

"Milady!" he grinned as he nodded a clumsy bow. "Ye've returned! Gawd, that is fine! Me missus is just puttin' out a good meal. Will ye be doin' us the honor to take it with us?"

"We'd be pleased, Almer." Richard smiled. "But first there are some matters we should discuss. Gervase has a splendid idea for tailoring that new plow."

"Heh?" Almer glanced at Gervase speculatively. "Well now," he grinned, "has Sir Gervase decided to smite his sword into a plowshare as the good book says?"

"Nay, I shall leave the matter to you, Almer," Gervase smiled as the men walked toward the smithy. "However I did have an idea..."

As the men disappeared Eve followed Sophie into the cottage. It was a large single room with a hard-packed dirt floor but it was swept and scrubbed to a neat orderliness. There was a bed against the far wall with a straw-filled mattress covered with furs and blankets and a large trestle table in the center of the room with long benches on either side. Two wooden chairs flanked the stone hearth where Martha, Almer's wife, was bent stirring a steaming pot hung on a hook over the fire. She looked up as they entered and her face brightened as she saw Sophie, then turned to a puzzled frown as she spied Eve at her side.

"Milady!" she gasped, recognizing Eve. She dipped a curtsy as the spoon in her hand dripped gravy onto the earthen floor.

Eve heard a sound and turned to find a small cradle at the end of the bed. She went over to the cradle where a baby whimpered then settled back in his sleep into heavy infant breathing.

"Oh, Martha," she whispered. "How wonderful! Is it a girl or a boy?"

"A boy, milady." Martha smiled, then added as a touch of pain passed over her hard working face, "God was good to us and blessed us with this late child to replace the one we lost."

A hard lump formed in Eve's throat as she recalled the hated vision of the small lifeless body clasped in his father's arms. Sophie changed the subject and plopped herself at the table, begging for a cup of cool water to save herself, she insisted, from expiring on the very spot.

The three women sat chatting and when the child woke and began to whimper, Martha scooped him up from his cradle, the baby's whimper rising into a lusty howl before she could even return with him to the table. She unlaced the front of her bodice and offered the babe her breast, all three women laughing delightedly as the child's cries were cut to a comic halt as he found the source of his dinner. As Eve watched the contented baby nurse, her mind flashed with the remembrance of the child she had seen by the edge of the road earlier.

"Sophie, did you see that boy we passed on the road?"

"What boy?"

"He was standing under a tree, just before we turned the bend to the south of the village. You did not see him?"

"Nay, lass, was their something wrong?"

"He looked as if he were starving! But I knew him before and I cannot believe that Richard would allow any child to come to that state! Even when Stephen was on the throne, Strongbow was able to care for his people!"

Sophie and Martha exchanged glances. "Lass, no one on Striguil's lands are starving," Sophie assured her. "Richard sees that none go without, in shelter or food."

"But I saw him!" Eve protested. "I do not think I shall ever forget that hunted look . . ."

"Milady, Sophie is right," Martha said. "The trouble came afore Lord Richard returned. In the year that he was gone 'twas a black time for us. Stephen's men took whatever they wanted and they came often. We spent most of the time hiding in the mountains so there was no way to farm the land, or seed to do it with. We lived off of what we could forage in the hills. Ye will not find any old ones in Striguil now and only the hardiest of the young survived. As for the ones who did, it will take 'em a long time to lose that look of hunger."

"But what of Richard's cousin—Rodger. He was to look after the lands!"

"Oh, he came a few times and stayed at Chepstow." Martha shrugged, shifting the babe in her lap. "I heard that 'e took what 'e wanted from the castle. We never saw 'im."

"You should have seen the lands when we returned, lass,"

Sophie added, shaking her head at the memory. "I'll never be forgetting the look on Richard's face when he saw it. But he's made of the same stuff as his father, to be sure. He wasted no time on bemoaning but took hold and began to set it to rights!"

"'Twill take a long time," Martha said. "Aye, years before he's able to put it all in seed again."

"That's it!" Eve exclaimed. "That is what has been bothering me all morning! The fields, they are so much smaller than I remembered! They used to run to the foothills, as far as the eye could see!" She looked at the two as she pondered the mystery. "Why does he not plant it now, when there is such need?"

"Eve, lass, that takes coin. As Martha said, Laird Robert took Chepstow of all that she had. When Richard returned he had only what he had gained in Normandy. It was a goodly amount but the land took it up like a ravenous animal and still bays for more. Striguil is building but it will take time."

Eve looked from one to the other in stunned amazement. Richard had put everything into the land. It would take time . . .

"Why, that bastard!" she whispered. Without warning she jumped up and fled from the cottage, leaving Martha to stare wide-eyed at Sophie, whose gaze followed Eve with a decided frown.

Sophie found her sitting on the stump of a tree near the edge of the forest in view of the charred remains of the inn. She was so engrossed in thought that she did not hear the older woman's approach until Sophie stopped beside her and set her hands on her hips as she looked at Eve's expression with dismay.

"Ye think ye've got it all figured out, don't ye?"

Eve's head snapped about and she glared accusingly at the Scotswoman. "You knew all along, didn't you? Ever since I told you about the bride-price! Why did you not tell me?"

"Because I know how you jump to conclusions," Sophie answered. "You're thinking right now that he did not return your dowery for being want'n' of the coin, are ye not?"

"Of course! He said that he had his reasons and now I know what they were! He had no choice!"

"You're wrong, lass. He'll have the coin soon. The crops will be good this year. If he didn't want ye he could have made the promise to yer father, aye, even borrowed the sum if he'd had the mind to set ye packing!"

"Oh, Sophie," she groaned, not hearing the words. "How

he must hate me! No wonder he wants revenge upon me—this now added to the other!"

"Eve, listen to me! Ye loved him once and ye know what kind of a man he is! Do ye think he's the kind who'll be bent upon revenge once the anger has passed? I've seen him with ye. He doesn't act like a man who hates ye, and ye'd know it too if ye weren't so blind!"

"But he does! Everything he has said to me . . ."

"Ah, and ye believe it, such the fool ye are! And what has he done to ye? Has he forced himself upon ye? Has he made ye miserable with his demands, humiliating ye before the others—or has he treated ye with respect and kindness and, aye, and honor as his wife?"

Eve raised her head slowly and looked at Sophie with doubt. "But—he has never said . . ."

"Ah! And ye expect it all from him! What have ye done to let him know how ye feel, except that ye hate him! Ah, don't be bristling at me, lass! Face yer own mistakes and the real reasons for them. Did ye ever ask yerself for the true reasons ye left Normandy? And before that, why did ye flee from him before yer marriage? What have ye been running from and what are ye running from now?"

"I don't want to be shuffled about like a pawn, without feelings, without a mind or thoughts of my own!"

"And where do ye hope to find the answer to that, love? Where else in the world do you think things will be different for ye?"

"I don't know," Eve answered wretchedly. "But it is not here."

"Where then?" Sophie pressed. "In Ireland? Ye told me that yer father would have sold you to O'Rourke as a chattel if ye had not obeyed him."

"And you think the answer is with Richard? He has no faith in me, Sophie, and in spite of what you say he has no love for me!"

"And you cannot give him the chance to find it, can ye? Eve, birds and animals accept what they know without question. But not people! You've had trouble between ye—how can you expect him not to question love? How can you expect him to give you more than you will give to him?" When Eve did not answer she sat down beside her and patted her hand. "Lass, ye grew up sheltered, pampered and spoiled. Aye, you know it so do not look at me that way. But inside of ye there was much more—a bright young woman with spirit and a need to be more than a pampered and spoiled young wife. Ye need to feel fulfilled and you've expected others, beginning with the father, and now Richard, to give it to you like a gift instead of realizing that it has to come from within you."

Eve's anger slowly abated as she heard Sophie's words echo to a time before. Hadn't Richard once brought her to realize the same thing? How easily she had forgotten it in the time past, with everything that had happened. Nay, she had not forgotten, but this time was different! "Sophie, what you say is true but now things have changed. How can I give in to him without forgetting all of my principles?"

"Eve, I do not know what principles ye mean unless you think that by giving him yer love ye demean yourself!"

"But my love is not what he wants, for he will not give it. He wants my obedience, nothing more."

"Lass, do not confuse your sexuality with weakness!" Sophie laughed softly. "Ye have a power ye have not even discovered yet. When ye find it, he will love ye again."

"Power?"

"Aye, lass. Men and women are different because it is meant to be. The relationship is served by the difference! Revel in being a woman! It does not demean or lessen you! It is in the search of each other, the discovery, that you will both find all that you seek. If you fight it, then nothing will remain except confusion and dissatisfaction for both of you!"

"Oh, Sophie, why am I so weak? Before I returned to England I made up my mind to face whatever was given me and see it through. But, as soon as I saw Richard again all my determination was swept away! All that I have been able to think of is how angry he makes me!"

"Ahhh, yer not weak, lass, just confused, and frightened. Meet him halfway, give him a chance! He won't disappoint ye!"

"How can you be so sure?" Eve asked ruefully.

"Trust me, lass. Nay, trust him. What have ye got to lose?"

"Only my soul," Eve whispered.

Eve walked along Chepstow's battlements savoring her solitude in the warmth of the July sun. She paused in her stroll and leaned her elbows on a parapet, letting her gaze wander across the river to the meadows and fields that stretched beyond its broad banks. The scrub oaks dotted the edge of the lazily drifting river, scattering the meadows to run to the craggy grey mountains in the distance.

During the past weeks she had spent hours thinking of what Sophie had said though they had not talked of it again. She had faced many truths, some not so pleasant. She had betrayed him, letter or no letter. She had run home to her father, not only to plead with him to reconsider his decision about their marriage, but to return to the only place where she had known safety. That too had been false. She had never, in all the years of growing up, accepted what her father had planned for her but she had never asked herself what she wanted. It was not until she had been uprooted, thrown unwillingly into a new life, that she had felt truly frustrated, though she realized now that the restlessness had always been there. And, with complete honesty she had finally come to grips with what she had been looking for.

Richard. There was no longer any question in her mind, no doubts. She loved him. She had never stopped loving him. Whatever else was important to fill her life he was part of it and without him nothing had any meaning. The completion of her soul, though he might be the source of destroying it. She could not accept, however much she might want to, Sophie's belief that he still loved her. The Scotswoman, in spite of her good intentions, was a romantic. Things were not that simple. You did not cause something to be just because you wanted it. Aye, he was kind and tender with her. He had brought little of his threats to bear though she did not doubt that he would be capable of it if she pressed him. So, perhaps he had forgiven her. But love, that was a different matter entirely.

She would love him, she couldn't help it, she wasn't sure that she wanted to help it if she could. But she would not cower and submit to him. She could not become what he wanted her to be, a simpering and meek example of submissive clay, molded to his purpose. Her love would have to remain within her, he would never know of it, she would never give him that to use against her.

It was hopeless. If there was not enough between them, there was now the conflict between their peoples. She was caught in the middle and she had meant what she had said to him in Bristol. She was Irish, and would always be. As she walked along the parapet, the warmth of the summer sun baking into her mind, pressing in a freshness of truth that came with the revelations about herself, she suddenly knew what she had to do. Just as she could not exclude the outside world from their lives, the only chance for them was freedom, a fresh start that would allow him to make decisions about her from the viewpoint of a new beginning. She would find Warwick and take him into her confidence—almost. He would help her to the solution.

As for the other part of her quandary, there was no answer. The conflict between their peoples was coming and she hadn't the vaguest idea of what could be done about it. She felt that her father was wrong and that the lack of unity among the people of Ireland made them open to invasion. Indeed, how could they hope to throw off the invader when they would not stop fighting among themselves? But she was only one woman, how could she do anything about it? If the gods were so inclined they would offer a way. Other than that she could only seek to find a solution to her more personal problem, and indeed, she may have found a way.

She left the battlements and wound along the close circular staircase that led below. As she reached the door to her chambers, Waverly came rushing breathlessly along the hallway toward her.

"Milady, I have been looking for you everywhere! We have a visitor and Lord Richard requests your presence in the hall!"

It was the first time that Richard had sent for her and she followed Waverly with some feeling of apprehension, wondering at the urgency of Waverly's manner. As she descended the stairs she halted abruptly, her heart quickening as she spied Miles still covered with the dust of his travels. He sat with Richard, Warwick and Gervase, and she hurried the few remaining steps, eager for the news she knew he brought with him from Erin.

"There you are," Richard said, looking up at her. "We have been waiting for you. Miles has brought us news."

"Is my father all right?" she asked as she took the chair next to her husband.

"He is well, milady."

"You were telling us of the landing," Richard said. "Was he well received?"

"Aye, Richard. In Okinselagh we encountered no resistance. Indeed, the people welcomed him eagerly though they were a bit stunned to find us in Dermot's company. Though Donnell had told the elders of Dermot's mission I do not think they thought that he would be successful."

"What of O'Conner and O'Rourke?" she asked. "I cannot believe that they accepted my father's return graciously, and with English company."

"Nay, they did not." Miles answered with a small smile. "Raymond, I'll take some more of that ale. My throat feels as if it was packed with dust." He took a long draught of the amber liquid and sighed at the relief it brought him, then threw himself into his story, which fell on eager ears. "They challenged us at Fid Dorcha. Gawd, but I've never seen such woods. There was no way to stay ahorse in its density and we had to lead the mounts single-file through most of it. Those damn Irish—ah, begging yer pardon, milady—they fight like animals! They have no weapons to speak of, using battle ax and clubs or stones, if nothing else is available. Those bloody woods are no place for a good English soldier to fight!"

"Why did you enter Fid Dorcha?" Eve asked with surprise. "Did my father not warn you of the dangers?"

"Nay, milady. In fact it was on his advice that we did so. Word had been sent from O'Conner requesting a parley. FitzStephen was willing, as it would give him the opportunity to measure the man."

Eve's eyebrows knitted thoughtfully. "'Twas Fid Dorcha that O'Conner last defeated him and drove him from Ferns. Miles, I know my father. The only reason he would lead you to parley with Rory in that place would be to recover his pride."

Richard glanced at Eve and his look became strange but he turned and prodded Miles to continue.

"As we were outnumbered, and generally at a disadvantage, we entreated for peace. We managed to retreat from the wood and met with O'Conner at its edge where we made camp. A week passed in negotiations and it looked as if both parties were agreeable to an end to the war, then and there. If O'Conner had been more successful in controlling his men, it might have. One night a part of O'Conner's men stole into our camp with their mind intent upon damage. If they had been English, we would have strung them up upon the spot for disobedience."

"How many were lost?" Richard asked grimly.

"Ten score of the Leinstermen and two of our knights." Richard swore. "Had you posted no guards?"

"Obviously not enough," Miles answered with chagrin.

"You underestimated your enemy," Richard growled. "Under the circumstances I am surprised that you did not lose more."

"I cannot explain it." Miles shrugged. "If the advantage had been ours we would have pressed for complete submission. Instead, they offered to come to terms."

"You're joking!" Warwick sputtered.

"If that were so, I would not be here to tell about it." Miles grinned. "O'Conner pressed Dermot for hostages and in return granted him the ten cantreds of Okinselagh without dispute. As for O'Rourke, he contented himself with accepting one hundred ounces of gold in retribution for the rape of his wife."

"Was that all?" Richard asked with amazement.

"Aye, nothing else. We were allowed to leave in peace."

"You not only underestimate the Irish," Eve offered with a wry smile, "you do not understand them, or their ways. You expect everyone to think as you do—typically English."

Richard glanced at her through half-closed lids but he turned back to Miles and asked dryly, "What happened next?"

"We returned to Ferns to find that Maurice Pendergast had landed with two ships of his Flemish men-at-arms and his archers. When Dermot realized that the reinforcements had arrived, he set to making plans with Sir Robert, who felt that Wexford should be our next target."

"What?" Eve cried. "But you had entreated for peace—you gave hostages to O'Conner!"

Miles glanced uncomfortably at Eve. "Aye, milady, but your father made it clear that he had no plans to submit. Maurice showed me the message Dermot sent him in Bristol. Here, I brought it with me to show you, Richard. 'Twas on the receipt of this message that Maurice set sail with his Flemish, milady."

He drew the message from his tunic and passed it to Richard who glanced at it briefly, then with a frown passed it to Eve. She took it, pale-faced, and scanned the contents. It was in her father's hand there was no doubt.

> Whoever shall wish for land or pence,
> Horses, trappings, or chargers,
> Gold or silver, I shall give them
> A very ample pay.
> Whoever may wish for soil or sod,
> Richly shall I enfeoff them.

Eve lay the parchment in her lap and looked up at Miles with tormented eyes. "Who were the hostages, Miles?" she asked softly.

Miles hesitated and looked to Richard for support. "Tell her," Richard said.

"Two freemen, milady—and—and the Rahdamma of Leinster and your father's youngest."

Eve felt her head swim as Miles confirmed her fears. She gripped the arms of her chair and felt suffocated by the constriction in her chest. "Enna and Conner!" she whispered in a gasp.

"Milady, when I left Ireland the word came that they were still alive!" Miles hastened. His words were true but he looked quickly away and Richard's eyes narrowed as he sensed that there was something Miles was not telling her.

"I do not hold hope for O'Conner's mercy," Eve said bitterly. "The lives of my brothers are forfeit."

"Perhaps not, milady. Your father claims lordship over Wexford by the right that it is not held by Irishmen but by Scandinavian foreigners of Ostmen. He means to drive them from Ireland."

"Do not think Rory to be so daft that he cannot see through that ploy!"

"Nay, Eve," Richard answered with a strange gentleness. "That is why I wanted you to be here. You must face the realities of what is happening. Donnell has done so and is doing what he can to establish the rights of Leinster."

Eve blinked as she tried to discern his meaning. "Donnell? What are you talking about?"

"Miles tells me that he lead the attack on Wexford."

"Donnell did this?" she gasped.

"Aye. He has not forgotten that the Ostmen were the first to withdraw their allegiance from your father when he was in trouble. Besides, what were his alternatives? Strategically, Wexford would lie at his back and FitzStephen is too good of a commander to leave it in hostile hands. What do you think Donnell felt to be the most preferable; for it to be an Irish or an English stronghold?"

Eve's expression clouded with doubt as she considered Richard's words. "So it is Irish, for the moment. How long shall that be, milords?" She didn't wait for an answer but pressed her next question to Miles. "Was my brother successful at Wexford?"

"Aye, milady, most definitely so. The townsmen came forth from the walls of the city numbering at least two thousand fully expecting, without doubt, to find hordes of naked Irish kerns armed with ancient weapons. Instead, they found ranks of armored knights with mail and shield and well-ordered Welsh longbowmen. They retired rather quickly within."

Warwick chuckled deeply and even Eve had to fight a smile at the presented picture of her people's ancient foe but Miles became immediately more serious.

"The first day of the siege did not go well as the town managed to defend from the turrets quite successfully. The next day FitzStephen allowed Donnell to go forth and with effort he managed to convince them to mediate with two of their bishops. They submitted to Dermot and gave hostages as good faith."

"I trust that FitzStephen did not withdraw," Richard said dryly.

"Nay, milord," Miles countered with a smile. "Sir Robert left the town well fortified—with Norman knights—hostages or no hostages. We then withdrew to Ferns to treat the wounded. When we arrived at Ferns we were greeted by most of Leinster's elders, assuring their loyalty to Dermot . . ."

"The spoils go to the victorious," Warwick muttered.

Miles shot him a rueful look. "Aye, they accepted us like old comrades. We spent little time there before we received a message that the King of Ossory was bringing a force through the Pass of Gowran to destroy us while we rested our troops. Donnell rallied a force of five thousand men and met Mac-Gillapatrick in the pass. He structured a barricade of triple fosse and vallum, crowning it with intertwined branches and set down to await the enemy."

"What of ours went with him?" Richard asked.

"Pendergast and his Flemish, Richard, though he gave Donnell the command—those damnable woods again . . ." He paused and his face grew suddenly pale as the memories of the battle flashed through his mind. He took a sharp swig on his tankard and ran his fingers through the thick mat of his auburn hair, reluctant to continue.

Richard watched his struggle, his eyes darkening with apprehension, "Tell us what happened, Miles."

"Sweet Jesus, Richard," Miles choked. "It was terrible. The battle began at daybreak and lasted well into dark. We managed to force our way through onto the plain, across to the valley of the Barrow. But MacGillapatrick managed to gather his men and reform at our rear, cutting off our retreat. Donnell retreated back through the woods, leaving Pendergast with forty-three of our men against MacGillapatrick's forces with woods and swamp at our flanks. We forced the men forward to the upper slopes of the hills while placing a small force of bowmen to ambush at the sides of the passes. Fortunately, MacGillapatrick was so intent upon pursuing Donnell that they became prey to our ambush and we were able to scatter them in a surprise of lances and spears. Dermot joined in at this point, eager to be in on the kill and—and—he . . ."

"He what, Miles?" Richard urged, noting the flush that swept over the knight's face.

"They—they took to the fallen with battle ax and—Gawd, Richard, I've never seen such savagery. They'd lop off the heads, laughing and crying prayers of praise, singing while they set to the task of dismembering and disemboweling the enemy. I watched man after man kneeling, pleading for mercy only to be struck down. And, they would—" He paused and swallowed hard, then gritted out the remaining words. "They would tear at the faces with their teeth . . ."

"Mother of God," Warwick swore.

Gervase and Raymond paled as they looked to Richard, whose jaw had tightened as he cleared his throat.

"The blood-covenant," Eve said, barely above a whisper. Five pairs of eyes turned to her and she flushed under their fierce disapproval. "It—it is an ancient custom. To discourage the ghosts of the slain one," she continued unwillingly. "By tasting the blood of the slain one, he becomes an ally instead of an enemy."

"You believe in this?" Richard asked sharply.

"Nay, of course not!" she snapped, then added more contritely, "nor did my father, or so I thought."

Richard's lip curled in disgust and he turned back to Miles. "Pendergast stood by and allowed this to happen?"

"He was as stunned as you are, Richard. Besides, we were helpless to stop it. As few as we were, we could only stand aside, on horse, and watch. However, when it was time to return to Ferns, Pendergast met with Dermot and informed him that he would be returning to Wales with his Flemish. He wanted nothing more to do with Ireland, or their customs. Following that he set out immediately for Wexford."

"Pendergast has returned?" Warwick asked, puzzled. "We heard nothing of it."

"Nay, Warwick. Pendergast's forces were battle-weary and, understandably, rather heavy of heart. They made their way slowly toward Wexford but found before reaching the coast that Dermot had sent word ahead that no aid was to be given to the English, but that they were to be stopped in any way that could be managed. No ship's captain would give them passage."

"They are trapped in Ireland?" Warwick roared as he struck the arm of his chair violently.

"Not exactly," Miles hesitated. "They—Pendergast retaliated by sending word to MacGillapatrick to offer him his service."

"Oh my God," Richard muttered. "Now we have Norman fighting Norman." He glanced at Eve and gritted a smile. "Well, it would seem, my love, that your father is not the only Irishman who would accept the services of the hated foreigner." He turned back to Miles. "Do you know why Maurice chose MacGillapatrick instead of O'Conner?"

"Aye, Richard, he made no secret of it. He meant to do Dermot as much disservice as he could. Dermot had a particular reason for hating MacGillapatrick as . . ." He paused and glanced at Eve. "Milady, God help me but I do not wish to be the one to give you this most grievous news . . . I beg you not to hold me accountable for it. O'Conner had given the hostages entrusted to him to Ossory and MacGillapatrick saw fit to avenge O'Conner for your father's unfaithfulness by—by blinding the Roydamma."

They heard Eve draw in her breath sharply and her face drained of color. She set her mouth tightly and said nothing, refusing to meet their sympathetic looks as she turned and stared into the crackling fire on the hearth.

"Is there more?" Richard asked grimly, drawing their attention to him. There was nothing anyone could say to ease her grief but he knew that she did not want their pity.

"Nay, Richard. FitzStephen set me on the first tide to bring you the news. When I left them, they were ensconced at Ferns and I believe that they will remain there for a time. FitzStephen awaits your counsel."

"For one, I want Pendergast home," Richard said, his voice edged with barely controlled anger. "Warwick, send word, to

Dermot as well, that this is to be done with haste. If there is any interference he will answer to me and I will enter Ireland as his enemy, make no doubt of it. Inform Pendergast that I will meet with him at St. Davids as soon as he arrives. Other dispatches will be sent with Miles and Gervase later but this is to go immediately."

With a sharp nod Warwick left the room hurriedly to find the chaplain, and Richard turned back to Miles. "You have done well, Miles. I realize the burden you've carried to bring us this news. Go now and rest and we will talk more of it later."

With a grim smile, Miles glanced at Eve and he too left with haste, followed by Gervase and Raymond who left tactfully without further words. The large room was soon settled in silence with only the sound of the crackling fire breaking the still quiet.

Richard watched her pale profile as she stared into the amber and orange flames and he fought the impulse to reach over and cover her small hand in his. He held back, afraid that if he were to do so she might suddenly shatter her composure, so they sat quietly, side by side, as he silently shared her grief. What could he say to her, after all? If he were to offer her sympathy she would probably fling it back at him with anger, denying any support he might offer. He knew that she disapproved of her father's actions but who could she give her loyalties to? The enemies of her clan? Certainly not the English. She had made her feelings most clear that she had no feelings of loyalty to his people. An unhappy smile pulled at his mouth as he thought of the similarities of their situations, though she would never realize it. The support for his lands had been taken from him when he needed it the most—as "reward" for his service to his country and king. One he had placed faith in, the one he had pledged his faith to for more years than he could remember, had betrayed him, wounded him dearly. Eve, he thought, you must harden. Perhaps, after all, there is no one, not another human being in which you might place your trust but yourself.

"I will help you," she said softly, interrupting his thoughts.

"What?"

"I—I said that I will help you." Her reply was almost a choked response.

"Why should you want to help me, Eve?" His tawny brows knitted with doubt as his grey eyes darkened.

"I do not expect you to understand, Richard."

The sound of his name on her lips tugged at him and he wanted to reach out for her but he held himself back, and kept his silence, as she struggled to explain.

"I do not agree with what my father has done but I am not willing to hand my people over to Henry. You said that you wanted me to accept reality, and I am. I told you before, my people pride and value their freedom above all else and if you will accept this reality you must know that you will never be their master. But, these values keep them from realizing the danger that threatens them." She looked up at him and smiled sadly. "You see, we have been threatened before, conquered before, but no one has ever desired to take that freedom. Enemies have been satisfied to plunder its riches and return home, or, as the Ostmen, build walled cities to shut out the people. I have no doubt that they feel that the English will do the same. But then, they do not understand the Norman!"

Her eyes glistened as she gave a short, brittle laugh. "You were amazed, all of you, when O'Conner had you within his grasp and let you go! But that is why, you see, he did not understand! We have always lived by a policy of divide and conquer. He felt that by taking hostages, as our custom, and leaving my father with only Okinselagh, his power had been reduced to that of a petty chieftain. But I do understand, all too well. Oh, aye, Richard, I have learned well as your wife! Your people will be different and that poor, trembling sod is so pitifully unaware of what is coming! I will help you because, God help me, I know now that it is inevitable, and you are our only hope. I have no choice but to place my trust in you."

He had listened quietly and with compassion, but when she stopped he pressed his question, "Eve, what are you asking of me?"

"Nothing." She smiled ruefully. "I am not asking you for anything, Richard. I expect that you will do whatever you feel you must. I know that you will be loyal to your king but—you see, I have no other choice. I must trust the man that you are. It sounds so ridiculous, but there is no other word for it—I must trust that you will be . . . fair." She rose from her chair and turned to face him with composure.

"If you will excuse me now we both have things to attend to. I must write a letter to Donnell and I would appreciate it being sent with Gervase." She began to turn away then paused. "There is one more thing. You should understand that I do not

hold you accountable for what has happened to Enna—or Conner. What occurred was totally due to the actions of my father.
He knew all too well what would be the result of his duplicity."

He watched with fascination as she walked from the room,
her shoulders squared back with a pride in her sorrow that
touched a different chord within him. When she had gone, he
slumped in his chair, rubbing his brow in careful thought. It
had come at last. She was no longer the wild, impulsive girl
as before, but now, braced against her despair, overridden with
concern for her people, she was a woman. He smiled. He tried
to stop it, but he smiled. Damnation, but if she wasn't the
woman he always knew she could become! But, had he seen
a glimmer of contempt in her eyes? Dear God, he thought,
why do things always come too late?

26

Warwick shouted terse orders to the rows of swordsmen who struck and parried their blows in mock combat on the large open field that lay just west of Chepstow's battlements. The mid-morning summer sun lay mercilessly upon the heavily-armored men as the sweat of their endeavors ran in rivulets from beneath their helms along muscled necks taut with the strain, under mail and leather corselets to further dampen already soaked gambesons, adding to their discomfort.

Warwick spied a young armiger fail to counter a stroke from his opponent that should have been easily deflected. He crossed the distance between them in a few angry strides and snatched the sword from the startled young squire.

"God's Breath, man! If the blow had been in earnest you would be greeting your ancestors at this moment! Have you learned nothing?" He proceeded to show the man how the parry should have been met, then passed the sword back to the chagrined young man and turned away, mumbling a profanity under his breath. His critical gaze swept down the rows of men and to Beaumont who was attempting to help another pair. As he turned away he muttered another profanity of frustration under his breath and looked up to find Richard standing at the edge of the field watching the proceedings. Glad for the respite, he wrenched his helm from his head and tossed back his coif to run his fingers through his dampened hair, his eyes sweeping over the swordsmen once again as Richard approached.

"How goes it?" Richard asked as he fought a smile over Warwick's ruffled expression.

"I think they'll be ready, Richard, but I'll have to drive them. Even the experienced ones seemed to have softened and as for the younger ones—"

"You sound like my old friend Kerwain," Richard grinned.

"I think I understand his frustration now," Warwick answered grimly. "I do not suppose you would reconsider your choice of master-of-the-sword."

"Not a chance!" Richard laughed, but became more solemn. "Who else could I entrust with this? I do not need to tell you the importance of having the men ready in time."

"Have you made a decision of when we will leave?" Warwick asked as he wiped his brow with a cloth from his tunic.

"Nay, but soon. From what I learned from Maurice the decision cannot be long delayed."

Warwick nodded silently as he rubbed the back of his neck. "Will you take Eve with you?"

Richard startled at the question, then frowned as he shook his head. "I have not decided."

"She has the right to go."

"I will determine that."

"Have you talked with her since your return from St. Davids?"

"Nay."

Warwick started to say something but held his tongue when he saw Richard's darkened look. "Has anything been heard from Henry?" he asked, changing the subject.

"Nay, but I am sure that word will reach him about what we are doing here—and my visit to Bristol. We will hear from him soon enough. Are you anxious for the confrontation?" He glanced at Warwick with a questioning smile.

"Nay! But as you said, it is certain to come. I would just as soon have it done with."

They stood in silence, watching the efforts on the field, and both flinched in unison at a few well-met blows.

"I think they will do," Richard murmured.

"Aye, for all my criticism, in battle ye'll not find better at your side. They'll come through."

He looked sideways at Richard, hesitating for a moment, then made a decision. "Richard, come with me. There is something I want to show you."

He ignored Richard's silent question as he called to Beaumont to take charge, then spun on his heels and gestured for

Richard to follow. They reached the armory which was set into the walls of the west end of the battlements and Warwick took the heavy ring of keys from his belt and inserted one into the massive lock in the thick oak door. As they stepped into the cool room Richard squinted against the sudden darkness but Warwick did not hesitate as he walked purposefully to the back of the long narrow room, making his way through the rows of weapons stacked neatly in readiness. As his eyes grew accustomed to the meager light from the slit windows high in the wall, Richard saw Warwick unlock a trunk against the far wall and swing back the heavy lid. He paused and looked back to where Richard stood.

"Close the door."

Richard closed it as Warwick struck a flint to a torch, lighting the oil-soaked rag, and stuck it back into its wall holder. He extracted something from the trunk's depths, setting it on a table under the lamp.

As Richard approached, his curiosity over his friend's odd behavior causing a frown, his eyes fixed on the object Warwick had placed on the table, and he froze. It was Eve's jewel box. He reached over and lifted the lid. The jewels gleamed and sparkled in the flickering light.

"Where did you get this?" he asked evenly.

"She gave it to me."

Richard looked up at Warwick with a start. "She gave it to you? Why?"

"She bid me to sell it, all of it, and give you the money."

"Why would she do that?" Richard was astounded.

"For Chepstow and Striguil, Richard," Warwick answered quietly. "To help you. And she bid me not to tell you where the money came from."

"And why did you?"

"Because I thought you should know. Besides, I had no intention of selling her things, even if you needed the money, which we both know you do not."

"Why did you not tell her that?"

"Because she was so in earnest—and it is for you to handle."

Richard closed the lid slowly as his brows furrowed in thought. "Put it back," he said quietly. He turned and left without another word.

Warwick stepped to the door and watched Richard striding to the hall, then he stopped halfway, stood for a moment, turned and walked in another direction to a small newly-constructed wooden building against the far wall of the keep. Warwick noted that his head was bent in thought and he sighed deeply as he turned to lock the door of the armory. If they would only talk to each other!

Richard opened the door to the wooden structure and stepped inside its dark enclosure, closing the door quickly behind him. The flutter of wings could be heard in protest to the sudden noise and he spoke in a soft, soothing voice, calming its occupants. He did not light a torch but stood quietly in the dark until his eyes grew accustomed to the light. As the occupants of the room began to take form, he smiled with pleasure, his own soul becoming soothed by what he saw. He stepped across the small span and pulled down a heavy leather glove from a shelf, pulling it on. Reaching out while talking in the same appeasing voice, he took a large, fierce bird from its perch onto his gloved hand. He talked quietly to the hooded falcon while stroking its silken feathers. He took comfort from its trust as it turned its head to the sound of his voice and fluffed itself, settling onto his hand.

"Ah, my lovely," he whispered. "Henry shall not have you, though he would try."

The gamebirds had been recently brought from Pembroke, the mews quickly constructed to receive its occupants in Richard's unwillingness to leave them behind. During an earlier visit to Pembroke Richard's Welsh birds had bested Henry's prized Norway falcons and Henry had not forgotten it. While Richard had made a gift of two of the birds to his king, Henry's eye had turned greedily to the rest.

Richard gently pulled the hood from the bird's head and smiled as the peregrine turned its head sideways and looked at him with a large yellow eye. He held tightly to the jesses tied to the bird's leg so that the falcon would not startle and fly about the small room, possibly injuring itself against the timbered roof.

"You would like to fly from me now, wouldn't you?" he smiled. "You are predictable, but then you are loyal too. Should I open the door and release you, you would take to the sky in search of prey, of freedom. But you would return, would you not, straightaway to me and of your own choice?"

The bird shifted its weight on his wrist and ruffled its feathers and blinked its yellow eye as if in answer to his question.

"If I could only be so sure of another," he murmured, stroking its feathers.

She had given her mother's jewels to aid Striguil. It astounded him. Could she have more feeling for his people than she claimed? He had thought of her constantly while he was away and was amazed at his own eagerness to return home. She had grown and there was little doubt in him now that she would be capable of handling what he expected of her. But her feelings toward him? That was another matter and he was not so sure. He had kept from her, telling himself that she needed time. He did not want to push her—but how much of his reserve had been due to fear of putting her to the test, that she would reject him? She might submit, but that was not enough; he wanted her heart too.

Sighing, he hooded the falcon and placed it back on its perch. He would have to face it sooner or later and time was growing short. He left the mews and returned to the hall only to find that she was nowhere about. He stopped one of the servants and inquired of her whereabouts and the man informed him that she had been seen earlier going into the stables.

"Was anyone with her?" he asked with a decided frown.

"Nay, milord."

He spun about and strode from the hall, his face flushed with anger. Damn! Had she taken it into her mind to ride alone? He had warned her about doing so, but it was typical that she would disregard his wishes!

When he entered the stable he was surprised to find that her mare was in her stall and there was no sign that another had been taken. Frowning, he reasoned that the man had been wrong and turned to leave when he was halted by a sound from above him. He looked up to the loft and heard the noise again. Someone was up there. Slowly it began to dawn on him and he shook his head in wonder. Was she still up to her old habits of escaping to haylofts to ponder her problems? A smile appeared on his tanned face and slowly spread into a wicked grin. He grabbed the ladder to the loft and ascended silently, pulling himself up at the top.

She was stretched out in the hay on her side, chewing on a piece of straw as she gazed from the window, obviously deeply lost in thought. He watched her for a long moment, almost unwilling to disturb her solitude—almost. He was entranced by her serene beauty, her hair drawn up in a coil at the back of her white neck where a few tendrils had escaped to lay softly curled about her ears and he could almost feel the silky texture under his fingers. Her waist lay narrow beneath the thin pale blue wool of her pelisse and rounded to the fullness of her hip where it clung to long and shapely legs that were stretched out full length, her small slippered feet peeking out from beneath the hem of her skirt as she wriggled them to scratch.

"May I join you?"

She startled with an audible gasp and jerked about. "Richard! You—you frightened me!" She sat up quickly, her cheeks pinking with embarrassment as he came to sit beside her. She brushed away the straw from the front of her pelisse, though the gesture was to little avail as it clung to her gown and hair and she glanced up to find him smiling at her.

"When did you get back?"

"This morning," he answered.

She blushed at the way his eyes were moving over her. "Did you see Pendergast? Is all well?" she pressed, wishing that he would not look at her in that way.

"As well as can be expected." He shrugged. He reached over and pulled a bit of straw from her hair. "Have you been well?"

"Aye, milord." She dropped her gaze from his with a rushing feeling of self-consciousness. He wouldn't! Her thoughts were becoming frantic. There was no mistaking the look in his eyes; it had little to do with his business in St. Davids. What had come over him? "I—I think that we best go now, Richard. I have dallied here too long, there is much to do . . ." she stammered.

"There is nothing that cannot wait." He grinned. "I find it rather pleasant. I've missed you."

"Have you?" She felt a rushing tingle at the inflection in his voice.

"Should I not? You are my wife."

"Aye—but—Richard . . ."

Her eyes widened as he reached over and pulled the pins from her hair, letting it tumble down her back and he ran his fingers into its thickness, then pulled her gently, but firmly, to him.

"Richard, please . . ." she barely said as his lips covered hers and he kissed her gently, with a coaxing tenderness that made her lips tremble. Her mind tumbled against what was happening; she wouldn't let him use her! She tried to remain stiff in his arms but her resistance ebbed. It was impossible to draw away from the way he was kissing her and she felt her own hunger begin to awaken. He pushed her back into the straw and his kiss deepened as he felt her begin to respond, his tongue probing hers as her lips opened under his gentle urging. His hand went to the laces on her bodice and he began to pull them apart, his lips traveling to the nape of her neck, and he heard her moan.

"Richard, nay, not here. Someone will find us!" she pleaded for reason, hoping that he would stop while something deeper, more urgent, prayed that he wouldn't.

"No one would dare," he chuckled softly. His hand slipped into the opened bodice and his fingers found her breast where they teased the nipple until it hardened in response and she cried softly, "Richard, please don't . . ."

"Hush." Her protest was weak and he could feel the desire that was beginning to grow in her and he knew that if nothing else, her needs, so long denied, were as strong as his own. A beginning, and he had no intention of not seeing it through.

He pulled the bodice apart and cupped a breast in his hand as his lips covered its tip, teasing and drawing from it until her breath quickened under his fingers. As her arms went up about his neck, pulling him against her, and she moaned softly, he lifted her skirt and his hand went beneath it, stroking the softness of her thighs, then the soft mound between them. He urged her slowly, patiently, giving her time to build, sensing that her mind was in contest with what was happening, allowing her time to rediscover her body and the feelings it was capable of offering. His tongue teased and licked her nipple as his fingers stroked her inner softness until she arched against him and her hands slipped beneath his tunic, caressing his back with a new urgency. But he held back, urging her further until he felt her moistness beneath his fingers and he knew she was ready. He slipped down his chanuses and pulled her beneath him, kissing her again as he poised at the entrance, then plunged deeply. At his entry she came up against him and drew in her breath, then began to move with him, meeting him with each movement until he felt her tense beneath him, then tremble in a final shudder. Only then did he let himself come. They were left gasping as he relaxed on his elbows and opened his eyes to look down at her.

"I told you I've missed you," he smiled.

"Apparently," she breathed, her body feeling languid and warm.

As he rolled off of her, with a kiss planted on her nose, she attempted to sit up but she felt weak in the middle and collapsed back into the straw. She heard him chuckle and he pulled down her skirts and drew her up onto his arms, kissing her lightly.

"Nothing like a tumble in the hay," he grinned. "And with a delightful bit of Irish fluff."

Her eyes flew open to glare at him with bright anger. She had lost herself, willingly from his first touch, but his ill-chosen words brought back her resolve and her doubts.

"Just another Irish to conquer, milord?" she snapped, jumping up. She looked down at his feet and she drew herself up haughtily. "You did not even remove your boots first!"

"We are in a hayloft, madam," he laughed. "Would you have had me disrobe you?"

She turned away from him with disdain and straightened her garments, then crossed to the ladder but he caught her arm at the edge of the loft. "Let me go first," he ordered, but she could still hear the humor in his voice. He descended the ladder and helped her down and as they took leave of the stable she would have walked on ahead but he took her hand. She glanced up at him at his touch but looked away quickly from the amused smile he offered her. As they walked across the courtyard to the hall, she missed a few steps as she paused to scratch her legs and rump. Seeing her dilemma, he chuckled and squeezed her hand affectionately.

"I think a bath would be in order, my love," he grinned. "Contrary to opinion, haylofts do not make the best love nest."

She shot a glare at him and would have offered a retort but they had entered the hall and she was dismayed to find that it was not empty. The men had finished their morning session and were gathered in the hall for mid-meal. It took but a moment to appraise the situation as straw still hung from both of them, and amused glances were exchanged and mouths drew into smiles. Eve felt her cheeks burn though the company was thoughtful enough to turn their attention back to their meal. Sophie came to meet them and, though she said nothing, Eve knew she had taken it all in as her eyes were sparkling with laughter and approval.

"Lass, Waverly is in the buttery and I fear he's in a dither. There is some problem with the stores and he would speak with ye about it. He's been looking for ye all morning." She fought a smile as her gaze swept over the two of them.

"All right, Sophie, I'll see to him as soon as I've had a bath," she sighed.

"You had better do it now, lass; he's in a right fit, he is."

"Go on," Richard offered evenly, though his grey eyes were crinkling with laughter. "I will see that the bath is readied for you."

She spun off and left the room in a huff and found Waverly in the buttery and though he frowned quizzically at her appearance, she was relieved that he made no mention of it since his attention was drawn to his own problems. To her dismay it took devilishly long to go over the tallies with him, checking each item in his typical painstaking detail, and she continually struggled not to scratch. After over an hour was spent, the shortages were found and she excused herself, with a relieved sigh, and sought out her chambers.

She was surprised to find that the door to her room lay open. The bath was not readied, as Richard had promised, but upon a second look her eyes widened in surprise. She whirled about and went back into the hall, stopping a serving girl who was rushing down the hall, intent upon her business.

"Millie, where are my things? My chambers have been emptied!"

"Why—milord told us to move yer things to his chambers, milady!" the girl said with surprise.

"He what?" She blinked, then glanced involuntarily down to the end of the hallway. The girl watched open-mouthed as Eve's face became flushed and she heard her mistress utter a profanity, spinning about to stride down the hallway.

It was true. She stood in the doorway to Richard's chamber as her eyes swept over her things which had been placed about his room. A tub had been set before the hearth and a fresh chemise lay on the chair beside it. She stepped into the room and shut the door quietly behind her, then looked back, realizing the significance of what he had done. He had not given her time to think when he had appeared in the loft. Her first reaction, finding him there, had been pleasure. She had missed him, terribly so, more than she could have imagined. She had gone to the loft, needing time alone to think, to consider her feelings toward him, and had been doing so when he had appeared so suddenly. She knew that when he had taken her into his arms she had wanted him to. She had given herself to him without letting herself think about it—pressing back her thoughts to his needed touch.

But her peace had been short-lived. He, himself, had seen to that. If he had meant to bring her back to the reality of their relationship by his crass comment, he had been ultimately successful. He owned her, he could do what he wanted with her. How could he be so tender one moment, and so heartless the next. For a foolish instant, as he made love to her, she had deluded herself into thinking that perhaps he did have some feelings for her after all. But love had nothing to do with it— he had possessed her, nothing more. And now, it was obvious that he expected her to be a wife to him in all ways. There would be no going back.

Could she handle it? She had responded to his lovemaking, and he knew it. Her own desires had been kept dormant for so long...Could she continue, having him make love to her, knowing that he only wanted her body while she needed so much more?

But he would give her no choice now; it was too late, she knew that with a certainty. Sighing, she moved to the tub and slowly discarded her garments, eager at last to have her bath. As she sank into the water she grabbed up the soap and began to scrub away the memories of the moments in the loft. At last, she leaned back against the edge of the tub and closed her eyes, letting the hot, sudsy water ease away some of her troubles.

She heard the door open and her eyes flew open to find Richard standing there, a smile on his face as he took in the scene before him. She should have expected it, she thought with a grimace, he probably timed it so that he would find her thus. She glanced down through half-closed lids and noted, with satisfaction, that the sudsy water covered her from his appraisal very nicely.

"I thought you would be through with your bath by now," He smiled as he removed his tunic and tossed it on the chest at the end of the bed.

"Indeed," she muttered and sank down deeper into the water.

He strolled over to the tub and sat down on its edge, folding his arms across his chest as he grinned down at her. "I see that you have been comfortably settled."

"Do I have a choice, milord?"

"None at all." His gaze passed down boldly to where the water swirled about the fullness of her breasts and the deep grey of his eyes twinkled as they leered at her. She tensed but he merely winked at her, then rose and took a chair next to the fire, where he stretched out his legs and yawned behind his hand. "When you are through, I would like to talk with you."

Talk? Her eyes opened widely with surprise but she managed to lower them again as he looked back at her. Had she read amusement there? She would not let herself look up again to find out.

"If you will hand me that cloth, I would appreciate it. This water is getting cold."

He said nothing but bent over to the chair across from him where the blanket had been laid and tossed it to her without comment. She pulled it about her as she rose from the tub and if she had looked she would have found his eyes following her with interest. The cloth fell away from her as she turned, and his eyes warmed as he noted the soft curve to her hips and her full, rounded breasts, their rosy tips pert and moist from her bath. He struggled with himself to remain where he was, as he felt his groin tighten and blood surge through his temples. God, she was beautiful. It had been so long since they had enjoyed ease in their relationship and he reflected with longing upon a time when he could have gone to her without hesitation, to be received with an eagerness to match his own.

When she finished dressing into a fresh chemise and robe, she turned back to find him staring into the fire. She crossed to him and took the chair next to his, curling her feet up under her as she bent her head to the side to catch his eyes.

"You wanted to talk with me, milord?"

Her formality irritated him but he swallowed the irritation. There was no point in beginning the conversation badly. "I have a decision to make, Eve, and you can be of help. For one, I need to know about Ferns, the lay of the country and exactly where your father would reconstruct his stonghold."

"Why do you wish to know?"

"Do not look so guarded. I will not ask anything of you that would betray your people. I would know these things myself in time but if you answer me thoughtfully we could save that time and many lives—and not just Norman."

"What has happened?" she asked with alarm.

"Nothing I did not expect, though I had hoped against it." He smirked. "When Pendergast received word that your father would allow him to leave Ireland, a decision made upon receipt of my message, O'Conner did his best to pursuade him to continue to remain and fight as his ally. When he realized that his entreaties fell on deaf ears, and Pendergast left for the coast, O'Conner changed his loyalties. He sent envoys to Dermot for a parley. They met and O'Conner urged your father to unite with him in driving all foreigners from Ireland, promising a strong alliance and more lands restored to him as the coup de resistance. We do not know what your father's answer was to O'Conner and I am concerned for FitzStephen and his men. My decision now must be to make sail for Ireland to protect our forces there or to hold for word from FitzStephen—if he is able to send it. Eve, you must know that if FitzStephen is harmed, I will be forced to act. I cannot allow them to think that they may harm a Norman without suffering the consequences. I would like to avoid what would happen in that event. Consider your answer most carefully, Eve, for I must know the truth. Would Dermot betray FitzStephen?"

Though they had made a bargain, and she had promised to help him, the weight of her decision struck her fully for the first time. She took a deep breath and raised her eyes to meet his. His question was reasonable and, though her heart was heavy, she did not shirk in her answer. "In honesty, Richard, I wonder if I am able to judge my father's mind any longer. I do not think he would betray FitzStephen. Moreover, Donnell and the elders would not allow it. Besides," she added with a grimace, "I think he has a greater plan for himself than to be O'Conner's ally—not to mention the fact that he would have to be O'Rourke's also and that he would never do. From what I have heard this past month I imagine he sees himself as ari-ri. He had always felt that it should have gone to our family and remained there. With the Norman as ally it is within his grasp. Nay, I do not think he will settle for O'Conner's offer."

There was a glimmer of respect in his eyes for her careful answer but he pressed forward, "Why would Donnell and the elders support FitzStephen against Dermot?"

The accusation behind his question was clear and she bristled at the inference. Could he not understand the line of loyalty of her people? "Because they would not betray an ally," she said firmly.

"They allowed Dermot to turn against Pendergast!" he snorted unbelievingly. "Why would they not against FitzStephen?"

"Pendergast was no longer an ally, Richard, and it was by his choice. Their honor would not allow them to turn against FitzStephen."

"Honor?" he gave a sharp laugh. She controlled her anger,

determined to make him understand, even a little. Everything depended upon him, he had to understand! "Richard, tell me, what you did when another man took all that you had, leaving you with little or nothing?"

He started at her question and his expression blackened, his mind turning involuntarily to Henry and he wondered what lay behind her question. "Why do you ask?" he said guardedly.

"Because I want you to try to understand! I think I know what you would do. You would fight him with everything you had until you regained what you had lost. Let me tell you what an Irishman would do, following our Brenhon Code, which is older than the laws you live by. Once robbed, the vanquished would sit on the doorstep of the one who had grieved him, there to fast until the offender paid him in full measure."

Richard digested her words for a moment, then threw back his head and laughed. "Fast! Good Lord, he is asking to starve to death! That is incredible. What is more, it is stupid!"

"Perhaps, by your reasoning." She smiled with satisfaction. "But I assure you that he will not. The price will be paid, in spite of your contempt, because it is a strong code that we live by. If the price is not met, then the accused will suffer a worse fate by his peers. He will be shunned and find himself an outcast all of his days, his penitence more terrible than anything you could have wrought with your sword! And all because of honor, Richard, an element you accuse us of not having!" As she saw him working the information, she smiled. "I tell you, Richard, FitzStephen will not be betrayed."

He looked at her silently for a long moment, his elbows resting on the arms of his chair as he rubbed his mouth thoughtfully against his clasped fingers. She saw his lips quiver in a hint of a smile.

"So be it." He smiled at long last. "Now, will you tell me another thing?"

"If I can." She returned his smile with relief.

"Your father has resettled to Ferns, and is rebuilding it, I would assume. FitzStephen is there with him and I must know how strong their fortifications could be against O'Conner. I do not think that I need to point out that regardless of your father's decision O'Conner may take issue with it. If he was to rebuild it with stronger defenses, where would it be?"

Her brow furrowed and he smiled at the way her head cocked to one side and she bit her lip as she strained to find the answer.

"My guess is that it would be an area known as the Duffry,"

she said at long last. "It lies just to the west near Mount Leinster."

"And why there?" he answered, forcing her to justify her answer.

"If he feared an attack, it would afford a natural defense. The area is surrounded by dense wood, mountains to its back, and protected by impenetrable marshes. It should be safe from O'Conner or Norman. Particularly Norman," she added with a mischievous smile.

He snorted in response to her comment but generally seemed pleased by her reasonings as he turned to stare into the fire, momentarily lost in his own thoughts. Finally, he spoke again in a low deliberate voice. "No matter what I choose to do, there are those who will condemn me, Eve."

"I know." She sighed, feeling the weight of his decisions as she could not have before. "There will be those on both sides."

"I am glad that you realize this, Eve," he said quietly, "for it will be the same for you if you return to Ireland with me."

She gaped at him. "I am to go with you?"

"Are you certain you wish to?" he asked, turning to look at her. "The way will not be easy. It is war that we will meet, not peace."

"I know," she whispered, "but if the choice is mine, I choose to go."

"So be it," he said softly. He looked at her for a long moment and then to her surprise, he grinned. "There is just one thing I would ask."

"What is that?"

"Never ask me to sit on Henry's doorstep. I'm afraid that I do not have that much faith."

She giggled, promising him that she would never ask it of him, but he became fixed upon the warmth of her eyes as she laughed, large green pools that seemed to invite him into their depths. Suddenly he reached out and pulled her from her chair and she squeaked as she found herself ensconced in his lap.

He pushed aside her robe and brushed the fullness of a breast with the back of his fingers as his gaze fell on her hungrily through the sheerness of her chemise.

"Richard—don't," she whispered pleadingly as she caught his wrist.

"Don't?" he repeated softly as he looked up at her. The pale startling grey of his eyes penetrated into hers as if he were searching for a truth, with a demand that made her lower her gaze. "Tell me the truth, Eve, do you really want me to stop? Look at me and tell me that you do not want me to touch you, ever again."

She closed her eyes and could feel his hand against her breast, though it lay still. Oh God, she could not live with his using her but could she live without his ever touching her again? He had reawakened her body to him and now he was asking her to make the decision. She opened her eyes, which were brimming with tears of a decision she could not utter, and looked up into his eyes.

He swept her into his arms and carried her to the bed where he removed her chemise and turned away to discard his own garments before coming to lay at her side. He looked down at her and brushed her hair away from her face with tenderness, then bent to kiss her lightly before raising his head to allow his gaze to move over her, caressing her body with his eyes.

"You are beautiful," he murmured softly, then followed his gaze with his hand over the softness of her body. "Eve, I have tried not to make demands upon you that would hurt you. I wanted you to come to me on your own," he said hoarsely, "but God's Breath, Eve, do you know how hard it has been not to touch you?"

As he bent to claim her lips, he did not see the tears that slipped from her eyes as she responded, her arms going about his neck as she gave herself up to him.

She awoke late in the morning to find that he had gone. She reached out and touched the pillow next to hers, still indented where his head had lain, and she felt a new rush of tears as she recalled the previous afternoon and night she had spent in his arms. She rose from the bed, feeling a weight of years that were beyond her. She picked her robe up off the floor where it had been discarded and wrapped it about her body, then crossed to the washstand and quickly bathed herself. He had been considerate and tender in his lovemaking, awakening in her body all the forgotten remembrances of her passions and his. If only . . . It had come so close to being perfect. More than once she had closed her eyes and pretended that it was as before and that he truly loved her again. As she sat at her dressing table in her chemise and pulled a comb through her hair, she suddenly stopped. Turning, she looked at the bed and chewed thoughtfully on the edge of the shell comb. It had come close! Surely he could not pretend what he had given her! Her heart began to beat wildly as she considered the possibility and she forced herself to be calm. Was it possible, in time . . . He no longer hated her, she could not believe that after yesterday, could he be beginning to . . . She jumped up and ran to the wardrobe, pawing through her gowns until she found the buttercup-yellow silk he had always favored. Once groomed, she left the chamber with a new lightness to her step and made her way down the corridor, smiling to herself with a guarded new hope. She felt like a maid again, seeking to be near the object of her heart, wanting just to be near him, though she knew he was yet unaware of her feelings. Just to be close to him, to see him and to hear the sound of his voice, and make him aware of her, to let him want her until she had had him.

She found him in the hall, sitting with the others about the dormant table. Intent upon their conversation, her entrance passed unnoticed and she contented herself with checking the haunch of venison which was turning on a spit over the fire, pausing to baste it from the kettle of juices nestled in the coals. Once done, she moved quietly to Richard's side where he sat on the edge of the table and listened to their banter of a recent hunting trip for boar, each topping the other with bigger lies of their expertise.

"Oh ho!" Beaumont laughed over Warwick's claims. He turned to Richard with a grin. "You were with him, Richard, will you confirm such boasts?"

"What can I say?" Richard shrugged good-naturedly. "If he says it is so, then it must be. Am I to deny the word of one who outweighs me by fifty stone? Nay, it must be as he said."

Richard's observation was greeted by a round of chortles from the knights, not the least from Warwick. Unconsiously, Richard put an arm on Eve's shoulder as she stood by his side while he continued to lay claim to Warwick's exploits. She startled at his touch, then realizing the naturalness of the gesture, she warmed with pleasure.

"We leave it to you, milady!" one of the knights laughed. "Will you judge the merits of our noble Warwick? Could he do what he claims?"

She was dismayed at the attention that was brought to her as Richard withdrew his arm but looking at him, she found that he too was waiting for her answer with interest and that his grey eyes were twinkling with amusement. She smiled warmly as she winked at Warwick.

"Noble sirs, while Sir Warwick outweighs me by far more than fifty stone I assure you that I do not fear from that gentle source. However, it is as my lord has said, for I would never doubt his word. Indeed, I would agree if he boasted of much more, for would a wise wife do otherwise?"

The men roared approvingly and she warmed to the smile and wink that Richard offered her as his arm went about her waist.

At that moment the door to the hall flew open and a porter entered breathlessly, his eyes flying about the hall until they found Richard. He crossed the room swiftly, his expression fairly bursting with his message.

"Milord, we have visitors! His Majesty approaches with a large party. I fear that they are only moments from the keep."

Richard exchanged a glance with Warwick but remained unruffled as he turned to Eve and said calmly, "Milady, see to the kitchens and inform them that our sovereign will be taking mid-meal with us. They are to prepare only what they have planned. Henry's tastes are simple and he will not notice if it is not other than our normal repast."

As Eve left the room, Richard settled into a chair and awaited Henry's arrival and the knights followed suit, wondering as to the earl's calmness in light of their impending visitors.

When the call was heard from without, Richard rose and went to the doors of the hall, throwing him back to receive his king. He stepped to the landing above the courtyard, a smile playing at his mouth as he watched Henry dismount and come up the steps. He bowed slightly, kissing Henry's offered ring, then straightened to look down upon the shorter man.

"I bid you welcome to Chepstow, milord."

"It is good to see you, Richard." Henry smiled broadly. "You have been keeping yourself from Westminster and I have missed you."

Richard escorted Henry into the hall, with the king's party following behind. "There has been much to keep me at Chepstow, Your Grace, but you had but to summon me and I would have obeyed. However, I had heard that you were in Normandy these months past."

"Aye, those damnable French have been keeping my attention," Henry replied, settling himself into a chair. His alert eyes swept over those gathered in the hall as he made note of Richard's company. "I noticed, as I crossed Striguil, that you have done well since your return. The lands are in fine repair."

"Aye, Your Grace," Richard agreed as he settled himself next to Henry. "The lands are mending and it is my hope that they will soon be completely restored."

"Beneath your able hands, I have no doubt," Henry offered graciously, nodding at Raymond, who had approached with a tankard of ale.

"How do things fare in France?" Richard asked.

"We will keep them at bay," Henry answered. "Though I must return soon to assure it."

At that moment Eve returned from the kitchens and Henry saw her immediately, his face breaking out into a grin. He rose from his chair and offered his hand as she knelt before him. "You look as lovely as ever, milady. It pleases me to see you with your husband again. May I assume that all goes well with you? If this rake is not treating you as he should, you must tell me!"

"Aye, Your Grace," she answered, aware of Richard's gaze upon her. "I am most content."

She saw him flinch, though it was barely perceptible, and a voice of warning went off inside of her. Was Henry surprised to find her happy, or to find her here at all! Had Richard a reason for sending her from the room before Henry's arrival? Had he wanted her appearance to come as a surprise?

Henry settled in his chair once again and gestured for Eve to sit by him. "Eleanor will be pleased to hear of your reconciliation! I fear that she was unable to make the journey, as she is again with child, but I will be pleased to convey the news to her."

The next hour passed uneventfully as the men exchanged light talk of other times, battles won and moments of pleasure, but as Eve listened she could sense an underlying tension that would have been missed by a less acute instinct. She listened, and watched, what passed between them as she tried to pick up a clue to what had changed their relationship so.

Suddenly, catching her off guard, Henry turned to her and smiled. "Milady, what have you heard from your father? I know that he has found aid with FitzStephen and his endeavors have been somewhat successful."

"Aye, Your Majesty, I understand that he has regained what is his and has returned to Ferns." She resisted the impulse to look at Richard, fearing that her words were unsuitable.

"And what of his plans, now that he has what he sought from me?" Henry asked with apparent innocence.

Instinctively, Eve knew that while she must not appear to avoid the question, she should not be caught in a lie. She had no way of knowing what Henry knew, yet her reply must appear natural and untutored. It did not help that Richard's hand rested on the arm of her chair, out of Henry's sight, and she started slightly as she felt his hand cover hers.

"I have no way of knowing my father's plans, Your Majesty. It has been his habit, in the past, to return to Ferns when he is well satisfied. I know that he has done so; therefore, I can only surmise that he is content with what he has accomplished." She relaxed as she felt the gentle pressure of Richard's hand.

"I am pleased that he is content." Henry smiled as he glanced from her to Richard. "It would seem that our Norman knights effected his return most handily. I was gratified when you came to me in Normandy, Lady Eve. I wish your father to consider me his friend. I understand all too well what it is like to have your future threatened by malcontents."

"Aye, Your Grace," she smiled. "I am certain that he is most grateful for your aid."

"Indeed," Henry replied, his pale eyes boring into hers. She managed to return his regard calmly and offered a gentle smile which belied the tingle of fear that she felt down her spine. She felt an unspoken challenge pass between Richard and Henry but outwardly they remained amiable, even pleased by each other's company.

"Tell me, Richard. I understand that you have recently returned from St. Davids." The suddenness of the change of subject startled Eve but Richard appeared to take the question serenely.

"Aye, Sire. It would seem that Rhys has misunderstood our treaty to be to his advantage, overly so. Though at our first meeting he appeared to understand that Pembroke lay in your trust—until the matter could be settled by you—he had taken full possession of it, and seemed to feel that it was by your word."

"The matter has not been settled, I assure you, Richard. But I am certain that you understand the difficulty of the situation. The holdings were given by Stephen and therefore must be reviewed as to their legality."

Eve drew in her breath silently and glanced at Richard who appeared to maintain his outward calm.

"I understand your position, Sire. You certainly cannot have it said of you that you show the favoritism that was favored by Stephen. My father's lands at Pembroke, not to mention the castle he built himself at Caermarthen, might well bring doubt to your word if they were left in my hands. I would not want it to be so on my account."

Eve startled. Caermarthen had been taken also? Henry had confiscated it also along with Pembroke when he knew full well that it had been given to Strongbow with full and legal license? Slowly, she began to see what was happening.

Henry flinched slightly at the mention of Caermarthen but he grinned broadly. "I appreciate your understanding, Richard, and that you offer no resistance to my decision. If all were as loyal as you, the tasks I must face would be far simpler."

"Whatever I might do to assist you, you have but to ask, Your Grace," Richard assured him with a smile.

Henry grunted but his heavy-lidded eyes narrowed as he peered at Richard and Eve trembled as she wondered if the defenses were to be lowered. "I will take you at your word, Richard. I will tell you now that I was more than a little disquieted to learn of the army you have been building and training here. It would not please me to learn that you plan to take Pembroke by force. The situation with the Welsh is tenuous, at best, and I will not have it flare by the actions of one of my nobles."

"When I gave you my oath, Sire, I gave it with a promise to be ever ready to come to your aid. I am not unaware, as you know, of your difficulties in France and I deem it my duty to have knights and men-at-arms in battle condition. Never, milord, did I entertain the notion of taking Pembroke by force— without your consent and prior advice. I would pledge that on my life. Besides, Pembroke was my father's, not mine, and as it was given him by Stephen, I hold it in little regard. But under your rule I am certain that there will be other opportunities for me, as given by Your Grace."

Henry laughed loudly at Richard's obvious flattery but Eve noted that it had not missed its mark. "Aye, Richard, there will be, I promise you! New conquests, new lands, with my blessing for those who serve me faithfully as you do! Moreover, I expect those under me to reason with such vision and I am pleased to find it in you!"

Richard returned Henry's merriment as he leaned forward across Eve to personally refill the king's tankard, then took up his own in a toast. "Then we understand that Pembroke is forgotten and I shall look to the day when, by my own merits, I shall replace it with conquests of my own!"

"Aye." Henry smiled, relaxing as he raised his tankard to meet Richard's. "To that let us drink, with my blessing to future endeavors!"

"And I shall take it, Sire," Richard murmured over his tankard.

Henry dallied at Chepstow for three more days before he took his leave, taking his departure at dawn as suddenly as he had come.

When Eve arose on that third morning, he was gone but it seemed that he had left a flurry of activity in his wake. Chepstow was abuzz with activity as she came into the hall to find the servants hurrying about, their arms laden with the burdens of preparation, the knights shouting orders to the men-at-arms who they felt were lagging under their terse orders. The courtyard looked like a make-shift encampment as wagons were being loaded from the kitchens and armory.

Eve had come into the hall in search of Sophie, wondering why the Scotswoman had not come to awaken her as was her custom when Richard had risen earlier, only to find the mayhem in full progress. She stopped a knight in his tasks to ask of Richard's whereabouts and the harried warrior gestured brusquely to the armory before returning to his lists, checking each item as it was loaded onto an already straining wagon.

She picked her way through the mass of men and horses, her growing alarm outweighing her puzzlement as she pondered the reason for the preparations. Had Henry ordered Richard to Normandy to help him against the French? He had stayed up late with Henry each night, thus she had not been able to speak with him at any length since Henry's arrival, so she could not know of his plans. But, it stood to reason, since each lord's first duty was to the sovereign in time of conflict. Eve's heart sunk as she considered the prospect of Richard's absence for months, perhaps longer, in Henry's service. She quailed at the thought of the long, dismal months in solitude, particularly in that they still had not been able to resolve their differences. As she remembered similar months in Normandy, spent in loneliness and worry for his safety, she quickened to cross the few remaining steps to the door of the armory.

She found him just inside the door, confering with one of his lieutenants, and she hesitated in the doorway, her dread heightened by finding him dressed in chain and mail, the three red chevrons blazing at her from his tunic.

He glanced up at her entrance and nodded a greeting as he completed his instructions to the other man. She was shocked to find the room nearly emptied. Stepping aside as the soldier took his leave, she looked up at Richard with dismay. "Richard, what is happening? Do you leave for France?"

"France?" He glanced at her with a puzzled frown, but smiled as he understood the question. "Nay, Henry has no need of my services. His armies are well staffed."

"Then what . . ."

"We go to Ireland," he answered simply.

"Ireland?" She was dumbfounded. The word barely formed on her lips before he laughed.

"Aye, milady, Ireland. But why do you look so stricken? I thought you would be pleased to be returning home." He smiled as he watched her face work with the news—her eyes seeming to grow impossibly larger with surprise.

"Henry has given you leave to Ireland? It—it is so sudden!"

"You heard him yourself, the night of his arrival."

"I did not hear him say . . ."

"He gave me his blessing to take new lands—and I am merely exercising his leave." In the light of the doorway she could see the amusement in his eyes as he awaited her response.

"You waste no time," she observed.

"We must be away before word reaches him. He is not yet so far removed that he cannot retrace his steps to halt us."

"But why not wait until he has returned to Normandy?"

"Eve, your father has been pressing me to come. The questions I put to you earlier helped me to determine how I would enter Ireland, but not whether or not I would. That had already been decided. Our time was overdue, as Henry delayed it. Now it is time."

She fingered the edge of the table thoughtfully as she considered the questions that had been plaguing her for the past three days. "Richard, why do you betray Henry?"

"I am not betraying him, Eve," he answered firmly. "Let it suffice to say that I no longer view the world in the black and white of my youth, but that I have learned to live in the grey areas in which my father dwelled for most of his life."

She looked up at him steadily. "And when did you learn that Henry was not a god? When he took Caermarthen from you as a reward for your service?"

"That was part of it," he answered honestly. "But only a

small part. There was another matter." He hesitated. "Trust me that I have my reasons for what I am doing. But do not mistake me, I still acknowledge that he is best for England and I will not be traitor."

"And Ireland?" she asked haltingly.

"The enemy is usually ourselves, Eve. In the long run we normally get what we deserve. I fear that if your people are to retain their present existence, they will have to fight for it, now or later."

"But why should they have to?" she cried. "Richard, freedom is theirs by right!"

"Is it? And who is to decide what is right, or even what is freedom? Your father, who fights to retain his kingdom and to gain more? Your people who change their loyalties with more ease than nature changes the seasons? The Pope, who feels that he is protecting the rights of the Church in Ireland while Henry feels he is best suited to bring Ireland to its ultimate greatness beneath his hand? Nay, Eve, the only thing that is certain is that each man has the right to fight for what he believes in, if he has the courage and the faith to see it through—and the willingness to sacrifice everything he has to do it."

There was nothing she could say in answer, but her heart heaved with foreboding as she asked quietly, "When will we leave?"

"By the first light of morning."

"What?" she cried. "But I cannot possibly be ready! I have had no warning!"

He laughed at her feminine concerns and reached out affectionately and touched her face. "You will be ready."

"I—I must know what to take with me!" she stammered. "How long will we be gone?"

But her innocent question struck a different response within him. He shifted uncomfortably as deep, bright emeralds shone up at him. She was overwhelmed by the prospect of returning to Ireland. Was she as eager to be rid of him? She had submitted; their nights of love, beginning in the loft, still warmed him in remembrance but had she responded to him only because she thought she had no choice? She was bound to him. What if she knew that she was to gain her freedom? He had begun to feel that they were finding a new measure of understanding. Would she discard it willingly? The thought settled into a cold feeling of fear in the pit of his gut. Accustomed to being in control of his feelings, the conflict only served his anger and he snapped with irritability, his voice more brusque than he intended.

"You will take all of your belongings, Eve. Do not leave anything; you will not be returning."

She drew in her breath sharply as his words, and the anger by which he spoke them, struck her as if he had delivered a blow with his fist. Oh God, what a fool she had been! Of course he would not leave her behind! He had planned this all along—to take her home, and leave her—to be rid of her once and for all! His revenge was at last complete—he had used her, worn her down until she had submitted—and now it was at an end! Her feelings dissolved into numb resolution and she turned away, her pride overcoming the deep wound he had inflicted.

"I will be ready, milord," she whispered, then left the armory without another word.

27

They left at daybreak. The long column was led by
fifty armored knights emblazoned with their coats-of-
arms and pennons of bright colors flying from lances,
followed by rows of over two hundred men-at-arms,
and wagons creaking from their burdens of tenting, weapons,
and foodstuffs.

Eve rode toward the middle of the column, her dark-blue,
fox-lined cloak drawn tight about her against the damp morning
fog, as she held a tight rein on her grey mare who danced
excitedly beneath her. She glanced sideways at Sophie and
stifled a smile as the Scotswoman was already shifting her
weight uncomfortably in the saddle. She had tried to convince
the older woman that she would be more comfortable riding
in one of the canvas-covered wagons with the other women,
but Sophie had rejected the suggestion curtly. She said that she
had no intention of passing the journey listening to idle chatter
but Eve suspected that her reasonings had taken another line.

Eve had not spoken with Richard since those last, terrible,
moments in the armory. He had come to bed late and she had
feigned sleep when she felt his weight upon the bed. Fortunately
he had made no move toward her and she was soon met with
the sound of heavy breathing as he fell almost immediately into
an exhausted slumber. He was gone when she had awakened,
to her great relief, but Sophie had come soon after. Their time
was taken with last-minute packing and though she said nothing, she could sense that Sophie was aware of her mood since

she would catch the Scotswoman watching her with a curious and bemused expression. When they had descended into the courtyard, Richard was there to meet them, and Eve caught Sophie watching them and knew that she was aware of the renewed tension between them as she saw her shake her head and roll her eyes unhappily. When she had insisted upon riding with her, more moments taken from their leaving as another horse had to be saddled, Eve knew that Sophie would not rest until she pried out the reasons for this latest unhappy development. Little good it would do her, Eve thought grimly as she now glanced at Sophie, not this time. She would not discuss it with her.

As the column made its way down the cliffs overlooking the winding river, they crossed the bridge and went out into the lush valley. Eve smiled, somewhat surprised at the villagers who had turned out to bid their farewells. They lined the road, rushing forward with gifts of flowers and cloth-wrapped foodstuffs, which they would press with eager hands to the departing knights and soldiers as they passed, shouting their good wishes for the bountiful return of Chepstow's men. They knew that if the campaign was successful, Striguil would see better days, the wealth filtering its way down to them, the enriched coffers keeping Striguil from years of hunger and lack of seed and cattle.

Richard was leaving ten of his best knights and ample men-at-arms to see to Striguil's needs in his absence, to be supervised under the able hands of his steward, so the day had taken on the atmosphere of a holiday. The children ran excitedly along the marchers, darting in and out to touch the knights, oblivious to the sharp hooves of the huge destriers that dwarfed the small forms. More than once a knight reached down to grasp a collar, pulling an urchin from under the horse's legs as the animal sidestepped, but it was done with laughter and good humor and not a hair was scathed in the departure.

If the body of fighting men seemed formidable to Eve as they left Striguil, she was soon awed as Richard executed his well-formed plans. Dipping into Wales, they marched southward through Caerwent, gathering forces of its famous archers, then on to Caerleon, where Roman legions had once gathered, their descendants eager to become part of what promised new hopes of wealth brought by the sword; then they marched on to the fortress of Cardiff, a magnificent battlement built by

Robert, Earl of Gloucester, son of Henry I, where men flocked to become part of the force that would be crossing the Irish sea.

They advanced through Morganwg to Neath, gathering Flemish soldiers all too eager for the excitement of battle, and through Strongbow's Caermarthen, where those still loyal to the deClares threw down Rhys arms and took up Richard's standard. At last, by mid-August, they reached Haverford where Maurice Pendergast awaited Richard's arrival. Now, with a force of over two hundred knights and a thousand men-at-arms, lancers and archers, they moved forward making final camp at Milford Haven, a city of tents and open fires, as they prepared for the crossing to Ireland.

Eve's red-and-gold striped tent of deClare colors was set up at the center of the camp, surrounded by the smaller ones of her ladies, the wives of Richard's knights. From the front of her tent Eve could see the banner of Richard's larger one, flying in the breeze from its crest, where Richard met with his commanders and lieutenants to prepare for the crossing and the campaign that would follow. As her maids prepared a bath for her, Eve watched the pennon flapping and snapping in the breeze and her mind turned to the conferences she knew were taking place beneath it. She had spoken with Richard only a few times on the march to the coast and then only for brief moments on matters of her welfare. She had met such moments with icy regard, speaking to him only in curt answers to his questions, aware of the coldness that would veil his own expression in response before he bolted forward to see to more pressing matters. Occasionally she had caught sight of him, the bright red chevrons easily picked out on their stark gold background of his tunic as he rode up and down the ranks on Taran.

As they approached the end of their journey, Eve had become more ill at ease, the reality of the Norman conquest which would soon descend upon her people heightening her dread with each passing hour. As she observed the hundreds upon hundreds of soldiers, eager to join their ranks with each farm, hamlet, and town they would pass through, any remaining hopes that she coveted for a peaceful solution drained away. It had been a faint hope, at best, but viewed from a distance she had allowed it. Now, standing at the center of the camp, her eyes passing over the multitudes of tents, the mass of men who made their way about the camp among triangles of lances and bows, she listened to the sounds of excited laughter intermixed with shouts and she realized unhappily what the fate of her people would soon be.

She had trusted Richard to be merciful, where another would not, and had prayed that he had the strength and ability to control the knights and men who served him. But would he? Perhaps she had been wrong about that as she had been about everything else. What was his true reason for aiding her father? To gain wealth? Undoubtedly. And, she suspected, to defy Henry, to gain back what he had taken from him. And at what cost? Certainly, Ireland would suffer for it.

One of her women pulled back the flap of the tent and informed her that the bath was ready. With a heavy sigh, Eve turned and ducked into the cool depths of the striped canvas. As she unlaced the bodice of her pelisse she was unaware of the trouble brewing in the larger striped tent, now silhouetted by the flaring brightness of orange and red hues of the setting sun. As she pulled the gown from her, two mounted knights were halted by the sentry at the edge of the camp; as she dropped her chemise from her hips and stepped into the water, the two, who had ridden hard from the north, were led, disgruntled, to a fire by a small tent at the edge of the temporary city, where a quick meal was prepared for them. As she sank into the warmth of the water, sighing in pleasure as it rushed soothingly over her weary shoulders, Richard looked up from his maps as Warwick, Pendergast and another knight of stature stepped into the tent, their faces grim.

Warwick handed a rolled parchment to Richard, then stood back as Richard broke the seal and scanned the contents.

"Is it what we feared?"

"Aye," Richard nodded as he finished the message and laid it on the table. "It is from Henry. He forbids the expedition."

"Damnation," Warwick muttered. "One more day and we would have been gone!"

Richard turned to the shorter of the other two, a middle-aged warrior with the beginnings of a paunch but still hard-muscled beneath his mail and with heavy, bristled eyebrows flecked with grey over black, fiery eyes. "Bertran, where are the messengers now?"

"They have been given a bed at the edge of the camp. They are well guarded. They will not be free to wander about."

"Good." Richard grunted as he gestured for the others to sit. "What did you tell them?"

"As little as possible." Pendergast grinned as he glanced at Bertran, while lowering his lean body into his chair. He removed his helm and wiped the sweat from his greying temples with the back of his hand. "Bertran told them that you and I had left for the Irish coast and that the rest were to follow on the first tide, just as you instructed."

"See that they remain at the edge of camp, at all costs."

"It will be done."

Later, when the others had left, Richard sank back into his chair and picked up a dagger which had been weighing down the edge of a map and began to play its tip against the surface of the war-table as he frowned in thought. Warwick watched him for a long moment, then shifted his weight and hooked his thumbs in his belt.

"Richard, it is not too late to turn back. You merely have to acknowledge Henry's order."

Richard looked up and smiled. "What order, my friend? But, in seriousness, Warwick, it is too late. It has been for a long time. There is no way that I would stop now."

"Have you told Eve about your agreement with Dermot?" Warwick asked suddenly, pleased at the way Richard startled at the question.

"Nay," Richard answered curtly, shooting a black glare at his friend.

"What can be served by your silence, Richard?" Warwick pressed. "Her life has been decided, she has the right to know."

"Nothing has been decided! Though you are correct in one thing; it is time that I talked with her."

Eve finished dressing, choosing a cool gown of cornflower-blue linen. Though she had just finished bathing, the heavy mugginess of the August evening made her skin feel damp and clammy. She waved aside the maid who picked up a starched linen coif, eyeing the object with distaste as she proceeded to twist her hair swiftly into a long heavy braid.

Sophie ducked into the tent as Eve tied off the end of the braid, her penetrating gaze taking in Eve's appearance with a quick glance. "Good, ye've finished with your bath. Richard would be waiting to have supper with him in his tent."

"Oh, he does, does he?" Eve snapped. "Just like that, I am summoned!"

Sophie cocked a brow at Eve's show of anger.

"All right, Sophie!" Eve said with a wave of her hand. "I will go. Heaven forbid that I should keep milord waiting!"

As she walked toward the large tent she nodded an absentminded greeting to those she passed, with a quick flash of a smile though her thoughts were occupied with what awaited her. The knights and soldiers who looked up regarded her appreciatively, their envy of Richard quickly disguised out of respect to their commander. And to the fact that none sought to feel the point of the earl's swift anger. But Eve did not notice the warmth behind those looks as her thoughts were fixed upon the large tent, the setting sun framing its outline in an aura of gold, accentuating the deClare pennon which waved nobly from its peak.

"Behold the conqueror," she thought wryly. She was determined, whatever his purpose, the evening would not be spent in idle chatter. Nor, this time, would he ply her for information without giving some himself. She would no longer allow him to use her, to make a fool of her, whatever happened!

As she approached the tent, the soldier standing guard at its entrance nodded sharply and drew back the flap for her to enter. She stepped inside, blinking for a moment as the flap dropped behind her and she sought to adjust her eyes to the darkness. Richard was lighting an oil lamp on the table and its meager, catching light began to throw distorted shadows on the sides of the huge tent. She glanced about, startled to note the contrast from her own quarters. A narrow cot, covered with wool blankets, stood to one side and there were backless camp chairs about the large map table, but aside from these and the stacks of charts and maps, and Richard's armor and sword heaped to one side, the tent was unencumbered by luxury. She realized, with bemusement, that Richard had spared nothing for her own richly appointed tent while he himself lived in spartan simplicity.

He looked up upon her entrance and smiled, his eyes lingering on the fullness of her breasts pressing tauntingly beneath the thin linen before he returned his attention to lighting the second lamp on the table.

"Welcome, milady."

"Greetings, milord," she said with equal formality, though with a touch more coldness.

"Please, sit down," he offered, gesturing to one of the chairs. "I have ordered a light supper for us. It will be here soon."

She was mildly surprised that they were to dine alone and

it added to her uneasiness as she took the nearest chair and waited.

He poured two goblets of spiced wine and handed her one, then settled into his chair directly across from her. "I hope that the journey has not been too uncomfortable for you."

"Nay, milord," she answered, affecting an equal casualness. It struck her odd, even while she tried to dismiss such thoughts, that after all that they had been through, they should now act as two who had barely just met. "The journey was less difficult for me than many others. I have been quite comfortable."

As he drew on his wine she watched his eyes in the flickering light but it was impossible to read them as they reflected the light, appearing almost silver. A soldier entered carrying a mazer of cheese, bread and roasted fowl, which he placed on the table. In a moment they were alone once again, the silence seeming even heavier than before. Eve had taken a few bitefuls of food when Richard's deep voice burst the silence, and she jumped involuntarily.

"Well, Eve, has it come to this, when we no longer have anything to say to one another?"

"Nay, milord," she smiled demurely, which she noted brought up a tawny perplexed brow. "I was only waiting for you to speak."

"Indeed," he replied, his eyes crinkling with amusement. "The journey must have exhausted you more than you will admit, *cherie*. Had I known it would effect such acquiescence I would have kept you to horse from the moment of our marriage."

Intent upon her resolve, she ignored the barb and reached over to refill his goblet. "Is there a particular reason that you have asked me to join you this evening, milord?"

"Must I have a reason beyond the company of a lovely supper companion?"

"You have forgone the pleasure before this night, milord," she countered. "Therefore, I must assume that there is another purpose to your invitation."

He stared at her for a protracted moment as he toyed with the stem of his goblet. "I have not requested your company before this as my duties were duty-bound elsewhere. However, tonight I have made time as there is a matter of some importance of which you must be made aware before we cross in the morning. You know that I sent Gervase to Ireland with Miles?"

"Aye, I am aware of it. You sent him to aid FitzStephen

and Montmorcey, who arrived there soon after Pendergast's return."

"Aye, but there was another purpose. He carried a message and two coffers to your father."

Puzzled, she waited for him to continue. She noticed that he shifted uncomfortably, as if reluctant to proceed.

"The message contained an answer to a proposition he made to me before he left Bristol. It regarded the two of us, Eve, and—one coffer contained your jewels, which I have returned to him for your keeping." Her mouth had dropped open in surprise and he waved it off, not wanting her to interrupt. "Your intent will not be forgotten, Eve, though it is the contents of the second coffer I wish to discuss. It contained your bride-price. It has been paid, Eve, and I wanted you to know before we left that you are free."

She had known that this moment would come, she had been prepared for it since her return to England, but now that it had arrived, it seemed unreal. It was over, truly and finally over. Her mind turned like a corkscrew, bending and twisting between realization and disbelief. As it fused into acceptance, she raised her gaze to him, meeting him with dry eyes and outward control she did not feel.

"So, I return home, unencumbered. It is well, Richard. I will not have to face my people as the wife of the conqueror but as an Irish subject. There will be no contest for my loyalties."

"I did not realize that there ever was," he smirked.

Her smile held a touch of sadness at his parry. "It would not be true to say that there was never a conflict. But it will not serve for us to speak of it now. I would rather discuss the future. Have you had word of what awaits us?"

Something inside of him twisted at the ease with which she had accepted the news. Had their marriage really meant so little to her? He had tried, and failed. The knowledge left him a little light-headed. "Who knows what the damnable Irish will do," he growled peevishly. "The last word was the Okinselagh awaits their saviors with open arms, all too ready to capitulate to a hand that will save them from O'Conner and O'Rourke regardless of the consequences, though I doubt that they have thought that far. As for Leinster, and the rest, they will give us little trouble in the end."

Her mouth tightened at his cruelty and she blinked repeatedly as she absorbed the shock. How could she ever have thought that he had begun to love her again? It had all been a nasty game, and he had won. Shaky, she rose from her chair and turned away from the uneaten meal, pausing only to establish a gracious exit in light of his rudeness.

"I thank you, milord, for the consideration you have shown me in the past months. I apologize if I have inconvenienced you or in any way have proved to be a burden. Now, if you will excuse me, I find that I am rather tired after all."

She left the tent, leaving him to stare after her. He rose and walked to the opening, then stood watching after her as her slender form disappeared among the tents.

"Damnation!" he swore, startling the guards who stood at either side; then he pulled the flap shut with an angry jerk.

28

On August 23, the eve of St. Bartholomew, the ships
sailed on silent waters into the fog-blanketed bay
known as the Passage. The channel lay due east of
Waterford, a triangle-shaped waterway that would
afford the fleet the quickest access to their final destination and
purpose. Camp was made a short distance from the landing
and riders were sent to inform Gervase and FitzStephen of their
arrival. It was Donnell who returned a party of soldiers to escort
them and the following morning they set out to join the forces
that would affect the history of Ireland.

As they rode into the camp, Eve's heart gripped both with
pain from the enormity of it, and with warmth as she recognized
the troops comprised of kerns, the Irish footsoldiers, spotting
familiar faces among them. As they approached the center of
the huge camp, they were met by Donnell, who stepped forward
with a pleased grin to help Eve dismount. She slipped to the
ground into his arms, throwing her arms about him.

"It is good to see you, little sister." He grinned, reddening
a little at her overt display of affection.

"And you!" She laughed. "You cannot realize how much!"
She glanced about and looked back at him with question. "Is
father not here to greet us?"

"Nay, he remains at Ferns for the time being." She caught
the look of concern that passed over his handsome face. "I fear
that you will find him much aged, Eve."

"But why?" she said with alarm. "Things have gone well
for him. What has happened?"

"Aye, we have done well," he shrugged. "But I fear that success has cost him more than he realized. He..."

Donnell stopped speaking and tensed as he stared past her shoulder at someone who was approaching. Eve turned about to find Richard standing at her elbow.

"You must be Donnell." Richard smiled, extending his arm, which Donnell grasped, obviously pleased that the earl would honor him as an equal before his men. "Eve has spoken of you often. I am pleased that at last we may meet."

"Aye, milord. And I in turn have heard much about you. We are glad that you are here."

"I have been told that your father is not well. I trust that it is not serious."

"I fear that it is serious enough to make him unable to greet you in person, milord. But he has asked me to convey his greetings to you and your men."

"Accepted," Richard smiled. "I shall look forward to seeing him again when is feeling better. Now, I should like to meet with you and the others. We have much to discuss. I understand that things have not been going well with Waterford."

Though his expression seemed casual, Richard's penetrating eyes caught the black look that darkened Donnell's blue ones for an instant and he stepped forward, taking Donnell's arm to lead him away.

"Perhaps we could sit and talk for a moment before we see the others. There, under those trees, it looks cool and inviting and I think I could use the respite."

Eve scampered after them, having no intention of being dismissed after such a brief reunion with her brother, and settled with them beneath the trees, well out of the hearing of those who were wandering about the camp. She was ready to argue if Richard attempted to send her away but he seemed not to notice her.

"Now, Donnell, I would like to hear it from you. I would know about the city and what has happened."

"Waterford is a triangular-shaped city, Richard, with well-fortified walls, the third side set against a wide river. The inhabitants are Ostmen, kinfolk of yours, though they have isolated themselves behind their walls for so long I suspect that they have forgotten the fierce legacy given by your common ancestors." He grinned.

Richard fought a smile at the observation. "Go on."

"You are aware that we took Wexford without much dif-

ficulty, and so it was with Waterford. When they heard of the
ease by which we captured their kin, they sent forth hostages
in submission, certain that they would be dealt with fairly."
He hesitated, uncertain of how to continue. Though anger was
clearly written on his face, he was obviously uncertain how
Richard would receive what he had to say.

"Tell me all of what happened, as you saw it," Richard
urged.

"I will say, milord, that there was some disagreement among
your men on the disposition of the hostages. Sir Gervase pleaded
on behalf of mercy, urging that they be held for ransom, but
the others claimed that it would show weakness and present
danger in the event of attack." Donnell became angrier as he
spoke, now making no attempt to hide his feelings. "The others
won out and the hostages, most of whom were the leading
members of the town, were executed. Their limbs were broken
and they were thrown from the walls of the city into the river."

Eve swallowed the bile that reached the back of her throat
and she glanced at Richard aghast, her own anger swelling
against the outrage. She saw his jaw tighten as he looked at
Donnell evenly, his eyes paling to silver.

"Who pressed for the deed?"

"Montmorcey and those with him, milord. Gervase,
FitzStephen and Miles were the strongest against it."

"Go on, what happened then?"

"When those in the city saw what happened, they fortified
the walls and repelled us handily. I assume that those in charge
expected complete submission after what they had seen and
they fought with a fury for which we were unprepared. Soon
we found ourselves defeated where we had thought ourselves
victorious."

Richard stood and walked away to the edge of the trees
where he stood in silent thought, his hands folded behind his
broad back. After a long moment, he turned back and nodded
to Donnell.

"Shall we join the others now?" he said calmly. Too calmly.
The back of Eve's neck tingled as she detected an element in
his voice and manner that only she recognized as intense anger,
boiling beneath the surface.

They crossed the clearing and Richard seemed not to notice
the men who saluted as he passed, his intent upon the tent they
approached. As they entered the war tent, the knights and lords
stood, greeting their commander with broad smiles and offers

of friendly greetings. Eve was amazed as Richard greeted each in turn, his manner friendly and casual, giving no evidence of the anger she knew he had felt only moments before. Only Gervase stood to one side, his manner one of remorse and reluctance to participate in the greetings. It did not go unnoticed by Richard, who nodded to the blond knight.

As Richard sat, the others settled into chairs about the large council table with Richard at its head. Eve took a chair to one side hoping that she would be forgotten in the shadows, thus allowed to remain. She startled as Richard smiled at her and proceeded to introduce her to those she had not formally met. She wondered as to his obvious intention to include her in the war council but she determined to hold her tongue, regardless of what was said, for fear that he would change his mind.

The proceedings were halted momentarily by Raymond, who blurted in, his arms full of rolls of maps. After he dropped them on the table, Raymond rushed to bring a tankard and ale to Richard, and he stumbled over a few of the knights seated on Richard's right in his anxiousness to serve his lord. Richard fought a smile behind his hand and nodded seriously at Raymond's well-intentioned efforts before finally turning his attention to the others.

"As we are recently arrived, I would know from each of you what has passed and of the situation at Waterford," he began with a light voice. "Montmorcey, perhaps you will begin."

"Ah, Richard, if only I could recount better news in celebration of your arrival," the lord began pompously, shifting his wide girth in his chair. "Unfortunately, I cannot as the news is grievous. The city is well-fortified, the citizens of the town repel us against every advance. I suspect that they had notice of our intent, as there is no other answer for it."

Eve held back a gasp of outrage over the bold lie and followed Richard's noncommittal gaze to FitzStephen, who had the decency to lower his eyes to the table.

"Tell me, Robert," Richard posed the question to FitzStephen as his eyes narrowed, "do you have anything to add?"

FitzStephen looked up from the table with a start. "I—the town is well-fortified, as Hervy says. We have laid them to siege but they repel us fiercely. They . . ."

As his voice trailed off, Richard picked it up. "I had it to believe that the Ostmen were smug and comfortable, unaccustomed to confrontation. They have resided within their walled cities for many years, growing fat and idle, and should be no contest for a well-armed Norman army. What has happened?"

There was an outburst of excuses from about the table, each attesting to the efforts of those present and the men they led until finally Richard rose, bringing them to an abrupt silence as he turned and leaned against the back of his chair, his grey eyes shining with pale anger as he spoke in a low, hard voice.

"Let me tell you how it shall be. What has occurred here will never happen again by any man in my company, or under my charge. Waterford has not fallen due to the same excessive cruelty that was laid upon our Irish allies you condemned with such vehemence. Have we proven ourselves to be less barbarous?"

Pendergast stepped forward from where he stood at the back wall, his arms folded across his chest, his jaw set firmly in anger as his hazel eyes darted about the room in support of Richard's words.

"In the future, no man shall act without my express approval," Richard continued, his eyes passing over each of the now rather chagrined occupants of the war-table, their protests cut to silence under his stern gaze. "Violation of this order shall mean immediate banishment without reward of conquest, or death if I deem the offense to be of a grievous nature.

"What is done here shall be the mark of a true Norman conquest. As with those who came with the Conqueror to England, your fathers and grandfathers, and as those who came into Normandy centuries before, we come to stay. Not to ravish and plunder the lands and the people, not to hide behind walls as our kinfolk, the Ostmen, have done, but to stay! To mingle with the blood of the Irish, to give them the best that is ours and to recognize what is theirs, to become part of this noble and rich land and join our mutual inheritance.

"You will understand that from this moment forward, we are not here as oppressors. Rather, our intent is to unite Ireland and become part of it, to assimilate ourselves into it. If any man here does not agree, he may depart now without recrimination. But, if you elect to stay, you will comply. Do you understand?"

Eve sat transfixed, completely stunned by his words. As others in the room recovered, bursts of comments broke out around the table, which he silenced with a wave of his hand. "You will be given the opportunity to choose. Once Waterford has fallen, Okinselagh and Leinster will be given up to Dermot and the first part of our task will be at a finish. You may decide then. If you opt to return to England, you will do freely with goodly payment to reward you for your trouble. But, if you decide to stay, you will do so with the commitment to Ireland as well as to England." He paused and looked meaningfully at each baron and knight in turn, then looked to Gervase. "Gervase, I shall meet with you, Donnell and each of the commanders in my tent. Some sense must be made out of this disaster."

He ignored the outburst of questions and strode from the tent, leaving their protests to fall into grumbles among themselves. Gervase and Pendergast strode to the entrance, their pleasure ill-concealed as they nodded to the commanders who rose to follow them.

Eve still stared at the spot where Richard had disappeared as she tried to make some sense of his words. The shock of what he had said still numbed her and, unlike the others, she was speechless. She startled as a hand was laid upon her arm and she looked up to find Donnell standing at her side.

"Come," he smiled. "I will take you to your tent. Do not sit there gawking, little sister. I must see to Richard and I have little time."

She rose in a half-trance and followed him from the tent, leaving the still disgruntled barons behind them. Halfway to their destination she caught her breath and spun to Donnell, grasping his arm in an attempt to halt his long strides.

"Donnell, what did he mean?"

"You heard him yourself," he smiled. "What more can I add."

"You knew about this?"

"Of course." He stopped and looked at her with mild surprise. "You actually had no inkling of it? Has he not told you anything?"

"Nay! Would I be asking you if he had?"

"Funny sort of marriage you have, Eve." He smirked as he stepped around a soldier who lay sleeping in the shadow of his tent. "Do you not talk with your husband?"

"He is not my husband!" she retorted, two-stepping to keep up with him.

He stopped abruptly and looked at her with surprise. "Not your husband? But—"

"Evidently you do not know everything, big brother," she snapped. "Or you would know that he returned the marriage portion. Did father not tell you?"

"Aye, I know that Gervase brought it but—" He looked at her oddly, suddenly unwilling to say more. He reached out and took her arm, his brows gathering into a deep frown. "What did he say when he told you that he had returned it?"

"Noth—nothing," she stammered. "Only that I was free, free to choose. Please, Donnell, you are hurting my arm!"

"And what did you say?" he growled, making no attempt to release her.

"I—I told him I was glad! What do you expect?" she cried. "Do you still love him?"

She gasped at him as she tried to wrench her arm free. Why was he acting like this? "What difference does it make? He doesn't want me, or why would he have returned it?"

"Do you love him?" he pressed.

"Aye! I love him, but I won't grovel before him!"

He released her arm suddenly and a grin replaced his blackened look so quickly that it startled her. "Good," he grunted, then pulled her after him.

"Donnell, what is the matter with you?" she hissed, angry with the way he had treated her.

"Nothing whatsoever, little sister." He laughed. "Everything is going to be just fine."

They had reached her tent and she turned on him. "Donnell, would you please tell me what is going on!"

"Hush, Eve," he growled under his breath. "The middle of the camp is not the place to discuss Richard's plans. Besides, little sister, there are some things I will not meddle in."

Before she could protest, he was gone. She knew it was useless to follow him, and the realization infuriated her. Did any of them have less at stake than she? Yet, she was delegated to pace the narrow confines of her tent while they decided the fate of her beloved Erin. Furious, she turned and entered the tent, resigned to help Sophie and her maids with the unpacking, unfortunately for them.

As the moon rose large and opulent over the sleeping camp, Eve stepped from her tent and leaned against a support pole, her eyes wandering about the dark shadows of the tents and men who were sleeping in the open air to escape the stuffy confines of their beds. Sophie had left her much earlier in the evening, throwing her hands in dismay over Eve's temper, as she promised to seek out the tent of another lady who would give her some peace. When the Scotswoman had gone, Eve had fallen into depression, with not a little guilt over her behavior.

She had not meant to take it out on one who had shown nothing but love and loyalty but, as is often the case, it is the one closest to us that suffers our unhappiness. Now that she was gone, Eve felt alone and lost. Her anger and indignation toward Richard had upheld her before but now she felt lonelier than she had ever felt before. Useless, what good was she? Richard did not want her, her people were in the midst of their greatest crisis, and what good was she? As before, she would move through her life, letting others effect what would happen about her, and she would stand in the vortex with no effect upon its outcome. If just once, for one moment, she could be a man! A great battle would be engaged on the morrow, while she . . .

At that moment her eyes landed on a young squire who passed by on hurried business for his lord. His pink cheeks, still untouched by his first beard, reddened deeper under the sudden, interested gaze of a beautiful lady who stood watching him from the doorway of her tent. He startled as a slow smile began on her lovely face and to his complete amazement, she gestured for him to come hither. Stunned, he glanced about, worried that someone might have seen. It was not unusual for a lady, bored and neglected by her husband, to dally with a young squire—but it had never happened to him. In fact, nothing had ever happened to him. He knew it was dangerous to refuse, he had heard stories from his fellow squires, while he pretended to know exactly what they were talking about, of the dangers of refusing the lady. Her manner of revenge could be as swift, if not as obvious, as that of her lord. Caught in the dilemma, yet trembling with the excitement of undiscovered pleasures, the squire swallowed nervously and, glancing about once again, accepted his fate and made his way to the tent into which the beautiful lady had disappeared.

Taran moved restlessly, tossing his great black head as he snorted in protest against the waiting. Richard held firmly back on the reins, the steel grey of his eyes narrowing beneath his helm as they moved along the walls of the city silhouetted against the orange and yellow aura of the rising sun. The sounds of creaking leather, as the knight beside him shifted in the saddle, seemed unreal against the almost total silence that accompanied the sunrise. It was as if the birds that usually greeted the morning in joyful chatter took part with the opposing armies, who studied each other in the awakening dawn. Richard looked up and down the lines of his men, satisfied as to their readiness. Baron, knight, and man-at-arm alike held the age-old expression of men prepared to do battle, the mixture of anticipation and dread heightened by the rushing adrenaline of excited fear.

Warwick moved his mount aside Richard's and they wordlessly made their way along the rows of men, circling the outer rim of the walled city, just out of reach of the bows and lances they could spot in readiness behind the parapets as the first rays of the sun caught an occasional flash of metal. They returned to where FitzStephen and Pendergast awaited, nodding grimly but with an excited anticipation of the coming battle.

"The hour grows late, Richard," Pendergast observed as he moved in his saddle. "The men grow restless and I worry about how long I can hold them before someone breaks."

"Your responsibility is to see that they do not," Richard warned. "The longer we wait, the more reckless they will become." He gestured to the walls. "By now they feel they have our positions fixed. I want you to reshift your men to just beyond a bow's reach there, north of the walls." He pointed with his gloved hand to the north angle of the city beneath two of the Danish towers that held points of the triangle. "Warwick will bring you the moment when Donnell is ready, but draw their attention! They must believe that the attack will come with you."

FitzStephen glanced at the city, then grinned with understanding as he moved away to shift his men to the north wall. He was followed quickly by Pendergast, though the latter had not the reasoning, as did FitzStephen, who had served enough years with Richard, and Strongbow before him, to grasp the subtleties of what was planned. Richard and Warwick pulled their mounts about and rode back the way they had come.

Donnell and Gervase waited in a small grove of trees with a large group of heavily mailed knights. Some carried immense battle axes, their blades hewed to a razor-edged sharpness. They pulled themselves to their feet as Richard and Warwick entered the grove, their eyes bright with an eagerness to be about their business. After a moment was spent in quick conversation with Gervase and Donnell, Warwick pulled the head of his destrier about and left the grove. A long, tenuous moment passed. Their heads jerked about in unison as the sound of the battle enjoined from beyond the trees and they went wordlessly to their waiting mounts, where their squires helped them to mount under the weight of their added mail.

Gervase settled into his saddle and pulled his helm over his head, adjusting the nose-guard. His blue eyes burned at Richard from beneath the helmet as he offered a cocky one-sided grin, "I suggest you do not dally, Richard, or the battle will be won before you have arrived."

"I will make haste to assure that I am part of it," Richard snorted with grim good humor. "Just see to it that you allow us the protection we need."

Gervase raised his broad sword in a brief salute and urged his destrier from the grove as Richard turned to the others who remained, his eyes sweeping critically over the waiting, mailed men and the battle axes they carried. "We move to the south behind Gervase's men. The object is to reach the wall and to your purpose with as few lost as possible. There will be time for each of you to use your swords later, remember that. It is your ability with the ax that is needed first and foremost. Do not allow the prospect of hand-to-hand combat to allow you to forget."

As they broke from the trees, the sights and sounds of the battle engulfed them. Forces had broken from the city to meet the enemy and Pendergast and FitzStephen had done their jobs well, as the bulk of the forces were met at the northern wall. But a contingent moved swiftly to the southern threat and the battle was enjoined when Richard managed to move his small group toward their objective. Gervase and Donnell moved steadily before them, engaged in combat, felling their opponents in a methodical progress that left Richard to wonder how the city could have offered any resistance at all. But soon he was in the middle of it. He saw the faces of the enemy surrounding him with wild-eyed assault, and he pressed Taran with his legs to release his hands from the reins to use his sword and shield, guiding the trained animal through the melee. He cut and thrust with a well-guided sword, striking down the foe with little resistance, aided by the razor-sharp hoofs of the destrier, which met the unarmored competitors, cutting them beneath him as they moved inch by inch toward their target.

Suddenly, an Ostman broke through his ranks, by sheer luck, gaining an advantage not held by his comrades. He came

in about Richard from the side and before Richard had gained
freedom from his last foe, struck with his club, grazing Taran's
shoulder. The animal faltered, screaming in pain, and nearly
fell, stumbling sideways before it regained its footing. Richard
turned instinctively, thrashing out with his blade on the unseen
foe and felt satisfaction as it struck its mark, sinking heavily
into flesh. As Richard swung Taran about, the weight of the
shifting animal pulled his sword from the impaled enemy, and
his eyes caught a glimpse of a slight figure in an orange tunic
and the vision of a white hand grasping the hilt of a short
sword. A nagging feeling of familiarity flashed through his
mind and he pulled Taran's head about as his eyes flickered
over the press of men. His attention was regained to the battle
as a sword flashed uncomfortably near Taran's sleek black neck
and his own sword moved in lightning speed to the source.

Having reached the wall, Richard moved the small band of
mail-clad knights beneath the object of their pursuit, while
Gervase moved his men about them in close protection. A small
house jutted out from the wall, its corner supported by a heavy
post no more than a foot from the wall. The men moved about
the post and raised their battle axes, some still stained with the
blood of those of the enemy who had managed to break through
the line of Gervase's man, and began to hack at the shuddering
timber in accurate and swift unison, each stroke cutting white
slivers which flew from the wood in measured sparks.

As the Ostmen realized the intent of the invaders, the barrage
gained a new fury and Richard drew his men back to meet the
intense rush that broke through Gervase's and Donnell's lines
in desperate attempt to reach the ax-wielding knights.

With blood-curdling ancient war cries, a tight group of Ostmen swooped down upon Richard, their eyes burning with
hatred at the gold tunic as if the three chevrons taunted their
weapons to their mark. His sword brought down the first two
unfortunate enough to reach him and Taran's hoofs struck out
effectively at the third, whose object was the smooth belly of
the animal.

In a distracting moment Richard spied the orange tunic of
his earlier disquiet. As he turned to find it he suddenly felt an
explosion of white-hot pain burst from his leg. He twisted about
and brought his sword over Taran's head in one swift motion,
its deadly intent directed to the object of that pain even before
he considered its source. In an unreality of incredibly slow
motion he watched the enemy's broad sword, which had sliced

into his thigh, come about in a fatal thrust to his neck and in that instant he knew it was too late, the sword would meet its mark before he could parry. As he numbed, bracing for the blow he was certain would come, his eyes focused vaporously on a dagger that seemed to emerge from the man's neck. The Ostman's lips drew back in a mocking grimace, his eyes fixed upon Richard in surprise. But, as he slumped to the ground, his bloodied sword still grasped tightly in his hand, Richard's eyes riveted upon the slender dagger and its jewel-encrusted hilt. Stunned with shock, his eyes flew over the melee, searching for an orange tunic among the dust and bodies of the fighting men.

Not finding the object of his search, he swore fiercely and urged Taran forward, as the huge destrier cut a path through the battle and he spotted a flash of orange leather. He watched with horror as it disappeared once again in the midst of the broil, lost from sight behind a rush of horsed knights. Feeling a rush of sickening despair, mixed with a heightened panic, he spurred Taran sharply in the flanks. The startled animal snorted with pain and fairly leaped over those nearest. Oblivious to the battle, Richard made his way to the spot. As Taran picked his way through the dead and dying, the battle having moved closer to the wall, he began to breathe slightly easier when he did not find the object of his search among the unfortunate.

"Richard, it's going!"

His head jerked about at the sound of Gervase's voice nearby and he followed the knight's arm to the wall where he saw the stone of the jutting house begin to crumble. Having completed their task, the knights had turned their axes into the battle and had made their way clear of the wall. It began to give way, the sound reverberating along the battlements like a rolling clap of thunder, gaining in rapid intensity until its sound brought the blood-stained men on the field to frozen, silent awe as they stared at the shifting stone, their weapons momentarily forgotten along with the enemy they faced. As the house came down, dragging a large portion of the wall with it, a huge breach suddenly opened like an enormous, gaping eye.

A new intensity of fighting began as suddenly as it had stopped, though all knew the battle had been decided at that moment. FitzStephen and Pendergast appeared from their positions, their forces now concentrated on the breach, their distraction at the north wall having served its purpose.

It was over before the sun began its descent, the late after-

noon light shadowing the silenced battlefield as men were set
to work burying the corpses and tending to the wounded.

Richard had moved through his duties, his stomach tightened in worry and dread, though he had made a swift, and
fortunately unfruitful, search through the battlefield. The order
was given out that there was to be no butchery on the defeated
town and though it was a mere reissuance of orders, there were
those among the Irish and the English who chose not to obey.
Sitric, the Norse leader of the Ostmen, was dragged to Ragh-
nall's tower and put to the sword. Richard's justice was swift.
The offenders were promptly hung in the town's main square
as an example of what would happen to those who chose to
ignore his orders. But many were to follow before the point
was made and it was a bloody victory.

As the remaining leaders of the town were found, they were
secured in a large stone and timber house Richard had taken
for his quarters, while FitzStephen and Pendergast set about
securing the town and establishing a garrison.

Aching with fatigue and from the throbbing wound in his
thigh, Richard made his way with a small band of knights
through the narrow cobblestone streets to his quarters. The city
was secured at last and he longed for a chance to bathe and
rest, to ease his exhausted body between clean, comfortable
sheets where he could pass undisturbed until morning. But he
knew that there were hours of work ahead, perhaps the most
distasteful of all, as he would face the haunted looks of hatred
from the conquered and spell their fate. His thoughts had been
numbed except to his responsibilities over the past hours and
now worry crept into his fatigue and his fingers rested on the
small dagger which he had retrieved from the battlefield and
now rested in his belt.

The small party passed an open market which only the day
before had been filled with hawkers and merchants selling their
wares and was now strewn with wounded men, whose moans
and crys of anguish filled the square, sounding off the stone
buildings in contest with the click of the destrier's hooves.
Richard's eyes passed over the tortured and the men who were
giving what aid they could to their desperate comrades. As he
began to look away, he did a double take and glanced back at
a small, slender figure who was bent over a groaning man-at-
arms with a severe head wound. The shadows of the market's
lath roof had hidden them from view momentarily but, as the

figure moved about, the broken rays of the late sun momentarily flashed on an orange tunic.

Richard pulled Taran abruptly to a halt, relief flooding over him as from beneath his helm his eyes fixed upon the figure. His mood changed to one of intense anger as he watched the figure move about the wounded, then almost as quickly he calmed and a smile began to play wickedly at the corners of his mouth.

He looked up at the sound of approaching horses to find Gervase nearing with a guard of knights. He sat back easily in his saddle and waited, feeling much of the earlier fatigue leave him. He found suddenly that he was actually looking forward to the rest of the day.

Gervase pulled his mount alongside of Richard and blinked at the amused smile Richard wore. He glanced down and looked himself over, wondering as to this friend's humor. Finding nothing out of order, and too exhausted to bother with it, he shrugged it off, feeling slightly irritable that Richard should be in such good humor when he was so tired.

"MacMurrough has arrived," he growled irascibly. "I took him to your quarters, he is waiting for you there."

"Good," Richard commented, still smiling.

Gervase gawked at him. "Damnation, Richard. If there is something amusing about today, I wish you would share it!"

Richard moved Taran abreast of Gervase and out of earshot of the others. His gaze settled over the street beyond them while his mouth worked with suppressed laughter. "Gervase, my old friend, it occurs to me that Raymond has his hands full with other matters and I am in need of a squire."

Puzzled, almost to the point of endurance, Gervase frowned blackly. "Do not look to me! I served my duty with your uncle!"

"Nay, not you," Richard chortled. "I have another in mind. Look you to the market shed and to a certain slender form clad in an orange tunic."

Still frowning, Gervase looked beyond Richard's shoulder. All at once Gervase's face fell into astonishment, his eyes widening into large circles as they gasped with shock from the shadows of his helm. "God's Breath! What is she doing here? How . . ."

"Bring the priests to tend the wounded." Richard smiled. "And send these others to rest. However, be sure that the 'squire' is brought to my service."

He finished with a smile, which Gervase now answered broadly, "Aye, milord, it shall be done with haste."

A full two hours were spent hearing the reports of the commanders and more were given to issuing orders as to the disposition of the city and its inhabitants. When the last had departed, Richard leaned wearily back in his chair and let his eyes wander idly over the large, comfortable room, the warmth of the fire behind him easing the soreness and fatigue from his back. Damn, but these Irish summer nights were cold, or was it something else that plagued him to a chill? He leaned his elbow on the arm of the chair and rubbed his forehead as he stifled a yawn. While he had listened to the grumbles and pleadings from his commanders, his mind had wandered to thoughts of Eve, and his anger had grown thinking of the danger she had placed herself in. When he had faced the fierce pride of the fallen leaders, as they had stood boldly before him, prepared for the outcome of his decision without asking for quarter, he had thought of her. He knew that it was her pride that had caused her to do what she had this day—as incredible as it was. It was her country, her people, and those they met in battle were more her enemy than his. Outrageous, but she did it. He should have suspected it, but it had never entered his mind.

His short conversation with Donnell had completely knocked the props out from under him. There had been a letter, taken by Gail and destroyed by her father. But more importantly, Donnell insisted that his sister still loved him! He said that she had admitted it! Why? Why did she not tell him, offer even the slightest hint that last night in Milford Haven? He knew the answer—it was the same reason that had caused him to hold back on the edge, not admitting his own feelings—pride. How much had that pride, from both of them, caused walls that might never be now breached?

He stretched out, planting his feet on the desk, and pursed his lips in careful thought. He had a point to make, and by God he would make it before all was done. If she wanted to play the role of the squire instead of the gentle, well-born lady, then so be it. Armed with new knowledge, he stretched back in his chair and waited.

With perfect timing Gervase opened the door and crossed to the table, throwing a sheaf of parchment on the desk. "These are the completed tallies of the stores you asked for. We were able to keep most of the warehouses from being burnt to the ground. With care the city should have enough provisions to see them to the next harvest."

"Excellent." Richard sighed. "Though I swear there will be more order in the future or I'll see every jackanape swinging from the gallows!"

"I think that they now understand what you mean, Richard."

He merely grunted in reply and stifled another yawn.

"I have news that might wake you up," Gervase grinned. "Your new squire awaits without."

Richard glanced up with interest and his eyes lost their weariness. "I wanted it done quietly," he cautioned.

"Never fear," Gervase chuckled. "She takes great care to keep those auburn tresses well tucked beneath that ridiculous cap she is wearing, and I suspect that she has bound herself. She is so involved with her game, and certain that she plays it well, that she has not even noticed the strange looks from the men as we passed, though I thought she was going to faint when I told her that you wanted to see her. I had to give the evil-eye to a few interested looks that caught her well-turned legs but I am certain that they just think that I bring you sport for an evening's merriment. That fact that you have issued an order that they are to hold themselves from the local wenches shouldn't bother them a bit."

Richard growled as he frowned at Gervase's amusement at his expense. "Where is Dermot?"

"He is waiting to see you." Gervase laughed. "To the discomfort of your new squire—who nearly fell apart when her father and brother entered the room, not to mention the company of our all-seeing Warwick. At the moment she is hiding in a corner. Who shall I bring in first?"

"Oh, hell, all of them!" Richard sighed. "Let us see what happens."

Though he had been forewarned, Richard was shocked at the change in Dermot's appearance. In the months since they had last met, Dermot had aged incredibly. Richard rose to greet the aging man but Dermot waved off the effort as he sought a chair for himself by the hearth.

"It has been a good day, Richard," he offered as he lowered himself into the chair. "You are to be commended for it. I've lived to see the Ostmen finished in Waterford and in Wexford and my lands returned. Aye, a good day."

Richard's first alarm relaxed at the sound of the strong, steady voice and the intense brightness of the older man's gaze. While Richard held no particular fondness for Dermot, there was a bargain made and Richard had every intention of seeing it to the end.

"You have your son to thank for our success, MacMurrough, as much as us," Richard offered, leaning back in his chair. "He did well today."

"Aye, he's a good lad," Dermot agreed, casting a satisfied and fond glance in Donnell's direction.

Richard caught a glimpse of an orange tunic as it entered the doorway to stand behind Warwick's broad frame and he stifled a smile. "Aye, MacMurrough, it has been a good day. We have returned your lands to you, as you say, and have effectively removed your old enemies, the Ostmen, from your lands. But we will not set the town to torch or leave it to be taken another day. It is a Norman custom to fortify and hold a city, once taken, and so it shall be done here."

Dermot nodded. "And I suppose ye'll be now wanting to discuss the rest of the terms in our agreement?"

"I expect you to fulfill your part of the bargain."

Dermot nodded to Donnell, who crossed to the table and extracted a parchment from his tunic and laid it on the table. "They have been signed, milord."

Richard looked at him keenly. "And how do you feel about what is written there, Donnell?" he asked softly. "Do not fear to answer me truthfully."

"I have agreed." Donnell straightened and looked at Richard uncompromisingly. "I do not deceive myself into thinking that we could have done it without your aid. Better you than O'Conner or O'Rourke."

"But I am English," Richard countered.

"Aye. But O'Conner would have sold Erin to Pendergast. I think that you are the better choice."

Richard's pale eyes narrowed as they regarded the young Irishman. "Why?"

"Because I believe that you might do what no one else has done."

"And that is?"

"Unite Ireland. Bring the clans under one rule with a common purpose. When that day comes we will have the strength to cast you out and make Erin ours."

The room tensed at Donnell's honesty and Richard heard a

small gasp from behind Warwick, but he merely threw back his head and broke into laughter. "Well said and I admire your ambitions! Donnell, I trust you to fight at my side and perhaps, with a little luck, you may realize your dreams! As we come to know each other better, you may find that our goals are not so different! Besides," he added, "it may prove easier than you think. With the blending of our customs, the manner of your dreams may come to you through my heirs."

He unrolled the parchment and dipped the pen into the ink, then scratched his signature across the bottom of the agreement. "It is done then, and well done," he said, folding up the parchment and rising to face them. "There is one more battle to face in this phase—the Ostmen cowering behind their thick, stone walls in Dublin. But we will discuss that on the morrow. I am greatly fatigued, as I know you are, so I bid you a pleasant good night."

As they took their leave, Eve attempted to follow but at the door her exit was blocked by Gervase, who was the last out and closed the door behind him.

"Lad," Richard said as he settled once again into his chair, "come and remove my boots."

Richard smiled as the slender shoulders tensed and her hands clenched at her sides. "Don't just stand there," he barked. "Come and do as you are bid!"

She turned about slowly with her face lowered beneath the brim of her cap, and crossed the room, rounding the table where she knelt before Richard, grasping the heel of his boot.

"Not like that," he growled. "Turn around."

As she turned and straightened, he thrust a foot through her legs and planted the other foot on her bottom. Startled, she grasped the heel of the offered boot and began to pull, the pressure of his other well-placed foot nearly throwing her to her knees as the boot came free.

"Well, come on, the other one!"

She backed up and accepted the other foot between her knees and her eyes flared as his stockinged foot pushed against her thinly clad buttocks. But, she huffed and pulled until the boot came free and she flung it angrily to the floor with the other one.

"That is no way to treat good leather, lad! Pick it up and see that they are well polished before morning."

She picked up the boots, keeping her back to him, as she nodded silently. The retrieved boots clutched to her breast, she glanced about for an escape and began to cross to the nearest door, but his voice stopped her midway.

"I did not give leave for you to go. Pour me some ale."

He could see her shoulders tremble with what he suspected was sheer rage and he fought a chuckle as she set the boots down—gently—and crossed to the table by the far window where a shaking hand poured him a measure. He leaned back in his chair, hooked his thumbs in his belt and regarded her with interest as she set the tankard before him, her eyes still downcast beneath the shadows of her cap. He smiled at the auburn tendrils that had escaped and were curled about her ears. "Tell me, what did you think of our guests?"

He saw her head jerk at the question and after a moment she shrugged her shoulders in answer.

"I asked you a question, I would like your answer," he pressed.

She cleared her throat uncomfortably and lowered her head more. "Me, milord?" she answered huskily. "I have no opinion."

He struggled not to burst out laughing at her attempt to disguise her voice. "Nonsense, everyone has an opinion and I would have yours. In fact, I think yours might be the most interesting of all." He had fully intended to press the game for much longer but he knew that he could not contain his laughter if he continued. "By the way, I have something of yours that I would like to return."

She blinked from beneath the cap as he removed something from his belt and tossed it onto the desk between them. She stared at the small, jeweled dagger for an interminable moment, then her eyes flew up to his, meeting bright grey eyes dancing with amusement.

"You knew!" she squealed. "All the time, you knew!" A white hand flew out at him in rage, reaching for a swipe at his laughing face. He grasped her handily, half pulling her across the desk.

"Nay, not all the time," he answered, his face inches from her own furious, flashing eyes. "Not until I saw that." He jerked his head to the dagger. "Oh, there was a moment before, when I spotted a familiar trim-waisted form in the melee, though my senses defied the reason of it. Madam, I have said it before, and now I am most certain of it—you are a fool."

His jaw twitched with momentary anger but he released her

wrist, nearly flinging her from the desk as he settled back into his chair to regard her coolly. As she caught her balance, and rubbed her wrist, her own anger met his with a matched intentness.

"Why?" she snarled. "Because I would not negate myself to a safe tent with the other women, waiting for word of the battle? This is my country, Richard, these are my people! I can fight and I proved it today! I bloodied my sword as well as the others!"

"Wonderful," he drawled. "That is what I have yearned for in my bed. A damned amazon!"

"Your bed!" she cried. "You dare to turn this to your needs? I am talking of battles and wars and you turn it to the comforts of your bed! You will have to find another wench to ease your needs, Richard, for my needs have turned elsewhere!"

"You never will realize the measure of power, will you?" he returned, barely controlling his anger.

"What are you talking about?" she snarled.

He rose from the chair and paced across the room, pausing at its center to face her, his emotions again in control. "Eve, I have an army of over four thousand men, well trained with weapons beyond the short sword. If you had fallen today, what would it have meant to the outcome of the battle?"

"I saved your life!" she threw at him. "What would it have meant to you if I had not been there?"

"While I hate to seem ungrateful, my love, in this particular case if you had remained with Sophie I would not have been distracted. Had my attention not been focused on you at that moment, I would not have been caught unaware. Now, answer my question: What would one life, yours, have meant?"

Unsettled by the truth that she had endangered his life, she cast her eyes to the floor and shook her head in answer.

"Exactly," he snapped. "Nothing, to the outcome of the battle itself. But your death would have changed the course of what I plan to do here."

Her eyes came up to his with surprise, open and unguarded with question. Oddly, he turned away and she was puzzled that he seemed suddenly uncomfortable, as if unwilling to continue. When he finally spoke again, she was startled at the softness to his voice.

"Do you remember the morning we were married at Hertford?"

"Of course," she snorted, but she was stunned by the question. "But what has that to do with this?"

"Everything," he answered tiredly. "You were forced into a marriage that was unagreeable to you—and the results saw its natural conclusion."

"Oh, Richard . . ." In the face of his admission she felt something stir within her. She could not let him accept full blame for what had happened between them, nor dismiss what joy he had given her. But, he glanced at her with a frown and shook his head, not letting her continue.

"Eve, you are free to choose the course you will follow. I gave you that when I returned your dowery." He glanced at her hesitatingly, then noticed for the first time the slump to her shoulders and the tired lines about her face. "Sit down, Eve. It's been a long day and you must be exhausted. Forgive me for not realizing it before." She took a chair gratefully but he could not know that the turn of the conversation had left her feeling more drained than anything that had happened before. She sought to control the trembling of her body, and seeing it he crossed to the table to pour her a goblet of spiced wine. Then he knelt before the hearth, set a poker into the flames, withdrew it and plunged it into the pewter goblet to warm the ruby-red contents.

"Here, drink this. It will warm and relax you." He handed her the goblet. "And remove that ridiculous cap. By the way, where did you come by those clothes?"

She glanced up at him and offered a sheepish smile. "I fear that an unsuspecting, and too-trusting, young squire awoke this morning with a mite of a headache . . ."

"You drugged him?" Richard said, astonished.

"Only a little."

He shook his head and mumbled a profanity under his breath. "And how did you manage the rest? Your—ah, disguise is not as concealing as you might have thought."

"Oh, that was easy." She brightened. "I merely waited until the fighting began. Once it had, no one had time to notice me."

He shot a look at her as he smiled grimly. "Except me. You seem rather proud of yourself. Damn it, Eve, you could have been killed! It's only by God's mercy that you weren't!"

"I am not ashamed of it, Richard. Nor should I be. You are fighting for wealth to save Chepstow. My people are fighting for their survival!"

"Are you so sure that I am not fighting for my survival?"

"What do you mean?"

"I will not deny that wealth gained here will help Chepstow, Eve. But there is more. I told you once that I no longer attempt to live in a world of black and white. Such a world does not exist in reality but only for the very young—those full of pure idealism and too often a generous dose of intolerance." He smiled sadly, his mind turning to the past. "It is amazing how much wisdom we gain when we view life from experience, how differently we see the same events."

"You're thinking of Strongbow."

"Aye." He leaned a hip on the table and rolled his tankard in his hands as he stared thoughtfully into the cup. "He once told me that when experience, and time, show us our errors, we either become embittered with disillusionment or we mature and gain wisdom by our mistakes."

She bit her lower lip and lowered her eyes from his, unable to face him as she thought she understood his meaning. "Have I embittered you so?" she asked softly.

"You?" he blinked at her with surprise.

"I . . . I never meant to betray you, Richard. I know that you will never believe me, I cannot expect you to now, but I truly never meant to hurt you."

"Oh, Eve, I let myself be hurt through lack of faith. I think we both were guilty of that error. But the matter was long ago settled, when I came to realize it. Earlier today, Donnell told me of the letter."

Her eyes jumped up to his. "He did? I—I am glad that you know of it at last. I would have told you myself but I did not think that you would believe me. If only my father had returned it to you, instead of . . . of using us!" He saw her cheeks redden with anger at the memory and she startled as she heard him snort a short, brittle laugh.

"Direct your anger where it is due, my love. We were all part of a game turned by an expert player. Tell me something. How did you manage to persuade Gail to see you home, and why did you even consider him?"

"Eleanor suggested him." She shrugged. "I could think of no other—no other who would not run to you with the news," she added sheepishly. "So I asked him, and he consented."

"You asked him," he repeated, cocking a brow. "And, with no more than a pretty request, he whisked you from Normandy, risking Henry's displeasure, not to mention that of Stephen's. A rather risky venture for one of Gail's ambitions, wouldn't you say?"

"He was well paid," she said tightly. "My father saw to that."

"Ah, you mean the small coffer of gold he displayed with such pleasure upon his return? Though he said you had paid him."

"He showed it to you?" she asked, shocked.

"With great relish. It was all I could do at the time not to crack his head." He darkened, remembering. "But, that is not the point. He left Ireland, post haste to return to Normandy, his journey across England as uneventful as the first. Henry, surprisingly, did not even seem to notice his absence. And I, like a fool, was so engrossed in my own feelings that I did not reason it out. Consider it, Eve. How was it done?"

Her mind turned with the question, her memory flashing on Eleanor, then the truth struck her. "Henry," she breathed. "He was part of it!"

"Not part, Eve," he corrected. "All of it."

"But why?" she cried, "what did he hope to gain?"

"You know Henry's ambition. In fact you were aware of it long before I was. I do not think he knew at the time exactly how he was going to use us but his instincts are good. Though he had nothing to do with the annulment, that was due to Stephen, he sensed that the time might come when you could prove to be a powerful pawn. He reasoned that you would leave me a letter, Eve. What he did not plan on was that Gail would take it, or that I would think you compromised. I think that he was rather surprised to find that I would not do anything to get you back. However, when your father came to him in Normandy, with you in tow, he knew that he had played the game well, just as he knew Dermot would come to me in the end."

"Then he is using us now!" she gasped.

"Not exactly." He grinned. "In fact he tried to stop the landing. It was not by his hand and I think he must be rather shaken to know that there is a large Norman army in Ireland without his leave. That in itself is worth what I have done."

Fear crept into her eyes as she digested what he was saying. "Richard, what is going to happen?"

"He will expect me to lay Ireland at his feet. That well may be the end result . . . but with a decided difference if I play it well, and given a little luck. He does not expect me to stay, and the news is bound to unsettle him, not to mention the barons, over five hundred knights, and three thousand soldiers who are pledged to remain also—not to conquer, my sweet, but to remain."

"Why would you want to stay, Richard?" she asked softly. "Your lands are in England and Normandy. Everything Strongbow worked for could be taken from you."

"Aye, they were my father's, *cherie*, to be used as pawns by Henry. However, if matters go well I will lose nothing, only gain far greater things, affected by myself. I suppose my dreams are now the same as Strongbow's, and his father before him when he left Normandy with the Conqueror. A new beginning, a new life.

"I have much to learn, Eve, and I will need your help. Until your people begin to act as one, to unify, they will never be secure. For now Henry is not free to concentrate on what happens here. What with the French, the Church's demands for a new crusade, not to mention Henry's unlimited ambitions for the whole of Europe, given enough time, with luck, we may succeed. But only if your people come to accept us and take what we have to offer—those same Norman traits you so heartily detest." He smiled.

"And you will see to that end, proving your point, by taking Ireland with the sword," she observed sadly.

He rose from the table and gave himself a moment before answering her question. "Eve, I will not deny that our position must be won, and held, by the sword if necessary. And I will not debate the wrong or right of it with you now. But I would rather use diplomacy, not the sword, as its effects are longer lasting. If I am to be successful, your people must see that I am sincere in my intent. Your father and I began to lay the groundwork in Bristol. He has named me as his successor to Leinster and Okinselagh."

"But how could he?" she cried. "He has no right! The council of elders must pick the successor!"

"They have agreed to it. Eve, remember, these are not normal times. My aim is for your people to see that I will not completely ignore their traditions, yet they must make the best that is Norman if they are to survive Henry's hand. Your father will remain king for as long as he lives, that I promise you. As for me, I have no desire to be king, but I will govern, have no doubt. But there is another matter, another part to the agreement and perhaps the most important of all. I have told you all of this because I want you to understand the weight of a decision you must make—one as I promised you, will be of your own free will. I want your people to understand—thoroughly—that we have come to stay. Tomorrow you will have to make a choice, an irrevocable one. You may return with your father to Ferns, and do whatever you will with your life, or you will marry me."

It took her a long, endless moment to focus on his last words before they struck her, stunning her senses. She stared at him blankly. "Marry you? What are you saying?"

"I believe I said it." He shrugged, turning away from her to pour himself another measure. "Others will follow. I have encouraged the men to take Irish brides."

She rose from her chair and moved shakily to the hearth, where she pretended to stare into the flames while she composed her spinning thoughts. Tears bit hotly behind her eyelids as she considered his cold proposal. She swore under her breath, angry that she had allowed him to hurt her again, and she bit on her lip as she flashed on the irony of her two marriage proposals from him, and their distasteful similarity. The first time was for the good of England and now this, supposedly for the good of Erin. Was love never to be part of anything for her? Swallowing, she struggled to keep her voice from trembling. "So, this is why you kept me with you all of these months. And I had thought it was for revenge for leaving you in Normandy! I do not understand why you give me a choice. If this is what you have decided and my father is in agreement, what more is there to be said? I'm to be bandied about again . . ."

She heard him cross the room to stand behind her and she gripped her hands tightly in front of her, praying that he would not touch her. She was terrified of her own emotions and she clenched her eyes tightly shut as she fought the trembling of her body from his nearness.

"Because I want you to have that choice. One that you did not have before."

The sound of his deep voice, sad and so uncomfortably close, sent reverberations down her spine in a bittersweet pain and she fought to hold back the tears.

"Eve, you have never trusted me, or anyone, I think. I want you as a whole being, with that trust. If you come to me now, you will do so willingly, without pressure from me or your father. Our world is falling apart and we do not know what will happen tomorrow—we may only have that one day. The only thing we can be sure of, and depend upon, is each other. We are really quite alone, you know, and—and I need you. I love you, Eve..."

She spun about to find his eyes burning with a deep grey emotion as they watched her with anticipation. For once, totally unveiled, they said everything she wanted to know, even more than his words. Her heart bursting, she threw her arms about his neck and laughed at his dumbfounded expression.

"Oh, Richard!" she laughed through her tears. "Why did you not say that before?"

29

The Norman barons and knights stood shoulder to
shoulder with their Irish counterparts in the Christ
Church of the Holy Trinity of Waterford that bright
August morning. The sanctuary had been bedecked
with the brightly colored standards of Norman and Irish, the
symbolism burning into the minds of those present. The initial
distrust of the Irish had eased somewhat as they found their
positions regained under the surprising generosity of the invader. Richard's orders had been firm—the Irish leaders were
given the ancient lands lost to the Ostmen and no Norman
would treat an Irishman as a subordinate but as an ally.

As to the marriage, while other high-born brides had been
given to English nobles in times passed, the ladies had gone
to live in their husband's lands. But word had spread quickly
that the earl was to remain. While it had not missed the thoughts
of the Irish that Eve would be bringing the earl a broad fifth
of Ireland to her marriage bed, they knew that this union would
not be as those that had gone before. The marriage was simply
unnecessary. The elders had agreed to Richard's succession
and the choice of his bride could only be as a gesture of good
faith—an affirmation of his pledge to Ireland.

The Irish watched with a begrudging awe and the Norman
nobles filled with pride as Richard stepped from a nearby room
to the altar, bedecked in glorious finery of royal-blue velvet
trimmed with silver braid, and brilliant jewels encrusted on his
tunic and hilt of his sword. The essence of Norman nobility

with all of its grandeur, the Irish felt an unhappy moment of intimidation—until their lady appeared.

If they had any doubt as to their own nobility, it lasted only for that moment before Eve entered the sanctuary. A ripple of appreciation moved across the company as she proceeded down the aisle to the altar where Richard waited, his eyes burning with pride and love. He had ordered the gown prepared for her in England, in strict secrecy, and no expence had been spared to assure the fact that she would out-meet the expectations of her people, and serve them proudly. She was clothed in golden brocade, encrusted with embroideries of seed pearls and trimmings of jewels. Her hair, held back in shining glory, but, loose in the Irish fashion, tumbling to her waist, was crowned with a diadem of jewels and pearls, confirming her position as an Irish princess. Richard's eyes flickered with surprise, then crinkled to a smile as he noticed that she had hung her dagger to her girdle. Her own confirmation of her position? In the solemnity of the occasion he fought a smile but his eyes fixed on hers with fierce devotion.

As she knelt with him before the altar, Eve's mind flashed involuntarily back to another time, so different than the one she was experiencing now. She recalled the trance she had moved through then, the unreality of that occasion when her only conscious thoughts were to flee. She glanced up at Richard to find him smiling down at her, his eyes filled with warmth and love that made her tremble. As she listened to the priest's words, his hand clasped hers in the folds of her gown, the warmth of his touch enfolding her in its reassuring presence. She watched his profile as he responded to the priest, uttering the words that would bind them, this time irrevocably. Was it really, actually happening? He loved her, wanted her, and needed her. And, for the first time she accepted it all, even the fact that she needed, wanted his protection.

She repeated her vows in turn, with an enthusiasm that brought a smile from him, then rose and accepted his kiss. A light, brief touch that filled her senses with its promise.

He took her elbow with a reassuring tightness as he escorted her from the sanctuary and into the brightness of the morning sun. The courtyard was crowded with the well-wishers and as they passed to the manor on the opposite side of the courtyard, a woman stepped out and threw a garland of flowers at their feet. Pausing, Richard bent to pick it up, whereupon he presented it to his bride and kissed her briefly to the gladdened cheer of the crowd before they proceeded to the waiting hall.

Richard had dispensed with the normal celebration in deference to the destroyed warehouses, knowing that the food stores would be sorely needed to face the coming winter. But the hall filled with well-wishers and the ale flowed freely, tankards raised in rapid toasts, and more was carried to those in the courtyard as all were encouraged to join in.

As an Irish lyre began to strum and the body turned to a gayful dance, Richard pulled Eve to one side and into his arms, the couple quickly forgotten in the revelry.

"I think I have had enough of this," he murmured huskily. "We have seen one marriage celebration and my mind is turned to other matters. Do you think that we will be missed?"

"If we are, who is to protest?" she laughed brightly. "I think that they will get along well without us."

He swept an arm about her waist and pulled her into the doorway nearby to the hall leading to the upper floor where their chamber awaited them. As he closed the door behind him, the merrymaking from the floor below silenced to a distant murmur, she turned back to him, her happiness shining. He stood, leaning against the door, watching her without saying a word. His face was clouded, his eyes a deep grey filled with emotion as they moved over her slender body with a blatant possessiveness. A small smile touched the corners of his mouth and suddenly she felt very self-conscious.

"Richard, please!" she laughed nervously. "Just don't stand there staring at me! You make me feel like an innocent about to be devoured!"

"Ah, but you are." He grinned.

"Hah!" she laughed. "You forget that I am no longer a maid, my love, but a twice-married old woman!"

"Not to me." He smiled. "Indeed, milady, you are even more lovely than first we met, if that is possible. And, I would hardly say that nineteen is old." He rolled his eyes heavenward with a wicked grin. "Ah, shall I ever forget that first meeting? There in the moonlight, with your bodice ripped and your..."

"Richard!" she blushed.

He chortled over her flush, entranced that she could still feel modesty between them, and anticipated many long pleasant hours ahead in wearing it away. Odd, he mused, they had been through so much, and still everything was so new between them. Smiling, he walked over to her slowly and pulled her into his arms, kissing her until they both felt heady and slightly breathless. His arm held her as a hand moved to the back of her gown and he slowly, methodically, began to undo the fastenings down her back. Pausing, he lifted an auburn tress from her shoulder and rubbed it between his fingers.

"It is like silk," he murmured, as if to himself. "So often when you would stand near me in the past, I yearned to reach out and touch it."

"Why did you not?" she teased.

"In fear of your reaction if I did."

"You, afraid?" She laughed lightly. "Are my claws so very sharp, Richard?"

"It was not your anger I feared, my sweet," he smiled, rubbing the back of his fingers against her cheek. "It was the indifference I could not have borne."

"Indifference?" she blinked. "Oh, Richard! Of all the emotions I have felt for you, there has never been indifference, or ever could there be!"

His mouth swooped down to find hers but to his amazement she turned her face away and her hands went up to his chest and she pushed him away from her. His face darkened to a puzzled scowl but she just smiled at him and turned away and went to stand by the bed. She pulled the coronet from her hair, dropping it to the floor, then pulled her heavy gown from her shoulders, letting it drop to her feet where she stepped daintily out of it, then she turned back to face him as her fingers went to the laces of her chemise. She untied them with slow deliberation as her eyes never left his, which were watching with fascination as her fingers moved down between her breasts. She pushed the garment from her shoulders, letting it cascade to her feet, her soft white body open to his gaze. He made good his promise and devoured it with his eyes, his gaze traveling slowly back up to be startled by her expression. Her eyes were open and inviting and they danced with an unmistakable mischief.

"Indifference, Richard?" she said softly. "Never."

He crossed to her and pulled her into his arms as the blood surged through his veins and for the first time in his life he felt himself tremble with anticipation. But she still held herself from him, her hands planted firmly on his chest as she pushed away. He watched, unreally, as she unhooked his belt and pulled on the laces of his tunic, and once unclothed, she pushed him back on the bed. His mind filled with confusion but it soon exploded with a pounding in his temples as she lay beside him

and began working her wonders. His brain whirled with her
intentions, tumbling at her brazenness and when he gasped, he
heard her soft, pleased laughter. With a growl he tossed her
over and met her eyes, which were afire with a brightness that
made him wonder. "God, I love you," he whispered, and his
mouth came down to cover hers. His hand trailed down over
her waist and hips to her thighs, forcing her legs apart as his
fingers went to the soft mound and began their play. His lips
and tongue caressed and teased her breasts until the nipples
hardened in response and then they traveled, slowly, tauntingly,
down the silkenness of her body, pausing to appraise her with
his eyes, drinking of her beauty in the soft morning light. They
turned, drew from the depths of each other, their bodies clothed
in warmth. Richard and Eve, two formed and fused as one,
one body, one like mind, one expanding and joined soul. The
sunrise of spirit, the dawning of hearts refound, brought together in mutual joining of ecstasy, sweet tense promise finally
bursting in a shattering explosion of release. They lay on the
bed in each other's arms, totally spent in the floating aftermath
of their love. No words were spoken, none were needed. Their
understanding was complete, their lives lighted to a new level
of being where everything was known, yet tantalized with the
wondrous promise of their future. Eve smiled as Richard buried
his face in the softness of her hair and nuzzled her ear. His
arm slipped under her as he pulled her even more closely. And
they slept.

They awoke much later and Richard made love to her again,
reveling in their time alone, stolen from the rupturing world
about them. The time was theirs, this one day if never another,
and there would be no other like it. They supped alone, nour-
ished more by the food of their mutual love than the repast
which lay between them, the trenchers soon left discarded as
they found the need for each other's arms, curling up in a chair
and clinging to each other in shared whispers. They talked
longingly of the future with unspoken agreement denying the
possibilities of anything that could destroy that promise. Plans
were made, beautiful, sweet plans not unlike countless lovers
before them. They lived a lifetime in one afternoon, more than
most over years of existing, living side by side. Nothing was
allowed to intrude. They sat for long, silent moments, drinking
of their love and future, grey depths drawing from deep emeralds, the sealed melding of souls.

She awoke as the soft light of dawn crept gently into their

bedchamber and opened her eyes to find Richard leaning on his arm, watching her. She smiled sleepily and reached up to touch his face, tracing her finger along his cheek to the corner of his mouth, where he took her hand gently in his and turned it to press his lips to its palm.

"Good morning, milord," she whispered. "Are you unable to sleep?"

"With you so near, need you ask?" He smiled. "I was watching you sleep. There's a rosy flush to your cheeks this morning, love. Could it be that you had too much sun of late?"

"It was not the sun that put it there, milord," she laughed softly.

He grinned and bent over to kiss her nose. "It is becoming. I shall do my best to keep it there."

His mouth moved down her neck to her shoulder and he pulled her to him as his lips moved to a breast. She gasped, then moaned in pleasure, arching her back to him. "There will be those waiting for you, milord. Have you time for this?" she breathed.

"We will make time," he whispered as his hand trailed down over her waist and hips to her thighs. "They can wait."

When she again awoke, the room was flooded with bright morning light. Before her eyes had opened her body filled with sweet remembrance of the day and night past and she turned, a smile on her lips, to reach for Richard. But the bed was empty. She rose on her elbow, glancing about the room with a terrifying feeling that it had only been a dream. But she saw their garments thrown carelessly about and she flushed with a contented happiness as she threw back the covers and leapt from the bed, eager to find him and begin a new day.

As she crossed through the main hall she startled at the room's disarray from the night's celebration. The servants moved slowly about, evidencing their own participation in the event, painfully doing their best to set the room to right. She stifled a smile, pleased that pleasure had been found in their day, that their peoples had found happiness in each other's company and that they had been the reason. Suddenly she laughed out loud, bringing some curious glances from the servants, as she realized that they had not been missed.

She paused at the closed door to the room Richard had taken for his council chambers and tapped lightly, pushing it open as she heard him bade her enter. A happy smile on her shining face, clearly filled with love, quickly faded and she bit her lip in embarrassment and dismay to find that he was not alone. Montmorcey was in the midst of speaking and he halted at her entrance. She reddened under the patient smiles from the men as they exchanged knowing glances. She started to mumble her excuses and backed from the room when she caught Richard's eyes.

He smiled warmly, apparently without the abashment she felt, and held out his hand for her as Montmorcey continued with what he had been saying before the interruption.

"We must take it by storm, Richard, it is the only way! They are certain to know that they are to be next and we must not give them time to prepare!"

Listening to Hervy's protests, Richard placed an arm about her and pulled her gently to him, placing a kiss on her forehead and murmuring a good morning. Eve smiled and leaned contentedly against his side, reveling in the feel of his strong arms about her.

"I beg to differ, Sir Hervy," Donnell protested. "Dublin is even more well-fortified than Waterford, or Wexford. A frontal attack can only meet with disaster. I should think you would have learned the folly of such a plan by now!"

Smarting under the obvious reference to his failure at Waterford, Hervy reddened and began to bluster an angry protest, but Richard brought him short.

"I agree that the city cannot be taken with the ease of the others, but it must be taken. Dublin is the key to the trading route and its position will guarantee the loyalty of Leinster. Also, it is the last firm stronghold of the Ostmen. As long as it stands in their hands, we will be faced with a constant threat against Wexford and Waterford. Dermot, you have been silent. What are your feelings?"

"You know my answer, as do all here. The Ostmen must be thrown from Ireland, once and for all. Once done, it will also bring an end to the slave trade with England—and restore my rights as high-king, as it rightfully should be. It must be taken, at all cost."

He leaned back in the chair, the short emotional speech seeming almost too much for him. Eve tensed with concern for her father as she noticed his hand tremble picking up his tankard.

"The question still remains of how to manage it," Donnell reminded them. "We will most certainly have the forces of Breffny, Uriel and Meath against us as well as the Ostmen.

To simply rush pell-mell toward the city is suicide! We would be cut off before we were halfway there!"

"What route would O'Conner expect you to take to Dublin?" Richard asked the young commander.

"Well," he paused thoughtfully, "the usual route would be by way of Clondalkin—up the Stanley."

"And not the usual course, but a less frequented one?" Richard urged.

Donnell thought for a long moment, his brow furrowed, "Through the Scako and Enniskerry." He crossed to the table where the maps were spread and traced the routes as the men gathered about, crowding to see.

"Then neither route is suitable," Richard said grimly as Donnell finished. "There must be an alternative, one that O'Rourke and O'Conner will not suspect. Success will depend upon our finding it."

"May I make a suggestion?"

All eyes turned to Eve as she stepped to the table and she ignored their looks of surprise, and in some instances, disapproval. "Donnell, do you remember the summer I visited Urlacam? Though both you and father protested because the way led through areas held by O'Rourke, Enna finally convinced you to allow me to go, promising that he could see me there safely."

She leaned over the maps and traced her finger along the mountain ridge through Okinselagh to Dublin. "There are narrow mountain passes along this ridge coming out below Glendalough, here. It will bring you in behind Dublin to the south. I am certain that O'Rourke will not suspect it as it is only a seldom-used mountain track. We had no trouble whatsoever."

"Sweet Holy Mother!" Donnell exclaimed excitedly. "That is it! She is right, Richard. Even I had forgotten that track! It will work, I am certain of it!"

"Then through Glendalough it shall be." Richard smiled, satisfied. Eve delighted in the wink he sent to her but she withdrew to a chair near the window as the men bent over the maps, sensing that this was not the time to press her luck. Besides, she was feeling proud and well-satisfied knowing that she had gained an important moment but she knew better than to expect to be included in their war council. That she was allowed to remain spoke their gratitude and, wisely, she accepted it gracefully.

The council wore on until well into the late afternoon, mid-meal being taken casually as they talked. At last, as the sun moved to bathe the room in soft lights of approaching sunset, their plans were made and one by one they took their leave. When the door closed behind the last, Eve rose and went to Richard where he sat on the edge of the table, lost in thought. She stepped into his arms, running her fingers over the worry creases in his brow, and he smiled, wrapping his arms about her.

"I was proud of you today, love. When you stepped forward I think you shook poor Montmorcey to his cross garters." He chuckled at the thought and kissed her lightly on the forehead. "But even more so when you took the chair by the window. He kept looking over his shoulder at you, expecting you to pounce upon the discussion. I think he has been so long with the queen."

"I had nothing more to say," she sniffed, raising a brow of mock indignation as she toyed with the laces on his tunic.

His own brows raised as his eyes flashed with amusement. "I am not Hervy, my love. I watched you and saw you struggling with yourself not to answer a question or take up with a point made. Do you deny it?"

She began to protest but smiled as she found him watching her keenly. "Nay, I do not deny it. But—but I did not want to embarrass you before your men."

His eyes widened with surprise. "That's a new thought." Then he laughed softly as he nuzzled her ear. "At last, I have found the secret to making you obedient. I merely have to keep you to your bed for a day and a night. It puts a rosiness to your cheeks and a dreaminess about you, not to mention a softness to your manner. The question is how I will find the time."

As he spoke, his hand had lifted her skirts and gone beneath, where it found its mark. Her eyes flew open and she gasped. Laughing, his other hand cupped her chin and he brought her lips up to his, drinking of their softness as they parted in response. His hand slipped down to the laces on her bodice and he began untying them, slipping a hand to the fullness of her breast.

"Richard, someone will come in," she gasped.

"No one will come," he said hoarsely, "They know you are here alone with me."

Standing between his legs, she felt him harden against her and her head swam dizzily in her awareness of his need for her. Her hands went between them and she pulled his chainse from his belt in a sudden urgency that matched his own. Soon rid of their clothing they found themselves on the narrow cot by the far wall and her hands went behind his head, pulling it to her breasts in a soft moan of pleasure as his lips took a taut nipple and his tongue began its play. He parted her legs and knelt between them, his hands slipping under her hips, bringing her up to him as he entered, plunging deeply in eager thrusts, moving within her until she arched her back with a small cry. They went at each other wildly, with a fierceness of passion that spelled their intense need of each other, both knowing that there would soon be leave-taking and they expressed their sorrow and desperation with their bodies. He would begin to withdraw slowly, then plunge deeper, drawing and giving, building them as she clung to his back, her nails digging into his hard flesh. She bit into his shoulder, causing him to grunt though it seemed to drive him to a greater urgency.

They reached their climax together, leaving them both gasping for breath, and tangled in each other's limbs. He rose up on his elbows to release her from his weight but she could still feel his heart pounding in his chest, in rhythm with her own. He bent his head and glanced down at the angry red mark she had left on his shoulder. Following his gaze, her eyes widened and she flushed, but she looked up to find him watching her, his eyes deeply grey with amusement.

"It seems that there are sides to you I have yet to see." His mouth twisted into a grin. "Is your aim to mark me as a warning to other wenches?"

She bristled at his humor and tried to push against his chest with her hands but he merely settled onto her, holding her firmly beneath him. "If I catch you with another, Richard deClare, you will find more than a mere blemish on your shoulder!"

He chuckled and bent down to kiss her nose. "Nevertheless, it will carry with me as a reminder of what I have waiting for me."

"When do you leave?" she asked softly, hating herself for the unbidden tears that began to burn at her eyelids.

He brushed his lips across each of her lids, then took her mouth tenderly before meeting her gaze again. "In two days," he murmured, regret clear in his voice. "And you must know that you will remain here."

"Aye, I know." She sighed. "I never expected less."

"As long as we understand one another," he replied sternly, his look reproachful. "I do not want to take Dublin and find you in the midst of the battle."

"You will not, milord." She smiled. "I promise you that I will remain here as the dutiful wife, waiting for her lord to return... at least this time," she added, mischievously.

He rolled her over and smacked her bottom with the flat of his hand, causing her to yelp. He jumped up and caught up her clothes, tossing them to her. She got up, rubbing her buttocks painfully, pouting as she noticed the grin he threw at her. Now dressed, he pulled a leg up on the table and sat back, his arms folded across his chest, his eyes passing over her before they came to rest on her full white breasts with their rosy, upturned tips. His eyes came up to meet hers, which were still glaring at him.

"Are you going to get dressed?" he smiled. "Or is this your way of asking for another ride? Give me a moment and I'll accommodate you."

He laughed at her outraged gasp and she spun about and began to struggle into her clothes. Amused by her typically feminine response of turning her back to him, he allowed his gaze to feast on her back and the gentle turn of her waist and her full delectable hips and long shapely legs. Quite a prize, he mused, overwhelmed that they had ever found each other.

When she finished dressing, she turned back to find him pouring them each a goblet of wine. She joined him at the table, taking a goblet from him, and then she sat back, pulling herself up on the heavy oak piece until her eyes were even with his. His manner had become serious and she sensed that there was something he wanted to speak with her about and he was not sure how to approach it.

"What is it Richard?" she whispered, reaching out to touch his face. "What is it that you want to tell me?"

He took a few steps away from her, as if the telling would be easier without her so near. He took a sip from his goblet, then lowered it, staring into its depths for a long moment. "Eve, if something should happen to me, now or at any time, I want you to return to Chepstow." She felt her heart leap into her throat at his words but she held back comment, knowing that he had to voice his thoughts. "You will be safe there, as you never will be here. There are those here who will call you traitor. And, there are others who would attempt to use you. We may have grievances against Henry, and you may find it hard to believe after what he has done, but he is fond of you, as is Eleanor. They would see to your safety, offering you their protection, and I think you know that those of Striguil would give their life for you. Moreover, if we are blessed enough to have a child"—his gaze wandered to her middle and she thought she caught an element of wistfulness in it—"Henry will see that my lands are kept for him—or her—" He smiled. "Whatever differences Henry and I have had, I have no doubt that he will do this. Do you promise me?"

She swallowed hard, fighting back the tears that hung like acid in her throat, and nodded, unable to speak.

"Good," he grunted. "That will make Warwick's and Gervase's way easier." He smiled at the question in her eyes. "They have had their instructions but both fully realize how difficult you can be."

"Oh, Richard," her voice broke and she glanced down at the goblet in her hands as the tears began to slide down her face. He was there in a moment and he took the goblet, setting it on the table, then an arm went about her as his hand went under her chin to lift her face to his.

"Don't cry," he said softly. "These things had to be said. It will help me to know that you will be safe. Now, dry your eyes and let's be to supper." He smiled. "I've worked up quite an appetite."

The two short days that remained before he left, in the moments they were able to take for themselves, were spent in impassioned lovemaking, each touch carefully placed as a memory to last for the length of their separation, while neither spoke again of the possibility that he might not return at all.

The morning of his departure she stood on the steps of the manor, looking up at him with tears that misted her eyes but ones that she would not allow to spill in her unwillingness to spoil their leave-taking or to humiliate him before his men. She smiled bravely, then removed a lace kerchief from her pocket and, descending the steps, tied it to Taran's bridle as a token. She saw his eyes gleam warmly from beneath his helm, then he leaned forward, catching her about the waist, sweeping her off her feet into his arms for a brief, impassioned embrace that bruised her lips in its urgency. After he set her upon the ground, she walked up the stairs to join the other ladies, and then she smiled bravely at him.

She thought of him now, in the weeks that he had been gone, not only with love and longing, but with gratitude. He had provided that she was to fulfill her position as his wife as mistress of Waterford, making decisions alongside the commanders, headed by Beaumont, he had left in the garrison. The people came to her, pleading their needs and any injustices they found under the Norman soldiers, and she became the buffer between her people and his own. Consequently, she found the days passing in merciful quickness, though the nights remained agonizingly empty.

One morning, three weeks after Richard's departure, Eve was sitting in her chambers, taking a quiet moment from her duties with Sophie. There was an urgent knocking at the door and, when Sophie jumped up to answer, one of the young serving girls burst in, her eyes wide with the news.

"Milady, we have visitors!" she cried. "Norman riders have entered the city!"

"News from Dublin!" Eve exclaimed, leaping from her chair. "Oh, Sophie, perhaps they are returning!"

She rushed from the room, her heart leaping with expectation, and down the stairs to the main hall. She was met at the foot of the staircase by Sir Beaumont and her chest gripped painfully. It was obvious by his expression that the news was not what she had hoped for.

"Milady, riders have arrived with messages for the earl. I told them that he is not here and they wish to speak with you," he said grimly. "They are from the king."

"Henry?" she gasped. "Did you tell them where Richard is?"

"Nay, milady. Only that he would be gone for a time. Will you see them?"

"Aye," she gritted. "Come with me."

Eve paused before the door to Richard's study, smoothed her gown and adjusted her coif as she braced herself to face the king's men, her mind bent with curiosity and caution. What could Henry want? The news would not be good, of that she was certain. Nodding to Beaumont, he opened the door for her and she swept past him and into the room. There were three men standing at the room's center, none of whom she recognized, but as a dark-haired man standing by the window turned at her entrance, she nearly cried out with shock.

"Sir Gail!" she gasped.

"My Lady," he said smoothly, in a voice that unsettled her.

He crossed and bent over her hand, which she could not very well refuse under the regard of the other men. "It is very good to see you once again."

It was all that she could do not to wrench her hand from his touch, as her skin rebelled from the feeling of his lips upon it. "What are you doing here?" she demanded.

Unruffled by the sharpness in her tone, he nodded toward the other men. "We carry dispatches from the king, milady... Ah, it is deClare once again, is it not? Or so I am led to believe. How surprised I was to find that you had wed the earl once again. To think that all of my efforts would come to this..."

"I have long since learned of your duplicity in the matter, Sir Gail," she snapped. "I think it best if we do not speak of it."

"As you wish." Gail nodded. "I understand that Earl Richard is not in Waterford at the moment. If you will be kind enough to tell me where he is, I have matters to discuss with him."

"Nay, Sir Gail, I shall not," she said tightly. "He is on business and will not return for a time but there is no need for you to wait. If you will leave the dispatches with me, I will see that he receives them."

"You are making this most difficult, Eve," Gail countered unpleasantly. "The messages are from the king and my instructions are to place them in no hand but Richard's."

"Then the wait will be a lengthy one," Eve said firmly.

"Oh, I think not." Gail smiled, his eyes moving slowly over her. "I am most certain that he will be returning here posthaste, for I cannot believe that he would leave such a beautiful bride for one moment longer than necessary."

She bridled at his boldness but answered with control as she turned to the other men, refusing to meet Gail's eyes. "You are welcome to take quarters in the city," she said. "But I warn you not to reenter this house again in my lord's absence."

The door had barely closed behind Gail and his companions when Eve rushed to Richard's desk and grabbed a pen and paper.

"A message for Richard?" Beaumont asked.

"Aye, Beaumont," she answered absentmindedly as she chewed on the end of the pen while composing her thoughts. "I must warn him. If messages are brought from Henry by Gail's hand, you may be sure that the contents bear no goodwill." Dipping the quill into the ink, she began to write, the only sound in the room now the scratching of the quill across the parchment. Moments later she laid the pen down and dusted the page with sand, then blew on it before folding it and sealing it with hot wax. She grasped up Richard's seal from the desk and pressed it into the still warm wax before rising and handing it to Beaumont, her expression grim. "Under no circumstances can this fall into the wrong hands. See that the rider is trustworthy and that he leaves undetected. Gail is certain to have men watching the gates. He is to give it to no one but Richard."

Beaumont nodded and started toward the door but she called to him in a last thought.

"Beaumont, there is one other thing. If Sir Gail is truly intent upon finding Richard, it would not take him long to learn of his whereabouts. You must post extra guards at the gates and the walls. He must not be allowed to leave Waterford."

The following morning Beaumont escorted Eve to the grain warehouses where they were to inspect the reconstructed buildings. The former burnt-out shells had been cleared away, the ground leveled and new thick-walled towers were being raised, their seams caulked with straw and clay. As they viewed the process, Eve cast a concerned look at Beaumont. "Will there be enough grain to fill these?"

"None from the city, milady, as it had all been stored before the buildings were set to torch. But, Richard has sent to Bristol to supplement the shortage. Our tallies suggest that other foodstuffs are adequate to see them through the winter. Richard has also sent to Chepstow for some of his own farmers to see to the plantings. The locals' methods seem—ah—rather primitive, milady, if you will forgive me for saying so. He hopes that a better yield may be realized with the coming season."

They left the granary and passed through the market, where the merchants had reconstructed new stalls for their endeavors, the past weeks of efforts having covered and healed the scars left from the battle. The air was rich with the aroma of cooking meat, vegetables, and the pungent odor of the spice traders' stalls, the mixture whetting Eve's appetite. She decided to sample their offerings but Beaumont declined and left to retrieve the horses. Eve drew a coin from her pocket and purchased a pastry coffin filled with spiced eel and dates. She strolled along under the awnings covering the stalls, listening to the din of chatter as the merchants argued and bartered with both sellers and customers. Pausing in the shadow of a leather-worker's stall, she nibbled on her meal and watched the muscled young artisan bevel a sword belt, mallet striking tool in a rythmical progression across the leather.

"Ah, aye, the role of noble lady of Waterford suits you well."

She whirled about to find Gail standing in a doorway nearby, leaning against the jam. It was apparent that he had been watching her for some time.

"What are you doing here?" she snapped.

"Where else could I be?" He smiled as he walked up so close that she could smell the heavy fragrance he wore. "It seems that I am not allowed to leave the city . . . but I don't suppose you would know anything about that. However, I do not find the prospect of remaining so near to you an unpleasant one. I saw you enter the granary and I wanted to talk with you—how fortunate that you sent your 'guard-dog' on ahead."

"He will be returning momentarily, Sir Gail. You had best leave." She turned but he stepped in front of her.

"It would have been better if you had told me where Richard is."

"Better for whom?" she hissed.

"For everyone concerned, my sweet. Nothing will be served by the delay. Henry's dispatches will say the same then as now, but the king's ire will only be increased if Richard attempts to ignore them—as he did before."

"Richard will make his own choices, Sir Gail, and I trust him to make the correct ones—for everyone concerned."

"And you?" Gail smiled. "You seem to shed your guilts quite easily. I must admit that I thought this all would have been harder for you."

Her eyes flashed and she stepped back as he made to take her hand. "What do you mean? You are talking nonsense!"

"Am I? What must your people think of you?" he countered, glancing about the square. "You have wed the infamous conqueror and most happily, it seems. But do not misunderstand me, I sympathize with you. One must do what one can to survive."

"These are not my people!" she snapped. "They are Ostmen. They were once conquerors of my people! They have suppressed Erin for . . ."

"Ah, the Ostmen," he said easily. "And will Richard stop with them. I wonder?"

She would not concede to him that many of her own people lived within the walls, nor had she any intention of discussing

Richard's plans with this vainglorious knight.

"Leave with me now, Eve," he said, suddenly grasping her arm. His expression had changed and he was looking at her with unmasked desire. "I will protect you, care for you! If you stay here I may not be able to help you . . ."

"Sir Gail!" she choked as she tried to wrench her arm free from the knight's grasp but he pulled her toward him, his fingers pressing into the soft flesh of her arm. At the sound of horses behind him, he reluctantly released his hold, his face blackening as Beaumont approached.

"One of these days you will not have one of Richard's lackeys about," he growled in a whisper. "Remember what I have said, Eve. Your only chance is to come with me."

She darted away from him to Sir Beaumont, who had dismounted and was watching the Norman knight with a concerned frown. "Has he been bothering you, milady?"

"Nay, Beaumont," she shook her head while trying to keep her voice light. She knew what Beaumont would do if she told him the truth and it would not go well if Henry's man was injured, or worse, while in their company. "Please, just take me back to the manor."

She awoke with a scream tearing from her throat, her eyes staring sightlessly into the blackened room, as a hand clasped over her mouth. She struggled and thrashed in terror but a heavy weight threw itself over her body and she bit against the hand, her eyes rolling wildly in terror.

"Damn!" There was a grunt of pain from the source of the offending hand and another took its place. "Dammit, Eve, it's me!"

At the sound of his familiar voice, she went limp but she pushed his hand aside and pushed at him. "Richard!" she hissed in anger and shock. "What are you doing here? And did you have to do this? You scared the wits out of me!"

"A necessity, my love." He gnashed as he shook his hand and bent it to the dim light from the window to examine it. "I received your message and you were quite right to send it. Did you know that Gail has his men placed around the house and at the gates? Just about now one should have returned to his place beneath our window. It would seem that our old friend does not trust us."

"He has posted guards?" she gasped, sitting up. "How dare he! Richard, I truly did not know!"

"No matter, I suspected that he would—so I came through the window when the guard had passed. I'm sorry that I frightened you but I did not want you to call out." His eyes flickered with interest as they moved over her in the dim moonlight. "Since when have you started sleeping in the buff?"

"Since the night of our wedding," she smiled. "Or had you not noticed?" She threw herself at him, nearly knocking him back on the foot of the bed, and covered his face and neck with kisses as she whispered a rapid stream of endearments, almost taking his breath.

"Shhh!" he cautioned, trying to control his laughter. "Would you have Gail's men pounding at our door?" He rolled her over and held her beneath him as his hands moved over her body. "Ah, but you do feel good, so warm and soft. Well worth the forced ride, *cherie*."

"Dublin!" she exclaimed in a soft cry. "What of Dublin?"

He sighed and turned on the bed, sitting up as he began to pull off his boots. "How your attention drifts. It is ours, did you expect less?"

"Tell me, what happened?" she prodded.

"Now?" He turned and looked at her over his shoulder. "I had my mind on other pursuits." His eyes passed over her naked form, fixing on her breasts with a wicked gleam.

She leaned forward on the bed and wrapped her arms about him from behind as she nuzzled his ear. "Please tell me, Richard."

"You make it difficult to think of battles, madam. If you want an answer to your question, you had better release me, and cover yourself."

She sat back on her knees, laughing softly as she wrapped a cover about her. "I'll be good. Now tell me."

"Your suggestion was a good one, Eve," he said as he pulled his tunic over his head. "We were able to approach the city without difficulty. I think they were rather surprised when the sun came up and they found us encamped about the walls." He chuckled at the memory as he pulled his chainse over his head and tossed it to the end of the bed with the tunic. "Envoys were sent from the city to negotiate a treaty. Evidently Waterford and Wexford had been noted by the citizens and the city could have been taken without shedding a drop of blood. It

was agreed upon that the city would give their allegiance and
would surrender thirty hostages in good faith and allow a garrison to be established . . ."

"Could have been?" Eve interrupted.

"Aye," Richard answered and she could hear the anger in
his voice. "I had posted Miles and his forces near the gates
with orders for them to hold their position. Evidently the three
days of negotiations proved too much for them and a contingent
rushed the city. Unprepared, it was taken easily but Haskulf
managed to escape in boats with some of his men, fleeing to
his kinfolk in the Hebrides. I fear that we have not felt the last
of that . . ."

"Miles' men did this?" she asked with shock.

"Not by his orders, thank God," Richard said grimly. "Or
I would have been forced to hang him with the rest. When he
tried to stop them, he was overpowered by two of his lieutenants
who were intent upon being the first to the spoils." He sighed
wearily. "I fear that it will take time before we weed out the
rotten ones, but it will be done."

"What of O'Conner and O'Rourke?"

"They withdrew their armies without any attempt to stop
us," he said with wonder, shaking his head. "Donnell felt that
Dublin's submission relieved them of any responsibility to the
city."

"He is right. By giving you hostages, they broke their oaths
to O'Conner."

"Now tell me of your news," he said, leaning across the
bed. "Has Gail given you any trouble?"

"He keeps to himself. But, Richard, he gives me the chills.
He is plotting something, I know it."

"Have you seen the dispatches?"

"Nay, he will show them to no one, not even Beaumont.
What do you think Henry wants?"

"We will know soon enough, but I have my suspicions. But
do not be afraid, love. It is nothing I haven't been waiting for."

"Did you come alone?"

"Warwick and Gervase are camped with their men a few
miles away. But I wanted to talk with you before I was forced
to meet with Gail. Talk, and other things." He grinned. He
reached up and pulled the cover from her slowly, then pulled
her down, this time without resistance, pushing her back into
the bedding. "Enough talk, love, the rest of the night is ours
and I plan to make the most of it."

"Then do not dally, milord, for dawn is approaching." She laughed softly, wrapping her arms about him.

"His majesty will remain in Bristol until he receives your assurance that you will withdraw your troops and return to England."

Richard ignored the look of satisfaction on Gail's face and stood calmly at the study window, watching the activity on the street below, his hands folded behind his back.

"Has Henry forgotten that we are in Ireland by his word?" he asked quietly. "I have his hand upon the letter giving his word to Dermot . . ."

"He has forgotten nothing, Richard! Including the fact that you are a traitor!"

"Traitor?" Richard turned his head to study Gail. "I think that to be your word and not Henry's, Sir Gail. I suggest that in the future you choose them with more care, if you value your neck."

Gail bristled at the threat, his fury increasing at the amused looks on Warwick's and Gervase's faces, though his real anger came from the fact that Eve should be witness. The fact that Richard had insisted that she remain had encouraged him to speak boldly—more than he had intended—and now he regretted his words but pride would not allow him to retract them.

"I had hoped that this matter could be settled without difficulty, Lord Richard, but nevertheless the message is clear—you will withdraw from Ireland! I am to remain here to see to Henry's interests while you are away. I assure you that when you return—to withdraw your army—I will have it in readiness."

Richard turned now and regarded Gail with the contempt he felt for the French knight, his voice cold with a dangerous element that left no doubt as to his meaning. "I will see to Henry, Sir Gail, and if you insist upon remaining, so be it. But understand me: no one under my command will take an order from you. Warwick will care for my interests in my absence—and that includes the 'removal' of anyone who attempts to interfere. If you do not agree, we can settle the matter here and now—this and past grievances."

Eve's eyes widened at the open reference to the past and she glanced from one to the other as they stood glaring at each other with open hatred. She saw Gail's face redden as he glanced at Warwick and Gervase, their expressions clearly showing their pleasure at the prospect of making good Richard's threats if the earl did not. She realized then that Richard had been baiting Gail to this purpose and now that the gauntlet had been thrown, she waited, unable to breathe, to see if Gail would pick it up.

Gail stared at Richard in barely controlled rage, realizing that he had been backed against a wall. He had no intention of risking the opportunities Henry had placed at his feet by engaging in a duel, with Richard, which he was almost certain to lose. He ignored, with difficulty, the open looks of contempt from Warwick and Gervase, brushing them off as best he could. But the woman, that was another thing—deClare would pay dearly for humiliating him before her. The day would come when she would look at him with the same open desire with which she now favored this bastard earl. He mentally pledged his life on it.

"Forgive me, milord, if I became somewhat overzealous," Gail answered smoothly. "While my words may have been ill-chosen, it was only due to my desire to carry out the orders of His Majesty. I assure you that they were never meant to offend."

"Of course," Richard answered with disgust. "But for now I think that enough has been said. Leave the dispatches and I will send you my answer in good time."

After Gail had departed, Eve retired to see to mid-meal, leaving the men to discuss Henry's dispatches. They contained what Gail had said, Henry was recalling the Norman army. If they did not comply, he promised to forfeit any lands held by the invaders in England and Wales and he would cut off any supplies from England to Irish ports.

"I think you have given our noble king cause to worry, Richard," Warwick commented as he scanned the dispatches for the second time. A hint of a smile curved his lips as he looked up. "Could he be concerned that we might be thinking of establishing a new kingdom in Ireland? I wonder what devil planted such thoughts in his head?"

"Perhaps it has something to do with the fact that the same noble knights who have given him such cause for concern in Wales now comfort themselves with deClare, FitzStephen and Pendergast." Gervase laughed.

"Enough," Richard commanded but he gave in to a small smile. "We are not out of the water yet. Henry's words are more than mere threats and we now face our biggest obstacle. The moment has come and it must be handled with the greatest diplomacy. Warwick, I trust you to use that same diplomacy in my absence. Do not anger Gail into acting rashly. Just keep him mollified."

"What of me, Richard?" Gervase asked. "Perhaps I should see to Dublin in your absence..."

"Nay, Gervase, you shall go with me to England. I trust Miles and Pendergast to see to the garrison there. Miles is anxious to make good and he should be given the chance. Besides, he will have Donnell to help once Dermot is resettled in Ferns."

"Have you told Eve what has happened?" Gervase frowned.

"Nay," Richard answered grimly. "Not all of it, only that we had taken Dublin and O'Conner and O'Rourke withdrew. She has had enough to think about now. Besides, I wanted Donnell to be here when I told her."

"Told me what?"

Eve stood in the doorway, looking from one to the other as Warwick and Gervase averted their eyes, and then she glanced at Richard, who sighed heavily as he gestured for the men to leave.

They took their leave, nodding at Eve as they passed with looks so filled with compassion that her eyes widened with dread, and she glanced at Richard.

"Tell me what?" she breathed as the door closed behind them. "Richard, what haven't you told me?"

He handed her into a chair, touching her face lightly with his fingers, then sat on the table edge in front of her, his face filled with regret in his unwillingness to hurt her. "Love, after Dublin fell, your father took his army into East Meath in pursuit of O'Rourke. He—he vowed he would not rest until O'Rourke had fallen and that ari-ri was his by ancestral right."

She had been staring at her hands while he spoke but when he paused, she looked up and drew in her breath, wincing at the pain she saw in his eyes. "Go on, Richard, tell me what he has done now."

"They went as far as Cavan, taking hostages as they went. When they entered his territories, O'Rourke went mad—demanding that O'Conner come to his aid and finish Dermot once and for all. O'Conner responded by sending a dispatch to your father. I have it here." He twisted around and shuffled through the papers on his desk until he found the message.

She sat back in the chair and read the contents, tensing more and more with each line.

> Contrary to the terms of our treaty you have invited a host of foreigners into this land. So long, however, as you confined your operations within your ancient kingdom of Leinster, we bore it patiently; but now, inasmuch as, unmindful of your oath and reckless of the fate of your hostages, you have passed the limits assigned and insolently crossed even your hereditary boundaries, for the future you must either restrain the eruptions of your foreign troops or I shall certainly send to you the decapitated head of your son.

"Son?" Eve gave a small, pitiful cry.

"Conner," Richard answered tightly. "We were unaware of it but he has been O'Conner's hostage since your father returned to Ireland." He paused but Eve's silence forced him to continue. "Your father returned that he would not stop until Ireland was his."

Eve looked away as silent tears rolled from her eyes and she bit her lip to keep from crying out. Conner, her gentle little brother. He had never harmed anyone . . .

Richard took her by the shoulders and pulled her up into his arms, holding her sob-wracked body tightly against him. He murmured softly to her, encouraging her to let it out, while his own chest tightened with pain and anger toward Dermot's folly.

"Donnell has seen your father to Ferns. I can only say that there is some demon that drives him to do what he does. He plunges recklessly, without listening to counsel, even his own. Once the deed is done—only then does he face his actions. He—he collapsed when the—when O'Conner's final message was sent. He seems not to be even aware that he caused it. I do not think he will be leaving Ferns again, Eve."

Pulling herself under control, Eve leaned back in Richard's arms and wiped her tears away with the back of her hand. "When you leave for Bristol, I shall go to Ferns. It is a time of grief that I must share with my family. Besides, Donnell will need help with him."

30

Gervase glanced sideways at Richard, amazed at the earl's control as Richard returned the king's smile.

"Sire," he said smoothly, "it was by your license, if I recall, that I crossed into Ireland to aid your liegeman Dermot in recovering his territories. Whatever lands I have had the good fortune to acquire, I owe them to your gracious favor and I shall hold them at your will and disposal."

Henry peered at Richard through half-closed lids like a cat watching its prey. He considered Richard's statement for a long moment, wondering what truth lay behind the words, then suddenly brushed them off with a wave of his hand.

"Indeed, my noble earl, I can find no fault with your statement and we have known each other too long to quibble." He paused and then threw back his head and laughed. "God, Richard, but you are a statesman! You use my own words against me, though we both know they were innocently given, until I find that I am arguing with myself! I would hate to lose you, Richard! Tell me, I have heard that many of your army have followed your example and have taken Irish brides. Is that true?"

"Aye, milord," Richard nodded. "They have chosen to do so and I have not contested it."

"I imagine," Henry observed with a cackle. "I am sure that you have not!" He stopped laughing suddenly and leaned his hands on the table between them, his eyes narrowing suspiciously. "Richard, we both know, in spite of your pretty words, that you plan to take Ireland for your own! Why not admit it and have done with it?"

Richard smiled at Henry's bluntness but he merely shrugged. "I do not deny that I find Ireland a pleasant place, Your Grace. It is my wife's home and she is content there. I am considering remaining, as are many of my men, but it has never been my intention to reject you as my king. I fought with you in Normandy, and at Wallingford, because I believed that you were the best for England, and my mind has not changed."

"Ah, you would remind me of past loyalties."

"Have I ever done other than to support you?" He paused for effect, then added quietly, "If a Norman army can bring Ireland together under my hand, why should you consider that it could be other than for your benefit?"

"Hummm," Henry mused. He picked up a sweetmeat from a tray on the table between them and nibbled at the morsel while never taking his eyes from Richard. "And if I were to order you home, Richard, what then? Would you obey?"

"Aye, milord," Richard answered, looking directly into Henry's eyes. "But you won't."

"Oh?" Henry paused with another sweetmeat halfway to his mouth. "And why is that?"

"Because if you do, you know that you will have lost the foothold I have gained. A full fifth of Ireland is now under Norman rule—a feat you have not had the time, or the armies, to bring about. If I were to now withdraw, the clans would close in the gap, stronger than before, and the next entry would not be achieved with such ease. You will not choose to lose that advantage."

Gervase held his breath as Henry glared at Richard. The king wiped his fingers carefully, almost thoughtfully, on a napkin, then tossed the cloth on the table as he turned away and walked to the high-arched windows that lined one full wall of the room. Catching his hands behind his broad back, he stared sightlessly into the courtyard below. Gervase felt his stomach flip as Henry turned about to again face Richard, who stood as before, calmly regarding his sovereign. When Henry smiled, Gervase suddenly felt the need to sit down.

"Damnation, Richard, you know that you are right! You've made your plans well and, begrudgingly, I admire your boldness. But do not let it go to your head—or you'll lose it! You may return and secure what you have done, in my name, of course. Naturally, to—ah, assure your continuing and un-questioning loyalty I shall continue to hold your lands in Eng-land, Wales and Normandy, in . . . shall we say, in trust. Make no mistake . . . If you should displease us, I will not hesitate to brand you outlaw, and all of those with you. The blockade I threatened can be effected quite easily."

"Of course, milord," Richard returned the smile. "I would not have thought it otherwise."

Henry snorted and waved off further discussion with his hand. "Enough said. You may go now but I will expect you tonight for supper."

Once outside, Gervase took a deep breath and glanced at Richard as they walked along the long corridor to their quarters. "Sweet Mother of God, Richard," Gervase muttered. "I have never heard such doubletalk."

"Then it is time you learned the fine art of negotiation, my friend." Richard chuckled. "One thing you must always re-member—particularly when 'negotiating' with someone in power, like Henry—never lie. Say anything, skirt around the truth, but never, never lie. Should you be tempted to, you will find yourself in a trap with your head in your hand as the result."

"I'll remember that." Gervase grinned. "I am certainly re-lieved that the past two weeks are over. I thought I'd go mad with the waiting."

"That is exactly why he kept us cooling our heels, Gervase. Each day passed was to his advantage."

"Well, I'm glad that you knew what you were doing. I thought for a moment that we had had it."

"What makes you think that I knew what I was doing?" Richard grinned.

"What?" Gervase gasped, halting in his steps. "Do you mean . . ."

"Never underestimate Henry, Gervase. You never know what he is going to do until he does it. I took a chance and I won. It is as simple as that. Oh, I had made my plans but I had no way of knowing until this moment if it would work. What is more, the contest is far from over and Ireland still hangs in the balance. If Henry ever thinks for a moment that we might be double-crossing him, his vengeance will be swift—and deadly. It must always appear that he has our full fealty."

FitzHarding had opened his coffers to entertain his king and court and the hall was adorned with all of the finery Sir Robert could offer. As Richard and Gervase descended the stairs for supper, Richard's brow arched in appreciation of Robert's efforts. He glanced at Gervase and smiled at the eager look on his friend's face as he appraised the brightly-gowned ladies of the court, eyeing them as a veritable feast set for his consumption.

Sir Robert awaited them at the foot of the steps with a pleased grin on his face. "Richard, I am delighted that things have worked out well for you!" he said, clapping Richard on the back.

Richard glanced at the older man with concern, his smile fading. "I did not realize that my business with Henry had been openly discussed."

"No one needed to tell me, my boy," he chuckled. "But it was not hard to reason. If Henry had been displeased with you, you both would now be rotting in my cellars."

"Point taken." Richard grinned.

"Well, enjoy yourselves, lads. If you need anything, anything at all, do not hesitate to ask."

"I find that I am looking forward to our stay in Bristol, after all," Gervase said as watched Sir Robert's departing back.

"Do not become too involved, Gervase," Richard warned with a smile. "We will be leaving England as soon as possible."

Well-coiffed heads bent together in hurried whispers as the two handsome men passed. Gervase turned a dazzling smile to the young women and was rewarded by a rush of giggles.

"Richard!" came a familiar voice and they turned to find Gwen making her way through the knot of nobles and their ladies.

"Gwen!" Richard caught the roll of Gervase's eyes but he concealed his own dismay and accepted her offered hand, brushing it with his lips. "I had not realized that you were with the court, Lady Gwen."

"Oh, aye!" she exclaimed. "After Gilbert's death, Leonore and I were at wit's end. But Henry, our dear sovereign, graciously offered to bring me to court. Oh, Richard, it is so exciting! Hertford was so drab and dismal by comparison!"

"I imagine," Richard mused as his eyes shot about the room. "Is Leonore here with you?"

"Oh, nay, she prefers to remain at Hertford, now that Henry

has returned it to the family. But she will be so sorry that she was not here to see you!" Gwen dropped her lashes coyly, as she added with emphasis, "I have missed you greatly, Richard." Richard tensed as she pressed herself boldly against his arm.

"Perhaps you have not heard, milady," Gervase interjected, his blue eyes dancing with mischief. "Our noble earl has remarried."

Gwen lost her composure for a moment and she blinked at Gervase and then back to Richard. "Remarried?" she stammered. "Who?"

"Our lady Eve," Gervase answered happily before Richard could speak.

"Eve!" she shrieked, causing heads to turn in their direction. "But, I thought . . ."

"Lady Eve and I were remarried in Dublin, milady," Richard said quickly, throwing a glare at Gervase who was sporting a most satisfied smile.

"Is she here with you?" Gwen asked, glancing about.

Richard fought a smile in spite of himself noting that Gwen's mask had fallen and her eyes sparked with hatred as she sought Eve in the crowd.

"Nay, she preferred to remain in Ireland."

"How unfortunate." Gwen brightened, her voice returning to the purr she had affected before. "We must do something to keep you from being lonely during your stay . . ."

"There is no chance that I shall be, milady," he assured her. "We will be returning to Ireland very soon. Now, if you will excuse us—I would not want to be found guilty of monopolizing your time when there are so many available swains to enjoy your company. Please give my best to Leonore."

Before she could protest, he bowed and took his leave, while she met his back with an ugly pout.

"Mark you, Gervase, I shall return the favor," Richard growled over the knight's happy chuckle.

"Oh, come now, Richard," Gervase laughed. "Do you deny that it gave you pleasure to see Gwen's reaction when she learned of your marriage?"

"I could have forsworn that pleasure. God, for a moment I feared that Leonore . . ." He stopped short when Gervase seemed to freeze to the spot, his face having drained to a deathly white as he stared at someone across the room. He followed Gervase's pained gaze, searching the crowd until his eyes came to rest on the object of Gervase's sudden, unsettled state. At the far side of the room Lord Severn stood talking with another earl and his fair, lovely daughter stood at his side.

"Are you going to talk with her?" he asked softly, feeling Gervase's pain.

"Nay," Gervase answered, the word coming out as more of a choke than a whisper. "There is no point."

"You love her. That would seem reason enough."

"You know better than that!" Gervase snapped. "Besides, she's probably married by now."

"One can easily find out," Richard offered calmly.

"Nay!" Gervase glared at Richard, then turned to walk away but Richard reached out and grasped his arm.

"Gervase, no matter how you feel you cannot leave. Henry expressly ordered us to attend supper and I will not risk everything now."

Gervase nodded miserably but to Richard's relief he did not argue. He regretted using such tactics but at least it had worked and Gervase had not bolted from the room. "If you think that you can stay out of trouble, I will pay our respects to Henry. Your presence should be enough. I hope so, as in your present mood I doubt that you could add anything to our cause."

He ignored the mumbled profanity Gervase offered and made his way through the crowd that surrounded the king, while hoping that Gervase would maintain good sense and not decide to leave after all.

Gervase did remain but made himself as inconspicuous as possible in Richard's absence. He dreaded the thought that Lavinia would spot him in the assembly. He did not think he could bear to talk with her, pretending indifference in light conversation while his very soul was in torment over even being in the same room with her. He stood in the shadows by a wall, unaware that he was glowering unhappily or of the surprised glances from the maidens that he had encouraged only moments before and now looked upon with indifferent eyes. When supper was announced, at long last, he made his way to his place at the table and sunk into his chair while willing himself, with great effort, not to look to where she was certain to be, at her father's side. His frown darkened blackly as the thought struck him that she would not be there, but by another, a lover or even a husband.

When he realized that Richard was taking his chair, he

looked up, a snide remark on his lips, only to have the comment freeze in his throat.

"Good evening, Gervase," Lavinia said as she slipped into the chair, her eyes sparkling with emotion, the deep cornflower blue he remembered with such longing.

"Lavinia . . ." he stammered.

"I think that you might enjoy Lavinia's company more than mine, Gervase," Richard said with a smile from where he stood behind Lavinia's chair. "As for me, there are some things I wish to discuss with Lord Severn. If you will excuse me."

Gervase followed him with a pained expression, then looked back at Lavinia. A multitude of words passed through his tortured mind but with horror he heard his voice crack as he asked weakly, "Have you been well?"

"Aye, very well," she answered softly, lowering her eyes with a smile at the intentness of his gaze.

"Is your father in Bristol to see Henry?"

"Nay, he is here to see Lord Robert. We . . . we were surprised to learn that—ah, others would be here . . . We hear that you have been most successful in Ireland, Gervase. The court talks of nothing else."

"Dermot has been restored to his lands," he said miserably.

"And Eve, is she well? I was overjoyed when I learned that she and Richard had been reunited . . . They . . . are so right for each other."

"She is well," he answered, his eyes moving hungrily over her lovely face. "She speaks of you often, and misses you as . . . very much."

"And I miss her." His eyes held hers for a long tortured moment, then she tore her gaze away. "Richard wears his responsibility well. Many a faint heart was caused by the knowledge that he had remarried," she said, glancing to where Richard sat with her father. "We understand that many of the Norman knights have taken Irish brides. Many of them . . ." she repeated as she toyed nervously with the links of her girdle.

When he did not answer, she swallowed hard, as tears began to sting her eyelids. "Have you, Gervase, taken a bride, I mean?"

"Me?" he asked, startled. "Nay, I should never—I mean, nay, I have not."

"You have not?" she looked up happily at the discovery, her eyes shining brightly by the unshed tears, the high color in her cheeks lending an almost transparent quality to her skin. Entranced, he felt his chest tighten in a sweet pain as he reached out impulsively and took her small hand in his. "And you, Lavinia?"

"Nay," she answered, lowering her eyes. Her hand tingled from his touch and she looked away quickly for fear that he would read her feelings and think her too bold. "My father and Earl Richard seem to have found a most important matter to discuss," she said lamely, looking in their direction as she gently pulled her hand from his.

"Aye," he murmured. She was not married! His heart soared with the news, his good humor restored as he happily sliced off a trencher of bread offered by the passing servants. He forced himself to put aside the fact that the meal, and evening, would end all too quickly and she would pass once again from his life. For the moment, the fact that she was here was enough, more than he had ever hoped, dreamed for.

As the supper came to a close and the lords and ladies polarized into small groups for gaming boards or to exchange bits of gossip or to stroll into the gardens for a tête-à-tête in the still warm October night, Gervase and Lavinia retreated to an isolated bench at the far side of the room, allowing them a bit of privacy from prying ears.

Not wanting to disturb their moment, Richard subjected himself to the boring company of a lesser noble who was holding forth on the merits of the French tournament which Henry had outlawed in England since coming to the throne. The proclamation had caused an outcry among the landless knights as the tournament had been a means of support during Stephen's reign. A defeated opponent's horse and armor became the property of the victor, not to mention the ransom, often a sizable one, that could be claimed from the defeated's family for the luckless opponent. But Henry remained adamant. Richard attempted to defend the king's decision, pointing out that the arts of war could be readily learned by normal methods of practice and that too many good men, sorely needed for England's defense, had been lost in the brutal combats. But the man would hear nothing of Richard's logic and continued to hold forth with dogmatic pomposity. Richard found his mind wandering. As he sought for an escape, the answer came from an unexpected source. There was a tug at his sleeve and he turned to find Henry's aide-de-camp at his elbow.

"His Majesty wishes to see you in his private chamber, Earl

Richard," the shorter man whispered to Richard's bent ear.

Richard looked about with surprise, unaware that Henry had left the gathering. Normally, the retirement of the king would signal the close of such festivities but it was not unlike Henry to leave unnoticed, allowing the court to remain.

Richard followed the man up the stairs and down the long corridor to the room where he had confronted Henry only a few hours earlier. His brows knitted into a puzzled frown as he pondered what matter could be of such importance for Henry to call for him at such a late hour. Had he reconsidered his earlier decision? Richard's stomach tightened into a knot at the prospect as he considered what new approach he might take.

The aide opened the door for Richard, closing it quietly behind him. Henry sat at a table across the large room, his head bent over piles of scattered papers. He looked up as the door closed.

"Come in, Richard, come in! I trust that I did not call you from anything important?"

"Nothing could have more importance than a summons from my king," Richard answered automatically.

"Sit down." Henry gestured to the chair across from him as he pushed the papers to one side. He sat back in the high-backed chair and regarded the Earl of Striguil for a long moment.

"Had you other matters to attend to in England before your return to Ireland?"

"Nay, milord. It was my intention to leave as soon as possible."

"Did you not plan to visit Chepstow?"

"I have word from my steward that all is well there, therefore it was not in my plans, sire. Have you reason that I should?"

"Nay, nay," Henry assured him, though his eyes narrowed thoughtfully. "I just wondered what your plans were. I have intercepted a dispatch, Richard."

Richard's neck tingled at Henry's choice of words. Intercepted? But he remained calm and waited for the king to continue.

"The dispatch was addressed to you, arriving by way of a ship that docked only hours ago." He sorted through the papers and extracted a small packet, which he turned idly in his hands.

Richard noticed at once that the seal had not been broken but he tensed as he recognized his name in Warwick's broad hand. Henry watched Richard's reaction and allowed himself a small smile. "Nay, I have not opened them." He reached across the table and handed it to Richard. "I do not doubt that you will tell me what the message contains."

The two men stared at each other and a long-forgotten moment of understanding passed between them. Richard knew that Henry was testing him and, while the seal was untouched, the man that carried it would have had information easily obtained by the king. He broke the seal, feeling Henry's eyes upon him as he opened the folded parchment and began to read.

The dispatch contained the worst possible news. As Henry watched he noted the tightening to Richard's jaw and the tensing of a muscle in his cheek. "I assume that the news is not good," he observed.

"Aye, milord," Richard answered tightly. "It could not be worse. Dermot is dead. O'Rourke and O'Conner have called for all Irish to unite against us in a siege of Dublin. The Archbishop of Dublin, O'Tool, has called on Gattred, the King of Man, to urge the Vikings of the Western Isles to blockade the city from the sea..."

He paused, unwilling to go further, rage building within him over the rest of Warwick's desperate message.

"There is more," Henry murmured, seeing Richard's dismay.

"Aye," Richard gritted, "Eve barely escaped from Ferns and managed to make her way to Carrick with FitzStephen. The castle was besieged and is now being held by O'Rourke—and Gail deMathiew."

"DeMathiew is part of this?" Henry's massive fist hit the table in an exploding fury.

"According to Warwick, he was behind it," Richard answered, bringing his emotions into a tightened control. "My ship had barely cleared the passage when Gail began to make his move. It would seem, Your Grace, that Sir Gail had his own plans when he came to Ireland."

Henry leaped from his chair and began to pace about the room, his hands clasped behind his broad neck as he walked with furious strides. He suddenly stopped short and whirled back on Richard, who was rereading the message, his voice thickened with his temper. "You have our leave to depart on the first tide. Do whatever you have to do to bring the matter under control."

"And Gail..." Richard asked, rising from his chair.

"I am sure that you will make the correct decision when the moment comes." Henry smirked.

Richard turned to leave but Henry stopped him as his hand reached for the latch.

"Richard, keep me informed. I would know that your lady is safe."

Richard nodded grimly and left the room.

"Damn! May that bastard's soul rot in hell!" Gervase struck the ship's railing.

Richard glanced at his friend through the thick fog which hung in swirling drapes about the ship as it moved in creaking slowness through the harbor. He had begun to make preparations to leave as soon as he had left Henry, ordering the needed supplies that had been held during Henry's blockade and supervising the loading of the ship. He had not sought out Gervase until a few hours before their departure, unwilling to dispel his friend's newfound happiness. Gervase had responded to Richard's message immediately, presenting himself at the ship within the hour. In the hurried preparations they had been unable to talk, and it was only now that Gervase learned the full contents of Warwick's message, and as the ship began its trek out of the harbor, the weight of it hit him full force.

"He says nothing about Eve or FitzStephen?"

"Nay, only that they are being held at Carrick."

"Richard, I would give my life . . ."

"I know. Let us hope that it is not too late to do something, though I hope that is not necessary." Richard leaned on the railing and stared at the water below him. "I do not think that Gail would harm them. They are valuable only while they are alive. If there is a way to get them out, we will find it. The other problem, of course, is that this has served to draw Henry's attention more acutely upon Ireland. I fear that it may be the excuse he has been looking for to leave England."

Gervase looked puzzled as he turned to Richard's comment. "What do you mean?"

Richard glanced at his friend and smirked at his bewildered expression. "Were you so occupied that you were unaware of what is being said at court? It was abuzz with the latest gossip. What did you and Lavinia talk about?"

He smiled at Gervase's chagrined expression. "Allow me

to acquaint you with the latest scandal, my friend, though it should not be treated lightly. Much has happened since we left for Ireland. It seems that, while in Normandy, Henry came to disagreement with the archbishop on some particular matter. Becket remained in London but the matter fumed. Finally, one evening while well within his cups, Henry threw an idle comment to his company that the one who could rid England of Tomas Becket's presence would be doing their king an invaluable service. Three knights present, the fools, took Henry at his word, obviously not understanding his outbursts. They took the next ship to England, making their way to London, and proceeded to murder Becket on the very steps of Canterbury's altar."

"What? My God, Richard!" Gervase went as pale as the fog drifting about his face.

"I know, Gervase, it's unbelievable. I met Becket on more than one occasion while in London. There is little to understand why he was able to bend Adrian's ear, when he was but a clerk, and turn our cause to Henry. The man was brilliant. His powers of speech and persuasion were incredible. He was the only man I ever saw who could outwit Henry in an argument—but I suppose it had something to do with his goodness. I recall one time feeling awe, and considerable fear, at watching the effect he had on all present . . ."

"Why fear?"

Richard pondered the question at length. "There was something . . . almost mystical about him, and frightening." He laughed nervously, as if the remembrance was very uncomfortable. "I realize it sounds ridiculous but it was as if he wore an aura of disaster about him. Somehow I remember associating it with Henry—and England." He waved off the comment, brushing it aside impatiently. "Spirits aside, Becket's death may surely affect Ireland, more than England."

"Why? What does it have to do with us?"

"Becket was popular with the people, Gervase. The climate in London is not particularly healthy for Henry at this time. His decision to see to Bristol was greatly in part to allow tempers to cool. If they do not, he may decide to leave England for a time. But, knowing Henry, he will not run—if he leaves England, he will have an excuse."

"So he will look for a reason to leave," Gervase reasoned. "One that has nothing to do with his problems of Becket's death!"

"Exactly. And I fear that Ireland may provide that excuse."

"Damn that Gail!" Gervase swore, repeating his earlier sentiments.

"Aye. Let us hope that we may settle the problems there before Henry decides that the climate is cooler in Ireland."

The remainder of the voyage passed with agonizing slowness as both men paced the deck of the ship, their eyes turned westward as they watched incessantly for a sign of land. They were both tense with apprehension for what news might await them, Gervase's fears exceeded only by Richard's, whose mind was tortured with thoughts of what might have befallen Eve. He wondered who he feared the most, Gail or her father's old enemy, O'Rourke. Gail would certainly hold her for his own purpose, quite possibly ransom, though he knew he might use Eve badly in the interim. But O'Rourke was an unknown quantity. His purpose could be nothing other than revenge. What better source of revenge than Dermot's most precious child and wife of the hated foreigner . . . His head pounded and he felt weak with fear, more terrifying fear than he had ever known possible.

Their waiting was finally rewarded as the ship approached land and made its way up the Passage, finally docking at Waterford. Without pausing to rest, the pair took to horse and rode, driving their mounts unmercifully, toward Waterford.

Upon arriving, Richard called a war council, not even taking time to change his dust-caked clothes as he awaited the barons' arrival. Food and drink were brought to them by a concerned Beaumont who, unwilling to look at the earl, stole uncomfortable glances at the agitated lord, who paced about the room, pausing occasionally to study the maps he had laid on the desk.

"God's Breath!" Richard cursed. "What is taking them so long?"

Just at that moment Warwick strode into the room, his relief over Richard's return intermingled with the grief lined into his face.

"Warwick, what news have you?" Richard blurted impatiently.

"Alas, Richard, nothing more than what I wrote to you. No messages have been sent from Carrick other than their demand that you withdraw your troops from Ireland . . ."

"And of Eve . . ."

"The castle is under siege. No one can get in or out, I promise you."

"Who is in charge?"

"Donnell, he would have no other."

Richard grunted and Warwick exchanged a sad look with Gervase. "However, Richard, Montmorcey has been pushing to attack . . ."

"Naturally," Richard snorted. "I trust that you have held him at bay?"

"Barely. But, blood of the gods, Richard, the waiting is the hardest! This time I am almost in sympathy with Hervy. I want that scrawny neck of Gail's between these hands . . ."

"Mark me well, Warwick; whatever happens, Gail is mine."

The door burst open and the barons entered, their appearances as disheveled as Richard's and Gervase's, having ridden hard to attend the council. They filtered into the room, each acknowledging Richard, facing him with their own feelings of guilt over what had happened. While his manner accused no one, each felt the burden of responsibility, as they had time and again in weeks past, each wondering if they had been more aware . . .

As they settled, Richard looked at each one, pausing at Pendergast and Miles, as if reading their thoughts. "My lords, no man here is accountable for what happened. I alone carry the blame. I should have reasoned that such would happen upon my departure and measures should have been taken to prevent it."

"Richard, you are too hard upon yourself," Pendergast interjected. "We all should have suspected."

"Indeed, I am not," Richard said grimly. "I had to answer Henry's summons but I should not have underestimated the Irish people's love of freedom or the ends to which they would go to effect it. They had no time to understand our intentions and why should they? We are the invaders. Adrian's Bull still burns in their minds. How could we expect them to see us without Henry's ambitions? But we must recoup what has been lost and it must be done quickly. Even now Henry may be forming an army to cross the sea—and I have reason to suspect that he may be doing so. Ireland must be firmly settled before he arrives and the clans must be prepared to give him their oath when he does so."

"Milord, the situation is desperate," Miles spoke up, chagrined in the fact that Richard had left him with Dublin to garrison. "The northern armies have amassed and are marching toward Dublin. I fear that we do not have nearly enough men to counter the attack."

"If Henry is coming, should we not wait for his support?" Montmorcey threw in. "Richard, it could be the answer, with his added forces . . ."

The room broke out in a mayhem of conversation, the overlaying opinion that since reinforcements were sorely needed, Henry could be the answer.

Richard silenced the room, waiting for calm before he continued. "Milords, you suggest that we should wait for Henry. Are his ambitions as our own? Would he allow us to make peace with the Irish, to build futures and new beginnings? What are we waiting for? Are we looking for help from our own people? Nay, such is our position, that to the Irish we are Englishmen, and to the English, Irishmen!"

There was total silence as the barons absorbed his words and he gave them time to do so, gazing at each in turn. Finally, it was Gervase who stepped forward and addressed them. "Richard is right. The only hope is by what we might effect. Those who will come with Henry will take these lands for England. Our purpose is twofold: to settle our futures and to unite the Irish under our banner, the two objects being one and the same. For me it is simple, I must risk everything, as there is nothing for me if I should fail."

The matter was then quickly settled as the barons, each in turn, came to agreement. The moment passed and the council turned its attention to the matters of how it could be effected. Miles, Walter deQuency, Maurice Pendergast, Meiler Fitz-Henry, Richard deMarreis, Walter deRidelisford, and Walter Bluet would take their forces against Dublin, while Richard, Gervase and Warwick would join Donnell's forces to take Carrick.

The details of the sieges were discussed in painstaking detail until the room darkened, and the candles lit and placed about the maps. Finally, the barons departed, one by one, each with their plans tossing about their heads, certain to keep each from sleep as they took exhausted to their beds.

As the last departed, leaving him alone with Warwick and Gervase, Richard collapsed into his chair, almost overcome with tension and fatigue and an overriding sense of worry.

"Richard, let me see you to your bed," Warwick said, more as an order than a request. "You must have some sleep."

"I will," Richard assured him, but made no move to leave the chair.

"We will save her," Warwick said bluntly, reading Richard's thoughts.

"Can you promise me that?" Richard snorted, glancing up at his friend. "Even now..."

"Richard, you cannot do this," Warwick barked, with more anger than he had intended.

"How can I help it? If I had only taken her with me..."

"She would not have gone. You know that."

"Richard, he is right," Gervase offered. "There was no way to foresee this, regardless of what you said to the barons. What is more, even if we had known, she still would have insisted upon being with Dermot."

"You cannot be of any use to her unless you get some rest. Come with me—now," Warwick insisted.

Richard glanced up at Warwick and flashed upon the memory of a small boy, hurrying to the bidding of that harsh, demanding voice. He smiled and rose wearily from his chair and started toward the door, pausing as he remembered something and turned back to Gervase, who was crossing to extinguish the candles.

"Gervase, there is something I meant to tell you. I apologize, my friend, for not telling you sooner. It is unforgivable but I allowed my own problems to push it to the back of my mind." He smiled as Gervase looked up with question. "It is good news."

"Good news?" Gervase snorted. "Among all of this? Seems unlikely."

"Not even the matter of your marriage to Lavinia?"

Gervase drew in his breath. "Marriage—to Lavinia?"

"Severn has been convinced that your hand is worthy. I have assigned you lands from Striguil and a parcel in Normandy. He has agreed that, along with what you will gain in Ireland, it is enough."

"Lands? Richard, I..."

"It is only what is due you, Gervase. Be happy, my friend."

As the door closed, Gervase gripped the edge of the table, his emotions a tossed mixture of joy for Richard's news and terrible sadness for what Richard carried.

31

Eve watched O'Rourke wolf down his meal while her stomach churned at the disgusting display. She wanted to close her eyes but she would not give O'Rourke the satisfaction, so she kept her face placid and her eyes as void of emotion as she could manage. She shifted her eyes to Gail and felt a chill ripple down her back to find him watching her. She shifted uncomfortably on the hard bench which had been placed at the center of the hall and dropped her gaze, pretending not to hear his deep-throated chuckle.

O'Rourke looked up from his meal and glanced from one to the other. He glared at Gail, wondering what the Norman knight had found humorous.

"How much longer will you insist upon this defiance, *cherie?*" Gail smiled as he leaned forward on the table and looked to where Eve sat. "Your refusal to sit at our table will only see you ill, as you cannot survive on the watered ale and coarse bread you choose as an alternative. Leave your bench and come sit by me . . ."

"Leave the wench be," O'Rourke growled as he stuffed his mouth with more of the roasted pigeon. "I'd sooner she starved at that. I have no need for Dermot's brat to share my supper."

It was on Gail's tongue to call O'Rourke a fool but he thought better of it as he watched the Irishman from the corner of his eyes. The man was enormous, with forearms the size of ham hocks, his body covered with coarse red hair crowned in an unkempt mop over heavy, bushy eyebrows. For all of his ominous size, matched only by his foul temper, his most alarming feature was the remainder of what was once his left eye. His face was drawn up to the mangled, empty socket in hideous scars which gave him the permanent expression of an angry sneer. Gail's gaze fell to O'Rourke's hands which were tearing at a haunch of venison and he felt slightly queasy as he realized that they could have the same effect upon him with very little effort. He began to wonder how he had ever come to be involved with this barbarian.

"May I remind you, O'Rourke, that the 'wench' will be of no use to us unless she is alive and well. She may be Dermot's daughter but she is also the wife of an English earl . . ."

"You said that bastard, deClare, would not be returning from England," O'Rourke growled, wiping his greasy hands on his leather tunic. "What difference does it make about the woman?"

"Must I explain to you again about English law?" Gail said wearily. "If Henry decides to dispose of Richard, and I have every reason to think that he will, all of the lady's properties and wealth will come under Henry's control as her guardian. Or, it will go to the one who takes her to the marriage bed. Do you understand now?"

"By Irish law the matter will be decided by the clans, my English friend," O'Rourke reminded him, swallowing a sloshing gulp of ale.

"We had a bargain . . ." Gail protested, his impatience with O'Rourke making him reckless.

"Perhaps I've changed my mind." O'Rourke grinned unpleasantly. "Why should I give what is rightly mine to any foreigner?" He glanced at Eve, who was pretending not to listen to the exchange. "Mayhaps I'll marry the wench myself, as second wife, then the matter will be settled on both sides."

Gail attempted to keep his voice calm. "Should you decide to do that, Henry will bring armies into Ireland that will make deClare's seem paltry by comparison. The only chance that we have is to assure him that I have the situation in control, and the lady is mine, duly wedded."

"Your concern for Ireland is overwhelming," O'Rourke spat.

"Sir Gail," Eve interrupted. "May I be allowed to retire?"

Gail's chest constricted as he heard his name on Eve's lips, spoken without the usual contempt that lay in her voice when she addressed him. Since their journey across Normandy and England, she had never been far from his mind. Each day had been sheer torture as he had tried to peel away her wall of aloofness and indifference. He had never thought that it could have happened to him. Women had been unimportant except for momentary pleasures, but he had fallen totally in love with her. When they had reached Ireland, he had spoken to Dermot, certain that her hand would be given to him, but Dermot had rejected him handily. He had rejected him! That barbarian, not much a cut above the animal who now sat next to him—had rejected a Norman knight! He had never forgiven Dermot the insult. But he had laid his plans well. Eve, Dermot's lands and power too, would soon be his—and he would not allow this scum to thwart his plans, now when they were so very close to success.

"Of course, milady," he said pleasantly, rising from his chair.

"You do not need to see me to my chambers, Sir Gail," Eve said quickly. "I am sure that you have more important matters to discuss with—O'Rourke." She could not keep the bitterness and hatred out of her voice as she spoke the name.

"Nay, lamb," he said smoothly as he took her arm. "I would not think of allowing you to go unescorted. He lowered his voice as he leaned down to her. "There are many in our company who would readily seek your favors without concerning themselves with your feelings on the matter. Nay, I shall most certainly see you to your room."

She shuddered at his touch but suffered it as she had no wish to draw O'Rourke's attention by a struggle. As they made their way through the dark halls of the mote-and-bailey castle, she thought to attempt, once again, to convince him to free Sophie and FitzStephen from where they had been locked away in another part of the castle. She could not even be certain that they were still alive, since she had not been allowed to see them since their capture. As they stepped into her room, she swayed slightly.

"My lord." She paused, touching her forehead as she appeared to feel faint.

"Are you ill?" he asked anxiously, his eyes darkening with concern.

"It is a small matter, milord," she answered weakly, "but one that causes some discomfort. Perhaps, if you would send my woman to me, she has means to help this malady..."

"And if I grant your request, will you keep your part of the bargain?" he asked, his eyes narrowing with suspicion.

"Nay," she hissed, drawing her arm away from his grasp. "I will never concede to that!"

"Then you will have to do without her," he said coldly. "You are a fool, Eve. Did you not hear O'Rourke's jest a moment ago? Would you prefer being his bride to mine?" His voice softened as he looked at her with an unmasked longing that startled her. "I would be generous with you, Eve. You would never want for anything..."

"Nay!" she cried, stepping back from him. "Never! I would sooner die than have you touch me!"

His face became hard as his eyes flashed with anger. "It may come to that, my sweet. How long do you think you will last as O'Rourke's bride? Perhaps I shall let him have you after all." He stepped toward her and she recoiled, panic rising in her as she saw his intentions all too clearly.

"If you lay a hand on me, I swear that I will kill myself, Gail!"

"At least I will have had this night, my dove."

"And tomorrow, what will you have then? Do you think that Henry will give you Ireland for what you have done? He does not look kindly on those who thwart his plans. It is only through me that you stand the slightest chance of achieving your purpose!"

He hesitated as his dark brows furrowed with doubt. "What do you mean. Are you making a proposal?"

"I need time to think," she answered, forcing herself to say what her mind would not even consider. "If it is true that... that Richard will not return, then..."

"I assure you that he will not," Gail smiled. "Henry made it plainly clear that he felt Richard had become too powerful. He suspected that Richard, and those with him, had plans to establish a separate kingdom in Ireland."

"Give me time, Gail. I—I promise that I will give you my decision soon."

"I am not a patient man, Eve, so do not be long." He turned away from her, pausing for a moment to sweep his hungry gaze over the length of her. "I will expect your answer tomorrow—I would prefer that you came willingly."

When he had left she sought a chair, lowering herself into it as her body trembled and she was no longer able to stand. She had managed to delay him, but what good was a day? She could not believe that Richard would not return—she would not! But how could she deny the possibility—she knew that

Henry was capable of anything. The thought of Gail's hands on her made her convulse in an involuntary spasm. But if he did not return, she knew, in spite of her words to Gail, that she would bear it. Not for herself but for the babe she carried. She would live for Richard's child. She was caught in a woman's trap that no man would ever experience, could begin to comprehend. Birth to death, fathers, husbands, sons, and even lovers, controlled their own lives. She did not have mastery even over her own death.

But there was one exception. If O'Rourke made his threat good. It had taken all of her control not to faint when he had uttered it, so effortlessly thrown as she clenched to the bench, her nails digging into the wood. She would not bring a child into the world under O'Rourke's hand, never! She rose heavily from the chair and crossed slowly to the window and looked out beyond the moat to the fields beyond, to the flickering lights of the torches interspersed among the camp of her brother's army. She would die, by her own hand, before she submitted to O'Rourke, and she would take the babe with her.

Oh, god, what if Richard did return, to find that she had died by her own hand? Faith, trust, the courage to wait for him, he would want that from her. She closed her eyes and she could hear the murmurings of ghosts past, the stirring of her ancestors as they claimed her soul, confirming her determination. "Your father's enemy," they whispered. "The murderer of your mother and your grandfather, your enemy!" Nay, O'Rourke would never lay a hand on the babe.

"Donnell," she said softly, opening her eyes. "You will understand, perhaps you alone. Make him understand . . . that I could not allow O'Rourke to touch me." A small smile touched her lips. "A shield of roses, Richard," she whispered. "All of my love will be there for you always. Its roots are deep, withstanding even winter's chill. I will find the strength to do what I must."

"Get up!"

Eve startled awake, blinking at the large form looming over her bed. A hand grasped her wrist and pulled her roughly from the covers.

"What are you doing?" she shrieked as Gail pulled her across the room. She stumbled and he yanked her up, half dragging her to the window where he thrust her about, his fingers digging into the soft flesh of her shoulders.

"Look!" he growled menacingly.

She looked out of the window, her mind straining to comprehend what he was demanding of her as her sleep-filled eyes swept over the encampment below. In the soft light of dawn there was something different and slowly her mind began to focus on what it was. It had grown. It was twice, nay, three times the size it had been the night before. Suddenly her breath caught and she gasped. There, at the center of the mushroomed camp, flew a large gold banner with three red chevrons, the flag catching and whipping in the sharp morning breeze.

"Aye," he snarled with hatred. "Your precious Richard, if that pennon can be believed."

"You believe it," she smiled. "I can smell the fear on you."

"Get dressed."

From the tone in his voice she knew better than to disobey and hastened into a woolen pelisse as he stood staring from the window. "What will you do now?" she said contemptuously when she had finished dressing. "Meet him on the field or remain behind these walls like the coward that you are?"

"Meet him on the field?" he smirked. "Would that I had the chance. He will not meet me in combat when he knows that O'Rourke holds you within."

"Then we will remain at siege." She wondered why he was here discussing this with her.

"With what?" he laughed shortly. "O'Rourke's army deserted before dawn, the sniveling cowards." He laughed again at her look of disbelief. "Aye, my sweet, they fled, groveling to the enemy even before the last tent had been set."

"What are you going to do?"

"Why, I am going to take you out of here. There are horses saddled and waiting at the south gate. If we . . ."

"Do you think that I would go with you now?" she gasped.

"Don't be obtuse!" he shouted, his rage building. "O'Rourke is in the hall fortifying himself with wine! How long do you think it will be before he comes for you? Do you think for a moment that he will let you live when his own life is forfeit, or that your death will be easy? He'll hang your body from the castle walls to torment Richard!" He saw her hesitate and his eyes turned strangely black and wild. "If you will not go with me for yourself—what of the child you carry—his child."

"You know? How?"

"I have eyes, love, though fortunately for you O'Rourke is

not so observant." His eyes went down to her middle and he looked up at her and smiled. "Now, will you come?"

She rushed to the wardrobe and grabbed a cloak, pulling it about her shoulders as she heard him laugh softly. As they stepped into the hall, Eve stopped, glancing down the darkened hallway. "Sophie!" she cried. "We must find Sophie!"

"There is no time!" he snapped. "He has no reason to harm her. She will be safe enough!"

"I will not leave without her!" Before he could stop her, she started running down the hall toward the end of the keep. He caught up with her at the end of the hallway and pulled her about, almost off of her feet.

"I tell you, we haven't time! Any moment he'll..." He stopped in midsentence and looked at her with a strange, quizzical expression. His mouth drew back in a soft smile and he began to say something but the words came out in a sigh, his expression changing to one of regret just before he seemed to crumble at her feet. She looked down at him, her eyes fixing with horror at the knife protruding from his back. She glanced up and then threw herself back against the wall, a mute cry suffocating her throat as O'Rourke stepped from the shadows, his eye leering at her like a lop-sided cyclops'.

Somehow she was able to move and with a hard yank she pulled her skirt hem from beneath Gail's body and in an instant she was fleeing. She ran to the stairs, as screams seemed to sound in her head, and the staircase appeared to float before her, though she felt her feet taking them one by one, as quickly as she dared without falling. Halfway to the bottom she slipped on the smooth worn wood, catching herself against the stair wall. Somehow she reached the bottom, not daring to look back as she glanced about for an escape. She measured the distance to the open doorway to the courtyard and knew immediately, as she heard his running footsteps from above, that she could not make it. Glancing frantically about she spied the screen to the buttery. She threw herself at it, falling the last few steps, crawling the rest of the way to where she crouched down behind the screen and pulled her skirts in, just as she heard him come down the steps. She tried not to breath, though her chest was heaving from exertion and fear. She waited, listening, but there was no sound except the beating of her own heart, which seemed to pound audibly. Had he left? Perhaps he thought she had made it to the courtyard! If he had run through the open door he would return in a moment. Seeing no sign of her, he was bound to come back. If only she could make it through the buttery and to the kitchens . . . Rising slowly, she stepped back and turned about, and her scream reverberated about the timbered hall. He stood at the other end and, when she turned about, he threw back his head, roaring in laughter.

"'Tis no good, MacMurrough!" His laughter stopped and his face contorted into an ugly sneer. "We shall both die today, though your death will see me some satisfaction, both before and by the act. In that, I shall have the satisfaction of knowing that Dermot shall pay to the very last. The last MacMurrough, and you shall die under my hand!"

"I shall not be the last," she hissed. "You are forgetting my brother and he shall have the last word, O'Rourke!"

"Your father's bastards do not interest me!" he roared. "Let us see, what is the name he has given himself? Kavanaugh, that's it, Donnell Kavanaugh! His seed shall never carry the name MacMurrough, and well it should be, for the name will be damned for as long as there is an Irish to remember it!"

"What are you talking about?" she shrieked. "You are lying!"

"Am I?" he sneered. "A deathbed confession, it was. Dermot, I heard, felt the need to exorcise himself as he lay dying, though evidently it was kept from you! Had to tell the boy that he was birthed by some wench he'd taken a fancy to—and had died welping him! Damned but I wanted to tell the tale myself! I was only waiting for the clans to name him heir—once Enna had been taken care of! Dermot cheated me of that pleasure but now I've been handed another!"

"How could you know? I don't believe you!"

"From your mother, of course! There had been rumors, and she merely confirmed them! Why do you think that I took her? Oh, she held out for a long time, surprising when she was such a little thing, but the truth came out in the end. Of course Enna and Conner had to be disposed of—but now the MacMurrough line is at an end!"

She grasped the screen to keep from falling as her mind whirled with the impact of what he was saying. Her mother, frail and gentle mother . . . Donnell not a MacMurrough . . . She straightened and looked up at him, her eyes gleaming with green hatred.

"You only used the treaties as an excuse, you meant to kill them all along . . ."

"Of course, and Dermot knew it, though he hoped that O'Conner would intercede."

She inched back from the screen and glanced at the open doorway.

"You'll never make it," he laughed.

She knew he was right and she looked about frantically for another escape. She saw it lying on the table and with a clear vision of what was certain to happen, knew that it was the only means available to her. She lunged at the dormant table, catching him unawares, as he had prepared himself to spring in the opposite direction toward the door. Catching up the knife from the table she backed toward the hearth, pressing the blade under her breast as she glared at him, her eyes shining with victory. Seeing her intention, he froze, his eyes fixed upon the blade as his face flushed to a blood-red.

"If I must die, O'Rourke, then it shall be by my own hand, and before you have laid a touch upon me. My last breath will be heaved with the satisfaction that the gods have helped me to rob you of your victory." With an odd feeling of pleasure, a waving lightness that seemed to waft about her, she watched O'Rourke's face distort with anger and she braced herself as she prepared to plunge the blade.

"Eve!"

Startled, her eyes shot to the open doorway, her astonished expression matched by O'Rourke's. Richard stood just inside the door, sword in hand, his face pale as his eyes fixed on the blade under her breast.

She cried out to him as the blade clattered to the floor but her attention was brought about by O'Rourke's blood-curdling cry. He lunged toward Eve and she cried out, bringing up her hands to defend herself but he brushed her aside as he flung himself at the battle-ax fixed to the wall by the hearth, wrenched it from its holder and spun about to face Richard. The two men circled each other, their eyes watching each other's movements, their hands fixed upon their weapons. Suddenly, O'Rourke brought his up with a sweep, the silver razor edge swinging over Richard's head for an instant before it fell. Richard jumped aside as he brought his broad sword about and the double-edged steel barely missed O'Rourke's arm as the Irishman feigned the pass. The silver-grey ax blade made another pass to Richard's left and he brought his blade about, neatly slicing into O'Rourke's arm. The Irishman gave a scream of pain but the wound did not stop him as he raised the ax before Richard could recover to parry. The blade seemed to stand for an interminable moment over Richard's head, its descent appearing

almost spectral as Richard watched it coming down upon him.
Then, with the same hallucinatory vision, just as the blade
would have driven home, accompanied by a scream from Eve,
O'Rourke leaped backwards. He fell to the floor, convulsing
in death throes with an ax blade and handle emerging from his
forehead. Richard spun about to find Donnell standing in the
doorway, his eyes fixed upon the convulsing body at Richard's
feet.

"He was mine," Donnell said calmly.

"And what if you had missed?" Richard countered, breathing heavily as he glanced back at O'Rourke's now still body.

"Then we both would have lost," Donnell smiled.

Richard chuckled and turned to Eve, who stood white-faced
by the hearth. "Are you all right?"

Laying in Richard's arms in the security of his tent, Eve felt
purged of the weeks of fear for his safety and her own. She
closed her eyes dreamily as he nibbled at her ear and traced a
light path of kisses down her cheek to her eagerly awaiting
mouth. Turning to him, her arms went up about his neck and
she pulled him to her. He pressed her down into the deep pile
of furs on which they lay, his hands roaming hungrily over her
breasts as he gently pushed aside her chemise, his lips finding
the tips of her breasts, his tongue tenderly roaming until she
moaned and arched her back to him. His hand searched downward, slipping beneath the chemise to her thighs, then up over
her slender hips to her belly, where it stopped. She felt his
body stiffen and he brought his head up with a jerk, his eyes
filled with questions as he looked down at her. His hand lay
still on her stomach and he glanced down at it, then shot a look
back to her, a tawny brow now arched with the unasked question.

"Aye, milord," she smiled, her eyes filled with happiness
and love as she nodded slightly. "There shall be a babe in the
late spring."

He looked back to where his hand lay with a look of wonder
and reverence, then his mouth widened into a grin and he swept
her into his arms.

O'Rourke's death brought the already weakened rebellion to a
halt. The clans braced themselves for the Norman's revenge

but Richard stunned the princes of Ireland by sending them tributes instead of armed bodies of knights. He made no request for hostages, asking instead for simple oaths of fealty.

To Murtough MacMurrough, Dermot's nephew and son of the murdered ari-ri, went Okinselagh. And Richard made Donnell seneschal of Leinster. Richard assured him that the honor was well deserved and not a gift meant to appease. With Murtough and Donnell the people would be allowed to retain their honor and would become a rallying force to strengthen the land for what was to come. Donnell balked at first, his confidence having been badly shaken by Dermot's deathbed confession, but Richard persevered in his desire to restore Donnell's confidence and because he knew that he was best fitted to the job. At last he accepted, to Richard's relief, as he warily watched the sea.

Richard's worst fears were finally realized as dispatches began arriving from Henry with greetings sent to the Irish princes. It took all of Richard's efforts as a statesman to appease the Irish leaders, drawing them together, plying his wiles to gain their trust, appealing to them with delicate diplomacy that they must unify. His efforts were barely realized before Henry brought his armada to the Irish shore.

Henry traveled from Waterford to Dublin, assuring the clans of his protection and that he would never allow the Anglo-Norman conquerors to place their boots upon the neck of Ireland. All he asked in return was their oaths to the English Crown. For their protection he had taken the ports, garrisoning them securely under the command of Hugh deLacy. While Henry named Richard Constable of Ireland, deLacy's presence was to assure Richard's continuing loyalty.

As a final act to the drama, Henry called the clans together for their oaths, unaware that riders were dispatched from Ferns to urge the clans to comply. Richard's greatest fear was that Henry would find reason to press his demands and thus find the need to remain for a time. They came one by one: Dermot MacCarty, King of Desmond; Connell O'Brian of Thomond; Donnell MacGillapatrick of Ossory: Melaghlin O'Phelan of Decies; Faelan MacFaelain of Offelan; O'Toole of Omurethy; Donnell MacGillamockolmag from the vale of Dublin; and Murrough O'Carroll, King of Uriel. Only O'Conner of Connaught, the ari-ri of Ireland, was conspicuously absent. Henry's rage over the high-king's absence was appeased only when Richard assured the king that O'Conner's absence was understandable, and even desirable. It was imperative, he explained, that the ari-ri be allowed to keep face. He could not be expected to participate with the princes who had formerly given their fealty to him. It had taken the greatest tact and soothing words to convince Henry of his wisdom but in the end Richard won out.

Eve stood by Richard's side in the hall at Dublin. The room was filled with the Irish princes and the Anglo-Norman. Henry sat on the dais at the front of the room listening attentively to the herald who was reading the proclamation to the assembly. She glanced up at Richard who was idly caressing her hand in the folds of her skirt and she wondered at the hint of a smile that he wore. Why was he so calm? Her own nerves were edged raw and she was stunned by the words the herald was reading. Did Henry seriously think that a few lines could change the history of custom that had been in existence for hundreds of years? Little had been left to their Brenhon Code: cohabitation with relations of blood or affinity were now outlawed; children would, in all cases, be catechized at the doors of the church; tithes would be paid to the parishes; church property would be kept from the secular; clerics were free of fines; and more, the final word, that all matters would be observed in the customs of the Anglican Church.

Eve was horrified. While no mention was made of the Papal Bull of Autibullar, these Constitutions of Cashel were certain to gain favor with the pope and secure Henry as overlord of Ireland. Henry, who had made a career of opposition to the power of the Church, was using the same to gain a firm foothold on Ireland!

She looked about, her alarm and outrage growing as each line was read. But the room was quiet and she noticed that her countrymen were accepting the news with surprising calm. Far too calmly. She wondered what each must be thinking, and feeling, as they heard Henry's demands, the end to their freedoms, under English rule. She trembled, unaware that she did so until she felt Richard's hand press hers gently and she glanced up to find him looking down at her with a smile. His eyes raised, subtlely, to another point in the room. She followed his gaze and she caught Donnell's eyes and to her shock, he winked at her. Her eyes shot from one Irish prince to another and slowly, very slowly, the meaning of Richard's smile, and Donnell's wink, began to dawn. Now she understood why Donnell and Gervase had been gone from Ferns for the weeks before Henry's arrival in Dublin, even to Gervase's leaving of his new bride in Eve's company. They had been prepared. They had been warned and counseled and their unity with the Anglo-Normans had been cemented to a single purpose against a common foe. It was a subtle difference she now saw in the room, one that fortunately went unmissed by Henry.

The corners of her lovely mouth pulled up into a soft smile as she leaned against Richard's arm and she squeezed his hand in return; then she listened to the rest of the declaration, her heart lightened and her courage restored.

Epilogue

Basking in a wash of contentment, Eve closed her eyes and pictured the scene about her. The new, large hall at Ferns, the friends who gathered about her before the crackling winter fire, and most of all, Richard. Her dearest, beloved Richard who sat in the chair next to hers, his long legs stretched out before him, his hands resting on his chest as they idly turned the goblet. Her hands moved to her swelling belly and the reality of its precious contents brought a smile to her face, as she opened her eyes and turned them to the babe's father.

He was there, returning her smile with a tenderness that swelled her heart with love and longing. She glanced to Warwick, with his ever-present tankard, and to Gervase whose bright blue eyes were fixed with a mixture of love and disbelief over his good fortune, his hand tightly clasped to Lavinia's. And to Sophie, who sat bent over her needlework.

The Scotswoman had been released from Carrick unharmed except that she had been so outraged that Eve had feared she would have a stroke. Sophie had ignored the fact that Fitz-Stephen had suffered worse injustices under O'Rourke's hand, as she had railed into Richard for not having rescued them sooner. Warwick, Donnell, and Gervase each had taken their turns at suffering her tongue-lashing. She had worn herself to the bone, pacing by the hour in the small confines of her prison-room, she had assured them. To the heaven-bent rolling of Richard's eyes, she had promised the lord-marchers that they would never be allowed to forget her trials.

Eve's gaze moved lovingly to Donnell where he stood leaning against the stone of the mantle, his face broken out in a huge grin as he listened to a comment from Warwick. He had taken the name of his mother, Kavanaugh, and she had no doubt that his seed would found a new and proud clan and be a credit to Ireland. He wore his new title with an ease that proved he was born to it and her concern for him had faded with each passing day.

The mention of Henry's name brought her out of her reverie and she focused on what Warwick was saying to Donnell.

"Aye, my friend, Henry would never have come to Ireland had the Pope's emissaries not been hot on his heels to hold him accountable for Becket's death. Now we are blessed with that damnable deLacy. Not only is he in charge of the ports of Dublin, Wexford and Waterford, but he'll be watching our every move and reporting it to Henry, mark my words."

"You must admit Henry played the game well, Warwick," Richard smiled lazily as he reached over and took Eve's hand. "He did not storm into Ireland as the oppressive conqueror but as the great friend of the Irish, the great appeaser, as he has done so successfully in Wales."

"Do you think that anyone believed it?"

"It was not important for them to believe it." Richard shrugged. "As long as they did not deny his position. The great protector, the stern repressor of the Anglo-Norman conquerors." Richard smirked. "Aye, it was played well. Thank God that the princes played their parts well or we never would have seen him out of Ireland."

"You do not need to worry about the clans, Warwick." Donnell grinned. "We Irish have played the 'game' too long to be taken in by festive displays. Though I must admit that Henry set an impressive table in our honor. We should be touched that he went to such pains..."

"While the pope may have been responsible for bringing Henry to Ireland, at least we can thank him for returning him to England." Warwick chortled. "If he had not begun inflicting penalties on Henry's dominions in Normandy, he might have decided to stay the whole of the year as he threatened."

"Good riddance!" Sophie mumbled, her head still bent over the tapestry on which she was working.

"Sophie! I did not think you were listening!" Eve laughed.

"Haven't missed a word, lass." Sophie glanced at her, over

the loom. "Though, if I've seemed unusually quiet 'tis only because my poor body is still in shock over the indignities it was forced to suffer of late." She ignored the heavy sighs and pressed on with her customary of-course-you've-missed-the-important-point tone of voice: "Henry cared less for the Holy Father's penalties, as just as they were. That man's never cared for the good of the Church. Nay, 'tis the duplicity of those traitorous barons, plotting to put the babe Henry on the throne, that rushed him back to England, mark my words!"

"You are both right," Richard said, rising from his chair to stretch. "And both reasons will keep him at bay for a time." He held out a hand to Eve. "I have need to take some air, milady. Will you walk with me?"

She took his hand and they left the hall, walking in silent company across the courtyard and through the gates where the sentry nodded in greeting. The air was heavy with a storm-threatening mugginess and the heavy cloud cover darkened the twilight to a smoky grey. The shadows of the trees and flora cast mirrored shapes about the landscape as the moon peeked occasionally from behind the thunderheads that were passing overhead. They paused on a knoll outside the walls where they could look out over the valley surrounding the manor and the thick dark forests beyond. Eve leaned back against Richard's hard form, smiling as she snuggled against him and he slipped his arms about her.

"If it could only remain as peaceful as it is now," she mused out loud, closing her eyes for a moment as if to confirm her thoughts. When he did not respond, she turned her head and looked up at him. "You are worried. Tell me."

He squeezed her gently and passed a hand down over her swollen belly but his gaze remained fixed out over the valley. "I did not want to spoil their mood, love, and I pray that their optimism will be realized."

"But you are not so certain, are you?" she asked.

"I wish that I were," he sighed. Releasing her he stepped away to lean his shoulder against a tree but reached out an arm to her and folded it about her shoulder as she came to lean against him. "They have forgotten how quickly Henry threw the embargo against our ports when he was displeased, or how effective it was in strangling us. I fear that it may prove to be England's policy toward Ireland. He did it when he had only suspicion to rule his emotions, to punish us, with no regard to how it might hurt the Irish people.

"Neither side understands the other, Eve. Nor do, I fear, they will make any attempt to do so. This is what I must try to effect. Henry does not realize that the Irish will throw off the yoke of their fealty with ease. They delude themselves into feeling secure because he is far away in England and Normandy. They will soon again begin fighting among themselves, taking Henry for granted, and find themselves in a vise from which they will never extract themselves, unless I can stop it. As for the king, and his heirs, well . . . they will strangle Ireland whenever they show evidence of independence as a unified people, unless he comes to see the advantage to a strong country here, as an ally. And, there is a new threat to consider. Eleanor has presented Henry with another son."

"Another son? But why would that be a threat to us?"

Richard looked down and smiled at her quizzical expression. "Because, my love, Henry will give his sons their place in England and in the continent. But what of this new one? Already, by way of nickname, they call him John Lackland—and Eleanor is clamoring for Henry to provide for her youngest chick."

"Ireland?" she gasped.

"It well could be."

"Oh, Richard, is it hopeless?" she cried, suddenly seeing the vision he was presenting.

"Nothing is ever hopeless, love," he answered, bending to brush a kiss on her hair. "You and I should know that better than anyone. You told me once, nay, twice, that no one would ever conquer the essence of Ireland. Standing here, at this place in time, how can we predict Ireland's future? Donnell will do his part. Whatever happens I know that clan Kavanaugh will take a great place in forming that future. As for us? I believe in the spirit I feel here. If our children can believe in it, there may be a chance. But, whatever happens, I swear to you, love, I will keep Henry from her shores for as long as I live. Perhaps, if the gods give me time, I can see her molded into the greatness she can become—the gods willing."